Born in 1950s Catholic Ireland, Maire lived in a Hindu family in India after marriage and was influenced by the similarities of worship in both cultures. She is currently living and working in London. The book took inspiration from an account of her sons' early lives and written for posterity. Maire's family have encouraged publication.

The Author with her sons – the real Jack and Matty

To Geraldine
Love always
Mary

For my beloved sons and their father

https://SITES.GOOGLE.COM/VIEW/GODDESS-DANA/HOME

Maire de Harpuir

THE CHILDREN OF THE GODDESS DANA

Book One: The Little Pink House

Book Two: The Tall Magnolia House

AUSTIN MACAULEY PUBLISHERS™
LONDON • CAMBRIDGE • NEW YORK • SHARJAH

A CIP catalogue record for this title is available from the British Library.

ISBN 978-1-78710-603-1 (Paperback)
ISBN 978-1-78710-604-8 (Hardback)
ISBN 978-1-78710-605-5 (E-Book)

www.austinmacauley.com

First Published (2018)
Austin Macauley Publishers Ltd.
25 Canada Square
Canary Wharf
London
E14 5LQ

Contents

Book One

THE LITTLE PINK HOUSE

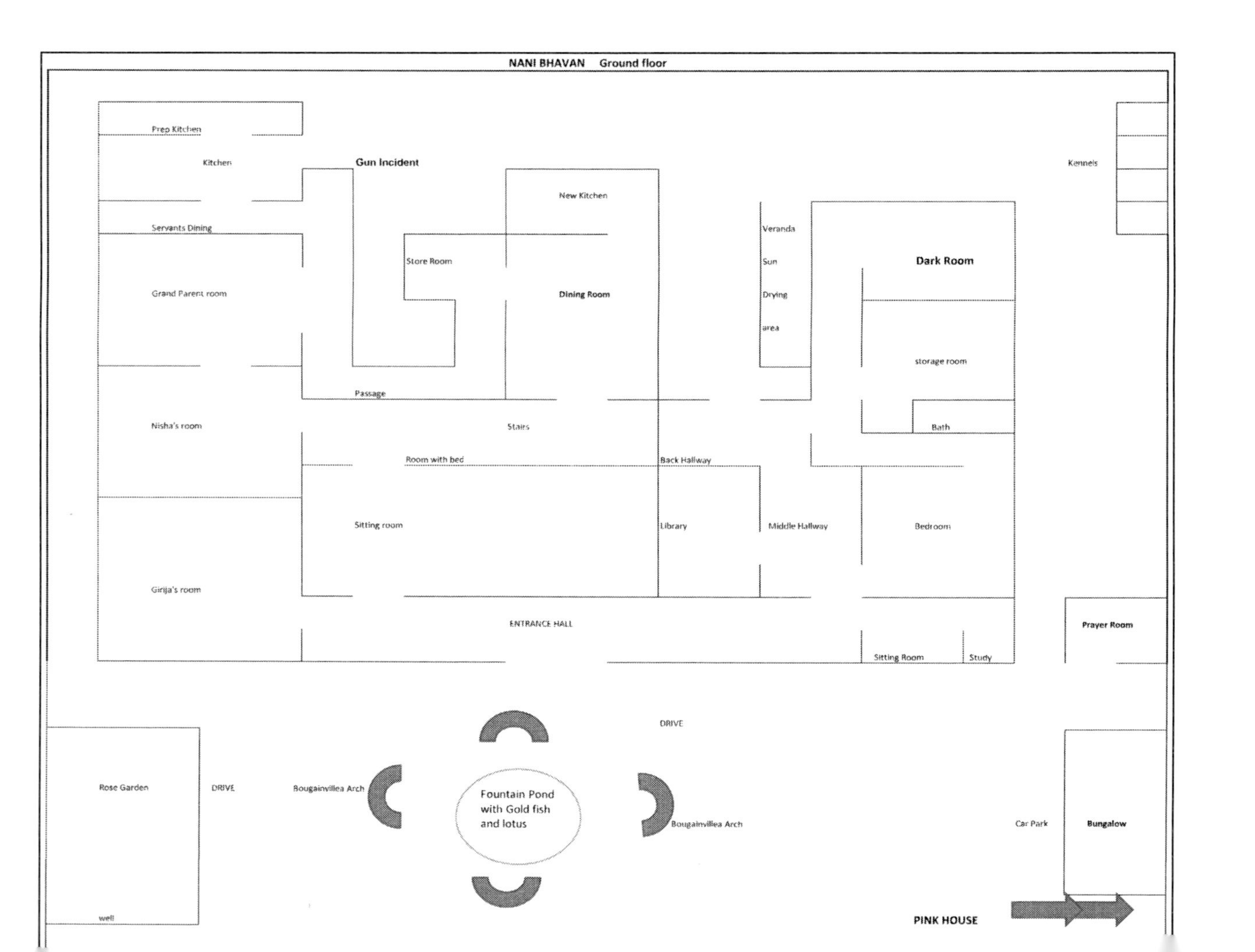
NANI BHAVAN Ground floor
Prep Kitchen
Kitchen
Gun Incident
New Kitchen
Kennels
Veranda
Sun
Drying
area
Dark Room
Servants Dining
Store Room
Grand Parent room
Dining Room
storage room
Passage
Nisha's room
Stairs
Bath
Room with bed
Back Hallway
Sitting room
Library
Middle Hallway
Bedroom
Girija's room
ENTRANCE HALL
Prayer Room
Sitting Room
Study
DRIVE
Rose Garden
DRIVE
Bougainvillea Arch
Fountain Pond
with Gold fish
and lotus
Bougainvillea Arch
Car Park
Bungalow
well
PINK HOUSE

DUSK

THE VAMPIRE ACTIVITY of mosquitoes had just begun. Jack felt a sharp sting on his ankle and automatically smacked his palm down on it, but missed. The mosquito buzzed angrily, loudly protesting the attack and swooped near Jack's head. He got up to put the fan on, feeling the clay tiles underneath his bare feet; they were cool, not slab-cold like the mosaic which was used in the newer parts of the houses.

As the large overhead fan creaked into life he could see, through the security bars of the window opposite the sofa, Grandmother on her way to the prayer room. He felt he didn't need the light just yet and went back to his notes and tattered textbook on Business Studies.

By the time dusk had engulfed the high ceiling and crept down over his books, Jack had decided that practical knowledge, well-structured with a bit of text book terminology would get him through the end of term exams. Not one to over-tax himself, he felt there was no need to consult the boring textbook a second time.

As he hauled himself into a sitting position and bent to gather his notes from the tiles, he noticed Aunt Saroj furtively looking into the shadows of the mango trees. Apparently satisfied, she briskly moved into the enclosed area between the bungalow and the garage to the prayer room door just beyond. Puzzled by her behaviour, Jack followed her path through the sitting room windows and on into the bedroom and through its windows. He knelt on the floor below the window sill which looked on to the prayer room door. The mosquitoes began their loud swoop and buzz attacks but he could not risk switching on the old fan; the wind-up cranking and wafting may be heard outside. He moved his feet every time the buzzing stopped, averting the imminent piercing. It was lucky he had on his long uniform trousers.

With his eyes peering just above the window sill and nose aware of the familiar old wood smell he wallowed briefly in the inveterate stability and love that surrounded him. His comfort was under constant attack; he moved his feet and arms to avoid the stinging bites. At the same time, the scene unfolding in the prayer room was piling on psychological discomfort as he watched his aunt. This was not the routine of prayer he was used to. She had removed the pin which secured the pleats of her sari and pierced the second finger of her right hand and drew blood. She smeared a circular dot on the deity in the picture on the altar. Then she squeezed more blood from the tiny wound and placed a bloodied, perfect, circular dot on her own forehead.

Amazed, stiff from squatting and dodging mosquitoes, Jack stood upright, hidden in the shadows at the side of the window, fingertips conscious of the deep grains in the painted wood. Aunt Saroj was quietly chanting, palms upturned and extended. In the bopping light of the oil lamp Jack could just distinguish the large picture of the Goddess Kali on which the blood had been smeared. Puzzled, he tried to remember where and if it had ever been in the prayer room. He tried to remember when he last used it. *The God Vishnu was always centre stage. She had not carried anything into the Prayer Room* – he was sure of that, he remembered she held up the pleats of her sari as she moved along the sandy drive. So where could the picture of one of the most powerful and dangerous Hindu Goddesses have come from?

As the chanting of sacred Sanskrit became a raucous whisper Jack's aunt began to dance. Jack was acutely aware of the smack of bare feet on the tiles, the tingle and ring of her gold bangles, the rustle of her starched cotton sari and all the time the frantic pace of the Sanskrit. Jack stood stock still, unwary of marauding mosquitoes. Then suddenly she was prostrate on the floor in front of the altar, with deep throaty invocations, then up on hands and knees, arching her back cat-like, then kneeling, arms up, stretched, begging, beseeching. Jack realised the sounds of dusk had disappeared: the buzz of deadly mosquitoes, the cawing crows, the piping crickets and the tweeting of little honey sucking birds had all been silenced!

It was then it began. A small cloud of fog formed in front of the altar and then the wraith appeared. Jack's half-choked scream made little noise considering its invocation but the wary aunt was at the prayer room door, hands on the door posts, large, wide, dark disseminating eyes scanning the dusk. Jack bent low, scurried towards the adjoining bathroom door and quietly bolted himself inside. He could hear the aunt as she leaped on to the walkway which was buttressed against the bungalow walls. He heard the clatter of the flung sitting room doors as they hit the walls on either side. She would have seen the school paraphernalia and have had no doubt as to who had been watching.

HUSH

SILENT AND SWIFT bare feet moved into the bedroom. Jack imagined her fingers splayed wide, pushing silently but powerfully on the bathroom door as she stood and waited in the darkness. Jack too stood and waited, scarcely breathing. His eyes surveyed the walls for ways of escape; there were none. The ventilation was composed of curlicue brick covered with lime plaster and years of paint. He listened: the sounds of nightfall had begun again. The mosquito horde continued their attack on his feet and arms. He rolled down his shirt sleeves, one roll-over at a time and buttoned the cuffs silently, not making a sound. She waited too. Jack hoped she wasn't conjuring more magic, evil, whatever it was… he tried to wipe the image of the wraith from his mind. *How could she be so… so disingenuous – far worse than that, so very wicked?*

Far away but increasing in velocity he could hear the voices of his mother and little brother.

'There's another one over here Matt,' came his mother's voice not more than three thick walls and twenty feet away.

'Thanks Mum. There's no point checking that bed; they never go over there.' Matty's voice came back assuredly and then both their voices faded away. Jack knew his brother was collecting his pet rabbit family to secure them in their hutch for the night, safe from snakes and the watch dogs.

That protected world next door, his home which he rarely inhabited in the evenings, spending most of his time at his grandfather's house, seemed under-appreciated as darkness and despair enveloped him.

He became aware of footsteps in the sand on the drive. He held his breath and listened: no sound from the other room. Then he heard Grandmother calling impatiently.

'Saroj, Saroj.'

'Here, Mother.' His aunt must have moved into the sitting room; her voice sounded further from the bathroom door.

'What are you doing in there?' Grandmother's voice came now from the front of the bungalow.

'Jack has been here, he left the fan on. I'll bring his books into the house,' replied his aunt. Jack could imagine her feigning annoyance and busying herself picking up his school books.

Then he heard the key turn in the lock. *Prisoner*, he thought, *out of danger only for now*. He unbolted the bathroom door and carefully peered round the door post; he watched mother and daughter through the opposite bedroom window as they strolled along the drive towards the front door of the main house where the wicker chairs were placed for the usual evening sit out. Aunt Saroj did not go into the house, instead she left his books on the wicker table and sat facing the front door of the bungalow, the only possible route of escape.

Back in the sitting room Jack switched on the fan again to protect himself from the mosquitoes and to cool his body; he could feel his shirt clinging to his back and chest in the humidity. He found a dark corner behind the doors and waited. From time to time he moved across behind the double doors to peer out the window from the deep shadows. Aunt Saroj sat there watching and waiting, like a lizard preparing to pounce on a cockroach. His mind was a desultory morass of petrified images and all the time the deep unease kept growing. He was no longer shivering with fear. He instinctively felt he had to keep that in check so he tried to rationalise his situation. Firstly, she had not actually seen him; only his books lay about on the sofa and floor and like she told Grandmother, *Jack left, leaving the fan switched on*. Jack mimed her Malayalam in his head.

Secondly, the key usually stayed in the door so that the watchman could allow visitors for Grandfather to wait in the bungalow. The drivers occasionally used it for the car cushions, mats, curtains and dusters. So all he had to do was wait… wait until the drivers began returning the cars for the night. He squatted and put one eye to the keyhole to see if the key was still in the lock – it was.

HOPE

WHILE HE WAITED, the wraith image stayed uppermost in his mind: every detail of his grandmother at her physical worst, grey skinny face, forlorn eyes, body weight halved, blouse hanging loose on her shoulders… *There has got to be a way to negate this terrible unreality that could become reality…* but in horror he realised it was the other way round. Grandmother had been complaining of pain in her stomach: everyone had been urging her to go to the doctor but she protested as usual, saying it was indigestion. *Did his aunt want Grandmother incapacitated or worse… dead? But why? It was unimaginable. How could mere wishes, thoughts or invocations cause things to actually happen? – Mind influence on particles, cosmic energy, quantum physics…* Jack was an avid reader but this was unbelievable. He could in no way fathom it, but he had seen the wraith – the power of it and it was working… *How did she do it?*

Jack thought about the night fogs he'd experienced in the Irish countryside. He revelled in the sudden eerie fog banks apparently appearing out of nowhere which engulfed the car, causing his mother to quickly change down several gears and have the car crawl with lights on dim – using the grass verge as a guide – and then just as suddenly they would have driven through it. That night, the fog was different; or was it smoke? Had his aunt opened some sort of a vortex or a portal?

Just then he heard the sound of a car horn at the gate. *Please let it be one of the family cars.* Jack mentally visualised one of the Ambassadors. It would be parked under the porch beside the bungalow. A visitor's car would wait in the drive, causing a distraction but not a possible means of escape. Whichever one it was, was better than what was happening in his mind.

He sprung up and peered out the window: *yeees,* it was Grandfather's car. It stopped, Grandfather got out; the driver closed the back door and got back in and started the engine, drove across to the bungalow and parked the car just outside. Grandfather went indoors but Jack's aunt stayed, watching.

Vishu the driver visited the staff bathroom and on returning began to clean the car. Jack waited until he had worked his way around to the side facing the bungalow windows. He then implored the driver not to react but to continue cleaning and polishing, which he did. Jack then ordered him to listen.

Jack was aware that Vishu had become accustomed to a myriad of situations and behaviours, working for so long with three generations of the family. As part of the third generation, Jack himself, at just twelve years old, regretfully knew that he was occasionally becoming a bit of a challenge for the driver but had not yet forced Vishu onto the fine line.

It wasn't enough for the faithful driver to enhance life for the past forty years by providing in-car entertainment on long journeys on pot-holed roads with his own brand of philosophy; Jack was aware that the second generation had stretched his forbearance and discretion to the limit.

ESCAPE

JACK INTENDED TO say he needed to get out without anyone seeing him. He had decided to pretend that he was playing a game but shocked himself when he began to speak. The truth tumbled out as the images turned into words: once he started talking he told the driver everything that had happened. To Jack's relief, Vishu naturally, in his wisdom, made all the right moves, keeping his head low when replying and occasionally moving to the other side of the car, opening doors, shaking mats, wiping, polishing and adjusting windscreen wipers.

Eventually Vishu opened the front door of the bungalow, stood there making a spectacle of wringing the water out of the cleaning cloth, briefly went inside and exited just as quickly, locking the door carefully. Jack's aunt watched all this with sheer concentration; the few seconds she missed was when Grandfather re-emerged from the house with Grandmother and a servant bearing a tea tray. In that second or two when wicker chairs were rearranged and teas handed out, Jack's agile body elbowed and kneed out of the bungalow door across the walk-way on his stomach, past the rubber-slippered feet of the driver and slid into the back seat of the car and rolled on to the floor.

Minutes later, as the driver closed the boot and headed off to the tea shop, the aunt, satisfied that the nephew was still hiding in the bungalow, settled in to have a cheerful chat. Jack, who normally took tea with his grandparents, was aware of how she always had an amusing story ready for her father who liked to have a jolly home. Meanwhile, with the upright part of the back seat replaced, Jack tried to make himself comfortable in the fairly large, wide but short space of the boot.

The wait was long, but he was out of the bungalow. The mosquitoes had ceased their frenzied attacks and night was quietly settling in. He was aware of a second Ambassador car being retuned, the basic mechanics of its engine throbbing as it was eased in behind the boot. Fortunately for Jack, it had not been reversed, otherwise the diesel fumes would have induced a fit of coughing. The driver of this car, Raju, was a young and whimsical fellow, not judicious, especially in the dire situation the day had become.

As the long minutes turned into an endless second hour, Jack realised there were other small mercies. Easing his body quietly around onto his back again, knees drawn up, he was thankful that his parents were at a reception as the eight-thirty dinner time had just passed. There was nobody to miss him. Aunt Saroj was the only person who knew his whereabouts, other than *The Merlin Driver*, thought Jack, smiling to himself; and Vishu had checkmated her.

TEMPLE

JACK FELL INTO an exhausted doze. The ordeal had drained his energy and now that he had a chance to escape he relaxed a little. He was jolted awake by the slap-bang of the heavy Ambassador door. The engine started up. He clamped his palms flat on to the roof of the boot as his body swayed from the motion on the drive. He was aware of his grandparents getting into the back seat and could even hear their conversation clearly:

'Where is my *mone*?' enquired Grandfather.

'Jack must be at the home,' replied Grandmother.

'He didn't come this evening?' asked Grandfather with what sounded like annoyance.

'He was here earlier, studying in the bungalow as usual. I don't know where he's got to,' explained Grandmother.

Then the engine started once again. The motion was swifter and bouncier. It left Jack grappling for a secure hold; the only thing to do was to change again on to one side and grip the spare wheel which was secured to the inside of the framework of the vehicle, beyond his head. This didn't stop his body below his waist from the discomfort of the bumps and sway on the bends as it twisted painfully. His shirt was sticky with sweat and perspiration, so also was his hair, especially around his face and neck. He knew it would be a short ride; his grandfather visited their family temple twice each day.

Jack was ready for the *bang-shudder* of the heavy car doors this time: *relax the body, hands on ears, but he must think fast*. Before he could formulate a plan there were three regularly spaced knocks on the metal of the boot. Jack waited and then responded with three of his own. The boot was lifted, letting in the blaring light from a near-by fluorescent street light.

'Get out, now, before I reverse the car and when I park get into the passenger seat,' whispered the driver, glancing out and around at the empty space at the temple approach. 'Quickly, there is nobody about now.'

Jack obeyed, stiffly scrambled out of the boot and stood feeling very vulnerable, glancing down the long road of the temple approach towards the houses at its end. There was nobody visible either outside or even at the curtained windows. The driver faced the car towards the road and Jack approached the passenger side feeling utterly defeated.

'Why are you taking me back there, Vishu brother?' asked Jack in Malayalam. He spoke this well but was weak at the script, mainly because he attended an English medium school in the Anglo-Indian quarters of his town.

'This is what you will say. You have been to the temple to pray to pass your exams. Then you got talking to "The Corpse", he is here every evening – you know Hari the cashew factory manager, with the half-closed eyelids?' Vishu spoke softly, confidentially, as he opened the passenger side door.

'Yes I know him, what's he have to do with anything?' Jack sensed hope.

'You were just saying goodnight to him when you spotted your grandfather's car and decided to come home with them.'

Jack began to understand.

'You are a saviour, Vishu brother, but what about Saroj Aunty?'

'What about her? You know nothing about anything that happened before dusk. You left for the temple after studying.' Vishu's eyes were smiling and shining in the street light as he stood holding the door, head bowed at a respectful angle, a servant and a sage. Jack felt that Vishu knew he needed help and he appeared glad to thwart whatever Jack's aunt had in store for him.

As he sat on the long front car seat Jack welcomed Vishu sitting at the other end of it as an interloper; he considered the surreptitiousness of how he had handled a dangerous situation but wondered why... was it just altruism or did he in his wisdom relish the danger of a challenge when his very livelihood was at stake?

They were the last visitors of the day. The middle-aged couple emerged from the temple, there was the usual loving, demonstrative greeting from Grandfather. The driver's story was readily accepted when Grandmother queried Jack's whereabouts. They both praised Jack's dedication and a warning followed from Grandfather, echoed by Grandmother, about wandering alone at night.

When the car turned into the road facing the main gates Jack noticed his father's car at the Little Pink House, his parents' home. As Jack bade his good nights, Grandmother worried about his textbooks. Feeling ecstatic, he requested her, in his most charming manner, to send them over to the Pink House with the watchman.

FINN

THE COB WAS still full of energy. She had completed the length of the track and back but Finn was still raring to go so she turned again, the firm sand of the track curving out in front of them, hugging the mainland with the dunes raised on the opposite side. She gave him the reins and prepared for a wild ride. It had been five days since he had been exercised, due to study pressure: she had to do well, prove to her parents she could pass her exams as well as take care of Finn. She was twelve years old and would start secondary school in September. She bent low, helmet almost at the same height as Finn's ears, heels tucked in, knees gripping the saddle and the reins loose, just threaded through her fingers. She could hear his breath, feel his muscles as they became one, slicing through air; if he stopped abruptly she would have kept on moving right over his head, but he had never done that even when startled by a wild animal, he always gave her time, a split-second of warning. Once she avoided a fall by clinging on to his powerful neck, managing to slide off and get her feet on solid ground as he danced sideways: he would never throw her.

It was on the way back while she kept one eye on the tide that Kate saw her: long dark hair, riding bareback except for a cloth across the horse's back. She kept pace with Kate and Finn, no stirrups, head lowered like her own, bare legs, feet enclosed in what looked like animal skins, bound with leather strips. *She is good,* thought Kate, *better than I am.* They kept the pace; her smile was challenging; animals straining, riders determined. Kate noted the bridle, the bit – there had to be a bit because she noted there were rings attached to the bridle – and then she had gone, vanished. Finn slowed as they neared the end of the sandy track. Kate dismounted: *was she imagining things*? She choose a time when the race horses from the local trainers had finished their morning exercise and rarely saw another human being on this or the St George's Channel side of the finger of land named the Borough. She took the reins and walked Finn back along the track, working out where the girl had disappeared. She would have noticed if the girl had driven her horse up into the dunes. She hadn't, there was no track – without one the horse would sink into the dry, fine sand. Kate decided she would walk back to the crossing, the tide was about to turn and she needed to get through the slim and on to the path before the water had covered it. She stopped and stood still, gazing at the channels of water between her and the mainland: they were not yet swelling and spilling salty water on to the pock-marked sand made by wiggling sea creatures. Satisfied, she continued to walk, examining to her right and left as she did. Finn was covered in sweat; no harm to let him dry off for a bit, she would need to mount to keep her feet dry for the crossing.

Then suddenly the girl reappeared, this time sitting up in the dunes, reins in one hand and her horse waiting below her.

Kate stood still and watched the confident, grinning girl. After a moment or two she turned Finn and traced the last few steps they had made and looked up into the dunes. No girl and no horse. *Why could she only see her in a certain area of the shore?* Kate walked forward and there the girl was, still smiling, a smile that was full of laughter. She stood and slid down into the cascading sand which she disturbed, moving down from the dune. Kate stood still as she approached and then she stopped as Finn began prancing and whinnying, pulling sideways on the reins in Kate's hand, causing her to grab it with both hands and follow him in a failed effort to control him. The cob could not be calmed and Kate felt he was trying to distance her from the girl who with a quick glance back in her direction looked perturbed. However she stayed still and did not follow them; Kate felt the girl understood animals. Nearer the tide mark Kate noticed the slow and steady coverage of water on sand. When Finn was calm enough to mount she did so but could not resist another glance. The girl stood there with her horse looking directly at Kate, with a sadness about her.

'Who are you?' Kate called out while urging Finn to be still and putting a little tension on the reins.

The girl shrugged her shoulders indicating she did not understand.

'*Tusa, ce he tussah?*' ('You, who are you?') she called out in Irish as Finn continued to resist control, moving sideways, backwards and all the while trying to get his head to flee.

The girl moved slightly forward, raising a hand to her ear. *She understands Irish,* Kate thought.

'*Caith is anim dom,*' ('I'm Kate,') she shouted.

'Medb,' the girl called back, placing a hand on her chest, a hopeful smile: 'Medb.' And then she was gone. Kate knew Finn had drawn her away from where the girl was and she allowed him to lead her along the path through the slime and home. From the far shore she scanned the dunes for the illusive Medb – Maeve – and patted Finn's neck, thinking: *You know more than you can tell me?*

PAST

 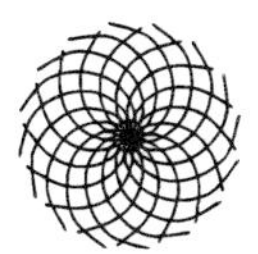

WHY WAS IT that one memory, the scene from the bungalow bedroom window, the beginning of the end although he didn't know it then, why was it more significant than all the other memories lived throughout a twelve-year childhood?

Jack stood and very occasionally shuffled forward as he waited in line to present his passport at an airport which he had used frequently as a child but which appeared different in the ten years he had been away. It was Trivandrum, the capital city of Kerala State, South India which now accepted international flights, and Jack was journeying back from London, England.

It was the sight of the Elephant God Ganapathi, a large stone idol that had invoked so powerfully the memory of his grandfather's bungalow and the mysteries that began to reveal themselves there.

His father, who was Indian by birth, showed signs of discomfort. Obviously adjusting to the moist heat, he had pulled the collar of his shirt back, away from his neck. The overhead fans helped a little, depending on where one stood, as the queue moved haltingly and very, very slowly forward. Everyone waited and waited, some fanning themselves with books, newspaper and even air tickets jutting out of their passports as they moved on a few centimetres every now and again. Jack felt he was back in the land where time stood still: even the entry slowed him down, the heat physically and the patience needed as the system ground slowly on his jet-lagged mind. On the other hand, he loved the wet heat; his T-shirt clung to his chest and back underneath his open-neck shirt. He relived the moment the plane door swung open and the invisible warmth enveloped the cabin in the same way that the heat from an oven door opening claimed him in a kitchen in a cooler hemisphere from time to time. Jack was back: years of a cold climate became the memory, he was back in mind as well as body.

As a way of avoiding the past Jack once again glanced at the statue of

Ganapathi and found himself smiling. Matty his little brother had always been fascinated by the Elephant God for as long as Jack could remember. Matty had brought most of his possessions from India whereas Jack could not bring himself to take anything that reminded him of his life with his grandfather, his father's father, for they shared a bond that was unbreakable, or so Jack thought. He tried to imagine the row of elephant gods on the shelves in Matty's tiny crowded bedroom, hours behind in London. He had ceramic ones, brass ones, a papier-mâché one and a beautiful resin one with the boy Ganapathi seated on his parents' knees: that was his favourite.

Then he remembered his mother in London with Matty, how she had fussed and reminded both Jack and his father about the danger from overhead fans or a badly directed air conditioner vent on Jack's childhood asthma. Coming from Irish farming folk his mother, conditioned by centuries of a compassionate Jesus type of Catholicism had never expected the jealousy and evil she witnessed in Kerala and fretted about the effects of the trip on Jack even though she didn't know the half of it. Her mind had been wiped clean of her ancient heritage as efficiently as dreams in the morning, but Jack knew how reality differed in different states of consciousness and he possessed certain knowledge that the Tuatha dé Danann was alive and well. Again the past had crept irritatingly into his mind.

After the 100-kilometre taxi drive Jack and his father reached Adoor, their home, where after his father Jack was the crown prince who should have inherited the goodwill and an industrial complex built up by his grandfather. He had employed over five thousand people in various industries. Jack and his brother Matty were aware of their legacy of expansion of an asset base of over ten million pounds and continued the philanthropy of their grandfather.

Early the next morning and after a good night's sleep in an air-conditioned room which his father needed, Jack took an auto rickshaw from the hotel. He skirted across the periphery of the busiest part of town, crossing the bridge and heading towards the open green area known as the *maidan*. He felt powerful and in control, unlike the forbidden auto trips he'd taken with Khalid or Akhill, his old school friends, and wondered if he could locate them. He had been a bad correspondent and preferred to leave the past in the past in his growing up years.

It bothered him that he was being treated like a Sahib and a tourist but no wonder... it wasn't just his appearance, it was his Malayalam that gave him away: it was juvenile and he hesitated, forgetting words. The weaving and jerking made by the auto rickshaw as it sped along congested roads made his body sway this way and that, causing his mind to become excited. This was life without regulations, this was how he liked it after the pressure and confinement of study for his degree. He had more than a vague idea of the way – he hadn't forgotten that. He remembered the name of the hospital near his grandfather's house and had asked the driver to drop him there; so far everything had gone his way. He got out of the auto rickshaw at the hospital and paid the driver. He wanted to walk the rest of the way at his own pace. He passed the tea stall where the drivers used to take their tea and stopped. A few more steps would take him to the smaller road which formed a T-junction with the main road and he knew as soon as he entered the junction the gates would loom up in front of him.

He expected disrepair. Matty had taken loads of footage on his trip the previous year to see his grandfather before he died. Jack didn't expect his entire youth to fill the space between the T-junction and the pink, blue and white cheerful gates that used to be so expertly swung at just the right motion to stay open as the cars sped through and close safely around him as the cars rolled around the drive. He lingered in the shade by the tall walls surrounding the neighbouring houses. Passers-by idled, both those who walked and cycled by and stared at the Sahib. Nobody knew him; he was just another tourist. No doubt they wondered why he was hanging around far from the town and the markets. He squatted down comfortably, his body revelling in the heat, still staring at the gates but living only the past, absolutely stuck in the past.

He could see the compound wall of the Little Pink House just across the road from his grandfather's house, the home he shared with his little brother and parents, but he had spent most of his young life with Grandfather in his house. From where he squatted in the shade he was captivated by the house. The gates had a little more rust on since Matty had taken the video. The white walls were streaked with grey and black by years of monsoon rain. They were so murky that Jack wondered if any maintenance had taken place since his grandmother died. The tiled roof of the bungalow was visible over the wall. That looked intact. From where he alternately stood and squatted in the shade that was all he could see. The roof of the bungalow symbolised the beginning of a mighty change, the beginning of the disintegration of his family.

A defiant enquiry from an old man startled him. 'What is it, what are you doing here?'

Jack stood up. The old man's chin pointed up towards Jack's face, the man's right hand also pointing up, fingers displayed in the shape of a vase. His other arm cradled a large jack-fruit.

'It's nothing,' replied Jack, turning away. He automatically used Malayalam.

'You're not from here, are you?' continued the old man.

'No.' Jack tried to get rid of him, get back inside his head, into the vast familiar and the incongruous, but the old man would not give up.

'Why then, why were you standing here all morning?' He walked along now, following Jack nearer to the gates.

'Who lives in there now?' Since the man wasn't to be shaken off, Jack instinctively became a visitor to his grandfather's house.

'Why do you want to know and what do you mean by now?' persisted the old man.

'Nothing, I used to know someone who lived there, that's all.' Jack was with the present and decided to be vague and play the old man at his own game.

'Who did you know then?' challenged the old man.

'Saroj.' Jack decided to be totally indirect by not mentioning his grandfather's name.

'Aah, the lady of the snakes,' replied the old man thoughtfully.

'Snakes?' queried Jack. 'I never heard that story!' he lied.

'It's not a story,' the old man replied indignantly.

Jack gave a little laugh, putting across that the old man was trying to fool him. He edged a little nearer to the gates, the memories of the snake Ekans in the Little Pink House taking on life again. He was guarded now and didn't dare look in the direction of the dereliction of the Little Pink House which he knew lay in a pile of rubble. It had been demolished since his brother took the footage. This man seemed too near, too careful to trust.

'You won't find her in there,' said the old man authoritatively.

'No? Where then?' asked Jack, looking back at the old man.

'Nobody knows, maybe dead,' the man replied automatically, without thought, all the while lost in his mind while rubbing the stubble on his chin with the forefinger of his right hand.

A teenage boy who had been cycling up and down the road added himself to the couple debating outside the empty house. He parked his bicycle by hanging one leg over the crossbar and propping himself up with the other leg. Jack didn't welcome the intrusion but the cultural habit brought another pleasant, familiar reminder. About the same time an equally ancient and lithe watchman slid his face between the quietly parting gates.

'This young Sahib wants to see the Snake Lady,' the old man said mischievously.

'No Snake Lady here, the bank owns this property,' came a now inquisitive watchman.

'Can I come in and look around?' Jack said in Malayalam. His anxiety overcame him and he leaned to see what the slit in the parted gates revealed.

'He speaks Malayalam,' explained the old man, clasping both palms together.

'Naturally, this was his home,' proclaimed the watchman, quietly confident, and with that he bowed deeply, joining his palms in a reverential *Namaste.*

Then it was Jack who needed to ask the questions, to be the intruder in his own legacy.

'Who are you?' Jack forgot about the parted gates.

'I will give you a clue, just one word... alchemy,' smiled the watchman.

Jack stared at the fungus-blackened pillars not seeing them and then remembered.

'But you were very tall then!' exclaimed Jack emerging from the memory.

'No, you were very small then,' replied the goldsmith.

Jack joined his palms and returned the *Namaste* with sincere respect, and apologised for not remembering.

'Your hair hasn't changed,' smiled Jack.

'How can a Sahib have owned this place?' an impatient and confused old man cut into their memories.

'What do you know? I was his grandmother's jeweller. When he was very little he and his mother would sit as I melted the broken gold ornaments and transformed them into liquid gold and then as it cooled into nuggets. You remember?' He nodded at Jack knowingly, apparently as happy in the memory as Jack was.

From across the road came the sound of English.

'Jack, is it Jack?' Through the gate in the wall where Jack had sheltered all morning from the sun came a more filled-out version of his Maths tutor. *Obviously no longer a student, perhaps a mother, as she held a small girl in her arms.*

'Kumari, you are the same but different – that's not making sense,' Jack shuffled awkwardly, using English, he blushed and looked down at his sandalled feet.

'You too, the same but very tall and very white,' said Kumari, beaming.

A brief exchange of life histories was all the old man would permit. He ordered the watchman to bring the keys to the Little Pink House, for his memories of the family who had lived there were misty but real. He shooed everyone out of the way and escorted Jack through the gates of the place he was least anxious to go.

Jack had minutes to protest, to assert his right to explore his grandfather's house but he allowed himself to be taken into the past through a different gate. He couldn't understand why he was permitting some things to happen to him, to relinquish control and go with the flow of other people's perception of his past. He consciously did not want to use his will to shape his destiny now, he instinctively handed it over to two old men. The Snake Aunt had both intentionally and inadvertently shaped part of the karmas of his entire family and the lives of those who depended on them for work, so why dispute the entrance with the goldsmith and an unknown neighbour?

NANI'S HOUSE

 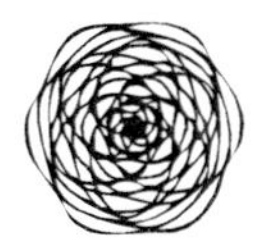

THE LITTLE PINK House lay scattered in its broken red brick and misshapen concrete plaster pieces with blotches of its faded pink paint visible here and there amongst the desolate rubble. The stained pink disturbed Jack: he felt it was saying, *I'm here, don't desert me*. Work had stopped for the new buyer due to a dispute. Apparently the deeds had been mysteriously taken from the bank to which it had been mortgaged at the same time that his aunt had sold it to Jack's cousin, her daughter, for one rupee. Jack couldn't help smiling to himself knowingly: his aunt's behaviour was so predictable. The goldsmith had relayed all this news quietly and with discretion, having rid them of the curious old man. He smiled subtly at Jack's smile. Jack did not envy his father's task at sorting out the jumbled mess of debts.

Jack felt sickened at the sight of the unnecessary destruction and the height of the weeds and long grass. He began to explore; the goldsmith, now turned watchman, cautioned him against entering deeper into the property as snakes were the new residents. He explained that his aunt appeared happier among the weeds which quickly over ran both gardens. This in turn became a habitat for snakes in particular who came to feast on the vermin who found a home in the undergrowth – rats and toads – and no visitors ever entered. Prior to that, Jack's aunt used to turn people away, claiming Jack's grandfather was busy or resting or not in the house. And so the beautiful gardens became a place of dread.

Jack turned and asked the goldsmith if he would take lunch with him at the smaller market where most of the fish, meat and vegetables were bought daily for both houses when he was still a child. The goldsmith was very grateful and willing to accept. Jack enquired if 'Chellapas' was still in business. He had a longing for their fried chicken which was an infrequent dinner treat at his grandfather's. Infrequent because his grandmother had explained to him when he asked to have it at least once a week, how excessive it would have been to send either the watchman or driver to buy it when it cost more than either earned in a week.

After a slow walk in the heat of the midday sun they reached the market and had vegetarian lunch. Jack talked mostly as his companion was very interested to know about London and his university and his new life, what his father did and what his mother did and when and if they were coming home.

It was evening when Jack peered through a gap in the rusted metalwork in one of the double gates which opened on to 'Nani's Home'. It was that time when the heat of the afternoon had reached its extremity for Kerala's rich, green and humid climate. Jack almost immediately slipped back into the past – as it was, as he imagined it always would be in his naivety as if he had been watching, as he often did, the evening routine… *The gardener scooped water with a watering can from the pond in the centre of the garden and sprinkled it over the four grass parterres which surrounded it. There was no other human in the pretty garden, just the sound of the water fountain spilling over and splashing down into the water in the pond, the water lilies seemingly oblivious, accepting the water as it formed itself into jewels in the valleys on their waxed leaves. It was still quite hot; even the roads outside the high walls were silent, just the occasional whisper of rubber flip- flops touching earth as a pedestrian passed and the quiet crunch of a cycle tyre on a stray pebble of tarmac as a lone cyclist passed by.*

His eyes were suddenly drawn to a flash of white among the hibiscus and bougainvillea shrubs which grew all around the garden walls. The night watchman had already arrived and was silently collecting and filling the steel basket with hibiscus flowers and the occasional rose for the temple for the evening offerings, probably making this his offering at the same time and thanking each shrub for the gift of its flower with love and respect. He imagined the two men going calmly on with their tasks without interacting.

He could just imagine the closed front door which he knew would be locked and then his eyes travelled up through the muscular mango branches of the tree nearest the gate to the windows upstairs and he thought again how pretty it all was – its name was 'Nani Bhavan' – which meant Nani's Home, the home of his great-grandmother. And then he thought of what went on inside as his mind slipped easily into the present again, the negative energy still clinging in the darkened, closed rooms and the watchers, he became aware of them again, they were there too, in the garden, beneath the canopy and the beauty of the mango trees, invisible, it was their garden too… thick with weeds and long grass.

The goldsmith-watchman stood by and allowed him to make his own pace into the past.

As the negativity pervaded Jack his eyes travelled to the guest bungalow and he was back… back home…

THE LITTLE PINK HOUSE

THE LITTLE PINK House nestled among the coconut trees with all the other houses. The coconut fronds made green, half-closed umbrellas high above the earth-coloured roofs and all rested quietly under the star-filled night sky, the warm air causing just a breath of movement on the sleeping, giant green fronds.

The nursery was on the east side of the Little Pink House. It was not a large room but it had a very high ceiling, so it was cool. The fan made its slow circular rounds sleepily, wafting the air gently over Jack's bed. He slept on his side with one arm outstretched: no covers, just his cotton, blue-striped pyjamas which had a square cut-out neck to avoid becoming too sweaty, for even in the dark the air was sticky hot inside.

The large, muscular snake was at the window, brushing and pushing against the mosquito netting with his sliding coils. The nursery had two tall windows but the snake always used the window which did not face the netted nursery door which was used between dusk and dawn to keep mosquitoes out. This would have been a much more exposed position for the snake, and it was just across the hall from Jack's parents' bedroom door which also had a netted and a wooden door.

The snake managed to wake the boy by using his head to lunge at the window netting until it made a ripping sound as the separated layers of Velcro which attached it to the window frame gave a little. His hisses disturbed Jack just enough to cause him to roll onto his back but not rouse him from a deep sleep. When the snake vibrated his tail against the netting or even the window frame for any length of time, Jack came out of the profundity of sleep. He felt his eyelids open and close again. Then his ears became aware of the *tud, tud* noise against the netting and he began to understand why he was waking up. It was dark, the street light outside the compound wall gave enough light to see the coils on the window ledge, the flat head kept low.

At first, the very sight of a hefty snake silhouetted against the whitewashed compound wall excited Jack: he felt there was no need to wake his father, just as he hadn't shared the prayer room experience with anyone other than the driver. He liked time to digest the complicated and make his own evaluations. The all-over feeling of reacting to a new situation, literally allowing himself to be swept along wherever it took him, and then he'd deal with it as the unknown changed: it was adventure at its best. Sometimes his body responded before his mind understood fully, mostly he just overruled his mind and went with the physical.

The knowledge of the limited types of anti-venom at the local hospitals flashed briefly into his mind and was quickly dismissed. The snake, although quite long – he reckoned, *maybe a metre and a half or longer* – was outside the netting and even though he was stabbing at the net with his forehead it did not give way: *he could not get in for now anyway.* Jack sat entranced, watching the snake, a wild and dangerous thing, right there on his window ledge a foot or two from his pillow, within touching distance.

This had become a nightly occurrence: Jack would roll over on his side facing the window while the snake undulated until Jack fell asleep again. The first morning he thought it may have been a dream and only remembered the snake when his mother remarked on the dark circles under his eyes at breakfast… *Was he up all night reading again?* A constant complaint of hers as the subject matter was not school textbooks.

The third night on and the snake was becoming a bit of a pain – Jack kept getting thoughts in his mind as if the snake was putting them there. He felt his mind was playing tricks on him due to the danger and the guilt at ignoring his impulse to tell his father.

Come on Little Lord, open the net for me, I can protect you, be your friend, have no fear, you have friends, no living person can hurt you. He'd crouch his head low, dark inanimate eyes ever fixed on Jack's.

Jack tried to stop the thoughts forming in his mind, he reasoned that if he understood what the snake wanted perhaps the snake understood his apprehension.

'*Nala*,' – 'Tomorrow,' – he said in Malayalam and briefly thought about tomorrow, before closing the shutters. He carefully hooked them and went back to sleep.

DISCLOSURE

ON THE FOURTH morning he decided to share the snake secret with his school friend Akhill, to sound him out. He was reluctant to tell his parents as he knew that would be the end of the nightly adventures. Khalid, the third member of the group, was not at school, fortunately, as Jack felt he would be much more proactive and this was a dangerous situation for a friend who hardly ever engaged his mind.

Akhill was short and although not obese, was fleshier than Jack. He was an only child and had a TV in his bedroom, something that was banned in Jack's home. Some days Akhill actually hallucinated due to lack of sleep and twenty-four-hour MTV, which was only broadcast on cable and which everyone loved, everyone who had it.

Akhill and Jack took their lunches at one of the homes next door to their school. For a small fee some families allowed children the use of their dining rooms, those who preferred to take their tiffins privately rather than eat on the school premises in the classrooms, where lunch was taken.

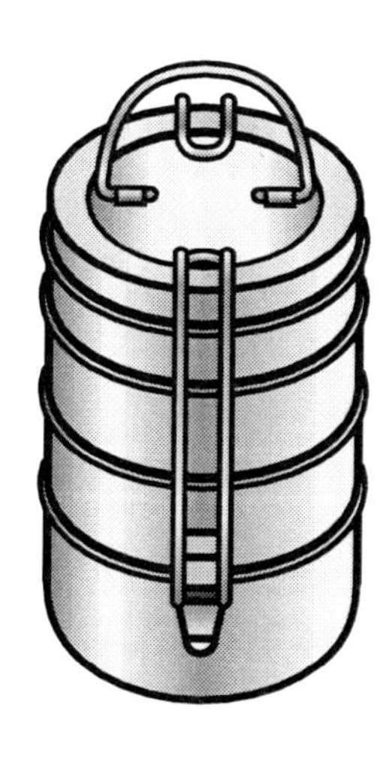

Their bearers collected the tiffins from their homes and cycled into the Christian enclave with the warm rice and curry in the circular, stacked steel containers forming cylinders which were deposited at the house ready for the hungry boys at mid-day. It was a tradition Jack's mother continued due to the discrepancy in food, most parents could only afford rice and pickle.

Akhill pushed his tiffin away the minute he heard about the snake. Apparently he was not able to digest the food: his excitement kept meeting the food on the way up, it was impossible to keep on pushing more rice into his mouth which would have to be swallowed into the block of exhilaration. Jack noticed and was not a little surprised at his friend's reaction.

The boys used English as Akhill's family came from another state and spoke a different language. Communication between peoples from different states all over India was in English.

'What if he gets in while you're asleep, Jack? You'd wake up just to feel the coils tightening round your chest. No… it's too risky, you must do something.'

'It's a young constrictor Akhill, I don't think he'd have the strength to crush my ribs. Anyway I'm not really sure what type of a snake it is yet,' Jack replied impatiently.

'Well… if it is a constrictor it could squeeze itself around your neck and then inject the paralysing venom… Anyway, how do you know if it really is or is not a constrictor? We never see them in town.' Akhill still couldn't believe a fairly large snake could stay unnoticed for so many days inside a garden with dogs.

'I checked it out in Grandfather's library, there was a book on Herpetology. I rechecked his markings with my reading lamp, I'm almost sure he is a constrictor but his markings are not exactly those of a python and if he is he will not have venom…' said Jack, just managing to over-ride the impulse to do the right thing, yet again.

'Wait, wait I read once… I think it was in *National Geographic*… that some constrictors have a venom which is not lethal… it stuns the prey… It showed a picture of a rat… while the animal is stunned the snake quickly twists and tightens its coils around the chest squeezing the breath out and then swallows it,' explained Akhill.

'Akhill do you know anything about telepathy?' Jack raced on, ignoring his friend's warning.

'Isn't that sending thoughts to another person?' Akhill enquired, pulling his tiffin closer.

'Yeah,' said Jack, surprised at the MTV man's knowledge.

'Why?' Akhill asked avidly, his eyes widening open, a handful of rice suspended halfway to his mouth.

'Well… I think I can hear him inside my head,' Jack said, half-regretting his veracity.

'Wow, man…' Akhill slapped the table causing the old woman dozing on the veranda to rouse up.

'Shush,' whispered Jack.

'What's he saying to you?' The tip of Akhill's nose was now almost touching Jack's from the far side of the table, as he leaned and stretched in an effort to extract even more information on the dangerous nocturnal visitor. The rice did not make it to his mouth.

'I think he's asking me to open the mosquito netting, or maybe I'm just imagining it,' said Jack, now reddening and truly embarrassed.

'Are you sending him back thoughts?' Akhill remained eager, enticing Jack to continue.

'No… I just speak to him in Malayalam, telling him to get lost mostly…' said Jack, feeling he had missed out on an opportunity to experiment with the wild beast, upset that he hadn't thought of it himself.

'I'm coming over this evening. Where is he during the day?' Akhill had immersed himself a little too deeply for Jack.

'We really have to be careful Akhill, I don't want Matty or Mum to become suspicious,' scrabbled Jack, who was no longer able to eat either and began layering the individual steel containers and inserted the bar through the handle to secure it as one carrier.

'We'll use a code name for him,' Akhill suggested enthusiastically, trying to mollify Jack.

'Like what… Kaa from *The Jungle Book*…?' It was getting too realistic for Jack, part of him wanted the python to be his own in the dark hours but he realised he needed to make sense of the snake's actual existence too.

'Com'on, that's not fair,' Akhill muttered, stung by Jack's jeering.

'OK, OK, I guess it'll be a help if we can talk about him openly,' Jack forfeited, not meaning to hurt his friend.

'E.K.A.N.S.,' said Akhill after sitting in silence for a while.

Jack, who still half-regretted sharing his secret with his friend, rose from the table.

'What?' Jack asked, crossing out of the veranda.

'Thanks Mrs Fernandez.'

'See you boys tomorrow,' the fully awake elderly woman replied in English, getting up.

'E.K.A.N.S.' repeated Akhill.

'That's the name for the snake?' queried Jack, one hand shoved into his white trouser pocket, eyebrows meeting.

'It's a code,' Akhill insisted, running to catch up with Jack's long stride.

'What? Like a cipher?' Jack turned towards Akhill as they neared the school gate.

'No, not that complicated, it's just "snake" spelled backwards,' said Akhill in an effort to be modest but failing to hide the superior look on his face.

'A mirror ambigram… Wow, yeah, great… OK, Ekans it is then,' Jack was silenced and thoroughly impressed with his friend who usually came across as superficial.

QUARRY

AS DARKNESS ROLLED over the Little Pink House and the sounds of nightfall began, the boys had been in Jack's room for over an hour hoping for and intent on sighting Ekans. Matty appeared in the doorway as the two boys sat on Jack's bed, their backs to him, staring through the netted window.

'Is that Dodo, do you see him?' fretfully Matty pushed the boys apart.

'Dodo, who's Dodo?' Akhill shot back at Jack, jumping aside, his nervousness apparent.

'Dodo is his pet rabbit,' said Jack quickly, trying to placate Akhill, following his line of thought.

'Is your rabbit missing?' enquired Akhill, now calmer but intensely interested.

'Yes, the watchman can't find him anywhere, neither can I. We've searched the whole garden, and the car shed, even the kennels, even though I know he wouldn't go in there.' Matty turned around and plonked down on the bed between the two older boys, totally dejected.

'What about Mrs Dodo and the litter?' Jack queried, trying to appear calm.

'They were out earlier and we put them in and then let Daddy Dodo out for a run, but now he's gone.' Matty's chin was on his chest, his words barely audible.

'Why can't they go out together? Are they divorced?' asked a now mildly more relaxed but sarcastic Akhill.

'Daddy Dodo eats his offspring,' replied Jack, eyes towards the ceiling, as he talked over the dispirited Matty's head. 'So he lives in the hutch alone until the rabbits are bigger.'

Mum appeared in the hall outside the netted door.

'Come on Matty, we'll find him tomorrow, he may have burrowed into the lawn and found a new home for himself. Let's go, it's supper time now.'

'Do you think he has? He never did it before, though,' replied Matty hopefully, allowing the netted door to swing closed as he was led towards the kitchen.

'Akhill your driver says it's time to go too,' Mum called back.

'You are going to have to do something now,' Akhill commanded, staring hard at Jack. It was obvious to both that the missing rabbit may have already been consumed as Jack realised the consequences of having the possibility of a python or some other type of deadly snake in the family garden.

'I know, I know, just one more night…' said Jack petulantly. He just wanted a little more time to try telepathy on the snake.

Jack woke in the middle of the night not to the sound of scales on wood or netting but by a horrendous scream, followed by the bang of a door and then animated whispers from his parents' bedroom. Before he reached the netted door, after checking his empty window-ledge his father was unlocking the front door and shouting at the sleeping watchman. He found his mother sitting on the edge of her bed, looking at her bolted bathroom door.

'What's wrong, Mum?' enquired Jack, dreading what he knew her answer would be but still clinging to the shadow of a hope that it might not be, all at the same time.

'There's a snake in the bathroom, a big one,' she replied looking up at him. *She didn't appear to be as shaken as he'd expected.*

'Did it bite you?' Jack moved closer focusing on her porcelain white ankles which were just visible below her kaftan. There was a weight inside his chest now and he was glad of the paralysis in his throat as he may have spilled everything like he had to Vishu less than a week ago because the same hopelessness enveloped him.

'No, no…' her words trailed off. 'He was just lying coiled up on the mat around the toilet,' she continued, not taking her eyes away from the tiny slit at the bottom of the bathroom door where it met the floor. 'I only managed to see him because the mat is yellow. If he'd been on the mosaic I wouldn't have seen him at all, the tiles are the same colour as his skin,' she continued with a vacuous expression, her Irish accent more pronounced.

Jack's father rushed by with a large wooden plank and pugnaciously locked himself in with the snake. Jack rushed against the bathroom door, banging on it with his fists, pleading with his father to come out. He could hear the watchman from his grandparents' house beseeching him from outside not to kill the snake, warning him in his dirge-voice of the consequences of killing a snake on home property. From inside came the clatter, bangs and shattering sounds as Jack's father supposedly walloped the broad board down on the evading snake. Jack's mother now joined him at the door, her face full of fear, she didn't implore him to stop as Jack was still begging, sometimes even pleading.

'That's the china toothbrush holder in smithereens,' remarked his mother quietly while chewing on her thumbnail, eyes wide, staring at Jack blankly.

'What?' Jack turned from the door giving her an astounded look, aware of the smashing china on the tiled floor as well as the frantic foot movement at the other side of the locked door. He wanted to shout at her but noticed she still had the inane expression. *It must be her way of coping*, he thought.

Just then the grandparents quietly and quickly joined mother and son outside the bathroom door. Jack lost all the pent-up frustration and began to implore his grandfather.

'Please make Dad come out, there's a snake in there, please Grandfather, please.'

It was whatever transacted between grandfather and son through that locked bathroom door that caused his father to emerge, sweating, shirtless with club in hand and uncharacteristic dishevelled hair.

Jack was numb all over. All he could understand was how reckless he had been. His mother could have been bitten, the deadly venom quickly quietening her if Akhill's theory was correct, possibly strangled in the silence of the night. The snake was young and if it was a python it would be large and strong enough to chock the life out of her if the coils were positioned correctly – and a python would instinctively know where.

Jack felt certain now that the snake had been Dodo's nemesis. He imagined the strangling muscles tightening with every exhaled breath and the sensors under the snake skin registering when his prey, Dodo's, pulse beat no more.

His father who knew nothing about snakes was protecting his family with a fight or flight reaction, and all because of his Jack's indulgence.

COMPREHENSION

 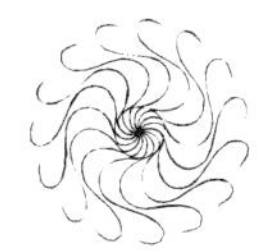

GRANDMOTHER JOINED JACK as he sat on the edge of the bed and patted his hand, 'It's all over son, it's all over. Your Dad is here, see.'

Jack was aware of his in-breaths, he was aware of the air-conditioner he was staring at, he was aware of Grandfather and his father in deep discussion and saw them pass the bedroom window as they headed out into the garden. He watched through the window as his mother offer tea which nobody accepted, *not without first brushing their teeth, didn't she know that!* But he knew she would go to the kitchen anyway and boil the electric kettle. It was like being underwater, muffled sounds and quietly life went on.

'Where's everyone, Grandmother?' he asked as he slowly emerged into the there and then.

'We're sending for the snake-catchers, the rubber estate-manager will go to Thiruvallur district of Tamil Nadu early in the morning. The Irulas will take the snake away in a sack and release it in the forest after draining some of the venom, if it has any,' she said in her quiet reassuring way.

It took some time for Jack to become himself again. His knees no longer shook, so he stood up and was aware of the cold floor. He headed out into the garden, slipper-less, followed by Grandmother. They joined the little congregation now gathered underneath the ventilations of the bathroom with the snake. Both watchmen and his father and Grandfather were quietly discussing while checking the sand and drains with torches. There was no trace in the sand that a weaving body would make and the metal covers over the drains had not been disturbed. When Jack heard next door's watchman, who was old, wizened and never reined in his tongue even with Grandmother, he made a vital but devastating connection.

'It's impossible for a snake to climb a vertical and smooth wall; however it got in, it wasn't through the ventilations or the drains.'

Jack had once more entered that bleak, fearful place, the realisation of a force working against their peaceful existence. The deadly lump in his stomach was hard and heavy again. If only he had connected the sight of the python with what he witnessed in the prayer room on that very first night, these near-death experiences would have been avoided. *The question now – was the snake meant for him or his mother? Or having had no results with him, was it then directed to his mother?* Jack walked trance-like towards the back veranda where his mother was seated in the wicker chair sipping from a mug of hot tea.

'Are you alright?' she enquired.

'I don't think I can face school tomorrow!' he said and meant it. The covert danger was omnipresent, deadening and dark on his mind.

'Don't worry,' she assured him. 'One day will not matter and Harvest Holidays are just round the corner. I'm sure you won't miss much.'

She seems to be back to normal, he thought. As he was about to move on, the rabbit image appeared and he turned to face her again.

'Mum – Dodo, do you think…'

'Probably,' she said. 'I was just thinking that too.'

'Matty will never get over this,' said Jack languidly, sitting down heavily on the wicker recliner.

'He can have the day off too. He'll be really into the Snake and Rat Catchers. Just don't mention Dodo, let him come to the possibility of the snake swallowing the rabbit himself. He'll get over it. The excitement of having a python in the bathroom will make up for the loss of Dodo.'

'Hope so,' Jack replied hopelessly, head hanging over his lap and cold, wet and dusty feet.

'How many times has Dodo nipped your toes over the years?' his mother began reminiscing.

'Yeah, I know,' Jack continued in a lamenting tone, musing guiltily over Dodo's attacks from underneath the armchair valance. Dodo had pounced and assaulted Jack's toes, just Jack's and nobody else's. Jack was too exhausted to remember the last time he did it. He would never do it again.

THE SNAKE CATCHERS

JACK RINSED HIS feet under the tap in his bathroom and lay down on the bed but couldn't sleep. His mind was too active, full of its own chatter about the snake, the prayer room and the phantom. The difficulty was that when Jack explored these events in his head it felt like they encompassed his very person, like a grey cloud; they were persistent and there was very little he could to rid himself of them. The thought of accepting the events felt as though they were suffocating him. He didn't want any of them to be real. Firstly, who should he confide in? His parents and grandparents would definitely not believe him, Jack, the reader of *Star Wars* novels. And then there was Akhill and Khalid, his friends: they were considered by his father to be the daftest friends. He could hear his father's voice in his head: *Jack manages to pick the worst people, ever since he was in kindergarten. Why can't he have the potential engineers or budding chemists… studious types? No, trust Jack not to do anything normal.*

And why should he anyway? Some of those geeks were the most boring people on earth and just because they came first in the class didn't mean they were intelligent, no, most of them were well-trained parrots, who learned by heart without sometimes the faintest idea of understanding what they were learning, whereas his friends Akhill and Khalid were smart when they wanted to be. Like himself they didn't overtax the brain with school stuff until about two weeks before an exam. What his Dad had overlooked was the fact that to get admission into his school you had to be a top ranker in the first place and the three of them were in the top ten in class.

Jack considered Akhill's interference when he had divulged the news of Ekans. Somehow or other it didn't feel right to expose the family secrets to him or Khalid either. The only other person was the driver Vishu, and there was a possibility that Vishu may feel Jack was exaggerating and Jack himself was reluctant to involve the driver and risk the loss of his job. No, it seemed to Jack that he was alone with the evil occupier; he wondered what it was all about.

Why would his aunt want to rid the family of his grandmother and himself or his mother?

The sounds of morning started at the Little Pink House. His bathroom was in demand as the one attached to the big bedroom was out of bounds. Matty was so excited that he wanted to climb on a ladder and peer into the bathroom from the outside to have a look at the snake, which was forbidden in case the snake could scale a ceramic tiled wall. So they waited and waited for Indian Tie to bring the Snake Catchers. Indian Tie was the rubber estate manager and highly respected in the family for his knowledge of all things rural and wild. He was only referred to as Indian Tie in the Little Pink House because Jack's mother couldn't pronounce and therefore couldn't remember Indian names very well in the beginning when she first came thirteen years earlier, so she used nicknames on a lot of people. There was Wobbly Aunty because she was a perfect round shape, with a moon-shaped face and a balloon tummy and she sort of wobbled like a skittle. There was Buddha Uncle who always sat naked from the waist up with his mundu made katcha-style. He did look like a Chinese Buddha; he had a shaven head and an enormous tummy. Then there was Toad Aunty because she too was fat and had an extra hanging large chin that made her toad-like. But Indian Tie was the most ambiguous name ever. Indian Tie wore a Khadi mundu which was see-through cotton and in a particular light his hips were visible. Jack's father had assured Jack's mother that the manager did wear underwear, a traditional type of underwear called an Indian Tie which comprised of a triangle of cotton with three strings, so from then on he was known as Indian Tie.

However this nicknaming hadn't gone as smoothly as Jack's mother had wished because his father had disclosed some of the funnier ones to Jack's aunt when she was on a visit many years ago, much to the annoyance of his mother who gave his father a scolding which resulted in one of his many sulking moods, referred to by the family as a 'chutty' mood. Grandmother confirmed he had always been prone to them: 'chutty' meant two cheeks like the round bottoms of the clay pots which were used on the traditional fires in the kitchens in Grandfather's house. Over the years Jack noted that the sulking had reduced from a week to about a day and around that time his father seemed to have them more frequently, not so much with him or his mother but more to do with the business and Grandfather, judging from snippets of conversation Jack had overheard.

All that morning the grey cloud felt like it clung to Jack and every time he needed to pass his parents' bedroom door the closed bathroom door stood large and the cloud felt like it was suffused with guilt which suffocated him.

After lunch his mother used Jack's bedroom for her nap as she didn't feel at ease in her own room. Around four o'clock when everyone was stirring again

Jack heard the bolt pull back on the gate and many voices in quiet conversation. He headed for the front door only to be beaten to it by Matty who was also on high alert, waiting and waiting for a glimpse of the snake.

Indian Tie was there with his deferential *Namaste* to Jack's mother and her translator. Jack noted his traditional garb while he translated: *more like a sanyasi than an estate manager, he wore no sandals and his heels were crevassed like an elephant's foot.* Matty – who was not used to seeing him as he generally visited Grandfather in the evenings when Grandfather came home from the office – now focused his stare at Indian Tie's mouth which had a sort of underbite with half his upper front teeth missing. Jack wished that Matty would not gawk so much but knew that Matty everything he did had intensity, and irritatingly the examination of the jaws continued.

Polite greetings finished, the Snake Catchers' elder stepped forward. He too was barefoot and very thin with a very dark skin which was deeply lined as was the skin of the other three men in the group. Questions were asked and answered but this time Jack could not understand the Snake Catcher and relied on Indian Tie to translate into Malayalam for him. This left Jack in a bit of a quandary as he was not supposed to have seen the snake and his mother had a poor description as she saw it only in the faint glow from the garden light which shone through the bathroom ventilations. He decided to have no input and therefore he learned nothing new about capturing the snake or anything else which interested him from the exchange. They all proceeded around to the back veranda where lime juice was taken and a plate of biscuits left untouched. By this time Matty had shifted his focus to the Snake Catcher's bag. While the men drank he whispered to Jack:

'Do you think there are any snakes inside it?'

'How should I know?' answered Jack, still under his grey cloud of responsibility. The questioning had made him nervous again.

As the boys followed the snake catchers through the big bedroom, Jack's mother called them back into the hall but Indian Tie urged her to let them come in, with calm hand signals conveying confidence in the Snake Catchers. Matty had stretched from behind the estate manager to watch the Snake Catcher who had squatted and had started to play a quiet but melodious tune on the tiniest flute that Jack had ever seen. The others did not move into the open door of the bathroom, instead staying beside the flute player and waiting.

Both Jack and Matty were mystified as the snake slid along the floor to the feet of the catchers. Jack's mother had been positioned behind the boys with a hand on both their shirts and when the snake appeared she tightened her grip as if to yank them out of the bedroom should the snake come through the door. The elder catcher bent low, caught the snake expertly and manoeuvred it to enclose it in his bag. As if this had not mesmerised Jack enough he found himself groping for the bed for he needed to sit. The snake he saw going into the bag was not the snake he had watched so keenly from his bedroom window for three nights running. This was a different snake. As the little throng left the room he quickly caught up with the estate manager and asked what type of snake it was. The manager had words with the Snake Catcher who wore the bag and even before a translation Jack saw him shake his head.

'This is a very unusual snake,' replied the manager as the Snake Catchers dispersed in the garden in search of more snakes.

'Has it venom?' questioned Jack.

'They don't know. It has teeth but they can't tell yet,' replied the manager and at the same time Jack could not help the feeling that the manager was being vague; but why did he not know, which was unusual for him. Or was the manager hiding something?

'Matty, stay on the veranda, it's safer to watch from here especially while they are playing the flute. Snakes could come from anywhere,' ordered their mother.

'But Daisy is out,' protested Matty, halfway down the steps.

'The snakes won't touch the dog while the flute is being played. Come up here, come on Matt, the best view of everything is from here,' she urged.

COBRA'S NEST

UNKNOWN TO JACK, it had been decided that the grounds in Grandfather's house were also to be checked. As Indian Tie came to bid goodbye, Jack realised they were going next door. The boys immediately begged to go too but Jack's mother would not let them go alone. However, by this time Jack's father had returned from the office. Too tired to play tennis after the night's events, he too joined the throng going to Nani Bhavan, along with the ayah who followed after being given instructions to lock the house.

It was there, at the very rear of the compound in the wood pile by the back wall, a place that Grandmother had begged Jack over and over never to play near, in that very place, it was discovered that nine young cobras and their mother lived: they had fed and grew. Jack would never again dismiss Grandmother's advice. The guilt of disregarding her, and the danger he had drawn Matty into only recently, shocked Jack like an unexpected slap. Matty and he had played games there in the afternoons when everyone else napped; sometimes the young girls from the kitchen would join in and weave coconut skirts and head dresses for them and teach them their games. Occasionally the boys would bring their carom board and play with the girls on the kitchen veranda in the shade only feet from killer venom.

The search intensified for the father cobra but he was not found, or perhaps he was not in the property, but in that search, fourteen more snakes of varying types were found and bagged. It was dusk by that time and so, alarmed by the sheer number of snakes, Grandmother asked if the catchers would search the house too. What Jack found strange about this was his aunt's objection: he could hear her berating his grandmother and eventually she approached his grandfather. However, Jack's father had been standing watching the search with him and he dismissed his aunt and her pleas. Jack ceased watching the catchers and followed the aunt into the house, but just as quickly he lost her. After searching every room downstairs and upstairs in the newer wing he noticed her creep out of one of the back doors which were normally closed, in the unused wing. He watched her through the dining room windows as she headed in the direction of one of the outhouses that had been already searched.

'Saroj, Saroj,' called Grandmother, and on seeing Jack she asked him to open up all the closed rooms and the library for the house search. So caught up with this, Jack did not have a chance to follow the aunt and the next time he saw her was in the big kitchen, directing the cook to prepare a meal for the snake catchers.

Later, while the adults sat and debated, around the dining room table, on the numbers of dangerous snakes and how they could exist in the grounds despite measures to keep the entire compound clean, having every inch swept every morning and the watch dogs prowl at night. Jack was now very sure his aunt was up to something very sinister and snakes were very much a part of it.

'What if Hemani or Aasha had been hurt?' Grandmother said quietly.

'Who?' enquired Jack's father.

'The cook and the small kitchen girl,' Jack's mother reminded him.

In all the years that Jack had disobeyed and played around the back near and often on the wood pile, even helping Aasha carry the wood in for the fires, he had never encountered even a young snake. Always aware of where he placed his feet and hands because of Grandmother's warnings, he had encountered nothing more threatening than a toad, the odd lizard and plenty of cockroaches. Grandfather was very particular about cleanliness, changing the sand all over the compound frequently and every inch of it was swept each morning. There had to be a reason for such an influx of snakes and listening to the adult conversation he heard some were those worshipped in Hinduism and some were considered unclean creatures.

Jack noted that his aunt had nothing to add to the conversation and his cousin Nisha appeared uninterested, even bored with the whole event, while her elder sister Girija helped Matty with books in the library which had been opened; even the bookcases had been checked for snakes.

HOLIDAYS

 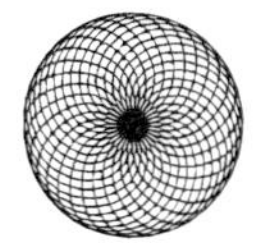

IT WAS THE Harvest Festival holidays and the aura of activity next door was tangible. Even before he was fully awake Jack could hear the gates yawn loudly on their hinges; the murmuring voices filed through with their head loads and skeleton men pulled laden, shafted carts, tugging them over the rises and slowing them on the dips in the side road leading to the front gates.

It was always the same flurry of preparation and like Christmas it never lost its magical anticipation. Jack had no need to get out of bed to watch the procession filtering into the garden, briskly moving along by the front of the bungalow, through the gate between the garage and the main house, which separated the garden from the back. Along by the kennels near the compound wall on one side and the original and now unused part of the house on the other, jutting out like the top horizontal line of a capital 'E' and rounding the corner, the middle part of the 'E' jutting out with the dining room and European kitchen which had been modified for his mother's arrival but never used by her. Then along and across between the house and the cow shed, the biogas digester on one side and finally the bottom line of the 'E' on the other, over towards the old kitchen veranda where the fires would be built, encased in quickly-laid brick square grates on which the huge brass vats would be stirred with paddles the size of sweeping brush handles.

When Jack was little he would nag his mother to have the night watchman take him across the road at just past the crack of dawn when the crows were rasping their *ka, kas* the loudest. Delighted, his grandfather would sit down with him on the mosaic stoop of the front door and watch. Grandfather would quietly scold him for not stopping to brush his teeth and never allowed him to have the forbidden tea until he did. His mother was strict regarding diet: it was juice, water or milk, no stimulants.

That morning his grandfather, as always, would be in the garden exercising by walking round and round the drive, a part-time spectator of the procession of food makers. In recent times Grandfather's mood had not been consistent, he would sometimes use critical vocabulary and it appeared to Jack that he felt the admonishing which had been dealt him caused his grandfather great anxiety; it was as if something compelled him to find fault, whereas before, he found fun. Sadly Jack rolled over and reached for his book. Luke Skywalker's world took precedence and anyway Nisha would not be up this early.

No, Onam would be confined to sitting on his own stoop the next morning with Matty and his mother as they watched Mary, the ayah, magic a *pookalam* on the concrete, from flower petals, rice flour, and dyed grains like rock salt – he kept forgetting to ask her what exactly the coloured tiny rocks were made of, all he knew was that she ordered them from the market with the rest of the groceries, so they must have been easily available. Every year the *pookalam* would be different, last year was a circle with elongated triangles merging at their smallest angle at the centre. Jack was amazed at the precision this young woman wove into her creation without the use of a string or any other instrument of measurement and how she graduated the colour and matched each section with what flower petals were available to her in the gardens. The accuracy, Jack felt, was nothing short of Fibonacci mathematics.

That year she did not ask for flowers from the next door garden. She, like Jack, had been made to feel the aunt's wrath when she went with the family for Sunday lunch. Mary had come to them when she was sixteen and Matty was still a toddler; she was Matty's ayah and slowly learned basic cooking and how to clean. She was saving her salary for her dowry, hoping to marry and have her own family. Jack's mother had romantic ideas about Anthony's son, who was the messenger for the factories and did the shopping for both the houses. His son was a trainee plumber and Christian like Mary, and Jack had to admit he did notice the shy, embarrassed exchanges between the two when Anthony's son was asked to come to repair dripping bathroom taps or the pipe from the well to the storage tank on the roof.

The thought of his mother reminded him of the staff gifts, all wrapped and piled on the desk in the middle hallway. Nobody wrapped Onam gifts and he somehow felt embarrassed for his mother as she gave out the pink paper enveloped gift to each domestic employee. Every gift was the same: a piece of fabric for the making of a shirt and a dhoti for men and a sari fabric for the blouse and a petticoat which matched the main colour of the sari for the women. She did this even for Jack's father's family. Jack considered how it must be impossible to eradicate certain habits.

COUSINS

THESE HOLIDAYS WERE different. It was the first time that his aunt and cousins were staying permanently. Previously they would come for a few days and go back to their home three hundred miles away near the Western Ghats.

Jack was delighted to have company nearer his own age, even if his favourite cousin Girija was a bit older. That wasn't the case with his younger cousin Nisha: she had a sense of humour too, but was moody and not a little devious. They shared the car to school; she was dropped off at the girl's school first and Jack and Matty continued on to the Christian enclave for four more miles.

Nisha was a reluctant riser and had problems. Jack had rare insights when they were getting on really well. It seemed that she wanted to share but would suddenly snap firmly the lid of her tin-box mind, locking whatever was on the tip of her tongue within, agitated as if she had to beat the word-thoughts back down, away from where they occasionally crept. She was good at concealment but there was a sad drip of disclosure when rarely she spoke of her absent father.

'Everyone says you look just like your father,' she'd say. 'And then they'd sigh.' This just heaped more guilt on what she called her refugee status.

She hated her new school and everybody in it.

'No friends and no prospects either, the stupid teacher can't even pronounce English properly, imagine, saying le-o-pard for leopard!' All this she proclaimed loudly and to everyone.

And then there was Grandmother.

'Grandmother the Reverend Mother, modesty in all things, no cream cakes from the bakery for tea, just bread which nobody eats and which is given to the dogs with milk for breakfast! And sardine curry for dinner, all bones and no fish and such a strong fishy smell.' Nisha accompanied this with a little shudder.

'Do I look like a bear?' she'd question Jack, eyes wide, arms spread and palms upwards.

'And as for the rice, always the healthy rose rice from Grandma's own paddy fields, never beautiful basmati. What happened to the days of biryiani?' she'd implore.

Her apt descriptions left Jack chuckling with amusement. It didn't bother him as he had most of his meals at home. He had never considered food a discomfort until he experienced Nisha's plight.

'Then nag, nag, nag even from Mummy. It was alright for her, she grew up here, she had all this order and correct behaviour before. No running through the house, no loud laughing…' she would lean her chin on the heel of her hand, the corners of her mouth arching down, and the large, beautiful eyes would blindly stare, lifeless.

Jack had suggested a sleep-over at his house the Little Pink House to give her a break but porridge and cornflakes for breakfast wasn't her thing either; she said the porridge sat like a stone in her stomach all morning. So Jack's mother would prepare dosa batter the night before if there was sufficient notice of a sleep-over, which was accepted by all except Grandmother who had her reservations on a cultural issue. It was a custom that certain cousins could marry in India and Jack and Nisha were such cousins but were unaware of it. Grandmother was reassured that they were still children and nothing like romance had entered their minds as yet.

It was more or less true: very young teenagers were not as sexually progressive as those in western cultures, as Jack discovered on his annual trips to Ireland. There he felt he got away with it by remaining quiet on the subject, through sheer ignorance. This inadvertently gave the impression he had a girlfriend but he was not going to talk about any aspect of the relationship either in a general or knowing manner.

SMOKE

DURING THE ONAM holidays businesses either closed or slowed for the week, except for the shops, which were crowded with people buying cloth for the making of clothes or actual ready-mades, clothing being the traditional gift exchanged and given to employees. This meant that Jack's father was at home longer in the mornings and at siesta time and would sometimes hold meetings in the Little Pink House. To avoid having to be quiet and leave Matty in peace as he preferred to be on his own, Jack decided to check out the activity next door.

Nisha and he had decided on a sleep-over at Grandmother's and he wanted to remind her to have the two rooms upstairs cleaned. Nisha usually shared a room with her mother on the ground floor next to his grandparents' bedroom but when Jack stayed over they had a room each upstairs. They played cards on the landing which was large enough to be used as a sitting room and had sofas and armchairs and a dining table since his mother lived there before he was born. As long as they didn't make too much noise and stayed off the balcony Grandmother, although not entirely happy, didn't grumble.

It was almost the end of September and the clouds were liquid black paint dissolving in watery sky motion and threatening even more monsoon rain. This meant shorter power cuts, lots of smelly towels which hung in the ironing room taking two to three days to dry and fans and air conditioners became redundant. It also meant everyone was sniffling or coughing due to colds and mosquitoes were everywhere; it seemed the whole place was sogging wet. The monsoon was needed and everyone hoped it would last much longer than in previous years.

Jack picked his way across the road which separated Nani Bhavan from the Little Pink House, lifting his trouser legs and avoiding puddles. There were a couple of drivers standing by the cars under the bungalow parapet. He threw an acknowledgement eye in their direction and they moved respectfully releasing their dhotis to fall to their feet as he passed.

Grandfather was in conference with a couple of men in the front hall so Jack nipped around through the side gate in the direction of the many back doors, all of which were open and busy. Kitchen girls struggled with weighed down steel containers. Grandmother was busy supervising the allocation of raw ingredients from the store room for the big cook up.

Jack wove a zig-zag path through all the labourers and the giant cooking vessels in the back yard and headed into the big traditional kitchen. He loved the atmosphere there created by the smoke from the open fires which darkened the walls on its way upwards to the exit through the specially constructed open roof tiles which lay exposed between the rafters. These were positioned directly over the fire grates. When the smoke ascended as it did every morning and forenoon those open roof tiles shone beams of light which mixed with the rising smoke. It was after lunch had been served and the kitchen was empty and the last of the smoke from the embers rose to mingle with the rays of light that Jack felt the place most hallowed. The light from above beamed down in several rays lighting up the gloom causing another worldly atmosphere. The occasional silent emergence from a darkened corner of a servant girl who gazed at Jack in the same way he gazed at the beams of light was often altogether unreal. Mostly he'd only become aware of the other soul when he'd had his fill of the image and turned to leave.

But not that day. The hired cook was already at work making his famous pathiris, he was beating and pushing the dough on the table and Jack gave him a wide welcoming smile, accompanied by his name receiving an equally heartfelt *Namaste* in return. Jack felt that the flaky, layered, circular and warm breads would go a long way in cheering Nisha up.

Jack moved on through the kitchen and into the next room with difficulty. This was a servants' dining room where the household and senior factory workers of Onam were fed. Here the clanging of brass and steel, the crowds of temporary workers sipping their warm tea and the conversations and disagreements as to whether the outside fires should be started with the lingering rain filled his head.

He pushed his way past it all and on into the corridor past the store room door, turned right into the corridor which ran along by the dining room and then into the open room leading to the drawing room and ground-floor bedrooms and stairs.

WATCHER

HE FOUND NISHA, eyelids half-closed, neck poking out of a kaftan and hair hanging tangled all around her face and shoulders, like a demoness. She was wandering zombie-like towards the dining room in search of breakfast. They always communicated in English ever since Jack was little and didn't speak Malayalam.

'You just up?' Jack asked.

Nisha didn't reply in words, just a sleepy 'Mmmm…', barely audible, and walked past him. Jack thought: *evidently forced to get up early again.*

Jack helped himself to a second breakfast. It was Vella Appam, his favourite: a fried-egg shape of ground rice flour and coconut milk with a little coconut alcohol to help the fermentation process. The result was delicious, a lithe appam with just a hint of the coconut vapour-like sweetness, like the effect of sherry in a trifle, but a totally different experience. He had three to Nisha's unfinished one!

Aunt Saroj appeared and immediately a strong exchange in Malayalam took place, most of it from the aunt who was pointing in the direction of their bathroom in imperative tones. Nisha's replies were mumbled and at first pleading, pitiful. Before too long she pushed back her dining chair causing it to scrape loudly on the mosaic floor. She washed her hands hastily and stormed out. It was the old familiar about not being bathed and dressed. Jack washed his hands and left without reminding Nisha about getting the upstairs rooms ready. With moods like those, the sleep-over could be sabotaged, it wasn't the time and anyway his aunt had nothing but baleful looks for him since the prayer room incident. He felt she too must sense his scrutiny and the loss of innocence in their relationship. He had never confronted her, or she him; confrontation was not practised in this family and anyway he considered Vishu's advice to be the safest – *know nothing.* But he watched her, tried to understand her and wondered why she really moved back home.

That night Jack's parents had been invited to dinner. Everyone got together early in the dining room for evening tea. There were lots of visitors, mainly family.

It was late when Grandfather's house returned to its normal quiet. Jack, and the pale face and dark-circled eyes of his little brother who had begged to be part of the sleep-over, fell into a deep sleep. It was about two when Jack woke, realising he hadn't taken up drinking water. His tongue was rough, arid and felt swollen and the roof of his mouth was parched. He reckoned if he was very quiet he could manage to open the middle door downstairs leading to the dining room and the water filter without frightening Grandmother. She didn't sleep very well, usually going into a deep sleep at five when Grandfather got up. She was always on the look out for burglars and even had a time-keeping machine installed at the furthest point from the front gate where the night watchman dozed, to ensure he did a round every fifteen minutes, the watchman would push a button which punched a hole in a square of paper. Grandmother would check the paper every morning after the night shift had left it on the ledge, inside the bars of the dining room windows.

Jack, barefoot, slowly moved downstairs. There was enough illumination coming through the windows from the garden lights to show the familiar architecture. Rounding into the room at the bottom of the stairs, he almost fell over two dining chairs placed in the shadows. Recovering his balance without having to fall across them, he moved on towards the double door. With a quick glance it was far too gloomy to see the outline of the bunch of keys on the side-board but as he neared the door, he realised it was closed but unbolted, which was unusual.

As he entered the hall leading to the dining room he looked about for the beam of Grandmother's torch near the windows; he expected to find her checking on the watchmen and the dogs from inside the house. But all was quiet. He entered the dining room, noticing that the doors leading to the first of the capital E house extensions were open. But then he remembered that one of the clerks from Nisha's father's factory had been discussing financing their Harvest bonuses with his grandfather that morning in the front hall. Grandfather had been running the factory for years after the death of Nisha's other Grandfather due to mismanagement by his aunt Saroj and Uncle Rajan. Jack didn't realise the clerk was staying over and wondered why he was not using the bungalow as employees usually did.

Jack carefully removed a silver beaker from the holder making sure it didn't jangle its neighbours, which would possibly wake Grandmother from her dozing. The dining room was the middle extension of the E shape and Grandmother's room was in the lower part of the E extension from the façade of the house and most of the windows were open despite the monsoon as the day had held up.

Jack filled his beaker by turning the tap on the filter halfway so that the water trickled from the spout, down the side of the beaker until it was full. He gulped it down thirstily and was about to have a refill when he heard a woman's laugh. Intrigued, he listened again, thinking it may be coming from the kitchens where the servant girls slept. Quietness reigned. Halfway through the trickle of the second beaker he became aware of murmurings. Turning off the tap, he listened intently in the stillness. For just a fleeting second or two he thought he saw a dark shadow appear and disappear next to the windows in the corridor which led towards the kitchen but he was distracted by the voices again; there was more than one person staying in the unused wing.

He put his beaker on the dining table and quietly crept back out into the hallway and headed past the double doors leading outside, noting that the bolt was home and padlock secure. On he crept towards the open double door leading up to the bedrooms in the first wing which extended along the other side of the dining room. The polished clay tiling on the stairs made it easy to move undetected, especially without sandals, but he touched the rail as he climbed for that extra bit of silent stability. As he rose, the flickering glow from perhaps a candle was visible as more of the open door of the bedroom facing the stairs came into view. Carefully he placed one foot over the next at each step. Jack was unaware, as he took that crucial next step, that this marked another revelation in the beginning of a battle of mind and soul for his very survival.

SECRETS

ON THAT STEP, just a few steps away from the landing, he froze transfixed. She stood with her back to him looking like the statue of the Goddess Tara. Her sari and blouse were on the floor around her feet like the Harvest Flower Mandala made from pink and white petals, radiating out into an increasing circle. Her figure was as perfect as the Goddess's, compact, tiny waist with the curve of a rounded breast just visible and all the time he was aware of the other unseen person. Jack became conscious that he was witness to bare flesh which was normally covered and private and which made him feel like an intruder. He turned and raced down the steps, missed the last three and stumbled out into the corridor, just managing to prevent himself from falling a second time in the gloom. As he regained physical balance he became aware of Grandmother standing silently in the dimness, hair loose and all around her like a black veil.

'What are you doing, son?' she whispered.

'I was thirsty and then I thought… I heard voices,' he prevaricated.

'Who is up there?' Grandmother was pushing him into a place he could not extract himself from without telling an obvious lie and disappointing her or telling the truth which he innately felt would hurt her. He looked down at his feet now writhing over each other in the physical attempt of avoidance.

She waited, very slowly curling and uncurling the fingers of both her hands which dangled on lifeless arms at each side of her white half-sari. He took a step towards her, pleading:

'Grandmother.'

Now nearer to her, he realised tears were running down her cheeks and he automatically reached out and hugged her, not having smelled her familiar Grandmother smell for a long while, the oil she used in her hair and the freshly laundered, starch smell of her half-sari. She patted him inertly on the back and then caught hold of his wrist and led him gently towards the room below the stairs.

'You have seen something that is wrong and will never happen here again.' She spoke quietly and slowly, with the tears still making little wet streams down each of her dry cheeks.

'That is why we will keep it a secret. It must remain a secret,' she whispered in her distress.

'There is no need to cry any more, Grandmother, it is our secret,' he tried to assure her. He wiped her cheeks with the sleeve of his pyjama and quietly went upstairs to his room leaving her sitting in her half stunned misery, reserving the questions for another time and some other person. The whole ethos of his family was quiet reserve.

The bedroom door gave its familiar squeak of complaint as he closed himself in. Matty was in a deep sleep, knees in the air as usual, arms outstretched above his head. It was fortunate he didn't follow Jack that night; it would be impossible to explain to an eight year-old the scene he had just witnessed. In the space of one week, life had revealed to Jack profound insights: secrets were not only to protect, they hurt and shamed. In the space of just one week, Jack had become acutely aware of the ambiguity of life. The secrets: one had caused hurt and shame, and more than that, how these secrets were revealed to him. The other secret was dangerous and beyond belief.

Jack lay down but couldn't sleep. He tried to siphon his thoughts and make sense of them. The image upstairs stayed foremost; no wonder Nisha was so secretive and upset. *Is the clerk a boyfriend? But why should that make Grandmother cry so hopelessly?*

Without the whirl of the fan he realised he could hear most of the sounds of the house, although muffled. Grandmother had not gone back to her room. At least an hour had passed and he reckoned she must be sitting at the bottom of the stairs weeping and waiting. He rolled over but sleep did not come. He watched the hours tick by on his watch face on the locker, using Matty's pen torch which he found after a quick forage in his brother's bag. Matt always carried a rucksack full of all types of mostly useless things and broken toys. Jack had been pleasantly surprised several times with what he could produce from the ubiquitous bag. The bag never stayed far away from him. That night he had pushed it into the small gap between the mattress and the foot board of his bed.

Suddenly there was the sound of a muffled argument. Jack flung his legs over the side of the bed and tiptoed to the bathroom door, carefully slid back the bolt, closed the door and sat down on the floor inside to listen. The bathroom ventilations were ideal for eavesdropping on the room below the stairs; Matt and he had hidden in there many times, locking themselves in while they listened to Grandmother ordering the ayahs to find them.

'What, what is this?' Jack heard his grandmother demand.

'I needed news of Rajan,' replied Aunt Saroj, Nisha's mother.

'Hmm… and what about the children? What if they saw what you were doing?' Grandmother went on.

'Nothing, what are you talking about?' came back his aunt's defiant voice.

More muffled conversation which Jack could not quite interpret, followed by a howl.

'Enough, enough,' pleaded the voice of his aunt, now sufficiently loud to hear.

Then he heard the sound of chair legs scraping the floor. Jack imagined Grandmother chasing his aunt around the room and – was it possible? – it sounded as if she was walloping her.

Nisha's bedroom door squeaked open. Jack jumped to his feet, standing underneath the ventilation in an effort to maximise what he could hear. The bathroom ventilations were at a right angle to those of the landing. Nisha must have stayed above on the landing, listening in the shadows at the top of the stairs as her voice didn't join in with the other two voices, nor did the confrontation below stop. Perhaps she had been a forlorn and silent witness for far too long?

Eventually the commotion below subsided and both Grandmother and Aunt went to their respective rooms. Jack waited and, as he guessed, heard Nisha slip back through the squeaking door from the shadows on the landing into the gloom within.

Grandmother took to the great-grandfather's bed for the rest of the holidays. This was a three-quarter size, very ornate carved rosewood bed which was kept in that room of confrontation and secrets below the stairs. For visitors and family alike this was not unusual as Grandmother suffered from hay fever.

For Jack, however, it meant the rest of the holiday was a subdued and non-eventful few days and the rains continued to pour down. He stayed at home pondering the strange events, the vulnerability of everyone, especially his grandmother. What was his aunt's scheme? Staying out of her way would not keep him safe. She appeared to be assailing the defenceless. He vowed to scrutinise her behaviour towards each member of the family and the servants, to uncover more clues. One thing was for sure, he needed advice and a very specialised type of help.

Unknown to Jack, the latent help visited the Little Pink House a couple of times each month; however, he didn't use it or didn't need to use it for a very long time. As September moved into October and the following month slid into the next Jack found that he was spending less and less time at his grandparents' house. He had never since gone to the Bungalow to do his homework; instead, he sat at the dining table in the Little Pink House leaving his school books undisturbed at one end of the table when it was dinner time which he ate with his parents. What was really curious during the months after the Harvest Festival was that Jack realised that his grandfather hardly ever called for him.

Since Jack was born, there were two mandatory visits to Nani Bhavan daily: one before Grandfather left for the office and a very long one each evening before Jack's bedtime. Since Jack grew and started school the visits were cut down to one, when Grandfather got back from the office each evening. Jack would sit beside his grandfather while his numerous visitors came and went each evening. Jack did not feel like going to Nani Bhavan as Girija and Nisha were no fun at all, both defiant in their different ways about the separation of their parents and apparently clinging to a hope of returning home.

Jack spent Christmas in the Taj Residency Hotel in Bangalore with his parents and little brother, returning with a tan and peeling skin from being too long in the swimming pool. Grandmother was horrified as Jack peeled the shedding tanned skin away from his body, revealing the lighter skin underneath and he got a scolding for spending too long in the sun without the protection of his shirt.

The school summer holidays were in March, April and May and he and his mother and Matty spent those hot months in Ireland with his Irish grandparents. Jack forgot what he had witnessed at times, especially in the different Irish culture, who would understand anyway about the strange happenings at home in India. One incident in particular did not make sense, though. It was something he found strange at the time. It happened after he witnessed the aunt in the Prayer Room, again one evening after school at his grandfather's house.

While he was in the library Nisha – who was his age, just like Kate, his Irish cousin – confronted him. Jack remembered clearly the unforeseen exchange.

'Get out,' Nisha hissed.

'What's the matter with you?' asked the startled Jack; she had crept in barefoot.

'Who gave you permission to come in here?' the words came out hard as stones through Nisha's tightly stretched lips.

'Grandmother gave me the keys,' said Jack, shifting from lying on his tummy on the cool tiles into cross-legged.

'I live here now and I say put the books away and leave.' She was standing over him in the gloom, Jack hadn't bothered to put the lights on; he had been reading with the dusky, fading light which filtered through the ventilation.

'You've gone mad,' said Jack. 'Get lost.'

'You want to see mad?' Nisha had asked as she picked up the *Inventions of the 21st century* hardback from the table. She held it by its large front cover, so that the heavy pages which had begun to pull on the binding gave a rip and yet another little rip.

Jack had given into her then, forgiving her, feeling sorry for her because of her predicament, being separated from her father and her home. But in retrospect he felt there was more to that incident.

He didn't feel the need to share this or anything else with Kate as he felt she would not relate to them. Kate was a first cousin too and she lived up the road from his Irish grandparents' house with his uncle and aunt and his other cousin, a boy of five called Nicholas. During that visit it was decided that Kate would come to stay with them in the Little Pink House in India when she got her school holidays, shortly after Jack and his family had returned.

KATE

JACK WAS AMBIVALENT about Kate's visit in view of the events of the previous nine months. He reassured himself with the thought that she was just a visitor and therefore no threat, unlike himself. *No, his aunt could not be subservient to him as heir, ever... Kate, on the other hand, was just another cousin, his mother's niece, the other side of his family. She was staying for a few months; her school opened again in September and she would be gone.*

All these thoughts began boring Jack and, worse, making him impatient with himself as he had come up with nothing more sustainable than the same old reassurances which kept floating around in his head while he waited in the arrivals and departure area of the Trivandrum Airport. He was glad of the glass partition dividing the arrivals from those waiting as it took his mind off the failure to convince himself as to why he hadn't confided in his mother his reservations about Kate's safety.

Even with Jack's height he could not distinguish Kate among the many fair-haired back-packers and few young, possibly European, American or Australian teens filing in from the customs area to collect their luggage among the majority, Indian parents and children back in India for their school holidays.

Finally he spotted her on the outer edges of the crowd at the luggage carousel being jostled to the edge every time she tried to penetrate in. Jack smiled to himself: Kate would have to learn to use her elbows and forget about any sort of a queuing system or European concepts of politeness in India.

Kate was average height for her age; she was just twelve days older than Jack and eight days older than Nisha who was four days older than Jack. She had a well-defined muscle structure. It was as she finally heaved a heavy suitcase off the carousel and on to a trolley which wouldn't stay still, that the pale, blue eyes found Jack's laughing brown ones. By then the hall was almost empty and a porter had begun nudging the large case onto the trolley while she held it steady. The young cousins embraced, causing a deal of consternation. Jack made a mental note to explain customs to Kate but not now.

At the car he should have sat up front with the driver but couldn't be bothered spending the following two hours talking to Kate in the back seat with his neck in a twist. He tipped the porter and jumped into to the back seat beside the red- and moist-faced Kate and told Vishu he could set off for home.

The discomfort of the humidity was just beginning to have its effects on Kate. Jack offered her the iced water from a water carrier his mother had provided and she drank thirstily. Jack noticed she already had a few freckles and the front of her hair was lightly bleached with the mild Irish sun owing to the outdoor life she lead galloping on Finn, her cob, through the sand dunes. Jack had spent his school holidays mostly indoors in Ireland just two months before; it was March and cold with gusty winds and everyone was pale from the lack of sun.

Jack introduced Vishu, first in English and then explained in Malayalam to the driver who bowed his head in the mirror. Kate joined her hands as if in prayer and made a *Namaste* in the mirror. She had been interested to learn about India and Jack's mother had given her a few greeting and dress tips and she would get plenty more, he thought. She mentioned she had changed into a cotton skirt as the flight neared Bombay before she transferred to the internal Indian Airlines carrier and remarked that she was really glad she did as she felt sticky all over although the air-conditioning was already chilling the sweat and reducing the redness.

Jack didn't feel the need to talk as Kate sat up intently, staring out of the front window, peering beyond the driver on the edge of her seat and occasionally turning for a better view of the traffic on the outskirts of the capital. Jack visualised how this ordinary scene of women rushing for overcrowded buses clutching the pleats in their brightly coloured saris, teenagers slowly walking in the direction of the college with armfuls of books, oxen grazing on the fallen spinach and cauliflower leaves in the market, must be a novelty for her. Jack pointed out a dhobi with his rectangle head-load of neatly pressed saris wrapped in someone else's bed sheet. Then the magnificence of an elephant, trunk curled around a bunch of coconut fronds, caught her attention.

'Why is he carrying the palms?' queried Kate.

'Lunch,' replied Jack.

'He's carrying his lunch!' enthused Kate, as the forward movement of the car caused the elephant to move from front windscreen, round by the passenger window. Finally kneeling against the back of the seat, Kate sucked in and soaked up the fascination through the back window watching the swaying tail, black hairs sticking out horizontally at its end.

'The tail is like a worn-out toilet brush!' she giggled.

'Kate, sit here, you will have a better view,' Jack said as he half stood and swung in behind the driver while Kate slid across to the other side of the back seat.

As they got on to the highway there was the blare of a bus horn which seemed to fade as it thrust forward, its lights flashing as it hurtled passed them.

'It's jammed with passengers, look... half of them look like they are hanging out of the windows,' exclaimed Kate, holding on to her blouse.

'That's nothing, look up on the roof,' urged Jack, smiling, pointing out three passengers who were gripping a rail which was attached to the roof just an inch or so above it with even more luggage.

'There is an entire family on that scooter,' called out Kate a little later as they over took a stick-like man walking oxen.

At a closed railway level crossing, the car stopped and she got out, stepping purposefully and looking about stroking and feeling the air as if she had arrived somewhere fascinating. The coconut trees intrigued her. Jack followed as she walked to a tea shop a little way along the road to see what was for sale. He assured her that there was nothing she would be interested in and explained about 'pan', which was betel leaf filled with either sweet or savoury spices, and narrated the story concerning pan and his mother when she first came to India. His mother had seen a man apparently spitting a whole mouthful of bright red blood on a street in Madras and drew his father's attention to it, panicked, and asked if the driver would stop and take the man to a hospital. Jack's father had to reassure her that the man had been chewing pan and the spices and herbs caused the red colour that looked like blood.

Kate watched as someone waited while the tea shop man filled and folded the betel leaf into a little parcel which the purchaser duly popped into his mouth and began to chew.

By that time Kate had begun to attract the attention of the increasing number of other travellers awaiting the passing train. A few young men who had got off their bicycles began to call her 'cat eyes' and made comments on the gold, blond and brown hair. Jack instinctively knew it was time to act as chaperone and encouraged her back to the car, explaining the lack of respect for western women and the part-curiosity of the locals who were gathered around the car and had begun questioning the driver as to who she was. Kate seemed only partly aware of the attention and exclaimed to Jack as she sat back into the now partly humid and cool car:

'It's like opening an oven door, the heat – I mean, it just engulfs you and makes you boil from the inside out.'

'I love it, the stickiness doesn't bother me, but it makes Mum irritable,' Jack told her.

THE LIZARDS

 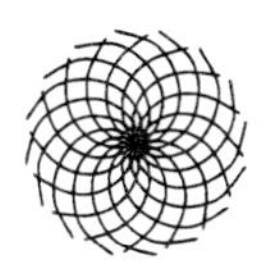

AND SO KATE happily settled into Jack's bedroom. The first couple of days she adjusted to the heat and familiarised herself with Indian life at the Little Pink House. She spent most of the time the boys were at school in the house with Jack's mother watching and consuming the domestic happenings. The dhobi's wife arrived before the car left with the boys for school. She took the bucket of soaked clothes to the washing stone, a rectangle of concrete with a sloped top to allow the water to run off. There was a tap beside it and it was situated to one side of the compound, the part of the garden beyond the cook's kitchen which was in one of the rooms attached to the Little Pink House. Radha literally beat the soaked clothes on the top part of the concrete rectangle after rubbing stains with soap.

Jack could see Kate's head and back as she sat intrigued on the steps of the back veranda watching the dunking of the beaten, soaped clothes into buckets of clean water as they were rinsed. Radha, who was very pretty, with skin almost the colour of teak wood, appeared self-conscious at the attention and Jack knew Kate would be sensitive to this but they could only communicate with their eyes and he didn't have time to explain that it was only the washing process that Kate was interested in.

The dhobi arrived later and ironed the clothes which had been washed the previous day; he used the work surface in the main kitchen as his ironing board. While this was in progress the gardener/watchman Divakaran swept and swabbed the floors. The shopping list was given to Anthony, a man who doubled as a messenger for the offices and factories as well as shopping for both houses. Then Mary the ayah cooked the rice for lunch and got ready the boys' tiffins to be taken to the houses near the school.

Jack felt that Kate slept a lot, especially in the afternoons when the bustle of the morning was over and the dhobi and his wife had left and the floors swept and damp-dusted. After lunch the house always went quiet. Once the ayah sat on the steps of the back veranda to comb her hair after her bath, Kate made her way to her bed and slept. Neither Jack nor Matty needed this siesta and waited impatiently at weekends for everyone else to get up.

Lizards fascinated Kate but not at first. Shortly after she had arrived she had rushed out of Jack's bedroom and sought the help of his mother.

'Aunt Elizabeth, will you come and look, there is the strangest little animal, like a crocodile crawling along the top of the wall,' she petitioned.

The boys and their mother exchanged puzzled looks but before Jack's danger radar had gone into action, his mother had explained that lizards were perfectly safe except for their urine or spittle, and of course, there was the unsightliness of the odd splatter of dark material on the paint. It was explained that food and drinks should be covered and a little crochet net with beads attached to weight it down was given for the water beaker beside her bed. And so Kate took to watching the *lizards*, their battles and their seemingly aimless scampering along the tops of the walls near the ceilings.

Kate found out the difficult way not to leave crumbs about, particularly in beds or sofas as the bites and inflammation and the itchy redness was just not worth it. The news of the availability of biscuits, Bombay mix, banana chips, any type of food in fact, spread instantly in the ant world and before long a trail would be seen and they lingered long after the food had been cleared away and the floor swabbed.

Matty had been keen to show Kate the baby elephant, which was no longer a baby. It had been gifted to a temple near the Residency which was a public park with a colonial-style building, a leftover of the British Raj and now a Government Guest House. On the third evening the boys took her to visit both these places; since they were very near their house, all three set off in a car with a driver.

After a brief look across the lake at the Residency, the children ascended the steps on to the long drive and got back into the car. The temple was beside a smaller lake and they watched the elephant which was tied nearby and also fettered.

'It keeps shifting its weight from one front foot to the other,' Kate remarked.

'Jack does that too,' said Matty with a sly smile and then quickly disappeared into the temple after depositing his sandals on the lower step.

It was pooja time and Jack explained to Kate that it was one of very few temples that only Hindus could enter. Kate was very interested to know about the whole complex, the outer walls and what the layout was inside. Jack had explained as best he could and promised they would visit their family temple erected by his great-grandfather and expanded by his grandfather on the way home.

'Matt's just gone in to see Ganesh,' Jack explained. 'Every time he comes to see the elephant he finishes off with a visit to Ganesh's *Sanctum Sanctorum.*'

'I guess that is the elephant-headed God,' smiled Kate.

Matty emerged shortly and Jack told him of their visit to their own temple.

'There is a Ganesh there too,' explained Matty, 'I'll show you.'

'Why are you so keen on him?' asked Kate as they piled into the car again, Jack up front with the driver and Kate with Matty chatting in the back.

'I don't really know, it's just that he's a little boy with a very strange father, I sort of feel sorry for him,' said Matty truthfully.

'Strange how?' asked Kate.

'Well Lord Siva, that's his father, knocked off Ganesh's head when he was a baby,' explained Matty.

'Heavens,' exclaimed Kate.

'Grandfather says Ganesh's head was burnt off by the sun god,' Jack intercepted.

'How did he end up with an elephant's head instead of his own?' Kate asked.

'When Siva realised Ganesh was his son he sent wise people all over in search of a head…' Matty stopped mid-sentence. 'What did Grandfather say about that, Jack?'

'He said Brahma – he's another powerful God –' Jack turned to explain to Kate, 'Brahma told Parvathi, that's Ganesh's mother, to find what she could to bring her son back to life and she found an elephant's head.'

'This is a Murugan temple, he's Ganesh's brother,' pointed Matty as the car came to a halt outside a very colourful, ornate and temple.

Kate followed the boys into the temple, leaving her rubber flip-flops outside in the sand. She copied all the movements her cousins made. In the first *Sanctum Sanctorum* there was a statue of a boy beside a peacock.

'That's Murugan, Ganesh's brother,' Matty repeated in a whisper. Next to it and to the right was a statue of a female goddess. The stone statue was dressed in silk, folded sari style. She had on gold jewellery with precious stones. The boys stood with their palms joined and when the Brahmin priest saw them he approached with a brass lamp containing a flame. The boys opened their palms but kept their thumbs intertwined above the flame and then brought their palms to their foreheads and over their heads. Kate copied and Jack felt it came as naturally to her as it did to his mother. The priest prayed in Sanskrit while anointing them with liquefied sandalwood and they moved on to Lord Siva's representation.

Jack whispered to Kate that he would explain later. Behind this was Ganesh's *Sanctum Sanctorum*. Matty reached up and rang the little bell which he could only reach by leaning on the threshold of the *Sanctum*: a bit of an intrusion, Jack always felt, but Matty never took heed. He felt and treated Lord Ganesh as if he was a brother, or so Jack thought.

Jack was satisfied that Kate had been shown the basics and she was taking advice from his mother on food and eating lots of yoghurt to feel cool inside. Kate felt hungry all the time as she was not sated with the new diet and had supper with Matty, which his mother cooked. Some evenings it was pizza, toasted cheese sandwiches or scotch pancakes with honey which the boys referred to as moon rocks. Not that they were anything but what they were meant to be; it was a name their father had used for them.

THE FAERIES

 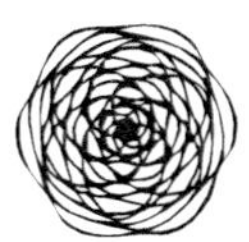

IT WAS ON the third night of Kate's stay that Jack became aware of murmurings emanating through the netted door of his bedroom. He stopped in the darkness of the hallway, forgetting about his planned rummage in the fridge. His parents had closed their bedroom door but Kate still used the netted one only; despite it being the rainy season, the weather was still too hot for her.

Jack slowly peered round from the position he had placed himself in beside the desk where he could see Kate who was seated cross-legged on the bed, apparently conversing with someone outside the bedroom window, the same window where Ekans had first appeared. Jack couldn't distinguish any meaning from the ebb and flow of the soft, strange monologue.

After only a minute of two he decided to make himself visible and touched the door frame. Kate spun round, startled, grasping her shirt; she had taken to wearing a cotton shirt and shalwar like a lot of local teenage girls her age. She wore them for comfort from the heat rather than a sense of fashion.

'Thank God it's you,' she exclaimed in a whisper. 'Come in, sit down.' She patted the bed.

'What's going on?' Jack strained to see out the window but couldn't see anyone. 'What are you murmuring to yourself? Are you homesick?' She had shown no indication that she was, but he decided to explore every possible approach to get an explanation.

'No, no, why would I be homesick?' She looked surprised.

'You were talking to yourself,' he explained.

'Was I?' Kate smiled and turned towards the window and bent her head. She was silent for what seemed a long time to Jack, whose impulses were getting the better of him.

'What's up then?' Jack decided the sensitive approach didn't work and went head on.

'I don't know if you remember a conversation we had last time you were at home about our great-great-uncle who died when he was our age?' she inclined her head over the opposite shoulder, looking directly and intently at him, speaking quietly.

Jack thought for a bit, turning his head to stare out the window.

'The one whose dog went on visiting all the houses the dead teenage uncle used to visit after he died?' Jack turned back to face her.

'Yes, him. Well… I often see him and talk to him… I'm clairvoyant…' Throughout this halting declaration she kept watching Jack carefully.

'Is that who you were talking to just now?' he asked after a little while in which he tried to arrange his thoughts to ensure his reaction appeared normal to her.

'No, no,' she smiled broadly. 'Michael speaks English not Gaelic. He lived in the twentieth century, and anyway I wouldn't expect him to ramble around these parts. He loves the fields and country roads and I've been trying to persuade him to pass over but he resists… as long as he is happy… I guess…' She rambled on as if she was explaining something as inconsequential as breakfast until she realised not everyone spoke to the dead as if they were the living.

There was an unfilled space between them as Jack tried to pretend to himself that it was normal to talk to long-dead relatives. Normally he and Kate connected quite well so he decided to go with her way of thinking or accept this new strangeness to see if he could understand her more. At the same time he tried to quell the fascination that was bubbling up inside his mind. None of this had been apparent during the several months they had played together over the years on his annual trips to Ireland, yet there were times that he felt distance had grown between them especially since they had grown up more; not so much distance, he considered… more… well, it felt like part of her eluded him sometimes…

'Who were you talking to then… and what was that language?' Jack asked, bewildered.

'The language is Irish… not as we learn and speak now, it's an earlier form. Your mum probably learnt a bit of it in its original Latin script before the Department of Education started the study through English script.' Jack was once again consoled by the thoughts of himself and Matty congratulating themselves that they didn't go to school in Ireland; if Irish got a fail mark in state exams, the entire exam would have to be repeated, every single subject even if a student got an A or B in the other subjects. Jack knew Kate was good at languages as he was but she put a lot more work into her French and had Latin at school as well as Irish, which was compulsory.

'If it wasn't a ghost… then who?' Jack asked.

'I was attempting to make sense of what the beings here were telling me.

You've heard of the Tuatha dé Danann?' she turned away from the window to face him again.

'Leprechauns,' replied Jack, eyebrows raised, with a smile of disbelief; he could not make himself even consider this, regardless of placating her.

'Well not as everyone visualises them… not little men dressed in green… that's the commercial and general interpretation. The real faeries, if you like.'

'And they are here, right here, outside the window, these faerie folk, speaking ancient Irish. Tell me, how do they like the weather, did the humidity affect their flight wings?' Jack was amazed, excited and found this incredible all at once and unknowingly had raised his whisper mockingly.

'Sheee… be quiet, you'll upset them,' she gave a quick glance out through the netted window, then got off the bed and stood nearer to it and began conversing in the strange guttural tongue in a soft, pacifying voice.

'I can't see a thing,' Jack whispered as he joined her.

'They say you're in danger, at least that's what I think they are saying,' she whispered.

This last statement began to resonate with Jack and he thought for a while.

'Alright…' Jack was more than grounded by this last statement. The thoughts of Ekans and the horror that went with him struck him hard and once again he decided to give her the benefit of the doubt.

'I have a question then.'

'They don't have to prove anything to you and anyway they are not leprechauns as you put it… they are not Irish, not the Tuatha dé Danann, these are *your* faerie folk, not mine,' Kate whispered indignantly.

'What do you mean by *my* faeries?' Jack's reasoning was once again losing its practical edge.

'From what I can understand these beings are similar to the Tuatha, they have the same Goddess – Dana – and the language is somewhat similar. I've been looking at the Hindi script in Matty's text book, it has a lot in common with ancient Irish script… I'm using the equivalent of pigeon language with them… their behaviour is very like the Tuatha though…' she trailed off, focusing out into the darkness again.

'Wait, wait… how long have you been talking to them?' Jack had that last-to-find-out feeling, he was somewhat peeved that she had not confided in him before. 'Do you see them all the time…?'

'I'm aware of all sorts of energies but it was very easy to distinguish these last night, we have set up a sort of dialogue and now I think they are trying to tell me that you are in danger, but I'm not sure…' Kate broke off, still staring out the window.

'My question should make that clear… or not, then.' Jack returned to his question again.

'OK, let's hear it then… keep it simple though… my translation skills are more intuitive than theoretical right now without my textbooks,' Kate concentrated.

'Ask them how the snake got in,' Jack took a deep breath.

'Just that, how the snake got in,' repeated Kate who turned towards the window again concentrating.

'The word for snake is easy, tense is giving me trouble and they didn't understand when I try to use it,' she said half to herself.

'Remember how we talked about Latin being similar in some ways to Malayalam and Hindi…' Jack waited for her to answer but she was thinking.

'Just use the nouns, put them together with verbs and forget about the tense.' he urged.

'That's what I'm doing,' she held up her hand to silence him.

Jack waited, peering out into the darkened garden, listening to Kate's soft guttural, halting speech but he could not hear the response however hard he listened.

'The snake was brought by a man who dropped it into the garden further down this wall, in the lane, not over the wall bordering the main road,' Kate's reply came back quickly as she pointed to the side of the house bordering the lane opposite the kitchen window, which set Jack's heart racing.

'Ask them who sent the man with the snake,' he pushed on.

'They say a blood relative from the generation above you. What's this all about?' It was Kate's turn to feel bewildered.

'I'll explain later, I have another question, ask them is the sender male or female,' he replied.

'Woman.' The answers were coming back quick and fast.

'Who placed the snake in the bathroom?' Jack nodded at Kate.

'They did.' Her answer came back and she looked as shocked as Jack.

'The evil devils,' the words spat off Jack's tongue. Kate grabbed Jack's arm as he turned to peer out into the shadows made by the street light.

'Don't curse them, they feel the negative energy, they don't have to understand your language to understand your meaning, they are much more intuitive than us.'

THE SPIRIT

JACK SAT DOWN heavily on the bed. He understood Kate's point. She remained at the window a little longer speaking softly and gently in the stillness that darkness brings. When she quietly joined him on the bed, he told her everything that had happened within the family. It took a while as he had to explain cultural aspects of family life in India. By the time he finished they were facing each other cross-legged on the bed, Kate at the pillow end and Jack at the foot end, bathed both in moon-light and street light.

'A lot of things make sense now,' Kate said, still thinking in the stillness.

'Like what?' whispered Jack. He was curious to know if it was her psychic skills or just plain human observation.

'Do you remember that first evening I came... we were invited to your grandparents for dinner? Afterwards as we sat in the garden... well... your aunt has what I can see as a type of entity, like a grey energy around her, I don't know how I can express it better... it sort of... well it frightened me... it hovers at her back mostly...'

'Like an aura?' put in Jack.

'Yes... no, it looks like it has become part of her aura but it is not normal, not like other people's auras,' replied Kate. 'An aura surrounds the person, this energy she has attached to hers is different... it's threatening... it's heavy and dark...'

'That was noted by them,' Jack put in quickly.

'What do you mean?' Kate didn't seem to understand how Jack was aware of negative energy undercurrents.

'My aunt kept on asking Nisha in Malayalam why you were staring at her,' he explained.

'I had never seen energy like it before. It will be a wake-up call for me from now on when dealing with your aunt, I must remember not to stare,' Kate said thoughtfully.

'It's important that I appear as if I know nothing of what has happened between you,' she said after some thought. 'You need a plan of action, though. Let's get our heads together tomorrow after you get back from school.' She seemed really tired.

'What's the point?' asked Jack, head bent. 'With the Goddess Dana's people helping my aunt, what chances have we got?'

'More than you think,' she smiled. 'The faerie folk have their own principles and pride; our job is to keep them on your side and more importantly try to understand their warnings.'

'Is that even a remote possibility?' Jack looked up.

'Not remote, real. They are already helping you,' she said.

They sat and talked some more and Kate explained how she began to understand and accept the other worlds, and after what seem ages she said, 'Now go away and let me sleep.'

Kate stretched out on the bed and rolled over on one side, gently pushing Jack to his feet.

'Want anything from the kitchen?' whispered Jack through the netted door his mind was in both existences. He needed the reassurance of the familiar but at the same time he felt comforted that his experience with Ekans was not in his mind; if Kate could not only accept but live with beings from other dimensions he reasoned it would be a necessity for him to accept their existence too.

'Good night… wait, how I get into the library next door?' she was sitting up again.

'Ask Mum. She'll get you in. Sure you don't want a sandwich?' Jack offered with a smile.

Kate pulled the sheet over her head and rolled on to her other side. But before he left the hall side of the netted bedroom door she had sprung up yet again.

'Jack, pssst, come here a minute will you?' she whispered loudly.

'What now?' He opened the door as quietly as he could and poked his face inside the room, conscious of the direction the sound his whispers would carry. He poked his face just inside the door frame conscious of making noise that may wake his mother.

'At your grandparents' house, in the room with the ornate bed, who is the old woman in the large black and white photo, she has a sari partly over her head?' She was alert again, describing with her hands.

'That's my great-grandmother, my grandfather's mother. Why?' He was curious.

'She never leaves the passage which runs along beside the dining room to the kitchens, all through dinner she was there and she even acknowledged me as we came back to the sitting room,' she said pensively. 'What's her name?'

'Nani. You know that makes so much sense to me,' Jack now advanced into the bedroom again and seated himself on the end of the bed, facing the window.

'What do you mean?' she drew up her legs and sat cross-legged again under the cotton bed cover focusing intently on her cousin.

'Before my grandparents renovated and extended the house that area used to be her bedroom and bathroom, you know the pantry with the freezer and fridge off the European kitchen, that whole area,' he explained.

'Yes, I know where you mean exactly…' she said quietly and then urged him on.

'You just mentioned that something made sense,' she reminded.

'I sometimes avoid that passage; actually, I've avoided it for years off and on and go to the kitchens through the dining room mostly,' he said still unsure of himself.

'Why?' she persisted in her soft tone.

'I have felt something there, just at the windows… for ages, and the night we had the sleepover last Onam, the one I told you about, I actually thought I saw a shadow move with the corner of my eye,' he said. 'It's frustrating when I cannot understand and interpret what I feel… or sense. Like I said, it's much more logical now, though.'

'Sounds like she's always been there,' replied Kate, pensive.

'What do you mean, always there?' questioned Jack.

'Well it's hard to say if she has crossed to the other-world or if she is just visiting; she could be hanging around like our great-uncle Michael.' She was still thoughtful.

'Does it matter?' questioned Jack.

'Some, mothers in particular, stay near to their living relatives especially if they are in trouble or danger and of course I'm thinking now of your aunt…' She trailed off.

'Yes,' was all he could say and then he asked, 'How can I communicate with her, I can feel coolness in the area too…'

'A very subtle cool is OK but if you ever feel intense cold, keep away.' She began to explain, but he cut in:

'Why?'

They were now facing each other; he had one leg bent and up on the bed.

'You wouldn't want to encourage a portal, an opening where wandering, lost spirits would bother you. How cold is it in the passage?' she asked.

'It's barely perceptible, so much so that I'm sometimes not sure whether I felt it or not,' he replied.

'That is Nani then, your grandparents have a friendly spirit,' she smiled. 'Try out the passage next time you're over there, pick a quiet time when you will not be disturbed and see what you feel or sense, make sure it is when the light is dim like twilight. It will be easier for you to see her in that type of light but don't focus too hard, just relax your eyes; she is a benevolent spirit, she might be able to help you. Now go away or you'll not be fit for school tomorrow and I'll end up sleeping all afternoon.'

Once again she lay down to sleep that night.

FRIDGE FEAST

JACK DIPPED HIS peeled banana into the plastic container of left-over chicken curry as he considered the strange nocturnal happenings – not just Kate's clairvoyance but the Ekans incident and everything else concerned with the now permanent stay of his aunt next door. The tiny sweet banana, flavoured with cold chicken curry gravy had been devoured in two mouthfuls and caused a need for something more to follow. Jack undid the aluminium foil in which the flat circular breads were wrapped and helped himself to one along with the remains of an onion and tomato salad.

He sat up on the counter top on which the dhobi did the ironing with the window over the sink at right angles to him. The bread took some time to chew, especially as it was cold, but with the satisfaction of the nurturing taste of the cooked fat, flour and water Jack began to remember incidences from his last trip to Ireland as he tried to come to terms with this new aspect of Kate.

He focused on their trips to the Ballyteige Bay which was her favourite haunt, an area of conservation not easily accessible. He would do the journey three or four times during his holidays in Ireland. It took half a day to get there and back to his grandmother's house, he walking, Kate sometimes on foot and sometimes mounted. She took her horse on to the firm sand on the inner side of the lagoon and galloped him for exercise while Jack had to catch up on foot or travel parallel on the ocean side of the sand dunes on the shingles which was slow going. Along this side the Atlantic winds split his thick black hair into temporary partings, ripping it at the very roots, dragging the forced partings this way and that. The odd shaped bits of driftwood occasionally took his interest and he wondered how the gulls kept their graceful flight up above in the wind torrents, seemingly correcting their flight now and again. He remembered his last visit: he had decided to relieve the boredom by bird-watching, particularly coastal visitors and on that day he could not make out whether it was a herring gull who had kept him company, as it was too high to spot the pink legs and of course with the bird just gliding he could not see if the grey markings were on its back to confirm that the call it made was indeed that of a herring gull.

Kate and Jack would get together at the Borough House – their meeting place – when she would pull out sandwiches from her saddle bag. They sat in the partial shelter of the ruins, rested for a while, talked and discussed and disagreed mostly on common subjects before starting the long trek home.

He felt that the silence of that place seemed to beckon Kate; she went there every day and he would be left alone especially since he had grown up, bored time after time. Matty still played with their little cousin Nicholas when they were not visiting other cousins from both sides of his mother's family. Also the time of year they spent in Ireland wasn't ideal as, depending when Easter fell, everyone his age was at school. Ever since Jack had started secondary school his parents decided the annual Irish trip had to be during the Indian summer holidays otherwise Jack would miss too much.

From the kitchen window of his grandmother's house Jack could just see the tips of the sand dunes on the Big Borough. He could never understand what drew Kate there, the quietness, the monotony of the landscape and the enveloping greyness of the place was just so uninteresting to him, even on sunny, warm days it was grey and the calls of the curlews sounded forlorn. But he felt he was beginning to understand, he stepped carefully among his memories and listened in their silence. There was a timelessness about the place.

At high tide Kate took the long route round to the big borough having to open and close metal gates made with hollow tubes through which the off shore winds made 'faerie music'. It was true, she had silenced his intense argument that modern religion, Christianity in particular had plagiarised Egyptian mythology versus her argument that mythology is life just repeating itself. As she closed the tubular gate she had ordered him to listen.

'Listen to what?' he had shouted back, his ears were cherry red and beginning to pain him badly from the wind which moved in slashes and slammed invisibly at them since they had rounded the last bend on the headland, there was no avoiding nature's energy there… except walking backwards he remembered.

'I can't hear anything except the wind,' he had called back to her but his words did not travel in her direction, instead they were split apart and disjointed sounds flung this way and that as he turned his back to the gusts. Her face was red too as she tied Finn's reins to the sturdy stem of a gorse bush a little way off which had grown bent almost at right angles from the constancy of the powerful gales. Finn had begun to graze and the sound of 'the music' was obviously being lost in the grasp and pull of the grass. They had both turned their backs to the force pushing against them and using gloved hands to silence their flapping anoraks he had heard the 'faerie music'. It was soft and distant and not without rhythm, like tiny flutes from strange existences playing unfamiliar music; but it was music made by the wind finding its way through the hollow tubes of a metal gate. He remembered smiling at her, wordless for once, trying to quell the scientific explanation to keep peace with her and allowed himself to accept another incalculable. It worked because she had beamed back at him, *how could she accept that?*

But then the memory of a tiny flute coaxing a snake across a bathroom floor swiftly filled his faithless mind and he let silence rule. Again he wondered if he had been a bit more convincing then and there, would she have let him in on her secret. In hindsight he felt she may have been using the gate music as an introduction to her second sight.

He remembered that as they moved on into the wind, the land sloped down and she had taken Finn and cantered along the beach where the tide had receded a bit and the sand was firm. He had noticed the wader birds as they dipped their curved sleek beaks into the mud, daintily lifting one leg and then another, and the lonely calls of unseen birds as she vanished round another headland.

How long had she been in touch with the Tuatha dé Danann? She had explained that she had felt them long before she could see them. And then that night in his room in India she answered all his questions with what seemed to him absolute honesty but she admitted her discomfort with her 'gift' and this last year in particular she said that for the first time in her life she knew what it was like not to feel confident within. Jack felt they had so much in common, the feeling of the earth moving below their feet like a slow-moving earthquake and she agreed with him that it felt as though their childhood was just a dream in comparison to where they found themselves then.

Kate had borrowed the words from a hymn to explain what the beginning of it felt like, to sense these other beings. At first it was hardly perceptible, she had explained: 'a touch as gentle as silence.' He was beginning to understand, trying to block urges to put his own limited scientific explanation on it and hoping his mind would just accept it without his natural instincts contradicting. He wondered again, had she tried to tell him last March of her developing ability? He felt as long as he could hold on to an emptiness inside his mind, which was difficult to achieve in any brain, then perhaps the incalculable knowledge might have come in to help him understand what was happening to her. To him it was late Stone Age history, he wouldn't go so far as categorising it as mythology, but realised it was real life for Kate and had become frighteningly so for him. Just because his sensory ability was human and limited did not mean that the other dimensions and their beings did not exist.

To help Jack understand, Kate had explained how she had been helped by the Rhubarb Couple. About a mile from his grandparents' house in Ireland there was an elderly couple, Macha and Magh, who lived in a small thatched cottage and they grew rhubarb which would be just coming at the time of year they spent in Ireland. Jack's mother was mad about it and he often accompanied Kate, he on an old bicycle belonging to his grandfather and Kate on Finn, to get a supply for his mother and Jack himself, for he too had developed a taste for it. Like his mother, he ate it stewed on his grandmother's brown bread for breakfast, in crumbles and in tarts. Finn was tied on a long rein outside Macha and Magh's field gate grazing while Kate and Jack followed Macha to the rhubarb patch by the side of the cottage. That night in India Kate reminded him of the elderly couple and she explained how Magh helped her distinguish the coloured blobs and orbs she sometimes saw. Magh explained that at puberty, when children develop, something happened to Kate which allowed her more perception than normal humans.

Jack felt he needed to get to a library or good bookshop, neither of which was possible in Adoor. He was sure this was something that could be explained by physics and totally destroyed by lack of proof. He considered Einstein's relativity, which would be one way of rationalising her experiences, but then there was Sheldrake's morphogenetic fields to consider… especially linking two mythical races… but was it more than mythology?

As he tipped the last piece of chewy bread into his mouth he began to formulate a plan. He stared blindly through the window at the compound wall outside. The idea began to click into place… Swami!

GURU

SWAMI WAS A family acquaintance who had surprised everyone by visiting Jack's mother about twice a month, in the evenings, at four, which was the usual time relatives and friends dropped in. The astonishment was due to the fact that Swami was a Brahman priest and although he came from the priestly cast he had spent his life as an engineer. He had lived in Northern Ireland for some years when he had worked at the Harland and Wolf shipyard. He was a worldly man now retired.

Not only did the discussions on religion and culture go on long past Jack's father's arrival after tennis at seven and Matty's bedtime, Swami and Jack's mother sat in the garden through dusk and marauding mosquitoes and long afterwards. Swami bridged the culture gap of East and West for her; Jack thought he understood why she still struggled with it, having been conditioned to her own culture for twenty-eight years. The Swami and his mum had a mutual respect; he even accepted toasted sandwiches which she stuffed with a local vegetable dish usually served with rice, as a tea time snack. Brahman priests rarely visited houses of lower castes, not to speak of other religions, and never ate food from non-vegetarian homes as it would be considered unclean.

Jack planned to include Swami, gradually, seeking advice as he was sure Kate would not find anything helpful in his grandfather's library, nothing she could interpret anyway, even if there were books written in Sanskrit nobody in the family read the five thousand year-old language. The next day he would explain to her all about Swami.

He hopped down from the countertop, closed the fridge door and headed upstairs to Matty's room, to his mattress on the floor, feeling more hopeful than he had in ages.

A couple of nights later that week, while Jack sat at the dining table in the Little Pink House, his mother announced that Swami and Kate had 'hit it off really well together' – that was the expression used at dinner to explain to Jack and his father that Kate had met Swami when he appeared for his regular visit. Jack's mother went on to explain that Kate had a very keen interest in yantras which were sacred geometrical drawings, way beyond the depth of Jack's mother's interest, so she had asked Swami to come more often during Kate's holidays which he agreed to, saying he was more than willing to enlighten such an earnest young woman.

And so it happened that Swami could be seen in the garden every evening of the week with the young girl and her sketch pad. Swami sat with the tips of his fingers meeting, forming and enclosing what appeared to be an invisible sphere and talking while the girl drew. She raised her head occasionally appeared to question, use her rubber and continue the scraping noises as charcoal scratched paper. Jack's mother plied them with trays of lime juice and snacks.

Hidden behind the heavy, dark green chick blinds of the veranda Jack relaxed with his glass of freshly squeezed lime juice, watching Swami and Kate who sat on white painted wicker chairs, in the only shaded area of the lawn. Shadows never lasted very long in this part of India because the sun's hospitable and beautiful state was short-lived. It mutated from blinding, scorching, radiating heat to a large, glowing, orange-red globe very quickly, before sinking out of sight, leaving its heat and the hush before the sounds of dusk.

Swami watched the cook arrive and take his ingredients to the outside kitchen where most of the non-vegetarian food was prepared. This might be the reason he took food from Jack's mother, as only she prepared food in the main kitchen, thought Jack, who pushed his school bag under the wicker recliner, and pulled his feet out of the cook's path as the latter made his way back and forth between both kitchens.

Jack continued to sip his lime juice, watched and contemplated, relaxed, slipping easily into the familiar and momentarily forgetting the dark undercurrents. The back veranda… he wondered why it was referred to as the back veranda, they didn't have a front veranda; *it must be an Irish concoction*, Jack mused. It was his mother's favourite spot except in the afternoons when the sun crept around to the back of the T-shaped house. It was then the chick blinds were lowered but the intensity of the heat made it unbearable for her to sit or lie there for very long. Jack on the other hand loved the sticky heat and often used the veranda while she read in her air-conditioned bedroom waiting for the extremity of the heat to fade a little. The bamboo slats, as well as keeping out the sun, created a womb-like shade, making it possible to see the lawn and the aviary clearly but not be seen. The Little Pink House sat at one end of a rectangle compound, with the lawn stretching out from its side and the veranda nestled in the angle of the T. Two sides hugged the house and two sides were open. Three broad, deep steps led down to the lawn from the south-westerly side, Jack remembered Matty managed to break his front teeth twice by falling up those steps. Jack yearned for life to be innocent again; he wondered if the darkness had always abounded. Perhaps he had been unaware of it until now. Was this what growing up was like? He longed to be Matty, who still lived in his safe, small world. It was more than just growing up, though: there was imminent danger too.

After Jack had explained who Swami was, both Kate and he felt it was time to share with him what was going on; not all of it, just to get his opinion on the snake and the wraith. Swami usually walked to the Little Pink House as part of his daily exercise and was given a lift home with one of the drivers. Jack had decided to take the drive home with Swami and speak to him where his parents and brother could not overhear.

This thought prodded Jack to change. He went upstairs and fetched his shorts and shirt from their temporary place in Matty's cupboard. Out of his uniform and feeling fairly satisfied with his plan, he realised how easily he had accepted Kate's *second sight*, which was how she referred to it. As he buttoned his shirt he wondered if Swami had understood that Kate's interest was in protection yantras only. She had gleaned enough information from the Tuatha dé Danann – no, *the Danavas*; he made a note to force his conscious mind to accept the concept of the beings outside his bedroom window as real, with their own world and identity. One way to do that was to give them their correct title. The Danavas had advised Kate, or at least that was what she understood, that there was a type of magic she could use for protection in the form of geometry.

She explained that this was not unusual: since the introduction of Christianity in Ireland people used the Christian symbols to protect themselves against the Tuatha dé Dananns' wrath. The Tuatha respected the other God and avoided the symbols. She was fascinated with the mathematics of the yantras and so was Jack: if Einstein and Wheeler believed all matter could be reduced to a geometric formula, that was proof enough for him. All this went through his head as the brothers in their different worlds physically shared the same room.

Matty was still in his uniform but already the He-Man castle was on the floor beside his cold milk and half-eaten biscuits, forgotten, as he arranged and rearranged the dolls into defence positions outside the plastic castle. Jack was aware of Matty's half-resentment to the intrusion in his bedroom but he knew Matty put up with him because he loved having his cousin staying with them at The Little Pink House. Sleep-overs were not common in Kerala and they rarely had anyone other than Nisha's recent couple of sleep-overs since she moved into their grandparents' house. Matty was more interested in horses than Jack and got on well with Kate; he longed to have her mastery of horses. This last visit to Ireland she allowed him to ride Finn who was a cob and gave him a few lessons, starting with the rising trot since he had grown a little taller. Next visit she would arrange riding lessons for him on a pony more suited to his size. All this ran through Jack's brain while he changed without ever speaking to Matty.

SENTENCE

LATER THAT NIGHT, on Swami's front veranda, Jack explained as briefly as he could his experiences of the wraith and much later the snake. Swami sank deeply into one of his well-worn wicker chairs and appeared to shrivel into the threadbare cushions he leaned against. There was a long silence as Jack waited for a reaction and then the advice he hoped would follow. But Swami was lost in thought, staring out into the darkness of the trees which he did not see. Jack was about to prompt conversation when Swami showed signs of communication…

'It's not going to finish with the snake,' Swami spoke quietly and gravely as if to himself.

'But we could try to stop it'? Jack stated intensely; he could not understand why Swami appeared so destroyed by it all.

'Greed and power… selfish ego… it is a pity…' Swami trailed off almost in a whisper, head bowed low as if he was examining the red tiled floor of his veranda. Jack felt Swami hadn't heard a word he had said.

'You speak as if it is already over,' Jack murmured; his face belied the incredulity he felt.

'I'm afraid it is… or will be…' Swami raised his head and looked straight into Jack's eyes. Swami's eyes were wide and sad and his blank stare more than his words disconcerted Jack.

'No, no… what about good triumphing over evil, all that… action and reaction – every action produces a reaction… cosmology?' Jack tried to concentrate, grasping for solutions but his mind would not co-operate. He failed to remember the solutions he found in Physics text books and his mouth just undermined his brain, spilling what must have sounded irrelevant words.

'There is a way to counter the forces she is using. Let's take physics, the theory of relativity for example, surely that would explain the wraith. A worm hole… that's it a worm hole, forget about how she manifested it… if we know what she is doing surely we can thwart it in some way, if not stop it.' Jack stood up and began to pace; the energy coming with his thoughts was palpable.

'Swami, don't tell me there is no way out of this.'

Jack sat down again but this time on the edge of the wicker chair next to Swami and facing towards him, intently. Swami who had been staring blindly at the floor again slowly turned towards Jack and gently placed his hand over Jack's which was gripping the curved woven wicker arm of the chair and he very quietly said

'I fear she is using dark, primitive forces; you will not be able to defeat them. Even protecting yourself from them will take a lot of ingenuity.'

Jack continued as if all that Swami had said was just a caution:

'Let's look at what we have, Swami. You are an engineer, a priest, an astrologer, you are knowledgeable, intelligent and wise. You perform prayer, believe in a higher force, let's start there then,' Jack hoped this plea would spark a little enthusiasm.

'Son, it is precisely because of all you say, my knowledge, my experience that I'm telling you to walk away,' Swami was becoming more animated; it was his turn to get up and pace.

'You know… convincing your father is going to be the hardest… where will he take you all… the west, yes, the west, that's it, across a vast amount of water…'

'Swami,' Jack interjected, standing now midway between Swami's two points of pacing. 'Swami hold on a minute, nobody is going anywhere… you have to stand up to it, I have to stand up to it, OK maybe Dad too and Mum…'

'Listen to me son,' Swami caught hold of Jack's arms above the elbows, a middle-aged, white-haired man looking up with hard, determined eyes at the tall youth, 'Let me tell you what you have to be ready for…' Swami's grip was firm and strong.

'The nagas you already have had a tiny taste of; if she can summon a serpent she can possibly send a dragon or more dangerous snakes. Somehow she has visited their underworld, the serpent-world; three of the lower worlds belong to the snakes according to the Varaha Purana. Some have three, five or ten heads and are known as creeping-creatures, they are swift and brutal.'

'You're frightening me now Swami. I'm listening…' Jack was beginning to feel trapped and it wasn't just Swami's grip, he knew he would not exaggerate.

'Listening…' Swami gripped even tighter and the words seemed to be ejected forcibly through his teeth. 'You haven't heard the half of it. There are countless forms of horror and death your aunt has at her disposal, if as I suspect she has immersed herself in the underworld. Have you heard of the Night-Wanderers? Among them are fiends and trolls, they can eat raw flesh and will not hesitate to eat a human. Others animate dead bodies, disturb sacrifices and harass honest people: here we call them Kutty Chathans. They are dwarfish in size with dark intent and ramble at night creating the vilest mischief, throwing stones and even faeces. And I haven't even started on the Ghouls and the stuck souls. She is interfering with the normal construction and moulding of powers that uphold the universe, for nothing more than gain.'

Jack pulled out of Swami's grip and turned to stare into the thick, dark shrubbery of his garden. Swami closed his eyes momentarily and stood near Jack, calmer, and waited for the realisation to sink in with the boy.

'It's hopeless then?' Jack, near tears, turned around and faced Swami but still needed to lean against the pillar of the veranda wall. 'I'm expected to run away like a coward.'

'No… not a coward,' Swami stepped forward. 'Your karma dictates you must move. It's easier to go with it. Go against it and you may end up having to spend even longer in misery or worse.'

'I can't just give up Swami, it's not fair… what she is doing, is it fair?' he asked the older man.

'It's not about fairness, it's about how to cope with the life you have chosen,' murmured Swami.

'I didn't choose this… the underworld… made to run for my life…'

'You've confided in your cousin?' Swami questioned after several minutes of silence.

Jack nodded.

'It's a good start… the protection yantras,' Swami seemed to be trying to get some reaction.

Jack just stared at the older man. He felt he shouldn't keep up the desultory mood any longer, he wasn't being fair on Swami.

'She's psychic,' said Jack after some time.

'I've never seen eyes like hers, your mother has blue eyes but her eyes are as luminous and pale and as varied as a lapis lazuli, very striking,' Swami sat down again heavily, lost in thought.

'Our grandfather's eyes were the same colour,' added Jack.

'The yantras were her idea?' Swami asked.

'The Little People advised her to use them,' replied Jack, unthinking, still leaning against the veranda pillar full of gloom.

'What Little People?' Swami was alert again.

'That's what they are called in Ireland. Some sort of night fairies… or they walk out at night time… you mentioned night walkers Swami, are they the same?' Despite the moroseness, Jack's mind made connections and so he questioned Swami as much as himself.

'No, not the same, no, no, if she encountered the Kutty Chattans she would have been terrified,' Swami said waving the index finger of his right hand. 'No… she must be able to source beings I've never ever heard of – and they're not malevolent?' he questioned Jack.

'They are not exactly pure either, they admitted they put the snake in the bathroom,' Jack became agitated.

'Ah, the lesser of two evils,' Swami said half to himself after pondering for ages. 'No, they are giving her good advice. You have protection,' Swami continued, engrossed again.

'Kate believes they can be of some help. She feels they are the beings of the Goddess Dana,' said Jack more hopeful at Swami's more positive attitude.

'The Goddess Dana,' repeated Swami completely self-occupied. Finally he sprang to his feet.

'Now you must go home, I have a lot of reading to do,' instructed Swami, gently touching the boy's arm. 'We need to meet up, all three, you me and Kate. Come to the beach tomorrow evening, mind use Vishu driver and appear as casual as you can. Goodnight, goodnight.'

Swami disappeared through his curtained front door, leaving Jack standing somewhat bewildered but hopeful on the dimly-lit veranda.

CLOUD PICTURES

ALTHOUGH SWAMI HAD chosen an innocuous get-together at the beach, lots of people visited the beach in the evenings to enjoy the breeze and the outdoors when the heat of the sun had died away to a lovely warmth. However, they didn't have the privacy Jack had hoped for. Jack's mother and Matty invited themselves along too. As twilight settled down on the little group seated on the sand and their game of spotting animal shapes in the clouds had to end, a game Jack's mother picked up from their Indian grandmother, Swami cleverly suggested a walk with the teenagers along the beach, leaving Matty and his mother bathing their feet in the advancing tide.

'Jack told me of your visitors or rather *our* visitors…' and Swami waited for Kate to react.

'Yes, he told me,' she replied and shortly continued. 'Do you think we can rely on the Danavas?'

'It is very difficult for me to… I don't know how to put it… I accept forces, energy, but I cannot see like you can.' Swami stood still. 'You have got a gift which Jack told me you have slowly come to recognise… and you can actually converse with these beings… in Hinduism we accept differing states of consciousness, but only monks and yogis can manipulate the energy through breathing techniques. They spend long hours in meditation to maintain the altered states of consciousness and even and only then see what you apparently see effortlessly. I can only make judgments on this subject by what is written.' Swami put this very succinctly, pausing to look at Kate and then began moving on again, stepping as methodically as the thoughts he had just expressed.

'I understand,' she replied.

Jack was quiet throughout this exchange for he was trying to come to terms with it all himself.

'You think they are the same race as the Goddess Dana in Ireland, the… the De Danann?' Swami asked after a while.

'Yes, many similarities, possibly the same age. They seem to adore horses and all things natural, like trees, land forms… they are tricky… wily and can be dangerous too…' she began explaining enthusiastically.

'I have done some research,' Swami added very quietly and warily. 'There is a theory that a root race that most Europeans, Indians, Iranians as well as Greeks, Celts, Hittites and Romans evolved from.'

'I remember vague references to it in history at school and after my experiences here it makes sense. The connection between the two different cultures, I mean.'

Kate stopped talking. Jack felt she was trying to control the certainty of her theory, trying not to push her beliefs. He understood she had no proof and only intuition rather than theory.

'But you, my dear, your ability, when did it begin?' Swami had stopped walking altogether and turned and looked Kate straight in the eye.

'I have always felt something or someone, actual touch as lithe as a down feather on my skin, and I saw orbs as a small child and lately I have begun seeing them again but now I can see spirits too.' She paused and then continued. 'As far back as I can remember I sensed another energy very close to me. When I was very small I thought it must be my Guardian Angel because I could feel her touch on any part of my body that wasn't covered. My arms or legs in summer, my cheek or hand in winter. It is a very lithe touch, like a duck down feather, barely perceptible. I saw orbs too and lately I have begun to see spirits and of course, the ancient ones,' she repeated. 'I think that I might have seen them when I was very little, it's difficult to know whether I have flash backs or actual memories,' she responded honestly and half in thought.

'How long have you been able to see them since you grew up?' Swami asked.

'Nearly a year,' she said and looked at Swami as if she was puzzled by his questions.

'I'm trying to understand how it is you get into your aura,' he urged, making it obvious to Jack that he was aware of what was transpiring between them both.

'Aura,' Kate repeated.

'Yes. You see, when you were little it was not unusual for you to see beings in other dimensions because you did not have the protection of you own auras.' Swami began. 'You, all of us, were open to everything in the entire energy field… but as we grow physically so also do we add on chakras and layers of aura… what I am wondering is why you are not like Jack for example… more grounded in the physical?' Swami was threading very carefully, gently.

'I don't know, actually what you say corresponds to a wise woman at home, she explained my second sight in the very same way as you have,' she said ,appearing well pleased with Swami's theories.

'Oh dear, I hope I haven't given you even more confidence,' Swami extended a hand to her upper arm.

'Confidence is exactly what I need now, it feels like it is how you explained, if that makes any sense,' she replied as if she willed him to dispense more of his book learning and his understanding of her. 'Please go on,' she added.

'I have a sort of theory…' he began again. 'We have layers of aura or energy around us. The first layer is known as the etheric layer and that is surrounded by the emotional and then that in turn by the mental layer and so on up to a seventh layer. The first three layers are concerned with the physical body and the last four layers with the spiritual side of a person.' Swami looked from one to the other, checking their comprehension.

'You mentioned spiritual aura a moment ago,' Kate said thoughtfully.

'Yes, my theory is that you have this unusual ability of being able to live in both dimensions,' he looked excitedly from one to the other. 'My theory is that the fifth layer of aura, the etheric layer, which is actually a negative space…' Swami looked directly at Jack to see if he had comprehended the physics of negative space. '… We are in the spiritual aura now… in this negative space the etheric aura of the physical body can exist. Tell me my dear, when you leave your physical body, how do you exit and re-enter?' he addressed Kate this time.

'It feels as though I come in and out through the top of my head,' she replied actually raising her hand up to her crown.

'Magnificent, wonderful, wonderful…' Swami clasped both palms together.

'This makes so much sense,' continued Swami to the mystified teenagers who stood before him with frozen smiles on their faces.

'Please explain,' pleaded Kate.

'You appear to be perfectly rooted in every other way, thus you live like any other human except for… I think the seal on the etheric auras and their corresponding chakras may allow you an enormous amount of access to the universal energy compared with myself or Jack for example,' and he beamed.

'Like an anomaly?' queried Kate.

'Yes. That's the only way I can make sense of it,' he said. 'It is fantastic for someone like me to actually meet someone like you who can interact with beings from another world,' he continued still beaming through his glasses.

'Why are they helping us, though?' questioned Jack who felt it was time to get down to business. 'I spoke with the Sanskrit teacher today at school. He told me the Goddess Dana is a Tantric goddess: why would her people work against Kali who is a Tantric goddess too? Aunt Saroj's incantations in the prayer room were to Kali and she appears to have gained her energy from that goddess.'

'I can only think that they are more evolved than us and want to maintain a balance which is being disturbed by your aunt who is not using the power for the greater good,' surmised Swami, now refocused. 'And that makes it a very dangerous place for both of you,' he continued, fixing his eyes on both of theirs in turn.

'Matty is heading down the beach in our direction,' warned Kate.

'We must be quick,' said Swami. 'I have found out from your driver, you do know Vishu lives near me?' questioned Swami, but continued on before the children could answer. 'I took the liberty of having a little chat with him about your aunt,' Swami raised an eyebrow in Jack's direction and again continued on: 'I found out the name of the temple she visits very frequently and when. It's a village temple where worship is very primitive and which suits her needs, I suspect.' He paused briefly, turning and waving to Matty and his mother as they advanced nearer the little group.

'Unfortunately her next trip is tomorrow night so that does not give us much time to plan anything. She leaves the driver and her chaperone a distance from the temple and so Vishu was not able to tell me anything more,' he finished.

With that the cluster of three became five and since it was nearing seven-thirty and bedtime for Matty, the little group headed towards the car leaving Swami to walk to his beachside home.

TEMPLE POOJA

JACK FOUND IT difficult to believe he was being tossed about in the boot of an Ambassador car again. He was sure he would have bruises afterwards and was fearful he might even throw up, though the driver had warned him not to eat for several hours before the trip. For once he was glad he actually took advice, having had only a glass of lime juice after school. What was really irritating more than the sudden jerks was the fact that he was wearing a lungi, a sarong for men. He had begun wearing them in bed in summer instead of pyjamas but was not good at keeping them on; they were simply tucked in at the waist and with all the rolling and tension in his stomach muscles trying to keep stable in the swaying caused by the moving car it was impossible to keep the cloth secure around his waist. He hoped he would manage it better when he was among the crowds attending the temple pooja he was bound for.

Kate and Jack had met in his bedroom around midnight to digest the information that Swami had gleaned from the driver. Between them they had formulated a plan to spy on the aunt, she in her etheric form with the Goddess Dana's people and Jack as a farmer.

The plan had been lengthy despite the short time they hand to prepare. Kate had been very clever, she suggested he dress as a labourer and had borrowed Ram's lungi from the car shed where he left it when he went home each evening. It was ingenious except when Jack wound it round his middle: two large feet and ankles stuck out underneath the wrap, it was too short but they had no choice except use it and hope it wouldn't be noticed. Jack's own lungi looked too clean and the cloth a more expensive weave, Kate had explained. They worried that his height might give him away so he practised leaning back on his heels; the lungi would conceal his bent knees. It smelled of soil and even Ram's sweat. Thinking of sweat he realised that he had begun to feel damp all around his hairline, something that neither Kate nor he had not considered. Normally Jack sweated profusely when he exercised which never made him feel uncomfortable but the skin of his face had been stained, also his arms as far as his elbows and feet and legs as far as his knees, with semi-dried tea leaves. Kate had applied more to his neck, ears and face as Jack was fair -skinned and needed to be invisible and blend with the crowds. He was very afraid that it may now be streaked so he dabbed his temples gently with the frill of the cushions from the chairs in the bungalow which Vishu had lined the boot floor with: it left a stain.

Both Vishu and Kate had to come up with a certain amount of inventive excuses to convince the curious of their irregular behaviour. Matty had walked in on Kate at the kitchen sink as she tied used tea leaves in a fine muslin cloth and needed to know what she was doing. She had been very resourceful and showed him how to make ordinary paper look like ancient documents by dying it with the damp tea leaves, explaining his Norman heritage and the knight Sir Thomas from whom they could trace their lineage. As usual for Matty he became fully engrossed; the He-Man castle and figures were back in the toy box and medieval Lego was scattered all over the dining table where Kate helped him build their own version of a Norman castle.

Vishu's inventiveness caused him a scolding but Jack reckoned he knew it would. Jack was so intent on their plan that he dismissed the thought of the danger it would put the driver in. He approached Vishu when the latter delivered Matty and himself home from school earlier that evening. To his relief the driver not only became implicit but agreed. In order to stow the lungi-clad, tanned Jack safely in the boot Vishu must forget to bring the car to the main house for Aunt Saroj's visit to the temple. So after he delivered Jack's grandfather home later on he simply parked the car outside the front door of the Little Pink House. Stowing Jack in the boot was easy enough as the front door of the Little Pink House was near the front gate and the watchman left his vigil to water the flowers and lawn at the back just before dusk and while Jack's father was out playing tennis and his mother was sat on the lawn with the Swami, the uneasy distraction. Kate's part of the plan was to contact him by phone when Jack's mother took her shower that morning and explain their arrangement. Swami forbade it in strong terms, Kate told Jack, and refused to be part of it as he felt it was far too dangerous especially with the aunt dabbling in the darker forces.

However, at four-fifteen Swami appeared at the front door of the Little Pink House and although reserved in attitude towards the children he did sit with Jack's mother for the departure of her eldest son in disguise and stayed there when Kate joined the not so human beings at the village temple later on that evening. When it was time for Jack, the farmer, to slip out of the Little Pink House Matty was busy squirrelling the newly completed Lego castle safely up in his bedroom and stayed arranging Lego knights on the battlements and in the castle keep. Everything had gone smoothly and to plan; Jack even overheard the scolding Vishu received as the aunt and her biddable cousin, a nervous chaperone, got into the back seat of the car. Once the engine started it drowned out the sound of their voices so he couldn't even distract himself by eavesdropping and spent time comforting himself with these thoughts and Kate's part when it came time for her to escape, trusting that the more dangerous time ahead would go without trouble.

He imagined her making her way through the blinds on the back veranda and turning left towards the lawn, she'd say she wasn't feeling well and would go and lie down in his bedroom. Swami, he hoped, would not give their plans away and Jack's mother would feel Kate's forehead and be contented that she wasn't feverish. Jack knew Kate had rested most of the afternoon as she knew she would need every ounce of energy for the night ride with the Goddess Dana's people who were agreeable to take her and even offered their protection.

Jack still had difficulty with the science of what Kate had to do. She explained at length to him the place at the far side of a lagoon, in the ruins of a burned-down cottage where she moved into her astral, or according to Swami her etheric, body just once before and entered a Shee, a faerie mount. She instinctively felt what she thought to be a vortex, in that deserted place among the sand dunes on a windswept Irish coast, that helped her traffic between the worlds. Jack once again pictured it in his mind; it was just visible from his Irish Grandmother's house. That led him to think about the mound, the Shee; he knew where it was, the general area anyway. He could locate it given a chance as he knew and could see the ruins of the Borough House from across the lagoon. Getting there was another matter as the whole area between the land and the borough was made up of slime and a type of quicksand. There were paths through it at low tide and finally a channel to cross before reaching the bay the short way. It was nearby in those ruins that Kate thought she used a portal or perhaps it was a permeable boundary between the existences and the race of spirit beings.

He thought over her reservations about not being close to Mother Earth this time: would Dana's people get her through the man-made barriers, the security bars on the bedroom window? She had discussed with them the possibility of leaving her inert flesh body lying in the sand outside, just under Jack's bedroom window, but after some thought realised the watchman would find the body and an alarm would be raised, doctors called, bites from mosquitoes and other night creatures and possibly damage caused, leaving her forever among the Tuatha or in this case the Danavas. All these unanswered problems and scenarios had been tossed back and forth between the two over and over without a safe conclusion in their preparation for the night's investigation after Jack got back from school.

Although Kate hadn't spent any length of time in her etheric body that first time in Ireland, being excited and afraid all at once, she made a conscious effort to reunite body and soul as quickly as she could. However, this time she would need an hour, and wondered if time passed more quickly as it did in Ireland once she was in the other world. All this, she had confided in Jack and all of it was dominating Jack's mind as he struggled with car sickness, creating a very uncomfortable state of uncertainty in both body and mind. Jack pictured her having her final words with the Good People, as they were known in Ireland, Dana's people awaiting her, outside his bedroom window, a young mare held by its bridle awaiting the etheric Kate, for they already had shown it to her.

Jack's body was bounced yet again as the car swerved and missed evading another pothole; the pain from the bounce and thud felt in Jack's ribs left a persistent ache. Was preserving his lifestyle worth this, worth endangering Kate's life? The enormity of what Kate had decided to do, the physical pain and nausea were pressing down on his reasoning and thought processes, he wanted to burst open the boot door and leap out and away from this dark, heavy situation. The nausea was almost overwhelming.

Perhaps Swami was right: to do nothing, accept his fate, just move with his parents when his father would eventually make the decision to leave as Swami had predicted he would. Kate had felt like he did: why give up without a fight, what right had another human being to decide his fate for him, decide he should be banished so that she could control the wealth? She would never be accepted running any of his grandfather's factories or offices, women just did not do that in Kerala society and anyway she knew nothing of how to create money but was a skilled squanderer.

Jack pulled the sarong across his legs and tried tucking it in once again. He began to remember Swami's reservations and how he had been so absolutely unconvinced by their plan, relayed by Kate and discussion avoided when he arrived at the Little Pink House earlier. The strategy that they had worked out the previous night between them, both of them, avoiding Swami's advice to Jack, was to concentrate on work to create protection. This was the first step, the only step of a plan of a battle of will and power, to put the aunt under surveillance.

Information is power, the heading of the *Economist* magazine which lay on the coffee table in the sitting room at the Little Pink House announced: the words flashed across his mind. The full extent of the meaning was designed for a commercial situation but was aptly applicable in this battle, as the wise, the psychic and the young went in pursuit of the greedy one.

PADDY FIELDS

 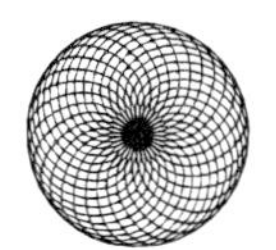

SUDDENLY THE CAR stopped. Jack prepared his ears for the slam after he heard the driver turn the handle of the back door to let his aunt out. The car started up again and was gently brought to a halt a little distance from the entrance to the temple which was beyond a raised walkway across paddy fields and into a dense coconut grove about seven minutes' walk away. Vishu kept up a monotonous conversation with the waiting chaperone, leaving the bonnet raised and then going to the boot to supposedly get car tools. Jack listened for the prearranged signals as well as the conversation about how air conditioners caused such difficulty for car engines. Vishu gestured to Jack who had crouched on hands and knees and hopped out, clutching his lungi to his waist. Darkness had fallen. The driver moved to the chaperone's window, wiping the engine oil from his hands with a rag and imparting gossip as to why he fully agreed with the aunt why air conditioners should not be fitted to cars and were only necessary because of the *Madama*, Jack's mother; she needed the comfort from the heat. This snitch of inside information caused the chaperone to focus intensely on what the driver had to say about the relationships in the inner family in the hope of getting more insight into the domestic goings on of her wealthy cousins.

Jack squatted by the back of the car for a minute and scanned the countryside; he had no difficulty arranging it in his head as per the driver's verbal map. He quickly arranged his sarong and made for the next ridge of land separating the damp paddy fields, less exposed further down from the temple entrance. It was easy enough to locate even in the darkness of the countryside and he hadn't spotted any other person; the ridge used by his aunt seemed to be the most used. Once on the ridge he walked on calmly, even though he didn't feel it, until he came to the grove of coconut trees. Here there was no path, just a dense forest of coconut trees under-planted with the green leafy plants of tapioca his own height, which he zig-zagged through as best he could, hoping not to disturb snakes. It was darker in there as the green umbrellas of the coconut trees so close together cut out the night light created by stars, so he walked as close to the edge of the thicket as he could and followed the sound of the drums coming from the temple.

Shortly he joined the edge of the crowd, all country folk. An old crone gave him an examining look; he slunk back a bit, remembering to bend at the knees to reduce his height as these people where not only mere shadows weight-wise, they were not very tall either. He automatically put his hand up to touch his hairline, being conscious of the dye, and had a brainwave to act as if he was half-witted. He looked shyly at the old woman and slunk further along the edge of the spectators and into the shadows away from the few florescent lights which had been attached vertically to wooden stakes nearer to the tiny temple entrance of which he had an excellent view.

His aunt was being given a lot of importance: she stood at the entrance to the temple which was just an ordinary door in a partially constructed foot high wall facing just one sanctum sanatorium, which Jack could not see into but had been told by Vishu that it was an idol of the village clay goddess.

A little girl, aged about seven Jack reckoned, held his aunt's hand. Now and then the aunt seemed to reassure her, swinging the arm back and forth and saying what Jack considered encouraging words, as the aunt beamed a smile in the child's direction but the child only stared wide-eyed into the crowd, *probably desperate to find her mother,* Jack thought.

Some men clad only from the waist down in white mundus motioned the aunt to a raised platform opposite to the *Sanctum Sanctorum*. Jack considered these were the priests of the tantric tradition which Swami had explained would perform blood sacrifice. The chanting was gathering pace and the drummers too lashed their tabalas, creating a frenzied build up as the aunt took her place on the dais. She kept a tight hold of the child's hand and took her place regally as the chanting by the temple priests and their attendants built and built, accompanied by the frenzied beating of the drums. Jack could clearly see the perspiration on the drummers' bare shoulders and foreheads. The crowd had become enveloped in the energy, joining in a repetitive chant. As it reached a crescendo Jack became aware of a machete rising in the air by a man clad only in khaki shorts. He supposed some goat or chicken was being beheaded, he could not see below waist level from where he stood. The drumming and chanting stopped momentarily.

The aunt let go of the child's hand and the child ran from the platform and into the crowd out of Jack's line of sight. The crowds let out a cry of trepidation. Eyes back on the aunt and for a brief moment Jack thought he saw his aunt's eyes roll right around in their sockets. Was she possessed? What had he missed when he looked away? He now realised she had changed. She stood imposingly, seemingly intoxicated with elation. The crowd appeared to be over their initial uncertainty and surged forward, touching her feet and garlanding her with flowers. She accepted the adoration and they parted to allow one of the priests to approach the dais and he anointed her with what Jack supposed was the fresh blood which he carried in a white enamel basin. Jack could just see the priest tilting the basin enough to let the rich red, velvet liquid, which, Jack imagined, felt warm, drain into his aunt's cupped palms which she raised to her mouth and drank.

Immediately a cry of approval arose from the worshippers standing behind the silent drummers who were in a semi-circle around her. Jack was trying to understand the reactions of the worshippers. He felt some sort of installation ceremony had taken place and hoped Swami would intrepid more from the ritual than he could. The drummers began again but with a less frenzied beat. A couple of women started dancing as if infatuated; their hair fell loosely over their backs and they began another sort of chant in rhythm with the drummers. Jack could distinguish the words.

Although Jack came from a Hindu family who were fish eaters and who occasionally added chicken to their diet, the sight of his aunt consuming warm blood from the freshly slaughtered and uncooked animal or bird caused his empty stomach to lurch and he could barely suppress the spasm as it reached his throat. He swallowed back hard and forced himself to look again at the woman, now fully alienated from him as she wiped the blood dribbles which had escaped from her palms from her chin. She then raised her arms and clapped her hands once and stepped into the dance. Jack recognised the steps: his father used to do it for Matty and himself for fun, boasting that he had been a better dancer than his sister when they were children. This was the dance of Lord Siva. Grandfather's stories also came to mind watching the spectacle, Jack remembered him saying the Goddess Kali sometimes became so caught up in her dance that she caused destruction and Lord Siva had to catch her ankle to stop her before she destroyed everything, including the whole of creation. Had this woman such grandiose ideas that she herself was part of the Goddess with all her dark powers? Destruction, yes, he knew who she wanted destroyed…

Like most people who were born into families who practised a religion, Jack attended the rituals, for him both Hindu and Catholic, but he did not know a great deal about either the Vedas or the Bible and had only a vague enquiring interest in their history. What he had just witnessed must be *the extremity of Hinduism,* he considered.

The temple priest who held the basin of blood approached the aunt and she stopped her manic dance. She followed him to the four corners of the temple and in each corner she dipped her finger into the blood, stooped and anointed the ground with it. *The four cardinal points*, thought Jack.

Just then an elderly man whom Jack had been aware of for some time from the corner of his eye moved closer to him rubbing his chin as he scrutinised Jack's face.

'You're not from around here?' he questioned.

'No,' replied Jack in Malayalam and began to move away in the direction of the forest of coconut trees, towards the car and safety. But the old man was persistent.

'Where do you come from then?' insisted the old man, hands now joined and relaxed behind his back but doggedly following Jack among the tapioca and coconut trunks. Jack was aware his Malayalam was accented and searched his mind for words that would rid him of the inquisitive old man without having to make a sentence.

'Go,' he hissed in Malayalam as he turned around to face the man and glared at his face as fiercely as he could. Then he turned and ran, holding his sarong but this only made the old man run too, following him. The old man was agile but soon got tired and began to shout out to the others back at the temple calling to them to come and catch the stranger. Jack hoped the drumming and chanting would drown out his shouting but was aware of answers shouted from far off. In that awful moment, Jack realised that the power his aunt had invoked was actually protecting her; he was being removed as a spectator, he could no longer spy on her.

Then suddenly the yelling stopped. Jack quickly glanced round to see the old man cower, abruptly he stared up as if he was afraid of something all around him, for he jumped from one spot to another and rubbed one arm then the other as he skipped seemingly to avoid some unpleasantness yet again. Jack relaxed and watched from behind the trunk of a coconut tree, he knew now he was not alone and longed to see the Goddess Dana's people and Kate.

He stared into the darkness of the coconut grove, but like the old man he could not see another being, just vegetation; but unlike the old man he couldn't feel anything. Then he became aware of a couple of men emerging out of the shadows near the old man; they approached him warily. He could hear them, they discussed the old man's behaviour. From their conversation Jack understood that they thought he had gone mad. Jack somehow knew he had to use this moment to escape and started to trace his way back to the edge of the grove in the darkness, always fearful of disturbing snakes.

AMBUSH

SOON JACK COULD make out the paddy fields again with the raised walkways between them but no sign of the car. He had no idea how far beyond the walkway he had used as an entrance to escape the old man but decided to retrace his way along the edge of the thicket. This had been a wise decision as from out of the murk he soon spotted the white car across the walkway on the road at the far side of the paddy fields. Jack stayed in the darkness of the forest and watched. A few people began to file along the raised walkways leading from the temple further along from where he was.

He was considering how to slip across without causing attention and before his aunt would arrive when a scream inches from his right ear erupted in the stillness and terrified him. He turned to find a monkey snout, teeth wide and bared. It loudly protested his presence. He knew not to tamper with monkeys as they generally lived side by side in the rural areas with people, occasionally stealing from their huts but generally cohabiting in wariness. He remembered being told never to feed one as scores of others would instantly appear begging incessantly. This one kept calling; reactively, Jack bent to grab the spine of a large coconut frond which lay drying among so much tall grass and dried leaves at his feet but it bent limp in his hand, a useless tool to protect himself. As he bent and grabbed he became aware of rustling and to his horror found himself surrounded by a whole troupe of monkeys, which was the result of the calls. He dropped the limp coconut spine and stood still remembering that these animals were not predatory by nature, they snatched cameras from tourists at temples but generally didn't bite unless provoked. At the same moment that he hoped his movement had not appeared aggressive he felt the powerful muscles of the large one land on to his back and instantly bite into his shoulder muscle. Straight away the others advanced on him as he screamed with pain and flailed hopelessly to dislodge the controlled cling of the brawny, screeching monkey. Jack was beyond horror. In a minute or two he would be shreds of flesh on bone among the dried leaves at his feet as the faces of monkeys with their incisors bared jumped and swung down on him. His aunt's retribution was almost complete. The last thought Jack had was for his parents.

As Jack waited for the next heavy grip and bite, probably at his throat, the feel of the monkey's overwhelming muscular strength and weight left his shoulder. Directly he saw them, or rather saw through them: the mounted ones, clad in what appeared to be katchas with split swords girded to their waists, carrying short, dagger-like swords and circular shields. They were so faint in the dimness a blue light outlined them, like a photo negative, but the energy was heavy and real. They partly materialised where the faint light broke through into the thicket and the monkeys fell away, becoming invisible among the trees and undergrowth again. Jack straightened slowly and watched this phantom army quietly march past on spectre horses with a beautiful young woman in the lead and a muscular, middle aged man who rode like a warrior of old and had a king's bearing.

Jack waited no longer, needing to be well clear of the small patch of jungle by the time the sprite army had passed. He sped along the raised ground not caring who noticed, feeling the warm blood on his right shoulder cause his shirt to stick to the skin. He bent low and crouched on the grassy verge near the car awaiting Vishu's signal. The boot was still open but the bonnet was shut. He could hear the chaperone urge Vishu to start up the engine and be in position and ready for his aunt when she emerged from the walkway further on. Jack was about to creep the last few feet towards the car and ease himself into the boot without the signal when Vishu emerged around the rear of the car and distracted the chaperone for the last time while Jack settled himself in the boot, carefully easing himself on to his left side to avoid the pain. His eyes met Vishu's and he knew all was understood as the driver placed the duster against the wound between Jack and the cushion to staunch the flow of blood. He shut the boot and Jack pressed his back against the cloth and the cushion remembering how his mother had dealt with grazed knees and particularly the minor puncture wounds of childhood. He was shivering but not due to fever; he knew it was sheer fright at how life could be so vulnerable. He had encountered nothing more dangerous than a few monkeys but they had the power and the will to tear him to pieces, for possibly their mistress was his aunt. He checked his imagination, *must not let it get out of control*; the monkey attack may or may not be coincidental.

As the car engine started and stopped and his aunt got in, the Danava army was uppermost in Jack's mind, not the monkey attack. He was also concerned about the wound and how to disguise it once home but that unreal army marching past with much more magnificence than any modern army on an Indian Independence Day parade overawed him. They were dignified, powerful beings seated erect on fine horses, which jerked their heads within the bridles and flicked their tails like tangible horses. He remembered the lady. Could it have been the Goddess Dana, she was the Tuatha's Mother Goddess and the Danavas' Mother Goddess was also Dana. Could it have been Kate? The riders were adult and the woman eighteen or older. She looked right into his eyes as they passed, he felt it more than saw it for he could not make out individual colours, more a radiance as they passed in the gloom lighted only by the glow of a night sky that penetrated the coconut canopy. More than the spectacle he remembered he actually heard them, the sound of the tack as the horses shook their manes.

The sway of the car was painful but his mind was full of the world which Kate had the ability to enter and exit. What a privilege: he longed for their midnight talk and wondered if she was already at the Little Pink House. As the journey wore on he realised his mind had focused on his rescue rather than the terror of the death he had just barely escaped.

THE AFTERMATH

 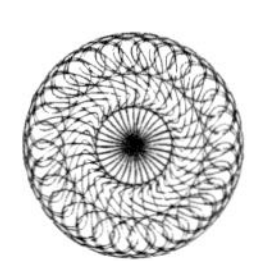

WHEN JACK FINALLY walked up the steps at the back veranda towards the dining room door of The Little Pink House he was met by Matty who looked stricken and pale and was agitated. He declared that Kate was dead. Jack ran through the dining room and pushed his way past the tight little group in the inner hallway, his grandparents and Nisha; the worried and startled look Swami wore hardened the concrete mass forming inside Jack's chest. He pressed past his Dad standing in the doorway to his room and over towards the bed with his mother cradling what appeared to be a lifeless Kate.

'What's the matter?' he demanded, catching hold of her warm hand, relieved that the colour was pink and not white and cold.

'She went for a rest and later on I couldn't rouse her,' his mother sounded as if she had a head cold and occasionally rubbed away a tear. 'Look, look at how limp she is…' and she held Kate's hand a small bit above the mattress, let go of it and watched it flop, lifeless, onto the mattress, the pads of her fingers sliding along the sheet straightening the hand as they touched down.

'I've taken her temperature, it's normal, her pulse is normal, maybe a little slow. We're waiting for Dr Krishna, I don't know what I am going to say to them in Ireland.' More tears rolled down her cheeks as she hugged the fair hair and squeezed Kate closer to her.

Jack knelt down on the floor close to Kate's head with his back towards the window. Her eyes didn't even stare, they didn't flicker or blink. Matty arrived at the foot of the bed and asked if she was dead. He must be facing the worst possible scenario, thought Jack; surely he understands she is unconscious, trying to reassure himself as well as identify with Matty's feelings in this horribly, loathsome circumstance that only he had unspoken knowledge of.

'No, noo she is not dead, she'll be alright,' cooed Grandmother as she joined Matty at the end of the bed, firstly reassuring him and then moving forward towards their mother repeating, 'She'll be alright, don't worry.'

'Look at her lips… what's that white… powder?' Jack's mother began examining Kate's mouth anxious at yet another mysterious symptom.

The shock and helpless energy of those in the doorway was pervading the very air in the Little Pink House and amidst this the hush of the bedroom. So many eyes focused on the lifeless body of the young girl willing her to wake.

Then there came the welcome and loud clang of the large bolt being drawn back on the gate and the throb of a diesel Ambassador car. Jack's father sped towards the front door and almost immediately the quiet, calm of Dr Krishna descended as he appeared with his serene smile. Everyone left the room except Jack's mother. They all quietly slipped into the dining room and carefully pulled out chairs from around the dining table and seated themselves silently.

Just as Grandfather had eased his mass into an armchair he rose and rolled up Jack's shirt.

'Son, what happened to you, what is this?' Grandfather was shocked beyond belief. Jack had forgotten about the bite and the blood.

'Ram, come and look at this.' He had no need to beckon Jack's father, for he was on his feet along with grandmother and Matty in seconds, all focused on the bloodied wound on Jack's right shoulder.

'Jack what happened… where did you get this… this is a bite… you've been bitten… how did it happen?' Jack's father had peered into the wound and begun taking off the shirt. Having taken out the non-bloodied side first he then carefully separated the cloth from the wound as Jack tensed and stiffened his back to avoid wriggling the muscles of his shoulder as the pain of the separation of the cloth from the sticky raw flesh wound caused the blood to trickle again.

Matty ran to the sideboard and struggled in his haste to get the first aid box free of the drawer, he pulled at the large drawer which he had not opened wide enough. Within seconds he started flinging dressings on to the table. Grandmother asked for 'Dettol' and Matty again ran to the cupboard under the kitchen sink.

'Is it one of the dogs?' queried Grandfather.

'No, not our dogs,' Jack imagined the vet putting down whichever dog he named and couldn't bear it because he knew that is what Grandfather would do.

By that time Matty had procured a plastic jug with some water in it for Grandmother who was commanding the first-aid part of the activity. She mixed in some 'Dettol' and dipped one of the dressings into the solution and interrupted the inquisition by warning Jack it might sting as she dabbed his wound. As she touched it, the thought came to him and he responded to his father's question halting between the tingling, needle-like sting of disinfectant on his raw flesh.

'Akhill and I met up at the Residency. We were exploring the wooded area down by the lake for a Biology project when a monkey sprang out of one of the trees on to my back and bit me.'

'Son, didn't we tell you not to go down there without an adult?' reminded Grandfather with his most disapproving face on.

'Didn't I tell you about the child snatchers, son, how can you be so careless?' Jack wished Grandmother would not scold and clean the wound at the same time, he really felt she was less gentle when she spoke.

'He'll have to have a tetanus,' added Jack's father. 'Krishna Aliyan is here, we'll have a word when he's ready.' This seemed to reassure the grandparents a little but the inquisition continued.

Jack avoided Swami's eyes completely as Swami stood up and headed for the little veranda.

'There are no monkeys near the Residency lake…' pondered Grandfather aloud.

Nisha had moved quietly to a chair facing Jack and the wide brown eyes stared right into his searchingly. *It takes a liar to recognise a liar*, thought Jack, thinking as quickly as he could whilst being tortured by Grandmother's wound cleaning. He didn't want to arouse any suspicion on the aunt's part caused by tales Nisha would carry, and she was an excellent embellisher.

'There have always been some in the wooded area across the lake,' Jack's father remarked.

'Yes, but they never cross the lake, very rarely have we had them on this side,' argued Grandfather.

Nisha's penetrating stare was unremitting, the wide, apparently innocent and uninterested eyes sensing the hidden truth that remained lost to the others.

Dr Krishna saved Jack having to invent more cover-ups: everyone looked up when he and Jack's mother appeared in the doorway of the dining room.

'All I can find are the mosquito bites on her ankles…' Dr Krishna stopped mid-sentence. There was anxiety radiating from a flustered mother; her eyes shot from the little pile of bloodied dressings on a newspaper on the dining table to the bloodied shirt and finally to the half-naked Jack.

'What…?' was all that emerged from her O-shaped mouth.

'Jack got bitten by a monkey,' provided Matty who wore an excited smile and hopped around Jack's chair and added 'at the Residency,' as if he anticipated his mother's question.

Dr Krishna began examining the wound at close quarters; Jack could feel the doctor's warm breath on his shoulder and was thankful that his touch was a lot gentler than Grandmother's.

'Are his tetanus jabs up to date?' quietly queried the pensive Doctor.

Jack's mother took her eyes from the wound and then Jack's face which appeared as unstressed as always except for the dark shadows under his eyes. She began to rummage in the side-board drawer from which Matty had taken the first aid box for her little green suede note book in which she kept a record of the boys' medical history. Jack rolled his eyes and thought to himself: *she'll never find anything in that.* Every time she needed to find out when boosters, etc. were due, she would end up berating herself for the messy chronological way she had made the entries over the years. Jack's history was in the first half of the notebook and Matty's was entered into the second part, also in chronological order. It meant having to find year dates by flicking through years of entries and then a lot of reading. *She should have placed the information under designated headings that would have been more practical,* Jack thought and wondered why he was even thinking about the green book when Kate was God knows where.

'I think he's covered,' Grandmother began talking to herself out loud. 'Remember the dog bite, wasn't that last year… or was it the year before? He had a course then.'

'I'm beyond thinking,' remarked Jack's mother as she continued to turn over page after page of the green notebook, scanning her notes. *She's probably beyond concentrating too,* thought Jack.

'It was the year before last,' interjected Jack, remembering how foolish he had been by facing the barking dog head on instead of jumping up on the church wall next to his school as his friends had done. He had read somewhere that this worked when confronted by a wild animal; regretfully it didn't work with pye-dogs.

'Ah, then he's alright,' reassured Dr Krishna. 'Just keep the wound covered until it heals but dress it every day. A monkey you say?… Maybe a course of antibiotics, that would be best,' and he sat down at the table and began to write on his prescription pad.

'What were you doing at the Residency? Out on that bike again alone…' Jack's mother's accused angrily; frustration had set in.

'I wasn't alone, I was with Akhill,' said Jack defiantly.

'Him… I might have known… you were at his house when you got the dog bite too…'

'No I was at school when I…' Jack had begun a defence.

'Leave it, leave it for now,' pleaded Jack's father. 'It could be a lot worse.'

'I don't think it needs to be stitched,' pondered Dr Krishna, peering at the wound again. 'The incisors have left deep puncture wounds; watch them, see that they heal from the inside out. I'll put hydrogen peroxide on the prescription.' He instructed Jack's mother on how to dress the wound.

'Should I try packing the deep ones?' she asked, peering at Jack's shoulder.

'No, they're too small, just soak the wound liberally with the hydrogen peroxide, that should do, he's healthy,' the Doctor said, calmly smiling at her.

Jack watched Matty slip through the dining room door in his invisible way. *Ever conscious, ever sensitive Matty, always aware of the unsaid and unseen.* Jack knew he was headed for Kate's room, she had been alone for some minutes now and he had been thinking of her between times too.

His mother had at last found the exact date of his tetanus vaccination and began clearing up the bloodied dressings from the dining room table. She offered Dr Krishna tea and headed to the kitchen, peering out at the pacing Swami as she passed the door leading to the veranda. From the corner of his eye Jack could see Grandmother hand Mary the ayah the bloodied shirt and give instructions for soaking.

As Dr Krishna and his father discussed how Jack would shower and his subsequent dressing procedure Matty flung himself literally into the dining room leaving the netted door to wallop against the open bedroom door and he announced with accomplishment:

'She's looking out through her eyes again.'

'What?' queried Grandfather. 'What's he saying?'

'Kate, Kate, she's moving her eyes... I think she is anyway...' and with that he disappeared in the direction of the netted door again.

Jack, his father and Dr Krishna were on their feet and Nisha slowly raised herself and called her grandmother. Swami's enquiring face poked into the light of the dining room.

Sure enough, Kate lay stunned on the bed – but she was reacting, smiling at Matty and her eyes moved as Jack and the entire household and visitors crowded into the little room. Dr Krishna moved over towards the bed.

'How are you feeling now?' he queried very gently.

'As if an elephant has walked all over me,' answered Kate weakly. Everyone laughed too loud; it was the relief.

'You must take some rest, you have some large swellings from the mosquito bites, your body might have overreacted, I've left a prescription for some medicines, you'll be alright,' he reassured in his quiet voice and bestowed his peaceful smile.

Jack wished everyone out of the room, he was desperate to know what happened to Kate but instead he was urged out by his mother and grandmother who said Kate had to rest.

GIRIJA

HAULING HIS MIND out of the past and into the now Jack remembered that the same night that Kate became unconscious and precisely when the family were collecting around the dining table at the Little Pink House and his wound was being exposed, Girija, Nisha's older sister slipped through the gates of the main house.

The night-watchmen, when later questioned, explained that Girija was heading in the direction of the gates of the Little Pink House, but the watchman at the Little Pink House being preoccupied with all the comings and goings never remembered letting her in or even seeing her. Jack empathised with his grandparents as they went from one house to another, from one disaster to another, from one unconscious teenage girl to the perilous absence of another.

Jack's family were privileged; they not only had Dr Krishna to call on when anyone suffered an ache or worse but they had a police inspector who was a cousin too. His presence was requested at the main house an hour after Kate's recovery, when Jack's grandparents had gone home to what they supposed would be a wind-down dinner after the anxiety of the evening. So while Kate rested and a watchful aunt regularly took her pulse and checked her breathing and made her move her toes, Jack arrived in the big living room of his grandparents' house to witness a discussion on the missing eighteen year-old.

'She never speaks,' Grandmother was saying, 'There is something troubling her, she's not happy. She used to be such a pleasant child.'

'She wants to be with Dad,' Nisha interjected, the first words had leaped out and the rest of the sentence just trailed away to silence, as she quelled it. Jack knew and understood how Nisha felt and believed she was right: Girija had probably gone home.

'This is your entire fault,' Grandmother began scolding Aunt Saroj.

'I went to the temple, I can't be expected to keep an eye on her twenty-four hours a day,' the aunt said, entreating eyes on Inspector Arun's, who immediately stood up and strutted authoritatively around the sitting room. The cane, held in his left hand, leaned obediently against the shoulder of his khaki uniform.

Jack noticed his aunt's hair was wet and hanging loose to dry and her sari had been changed. *She had bathed, not to avoid polluting the house with fresh blood but to hide her dark magic,* he thought.

'I think Nisha has made a valid point, she has probably taken the night train home. Saroj, ring Ravi and ask him to check the station in the morning,' the Inspector ordered with the full clout his uniform could command. Aunt Saroj obediently went to make the call. Jack knew she would be relieved to be out of the spotlight of responsibility as he felt his aunt probably knew a public lecture from Grandmother on separation in marriage was imminent.

Jack felt like slapping the police inspector and he knew his father was barely tolerating them. Surely he could phone ahead and have a plain-clothes police officer board the train at one of the stops to try and locate Girija without spooking her. Jack kept his mouth shut as Grandmother formed the words for the thoughts in his head.

'Arun, can't you have someone from Alleppy or Cochin board the train and search for her?'

'Aunty the sight of the uniform searching would only frighten her. What if she decided to get off the train at Trichur? I'm sure she doesn't have much money and even if she has enough to go to a hotel, anything might happen to a young woman without a chaperone.'

His words formed the only answer his poor mind was capable of and he was so proud of them, but they only made Grandmother and Nisha feel even more uneasy. Jack noticed Nisha sitting on a stool, head bent – hands clinging together, extending out beyond her knees, which were supporting her elbows – and her large, brown eyes wide with anxiety. Lately he noticed that she crept into the corners of a room and sat on low stools when the family gathered together as if she was drawing attention to herself by appearing to quietly tuck herself away. She usually kept her head down, literally, but was communicative unlike Girija who never made an effort to join in and remained sullen. This new Girija was so different from the Girija who had spoiled him and played with him when she spent her holidays with Grandmother.

Later as they walked back to the Little Pink House together Jack half-listened as his father cautioned him about taking his bicycle out with Akhill, with particular reference to the body snatchers, why they did it and how unscrupulous people from other countries would pay any amount for body organs regardless of the children who died during and after harvesting.

'I'm sure Akhill's parents feel the same as we do. Just because you are big and strong doesn't mean you are safe. These people move around in gangs, you would be powerless if five or six men tried to grab you!' insisted his father. 'Jack are you listening to me?'

'Yes Dad, I promise we'll use Grandfather's drive for cycling in future,' placated Jack.

'Why can't Girija or even Nisha stay with their father? I can't imagine having to move from here if we had the same situation. Nobody can blame her for running home. Is it a law that children should stay with their mother in separation or divorce?' questioned Jack.

'Even though your uncle is at home most of the time he would not be prepared to take care of not only one teenage girl but two and remember they both will have arranged marriages. Good families would prefer if they were from a stable home. It would be impossible to have a young man from a good family marry either of them if they were to live with their father.'

'By good you mean rich?' queried Jack.

'No, oh no,' explained his father. 'After your aunt's failed marriage, never again in this family. No, by good I mean the young men should have a profession and be employed and come from decent families.'

'Will Matty and I have arranged marriages?' asked Jack very quietly.

'It will be up to you what you do about marriage,' replied his father, smiling.

They had reached the front door of the Little Pink House. His mother was standing there silhouetted in the darkness; most of the lights were off.

'What news?' she asked.

'She's probably gone home,' Jack's father replied as Jack slipped by her on his way towards Kate's room, only to be hauled around by the arm on the uninjured side and directed upstairs.

'She's alright. She needs a lot of rest. You can catch up after school tomorrow evening.'

Tomorrow evening, thought Jack as he headed up the spiral staircase into Matty territory.

KATE'S TRANSITION

THE NEXT MORNING, as Jack came down the stairs from Matty's room, he noticed that Kate's bedroom door was still closed. Jack's mother reassured him that she was still fast asleep, emphasising a second time *a normal sleep*. After having a heavier and more sealed dressing applied to his wound, '*to keep out infection*', his mother said, he and Matty got into the car waiting outside the front door and set off for school. Jack was in no mood for talking, he felt he just wanted to let things settle in his mind; there was such a lot of energy and activity in his habitually monastery-like two homes that he needed to understand it and be in control of his mind. The monkey attack was fresh in his mind and he still felt physically exhausted at the thought of what had happened. He tried to come to terms with the realisation that he could have died.

The day at school, away from the turbulent environment, had given him a fresh view of everything that had happened. Driver Vishu always drove his grandfather so he had no news whatsoever from home all that day.

When Jack arrived home in the evening with Matty, their mother was asked in chorus, 'How's Kate?'

'Look out into the garden.' She motioned them to the dining room window which looked out along the lawn towards the whitewashed wall bordering their neighbour's house.

There sitting in his usual spot was Swami and facing him was the prone Kate, resting on the wicker recliner. The driver struggled with school bags and lunch tiffins and was left to his mother; Jack almost knocked Matty over the edge of the veranda as they both jostled through the dining room door and rushed towards the shaded spot on the lawn.

'Careful,' called their mother and then instructed the driver to leave the bags in the inner hall and the tiffins in the kitchen. She followed with a tray heavy with glasses of lime juice, cold milk and snacks.

Matty settled himself down on the grass beside Kate's recliner.

'I'm fine,' she said. 'Your mother will not let me move. That's why I'm stretched out like this.'

Jack helped himself to a lime juice before his mother had time to set the tray on the table and settled himself on the grass with his back against the white-washed wall. He knew he would have to wait before he could talk to Kate and Swami but the relief he felt at seeing her normal again enabled him to take the first relaxed breath of the day.

Matty as always had to be reminded to drink his milk and then encouraged to eat his biscuit but after a short while listening to mundane conversation he slipped silently away. Shortly afterwards the ayah beckoned to Jack's mother and announced the cook's arrival and so they were finally alone.

'What happened last night?' Jack directed his question to Kate; at the same time, he considered that both Swami and Kate probably had gone over the event but he didn't want a synopsis, he wanted to know everything.

'I've just been explaining to Swami… I'm remembering in bits and pieces… the more I think about it, the more it comes back. They insisted I stay with them,' she added, seeming to be struggling, trying to make sense of the journey herself.

'What…' was all Jack could form for his next question. 'Was this before you rescued me from the monkeys or after? Did they ask for payment, a fee from you, for the help they had given?' More questions formed as his brain tried to understand primitive minds, things he had read on ancient cultures; some must have an explanation as to why she was trapped for so long.

'I'll start again, at the beginning. They arrived at the window as arranged and I went over our plan, to take me to where you went. So I shut the bedroom door, lay on the bed and concentrated my mind and was outside with them instantly, except when you are out there the house is not a house as we know it…'

Jack couldn't help but look puzzled and she tried to clarify.

'Remember I was worried about the security bars on the window,' she urged him to recall their conversation after the beach.

'Yesss…' he remembered.

'Well I just walked through the bedroom wall and didn't feel a thing, it was as if it didn't exist and of course it didn't once I was outside the material,' she explained, beaming, and sat upright.

'Wow,' was all Jack could say as his mind failed to find a credible meaning but the pained look remained on his face.

'I think she can slip into other dimensions without any preparation,' put in Swami as a way of explanation. 'Something like… Astral travel is the nearest imaginable understanding I can come up with for now. While here in our world she is clairvoyant and can see spirits and sometimes the other world and of course The Little People; Kate explained to me they are known in Ireland and their world in the Sidhes,' Swami said in his pensive way.

'She appears to have access to both worlds at once,' he added, his shoulders leaning forward slightly.

'Sort of like an out-of-body or near-death experience,' suggested Jack.

'How do you know about that?' asked Kate, keenly interested.

'Last time we were in Ireland, I heard the great-uncle, you know the one who had the heart operation, explain to Mum what had happened to him during the operation. Mum said he had an out-of-body experience and that a lot of patients report seeing surgeons work on their bodies,' Jack explained. He was trying to rationalise her experiences to himself.

'But he had to be resuscitated Jack, he was lucky to survive the operation, his out-of-body experience... must have been while he died...' she trailed off ,looking at Swami.

'She is right, Jack, your uncle could only have the out-of-body experience if he briefly passed away,' Swami confirmed and after a little while thinking he continued, 'or there is another explanation: it could have been the medications he had. A shaman will take drugs to facilitate entry into the other world. Are you aware that you are leaving your body, my dear? Are you aware of being two different... how can I explain myself... do you feel separated from your physical body?

'No. I feel older, though...' she replied thoughtfully,

'But don't you feel you want to get back to something?' asked Jack, partially following their conversation.

'It's the same as it is when I am complete, like now, I feel the same and what I want to get back to is where I came from... at home, when I first went into the Sheidhe and last night, I just wanted to get back to a location, not back into my body because it feels as if I am one... I don't feel a separation. Just as in a dream Jack, do you feel separated from yourself in a dream?' she asked him.

'No,' Jack answered after reflecting for some time, trying to remember his last dream.

'There is no change for me Jack, no... transition,' she added.

'There is no easy explanation for this, you would imagine Kate would be discarnate in the other world, but she had a corporeal form. It cannot be compared to near-death or out-of-body experiences, although I understand how you came to the comparison,' Swami said into the silence after some time during which everyone appeared deep in thought.

Dusk began to descend over the Little Pink House and its garden. The pillaging activity of mosquitoes began. Kate enclosed her hands inside the sleeves of her shirt, monk-like, and pushed her pale, bare feet underneath a cushion. Jack smacked his neck from time to time, forestalling a sting. Swami sat Zen-like; the mosquitoes appeared not to bother him.

THE DEBRIEFING

'DID THEY HOLD you captive there and then?' queried Jack, lost but hopeful that meaning and understanding would come with the unfolding of the whole escapade.

'Oh no, not at all, they were very hospitable…' her eyes lost their focus as she appeared to remember more.

'What is it my dear?' Swami spoke softly.

'Things are coming back more vividly. When I was my etheric self, maybe my future self, their time is not linear, I was about eighteen and my hair was much longer,' she spoke very slowly as if thinking, half to herself, at the same time removing her hands from her sleeves and running her right hand down an imaginary long plait on her left shoulder.

'So it was you,' exclaimed Jack.

'What… what do you mean… was me?' Kate looked puzzled as he scooched along the grass coming closer to the foot of the wicker recliner.

'Do you remember distracting the old man who was chasing me and shouting?' asked Jack.

'Well not me, it was the sylphs Tuatha, I should say Danavas, who were responsible for that, actually the upanayika or devas,' she replied thinking, her brow causing the skin above the bridge of her nose to crinkle.

'The small beings with very pointed ears, elongated faces and transparent wings, really fine, finer than a butterfly's?' he asked.

'Yes, but how did…?' her mouth remained open and her brow squeezed again into a furrow.

Swami was bent forward, listening intently.

'Deep in the thicket the sky cast more shadows than light,' Jack explained. 'I had filches of the army, well… it seemed like an army… when they moved into the light, just snitches but enough to discern the beings…'

'That's amazing, so you think you were briefly in my dimension?' Kate appeared to study the aviary without seeing it.

'Out in the country and on a moonless night it might be easier to actually move between dimensions; he wasn't in it but had a brief sight of it,' explained Swami, more to himself. 'It was after all a black moon and the night before Friday which is a day used to call on creatures from the underworld.'

'What's that got to do with it, Swami?' asked Jack.

'Well with… a waned moon… and after all there were the invocations at the temple nearby!' he became aware he had two avid listeners. 'Well, what I'm saying is, the veil between worlds was thinner and therefore… the night was especially chosen by your aunt.' Swami seemed to search for a clearer way to express his interpretation.

'The black moon, as we call it, is the time when the darker forces are beckoned from the underworld, therefore the boundary was permeable, allowing an exchange between worlds – the materialisation of the people of the Goddess Dana for you, Jack,' Swami paused and looked at Jack, then continued. 'There is nothing terribly wrong with the creatures of the underworld if a balance is kept between them and the world of light, but your aunt is using their powers in an unbalanced way, namely, for personal gain. So there are portals open that wouldn't normally be there, that might explain, Jack, as I have said, how you saw the Goddess Dana's people. But there is another explanation also: Jack, you may have been in an expanded state of consciousness which would open up your latent sensory perception abilities.'

'How can Kate get through at will then?' questioned Jack. 'I can't get a grasp on how these dimensions are in my reality. What I saw… just happened.'

'You have heard of the collective conscious haven't you?' Swami's eyebrows moved above his spectacle frames.

'Vaguely,' replied Jack, adjusting one leg into a more comfortable position on the grass.

'We all have conscious states and unconscious states,' explained Swami.

'Unconsciousness is like an anaesthetic,' burst in Jack.

'Not exactly,' interjected Kate. 'We have both in our normal state.'

'I didn't know that,' replied Jack quietly, somewhat impressed by Kate.

'Is it our dreaming state then?' asked a confused Jack.

'Yes that's part of it, dreams send you coded messages. Our psyche is in the unconscious mind,' explained Kate.

'Or is it?' put in Swami. 'It is not part of our conscious mind but influences it, like the dreams you just mentioned.'

'I'm just going along with this for now, I don't really understand it,' said Jack, moving his head from side to side, looking at the grass, totally lost.

'Now, the unconscious or psyche mind is primordial and therefore in touch with the cosmos and therefore…' Swami put heavy emphasis on the last word. 'Precognition, which the conscious mind cannot access, but together they work beautifully as the conscious mind has the ability to evaluate, calculates and makes judgments,' Swami continued as if Jack hadn't spoken at all.

'Precognition… can Kate see into the future then?' put in Jack who felt he could not dismiss the dimension theory because he had actually witnessed it but at the same time he was unable to relate it to the tangible.

'No, that is just another part of it… Kate and I have gone slightly off focus, we had been discussing precognition before you arrived. You know how it is you start looking up a word in a dictionary and get side-tracked on finding something else interesting on the way. We had been discussing the role of dreams and consciousness and how their metaphors can give us warnings. For now let's simplify things: Kate can enter and exit other dimensions where time is not linear. Not only dimensions, but she can interact with the beings that inhabit them.'

'That is so well put, Swami,' beamed Kate.

'How do you know all of this, Swami?' asked Jack.

'From a very ancient Ayurvedic text known as *Caraka Samhita*,' replied Swami.

'I don't know how to be aware of this… as a person, as a human… do I start remembering my dreams and analysing them for messages? I forget most of them immediately anyway…' Jack trailed off.

'Nearly all of us humans are not aware of our unconscious mind but you have a beautiful example here in your cousin. While in the thicket you may have been in a heightened state of awareness that is one way of explaining how you may have seen the Devas and Dana's army.' Now it was Swami's turn to be incandescent.

'What…?' was all Jack could say again and yet he began to understand as Swami and Kate waited patiently with smiles, knowing smiles that seemed to be opening cracks of understanding.

'I think I know how she got out there now,' he smiled. 'I knew there had to be a scientific explanation for the clairvoyant, clair-auditory – Kate's ability to hear beings from other dimensions – and clair-sensory, her ability to feel these beings. Your unconscious mind works with your conscious mind in a more direct way than with us…' he beamed, looking at Kate.

'Normally this would cause mental health problems,' explained Swami. 'But with Kate they work in a very extraordinary way. You see, son, your awareness is tied up very much with your body and your mind. All the while you are surrounded by what is called an aura, layers of energy, remember we talked about this earlier, Kate's whole being enters her etheric aura when she participates in the other world. You and I and most people cannot do that without using drugs like a shaman or removing the mind and the physical like a yogi. Kate is in all of herself, or has become aware of being in all of herself, meaning her auras, unhindered by her psychophysical aspect, therefore she literally moves at will, like you just said between worlds.'

THE WORLD OF THE TUATHA DÉ DANANN

 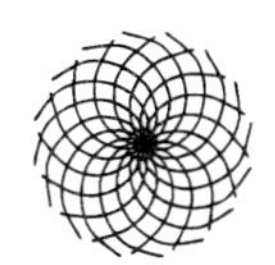

'JACK, YOU KNOW Keeragh House?' Kate continued. 'Until I came here, I always assumed there was a vortex there as that was the only place I could actually see the Tuatha dé Danann, never at home in my bedroom or in the stable, nowhere, only out on the bay. I could feel them and knew when they were around but had never seen them any place other than on the bay. Now I understand that there isn't a vortex there, I'm just psychic... extrasensory aware if you like, at times... or most of the time actually as Swami has explained through my auras and consciousness. The reason I could only see them in that deserted place was... probably for my benefit, my reaction to them. If, for instance, they had shown themselves to me at home I would have been frightened. For some reason I could see them outside your bedroom window and I wasn't frightened, I've just slowly come to accept them... I guess.' She strove to simplify the phenomenon for both of them, although she addressed Jack.

'For instance, that's a word Granda used,' Jack said, referring to his deceased maternal grandfather.

'Yeah, I know, that's probably how I picked it up,' Kate replied wistfully.

'Have you even seen him... when you... when you are...' Lost for a descriptive word, Jack trailed off.

'When I'm out there,' Kate followed this with a little excited laugh. She was just as much coming to terms with her abilities as Jack was. 'No, strangely no... but then I haven't been doing this... actually understanding it very much until I came here...' she said after looking at an empathising Swami.

'But there is a huge difference in being psychic and travelling in different dimensions!' Jack added; he still had to struggle with her being two different beings at once.

'Think back to our conversation on the unconscious mind, remember…' It was Swami who in his quiet way settled Jack's misgivings.

'But the Tuatha dé Danann are only found in Ireland, it's a recognised fact: they are the Irish version of what other nations know as fairies. Are you blowing that myth to pieces?' Jack asked.

'The Danavas are not the Tuatha dé Danann but very similar. Swami and I have been discussing the Goddess Dana. In Hinduism she is the mother of the Danavas, supernatural beings who dwell in the underworld to which they were banished due to their cruelty. The Irish De Danann are also the people of the Goddess Dana who forfeited the part of Ireland above ground to the Gales who invaded and defeated them. They live underground too or so the myth tells us, in the faerie mounds or Sidhes. There are other similarities: both goddesses are mothers of gods. Swami says the Danavas were highly intellectual, or should I say are,' she looked to Swami as if to confirm the new evidence or her understanding of it; 'they were very early people born from Daksa and Kasyapa. In Irish mythology Dana, like I just said, is a mother of gods, she is also known as Anu in Ireland, she is a water goddess and has rivers named after her. Swami made a connection here. The Danube was first recorded as Danuvius and the Rhone as Rhodanus: see Jack, the word Dana is in the prefix of Danuvius and a suffix in Rhodanus as anu.' She turned to Swami, who nodded in confirmation.

'Yes I know, you've said it twice now, I'm making the connection, we talked and agreed about the cradle of civilisation before. What I want to know about are the Sidhes,' questioned Jack.

'They are literally mounds of earth, they are to be found all over Ireland even now. The Tuatha live in some of them, it is believed that each Tuatha god was assigned one when they were defeated. I was in a small one at home; others are, I imagine, as large as the one I was in last night, the mound acting as the portal to the underworld. It is not clear what they were used for centuries ago, certainly they were not all used as burial chambers, as stone age people were cremated. Some scholars believe the druids used them for their magic as temples. And that's another thing they have in common, they live in the underworld or underground – and that's not all, listen to this,' Kate drew breath. 'Swami told me of the Danavas' King Maya: he was a famous architect.'

She again looked to Swami for confirmation and the speed of her dialogue portrayed her excitement.

'Are you with me?' She looked at Jack. 'And in Ireland, the Tuatha had Goibniu, the Smith God who was one of the seven chieftains of the Tuatha and with Luchta, the wright and Credne, the bronze worker are known as the three Gods of Danu. So many similarities, too many similarities to dismiss a connection,' she said, sinking into her cushions, tired with the excitement of discovery and its articulation. And then she was off again, ignoring Swami's raised palm which seemed to urge calm.

'Their worlds, underworld or Aos Dana, the Sidhe, are immense domains, with dwellings and… I'm sure it's the same Goddess Jack… and the same people.'

'Alright, alright I accept your theory…' Kate threw a look at Jack which caused him to quantify his statement. 'I accept your *reality*.' He paused and looked up at them both. 'Could we get back to what happened and why you were unconscious… or out of your body for so long?'

Jack rose and seated himself in one of the wicker chairs; darkness had fallen and the mosquito attacks had abated somewhat.

'As I said, I was treated with great respect and given immense importance,' replied Kate, bringing her head up from her cushions again. 'After the monkeys nearly killed you, the Danavas waited just inside the thicket and saw you stowed in the car boot. Once you were safe I faced the leader, the one you described, and asked him, with respect, to take me back. He didn't reply, just called out what appeared to be a command and the troupe set off. When I felt that we were riding for far longer than it took to arrive at the village temple I spoke to him as best I could. I asked where we were going and he told me to the Well of Wisdom. When I asked him why, he told me it was the only place I could pass to their land, their realm, where they were most powerful. You can imagine how shocked I was,' Kate put her hand on the centre of her chest as if she was re-living the experience.

'I tried to appear confident as I once again asked to be taken back from where I came, adding that perhaps I might visit their kingdom some other time. He ignored me so I pulled the reins and dismounted. He stopped as did the Devas or sylphs or whatever they are, they flew with those mounted and they formed a circle around me, forming two rings, the inner ring facing in and the outer ring facing out and watchful as if on guard. This commander or whoever he was… a type of leader, I suppose, told me we were passing through danger in the underworld and he was unable to protect me. I had to believe him especially after the old man driving you away from the temple, followed by the monkey attacks,' Kate explained as if defensive.

'Your aunt had invoked the Nagas or serpents and an enormous dark Goddess; I actually witnessed the energy in the temple and as soon as the priest anointed the aunt the protection started. In other words your aunt is protected so anyone who is against her interests will be wiped away. That explained the old man dogging you and then of course the violent monkey attack,' Kate conveyed exhaustion and fear and took a sip of lime juice.

'Kate has explained what happened at the temple,' Swami put in. 'This time of the year the villagers invoke a dark goddess, like the smallpox Goddess who wards off the disease. A young girl is chosen to be an incarnation of the Goddess, but your aunt let go of her hand before the actual incarnation took place.'

'That explains the unease of the villagers when the child ran back to her mother,' said Jack.

'Precisely. Somehow your aunt made the child uncomfortable and had planned all along to be the recipient of the Goddess, in other words her power,' said Swami.

'She certainly seems to have really powerful protection,' agreed Jack, 'and the villagers accepted her as their living Goddess.'

'Not only protection son, she has power and we don't have to speculate how she will use it, you have witnessed it yourself in the prayer room,' warned Swami.

'But how does it work Swami? How can a statue of an idol become powerful?' Jack puzzled yet again.

'In the other world, son, there are good and bad entities, just as there are what we compartmentalise here as good and bad people here in our world. These entities have power or energy and can pass into an inanimate object like a statue or indeed a person, just like what you witnessed happen at the temple. Think about it, son, when you go to Ireland you must have noticed how statues are venerated and cures for all sorts attributed to them. People's prayer which is their consciousness requests the healing energy of Jesus and Mother Mary into a holy place and it therefore attracts that type of energy. You know how energy never stands still, always moving and changing.' Swami had leaned forward; the connection between the wise and the searcher was physically centimetres apart, so enwrapped were they in the exchange.

'I haven't witnessed any cures in Ireland, people light candles in front of statues in churches after and before mass but I have heard my grandmother talking about someone who was cured of an illness in Lourdes in France,' Jack replied, if not in full understanding of Swami's explanation at least offering evidence of good energy.

'Your aunt is playing with something very dangerous, energy or a dark power, I don't have to explain to a physicist about action and reaction, it is that simple, for every action she takes there will be a reaction. Since her intent is entirely selfish then there will be a negative reaction… for herself as well as everyone else I fear…' Swami's words faded into the night.

Rousing himself, he continued, 'Your aunt has undergone an initiation: from now on she will work with that energy to strengthen it… I fear she may have another ritual space, other than the prayer room, somewhere away from prying eyes to execute the rituals and with implements.'

'You speak a lot about energy, Swami: do you mean demons, is she working with energy that is defined, namely demons?' Jack asked.

'More likely she will use curses; although she can use demons, they tend to be unreliable in the sense that… for example if we identified a particular dark force and offered it energy in our way, it can go with the highest bidder. However, curses are safer from her point of view. She would bind a deva, or an angel,' he looked at Kate. 'If she practised dark magic and attached it to a person. Unbinding a curse is very, very difficult for any but the most skilled.'

'We have drifted off course again,' said Kate slowly and quietly. Like Jack ,she seemed to be absorbing the enormity of what was taking place within the family.

'Will I get back to why I got stuck last night?' The elderly and the youth both nodded.

'Swami knows and feels that in normal circumstances the Danavas would not have dealings with either the dark force or snakes but they had taken a stand by involving themselves with us and they would be perceived as a threat. After the car left and looking back at what happened now, we, the Danavas and myself, obviously needed to be safe and quick. I had no choice but to agree with them. And so we rode out of the underworld and into their world through the Well of Wisdom,' Kate continued; when she finished she reached again for her glass of lime juice.

'Where was this Well of Wisdom?' queried Jack. 'What did it look like?'

'Not like a well anyway, more like a pond… like your garden pond actually…' she said thoughtfully, sipping the lime juice.

'What, the pond next door?' replied Jack, adjusting himself straight up against the back of the wicker chair, leaning away from the side where the wound was.

'Yes, if you could imagine it without the paint and decorations, I remember it was the same height as I prepared myself and the horse to jump the rocks into the water which was so unlike a regular well, as I said, about the height of the pond in the garden next door,' she spoke but remained in her memories.

'Did you go underwater, did you have to swim, how did you breathe?' Jack's elbows were leaning purposefully on his chair as he bent forward again, imagining Kate descending through water to the other world; the goddess was a water goddess and his mind began conjuring up visions of merpeople.

'No, you don't understand, as soon as we hit the water the scene changed. I remember a wall of water in front of me and the water in the pond, which was a natural pool, which was only about knee-high. I followed the procession in behind what must have been a waterfall and on through a passage into the rocks which sloped down and down. Once in the entrance at the back of the waterfall there was no starlight and I never again saw natural light until I woke up here this morning.' She remained in her thoughts as if Jack's questions were stimulating memories she had not remembered before.

'Are you saying that's all you remember?' persisted Jack.

'No, I remember everything now,' she replied, sitting up again and focusing directly on him. 'I remember the city, the people or beings, the atmosphere of contentment… even happiness.'

'What was it like, wasn't it stuffy, you were underground?' Jack was intrigued.

'Breathing wasn't a problem, and I got used to the glow, yes, it was a sort of glow,' she said. 'Can you imagine Petra in Jordan? If you can picture that in your mind, the architecture, but without the sunshine, more of an iridescent light, then you can understand what I saw,' she turned to Swami.

'You know of Petra?'

'Oh yes, I think I can visualise exactly what you experienced,' he assured her.

'I've no idea of how long I stayed there, their time is very different from human time, it moves fast and they do not age. In Ireland we refer to it as Tir na Og, the land of youth. I can only assure you I was there as the similarity of the beings I met in the Sidhe at home and these are unmistakable,' she had the glazed-over stare again but continued talking, aware of her two anxious companions.

'The commander took me to his home where his wife and daughter treated me with curiously but kindliness too. I was given clothes and shown to a bath area. Oh you should have seen it, water fell from the wall of rock into a tiny pool, a natural mini-waterfall, I remember tasting it; it was cool and crystal clear like spring water. For a moment I forgot about Magh's warning and realised I had swallowed the water,' Kate relayed the shock she had felt.

'Why,' asked Jack.

'She warned me never to eat or drink the faerie food unless you take salt beforehand,' explained Kate, 'otherwise you can be trapped in their world forever.'

'So that was what was on your lips when you were unconscious,' smiled Jack.

'Was it noticeable? I took it in water before I went into my etheric self,' she explained.

'Only my mother noticed, but she had been examining you all over for signs of what might be wrong,' replied Jack.

Reassured, Kate continued to relate her adventure, 'The walls were carved out of the rocks, not dark as you would imagine but various shades of pink and white marble. Roots of trees were carved into Romanesque-type arches along long corridors and also in large rooms, the roots extended downwards forming pillars, like a Banyan tree except much wider. I tried and failed to locate the source of the white and bluish light which made the jewels like amethyst sparkle in the rocks which were not marble, maybe quartz, yes pink quartz. At first I imagined it was magic; in Ireland the Tuatha dé Danann are famous for their magic. I had been inside a Sidhe only once before at home as I told you.'

Kate had been talking so long she looked to her audience for reassurance that she had not lost them in her monologue and then she continued.

'But this was different from the Sidhe, this was a whole city, the Sidhe I briefly went to visit was just one home, maybe it was the different terrain but the light was more yellow in Ireland…' she stopped as if she was assimilating the experience and seemed to work out the comparison. Then, once again refocused, she continued.

'I felt I should protest and somehow demonstrate that I needed to leave but I was aware I might offend them, so I complied and when I had bathed food was served, bread, honey and fish. I think it may have been grilled salmon or trout and some sort of wine to drink, more flower than grape I'd say, not that I am an expert. Afterwards I was shown to a room with a bed and although protest was on my lips I never uttered a word, somehow I felt safe. I was very tired so I slept, for how long I have no idea.' Kate sipped from her glass again which she held on her lap with both her hands, fingers intertwined around the glass as if she was gripping the reality of what she had done and where she had been and what she had seen.

PHYSICS

 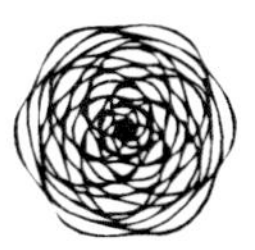

KATE CONTINUED. 'AFTER the sleep I was given milk and more bread and honey. The daughter, her name was Usha I think, she was friendly and patient with my language so I enquired about the light source. With the help of diagrams for which she used a stiletto which looked like it was made from antler – it fluoresced under the ultraviolet light – she drew with it on a tray of white sand and I could understand that they build their dwellings and cities on energy lines, "Prana" you call it; we call them "ley lines" at home,' she said, as if she needed to confirm the comparison to her companions. She turned towards Swami and appeared to be seeking his concurrence.

'Yes I'm very interested in this, please continue my dear,' he replied, now tilted forward like Jack.

'They allow the "pranic" beam to pass through an opening which is aligned to take the light coming from the sun at precise angles into a cruciform room at the end of a long tunnel. This in turn appears to be geometrically aligned with several earth stars which the girl drew like two interlocking equilateral triangles,' Kate broke off and looked straight at Jack. 'Like the Laxmi yantra,' she turned to Swami. 'Or Siva's drum is another version but used and drawn differently,' she said, sitting upright again as if she had only made the connection.

'Yes, I know the part of the drawing, the sacred feminine,' Jack replied, giving her a clear assurance that she was making sense of what she appeared to only partly understand.

'First the pranic beam passes through large quartz rocks where the light is split which activates the sub-atomic particles of the quartz and bends the energy on its journey. Like a cyclotron I guess, my physics isn't up to scratch. These sub-atomic particles become very large in the process. The beam accelerates the earth star forces and the geometric structures within the room which is crystal shaped with all its facets. They use reflectors to concentrate the solar wind and this is their energy source, in a nutshell,' Kate finished and lay back on her cushions.

'But they live in the other world, underground…' Jack questioned, puzzled. 'How can they get the sun?'

'I asked that very same question,' replied Kate, the index finger of her right hand held up against the glass, the level of the juice hardly diminished.

'The room is near the top of Sidhe with the opening which has access to the sun,' she replied.

'But where and how?' asked Jack.

'That was all I had time for. While I was eating the commander appeared and between my fishing for words and his impatient monosyllabic replies I understood that it was time to leave,' she said.

'Do you remember how you got back?' questioned Jack.

'I had a different horse but he was easy to handle. We left the city by entering into a narrow passage within the rock or mountain or below earth, wherever I was. The passage was a bit claustrophobic, there was only enough room for a single animal, at places my knees touched the walls of the passage. I was aware of a steep climb which took some time; again, I have no way of comparing it with our time. We emerged behind the waterfall but when I entered it seemed to be still night.' She appeared puzzled as if she was still trying to figure it all out.

'No army, just you and the commander?' Jack put in.

'We were surrounded by those Devas or Angels; I have not seen them with the Tuatha at home,' replied Kate. 'They either act as radar or are protective, maybe both. I also had the feeling that two beings traversing the underworld would draw less attention than an army. I had begun to understand the commander's reasoning.'

'The Angels may be Devas, they are very broadly speaking our version of Angels. It is all fascinating, absolutely fascinating,' uttered Swami as he rose to greet Jack's father who unknown to the teenagers was approaching them on the lawn.

It was fully dark, the outside lights had been switched on but the trio had not noticed sunset, the mosquitoes or the other sounds of dusk. Jack's father settled into a conversation with Swami and both teenagers sauntered slowly across the lawn towards the veranda. Jack's father called out for Jack to take the tray into the kitchen where his mother was preparing supper for Matty who was still forced to maintain an eight o'clock bedtime. There was no place they could sit and talk privately so they exchanged glances as Jack was reminded about homework and Kate headed towards the sitting room and the air conditioner. As was normal for South India the house had absorbed the heat of the day and was oven-like inside.

SACRED GEOMETRY

THE FOLLOWING DAY was a Saturday and Jack and Kate spent what was left of the forenoon in the big sitting room with the air conditioner switched on; not that it was unduly hot, even though the sun came in through the front windows in the morning, but the low hum combined with their quiet conversation made it impossible for anyone like Matty to eavesdrop at the doors.

Jack's mind was anarchic: he had spent most of the night awake having to acquiesce to the reality of a sentient cousin and the discomfort of the truth which lay beyond Kate's travels between dimensions. Actual trips into the other world, an eternal world and what was occurring there which actually impacted on what was happening in his world. Cairns, dolmens, incantations... having to accept all that as real... by the time the glow of dawn started in the eastern sky he had fallen into a deep sleep which lasted until midday.

Too late for breakfast he began a search for Kate and found her in the sitting room which had an air conditioner, with the windows still open to the increasing heat. Amidst the familiarity of domesticity he had experienced in the search for her he was eased again into a kind of confident security and with it Kate's reality. He felt he could cope with the many strange situations he found himself suddenly thrust into. He was sure they needed to plot a way forward but before that he suggested to Kate that they should collate what information they had about his aunt and talk about protection.

'Good afternoon,' murmured Kate, lifting her head from Swami's ancient book.

'I need to talk, help me close the shutters I'm switching on the air conditioner,' Jack busied himself looping the hooks on the shutters' home.

Before even sitting he launched into what was foremost in his mind.

'The fact is clear that Aunt Saroj has stirred some awful power which is working for her and therefore against us,' Jack made it sound like a declaration.

'A dangerous and unquantified power,' agreed Kate.

'I saw the wraith and you could see a Dark Goddess energy protecting her,' he continued as if defining the obstacles. 'Even if we do nothing she will still get rid of us somehow… I'm thinking of the wraith and grandmother.'

'But that's it,' replied Kate. 'It's downright dangerous. Without the Danavas last night… I dread to think what might have happened to you… how would you be found…? Vishu would have to go home when your aunt emerged from the temple…' Kate broke off.

'How can we draw her out, how can we test her… just to see how powerful she really is?' Jack seemed to be thinking aloud as he settled himself on one of the armchairs.

'I don't think we should do that, I don't like it. We need protection; how can you really think of such a thing after what happened to you last night?' interjected Kate.

'Does Swami feel the yantras are powerful enough?' questioned Jack, to cover up the rashness of his statement. The two sat at right angles to each other, Jack in an armchair and Kate occupying the near end of a sofa, consciously keeping their voices low.

'Swami is our oracle, isn't he? His knowledge combined with the advice from the Danavas with the devas or upanayika has given us valuable information and don't forget, information is power,' mused Kate, appearing to lighten her negative mood.

'Yes but what did he say, did you have a chance to talk about protection? I had no opportunity to be with him alone because of school,' replied Jack impatiently.

'What Swami advised is to use the Tripurasundari yantra because your aunt invoked a tantric goddess. If we use the diagram of nine intersecting triangles, I think he called it Srichakra and say the 'Srividya Mantra' while drawing it we should have protection as he advised by using the dual form of the cosmos to counter the Dark Goddess's destruction by placing a purer manifestation of the Goddess like Laksmi in her path,' Kate slowly explained, eyes on the ceiling as if she was checking herself for accuracy. 'At least I think that is his reasoning, sort of cancelling evil with good.'

'Can you say the mantra?' queried Jack.

'I'm working on it, it's got fifteen syllables, Swami wrote it out in English and translated it as well which helps a lot in remembering it,' she said, pleased with herself.

'I hope it works, I'm not sure… Grandfather told me that God Vishnu was the preserver?' said Jack thoughtfully. 'This feels too… simple.'

'Vishnu is, but Swami explained that every God in Hinduism has a consort who consolidates the powers and Vishnu's cohesive power is coupled with

Laksmi who is the Goddess of "hundreds and thousands", so his thinking is that when Laksmi needs to hold everything together the God will be there in their dual form.' Kate went on, 'Oh by the way, you are going to have to learn yantras and remember mantras too.'

'I still find it difficult to believe that geometry and language, whatever the language, can contain power, enough to ward off the Dark Goddess,' said Jack doubtfully.

'I think I understand it and I'm trying to believe in it. Think of it as your soul remembering how to be in contact with the elements, even with nature, don't try to rationalise it so much, try to feel it more. Have you ever heard of Kabala?' she queried.

'Vaguely, is it Jewish?' he looked up.

'Yes, Jewish folklore,' she confirmed.

'But what's that got to do…' he trailed off as she had raised the silencing finger.

'The Hebrew alphabets are sacred as they have energy. When they are said out loud the cosmic power is activated and create a sonic vibration pattern, an unseen power which can be used to restore balance for example,' she explained with that raised-eyebrow, all-knowing look.

'What or where did you find that out and what has it got to do…?' Once again he was silenced.

'You know we have readings from the Old and the New Testaments at Mass?' she questioned, eyes squarely focused on Jack, eyebrows still raised questioningly.

'Yee-ees,' he countered with a slight mock in his voice.

'There was something about "The Word" which got me thinking…'

He cut her off mid-explanation.

'In the beginning was the Word, the Word was with God, I know, I know, but I'm still lost.' Jack spread his arms wide apart and flung one leg up on to the arm of the chair, impatient with what seemed to take ages to get to a point.

'Yes,' Kate seemed surprised. 'Well let me speak then because you need two explanations now. Firstly the Word lead me to Genesis and the Old Testament and then on to all things Hebrew. The Hebrew alphabets are sacred as they have energy as I just said. Secondly, this made sense when Swami spoke about the mantras having the same effect and working in the exact same way,' she nodded her head in confirmation of his understanding.

'Sonic vibrations, alright I get that but I'm not at all clear on the yantra. Having just the female representation may not be enough. After all, this Dark Goddess is also feminine energy and extreme primitive energy. So there is imbalance. Too much receptive energy, "Yin" and no "Yang" and all that,' he questioned her.

'You have a point,' Kate replied thoughtfully and began leafing through her sketch pad and a very old, well-used book with yantras in Sanskrit which Swami had lent her, both of which accompanied her almost everywhere.

She spent some minutes searching and scratching the crown of her head and looking at the cupboards but not seeing them when finally she raised the finger again.

'What, what?' Jack queried, still impatient with her. Impatient with sitting around.

'The Raja Yantra,' she said triumphantly, a serene smile spreading over her face.

'Raja Yantra,' he replied, causing a crease in the skin between his eyes.

'Yes, I'll have to check it with Swami, though,' she told him assuredly. 'Look, let me explain,' and Kate took out one of her drawings, carefully working from inside the drawing to the outside straight lines, explaining the meaning of the geometry slowly, while he silently nodded, all the while sat upright and she bent over the paper.

'I'm hopeless at drawing,' his voice betrayed the doubt that kept on creeping back.

'But you're good at Maths,' she quickly pointed out and the positivity in her tone encouraged him to focus once again.

'It's all about the Maths,' Kate said; her determination was catching hold of his reluctance and he considered that he should trust her instincts. After all, her essential nature was one of consciousness, if what he had heard the previous evening was a true assessment. He realised he had to go beyond the rational mind and access an expanded state of consciousness and if delving into this system would protect him then he would learn 'Yantras and Mantras'.

'I'm going to have to practise this in order to remember it,' he interjected, 'and what about size, is that a factor?'

'Very much so,' she confirmed; the sharp focus of her eyes instilled the importance. 'You may have to stand within it, so think proportions.'

'You know, traditionally these are cast in rice flour, leaked from the palm of a hand on to the ground; that would take practice…' he was thinking out loud, remembering Akhill's mother's daily rituals.

'No, that wouldn't work,' Kate interjected. 'First of all you may have to cast one on the spot, you can't carry around a packet of rice flour.'

'Exactly,' he agreed. 'Then how will this thing work?' and he flung himself back against the back of the armchair again.

'We'll use chalk,' she said as the 'light bulb' look slowly began to emerge.

'Chalk,' he repeated in a disgusted tone. 'And that's going to keep the snakes and black energy and God only knows what else… all at bay!'

'Chalk to practise,' she exclaimed. 'You're going to have to know how to cast one in seconds and even to protect the house you will need to cast them every day after I have gone to Ireland, so you'll have to learn them pat.'

'So-o, where are we going to practise then?' he challenged her.

'Well I… only the front porch and the car shed floor are concrete and wide enough…' She was thinking and talking.

'Oh yeah, and how are you going to explain what it is and why?' He stood up and folded his arms across his chest.

With that there was a metal protest from the mechanism in the door handle between the little sitting room and the air-conditioned room as Matty burst in without fully turning the door handle.

'Got any chalk, Matty?' she queried as Jack stood stock still in amazement at her coolness.

'Yes, what do you want it for?' asked an interested Matty.

'You know Swami has been teaching me drawings, I want to make big ones,' Kate replied, Jack still bewildered at her composure.

'Can I learn too?' asked Matty.

'I think you should definitely know how to cast them,' agreed Kate as she passed Jack with a knowing look on her way out.

'Cast, what does cast mean?' asked Matty, following his cousin into the adjoining little sitting room and beyond.

'Did I say cast, I meant draw,' Jack heard her reply as their voices faded. *How could she be so positive with so much negative evidence around them. The alternative was no less acceptable, remembering Swami's words: leave his home, his existence, how could he make another existence? He'd have to change, everyone would change, even school, friends. He couldn't imagine the effect it would have on Matty. Why should they, be ejected from the life they were born into? It wasn't fair.* He pulled himself out of the comfort of the armchair, the drone of the air conditioner had ceased. *Another power cut,* he thought, and flicked up the switch beside the machine on the wall. He felt he had to drag his heavy mind into Kate's optimism and followed in her direction. He had no other option.

FRIENDS

THEY DECIDED THAT they would practise casting yantras under the shade of the front porch as the sun was shining directly into the car shed and that would have been far too uncomfortable.

'Let's place it in front of the door,' suggested Kate. Jack felt that the position she chose was not random.

'But the cars are parked here and the tyres will be right on top of it,' protested Matty.

'No matter where we draw it in this area, it will have part of the car on it,' reasoned Jack.

'It's only a practice one,' put in Kate who was walking and measuring in steps. 'Jack, will you stand in the centre of the concrete? Matty, mark four corners radiating out from Jack roughly equal distance away from him.'

Kate stood pointing and was so engrossed in her mind that Jack considered she was unaware that Matty may not have been up to the job.

'Why does he have to stand in the centre? ' asked Matty who hadn't moved.

'Well, because... let's make it to scale... it fits him.' She seemed lost in her evasiveness and unable to conjure up credible facts to convince Matty. Jack knew her head was full of geometry.

'So mine should be smaller then?' Matty questioned.

'I don't think it matters Matty, it's just that Jack is the tallest of us... and I think... we should make a really big one,' she began to mark four corners and Matty was satisfied at last.

'Hold on a minute,' put in Jack. 'We have to start in the centre, decide the proportions from the centre out, it will not work the other way. Matty will you get a ruler or a stick and some string?'

'What for?' Matty asked as Jack knelt down in the centre of the porch.

'To measure Matt,' answered Kate; she understood exactly how Jack was thinking.

By the time it took Matty to get his bag the kneeling teenagers were deep in consultation pointing and plotting their marks, referring to Swami's text book and Kate to her sketch pad. Matty produced a kite handle with white kite thread wound round it.

'Where did you get that?' demanded Jack as it was obviously not from an Indian kite.

'You know the cousins... with all the little children, who came to visit when we were in Ireland, this year?' temporised Matty.

'Yeah' replied Jack slowly, for dark thoughts about Matty were gradually but surely creeping into his mind.

'Well the smallest boy and girl had a fight over who should fly the kite, remember the kite... and the boy won but the girl came back with scissors when everyone had gone inside and she cut the string and the kite flew away and the boy just threw down the handle on the grass and went to tell his mother,' submitted Matty sheepishly.

'And... and you took it. I can't believe you brought this all the way to India!' Jack was kneeling upright almost at eye-level with Matty, astonished at how petty Matt could be but at the same time dumbfounded at his ingenuity. Jack couldn't stop a massive smile breaking out all over his face as he looked at the scrunched up little face of his brother, who on seeing his big brother identify with him immediately changed his unease to a nonchalant smile.

'Leave Matt alone, he's just recycling, aren't you Matt?' put in Kate.

'We need something to tie the string to,' said Jack, reaching for Matty's bag.

'Can I borrow your pen torch that's about the right thickness and nearly the right length?' But before he could get his hand inside Matty's bag, Matty had snatched it to his chest.

'No, not my torch... I'll get you something, just wait,' said Matty as he disappeared away from the strongly sunlit porch and into the shade beyond the front door.

'What a character,' remarked Jack to Kate.

'Ah, he's cute,' said Kate adoringly as she knelt upright, taking her focus off the little box of broken bits of chalk, her fingers covered in chalk dust.

Within what seemed seconds Matty was back clutching a wooden spoon, obviously from the kitchen.

'Perfect,' said Jack taking the spoon then tying the twine mid-way on its handle.

Matty sat on the cool steps as the older children worked and debated measurements often referring to the smaller drawing. The boys' mother came, looked and left apparently satisfied that the children were occupied. All the while Kate patiently answered Matty's questions and explained the meaning of the geometry step by step, line by line, lotus flower by lotus flower, circle by circle. She suggested that Matty squat in the middle as they moved outwards filling in the double lines until it was finished. Matty, having been sent to the kitchen for water and, later, to ask for glasses of lime juice as it was almost the hottest part of the day, seemed delighted to have a part in the drawing at last.

As they all knelt on the outside of three of the four sides of the yantra there was noise at the gate and Jack turned to find the faces of his friends grinning at him through the bars.

'Hey man...' said Khalid.

'What are you doing here?' asked Jack who tried to sound friendly and cover his annoyance as he walked towards the gate. Kate and Matty stood up too, surprised at the appearance of Jack's friends. Both Khalid and Akhill had been nagging Jack to introduce them to Kate since she arrived. He wanted to avoid it but hadn't time to give the subject enough thought. He wondered how he would make the visit short as Kate did not like being stared at and that was exactly what those two would do. The watchman came running without even been summoned to undo the padlock and admit the unwanted visitors. Jack's introductions were uneasy and halting and Kate's *Namaste* was also out of place. Khalid pushed the boundaries by extending his hand for a handshake which was ignored as Kate was by that time fully informed on Indian etiquette. The boys openly stood staring at her and the watchman stood dutifully by the gate, piling on even more awkwardness. Eventually Akhill, who Jack noticed had a high colour, broke through the tangled atmosphere.

'My mum can teach you if you are interested,' he stepped in Kate's direction and addressed her as he looked down at the finished yantra.

'Yes, if you are sure she wouldn't mind. I'm obviously not Hindu, but I am very interested to learn and understand how it should be formed properly,' she offered enthusiastically.

Jack knew she would take up the offer, as he like her knew that the more authentic the yantras were the more power they carried. He watched as Akhill suggested they go inside as Kate's face was shiny, red with sweat and she agreed. They went into the hallway, Kate asking Akhill if he knew how to do yantras. Jack noticed Matty as always on the perimeter of the gathering, observing and assimilating, seeing his brother's control slowly ebbing away.

'Is she a witch, man?' Khalid's insane question both irritated and reminded Jack of his uncomfortable situation.

'What?' Jack responded turning to face him threateningly, which was lost on Khalid.

'The eyes man, the eyes, not cat's eyes, weird eyes man,' Khalid went on as if talking to himself. Out of the corner of his eye Jack noticed Matt's broad smile which helped him regain some control over himself, as he squared up against the peace-loving but insensitive Khalid who was more than capable of physically leaving painful marks on Jack.

'Matty why don't you take Khalid to see the new family of rabbits and show him the new hatchlings in the bird cage too?' Jack proffered, hoping that Khalid would be interested.

'New babies then, lots of them?' remarked Khalid, addressing Matty.

Jack wasn't sure if Khalid was looking for a loophole or actually interested; it was difficult with Khalid, there was more to him than what appeared on the surface.

'And Betty had eleven puppies,' put in Matty proudly.

'Who's Betty?' asked Khalid.

'She's a Great Dane and nobody can go near the puppies except my mother as Betty is a watchdog and very fierce, especially now that she has the pups. We can have a look that's all,' warned Matty as they set out towards the kennel.

Relieved, Jack bounded into the house and found the other two on the back veranda chatting away and his mother in the kitchen making lime juice for the visitors; he relaxed a bit and tried to let go control. He sat down on the wicker recliner and hearing voices he was aware that the kennel visit was over and Matty and Khalid were making their way round the house to the back and the hutch. When the juice, Khalid and Matty arrived, the veranda was too small to contain everyone comfortably, so Jack took his friends to play the newly acquired games from Ireland on his beloved Amstrad computer in the big sitting room, leaving Matty and Kate to themselves on the veranda.

SHAPE SHIFTER

LATER THAT SAME afternoon when everyone was having their siestas Kate remained in the large sitting room with the air conditioner switched on, lying on her side on one of the sofas with her sketch pad propped up against the coffee table, eyeing it and using her free hand to trace the symbols in the air. Jack was sprawled in a nearby armchair, one leg dangling over an arm, watching a Malayalam movie.

'Oh, by the way…' she lowered her voice. 'Are you really into that?' She leaned up and eased herself into a sitting position with her legs curled to one side on the cushions.

'No, seen it before, it's Nisha's and I must remember to give it back,' he lowered the volume and sat upright, laying the remote on the glass-topped coffee table.

'I have something really serious to tell you and I'm afraid it might be a bit of a shock,' she said quietly. 'The snake in the bathroom, the one your mother found… if I have understood the Danava commander correctly, it was him.'

'Him, him… what do you mean him?' Jack was shocked and totally lost to the meaning of her statement at first and shot up from the armchair. 'You mean he put it there?'

'No, he was the snake… they shape shift… his totem animal is a snake and he was trying to warn your mother by appealing to her innate nature as her animal is also a snake but…' halting at first she trailed off as Jack was so obviously confounded by this.

'What it means is they can alter their appearance to become their totem animal,' she spoke with quiet and care.

'What are you saying, my mother is a leprechaun?' he began pacing short distances across the sitting room carpet and thinking; his hand covered his mouth in shock.

'No, no, not at all, the Danava shape shifted, just as the Tuatha do…' she quickly placed herself in front of him, interrupting the pacing.

'No, you clearly said my mother's… something, animal… was a snake,' he said adamantly.

'Look,' she paused. 'We all have totem animals, we're just not aware of them or haven't developed ourselves to recognise them within…'

'God, Kate, this is too much,' he sank down on one of the sofas, hands clasped in front of him. 'Are you saying she is like you then? All that sitting on the back veranda at night – can she commune with these beings? Does she travel like you? What?' He realised he was losing control of himself and he was aware Kate knew too. She was right, it was a shock.

'None of those things,' she said, gently easing herself on to the cushion next to him. 'If she ever had even a little bit of what I have developed she has forgotten it, the Danava commander confirmed that,' Kate held Jack's arm, trying to imbue some understanding.

'He says she sits in the dark because she is unhappy… lonely I think is what he meant… At night she finds herself in the quiet and the dark, you haven't realised what beautiful skies you have here at night, full of stars, she probably gets some peace watching the sky and it's lovely and cool then.' Kate stared into his face but Jack was focused on his hands.

'What has she to be unhappy about?' eventually he said, quietly as if to himself.

'I don't know, the Danava pick up on vibrations I guess,' Kate seemed to be trying to offer something plausible.

'Listen, you've had a bit of a shock, we'll talk later,' she said.

He felt she was giving up and he couldn't take down the wall that was between them either but he still did not want to be left with his mind like this.

'I can't forget about any of this, it's complicated, I need to get my head around it… so my mother is alright, just a normal mother, is that what you are telling me?' Jack turned his head to look straight into her eyes.

'Yes, I wouldn't hide anything like that, especially not now when you are all under threat.' There was conviction in her every word and he believed her.

Jack's brain felt like a greenish grey morass; the inside of the bio-digester tank in his grandfather's backyard came to mind. He was sickened but no longer needed to quell the panic within.

'But how would he warn her… my mother, in his snake form?' But he didn't wait for her to answer.

'He was trying to communicate with me too…' Jack continued to think out loud and she waited as he added.

'And I blanked him out?' he asked incredulously of Kate.

'You were not to know, very few people have the gift…' she tried to comfort him.

'And my father almost beat him to death,' Jack was now upright and pacing again full of remorse. He halted suddenly.

'But you told me that a man had dropped the snake over the compound wall. If he can shape shift why did he need human intervention?' Jack stood puzzling.

'He took the place of the snake which was meant to do you harm,' Kate continued.

'Yes, I remember now, the snake… the snake catchers took away was not Ekans. It was a different snake Kate, I remember, I think I understand,' he said a little excitedly.

'Look, just take this much in, it's difficult I know, but think about its positive side, you have their protection, they are watching out for you,' she said.

'What good is that when I cannot intrepid their signals or anything about them…?' he said quietly, thinking how he would have handled Ekans differently, realising he had learned from it and noted that he must in future use more of his senses and instinct. *Even Akhill had been more aware than he had.*

'How do you know this, did you know from the beginning… when precisely?' he questioned, more relaxed.

'They were outside the window last night, I'm still struggling with the language, but they tried to tell me the night you asked the questions but I didn't understand them then, I have a rapport now and this fits in, it feels right,' she said.

'Do they know anything else?' he asked.

'They will not be asked to do harm here again since their help at the temple has placed them in our camp,' she replied.

'Did they say that, or are you guessing?' he questioned.

'They told me,' she replied.

THE GUN

IT WAS ABOUT half past midday the following day, Sunday, and everyone at the Little Pink House wandered lazily across the road in the searing heat to Nani's Home for the customary Sunday family lunch.

Grandmother was resting on the ornate great-grandfather bed in the room leading upstairs when they arrived. She was not just resting, she looked shrunken with her face furrowed with pain lines. Grandfather wandered into the room with the rest of Jack's family from the front hall where he had been reading the Sunday papers, quietly concerned, and related in Malayalam to Jack's father that she would not have the doctor. Just as Grandfather finished emptying his worried mind Aunt Saroj came out of her bedroom and echoed his words in a loud rebuking manner.

Grandmother just closed her eyes while this went on as if she was ignoring it. Soon the adults were seated around the little table in the centre of the room in silent apprehension, while the children quietly sat on the low ledge of the sideboard underneath the staircase. Nisha was not to be seen. Jack felt she was lurking inside her mother's room listening as always. And he was right, as soon as Grandmother agreed to have Dr Krishna visit in the evening after gentle persuasion from Jack's father and Grandfather and when the adults began their slow journey in the direction of the dining room again, she appeared, sliding through the small opening she made with the bedroom door. The children stood up as Grandmother was led past by Aunt Saroj.

'Are you better now?' she enquired of Kate.

'Much better, thank you Grandmother. I'm sorry you're not feeling well.' Kate advanced a little nearer to Grandmother who just gave a weak and what appeared to Jack a hopeless nod. Aunt Saroj urged Grandmother to walk on towards the dining room in Malayalam.

'Hi Nisha.' Kate had noticed her sliding silently into the tail end of the procession.

'Any news of Girija? enquired Jack.

'Dad wants her to come here but she wants to stay with him,' replied Nisha without emotion, head down, her eyes examining the floor as they sauntered on.

'What do you think will happen?' asked Jack.

Nisha just shrugged her shoulders.

That's it; the shutters have come down, thought Jack, *end of conversation*. Kate and Matty were sensitive enough to keep their mouths shut too.

Lunch was subdued; Grandmother just picked at a little serving of rice with curry but no fish or chicken. Everyone just ate quietly. Grandfather and Jack's father occasionally exchanged odd bits of business news: the fall in the market of processed cashew nuts, the date of the next shipment of tin plate. They had just got on to the strike caused by the new conveyor belt at the brick factory when the doorbell rang.

'Who could that be?' wondered Aunt Saroj aloud in Malayalam and ordered Nisha to go and unlock the front door. As Nisha rolled her eyes unwillingly Matty sprang up from his place and grabbed the keys with his left hand without washing his right and sprinted out into the hall. He didn't speak Malayalam as well as Jack but he understood it very well.

It only took a minute or two for Matty to silently appear in the double door way of the dining room. Nobody heard him arrive, he just stood there with his arms raised in the air and a noiseless terrified look on his now ivory-white face. Everyone seemed to notice him at once and Jack immediately stood up but as he began to move he became aware of the two long barrels of a shotgun. They came into view inches from Matty's back.

Jack's father rose to his feet but before he could make a move Girija appeared behind Matty in full view, the butt of the gun wedged into her shoulder and her finger curled around the trigger, eyes aligned along the barrels; she appeared to know exactly what she could do.

'If anyone comes near me, he gets the first cartridge, straight into his spine,' she hissed.

'Why Girija? What's the matter Girija? What is it you want? We can organise whatever it is you need,' implored Jack's father, still standing.

All these exchanges were in Malayalam as Jack shot a look towards Kate but this didn't need translating. The pleading tone of his father's voice and the commanding attitude of the girl conveyed obvious meaning from the sound they made.

'Give me my evil mother and this one goes free,' spat Girija and she pushed the tip of the barrels into Matty's back, causing him to stumble forward into the dining room.

Everyone turned their heads towards Jack's father again; Jack quickly glanced at Nisha whose eyes were so prominent and wide he felt they may actually pop out.

'Why do you want her, do you want her to go back to your father?' queried Jack's father. Jack could see he was trying to penetrate beneath the surface but Girija's next retort exposed his failure to placate her.

'You are forcing me to kill two people,' came her determined retort. Matty took another dig from the gun barrels and was forced forward along by the side of the dining table nearer to Aunt Saroj's chair.

Jack's mother's mouth was in a straight line, her skin was ash-white and somehow grey shadows made two downward channels under her eyes. Jack was thankful she kept herself still and silent as her eyes stayed fixed on her youngest son.

'Alright, alright…' Jack's father asked Aunt Saroj to stand up.

Jack looked at her; she was clearly terrified and pale but couldn't or wouldn't move. Nisha leaped up and shouted at Girija to stop everything.

'Little weasel, condoning the filth,' was all she spat back at Nisha, but she had reached her mother's place at the table and the gun was pointed straight at her mother's right ear. Matty slid back behind Girija; everyone including Girija noticed but nothing was said or done to prevent his move.

'Get up, witch,' growled Girija. Aunt Saroj placed both hands on the table and hauled herself into a standing position.

'Out to the back, time for a sacrifice, mother… a blood sacrifice,' sneered Girija.

Jack was aware that Girija sounded quite insane. At that moment he knew for sure that he, Kate and Swami were not the only ones who knew the truth of what was going on. He wished Kate understood the words as he swiped quick glances in her direction, he realised something was happening with his aunt's entity as Kate's eyes seemed to be following something near the ceiling above Aunt Saroj's head. *How would the dark Goddess protect her?* Jack wondered.

Girija then urged Aunt Saroj to move slowly towards the double door at the other end of the dining room with the barrels of the gun. Grandfather's pleas sounded disturbed and alarmed but he did not stand up, just ended up burying his head in his arms on the table as he was ignored and his eldest child did a death walk silently past his chair.

'What madness is this?' he queried of Grandmother who was about to faint from fright and physical weakness. As mother and daughter passed from the new kitchen into the passage leading to the servants dining room Jack's father issued a forceful whisper to Jack.

'Call Dr Krishna,' he commanded, but Jack passed the same command to

Nisha who didn't move. Jack's father ran to hold Grandmother as she looked as if she would slide off her chair. He commanded Jack's mother to help support her, instructing her to take her to her room and ordering Grandfather to follow. While the bewildered grandparents were being swept to safety Jack and Kate followed the captive Aunt Saroj and Girija who were proceeding through the main kitchen as the two cousins peeped round the door frame to see three servant women – Mary, their ayah, Hemani, Grandmother's cook and the little kitchen girl Aasha – pinned against the wall, wide-eyed and motionless in the servants' dining room as mother and daughter vanished through the kitchen door beyond and out on to the veranda.

Neither Jack nor Kate spoke, just sped silently into each room and space the preceding two had entered and exited from. Finally peering round the window frame of the small lower kitchen used for grinding coconut and spices, they could clearly see the captive and her prey heading towards the outhouse used for grinding the rice into powder. Aunt Saroj began to speak.

'If you want all of us to go back there… then I will… if you spare my life… I promise I will…' she tried desperately.

'Promise… you don't know the meaning of a promise,' Girija jeered.

Jack whispered a translation for Kate, they were in gunshot range but partially concealed behind the trellised screen windows and could duck if needed. They could also escape through the house quicker than Girija could come around the building to get in through the kitchen door if they were spotted, Jack calculated.

'I will do it for you now, whatever you want…' Aunt Saroj had stopped walking near the entrance to the outhouse but didn't turn around.

'When have you ever done anything for anyone in your whole life? You are so selfish and greedy you are not even aware of it,' Girija seemed to be talking to herself, her voice had dropped an octave or two.

'I want to stay alive… I will do anything you ask me to now… I'll even go back to your father…' Aunt Saroj appeared to be crying; her shoulders gave a little shudder.

'No, no… stop that, more lies. Stop it, stop it, stop it,' Girija appeared to be losing control but then added quietly:

'He's penniless; otherwise why would you be here?' Emotions were seemingly bursting out of Girija and Jack felt she too was crying as she wiped her eyes with the sleeve of her shirt she had been supporting the barrel with.

'Why can't you be satisfied with what Grandfather sends us? We've plenty of food and clothes and our school fees are paid… why can't you be happy with that…? You lack absolutely nothing.' Actual conversation from Girija: Jack felt so sorry for her and for Nisha.

Jack continued to translate for Kate.

'This is pathetic, someone has to help Girija… she's out there facing the monster all alone…' Kate said, exasperated.

'Girija is too jittery, I don't think we should go out there…' replied Jack with just as much unease.

'Well I'm not leaving her on her own…' said Kate adamantly.

'What are you doing?' asked Jack as he watched her close her eyes and place herself into a sitting position, legs folded in a Padma Asana on the tiled floor with her back ram rod straight. Jack did not get an answer. He knew he should not interrupt Kate whatever she was doing; she looked as if she was meditating.

'I've never done this before… but someone has to help her…' continued Kate after only a minute or two. She turned herself on to her knees again and watched the scene outside the window.

Aunt Saroj chose this moment to turn and face her daughter, she was squinting, the volcano heat of the midday sun was in her eyes so Jack felt safe in their viewing position.

'And leave all this to the foreigners…' her arms were stretched down and open asking for an answer.

'Foreigners, what foreigners? Who are you talking about?' Girija appeared to be genuinely puzzled.

'My brother, your so-called cousins, your aunt… that white woman, does she look like family, is she your blood? And very soon there will be more of them, what about the one who just arrived… do you think they will be thinking of your school fees…?'

Jack was too shocked to translate but he knew Kate had got the gist of it from the few words of English used.

'Kate? She's only here for her summer holidays… and as for Jack and Matty ,they are the rightful inheritors… are Nisha and I going to run factories…? What greed, Mother… get into the shed, I'll pull the trigger there, less mess… Jack felt Girija had slipped into her hopelessness again as she realised her mother's base instincts would always rule.

'What did you do just now?' whispered Jack.

'I tried to channel some help from the Danavas, they are nowhere to be seen, I haven't done it before, Magh told me about it, how I could use it in times of danger…' replied Kate, peering just above the window ledge.

'Why isn't her entity helping her? Can you see it?' queried Jack.

'Go, Mother,' shouted Girija as Aunt Saroj looked to be searching for an idea or words.

'There seems to be some confusion… it's hovering nearby… look at the top most leaves of the shrub near your aunt, watch how only those top leaves move and not the whole shrub,' explained Kate.

'The curry tree?' confirmed Jack. 'Yes, I see the movement,' replied Jack thoughtfully. 'But where is her dark goddess?'

Just then an eagle landed on the lower branch of the nearby Jack Fruit tree.

Jack noticed the smile on Kate's lips as she turned to him.

'A shape shifter,' she whispered.

'Are you sure?' asked Jack.

'Yes, my arms have a terrible ache…' she said.

'How can you feel what he feels?' asked Jack.

'I don't know, I never felt this before but I'm sure he is a shape shifter,' she said. 'He has probably flown a long distance or is not used to using his arms as wings. This is really strange.'

They were distracted by the threatening sound of Girija's voice from outside again.

'No spells, Mother, don't try it, I've worked it out, I can squeeze the trigger in less than a second, you cannot summon your evil quicker than that.' The strangled words emerged from Girija between heavy sobs as once again the tears coursed down her cheeks, quickly chased by her sleeve.

With that the aunt turned towards the door of the outhouse. As they began to move away from the kitchen window Jack became aware of his father creeping barefooted in the sand towards Girija's back, mundu tucked up and in. He had come through the garden and through the gate which separated the front of the house from the back area. Through the side window of the little kitchen Matty could be seen lurking far away behind his father, moving from one coconut trunk to the next nearest one having obviously received instructions to keep away but at the same time unable to quell the dread of danger for his father.

They moved stealthily past the kennels for fear of causing the dogs to bark and alerting Girija. The dogs were lying down, dozing after their meal of turmeric rice and meat. Kate had seen them too, eyes moving from the sleeping dogs inside their kennels to her uncle and cousin behind him. Slowly and silently Jack's father reached the back veranda. Jack and Kate both rose up from their crouched positions and went in the direction of the kitchen door together to come face to face with Nisha, just standing there, blocking their exit. She had been listening as always with the deadly knowing look on her face. Realisation came to Jack and Kate at once: had she heard too much even though the cousins had been whispering, did she realise Kate had 'the gift' and knew they had heard the entire conversation between her mother and sister? As she silently watched Jack's father advance nearer and nearer his heartbroken and dangerous niece, her eyes swivelled from that scene to Jack and Kate but she remained silent, she appeared to want it stopped as much as everyone else did.

Amid this tension there was a deafening shot as Girija had obviously pulled the trigger. The servant women who had crept into the big kitchen behind Nisha let out high pitched shrieks and screams. The children stood paralysed holding their breaths, only eyes moved as Jack's father sprang from behind, grabbing the barrels of the gun just in time to tilt them skyward. Girija wrestled and kicked and bit but Jack burst through both doors and grabbed her around the waist as his father extracted the large gun from her grasping hands, uncurling finger after finger. Jack finally managed to haul her backwards as she let go of the heavy gun into her uncle's controlled grip.

Both Nisha and Kate ran to help Jack but Girija realised she was defeated and slumped in a sobbing heap into the burning sand. Aunt Saroj picked herself up dazed, she seemed amazed that she was actually alive. She shook the sand from her sari pleats and walked passed her brother, broken daughter and the little group around her into the darkness of the kitchen while the children clustered closer to Girija.

'Let's bring her inside,' ordered Kate.

Jack placed an arm under Girija's armpit and Kate placed hers under the other to try to lift her slumped body up from the ground.

'Mind...' ordered Nisha, pushing Jack away.

He knew she was using the customs as a way of excluding them, closing up tight as too much had escaped that day. However, she still needed Kate to take the spectacle away from the prying eyes of the servants as by then the watchman and the lone Sunday driver had come to find out where the noise had come from and even a head or two appeared over the high compound wall from the neighbouring houses. Jack's father had opened one of the side doors and beckoned them to lead her into the house through those, sparing Girija the stares.

Once inside Jack's father directed the sad little group towards Girija's bedroom which was at the front of the house. Aunt Saroj was nowhere to be seen, neither was Grandmother or Jack's mother. They silently led the mutedly, distraught young woman through the room which led upstairs with Jack and Matty at the rear.

'Take her out of here,' whispered Grandfather to Jack, indicating Kate with a dismissive wave of his hand.

By the time Jack caught up with the girls they were through the sitting room and almost at Girija's bedroom door.

'Let's go,' Jack said to Kate; she was perceptive enough to read a hidden meaning in his voice.

'Come on Matt,' Jack said quietly to Matty.

As they left Jack could hear his father discussing suicide with his grandfather and how Nisha or someone else perhaps a nurse should stay with Girija at all times. What Jack couldn't forget was the attitude of his grandfather towards Kate. It was revealing and it hurt deeply, much more than what had transpired at the back of the kitchen between Girija and her mother.

'What'll happen to Girija now?' queried Matty as they all walked passed the car parked near the front door.

'I think Dad's going to get her help… see a doctor or something,' replied Jack, his mind on the black car.

'Whose car is that?'

'Girija's. Why did she want to shoot Aunt Saroj?' pursued Matty.

'Who knows, probably had a fight over the separation or something…' said Jack evasively. 'Did Girija drive that car three hundred miles alone?' Jack continued to question Matty.

'I guess so,' said Matty shrugging.

'Did she have the gun pointed at you when you opened the door?' questioned Jack.

'No, she had it rolled up in a straw mat, otherwise the watchman would not have let her in,' replied Matty who appeared nonchalant.

'So when did she point it at you?' pushed Jack.

'After locking the front door she unrolled the mat and just told me to put my arms in the air and be very quiet and walk towards the dining room,' he said jauntily. 'Do you think she really would have killed Aunt Saroj?' – still oblivious to the danger he had been in.

'No, she was probably just angry with her and wanted to make her go back to Uncle Rajan,' said Jack hoping it would be convincing enough for Matty as he tended to agonise over everything, little things and big things.

'But she pulled the trigger though… so she really did mean to kill her,' Matty persisted and reasoned to himself and the other two.

'Your Dad caused the trigger to fire when he grabbed the rifle,' interjected Kate. They waited inside the garden of the main house on the instructions of the watchman. He crossed the road to open their gate on the other side thus avoiding passing cyclists and pedestrians who might loiter about and question the sound from the shot gun.

'But she put real cartridges in it?' insisted Matty.

'Otherwise she probably felt her mother would not believe she was really serious, I guess,' replied Kate. 'I don't know, it's complex,' Kate shrugged as she continued, trying to minimise the effects on Matty.

'What's complex mean?' queried Matty.

'Not clear,' replied Kate.

'That's for sure,' finished Matty as their mother joined them.

'You dismissed too?' questioned Jack.

'They'll settle things among themselves… anyway I wanted to see how you all were. Let's put on the air conditioner and cool down a bit, it's roasting,' and she unlocked their front door.

COOL DOWN

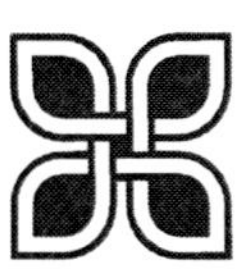 

THERE WERE SIX windows on the large sitting room in the Little Pink House so everyone had a window or two to hook shutters closed and draw the curtains. Jack's mother switched on the air conditioner to shelter, cool down and relax from the powerful discomfort of the afternoon heat.

'Thank God the power is back,' she remarked as she sat down on one of the sofas beside Matty. 'You'll have to man the generator if it goes again,' she ordered Jack.

'Is Grandmother shocked?' queried Kate, 'She doesn't look very well.'

'I think she's so unwell, that today was just another problem with Aunt Saroj's family, but of course it is an enormous problem,' replied Jack's mother.

'Girija is not mad, Mum,' insisted Jack.

'No, no, of course not. But she is very upset about something,' she replied and added, 'Nisha is coping better.'

'Maybe Nisha is doing what Aunt Saroj wants her to,' said Jack, trying to direct the conversation.

'Yes, they seem to get along together most of the time,' replied his mother. 'Poor Girija seems so lost.'

'Nisha – she buries bottles,' said Matty quietly.

'Bottles, what sort of bottles and how do you know?' Jack's mother was now bolt upright questioning the self-conscious Matty.

'You know the little tree here,' and Matty pointed towards one of the shuttered windows, 'the one Dad planted because you liked the pink flowers.'

'Yes,' his mother replied as Jack's brain shot into gear. 'But how do you know?' she asked again.

'I saw her,' Matty said, looking around at the other two.

'Saw her when?' asked Jack.

'When she had the sleep-over,' Matty replied. 'Betty woke me barking, I was afraid someone was trying to get in.' Unusually for Matty, he began to talk as if he felt he had to convince everyone.

'I'm in the highest bedroom, the crow's nest so that makes me the look out, so I looked out and saw her digging the sand with her hands and putting a bottle in the hole. But Betty kept bothering her and making a howl-like noise. When I went to take it out I found another bottle,' explained Matty cleverly.

'Where was the watchman?' questioned his mother.

'He was sleeping in the car shed, I went to the bathroom window and checked,' Matty continued to convince his amazed audience.

'What did you do with the bottles, Matt?' Jack was on the edge of his armchair.

'I kept them because they have really nice metal pieces in them with markings on. Do you want to see them? They are in my room,' and with that he sprinted out of the sitting room.

'I don't like the sound of this,' remarked Jack's mother as she rested back against the sofa again. 'I don't expect they will have best wishes in them.'

'What do you mean?' queried Kate.

'They contain usually a mixture of Muslim and Hindu, sometimes Christian, inscriptions invoking bad luck on the receiver and are usually buried in gardens and business premises by rival business people. Obviously Aunt Saroj isn't too keen on us,' surmised Jack's mother with raised eyebrows.

'No she is definitely not, we were referred to as foreigners in the argument she had with Girija outside the kitchen before Dad took the gun. Apparently she feels she should not have to share with Dad, you or Matt and me and is afraid more relatives from Ireland will materialise soon,' explained Jack, his eyebrows rose indicating the madness of it.

Before his mother could reply Matty burst into the room closing the door behind him. He had two small amber-coloured bottles, like tablet bottles from a chemist with metal screw-on lids which were bound with cotton and a thread and sealed with a sort of resin.

'Do you think it is very old, like buried treasure Nisha has found somewhere, maybe at her home and brought with her for safe keeping?' he asked excitedly.

'No, it's not very old Matty and it's not valuable,' his mother responded quietly.

'You'll have to give it to Dad, he knows someone who will be able to open them and read what is written on the silver or copper scrolls inside, it is difficult to know what type of metal it is due to the colour of the bottle!' their mother said, holding them up to the lamp which she had switched on.

'Oh, can't I have them back?' begged Matty.

'Not now Matty, maybe later,' she replied. 'But let's keep it a secret; no one needs to know that the bottles have been dug up.'

'Why?' questioned Matty.

'Well... If it's something nice then... it's OK, isn't it?' she struggled for words.

'What if it is bad?' queried Matty sombrely.

'If you are good and you don't believe in bad things then it can do you no harm,' she replied, but didn't convince anyone.

RESCUE

A WEEK HAD passed and both Jack and Kate's concern for Girija became more and more urgent. She had been unresponsive, even at the psychiatrists in the capital Trivandrum. Jack's father took her along with her mother who was apparently unwilling at first and later gave into pressure from Grandfather but remained detached. Blood tests had been taken, chemicals assessed and medications ordered. Jack and Kate both knew none of this was necessary but they also believed that adults felt they had to do something and find solutions. They truly felt that if they could support Girija, especially with their insight, it might help her, give her hope. The difficulty was access. Kate had visited on the Tuesday morning, allowing life to settle down after the Sunday incident. She had chosen a time when everyone was at school, especially Nisha but Aunt Saroj had not allowed her past the hallway and dispatched her when she tried to linger by enquiring after Grandmother. Kate tried again on the Thursday morning with Nisha out of the way after the visit to the doctor but once again she failed to reach Girija.

'I was just feet away from her, she was on the other side of a door and I couldn't get in and Girija would not or could not get out. Her mother has incarcerated her, fairly and squarely she is imprisoned. This is against the law where I come from, you know,' Kate emphasised as she passed back and forth on the small back veranda, confident in speaking out loud as Jack's mother's air conditioner was switched on. The ayah Mary was in the garden combing her hair after her shower and she did not speak English. It was a Saturday after lunch and Matty had left to visit a school friend and his father was at work.

'Well, consider this: what if she has given up and can't be bothered to talk to anyone, even us? Remember, she was not herself before she ran away,' Jack countered. He was sprawled across the recliner; the chick blinds made their slat shadows across his face.

'I'm sure I could get through to her if I had just five minutes with her,' Kate went on with certainty. She suddenly came to a halt and eased herself cross-legged into the hanging wicker chair which was suspended by a chain from the ceiling of the veranda.

Jack waited for the 'light bulb' finger to come up but she remained pensive and irritated for several minutes, playing with rubber bands which she entwined and separated. Slowly the finger activity died down; her hands lay still on her lap and her gaze was lost inside the house. Finally, she swivelled both eyes in his direction with a naughty grin on her face.

'What now?' he questioned, excited at the prospect of action but uneasy as he eased himself off his sore shoulder, the memory of the half-healed monkey bite still fresh in his mind.

'The Danavas,' she said quietly, 'I'm sure I can do it without them… or maybe not.'

He knew immediately what she was thinking.

'How is Girija going to see you, how will she know you are with her? I had only glimpses of you in your etheric body and that was because the conditions were right or there. Remember, there was a portal that night,' Jack reminded her.

'No, no, I need the Danavas, or at least the Devas,' she carried on talking out loud to herself, as if she was running something through her brain.

'Kate, Kate, listen to me,' Jack sat up and pulled the hanging chair around so that she was facing him.

She focused quizzically on his face momentarily but she still did not see him.

'You have to come too,' she said still talking to herself.

'Think, how are you going to talk to me, your physical body will be here… in my room… lying inert on the bed?' He had raised his voice and spoke every word slowly as if she couldn't understand his language.

'This is a good plan.' She seemed to be fully focused on what was in her head not on him.

He let go of the chair and looked around, annoyed that Kate had not heard one word he had said and he found the ayah watching them intently; probably his closeness to Kate or his voice caused her to be interested.

'Listen.' Kate spoke so quietly that the wicker squealed as Jack sat cross-legged on the recliner again and waited with reluctance for her plan, still looking out through the chicks, head turned away from her.

'Jack look at me,' she began and waited for him to turn his head. 'We have to ask the Danavas to help us, sorry the Devas; by involving them again we kill two birds with one stone.'

'What?' he quizzed. 'They were not much help when Girija had the gun.'

'Yeah, I know... I don't understand what's going on with them, they haven't been at the window for ages either,' she disclosed.

'So we can't rely on them, can we?' he asked her.

'They can protect Girija from whatever spells her mother may have cast on her,' Kate whispered.

'And the second bird?' he questioned with a fed-up expression.

'What?' she queried. 'Oh yes, they use crystals for healing. Usha is a healer or an apprentice healer. They can heal Girija.'

'You are assuming a lot. What if Girija is too ill? What if I can't convince her that you are with her inside her room? What if the Danavas don't show up?' he protested.

'She's not ill and you know it,' Kate shot back and the normally cool blue eyes seemed to give off lapis sparks.

'What's the plan then?' Jack hadn't anything to offer himself so he listened.

'The Devas will put the watchmen to sleep tonight and if the Danavas will co-operate and permit Usha to come... I will have to be in etheric form to gain access. What I need you to do is somehow get Girija focused and explain how we can help her and more than anything reassure her and plan a way out for her.' Kate was very intent.

'You said put the watchmen to sleep, why? They can't see you anyway,' Jack asked, still puzzled.

'I know that, but they can see you,' Kate explained. 'Once they are asleep I will pass the next door's keys to you to let yourself in and out again.'

'What about Mum? She wanders around the house at night, even comes out here to sit in the cool.' His reluctance had begun to dissipate, he noticed, and he began to submerge himself, but vigilantly.

'I will get the Devas to spread a little essence in her room and Matty's too. Look, I've got something to show you which Usha gave me, remember I told you she is a healer; she uses quartz crystal.' Kate reached into the pocket of her shalvar. She pulled out a tumble quartz stone and held it in the palm of her hand.

'How did you bring that across to this world?' he asked amazed.

'And I have plenty more,' she continued with a mischievous grin.

'Yes, but how? You were in your etheric aura, nothing solid or tangible... Oh Kate, I really don't understand how you could bring these crystals from the other world,' asked Jack, confounded.

'I don't either but I have placed one in all your bedrooms for protection; apparently some of them have Devas dwelling inside them,' she said excitedly.

'Are you saying you can activate them and make Mum and Matty sleep?' Jack asked.

'Well, according to Usha it can be done: not only induce sleep but protect them too… like I said this is my primary use of energy… activate these Sigils. I'm going to have to place some in the garage so the watchman sleeps and the two watchmen next door…' replied Kate, thinking and organising at the same time.

'So you're sure you can activate them to do more than protection?' Jack asked, doubt flooding his mind.

'Well that's the theory. It's the first time for me, let's see if I can do it… let's see if the Danavans will co-operate and let me have access to Usha,' she said without any hint of the doubt that clouded Jack's thoughts.

'You know, there is real hope for Girija,' Jack said, looking up at her. 'I overheard Mum talking to Dad about a girls' college in Ernakalum and how Girija could go there and stay on campus while she studies for her degree. She would spend holiday time between here and her father's and somehow build a normal life for herself,' Jack said meditatively.

'Now you're talking, that's exactly what you have to say to her, give her hope and at the same time encourage your mother to impress this on your father.' Kate unfolded her legs, stood up and replaced the tumble crystals in her pocket.

'What now?' he asked.

'I have to get in touch with the Danavas and I can't do it here,' she said, placing her eyes on the ayah.

'Kate,' he called after her as she entered the dining room door.

'What?' she said as she half turned round.

'Don't bolt the door, just in case.' He still had not gotten over the experience of the first night after the temple trip.

'I have to; if anything were to go wrong, having the door open wouldn't matter anyway. If it is bolted everyone will just think I'm asleep,' Kate said and disappeared.

NIGHT BEINGS

 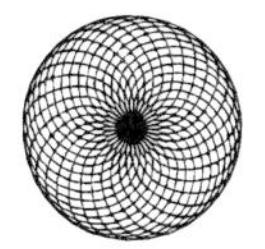

A FEW NIGHTS later Jack sat in the dining room with school paraphernalia scattered all over one end of the table and waited for the signs of bed-time activities to abate. When finally he heard the bolt on his parents' bathroom door being struck home a final time he leaped quietly up and peered out the dining room window to see that their light had been extinguished, their bedroom windows being at right angles to the dining room. He slipped through the double doors leading into the kitchen, unhooked the key for the kitchen back door from the key holder and snuck out onto the back veranda. This door was normally bolted on the inside and secured with a padlock; he hoped that they would not be robbed that night as there was no way of securing the door from the outside. He quickly located Betty who was on night duty, alternating her patrols with the care of her puppies in the kennel; ever watchful, she keened and licked them and raised her head at the same time as Jack rounded towards the front of the Little Pink House.

He wondered what form Kate was in but never doubted she would follow their plan meticulously; her door had been closed and the netted door too as he peered through the ventilation from his position at the dining table. The urge to see if she was in her sleeping state, lying flat on his bed, had to be quelled; he would have to trust that she was already outside and the Devas would do as they had promised her.

Jack had waited at the gate for no more than a few seconds when the bunch of keys came hurtling out of the air above his head from the road side of the gate. He managed to grasp them just, by clasping the largest key between the fingers of both hands while the others jangled briefly on the ring as he interrupted their arch of flight, the weight of the loose keys pulling on the key barely grasped between the tips of his fingers. He bent and peered through the bars of the gate but could see nothing. He undid the padlock and eased himself outside on to the street, wrapped the chain around the metal upright bars where both gates met, clicked the padlock secure and rotated it to hang on the inside of the gate to avoid suspicion.

With the keys stuffed tightly into the pocket of his khaki shorts so as to avoid any sound, he glanced quickly at the lawyer's house next door where he had Maths tuition from Kumari, his neighbour's college-going daughter. All was still there, just one faint light bulb lighting up their veranda visible above the compound walls. He darted across the road and placed himself where the gates met, expecting another haphazard flight of keys, feeling entirely exposed in the waxing light of an almost full moon. Instead a *jingle jangle* alerted him halfway down the gate. He bent and saw the key-ring suspended in air at thigh level and as soon as they began to be raised he prepared himself to receive them. This time he was ready for them. The aim was careful and the arch of flight not so high and he caught the bigger bunch with ease. He reminded himself to ask Kate how she managed to move solid objects in her etheric form; *however she did it, she was improving,* he thought.

Once the second gate was bolted with another padlock secured he left the keys near the hand and underneath one of the sleeping watchmen's dhoti. He waited there; in that position he would not have been seen from any part of Nani Bhavan and he plotted his next move, at the same time squinting and peering to see if he could detect any movement between the trees or among the shrubs in the garden. He had hoped to see the signs or traces of Danavas or Upanayika or at least have some indication of where exactly Kate was.

After waiting a minute or two he skirted halfway round the little box hedge which enclosed the pond and the four grass parterres in an ellipse, crouching low, pausing in the shadows of the mango trees to scan the next safe destination and to detect the other-worldly people or any sign he might recognise from Kate. He thought he heard a whisper from above but it was just a sough, as a gentle wind moved the leaves on the mango trees. There, positioned like a sphinx, was their Irish wolfhound with his head resting on his paws, his eyes on Jack. He didn't move. Jack had very little to do with him since their Irish grandfather had banned him from the Little Pink House. Shane was a pet, imported from a London kennel as a pup, but there was no convincing his grandfather that it was not a dangerous breed. He felt they were unpredictable, having experience of the large dogs devouring lambs on farms in Ireland. So Jack's parents decided to err on the side of caution and Shane was allowed in the Little Pink House only when Jack's mother was around to supervise. Even she had tired of his habit of vomiting and then eating his sick as it meant she had to disinfect constantly, so he was relegated to watchdog, spending most days in the kennels; but most importantly, he was the father of Betty's puppies.

Everything else remained tranquil too, so Jack took up a position under an arbour which was densely covered with Bougainvillea. This was as close to Girija's bedroom windows as he could get without being detected by any human inside the house. He waited in the silence of the thick cover of leaves, pastel-coloured, tissue-paper flowers and sharp thrones for several minutes and watched the movement of the two Alsatians, having realised that they would sense activity that he could not and remembering Kate's story about their long-dead great-great-uncle Michael's ghost walking his dog.

All the while that Jack had been hidden under the Bougainvillea the dogs had sat to attention on the lawn underneath Girija's window. He realised that for watchdogs they had shown little interest in him when he opened the gate. Every so often their ears appeared to point skywards and they shifted their weight from one front paw to the other as they did when a treat might be imminent. Whatever activity they sensed, it did not threaten them; in fact, they seemed quite at ease, although alert.

Reassured by this, Jack decided that one quick sprint would take him to the side window of Girija's bedroom out of the observable garden light and into the shadows of the top bar of the capital E which made up Nani Bhavan. And so he picked the next moment and did it. This time he felt something: a matrix of energy, hardly a resistance, but he had just run through or very close to something invisible to him. He watched the reaction of the dogs when he halted in the shadows at the side of the house; they mercifully had not barked but now stood on all four legs and remained in the same position, ears pointed upwards, tongues lolling out and panting peacefully. They were still at ease.

He crept towards the lower corner of the window to peer into the room, bathed in duskiness by the garden light which cast the shadow of the mosquito net frame across the bed. Girija was not on the bed so he gazed into the shadows of the corners of the room; but it was in a sort of twilight so he could not make out anything or anyone.

He scrutinised the outside again but could detect nothing out of the ordinary. The dogs had sat on their hindquarters again and continued to pant contentedly with their stare in the same direction, currently his direction. After another glimpse into the quiet room he decided he should call out Girija's name softly and begun positioning his face as close as he could to the security bars and the netting, so close he could smell the dust in the metal mesh of the mosquito net. As he carefully considered how his voice would travel in the quiet of the night Girija's voice caused him to pull away in fright from the window.

'Get away from here fast,' her commanded whisper was urgent.

'I'm here to help,' Jack whispered a little too loud, recovering from the shock.

'I know, it's too dangerous, leave… now,' this last part she said in Malayalam as if to emphasise her words. She moved in front of the window and he could see her: she must have been huddled or stood in the corner near the window all the time.

WARRIOR

'YOU DON'T UNDERSTAND, I've got help...' He couldn't continue as she grabbed and then clung to the frame of the mosquito netting with a half-pleading, half-terrified expression, causing the wooden frame to rattle in its holding within the window frame. She called out in Malayalam to someone beyond and to Jack's right.

'Don't touch him...' Then in English, 'Please let him go...'

Almost immediately Jack's attention was brought outside: the dogs were snarling and upright on four legs and advanced in his direction but not focused on him. They began to bark viciously and continued to press forward and then back a bit as if they were wary. Jack's startled stare shot back to the window and then sped in the direction of his petrified cousin's to his aunt. It was a sight he was not prepared for. The expression in her eyes was raw, even bloodshot from what he could make out from the edge of the light of the garden lamp as she proceeded on him out of the shadows from the opposite direction.

Jack began backing away from the window in the direction of the lawn and the dogs, all the time riveted on the creature his aunt had become. He tried desperately to wipe clean from his mind her capabilities, as sheer dread took hold of him and his legs became weak. The sight of her did not help at all. Her hip-length black hair was loose, her neck and chest were covered with many garlands of dead jasmine and a chrysanthemum: *all dead flowers and where was her sari?* She wore a red dhoti tucked up like the men who climbed the coconut trees with her sari blouse and when she sneered and laughed at him he could actually feel her scorn filling the entire miasma. But worst of all she carried a scythe.

'Always found where you have no right to be,' the aunt derided with confidence and followed the words by a dramatised pitiful look.

Jack lost his footing for a second, mainly as his knees gave way completely with petrifaction. He tried to rebalance and at the same moment he noticed a line appearing in the sand which continued to make a junction with another line coming forward from the direction of the lawn. Kate: she was there trying to remind him to focus. He instantly judged the scale and began on the circle that would become the middle of the yantra with his forefinger but a gruesome cackle followed by a snort distracted him and he glanced up to find the aunt had advanced to the very edge of the yantra. All around him the outer circles were forming in the sand, even the lotus shapes, and all he could think of was that they needed double edges and no time.

'Clever boy, are you drawing magic sonny?' the aunt placed emphasis on the word *son*, mocking him. It was how his grandparents addressed him.

'Stand back, I'm warning you,' Jack shot back at her stolidly with as much disrespect as he could muster.

This brought on another bout of guffaws followed by a loud grunt and all the while Jack continued the sacred geometry with his invisible cousin drawing visible lines in the sand. But no matter how quickly they worked; it was impossible to complete it in mere seconds as the aunt stepped forward and kicked sand over the outer line nearest to her. He continued to work mainly in the centre and the line which was covered by sand became visible again. This caused the aunt more dismay and she trampled the sand over a far greater area of the outer line of the yantra menacingly.

'I'm warning you… stop it now. Your little magic tricks are nothing to what I can call up.' She spoke as if it was a directive, but Jack, without looking, knew also that she was becoming emotional and he hoped she would lose her temper, which he considered an advantage. He was working on the extra line which surrounded each drawing within the yantra, mustering his strength at the same time while his invisible help drew and redrew the lines which were being destroyed. It was impossible for him to concentrate on the mantra as well as staying clear of the scythe. As he stood up and jumped over the inner circle, thus placing himself within the outer square of the yantra, the interloper advanced inside it, seething with hate, and raised her scythe. Jack stepped backwards, avoiding the lotus shape representing the God Vishnu with nothing to protect himself. But then and at once both were distracted by Girija shouting: she had come out and with a type of supremacy she walked down the steps, leaving the front door open. She advanced fearlessly towards her mother, warning her and threatening her in Malayalam:

'What is wrong with you, are you going to murder your own nephew?' She stopped outside the yantra's outer lines.

The mother swung round, awash with infuriation and pointed the scythe at her daughter, just inches away from her face.

'You… useless,' she spat and she stepped on top of the outer double lines of the yantra and placed the tip of the point of the blade on Girija's throat who backed in the direction of the front of the house.

Jack was about to complete the Laxmi Hiram within the triangle representing fire but became rooted to the spot. The lines completing the outer part of the yantra had been redrawn as the aunt stepped out. Jack was able to take this in, as his body became paralysed while his mind tried to configure whether he should complete the yantra with the sacred Sanskrit or wrestle the weapon away from his aunt. That curved blade would do far more damage than a straight blade; once plunged into a body it could only be withdrawn by taking part of the inner organs out with its hook-like arc.

Quickly his mind had cleared and he stepped forward ready to lunge at the aunt but in that process another figure appeared with a short sword not unlike a long dagger. He was older and a little taller than Jack and carried a buckler. He intercepted his aunt's perusal of Girija who fled in Jack's direction. Jack put his arms around the shivering Girija and looked around to see if there were more of them but the garden was quiet; the dogs were on guard near the two as they squared up against each other.

The aunt made the first charge but was blocked by the short blade. She pulled back her blade and made an upward stab, causing the warrior to jump backwards and clear of the point of her blade. He became more aggressive and moved about a lot. Jack was amazed at his aunt's strength and later her stamina as the fight continued across in front of the house and way over and underneath the car porch at the bungalow.

'What if she kills him?' worried Girija.

'Or *he* kills *her* – how are we going to explain that?' replied Jack as they both moved round the far end of the box hedge in order to get a better view as the fierce fight continued.

'I don't care, we would all be free again,' she said, shaking her head slowly from side to side. But then she gasped as her mother inflicted a wound on the sword man's left arm.

'Oh Vishnu please protect him,' she pleaded with her palms together.

'Wait... do you know who this fellow is?' asked Jack, aghast.

'A little bit,' she whispered, her hands clasped near to her chin. She watched the battle intently, closing her eyes when the fighter seemed to be merely protecting himself, but she prayed all the time.

'Who is he?' demanded Jack. All sorts of things were going through his head: was she psychic too? Or maybe he was real – but in those clothes! Jack felt, at first, that because the warrior appeared out of nowhere he may have been a Danava, but now he wasn't so sure.

'I don't think you would believe me if I told you,' she replied as she alternately watched and squeezed her eyes shut.

'Listen, I've had a shape shifting snake on my window and in our bathroom, I've been almost torn to death by a flock of feral monkeys, I'm ready to listen to anything,' he said with one eye on the two who were retracing their battle steps and had entered the area where the prayer room was. The aunt's blows were laborious and there was the sound of metal clangour echoing through the night.

'So you understand then what is going on?' she nodded at him.

'Is he Danava?' demanded Jack as the teenagers advanced along the drive towards the prayer room where Aunt Saroj was wildly stabbing with her weapon and her opponent seemed to be barely evading and protecting himself. Jack noticed his wound was oozing a type of ichor.

'She has him cornered,' wailed Girija and grasped Jack's arm.

'Is he or isn't he?' insisted Jack.

'I don't know what Danava is,' cried Girija. 'He says he is De Danann. Yes, yes he is then... but he can be mortal for short periods. See, nobody can outfight her... her strength... it's got to be more than the Goddess Jyestha. My mother has got some powerful dark energy...' Girija was close to tears of despair, pointing at her warrior mother.

'Yes she has and it is primitive and deadly, her temple visits are to a village temple...' Jack had begun to explain but then:

'Wait, just wait there a minute,' urged Jack as he set off in the opposite direction, back to the yantra. It was complete except for the Laxhmi Hirm.

FRAGRANCE AND LIGHT

JACK KNEW THIS little bit of sacred Sanskrit so well: he had practised it all over his notebooks during the classes that wearied him at school, and as he bent to write with his finger a gasp from Girija caused him to look in the direction of the drive to witness the sword fighter disappear into thin air and a dangerous cobra rise from the sand and bite his aunt on her left calf. She screamed and slashed down all at once, half-irascible and half in pain but the snake eluded her and disappeared into the shadows near the box hedge. To Jack's dismay the venom had no effect on her and the aunt once again had targeted Girija who stood frozen in the middle of the drive. He turned his head and focused with all his might on the triangle representing fire at the very centre of the yantra and as he prayed the most meaningful words of the mantra he drew the sacred Laxhmi Hirm. Rising, he realised for the second time that night Girija had a blade at her throat. He shouted with as much hubris as he could summon up:

'Leave her.' This distracted the aunt and drew her attention on him but not for very long. He noticed her mouth open and she wore an ambivalent look rather than the previous contemptuous looks which she had cast over the teenagers. At the same time he felt warmth surround him – he was still within the yantra – and a beautiful smell, extremely subtle and like roses but even more delicate, barely perceptible. He also felt safe as if nothing fazed him and as he followed his aunt's gaze he turned to find a glow, a luminous, translucent red glow with the colour gold shimmering within it. Girija seemed to notice it too and ran to join him within the yantra.

Girija's sudden flit appeared to jerk her mother out of the reverie and, the trance over with, the aunt began to dance, holding her big knife high and repeating a monotonous invocation not unlike what Jack had witnessed in the prayer room, only this time he didn't hear the slap of the sole of her foot on tiles but saw it raise dust from the white sand on the drive. The dance was even more energetic than the earlier one he had seen and this time she had the big curved dagger. As the dust rose from the white riverbed sand it clung to her sweaty skin and gave her an ashen colour which made her appear like something Jack imagined would come from a cremation ground. He looked at Girija but she was confident like him, obviously protected by the energy or essence within the yantra. The incantations became urgent and loud in rhythm with the dance.

The teenage cousins stood and watched the spectacle for a little longer and just as Jack felt he had his volition back he noticed Girija sniffing and at the same time he could discern an acrid stench and with that a leviathan rose up behind the aunt who still pranced, stamped and invoked.

An enormous hag became clear as the two cousins stared in disbelief while the aunt glowered and continued the petition. Held in each arm as a mother would cradle two babies, this ugly giant held a human-sized woman and a man with the head of a buffalo. He held a large truncheon against his right shoulder and was naked except for a small cover over his genitals. The leviathan stopped growing when it was as tall as the house. She wore no blouse, just a girdle below an overweight stomach. She stank and was the ugliest being that Jack could even imagine.

'She must be a troll', he said out loud; he no longer had control of his mind.

'That's the Goddess Jyestha,' Girija responded automatically in a languid and unsteady voice as if her mind too was on autopilot.

With that the monster's two offspring were set down on the drive; the male bent his horned head towards the two cousins and began moving in their direction. Both Jack and Girija clasped each other's hands automatically; with a glance Jack noticed that, like him, she appeared to be drained of all mental ability and Jack could feel her shudder which hindered him even more as the beast reached the outer edge of the yantra.

Swami's porch and his dire warnings flashed briefly through Jack's partially inoperable mind and almost at the same instant the Danava or De Danann warrior burst into his actual vision for the second time that night. He gave Girija what looked like a silver ring and instructed her in what sounded to Jack like the guttural language Kate spoke to the Danavas outside his window.

'What did he say?' Jack shot at her quickly, not looking at her, just feeling her terror, his eyes fixed on the truncheon and the horns of the buffalo man, how its hair had a natural parting on its broad forehead: what a powerful broad forehead, Jack imagined colliding with it.

'It will make me invisible if I put it on,' Girija's shaken voice said as the warrior bent forward sword and buckler ready to defend them against the man buffalo. Neither took their eyes off the scene just inches in front of them.

'And Jack, what about you?' she asked in trepidation and anxiety.

'Put it on,' was all Jack managed to say as the buffalo-headed man ran at the warrior.

'Put on the ring,' shouted Jack.

'But…' and he pushed it on her finger before she could protest more and with that she disappeared.

Meanwhile the Danava or De Danann with no sign of the previous wound or ichor stain was stabbing at the man bull, dancing in this direction and then the other and when the creature bent low to come in for the attack and when he had the chance, he tried to take aim at the top of the buffalo's head, beyond that forehead. Jack quickly glanced at the aunt who continued to dance in front of the troll-like being; the woman had joined in the rhythmic dance on the drive. Girija appeared for an instant still at Jack's side and then just as quickly disappeared again. For some reason Jack's attention was brought to the front door where stood the forlorn outline of his grandmother, clinging on to one of the closed double doors which had remained bolted when Girija came out. He wondered if she could see as much as he did and judging from her expression she did, she held the fall of her half sari to her face to protect against the stench. The buffalo man bawled a terrifying roar like a bull, causing Jack again to focus on the battle. The dogs yowled, not just the Alsatians but the Irish wolfhound and the neighbouring dogs. Jack remembered his grandmother had told him this happened when a death was imminent. Jack hoped the warrior would not feel disconcerted by this despite the fact that the creature came at him at a run once again.

At that very minute there was a rumble from the well in the corner of the garden nearest Jack and then another at the pond in the very centre of the garden and then a second much louder thunder from the pond. Before Jack could draw breath, the water burst high with vigour from the fountain, spewed upwards high above the mango canopy and then bent in the direction of the drive near the front door and the torrent soaked the dancing aunt as it descended to earth. At first Jack felt there was an earthquake but his common sense told him these only happened in Northern India. The rumble stopped but the water continued to spew up and out in vast volumes while the water in the pond churned and churned.

The aunt screeched as the deluge of what Jack knew would be cold water cascaded on top of her and she ran towards the house with both arms still raised as she thrashed the air above her head with her weapon. Jack was relieved that the blade had been flung down as she passed Grandmother who moved out of her way just in time. The Goddess Jyestha gathered up her progeny who sprang into her arms and instantly disappeared along with the warrior. At almost the same moment Girija reappeared and the fountain became silent, the water no longer disturbed. Both cousins stepped out of the yantra on to the drive and walked silently side by side and stood staring at the drenched sand of the drive, looking at the puddles which formed in the tyre tracks as though they needed confirmation of what just had happened.

'It must have been the shock of the cold water that stopped her dancing and chanting…' said Jack aloud but to himself. The sound of his own voice made him aware of his surroundings. The garden was once again quiet, except for the yantra and he glanced back to see if it actually existed and again at the wet patch on the drive. He failed to understand what had just happened although the exhaustion that he had begun to feel assured him that it had been no dream.

'The Goddess terrified me…' replied Girija quietly.

'She didn't move, it was the buffalo oh… I really thought we were finished…' Jack didn't continue; he didn't need to.

There was a moan from inside the front door and then Jack remembered.

'Grandmother,' he said looking at Girija.

'Where?' Girija asked.

'Inside, near the door,' he said on his way up the steps.

He found her with her shoulders and head slumped against the closed door with the lower part of her body and her legs sprawled out across the floor.

'Oh son,' she cried, 'you are alright and Girija too,' and she tried to haul herself up but her heels were not strong enough to give her any leverage.

'Grandmother don't do anything, we'll help you up.' Both the children hooked an arm under their grandmother's and with great difficulty the two got her standing and then eased her onto one of the sofas. Girija sat beside her and rubbed the hand nearest to her as Grandmother was frozen cold; Jack sat opposite leaning forward, focused on his grandmother.

'The fountain has been making all sorts of noises lately, sometimes no water comes out…' Grandmother went on in a shaky voice. 'I'm very glad nobody came to repair it,' she said quietly and then she looked up at the teenagers.

'I don't understand how it stopped her, though…' said Jack without reflection. He didn't care anymore; he was beyond thought.

'And when the dancing and chanting stopped, the Goddess disappeared,' Girija put in and then quickly added, 'Where is she now?' she asked her grandmother in Malayalam.

The words uttered were reactive and without much consideration, normal after a shocking experience. However this particular question caused everyone's mind to focus on the present.

'Having a bath, she's always taking baths,' Grandmother said.

'Will you both be alright with her?' questioned Jack, looking from one to the other.

'What was that big being?' asked Grandmother.

'That's the Goddess of misfortune, her name is Jyestha,' explained Girija. 'There is a temple dedicated to her near where we live, my mother has always worshipped there. But I never imagined she could invoke her like that.'

'I have never heard of her,' said Grandmother.

'But why worship a Goddess of misfortune?' asked Jack.

'Don't ask me, I don't understand my own mother,' replied Girija, shaking her head, 'all I know is that Goddess Jyestha is the elder sister of the Goddess Laxmi.'

'But that makes sense,' said Jack. 'I had cast a Raja Yantra which contains the powers of Laxmi and Vishnu. Your Mum is clever... To counter any effect of the yantra she invoked Laksmi's elder sister with the two dangerous offspring.'

'Just help me back to my room, son, I don't think I can listen to any more after what I have witnessed this night. You go home then... please...' she pleaded, looking Jack straight in the eye. Jack felt she knew tonight would not have happened if he had stayed at home; she was sure of it, he knew it too and one glance at Girija told him she knew it also.

And so they began the slow procession from the front to the back of the house, Grandmother stepping that little bit stronger the more they moved. Grandfather was in deep sleep as they eased her on to her bed and Girija bent to take off her slippers. Jack noticed how little her ankles and feet were as he eased both her legs onto the bed as she sunk back on her pillows. They slipped out the bedroom door and headed in the direction of the front door again; Girija held the door as if ready to lock it and as Jack began to descent the steps he looked back at her and said, 'We have to talk.'

'And we will,' she replied with assurance.

HOME

AS JACK WALKED out on to the drive he suddenly felt a slump that only illness or exhaustion could cause. He looked once again at the damp sand of the drive and paused a moment to pick up the scythe. Feeling that someone was watching him he turned to find a curtain move in the small sitting room in the older part of the house. *Nisha,* he thought; he reasoned that she had overheard the conversation between himself, his grandmother and Girija. Always watching and waiting and peering out of her fearful world at what must have been an even more faltering one. He walked on and thought of the other-worldly creatures. Kate's world seemed to jump right into his mind when he confronted himself with the mechanics of getting the keys to the watchmen. They were both still asleep so Jack removed the keys from where he had placed them earlier, wondering what time it actually was. No need to advance the watch punch at the far end of the compound as Grandmother knew the watchmen were nowhere to be seen and Jack considered that she would prefer they didn't know. He placed the scythe on the walkway beside the sleeping bodies; he considered that they would know where to leave it for the gardener with the other tools in one of the outhouses; he was too tired to put it there himself.

As he locked the padlock he waited but there was no sign of Kate, so he put his arm between the middle bars of the gate and stretched as much as it was possible and tossed the keys as far away from the gate as he could aim from an awkward position. While he did this a cynical smile crossed his lips: *why lock ourselves in when the real monster was among us*? As he was about to raise himself up, the keys magically levitated and floated to the hand of one of the sleeping watchmen and rested on the walkway beside it.

Jack crossed the road, let himself in and delivered a second set of keys to the car-shed, to another sleeping watchman. Betty had been at the gate anxious at first but lavish with her welcome once he gave her a chance to recognise him. Jack noticed that there was a form seated on the back veranda and as he sheepishly headed towards the steps he desperately tried to invent a lie for his mother, only to find Kate grinning at him.

'Whee... what a relief,' Jack's hand automatically flew to his chest. 'I thought you were Mum,' he whispered as he flung himself down on the recliner.

'What a night,' he continued in a whisper, aware that they were very near his parents' open bedroom windows.

'I really feared for all of us when the Goddess Jyestha appeared and worse still that buffalo-headed son of hers...' exclaimed Kate in an animated whisper who appeared to Jack to be less exhausted and as usual for her able to accept the unbelievable.

'Wait wait wait, how do you know her name?' he questioned, now sitting right up.

'Remember, I was with the Danavas!' she whispered with an attitude that said, *Why wouldn't I know? Clever of your aunt to invoke the Goddess Laksmi's elder sister, though.*

'Yes for several minutes on several occasions tonight I really thought I was gone. I'm so tired... I do think they could have been a bit more proactive though...' he whispered as if holding her to account for their lack of help.

'They couldn't appear to alienate the more powerful of the underworld...the shape shifter did well despite his injury...' she began.

'Only when Girija was in danger!' pointed out Jack.

'Even he had to be more defensive rather the offensive with your aunt,' defended Kate.

'What about Girija...?' Jack's whisper was cut short by his mother's voice coming through the dining room window behind him and this time it felt as if his heart really did stop.

'What are you two doing out there at this time of night?... and Jack, tomorrow is a school day...what on earth...?' She didn't finish and in another second appeared at the kitchen door and herded them in through the house.

As they both scurried in the direction of their rooms Jack could hear the sound of the bolt and the lock on the kitchen door. He whispered a question to Kate, 'Looks as if the Devas sleep essence has worn off?' Kate quickly closed the net door and then the bedroom door as Jack in his weary state still managed to take two steps at a time up the stairs to avoid the antagonist below.

STIR CRAZY

THE WEEKEND CAME and went and at the family Sunday lunch there were two remarkable changes. Firstly, Grandmother, although lying on the ornate bed in the room with the stairs when everyone sauntered in, did not need help to get up and walk to the dining room when lunch was served. Secondly, just as the men folk and children were about to pull out their chairs and Jack's aunt and mother had begun serving portions of a myriad of vegetable dishes onto everyone's side plates, Girija seated herself next to Nisha on the opposite side of the table to Jack's family. Nobody said anything to her but there was the feeling of *the elephant in the room*, Jack thought; he gave her a grin of encouragement. Despite that, everything went smoothly: Jack had been extraordinarily helpful at passing dishes and the water jug and even took the bother of passing everyone extra papadams when he helped himself.

Sitting on the same side of the table as Kate was disadvantageous for Jack. What he really wanted to know was if Kate had been watching his aunt's entity as she was unusually subdued. She barely answered the rare question that was sent in her direction and then it was mostly domestic and from Grandmother. The aunt appeared no longer to be the centre of attention and did nothing to include herself; she usually engaged Grandfather with a comical narrative and he in turn indulged her. That Sunday Jack found her left on the margins.

Grandfather was always the first to finish lunch; he washed his hands and mouth at the dining room sink and headed off in the direction of the big sitting room to make phone calls. Sometimes the adults lingered and talked and that Sunday it was a mixture of both. Jack's aunt busied herself organising the kitchen staff and the leftover food; Jack's father and grandmother talked about someone in the family. After washing her hands Jack noticed that Kate lingered and remarked on Girija's shirt and shalwar while she was waiting in line for the wash basin. He was reassured to see Girija's ready response and a conversation started up on tailors. Nisha was having none of it, though: she pushed past the girls at the sink in a glum mood, telling them almost rudely in Malayalam to mind out. After she finished at the sink she did not leave the room but waited by one of the dining chairs near the dining room doors on the way out, gloomy eyes on Kate and Girija who had begun to move in that direction. Jack remained just behind the two girls as they moved along the passageway in an animated talk about cotton and terry cotton fabrics. Nisha sulked, sauntering along with the others and when Kate waved quietly into the passage leading into the kitchens she moved forward

'What are you doing?' Nisha shot the words at Kate.

'Nothing,' replied Kate.

Jack reasoned that Kate had seen Great-Grandmother's spirit in the passageway.

'You waved at someone, don't try to deny it.' Nisha had placed herself face to face with Kate at the junction of the two passages.

'I was simply swatting a mosquito,' Kate lied.

'What does it matter Nisha?' put in Girija.

'Don't think you can treat my mother with disrespect.' Nisha's words were threatening.

'Your mother is in the kitchen, she was not in the passage,' came Kate's calm reply.

Jack felt that Nisha felt threatened by Girija's friendship with Kate and he felt that she probably sensed she should support her mother in defeat as well; that would explain her sensitivity and aggression. By this time the adults had caught up and the teenagers moved on, everyone went in different directions for their beds and a siesta.

There followed almost two weeks of torrential rain and washing had to be suspended as temporary lines of damp clothes hung in the outhouses for days and never dried, just developed stale odours instead. After school Jack would find Kate curled up in an armchair reading or writing letters to Ireland dressed in her jeans and at night she was even cold enough to add a cardigan. His mother stopped bringing woollens to India as they just got eaten by moths; she used the traditional shawl to keep the chill out in the evenings.

There was also the annual horrendous encounter with his mother over destroying his school shoes. He couldn't help it; every year since he was five Jack would roll up his uniform trousers at school and delight in jumping into muddy water-filled potholes. Even though he knew his mother would not restrain herself in front of Kate he went ahead and spent a whole lunch hour destroying his shoes with Khalid and Akhill and another wayward bunch of fellows on the very first day of the monsoon. After the shouting subsided – during which his father had tried to intervene as happened every year and as always was ignored and left to find peace in a quieter room – Jack joined Kate in his bedroom. He thought he would apologise but she was sitting facing the window as if the heated exchange was normal and he wondered if it rained on the Danavas. He joined her but all she said was:

'Now I understand how it must have been for Noah and his ark. I have never seen so much rain and water and I come from Ireland!' She continued to stare out the window.

Jack shook his head and thought to himself, *Mum out there still mumbling about waste and cost and her niece in here thinking on the Old Testament… even homework has to be better than this.*

With that he left the room and found his school bag in the thankfully empty hall, his warring mother elsewhere. He flung the bag on the dining room table and with a sigh slid the books out through its open mouth.

THE UNFORESEEN VISITOR

THERE HAD BEEN no escape for Jack during all of this. When he was young he would spend a little time after school with his grandparents making his grandmother laugh and when his grandfather arrived from the office he pushed the boundaries set at home and always got away with it; he defied all the quiet, loving advice his grandparents patiently conferred while they gently brushed his arm.

Too old for this behaviour, he had been restless as usual, unable to sit still, powerless to discuss anything with Kate as there was no way of drowning their conversation with the air conditioner; they didn't need the cold air. The windows and shutters were all closed against the rain and most of the older rooms had ventilation slits so there was little or no privacy except in the 'Crow's Nest' – Matty's room – and Matty was always there when he wasn't at school.

Kate seemed to be more interested in Matty anyway. She helped him set up the big torches and they both lit candles from six in the evening till bedtime and after, instead of asking the watchman to turn on the generator for lighting during the power cuts, preferring the atmospheric candle light. Kate and Matty had been working on a leprechaun game based on Snakes and Ladders. They had Sellotaped four sheets of white A4 paper together and Kate had drawn an outline of a very large shamrock. The aim of the game was to rescue the children who were stolen by the leprechauns to work in gold mines. Every evening after school they both worked on the obstacles in their underground mine as Kate drew passages, piles of stones, menacing-looking leprechauns and Matty filled in the tiny drawings with coloured pencils within the shamrock. They invited Jack almost every evening but he could not forget the awful night in the garden and needed to discuss it so badly with Kate.

The wind with sheets of rain tossed the heads of the older giant coconut trees this way and that in the semi-darkness. Kate got a great deal of pleasure out of the wildness of the storm while Jack's mother watched the wavering candle flames which almost extinguished with draughts from the wall ventilations while she tolerated the candles, aware that the children needed to occupy themselves.

When she was on her own Jack noticed that Kate opened the shutters and let the oversized raindrops storm their way through the security bars and splash her face. Jack felt it was alright for her, able as she was to accept her multi-dimensions but he needed to talk and plan. He was desperate to get some input on the powers in the garden that night but he honestly knew that Kate would not have the answers to most of his questions; he needed Swami for the Goddess explanations for a start. Just because his aunt was defeated did not mean Girija or anyone was safe. Jack knew the aunt would bide her time to plot.

Just as life seemed to become intolerable with wetness and the permanent shawl-wrapped silhouette of his mother on the back veranda, the rain stopped one evening and for a very short time it was grey and damp like Ireland, but in the morning the sun appeared again. Quickly the puddles dried up and it was as if the rains had been something imagined as life took on its constant, familiar feel again.

It was one of those evenings when Swami resumed his visits; he still had a sniffle from the tail-end of a flu he had developed during the cold weather the rain brought. He nursed a cup of warm tea instead of cold lime juice, Jack noticed when he returned from school.

Jack took his lime juice straight out to the lawn to join Swami and Kate, grabbing a couple of homemade chocolate biscuits on the way. He was thankful that Matty had early Hindi tuition with Kumari their neighbour and left him inside at the dining room table with his mother watching the half-interest he had in his milk and biscuits.

Jack wanted to launch straight into the new phenomenon: the Danava who could make himself mortal. Kate had no satisfactory explanation for it except perhaps, she felt, it was the reverse of what she herself had the ability to do. When Jack explained that Girija used the words De Danann not Danava, Kate pointed out that his clothes were more Tuatha dé Danann than Danava. First of all he wore a kilt, not a katcha.

'Who did you speak to when you asked for help?' asked Jack.

'The ones who come to the window, you know the ones who ride with the leader. Why?' Kate asked.

'I don't understand how the warrior fits in to any of this, is he one of them or is he a Tuatha? Jack asked.

'How could he be a Tuatha dé Danann?' Kate's voice faded and her face reddened. She appeared dismayed.

'What's the matter Kate?' asked Swami.

'He could very well be a Tuatha,' she replied, thinking, and then continued, 'Remember when Girija confronted your aunt with the gun? At the back of the house I tried to channel help from the Danavas.'

'The eagle, your arms ached,' said Jack.

'I have applied what Magh told me to the Danavas; although they are very similar they may not be exactly the same. I'm obviously not experienced in what I'm doing, in other words I really don't know what I am doing,' she said fearfully.

'Don't panic,' put in Swami, 'he helped you on that awful night when the Danavas just stood by.'

'But he must be in contact with Girija. Jack said she knew him, called him even by his name. What was it, Jack?' she asked anxiously.

'I can't remember,' he said, thinking.

'What are we going to do? I could have upset a balance. Was that the reason why the Danavas did not help, do they feel that the warrior is an interloper? This is an awful mess, I'm going to have to talk with them – that is, if they come again. I'll have to be in my etheric self just like when I asked them for help.' Kate was agitated and had almost worked herself into a frenzy.

'Be careful,' urged Swami. 'When you are etheric we cannot help you or even guess where you are.'

Swami had nothing to add to reassure them but strongly suggested that they adhere to a policy of non-intervention from now on after hearing Kate's account of the aunt and her black *Moorthy*. They both listened politely to Swami who having heard all that had happened on that night for the first time was fearful for Jack and Girija's life. The teenagers hoped he would not demand a promise from them; Jack thought that *Kate would have to get to the bottom of who the warrior was.*

Jack noticed that when Kate felt the warnings were given enough attention she related the Irish story of Oisin who lived in a Sidhe with Niamh to explain the De Danann warrior but that had not come near to a rationalisation of what had occurred or anything else to do with their De Danann warrior as he seemed unaffected by becoming mortal. Jack related the wound and ichor to Swami. Like Jack, Kate had not been aware that the warrior had a relationship with Girija.

'He had red hair, he is not a Danava – and the kilt,' Jack put in.

'I noticed that, the hair,' replied Kate, 'but some of the Danava warriors henna their hair, especially the older ones, so I wasn't sure. There was so much unexpected turmoil.'

'His skin is fairer too,' Jack said as if thinking aloud. 'Too light… it was weather-beaten but definitely naturally fair.'

'How could you tell? We had only the garden lighting which is not very bright,' replied Kate.

'I noticed when he fought the aunt underneath the car porch near the bungalow, the tube lights are fairly bright there,' Jack replied.

The conversation continued about the Goddess Jyestha's disappearance and Jack let it flow as it was one of the many unexplained incidents of that night.

'Swami has given an entirely different explanation for the fountain eruption,' said Kate to Jack as he seated himself on a wicker chair.

'We figured it may have been the work of the Danavas?' questioned Jack, looking at Swami devouring the remaining biscuit in two bites.

'And you might be correct. However, Kate told me you were aware of a benevolent energy within the yantra. You are familiar with the image of Laksmi seated on a lotus with elephants sprinkling her with water?' questioned Swami.

Jack nodded but Kate looked puzzled.

'I'll get one for you,' Jack said to Kate. 'Actually that exact picture is in the prayer room next door.'

'This image is so strong in my mind,' said Swami as if searching for words to make his theory credible, continuing: 'you see water is seen in every culture as cleansing and that's why I am of the mind that it was Laxmi. Jyestha, her sister, exists only in filth and dirt. It was one way of getting rid of her by pouring water all over her.'

'What you are really saying is that the water which fell on Saroj purified her because the water from the elephants which sprinkled Laksmi was a sort of consecration, a baptism, and you are connecting it with Jack having invoked her within the yantra?' mused Kate, who seemed unconvinced.

'Were you aware of the Danava plan. You mentioned that there was great number of them. Might they have engineered the water between the well and the fountain in some way? After all the well is the source for the fountain,' Swami asked, still half in his mind.

'Not that I was aware of but then I worked alone, concentrating on the yantra.' She trailed off momentarily.

'You know she was waiting for you,' Kate said, looking at Jack. 'Your aunt somehow knew you would come: I would like to know how.' She pondered, aware she was deviating but Jack considered she felt it was important as neither of them had thought of the possibility before.

'Why do you think that?' asked Jack, puzzled.

'When I reached the garden next door I was shocked to see so many armed Danavas. I mean, I had asked for support and I thought perhaps the Devas would be enough, I didn't expect the one we call the commander would come, not with a small retinue; but the garden was teaming with them. The commander mostly spoke with me, he told me they expected what he termed difficulties. By then the Devas had given Jack the keys to the gate and he was in the garden so it was too late for me to warn him.' This last sentence she addressed to Swami.

'Could you see Saroj at that stage?' queried Jack.

'No, I was as surprised as you were and the strange thing was that the Danava army was positioned all along that wall, the wall which stretches round the back of the compound and in front of Girija's room,' she said.

'I felt there had to be something or someone there,' replied Jack. 'The dogs were focused on that area.' He suddenly shot upright.

'What if she wasn't expecting us? What if it was sheer coincidence that we planned to help Girija on the same night she may have planned to kill or maim her?' He was cut off by Kate.

'How could she explain that?' questioned Kate, the sharpness of her retort revealing her disbelief.

'Well you must have seen how she came after Girija, twice she had that blade at her throat,' Jack defended his theory. 'I think she is power-crazed, capable of anything at time like that.'

'Maybe she knows about the warrior, he obviously protected Girija in some way,' added Kate. 'Saroj's open hostility would make sense then.'

'Whatever it is or it isn't, it's getting too dangerous,' interpolated Swami in his measured way.

'But we have controlled her, maybe even put a large dent in her confidence... hopefully made her realise that to have things her way is not going to be so easy,' said Jack with confidence and true conviction.

'I don't think we have put a stop to her, in fact I am sure she will not give up,' Swami added after a little pause to reflect, in the silence of his companions' non-agreement and then he explained about Saroj's nature and reality.

'Even so, what is more important, we have got help,' Jack said, smiling at Swami, and tried to rally him again.

'And, and not just Danavas,' Kate had her finger up again and her eyes sparkled; she seemed to be raising the energy by catching some of Jack's optimism.

'The whole garden was full. Oh Jack, I forgot to tell you. As well as the Danavas there were elementals and your great-grandmother and she had a lot of spirit people with her as well as angels. The angel orbs kept coming and literally depositing spirits. I suspect they must be family,' Kate continued.

Swami had raised his hand again and he seemed about to dispense more caution when from the front of the house Girija was seen passing the pink walls of the bathroom of the snake, in their direction. Kate and Jack stared at each other for about a second and then got up jointly to welcome her.

'Sit down Girija, we're so glad you came,' said Kate as Jack moved away from his chair, proffered it to Girija and dragged another one over the tufts of grass and into the circle.

Girija joined her hands at chest level and bowed towards Swami who did likewise. She then sat. There was silence. Jack who sat facing the back veranda of the Little Pink House prayed that his mother would not come out to offer food and drink and worry Girija; he could actually see her watching them through the dining room window and to his relief she stayed inside the house.

SANCTUARY

 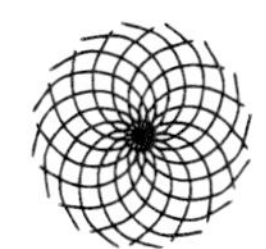

THERE FOLLOWED A silence which Kate quite quickly broke; she addressed the sensitive subject straight up in her casual way.

'Girija, we were fascinated with the young warrior; but more than that, Jack says you know him,' Kate looked at Girija intently.

'Not nearly as fascinated as I was that he knows you, Kate, and that you can visit his home and the homes of similar beings,' came Girija's rapid reply but it was without malice, Jack noted. This was not the broken young woman that lay crumpled in the hot sand only a month ago after threatening to kill her own mother. The three exchanged speedy glances and then focused once again on the radiant young woman with a triumphant, half-mischievous smile.

'I'm psychic,' admitted Kate. 'I don't actually know the warrior and although I can see the people of the Goddess Dana here and in Ireland I have hardly any experience in communicating and understanding them.'

'He told me you summoned him to help me,' replied Girija.

'I did so, yes but inadvertently,' Kate said. 'There is a similar race of beings at home, in Ireland who share a culture akin to the Danavas,' she said sincerely, reaching out to Girija and then she added: 'I was trying to get Danava help, not the Tuatha dé Danann's help.' The last word limped out, betraying Kate's confusion.

'I'm very grateful,' said Girija.

'Why are they helping us?' Jack very carefully put in, mindful not to change the genial atmosphere that had developed among them all.

'I know why Ailill has helped me, it is because of you two,' Girija paused and looked at Kate and then Jack.

'Us?' replied Kate, 'As I have said, we didn't know him, he was a mistake.'

'They only make themselves visible when they want to communicate with you,' explained Girija, completely ignoring Kate's last sentence. 'He was here and heard you both plan to come and talk with me and was aware of your request for help, Kate. Oh by the way, thank you for your attempts to visit me on the days my mother stopped you.'

'We didn't want you to take the medicine, we knew there was nothing wrong with you…' Jack felt that perhaps he may have overstepped the boundaries of comfort and he swiftly added, 'I saw your mother in the prayer room nearly eight months ago; I think she is destroying Grandmother so that she can control Grandfather.'

'Yes, I'm sure of it,' Girija nodded, convinced. 'And she wants to get rid of you and your family too. She manipulates Grandfather with never-ending tales of her own outlook on life,' she paused, 'and by the way Jack, I have been giving the medicines to Ailill to dispose of.'

'How can your grandfather be so naive?' asked Kate, totally confounded.

'My mother emphasises her miserable state, how intolerable life was with my father and how she is left in a pathetic state, having Nisha me and a husband who is unfit to fund dowries for us. Grandfather, as you know is very socially conscious and is afraid of scandal. Grandmother, on the other hand, is level-headed and sees right through her. You should just see how badly she treats Grandmother: she calls her an old woman and threatens her.' Girija trailed off, tears welling up in her eyes.

'Do you get threatened too?' asked Kate.

Jack felt Kate was pushing it but remained quiet in the shame and intensity of the moment.

'Yes.' She wiped her eyes with the scarf which was worn with her shirt and shalwar.

Everyone looked down at their sandals.

'We're going to put a stop to her,' Jack said quietly and with as much conviction as he could muster in the gloom of the confirmation they already knew.

'This Goddess she invoked,' Swami spoke softly and for the first time to Girija, 'I have never heard of her.'

'Jyestha, yes. There is a temple to her very near where we live at the foot of the Western Ghats, I believe it is the only one in all of India. My mother has worshipped there since I can remember,' replied Girija, in control again.

'What does the De Danann Warrior say about your mother's powers, can he control her?' Jack penetrated a bit further, having noted Girija's control.

'They have no control over her actions, they can control the consequences as you saw the night of the… that night,' she trailed off again.

'That was why Ailill's fight with your mother was mostly defensive?' confirmed Kate.

'Yes, but she did not know that,' Girija replied.

'I suspect she is plotting again, although she was very quiet at lunch on Sunday?' questioned Jack.

'She has been quiet, no trips to the temple in the countryside. She leaves Grandmother and me alone but she sits with Grandfather in the hall which is just outside my bedroom door and she brainwashes him,' said Girija.

'I don't understand,' put in Kate, agitated. 'My father would believe my mother before he would take *my* word for anything.' She looked up at Jack who nodded and then at Girija.

'And, and your grandmother witnessed what went on in the garden that night, I just don't understand it,' Kate said, shaking her head.

'Our grandfather would believe our grandmother for only as long as it would take for my mother to conjure up a story to make Grandmother's account look forged,' said Girija who thought for a while and then added, 'Look at our situation from our grandparents' point of view, what can they do with her?'

Girija looked at Kate. 'Socially she has disgraced them by returning home with two daughters to be married. She would not move to one of the rented properties as she would not have the same status as living next door and more than that our grandparents would have no control over her boyfriends which would bring even more scandal on them. Her position is a strong one and she knows it and exploits it.'

'She is right,' added Swami, head bowed.

'The society here is not as free and forgiving as yours, Kate,' said Girija quietly.

'It's still unfair,' put in Jack gloomily.

'It wouldn't be really that much different for someone high up in society in a western country,' said Girija.

'Money brings out the worst in people,' added Swami.

'Where do we go from here? We cannot just give in.' Kate tried to raise the hopeless vibes that surrounded them; she looked from one to the other to Swami, but there was no response.

'You spoke of your mother getting rid of your grandmother, how much danger do you feel you are in?' Kate addressed Girija, ignoring their inertia with her 'ready to deal with whatever the future held' approach.

Girija just looked bland and Kate continued.

'Would she harm you? I cannot help remembering what she did in the garden that night.'

'Provoked, she would have very little control, her instincts are basic not intellectual...' Girija trailed off again, in thought but not fearful.

'Would Ailill be able to protect you at all times like on that night?' questioned Kate.

'I think so... I hope so,' she replied, lost in thought.

Jack felt he should send Kate a signal to stop her probing. He realised that neither he nor Kate had any idea of the danger the fundamental nature of her questions were having on Girija's mentality.

'When did he first appear to you?' Kate was incessant.

'The night I tried to shoot Mummy,' she said, raising her head and looking at Kate defiantly as if it took a great effort just to say it.

Jack felt that Kate had gone too far. Girija had just referred to her mother as Mummy: the natural right that a child had, regardless of age, had been taken from Girija. She had never known a mother figure that one could rely on completely, yet the very word Mummy betrayed her need for that love. He looked at Swami: his head was bowed but Jack noticed his eyes darting this way and that; they had all felt Girija's natural anguish.

'Did you get a fright?' Kate continued with what seemed a type of distraction, Jack felt.

'Yes and no. I was very upset that night and thought I had gone mad,' Girija seemed to be able to release more of her feelings. She said it with a slight embarrassed smile.

The pretty, honey-skinned young woman played with the fingers of each hand which lay on her lap and continued to speak in her effortless English. Jack knew that unlike Nisha she had been sent to boarding school when she was eight years old and this was responsible for her fluency. Like him, her Malayalam was not as good. After a pause when she kept her eyes on her fingers she continued.

'He stayed very still in the darkened room and for such a long time I realised that he was neither an apparition nor a ghost. Eventually… and more to prove to myself that I was not insane I spoke to him in Malayalam. He gestured that he did not understand so I tried English and he shook his head and moved nearer to me. Finally I tried Sanskrit which is far worse than my Malayalam; he seemed to recognise words. That is how we communicate, hit and miss, most of the time patching together nouns with verbs,' she smiled.

'But that's how I manage!' interjected Kate. 'I use Irish, a very rudimentary form of it. Swami and I have talked about the similarities between the Celtic languages and the Aryan language; they must come from the same root.'

'But you can see them Kate, I can't, and Ailill can be mortal for short periods only. Is he here or any of them now?' she answered and followed Kate's question with another question, rather than her comment on the language.

'No,' Kate replied after adjusting her sight and scanning the garden.

'He asked me to come and talk to you,' Girija said after a little while.

'He was right,' encouraged Jack. 'Have you any idea how much we all care for you here? You could stay here when you go to college Girija, in my room, Kate's room.'

'But Uncle took me to see the psychiatrist. I was so frightened my mother and he would have me committed to a psychiatric hospital,' she openly spoke and Jack could see the family, his family, from her perspective and he understood her alarm.

The silent guilt on both Jack and Kate's faces revealed their empathy and worse still, Jack felt, their powerlessness and Girija's helplessness in the situation.

'If my mother convinces our grandfather that I should be admitted into a mental asylum it would not take much to have Uncle convinced,' Girija continued.

'She's right,' put in Swami. He didn't need to: Kate and Jack had seen it happen with the psychiatrist's visit.

'My parents want you to go back to college in Ernakalum and spend the holidays between here and your father's,' Jack tried to convince Girija.

'How do you know that?' she asked.

'I overheard them talk about you,' he replied.

'I don't think Grandfather would like the idea of me living here,' she trailed off.

'You will just have to do it Chechi,' said Jack determinedly. 'You would be a lot safer here than over there and it's only for some of the holidays anyway.'

Girija didn't seem convinced but Jack went confidently on.

'I think you should assert yourself more, you could come over here when you feel like it; Kate is here while I'm at school. Let's start talking about college,' Jack didn't finish his flow as he saw Nisha and his mother appear on the back veranda.

Girija followed Jack's gaze and by then Nisha had almost reached the seated group. She hardly acknowledged anyone, she kept her eyes on the lawn and made a nod in Swami's direction. She stood near the side of Girija's chair and told her she was to go home in Malayalam. Jack couldn't help but think that she was more withdrawn than usual. Girija didn't move but this only caused Nisha to repeat her request. Kate jumped up and offered her chair to Nisha who half-turned away from her and said in English, 'No, thank you, Kate.'

'I will tell Mummy you will not come,' Nisha said sharply to Girija in Malayalam half under her breath and strode off. Jack understood the threat in her parting words.

'I must go,' was all Girija said as she walked after Nisha in the direction she had come in around the side of the Little Pink House.

Kate followed her and Jack could hear her make plans for another visit.

'She is in a very precarious position,' said Swami quietly.

'Both she and Grandmother,' said Jack.

BIRTHDAYS

 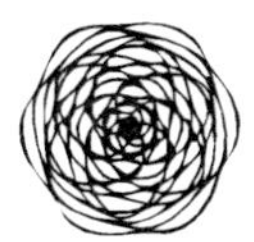

IT SO HAPPENED that Jack shared his birthday, not the actual date but the month, with two cousins. His birthday fell on the fourth of July, Nisha's was the eighth and Kate's was the sixteenth and it was decided that a date in between would be the day of celebration for all three birthdays. This was put to the children first by Jack's mother; she felt that the gun incident was well and truly in what seemed to be the distant past or, as she said, it felt as though it had happened a very long time ago and Girija was out and about again and so it was time they all got together especially as Grandmother although tired, had gained a little weight.

However, as the month advanced Grandfather's input became more pronounced: he pointed out that the rains were not as persistent as previous monsoons. He insisted that the get-together expanded into a much bigger party, so much so that the guests would need to spill out into the garden at the Little Pink House in order to be accommodated. Close relatives and their children were invited: in India a party or wedding invitation included the whole family.

Word was sent to the cook who prepared the harvest festival food; he was asked to come on an evening when Jack's father was present to translate. Menus were discussed; eventually final numbers were extracted from Grandfather by Jack's father and given over the phone between Nani Bhavan and the Little Pink House and the cook in turn dropped off his list a few days later. As with most large birthday and Christmas parties Jack's mother gave, the cooking had to be done at Nani Bhavan as the kitchens were not only larger but all the massive cooking vessels were there too. This was all discussed on the following Sunday when they gathered for lunch. Grandfather was delighted, Jack noted: as always he couldn't wait for some sort of upbeat activity. He joined in Christmas parties big and small at the Little Pink House over the years with plenty of enthusiasm; his Hinduism was inclusive of other faiths.

Grandmother took all this in her calm way; she, like Jack's father, never got excited about anything and they both seemed to derive a quiet contentment as they surveyed the animation among family members while they reacted to the plans. In retrospect, Jack felt that this had been the last time that the family was as it should have been and always was before.

He watched the silent aunt as they sat around the lunch table. He cast his eyes on Nisha too: both were glum in contrast to Kate and Girija who sat opposite each other and were in the midst of plans for a shopping trip. Fabric was needed for a skirt and blouse for Kate. Teenage girls wore floor-length skirts with knife pleats with a fitted short-sleeved blouse that covered the waist of the skirt; Jack's mother had treated Kate to one but they had never got around to shopping for the fabric. Now that there was a party planned the fabric would be silk and there was a lot of discussion about colour at the Little Pink House and again with Girija. Nisha kept her head averted from her sister and appeared bored with the conversation.

A few evenings afterwards Jack, on arriving home from school, found Kate angrily pacing on the small space of the back veranda. After Matty left for tuition she explained that she had gone next door to meet up with Girija to go shopping but even though the driver had been told earlier that a car was needed the girls were left abandoned. There were cars but no drivers.

'She's up to her mischief again,' was all Jack said to her blustery outburst.

'You think Saroj had something to do with it?' Kate said, bending over and pointing that finger at Jack.

'She has been too quiet for too long. I knew it wouldn't last, this is her typical meddling. Ask Mum,' he said.

'I did and yes, she said it was painfully familiar,' Kate said.

'Mum has a way around it, you know,' said Jack with a twinkle in his eye.

'Yeah, I know, she told me, the element of surprise. Anyway, she says she will book your driver one morning before he leaves for school, but the car has to collect your father from the tennis club so we will not have long to shop. This incident has made me more determined to be more assertive, I will go next door and plan the day with Girija and bother your aunt in the process,' she said in better form.

'I'm a bit surprised that you two are going out without an adult chaperone,' he said.

'Your mum warned me that your aunt would use it as an excuse to stop the trip and probably that's how she actually convinced your grandfather to send the drivers home early this evening, possibly?' she said, hesitating. Jack knew the guilt that Kate would carry by wrongly misjudging another and the proof she lacked now was seeping through the frustration of having to abandon her shopping trip.

It was also around this time that Jack remembered another pleasant incident. The Little Pink House was reverting more and more into its quiet existence after school as Kate spent more time with Girija next door. The quietness of the House reminded Jack that Kate was more than halfway through her holidays and soon she would be gone altogether.

The Little Pink House was always too quiet for him so he decided to do his homework at his grandfather's house. On his way to the bungalow he was distracted by giggling coming from the window of the little sitting room at Nani Bhavan. He left his school bag on the walkway surrounding the bungalow and advanced on the fish tanks which were below the study window adjoining the sitting room. In there, seated behind Grandmother's sewing machine, was Thankamma, the most famous blouse-maker in Adoor with a shameful grin and an occasional laugh which she shared with the women whom she was in close communication with through the double doors in the adjacent room.

Jack listened to the exchange which Girija translated for Kate and he discovered that the blouse-maker had kissed Kate's tummy when she was taking her measurements for her new skirt and blouse. Girija was in the process of explaining that the blouse-maker meant no harm; she simply loved fair skin. Jack peeped through the sitting room window to find his grandmother seated in one of the big armchairs with a quiet smile as she shared with the girls the humour which even Nisha got while Girija tried to assuage Kate's shock and discomfort. Jack could see Kate's struggle to understand the comedy as she sat with both her arms wrapped tightly around her chest pushed into the corner of a sofa she shared with Girija which seemed to cause Nisha and Girija to giggle even more.

Jack silently slipped away from the house, remembering earlier gatherings with his mother, grandmother and aunt sitting talking, being measured and adjusting the fabrics to be made into blouses at Onam which were past but not forgotten. The blouse-maker would complain of exhaustion and rightly so as more and more pieces of fabric were produced to be worked into perfectly fitting blouses.

It reminded him as he mounted the steps into the bungalow that all those memories and this new one would soon join many others and never really disappear; they were like precious glimpses of heaven and he wished he could relive the incidents at each recall rather than just the mere distant pleasure that we humans are allowed on the earth journey.

And so the birthday party came and went. Kate's much talked-about and at one time impossible-to-purchase outfit was turquoise which gave her eyes an even more other-worldly look. Jack hoped that she would fit in and that people would not react to her as Khalid had. Girija braided her hair like Nisha's and her own and she wore the ubiquitous bunch of jasmine at the nape of her neck.

Girija had used plenty of kohl around Kate's eyes, something that Jack found wrong: the starkness of the black on the white skin just didn't seem to go as well as it did on honey skin but it was the fashion and Kate appeared to be pleased but nervous with so much attention on her.

Girija was in great form and looked pretty as always but she wore a traditional Kerala sari which made Jack feel she was making some sort of a statement but he couldn't fathom what exactly. The weather held up and although it was overcast it was dry and most people sat chatting in the garden with the elder aunties in both sitting rooms. Jack noticed that Kate spent a lot of time with Khalid's mother and grandmother and she later told him how friendly they were; others either did not understand her accent or were too shy of her to converse. Jack knew from experience with his mother that people were self-conscious of their English and no amount of kohl or dress could change the difference people saw in them.

There was only one awkward incident, which Jack felt was caused by Aunt Saroj. Jack, who was asked to eat last with his mother after helping her serve the food, found her fuming in the kitchen. Apparently Grandmother and the aunt were having a fast day which was traditionally broken with a light vegetarian meal at night and nobody had told Jack's mother this. So while everyone sat enjoying lamb biryiani Grandmother and Aunt Saroj sat looking pitiful and neglected with all the relatives asking why, making his mother appear cruel and thoughtless.

'Your grandmother should not be fasting anyway with her complaint,' protested his mother as she piled more fried chicken on to a serving dish for Jack to offer the guests. Jack's father saved face by sending someone next door for the temple rice which was sent to the house after a special Pooja was conducted after evening prayers. Soon both the fasting ladies were helping themselves to curd rice and scandal had been averted but it seemed to take Jack's mother some time to calm herself as he witnessed her sarcasm when she took her chair next to the aunt's in the garden to eat.

It was much later that night, when everyone had left and Jack's parents had gone to bed, leaving the two teenagers on the back veranda with strict and repeated instructions on locking up, that Jack began to understand to his absolute horror what Girija had planned for herself.

THE REALM OF THE FAERIE

 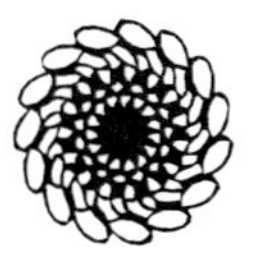

JACK AND KATE had talked about the difficulties of mingling at the party; Jack brought it up as he was aware of her frozen smile, bored look, stood on the edge of groups who naturally were conversing in Malayalam. After discussions, the joint conclusion was that it was mandatory to know the language in order to integrate into a society.

When finally, Matty, who had been listening to this seated in a wicker child chair, had been led upstairs by his mother and Jack's father had settled into bed, Jack felt in retrospect that Kate carefully introduced the subject of Girija.

'Why did she wear a traditional sari, though? I felt she had a meaning or a message,' he answered in reply to Kate's question of how well she looked.

'She did; did you notice the crystal she wore?' Kate asked, looking directly at Jack.

'No. Was there a significance?' he asked in answer.

'Have you ever been to the bank, into the vault where the safe deposit boxes are?' Kate asked.

'Yes, years ago with Grandmother. Why?' Jack was becoming more and more puzzled as their conversation had become more question-and-answer.

'I don't know if you are aware but your aunt had an overnight stay in Dr Krishna's Nursing Home last week for some sort of a procedure and while she was away Girija asked your grandmother if she could go to the bank to take out some jewellery. I think your grandmother thought it was for the party, well I did too until a few days ago,' Kate said, trailing off.

'So?' Jack was lost in what he considered to be simply evasiveness and became impatient.

'First of all, and I know I'm deviating here, I have never seen so much jewellery in all my life, sort of heaped all together in that tin box, like an Aladdin's treasure,' Kate explained with her hands, fingers splayed out as if they were weaving through a mound of gold ornaments.

'Yeah I know, but what's…?' he began again, only to be cut short.

'Well your grandmother wanted Girija to take out a set of garnets but Girija kept evading her and rooting around the deposit box until she found a very long gold chain and then more searching and eventually she found, maybe she knew it, I don't know but she asked your grandmother if she could wear the chain with a beautiful crystal, oval with a hint of gold. Well your grandmother seemed as perplexed as I was but she agreed and produced her key and had the bank assistant come and lock the deposit box with his key and we left.'

'Kate,' Jack began again.

'I'm coming to the point,' she said, both her hands palms down as if physically aligning her thoughts.

'This is not easy to say, to tell you, but Girija wanted me to be the one to tell you.' She quickly looked to see if the light was still on in Jack's parents' bedroom; he turned too and could hear the quiet murmur of their voices.

'This is becoming like the first night I heard you talk to the Danavas,' he said in a jokey way, trying to quell his apprehension.

'It's much worse than that, Jack,' Kate said, deadly serious, which wiped the grin from his face. Jack could feel the trepidation rise in his throat.

'Is it Grandmother?' he began fishing around for the very worst he could imagine.

'It's Girija, she is going to live with the De Danann,' Kate blurted out and waited, staring at him. He knew she had tried to break this news in a better way but didn't know how.

'The De Danann live in another existence, not ours, how can she do that?' he asked, now focused, and realisation slowly crept into his understanding and silenced him. He rose and walked down the steps of the veranda towards the aviary and into the shadow of the coconut tree fronds which stood growing beside it. With his back against the wall he stared out of the duskiness at Kate who stood up, above on the veranda and faced him. That sickening feeling was back in his stomach again but with even more intensity than the night the snake got into his parents' bathroom and Dodo had disappeared for ever.

'The only way she can enter their world is to die!' he said quietly, half in exclamation, half in the hope that Kate knew of a better way as she moved stealthily down the steps where she reached him by the aviary.

'No, she can't do that, she would be lost from him for ever if she did that. She would go to Tir na Og or the Summer Lands or wherever you believe the dead go but she could not be with the De Danann,' Kate whispered.

'How then?' he asked.

'I don't know how it works exactly but I have heard stories at home of…

disappearances and untouched bodies of young girls found near Sidhes.' She trailed off.

'She will die then?' he questioned, perplexed.

'Only her physical body, I think the etheric body and the other bodies live on provided they are not destroyed,' Kate answered.

'It's because of her situation, we've got to talk her out of it,' after some time he said; desperation had begun to well up.

'I thought so too at first but I've spent days talking to her, over and over everything, all the possibilities of life here with him,' Kate whispered for fear any other mortal should hear such a plan.

'Wait, wait are you saying she is going because of Ailill?' Jack demanded.

'Both reasons maybe. I don't know, I'm shocked, but it looks like she has thought it through and has a plan, like the sari tonight: that was her last night at a family gathering, a sort of goodbye and the crystal has something to do with crossing to their domain or is it her connection with her human life here, I forget. I think she said it's to keep her grounded in case she changes her mind, or something.' Kate pushed Betty away, telling her not to dribble on her silk skirt and walked back to the veranda where the dog sprawled out on the cold mosaic and Kate sat down carefully as if she was sitting on something sharp on the recliner.

'This is so unfair Kate, that Girija should be pushed into a corner, to be forced to make such a drastic decision,' Jack said quietly after seating himself once again in the armchair on the veranda facing her.

'Well you see that may not be it exactly. I think she has become quite attached to Ailill in a romantic way and I argued with her that she could live a natural and normal life here as she was meant to, get a job after university – you know she is really interested in doing medicine and like me she loves biology. I pointed out that since he can spend time in the mortal world, she does not have to marry and I reminded her of how many career women never married and even the few women in the family who never did, your great-aunt for example. I explained and agreed with Girija that Ailill couldn't be with her always and he wouldn't age as she would but so far, I have not managed to persuade her,' Kate trailed off.

'It's my fault, I can't give her the assurance she needs that she will be protected from her mother,' Jack said, his head bent towards the floor.

'If it's anyone fault it's mine, if I had never come here… you and she would be completely unaware of the Danavas and the Tuatha dé Danann,' Kate replied, equally veracious, swallowing hard.

'No, I'm glad you came, I'm glad too you have the gift… I'm sure Girija has more confidence knowing there is help out there, as I did in the garden the night of that terrible Goddess. No Kate, I think as Swami told me in the beginning it was all meant to be… All except this… that is,' he added ponderously.

'Let's go to bed,' Kate said after a little while longer in the edgy bleakness.

'Should we tell Swami?' asked Jack as Kate quietly turned the key in the padlock on the inside of the kitchen door.

'Yes. But no one else,' said Kate stolidly.

THE QUAGMIRE

JACK AWOKE THE next morning which was a Saturday and almost instantly the tenebrous thoughts took priority inside his head. Matty was already awake consulting his book on Greeks and Romans which he put down every so often to adjust the armour on his Ninja Turtle models and then he would resume reading or possibly consulting the illustrations, particularly the armour. A sluggishness overcame Jack and he rolled over on his mattress to face the wall; he did not want to talk to Kate and especially not to Girija, he could not form the words for a confrontation with Girija for fear they would manifest the unthinkable. There was no certain indictment, he could make no judgement, certainly no approbation and worse no solution for Girija's audacious plan.

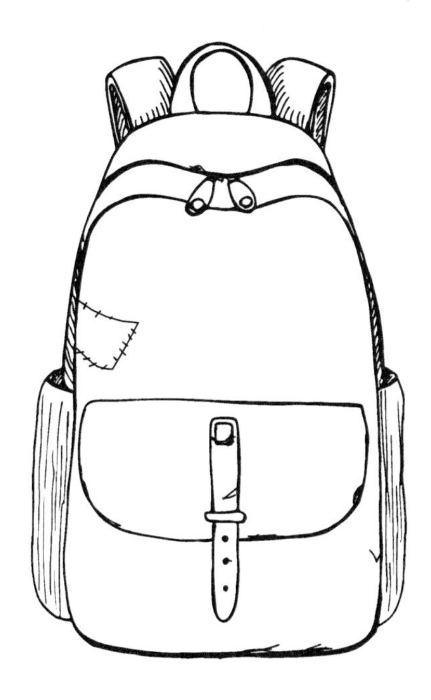

Everyone cherished Girija including himself, everyone except the person who mattered most. All his life he had looked up to her; she had all the qualities he hadn't, imperturbable and eager to help Grandmother when she stayed at Nani Bhavan, clement with his naughtiness and restlessness and erudite when he plied her with questions. Something terrible had withered her spirit, her very soul, his beautiful Chechi, now a genial young woman. What was she so afraid of to have to decide on such a chaotic path?

Even distressed days move on as that one did, with Kate and Jack more comfortable avoiding each other. Both languidly joined the rest of the family as they sauntered across the road to Sunday lunch the following day; they had nothing to say to each other about the heavy weight they secretly bore.

Once indoors everyone including Nisha had the remains of the light spirits the party had made which seemed to integrate the family, except the aunt who simply simpered when Grandfather teased Matty about his ragged bag. Jack watched Girija in particular, who radiated happiness. However, Jack's spirits lifted before lunch; everyone gathered in the room with the stairs where Grandmother was resting on the ornate great-grandfather bed. The adults sat around the table as usual and Grandfather announced that everyone was going to Madras the following week.

'Everyone?' repeated Matty and actually jumped up and forgot his bag which rolled on to the floor; the flap fell open and out rolled a ball made of elastic bands. Jack understood why Matty needed to clarify: there were no school holidays the following week, their trips to Ireland and weekends away were always when there was no school. Jack next turned his eyes towards his mother and witnessed the look of amazement she shared with his father.

Grandfather went on to say that as well as a holiday Grandmother was going to see a stomach specialist in one of the big hospitals there so that they could finally get to the bottom of her complaints. The realisation of all this quietly established itself on all the children as Jack's father began to discuss the dates with Grandfather and from the Malayalam conversation Jack deduced that a date had been set for Grandmother to see the specialist and the flights would be organised a day or two ahead so that she could have a couple of days' rest before the hospital visit as there would be tests and she had very little energy.

It was a short week at school. The flights had been booked for the Wednesday and the logistics of cars for the entire family – who travelled in which car – had to be worked out as well as a room booked in Trivandrum for Grandmother and Grandfather the previous day so that she would be rested and be strong enough for the flight the following day.

At the Little Pink House packing and prioritising laundry was Jack's mother's main chore. Kate was visibly excited as was Matty because Grandfather had promised a trip to Mahabalipuram, the ancient temple complex half buried under the sea. Matty could not concentrate; he told Jack as he consulted him about what he should bring for the trip to the temples, the bag had been packed and unpacked several times by Tuesday evening when Kate joined them in the Crow's Nest. Matty referred to his bedroom as the Crow's Nest because he had a 360-degree view of the entire property, Nani Bhavan and other properties, if he included all the bedroom windows and bathroom ventilations.

'Remember it's much hotter than here,' reminded Kate.

'Hotter but dryer,' put in Jack.

'I don't know how I'm going to be able to stand it,' exclaimed Kate, pulling at the neck of her shirt; it was that time of the day when the brick and concrete had absorbed all the heat of the blazing sun.

'Believe me it is easier than here, you'll see, ask Mum,' said Jack confidently.

'Well, what should I pack?' asked Matty again after the exchange finished. His hair was damp with perspiration, all around the hairline and had formed very wet, very short tendrils, his hair being less thick than Jack's.

'That hat looks just right,' said Kate as she pointed at the battered green safari hat which Jack's father had brought Jack back from Kenya and which no longer fitted him.

'Your room is so hot Matt, can we go downstairs to mine, it's much cooler?' pleaded Kate.

'Why aren't you packed?' asked Matty, looking around as all three clambered down the stairs.

'Your mum has put my clothes in with yours and I'll just bring my water and a sun hat in this,' and Kate pointed to a large basket-type bag she had bought on one of her shopping trips with Girija.

'That's great,' said Matty, having a good look inside. 'You've got the mosquito cream, I need some too…' he said and he began a rummage.

'Your mother will have all that in the toilet bag, she has a massive one, I saw her putting calamine lotion and all sorts into it earlier,' replied Kate and she jumped up and snatched back her bag.

And so everything went to plan: the children had three days off school, Nisha, Jack and Matty. Grandmother was booked in to have tests on the Friday and Saturday and the doctor had agreed to meet with her on Sunday. All going well, everyone would return on the Sunday, all except the grandparent sand Aunt Saroj, as Grandmother may need to rest or have treatment so their tickets were left open.

The next day two cars entered the drive at the Mascot Hotel in Trivandrum and after depositing their passengers at the entrance parked alongside Grandfather's car. Jack noticed that Kate spent ages staring at the large painting of Abraham about to slay Isaac which dominated the lobby while his father enquired where to find Grandfather's room. The desperation of the father about to slay his son was portrayed all too starkly for the teenagers who were in their own quagmire of anxiety.

'I just didn't expect to see a biblical painting like this here,' Kate explained to Jack as he stood silently empathising with her, neither able to express their fraught feelings, both identifying with the father in the painting like never before.

They all converged on the grandparents' room in a slow procession as the heat took its toll; shortly tea was arranged. This was a mini meal of sandwiches, cutlets, salad and cakes. Jack noticed that Kate took the sandwiches and realised that it was something his family never had in India, only the occasional toasted sandwiches which his mother fed to Swami. He realised how much she must be missing certain foods and also realised something much more urgent: that he had not told Swami the latest developments. This whirlwind trip together with school had not only knocked Girija into the background but also Swami.

Grandfather was also delving hungrily into the platter of sandwiches and when Kate went out on the large balcony, now sufficiently cool, Jack slowly followed her.

'I talked to Swami on Tuesday, he had to leave early for some meeting, I didn't have a chance to tell you, actually forgot about it, which is unbelievable considering what's going on with Girija,' Kate said, throwing an eye to make sure the bedroom windows were closed. With that, Matty, Grandfather and Girija joined them and soon Nisha, too. The trip, even though it was for Grandmother, had somehow loosened Nisha from the dark pit she seemed to want to inhabit and she was slowly creeping out into the light, it seemed to Jack as he watched her try to join in with the group looking out over the hotel grounds, for Matty had noticed the playground and remembered how Jack had broken his arm there when they were very little.

'No time for the playground today son, we have to leave very soon for the airport,' reminded Grandfather and went inside again.

Matty's bag seem to cause Grandfather a great deal of annoyance: at the airport he urged their mother to go to the airport shop see if she could buy a new one and throw the dirty one away or failing that have it put into the hold with the suitcases but she explained that Matty even slept with it and because there was nothing else to do while waiting to board everyone started to tease Matty.

'That's because it's a Crane Bag, isn't it Matt?' said Kate who came to his rescue.

'What's a Crane Bag?' asked Matty, relieved at not having an audience.

'If you come over here I'll tell you,' she said, curling her finger in everyone's direction except the adults.

Everyone followed including Nisha and they all stood around her in a corner as there were no vacant seats.

'Well… the Crane Bag?' reminded Matty.

'Oh yes, well, let me think, yes… centuries ago the Sea God Manannan kept one in his house and in it were his treasures: a knife, his shirt and a belt made of skin from a great whale… and whole load of other things, a helmet and bones I think, I'm sorry Matt I can't remember it all,' said Kate, thinking.

'But why was it called a Crane Bag?' asked Matty.

'Because it was made out of the skin of a crane, you know the bird with the long neck and long legs,' replied Kate.

'Uch,' exclaimed Nisha, turning her head to one side.

'Great,' replied Matty with a gleam.

'That's not all though,' added Kate whimsically, urged on by Matty's reaction, Jack felt.

'What?' Matty asked.

'The crane skin was actually the skin of a girl called Aoife who was in love with the son of the Sea God Manannan, you know the one I told you about,' she said with a storyteller's glint in her eyes.

'I can't listen to any more,' said Nisha and left to join the adults, casting an eye in the direction of Matty's grubby bag.

'It's only an Irish myth,' said Kate defensively.

'She's easily upset,' explained Girija.

'But I don't understand how that can be,' said Matty. 'How can it be both skins?'

'Easy,' replied Kate. 'Some jealous person turned Aoife into a crane.'

'Even better,' exclaimed Matty while he stroked his murky canvas rucksack affectionately, and Jack exchanged a raised-eyebrow glance with Girija.

THE GOD VISHNU

THE CHILDREN RACED along the beach. It was relatively quiet along that part: no canoes or fishermen about, not even visitors at the ancient temples and stone structures which were visible further along the sea front. Jack had been at the carvings a long time ago with his parents and an English visitor who had come to Madras to see his father but that day they had been promised an explanation of the carvings by Grandfather who loved to explain Hindu mythology. Matty was particularly interested in this as history from any period or civilisation was his favourite subject so he stayed close to Grandfather with the intention of soaking up every bit he uttered.

Jack kicked his sandals off and Nisha followed; they both ran to the water's edge. Kate joined Jack's parents and Aunt Saroj as they sauntered on towards the ruins apparently in no hurry to experience the enveloping freedom and actual relief that the deserted beach invoked in Jack and Nisha. The beach sloped slightly but the wet sand was firm and they ran towards the little waves which reached up and rolled in and in swishing urgent whispers then disappeared. Jack jumped into the vanishing wave mark and waited for the next small wave to come sloshing to its end; the water was tingling cool, sand grains moved between his toes and he felt his heels sink very slightly into the shifting sand as the sea water rolled back down the beach. He made more footprints with the help of the tiny waves and then he squatted, sinking his fingers into the wet sand and waited for another wave to wash over, experiencing the tingling, shifting feeling in his fingers as well as his toes, the ebb and flow of the tide causing a slight disorientation.

He was acutely aware of nature's draw and its healing and he remembered to look and see what effect it had on Nisha. She seemed oblivious to the others as she stood swishing the tiny waves with one foot before they broke. He was satisfied that she was free of the sinister and uncertain life imposed on her even if it was only for a few minutes. He felt an affinity with her; they both carried so much dark matter in their heads, too much; and now, like him, she had lost her inhibition and was free momentarily. For some time he considered how positive it was that she was able to feel natural as he went on playing with the tide.

She had done a remarkable thing on the second evening of their stay at the Woodlands Hotel where they rented three separate cottages. Nisha had joined his mother, Kate and Girija at the beauty salon to have their hair trimmed. However, Nisha appeared back at the cottages without her long hair; she had had it cut right off in a style almost as short as a boy. Jack wondered if this was an act of defiance, or was it an adjustment to her life without her father? She did look pretty and very self-conscious and had been reassured both by Kate and Girija as well as his mother who he knew realised the effect of the haircut. Grandmother and Nisha's own mother were shocked and didn't try to hide it.

Much later, the fading and again a near sound on the wind, 'Jack, Jaack, Jaack', from way off alerted him. It was the voice of his mother calling to him. Everyone, although meandering along, had almost reached the ruins; even Nisha had caught up with the women's group.

They were near the shore temple by the time Jack reached the still sauntering group, Grandfather and Matty in the lead. Matty was in explorer mode: he wore Jack's battered safari hat and the ubiquitous rucksack sat squarely on his back; layered on top of the strap of his water container was the strap of a pair of binoculars forming an 'X' across his chest. Jack wondered what Matty had eventually packed inside the newly named Crane Bag. He could hear Grandfather's familiar animated voice explaining to Matty the meanings of the symbols within the carvings. It was not often in those days that Grandfather got any member of the family to listen to his religious stories. Matty was touching the carvings with his fingers while he listened intently to Grandfather. Kate and his mother had joined them and a little group formed with Grandfather as a guide facing the enormous, thousands-of-years-old, beautifully-carved stone reclaimed from the sea.

'There had been no water left in the world due to a series of droughts, so King Bhagiratha prayed for water. God let the large river Ganges descend to earth but warned that it was so heavy it may destroy the whole earth.' Grandfather checked his little group and continued, 'Lord Siva was persuaded to break the fall of the river with his head. The water caught in his thick hair and by the time it reached the Himalayan Mountains it has lost its dangerous force. That is why we consider the Ganges a sacred river,' he explained while pointing.

Jack remembered the story and decided to look over the carvings later to see if he could decipher the meaning himself. His father was standing patiently nearby in the shade of a carved vehicle with so much detail that even the wheels had been fashioned out of stone. Aunt Saroj and Nisha could just be seen passing between the many giant stone carvings together.

Jack began to explore what looked like a very small, half-sunken temple – a rectangle which appeared to be half-buried in the sand. The opening was still tall enough for an adult to enter. He stood outside one foot on a sea- and sand-worn engraved stone that served as a step. He felt the smooth curve of the imprinted stone door jamb and peered right into the gloom: it felt strange, not uncomfortable, just different, but with a sense of caution he stepped inside, wondering if he should have left his sandals outside. After all, it had been sacred ground for many thousands of years. Then he reconsidered: if the family moved on, his sandals may be stolen and he felt the temple was no longer used for worship so he left them on. He noticed a gap in the stonework high up on the wall which beamed the outside light onto the floor of the temple which was uneven; large smooth stones and actual rocks filled in with layers of sand over centuries.

Jack rather abruptly noticed the life-size statue of the reclining Vishnu, positioned on the left side at Jack's feet. It came as a shock, somehow unexpected, the God's peaceful gaze seemed to watch Jack no matter where he stood. He experienced that inexplicable feeling again, as if the stone God knew what was going on in his mind. It was not quite fascinating, definitely not comfortable ,but not uncomfortable enough to make him want to leave.

Back in front of it he examined the carved stone statue from where he stood. It was in remarkably good condition: there was a bit chipped off one of the hands and the crown and the shoulder, but Jack noticed that they had been smoothed by sea spray and sandy winds; it looked complete. Jack sat down cross-legged, captivated by the feeling of being quietly observed. After a minute or two looking around, he realised there really wasn't much room in the little temple; it must have been part of a larger complex. *Perhaps this was the Sanctum Sanctorum,* he wondered. He felt there was nothing else to check out from what he could now see well as his eyes had adjusted with the light coming in through the gap and the door. He found it difficult to leave the presence of the statue. This was the Vishnu of Grandfather's stories: everything was as he said, crown, garland, four arms, and the tranquillity, and even the discus and conch shell in his hands.

Then Jack remembered that in the story there was the King of the Snakes and leaning forward began searching the wall at the back of the statue for signs of protrusions in the stone work, a damaged stone carving perhaps, in an effort to find a representation of the five headed snake. Leaning forward, he could see only the stone blocks which made up the walls of the building. Straightening up, he considered again the story: the arch of the great snake would not be behind the statue but on the wall at right angles to where Vishnu's head rested. He turned and looked and decided he was too far away to examine the wall. As he rotated to get upright, the light disappeared completely from the temple. At first he thought he had temporarily blocked it by shifting and searched behind to find the slit between the stones, but the floor of the little temple was moving in a rolling motion. Jack tried to steady himself by getting into a sitting position again and thought about the door and turned his head to search for it but it was very dark. He could only take in the feel of the rough but consistent floor – not rocks and sand, more like very hard toenails… it was as he turned his head that the yellow eyes of a monster glared from behind the snout and fangs of a gigantic snake.

Jack shot backwards, leaned back as far as possible from the warm breath that came intermittently from the massive mottled nostrils, his arms propping him up. The floor was still rolling; he realised he had not been breathing, he was afraid to breathe, not able to breathe. He could not make his eyes or mind move away from those unblinking, unpredictable yellow glares. The fangs and the dribbles, the thought of the powerful venom, and all the while the rolling floor, underneath his palms, he realised, was actually the snake body! As his sight became adjusted to the darkness once again he made out distant lights – no, eyes which were surrounded by shadow shapes, the other four heads of the King Naga, all the while not taking his eyes away from the monster head centimetres away from his face, he was prey, like the pet rabbit for Ekans. *Make it stop. Go away*, no voice came: his mouth was carved open, motionless like his breathing, dry, not even a squeak from his throat which seemed paralyzed in stone. While his eyes stayed fixed on the jaundiced glare, his mind was aware of the forked tongue which kept darting in and out of that mouth, sensing and relaying information to the monster brain.

The giant head swayed and pulled back and upwards and with it two shadows each side, their eyes occasionally flickering yellow lights in the distance as the eyelids opened and closed. Somehow this movement triggered Jack's mind: he became aware of his body; he moved his legs underneath him but as he did, the terrible head swooped low again, hissed and bared the mucous-covered fangs. He could see right into the breathing holes each side of the snout, the forked tongue swished out all around and almost touched his knees, sensed and sent information, the magnificence of the scales which was diminished now by terror.

Jack closed his eyes and waited for the piercing fang, he forced images of the hinged jaw right out of his mind. But they stayed, that jaw, which would open very wide and unhinge for the passage of his head and the rest of his body to be swallowed whole. He waited but was very careful not to move even a finger;

didn't even feel, didn't think, he just was, it was easy to stay paralyzed, he felt as dry and as inanimate as the rocks of the temple. He kept his eyes closed tightly and waited in the quiet, heard only the thumping of his heart and the sliding of the giant coils, felt only the movement beneath his legs, like a bouncy castle he had been on in Ireland, except the canopy and entire structure was a monster and he couldn't dare stand up and bounce on that floor.

Another thought came: Vishnu. If the snake was real the God had to be real! Vishnu the protector or preserver, which one…? Grandmother had said too long ago. Jack pictured him in his mind, not in stone but in flesh; though the peace didn't come, he managed to keep hold of the reclining Vishnu, yellow mundu, garland, crown…

After a time, Jack couldn't remember how long, he opened his eyes, just an infinitesimal movement, hardly a slit, the coils still rolled a little but the yellow was a brilliant yellow, like canary yellow he thought, not the yellow with a slit pupil. He slowly lifted the lids higher and higher, without any movement of his head, or mouth, taking slight quiet short breaths.

There was the human man, lying peacefully, not as round as Dad, maybe shorter, long black hair, crown and four arms. Above it Jack was aware of the King Naga, he didn't move his head or even glance up. He kept his eyes in an absolute stare on the God Vishnu. He instinctively felt that if he continued like that he would keep the Naga at bay. *Was this what Kate meant when she urged him to try and connect with his soul and nature, what was he looking at, where was he?* He felt part of myth and religion all at once, trapped as he was in the stone structure of ages old. He longed to get back to humanity, away from danger, away from living on a knife-edge…

INJECTIONS

JACK FELT CONSCIOUSNESS creep back. It came and it went. He was trapped in stone and again, much later, he was aware of the firmness of bed sheets and it was air-conditioned cool. He raised his eyelids just a little: there was white light all around so he opened the lids fully. Very near on the left was what looked like a steel drip stand with a plastic bag of clear liquid just in sight and then he became aware of the needle in his arm. He moved his head a little and his mother came into view. She sprang on him and grasped his bandaged wrist, counting pulses no doubt, he thought.

'Jack can you see me… can you hear me?' she questioned with urgency.

'Where am I?' he asked.

'You're in hospital,' she replied.

'Why… what's wrong?' he asked.

'We found you collapsed half in and half out of one of the ruins yesterday… don't you remember?' she explained and asked all at once.

'The snake, the giant snake…' he began.

'No, no snake venom in your blood, they tested for that last night… did you see a snake?' she asked, more concerned.

'No, I think I had a dream,' he replied, quickly recovering his senses.

'You were certainly doing battle with something awful all night,' she said.

'Was I… did I talk in my sleep?' he asked a little anxious.

'Not talk so much as whimpering and then you tensed up and twisted and turned… the whole night long,' she explained.

'What's the drip for?' he asked.

'You were not responding to any of the neurological tests, just like Kate… remember… just a sort of nightmare throughout the night, so the neurologist felt it was better to keep the vein open… and we couldn't get you to drink, so it kept you hydrated,' she explained.

'I'm alright now. Can I go back to the Woodlands?' he asked, trying to pull himself forward.

'You'll have to be checked over by the doctors first, be formally discharged. I'm going to find your father to tell him the good news,' she said

'Is Dad here too?' Jack asked.

'He's with your grandmother, they have taken her for a scan,' she explained as if unconvinced of Jack's state of mind, probing his face again for signs of ill-health.

'Oh I forgot, Grandmother's investigations,' he said as reality settled in.

'How could you remember anything, the state you were in?' his mother reminded him, at once reassuring him and satisfying herself that he was fully lucid. She opened the door to leave.

'Can you get me something to eat on the way, I'm starving,' he said. 'And I'm dying to go to the bathroom.' With that he swung his legs over the side of the bed.

'Hold on a minute, wait… let me organise the drip stand,' protested his mother, dashing back into the room.

Within an hour or two Jack found himself sitting upright, feeling full and almost fit in his grandmother's room. He found out that both had been admitted the previous night, Grandmother for her tests and himself through Accident & Emergency. Grandmother looked tired and drawn but smiled when she asked what happened to him.

'It must have been the heat… he collapsed,' interjected Grandfather who had been waiting patiently with Jack's father following Grandmother as she had been taken from one test area to the next. He was agitated and impatient with worry for her and to Jack's relief his lack of probing into the temple incident suited him.

A little later as the lift doors opened into the hospital lobby and he saw the familiar silhouette of the hired driver who left to fetch the car. Jack felt the full effect of his unconscious night; his knees felt weak away from the support of the hospital bed and chair.

Jack's mother ordered him to bed as soon as they reached the Woodlands cottage they shared and orders were given for restrictive access. Tucked in once again between white sheets and the air conditioner on a not-too-cool setting, Jack complained of being on his own and Matty was allowed in.

'Kate, Girija and Nisha are in the sitting room but Mum will not let them in to see you,' Matty told him in a discreet voice.

'I'm just a bit tired Matt, I don't know why she is making such a fuss,' Jack exclaimed.

'Nisha said a giant snake bit you; will you show me the fang marks?' whispered Matty.

'Where did she get that idea? I wasn't bitten,' exclaimed Jack.

'She said she saw you go inside one of the temples that had a nest of snakes, she told me,' Matty insisted.

'She's trying to frighten you, Matt, take no notice of her stories,' reassured Jack.

'But I know… I found you… you were hanging over the step of the temple, half in and half out of it and I couldn't wake you up… and Dad and Mum had to carry you to the car… and Dad drove so fast, Mum had to tell him to slow down, that the wheels of the car were not touching the road… and you just lay across the back seat with Mum holding your head and she had me help her search you for snake bites but we didn't find any… it was awful…'

'There were no snake bites Matt, they checked at the hospital,' Jack reaffirmed.

'I know… Mum rang us at night and told us. What was wrong with you Jack, why did you faint if you weren't bitten?' asked Matty, still perplexed.

'I don't know, one minute I was looking at the statue and the next minute… I woke up in hospital,' Jack prevaricated.

'Grandfather said it was the heat and maybe you were hungry too; were you hungry Jack?' asked Matty enquiringly, still not at ease with so much speculation.

'Don't remember, but now that you mention food, will you ask Mum to order a dosa for me?' he asked Matty.

Matty jumped off the bed and eagerly ran to the bedroom door. He had no sooner opened it than two faces peeped round it, Girija and Kate. They were instantly intercepted by his mother.

'One at a time please girls,' she said apologetically.

'Nisha and I will come back in the evening,' said Girija and she slipped away from the door. Kate slunk in with a backward glance at Jack's mother who was on the phone to room service.

'What happened to you?' she asked quietly and seated herself carefully on a chair near Jack.

'I think Saroj had something to do with it,' he half-whispered.

'How and what?' she looked puzzled.

'Think Kate, yesterday at the temples Saroj and Nisha were not with Grandfather and your group, they were not with Dad… and just now Matty told me that Nisha told him a big snake bit me,' he said hauling himself upright against the pillows.

'What snake Jack? I didn't hear anything about a snake and I have been with the girls all the time especially since we got back,' she said.

'You know the structure I was in, the half-sunken small temple?' He looked at her to confirm that she was fully focused as she kept looking in the direction of the door.

'Yeah of course, the one Matty found you in,' she said, slightly annoyed at having to reassure him she could listen intently as well as watch out for his mother.

'I had an encounter with Ananda.' It was a statement: it was the only way he could put it for he struggled to make sense out of it himself; the words were gulped out.

'The mythical five-headed snake Vishnu reclines on,' she said slowly.

'It's no myth Kate... believe me...' he said as the fear crept into his chest again.

'In Swami's book it is written that Vishnu is the only one who can control that serpent...' she trailed off, thinking.

'I really thought I was done for Kate, I really did.' He took a breath and sank into the pillows.

'I can't figure it out though... Ananda is not... or maybe it is... are all serpents from the underworld?' she asked thinking. He could see her struggle with these opposites as he had done since he regained consciousness.

'At first it was aggressive and threatening or maybe it was defensive... it was only when I saw the God... Vishnu that it pulled back...' he spoke as he remembered, disjointed, thinking as he spoke and relived it.

'Wait, wait, slow down Jack, I don't think I'm getting the whole of what you said happened to you, the God Vishnu?' she said and looked totally shook. 'Start at the beginning, from the very beginning. Remember, I was not with you since we got out of the cars near the beach.'

And he told her everything in detail, slowly, carefully in whispered tones; this was not something he wanted Matty or his mother to know.

'You know what I think Jack,' she said at last after a long period of silent contemplation while Jack felt a wave of physical weakness wash over him again. 'I think your aunt may have sent a serpent like Ekans but...'

She seemed to need more reflection.

'You remember how the Danava commander shape shifted into a snake and got rid of Ekans and how he tried to warn your mother...' she said and checked that Jack was following her line of thought.

'I think your aunt has called up her aboriginal demon tribes again and this time she sent you a monster snake,' she said as Jack cut her off.

'But it was always Ananda, I could see the shape of the other heads and their eyes in the darkness, Kate...' he began, desperate that she must not misunderstand anything that happened and therefore interpret it correctly.

'Yes I know, but Ananda is only sublime when he is with Vishnu and in your state of… possibly expanded consciousness there and then you somehow connected with the concept of Vishnu and all that he stands for and the monster serpent took on that role… or was forced in to a submissive role. It's somehow got to do with the mental aura manifesting your thoughts into reality… I can't really grasp it, Swami knows all about it,' she explained.

There was knock on the door and a waiter appeared carrying a tray. Kate was encouraged to leave; Jack heard his mother tell her that after he had eaten he would be taking a nap and to check back in the evening. He was so tired again that he didn't feel like eating the dosas but he felt that both Matty and his mother gauged his health on his desire for food. They watched while he tore off some of the crispy pancake-like dosa and dipped it in the coconut chutney and ate it. The more he ate the hungrier he became so he had no bother finishing all that was ordered, especially the mango lassi. As the tray was lifted away he was made to scooch down between the sheets and was tucked in again and fell into a natural and heavy sleep even before the bedroom door had closed.

A TERRIBLE TRUTH

JACK WOKE UP rested and energised. The cottage was empty so he decided to check one of the other cottages to find out where everyone was. The hotel had a temple and it was situated just outside the cottage Jack shared with his family. Hotel guests were coming for evening prayers and the priest was performing Pooja, ringing the bell and chanting. Among the worshippers was Matty inspecting a large mural of the God, Ganesh. Nearby his mother and the girls were gazing into the window of the small shop just beyond the cottage complex. Everyone converged on him at once, his mother checking his forehead for fever. Satisfied, she announced that Jack's father had sent back the hired car from the hospital where he was staying with Aunt Saroj and Grandfather waiting for the gastro-enterologist to give them the results of the scan and the other tests as they were anxious to know about the results and how many more tests may be needed. Jack's mother's plan was that they should go to the Breeze Hotel for supper. Jack knew it well: every time they came to Madras they stayed at the Woodlands Hotel but had supper at the Breeze not only because it was non-vegetarian but because it was near the beach and really had a lovely cool breeze at that time of the evening. It had a playground near the outside dining area where his parents used to sit and watch himself and Matty play when they were much younger.

Jack found it strange that Girija spent most of that evening sitting at the table with his mother while Nisha and Matty played on the swings, Nisha continuing to swing when Matty took a go on the slide. Kate had signalled Jack when the meal was over and he joined her as unobtrusively as he could a little while later. His mother called out that they were not to go to the beach and to stay in the hotel grounds. Kate waved reassuringly and sat on a bench just on the edge of the sand where Jack joined her.

'Are you OK?' she asked.

'Yes I'm fine, I had a long sleep this afternoon and I'm strong again,' he said.

'How come Girija is spending so much time with Mum? Don't get me wrong, I'm glad they are bonding, but still…' he trailed off, his gaze on the tables.

'She may be giving us space,' said Kate as she turned her head towards Jack and looked right into his eyes.

'No, no… what now? It can't be worse than what you have told me already,' he exclaimed.

'No, not worse… it's just that… she has told someone else,' said Kate, still looking at him.

'Who?' Jack asked, mystified, looking at Nisha as she played with Matty, – surely not, and certainly not her own mother. 'My mother?' he asked, alarmed, changing his gaze from the playground back to the tables again.

'You must be joking!' said Kate, looking at him as if he had lost his reason. 'The very last person she would tell is your mother and anyway with her background, she would see it as nothing else but pure suicide.'

'Well isn't it?' reminded Jack who momentarily lost the theme of their conversation and said out loud what he really felt.

'Do you think that anyone contemplating suicide would look so happy?' asked Kate.

'What are you saying? Do you really think what she is going to do is rational?' Jack became exasperated and stood up and began to pace.

'Sit down, will you, or your mother will be over here checking you out again for all sorts of ailments,' she ordered.

He calmed himself and sat once again on the bench.

'Who has she told then?' he asked after a little while.

'Your grandmother,' was all Kate said and gazed at the playground, returning Matty's wave.

'I saw her this morning, she was between tests, waiting for the scan, she looked drawn and so tired, I thought it was the effects of having all the tests but now I know why,' he said. Kate seemed to wait until this news had settled.

'Why did she need to tell Grandmother?' he asked quietly and thoughtfully. He felt defeated; it seemed that Girija was determined and there was nothing he could do.

'I think she knows something we don't,' replied Kate.

'That's why she didn't come to Mahabalipuram, isn't it?' he asked.

'Yes,' confirmed Kate.

'But why Grandmother, and especially now when she is not healthy?' he asked again. And then 'What sort of information do you think she has, is it from the De Danann?' he enquired.

'I suspect it is, he visits her here you know!' she said.

'Great… there's no getting away from him, is there?' he said sarcastically.

With that Matty and Nisha appeared on the scene and pulled Kate towards the playground. Jack wandered towards the tables, hands dug deep into his pockets and gave Girija the most piercing look ever. She held his look stoically. There was no opportunity for Jack to confront Girija either about her decision or why she informed Grandmother of it but within an hour it had become clearer to him.

When they arrived back at the cottages they found that Grandfather had returned and Jack's father's normal imperturbable mood was anything but that, although he said nothing to them. It seemed that he had been pacing a lot and asked the children in a clipped way to wait at their cottage while he spoke to their mother. When she finally came to join them she dithered in the doorway and looked at all five enquiring faces individually. She slowly sat down on one of the sofas beside Matty with great equanimity which was unusual for her and caused Jack a great deal of unease.

'Grandfather is a bit upset… the news from the hospital is not good,' she said and examined all the faces in turn again. There was silence and after a while she continued.

'Grandmother may have something seriously wrong and tomorrow she will have a biopsy,'

'What's a biopsy?' asked Matty.

'A little bit of her inside will be taken out and examined under the microscope and then they will be able to say what it is and hopefully treat it,' she explained. Silence followed.

'Will it hurt?' asked Matty.

'No, she will be given something for that,' replied their mother.

After a little while during which nobody spoke she stood up.

'Jack, would you sleep in Grandfather's cottage tonight, he's a little upset and Girija, would you share with Nisha and Kate as your mum will be at the hospital with Grandmother?' she said and at once everyone got up from their game, or rather Matty's Leprechaun game which he and Kate had devised during the quiet days of the monsoon, Matty had produced the crumpled, Sellotaped sheets from his bag, along with a dice and a plastic container belonging to a roll of film.

As she walked Jack back to his grandfather's cottage he enticed more information from his mother and it wasn't what he wanted to hear. Grandmother had cancer and it had spread to more than one organ, possibly three: the biopsy would show what type it was but the outlook was not positive. He talked about how it would be with Grandfather and she told him he was in denial and to go along with whatever he said.

NANI BHAVAN

THE FLIGHT BACK to Kerala was ponderous. Grandmother had the biopsy on the Saturday and on Sunday the Consultant gave his conclusion at the same time Girija, Jack's mother, Matty, Nisha, Kate and Jack boarded their flight at Madras airport. Matty had a look around the airport shop but nobody else was in the mood. By then everyone except Matty had been told what Grandmother really had. It had been explained that this information was not to be passed on to Matty at that time in order to mitigate its effect. It had been decided that Jack, Matty, their mother and Kate would move into Nani Bhavan until Grandmother and everyone else returned, as there was not enough space in the Little Pink House to accommodate all the teenagers.

Only one car met them at the airport and Jack couldn't help comparing it with their outward journey, the anticipation of the ruins and everything else a holiday promised. Matty was pinioned in the front seat between Jack and the driver and soon fell asleep, his head lolling from Jack's forearm to the driver's with the movement of the car. The girls and his mother were tightly seated in the back and there was no conversation whatsoever.

Phone calls had been made and the two rooms upstairs at Nani Bhavan had been cleaned and made ready for their return. Jack and Matty were to share the big room and their mother moved into their father's room. Girija shared with Nisha and Kate took Girija's room overlooking the garden at the front of the house.

Jack felt the habitually quiet Nani Bhavan did not know what had hit it. That evening his mother sorted clothes to bring from the Little Pink House for them and nagged them to organise their school bags for the morning. The library had been thrown open. Matty had pestered incessantly for the keys after arriving from the airport as his mother and the girls headed off for their naps. Reluctantly she gave in and both brothers settled on the cool tiled floor for the afternoon, searching and reading and then searching again and digressing more and more from their original quests and for a while Jack forgot about his troubles.

Girija was the first one to rise and Jack watched her as she entered the dining room for tea. He hauled himself off the floor and followed. He was not really interested in the tea but he needed to talk to her.

'Girija, do you mind checking on the cows with me?' he asked and inclined his head towards the open window which looked in on the library across the hall where Matty was still sprawled out on his tummy on the tiles, engrossed in a bound book of his father's old imported comics.

'Not at all,' she said obligingly, returning his hard stare, straight into his eyes.

They both took their silver beakers full of steaming hot tea and headed towards the corridor which led to the kitchen and then out into the back yard. When they were at a safe distance from any part of the main house Jack confronted her.

'You were not surprised at Grandmother's diagnosis, were you?' he asked; he had decided to take a surreptitious route.

'No,' was all she answered.

'Did you know what the diagnosis was?' he asked, aware that she was not eager to talk.

'I didn't know what the diagnosis was but I know she will not be with you for very long,' she said and turned to face him. 'I'm sorry Jack.'

'She's going to die, isn't she?' he said the words.

'Yes,' she replied, looking into her tea.

'And you have decided to die too?' he asked.

'No, I'm not going to die Jack,' she said firmly, her eyes on him again.

'What's the difference?' he asked and mustered as much control as he could when he really wanted to scream at her.

'I think you know. Kate must have explained it,' she said, closing in on him.

'She did, but it's the same as Grandmother, you cannot come and go like Kate does, once you're gone you're gone... forever... how do you know you will not be lost in some space between worlds...? Chechi, we do not know enough about it...' he said and he was aware that he had almost lost control of his outward calm and the careful conversation plan he started out with.

'Kate moves in and out of other worlds with only her etheric aura, I take my entire self with me.' She was still calm, almost ready for the argument.

'Jack, please understand that our aura comes before our physical body. My aura will survive in a different world, and therefore, I will survive. Remember your physics: no space exists without an energy field; my body, your body is living in a world of energy and I can exist without it in another dimension. I don't need the physical body, I will have my energy field. It's not like grandmother, her aura has been weakened which caused the physical diseases she has now. She will go to the spirit world. Kate told me you felt you saw Great-grandmother Nani, she may be waiting to take her.'

'What about your body, what do you plan to do with it when the time comes?' he said with as much veracity as he could as he tried the shock approach sickened by her theory and absolutely unconvinced by it.

'Yes, I'm sorry about that, everyone should have an alibi in case the police suspect trouble,' she said without any loss of composure.

He could say no more, he could take no more, so he placed his silver beaker full of untouched tea on the washing stone very carefully as if he was striving to maintain some control, at least over the beaker of tea, and he left her. He walked away all along by the back of the house towards the gate leading to the garden, past the bungalow and into the garden of the Little Pink House, but there was no escape: the horror of everything was exploding very painfully inside his head. The wraith in the prayer room – is Girija sick too? Is this life in another world real or has it been induced? Swami told him there was a law against black magic: if it could be proved it could be tried in a court, but he had no proof.

Kate knew what the aunt was up to, so did Girija and Nisha but neither Nisha nor the driver Vishu would appear as witnesses if Jack could make a court case. Kate's statements and testimonies would be torn to shreds by a good solicitor and Grandfather would hire the best to defend his daughter. It would be too easy to undermine Girija's evidence after the gun incident and that left himself, a minor with just the prayer room, temple incident and the appearance of a giant ogre in the middle of the night in a garden he was not supposed to be in and his aunt would deny she held a machete; they would put it down to a sleepwalking.

He sat on the back veranda. The cushions had been taken inside; the watchman was watering the lawn but he hardly noticed him. He dared to think what life would be like without these two women. Girija he saw only intermittently, so he probably would not miss her that much except for the way she planned to leave and, worse, the finality of it. Grandmother was another matter, though: she was not old, only sixty; it felt old to Jack but it was not old-old, like Swami or even Grandfather who was seventy.

Matty appeared with Daisy the Labrador in tow, to Jack's relief: he was sick of the thoughts inside his mind.

'What're you doing here, Matt?' he asked, as Matty always had a purpose.

'Will you help me catch the rabbits and Mrs Dodo?' he asked.

'Do you need to put them in?' Jack asked.

'I don't trust Betty, she is a watchdog, not like Daisy,' he said as he patted the head of the panting dog who always looked as though she was laughing. She in turn moved in closer to him.

'Right… where do we start?' asked Jack.

'Well Mrs Dodo is usually chewing and grazing on the lawn, so you get her and I'll collect up the young Dodos,' Matty said, flinging the Crane Bag on the steps and setting off in the direction of the flower beds surrounding the cook's kitchen.

THE WALK MEETINGS

 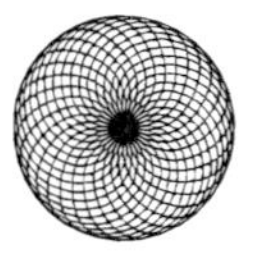

THE SCHOOL WEEK went quickly enough. Jack's desultory mood continued: he explained to his friends that his grandmother was seriously ill and that seemed to placate them. There was even an abatement of jokes except for the sporadic escape which died slowly without his participation. Word had come from the hospital that Grandmother was suffering from a most aggressive form of malignant cancer and was at the end stage and Grandfather had insisted that she should have an operation to see if there was any hope of a cure.

As if this news was not bad enough, existence became worse still for Jack as it was almost impossible to speak to Kate in the big house as there were so many ways of being overheard. Every room had openings in the walls; some rooms, especially if centrally situated, had openwork on three sides to allow air to flow freely through and cool the inside of the house. Kate also seemed to be disassociating herself ever so slightly from Jack and spent a lot of time with Girija, or at least that's what it felt like.

When, finally, on the third night they found a way of talking without being overheard Kate explained that she had invited Swami to visit when Nisha was at school and she hoped he would be able to dissuade Girija or have some evidence that what she had planned was not a solution, or at least get her to look again at her decision in a different light. Apparently it had taken a lot for Girija to agree to even discuss it with Swami. While all this was being exchanged Jack and Kate kept on walking round and round the box hedge which surrounded the pond area. Earlier Kate announced that she needed exercise when Matty set off for Hindi tuition. They spoke when they left the bungalow and headed towards the well and then had to change the subject which they agreed would be music videos – the Pet Shop Boys on the first round, Meat Loaf on the second – as they passed along the drive at the front of the house, near the open windows.

Nisha was sitting out alone, Girija was nowhere to be seen and his mother was organising Matty's supper and night meal for the others at the back of the house. This wasn't very satisfactory for Jack as he had to explain the law against black magic to Kate in instalments. He urged her to discuss it with Swami and Girija separately and get their views on the feasibility of a defence. He tried to impress upon her the importance of a deep discussion with Swami on the subject and insisted that he was sure Swami had told him it was an offence punishable by law, possibly carrying a jail sentence.

'Your plan is to put your aunt in jail?' asked Kate, perplexed.

'It's too late for Grandmother, we can try to save Girija,' he stated more than said and tried to look a lot more positive than he felt.

'Jack, I don't know if you know it, but what you are thinking of doing is enormous,' she said and slowed to a stop in the safe area of the drive.

'Convince Girija and then we'll start on the adults one by one…' he began.

'What if Girija leaves anyway?' she asked, looking up into his eyes.

'Well let's find out about the black magic charge first,' he said.

Kate seemed to need to sit down to digest all of what was said so they joined Nisha who had been sitting watching them on the wicker chairs, which were arranged as they were, every evening.

WHITE ANT INVASION

AND SO THE week wore on, every day filled with even more gloom as Kate reported Swami's reaction to Jack's litigious solution. In the honest moments Jack knew that it was a long shot but if he dismissed the plan it left him without any resource whatsoever, and in clinging on he annoyed Kate. She assured him that the law was still on the statute books – it was an offence to practise black magic – but as he more or less expected, Swami felt too that proof was the main problem and the fact that all the cousins except Girija were minors.

Swami had made no impression on Girija either but during their exchange Kate discovered information which Swami had predicted at the very beginning of the disturbance to Jack's peaceful existence. Girija had assured Swami that Grandmother's life was fading and her mother's focus would turn to her brother, Jack's father, as he was the only other real threat to her power over Grandfather.

It was difficult to thrash out any of this with Kate in the snippets they could manage in the now regular nightly exercise of walking round and round the drive. Jack was left to live with all these unbelievable events in the darkness within his mind. The move that Swami had suggested he and his family should make nearly three months ago seemed to be the only way out. So the unthinkable had become several painful realities: life elsewhere, no Grandmother and worse still, the horror of what Girija had planned.

On the Friday evening, just before Matty was called to have his supper, a very unpleasant discovery was made which in turn led to a terrible incident which uncovered the extent of the aunt's malefic intent: this dreadful presence was within the house.

It was just as dusk had ended and Matty had been disturbed by his mother's continuous calls to take his bath and have his supper, he reluctantly agreed to leave his comfortable position sprawled out on the tea-planter's chair in the front hall underneath a fan. Eventually Matty dismounted from the extended arms of the chair on which he had his legs positioned and called back to her that he was getting one more book from the library to take upstairs. Matty proceeded to unlock the third bookcase and after switching on the light to see if there was any type of reading material in there that might interest him he made that nasty discovery.

A very heavy blue-bound encyclopaedia on the third shelf drew Matty's attention. It was just in reach and he needed to manipulate the spine to dislodge it from its snug fit between two volumes of *Inventions of the 20th century*, which he did, but it almost fell on top of him due to its weight and location and ended up on the floor. Its pages fell open to reveal nibbled edges and gnaw holes throughout. Puzzled, he took it to the dining room and showed it to his mother who immediately searched the bookcase to find that it had been invaded by termites. So the room was shut off and word was spread that no one should open the doors or ventilations until the morning when all hands were needed to empty the bookcases and place every single book in the searing heat of the sun.

Saturday morning turned out to be a rescue mission. Girija and Kate organised separate areas in the sand outside for damaged and undamaged books while Nisha and Matty ran back and forth between the library and the back yard with arms full of books and Jack emptied the bookcases, examining the books for signs of damage and allocating them to the runners. All the books had been placed in the sun by lunchtime and the disinfectant bought. This was sprayed all over the library, particularly on the wood to prevent termite damage to the bookcases, ventilations and doors, table and chairs. Grandmother's houseboy took charge of the spraying after lunch had been served and all the food in the vicinity had been cleared away. He covered his nose and mouth with a cloth not dissimilar to a tea towel and tied it at the back of his head, closed off the room and sprayed. He emerged some time later through a haze of disinfectant and locked the door.

While Jack and Matty's mother had her siesta, Jack, Kate and Nisha joined Matty on one of the shaded verandas leading into the back yard and stretched out on the tiled floor in the balmy heat and lazily watched Matty using a magnifying glass on the undamaged comic books; one after another he checked them for termites and replaced them in the burning sun.

That evening Jack's mother decided that due to the severity of the white ant invasion in the library it would be necessary to check the dark room and all the adjoining rooms at ground level that were normally closed off at Nani Bhavan. By locking the unused part of the house it saved Grandmother the bother of having to search underneath beds and inside cupboards for would-be thieves who may have crept into the grounds during the day and who would lie in hiding until everyone had gone to bed to do their work.

Kate was the only other person, other than Grandmother, who was aware of what the upstairs of the closed wing had been in use for not so long ago and Jack understood that she was thinking of just that incident when he exchanged a look with her.

The books spent the night on tables in the hallway outside the locked library door; this time the children were less enthusiastic about carrying so many books back into the house again but their mother made a mission of the chore. Sunday morning was designated as the day to open up the unused wing.

DARK PORTAL

AFTER TRYING A third key, which resembled the key of the library door, the little group, around Jack's mother, heard a rusty, metallic, disrupted winding followed by another rotation by their mother and then an uncertain tick. The door responded to a gentle push and swung easily open.

'Mum, you know we can get in through the door at the end of the hall,' Jack reminded his mother, pointing towards the back of the house.

'Yes I know that, but I have never seen that door open and I'm not even sure if the key for it is on this ring,' she replied as she unbolted the double door which had just been released from the one which held the lock.

'It's open at Onam,' reminded Jack.

'Yes, it probably is,' she said. 'I'm just not used to so many keys and there are two bunches. Let me have a go,' she said and left in the direction of the back of the house to the hall that ran half the length of the house parallel with the front. Meanwhile Matty and Nisha had entered the first room which was a large bedroom. Jack stood back to allow Kate through the doors and saw the room from her perspective as she moved slowly in on the red-tiled floor. He knew she would be using more than her five senses to perceive the environment.

'This used to be my grandparents' bedroom when Dad was little,' he explained. She had been looking at the two wooden single beds pushed together and placed directly underneath an enormous ceiling fan in the centre of the room. Jack explained that the rectangle frame with hooks which was behind the heads of the beds was to hang clothes on.

Nisha had begun to unhook and open the shutters of the two large windows which were opposite the door. She flung them open and in the process swiped off clawing cobwebs and uttered sounds of disgust as she tried to dislodge the webs from her hair and her hands. Sunlight flared into the previously monochrome room, giving it an appearance of life. Kate moved to the corner having noticed a large very old iron safe and looked at Jack.

'Grandmother keeps most of the jewellery in the bank nowadays,' he explained. Beside the safe was a hospital-version weighing scale and Jack felt he had to explain this too. 'Everyone tends to be a little heavy…' he trailed off as Matty had left the room through another door near the windows.

'Matty, be careful of the electricity down there… it may not work,' Jack shouted.

'We're supposed to be looking for white ants,' reminded Nisha in sort of grumble as she pulled off a sheet and turned one of the mattresses over on to the bed next to it.

'Sorry Nisha,' began Kate as she joined her. 'What are we looking for?'

'Holes,' replied Jack.

'Not just holes,' Nisha whinged and rolled her large wide eyes in Kate's direction: 'Small white insects.'

'Like tiny flies but they wiggle like worms, more silver than white,' explained Jack. 'I must check on Matt, there are shocks here from the electric switches and he doesn't know the dark room very well,' and he disappeared through the door after Matty.

'You're getting out of work… this is not fair,' Jack heard Nisha call after him in Malayalam.

Jack had enough light from the adjoining bedroom door to see into the passage. Opposite to the door was the bathroom door, which had a bath rather than a shower, a separate toilet and a dressing room. The door was closed so he knew Matty had not gone in there. He proceeded on left, away from the outer wall of the top of the capital E which made up Nani Bhavan; he had just enough light to see the passage turn right and he wondered, *how had Matty found his way along there?* He did have his bag and therefore his tools, his torch, Jack remembered.

Jack continued along this passage with outstretched arms, hands just reaching both sides of the passage walls. He could hear his mother trying the lock and knew he must be near the door which she still hadn't managed to get open. That would have provided a little light from the hall outside which had a skylight.

'Matt, where are you?' Jack called out.

'Over here,' came Matty's reply which was fairly near.

With that the door opened and Jack could see the dark room door, just about. Matty straightened himself. He had been peering at the door lock with his pen torch.

'Now I know which one it is,' exclaimed their mother who stood in a sort of *Moses at the Red Sea* pose, arms spread wide and draped in a kaftan with a small key held in one hand while the others dangled on the same ring. She stepped into the hallway and began looking for a light switch by pawing the walls.

'There's one near the door to your right,' explained Jack.

'Found it... Ouch,' she leaped back, grasping her right wrist as a light flickered on. 'Nobody is to touch the switches down here, do you hear me Matty?' she emphasised his name, still hugging her tingling fingers and rubbing the ache in her right arm.

'I'm listening, are you all right?' he asked.

'I'm wearing my rubber flip flops, I think that may have helped,' she said and began to examine the lock on the dark room door in an effort to match a key with it.

'What happened?' asked Kate. The girls immediately appeared on the scene and Jack couldn't help notice that Nisha wore a very anxious look.

'Don't touch the electrics,' repeated Jack's mother. 'I've just had a nasty shock; it went right up my arm.'

'Here Mum, give me the keys,' ordered Jack and began to try the lock on the door of the dark room.

'Did you check the bedroom yet?' Mum asked the girls.

'Just the mattresses,' replied Kate, looking at Nisha who nodded.

'Nisha, would you find Babu and ask him to take the mattresses out into the sun?' Mum asked, continuing to rub her right arm.

Nisha obediently left through the open passage door.

'Why is it called the dark room?' asked Kate.

'When we get the door open you'll see it has no natural light of its own,' Jack's mother explained.

There was the sound of voices in the outer corridor as Nisha arrived with Babu and another bearer in tow and in Malayalam ordered the removal of the mattresses. By the time she joined the others Girija had also appeared and Jack had opened the door. The pale small beam from Matty's torch bounced off Grandmother's collection of steel vessels.

'The electrics are alive, Girija,' warned Jack's mother. She removed her rubber slipper and stood heron-like on one foot and asked Matty to direct his beam near the door. When she found the electric switch she pushed down the leaver with her flip-flop but there was just crackling from the switch and no light came on. She flicked it back up again and asked Matty to fetch a couple of the large torches they used during power cuts.

'It's like an Aladdin's cave,' remarked Kate, peering in at the silhouettes of the large silver prayer lamps and round-bottomed steel containers with curled lips as she moved the beam of the small torch here and there.

Jack noticed that Nisha moved back; she was uncomfortable. Maybe she felt that Kate was valuing the wealth, which he knew was not the case but the strangest things threatened Nisha. He instinctively felt that Nisha, like her mother, considered Kate an intruder.

When Matty arrived with two large torches Jack's mother organised the removal of all the lamps and cooking and storage vessels. Since none of these could be damaged by termites they were placed in the hallway between the library and the bedroom with the safe. The plan was to have the dark room swept, swabbed and disinfected. When it was empty the torches were carried further along the corridor to the very end of the top of the capital E on the ground floor. This was a square space with just a small, oval-shaped ventilation at ceiling level covered with wire mesh. Here the large brass cooking vessels were stored upright against the walls. Jack's mother asked him to translate instructions for Babu to roll them along clean and roll them back again. With that she headed towards the bedroom and began examining the wood with her glasses on.

'What about upstairs, Mum?' asked Jack when he joined her?

'That was used last Onam; someone stayed over so it would have been cleaned then,' she replied.

'Would you open the library and start categorising the books and sort them?' she said to Jack.

'Girls give him a hand, it will take ages,' she said, looking at all three girls at once.

'Matty you cannot put anything too damaged back, you might just spread the bugs, do you understand?' she stood up from squatting, having examined the legs of the beds.

Everyone left her quickly and quietly; nobody wanted the job of hunting for evidence of the white ants.

And so the morning wore on with various people disappearing at various times to have their baths. By lunchtime, when the heat had begun to suffocate despite having all the windows and ventilations open, Jack felt weary. They had to move the steel and silver off the tables in the hall between the library and the now open bedroom to make room for the various categories of books. The steel was piled in rows outside the door leading into the closed wing in the hallway with the skylight at the back of the house.

It was at that time when Jack stood akimbo, alone in the library – viewing the open bookcases, trying to decide which category he should place in which bookcase – that he partly overheard a clandestine conversation between the houseboy Babu and Nisha. The half-whispered, intermittent, argumentative voices came from the direction of the dark room. Jack crept closer and hid in the hall between the bedroom being aired and its bathroom; he could always slip into the bathroom or toilet if they came in his direction, he thought.

Pressed silently against the wall he became aware of a breeze which was so heavy with the heat of the midday sun that it never reached the library. In this position he could hear them better – and what were they talking about?

'Where should I put them?' asked what sounded like the frustrated houseboy Babu.

'In one of the outhouses,' ordered an impatient and hurried Nisha.

'The kitchen girls will find them; they use the outhouses for grinding the rice,' he protested.

'The men's toilet,' she proffered.

'The drivers use them and the watchmen… the milkman and the gardeners… anyone can go in there…' he remonstrated.

Then after another short pause…

'Chechi could take them upstairs,' Babu suggested.

'Auntie has the keys,' replied Nisha.

'She left them on the cupboard in that room,' he said and the voices moved so near that Jack moved closer to the bathroom door; clearly Babu must have pointed so they would be in the doorway leading into the outer hall, Jack thought.

'I have to do everything,' griped Nisha and Jack could hear her flip-flops slap against the soles of her feet as she apparently marched away towards the room with the great-grandfather bed in it. Jack did not hear Babu's bare feet leave; instead, he heard the rustle of the brooms and the clang of his metal bucket head away in the direction of the kitchen, he hoped, as by this time all the cleaning should have been finished.

Nisha did not return immediately. As Jack crept round the corner nearer to the door with the faulty light switch, he could see her talking to Girija and Kate who were watching Hindi song videos on the television. He slipped past the doorway and on into the open area beyond the dark room. The tiled floor had been swept and washed; it was still damp. In one corner was paraphernalia and on closer inspection Jack discovered it was prayer things.

Jack bent and picked them up one by one, raising them to the oval ventilation to examine them in more light. They were old and well-used, stained with oil and soot; they were made of clay and really filthy. The lamp was just a little saucer with a beak for the wick, in fact it had a half-burned wick still in it as well as several dead ants and a fly; the oil must have evaporated, he thought. *Grandmother used these, hundreds of them on Karthika, the festival of lights. She placed them all along the front of the house at ground level and all along the railings on the balcony upstairs and she would never use something as grim as this,* thought Jack. There was an incense holder and a small crude statue; this was slimy with a build-up of muck of some kind and even though it was old without any carving, Jack could not mistake the shape of the Goddess Jyestha with her bull-headed son resting on one arm and her daughter on the other.

He put it down quickly; memories of the monster ogre of the night in the garden almost overwhelmed him. He needed to get out of the place and quickly left without giving much attention to the rest of the stuff, including the red katcha his aunt wore on that awful night.

JYESTHA'S SON

 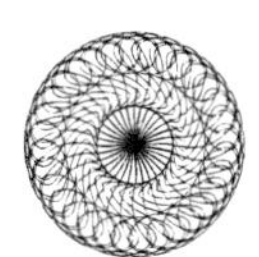

THE SEATING ARRANGEMENTS were a little different with the new occupants of Nani Bhavan. Jack's mother sat between both sons at one side of the dining room table while Kate joined Girija and Nisha on the other side at meal times. Nobody used Grandfather's chair at the head of the table. On that particular Sunday it turned out to be an opportunity for Jack as it meant he could signal Kate without causing any interest from the others. A frown, a nod, eye movements unrelated to the conversation would be enough to alert Kate and after lunch she slipped upstairs to the big bedroom where Jack was waiting for her alone.

'I found out where she performs most of the black prayers, her rituals,' Jack began as soon as Kate had closed the door.

'Whew, it's boiling up here, why can't we put on the air conditioner?' asked Kate as she advanced in the direction of the knobs.

'It's not working properly and Mum has forbidden us from using it,' explained Jack. 'Didn't you hear what I said?'

'What did you find and where?' she asked and plonked herself into an armchair near one of the large windows and began fanning herself with a book which she took from the nearby dressing table. Jack couldn't help the feeling that he was harping on about the aunt – or was it that Kate had become complacent this week, living as they had without evidence of malice and fear?

'You know, the square area beyond the dark room.' He waited until he was sure it had registered with her. 'Well, there was some primitive stuff on the floor but among it was the statue of the Goddess Jyestha.'

'We went in there with your mother when she organised the cleaning, there were only some very large copper pots, I know the light was not good but other than checking for cobwebs I didn't notice anything else,' she replied, thinking.

'That's it, the passage and the pot area had no cobwebs, a sign that it is in use. And… and the stuff must have been hidden behind the pots because I didn't notice it then either; it was only when I heard Nisha and Babu arguing that I had a look round,' he explained.

'Why were they arguing?' asked Kate.

'Well something else that shook me a little was the fact that Babu is her helper, or more precisely he was probably coerced into doing what she wanted or else lose his job… you know he has worked for Grandmother for years and he always seemed so loyal…' Jack thought out loud, 'anyway Nisha and he were arguing over who should hide the stuff…'

'Wait, wait then, both of them knew what she was up to or at least that she is up to no good. I'm sure she wouldn't divulge all her plans to either of them but use them when needed…' trailed off Kate who had jerked upright from her previously sprawled position.

'Well I told you that since the snake incident at Mahabalipuram,' reminded Jack. 'Remember Nisha told Matt…'

'Yes… she would cover up for her mother… but to tell Matt about it gives me the impression that she is now part of it, she actually boasted confidently that you had snake bite… and no remorse…' Kate considered all this and then: 'Let's have a look.'

'We'll go down separately, you go through the library but have a look out for the others, particularly Nisha; she doesn't take a nap and Babu could just materialise in any part of the house. Remember, he'll be barefoot, you will not hear him coming,' he whispered as they neared the bedroom door.

About five minutes later Kate appeared in the passage leading from the bedroom in the closed wing just as Jack came through the door from the corridor at the back of the house. They moved stealthily into the space beyond the dark room with scarcely enough light and Jack began searching in the gloom for the statue but it was nowhere to be found, or any of the other stuff.

'Nisha must have got to it,' whispered Kate and with that they both headed out to the long corridor again to see if the lock was open on the upstairs bedroom over the dark room. To their amazement the lock was on.

'She's quick,' was all Kate said.

They both headed towards the library and Jack began to explain his layout for the books as soon as he saw Matty kneeling on the floor in front of one of the bookcases, busily replacing the bound comic books on the bottom shelves.

'Wait Matt, I thought they should go in with English Literature, in that one over there,' explained Jack.

'Well, where is the children's section then?' asked Matty.

'We really haven't enough to make a Children's Section Matt,' continued Jack.

'If we bring over all our books we would,' suggested Matty.

'I don't think that will work, Matt,' he began.

'Why not?' insisted Matty.

'Listen you two, I'm going for my nap… I'll talk later, Jack…' said Kate as she lolled out of the library, hunchbacked, heavy with sleep.

TERROR IN THE DARK ROOM

JACK WENT IN search of help. Matty could not fetch all the books for re-stacking; it was not physically possible and his mother had reminded him that Babu, Hemani the cook and Aasha had their own work to do, since Francis and Mary had been given leave from the Little Pink House. The only other person who was not napping was Nisha and it took a lot of persuasion to haul Nisha away from the Hindi music videos.

'I don't see why I should have anything to do with the library.' She was truculent and she dragged her feet literally and unwillingly on their way to the library.

'How can you say that? You live here,' Jack stopped outside the dining room doors and rounded on her. To be honest he was thinking of how she had outwitted him with the ritual paraphernalia, which angered him: she was helping to destroy her own family whether she was aware of the consequences or not.

'Have you ever seen me read any of the books?' she asked defiantly.

'When you get into pre-degree you will need reference books,' insisted Jack.

'I'm not going to study English Literature, the Bible and I've certainly no use for those encyclopaedias,' she said emphatically and turned and marched defiantly back to the TV. And then the final dig: 'I shall take commerce like you, Jack, I will be studying for a Bachelor of Commerce.'

On returning to the library Jack was on his own. Matty had the last shelf in two bookcases filled with the bound comic books and he hadn't done a bad job. The classic comics were in one bookcase and *Richie Rich*, *The Phantom* and miscellaneous in another. Jack decided to make a start and, taking the books which Girija and Kate had placed spine up on the tables in the hall way, he began to replace the *Complete Works of Shakespeare*, the English poets and writers in the same bookcase where Matty had put his classic comic collection.

The House was so very quiet at that time of the day. Nisha was back in front of the TV but had the volume on low. Jack could just hear the music: it was loud enough for him to be able to recognise popular songs. After a couple of trips between both rooms ,one of the bookcases had two shelves full at the top and the bottom shelf. It was as Jack was on his way for another armful that it seemed to him that Matty literally fell out of nowhere on top of all the steel vessels in the long hallway. It felt like the quiet was blown apart as round-bottomed steel pots fell against their neighbours and tumbled onto the tiled floor like skittles, loudly knocking against the steel and silver salvers which had been placed upright against the walls and which in turn rolled, wobbled and collided with stacked steel servers, beakers, small steel serving bowls and landed right on to the floor over a large area with more clamour and reverberation than church bells.

When Jack reached the scene Matty was picking himself up but it was the terror in his expression that alarmed Jack.

'Matt don't worry, Mum will not hear, she has the air conditioner on in her room, we'll tidy it up...' Jack said in an effort to reassure him but the eight year-old began to run.

'Matt, Matt listen man...' Jack intercepted Matty near the dining room doors where the last of the steel plates had rolled. Matty was frantic and desperate and fought Jack who had to grip him firmly round the waist.

'Matt, wait... ouch, Matt now you're hurting me...' as he tightened his grip on the smaller boy, mindful that he may squeeze him too tight.

Matty dug his nails into Jack's arms which had no effect. Matty continued to bite and dig in his nails and during this Jack realised that Matty was not speaking so he released him but held him by both his forearms.

'What is it Matt?' asked Jack. 'Why can't you tell me?'

The frightened boy kept his eyes fixated on the door leading into the closed wing.

'Did you see something Matt?' asked Jack, trying to be calm.

Matty nodded his head but the wild look remained in his eyes and he began to pull away again.

'Shadow...' Matty said and he pulled one arm free and then, 'The Minotaur, the Minotaur... let me go... I saw a shadow of the Minotaur...

Jack let go of his brother's remaining wrist as the realisation settled in. His instinct was to reassure Matty that it was a Greek myth but his mouth would not open. Matty had reached Nisha at this point: she was standing in the door way staring petrified at Jack and he knew that she knew it was not the Minotaur but Jyestha's son and Matty must have seen it. Both Kate and Girija appeared on the scene, obviously shaken out of their sleep by the clangour. The very last thing that Jack saw and heard before he entered the passageway leading to the dark room and beyond were Kate's instructions to Matty.

'Do you remember the hiding place you told me about?' she asked Matty.

He nodded as he didn't seem able to utter words and his eyes stayed fixed on the rarely open door leading to the dark passage.

'Wait there for our signal, you do remember the signal we had for the leprechaun game, don't you?' she reconfirmed very calm and very firmly.

Matty nodded again.

'Go,' she said. Matty ran upstairs, taking two steps at a time. The last that Jack saw of him was his head sticking over the balancer.

'What about Mum?' Matty asked.

'She'll be OK,' Kate assured him with a smile and with that he disappeared.

NEAR-DEATH ENCOUNTER

'JACK, WAIT,' INSISTED Girija as she passed Nisha and came closer to the door which Jack had just stepped through. He gave one quick glance backwards and saw Kate pick her steps between the catastrophe of scattered steel and silver.

'Jack,' she called. He recognised the firmness she gave the word and knew she was reminding him he had no protection, both of them aware of Nisha's presence.

'Matt said he only saw a shadow…' he called back and advanced into the corridor which was partially lit by the refracted light coming from the skylight in the outer corridor.

At first everything was normal just as it was in the morning when he had eavesdropped on Nisha and Babu. That thought gave him confidence so he advanced on towards the dark room, stood and listened and in the silence he summoned the courage to peer around the door. The room was empty but in that light he could not even distinguish the corners of the room and the fear in his body prevented him from going in to explore more. He came forward but spooked himself when his toe hit against something. He stood without moving for a moment, tried to calm himself and distinguish what his right big toe had felt and after a while he realised it was the canvas of Matty's bag. Jack bent to feel it and recognised the leather straps and buckles. He picked it up and when he joined the corridor again to his left where the girls had gathered in the rarely used doorway Girija and Nisha had wide-eyed stares and stood mutedly as did Kate, slightly inside the corridor in front of the girls. Jack tossed the bag at Kate who caught it and passed it back to the girls.

Jack turned right to check out the area beyond the dark room and was partly encouraged by the faint light which came through the oval ventilation. It was as he and Kate had found it after lunch. He held up his arms and hands to the girls when he turned to leave, indicating nothing strange there. As Jack began to leave there was a loud bovine bawl followed by screams from all three girls. It didn't come from the cow shed; it was in the immediate vicinity. Jack knew the sound came from the dark room and within seconds the buffalo head appeared.

It was truly fearful, so large in the confined space and the man, his body much taller than Jack remembered on the terrible night in the garden. The horns; Jack could not take his eyes from the sharp tips of the potent spikes of the beast. It was angry, it had froth at its mouth; some of it formed into little bubbles where it was copious. Jack's eyes followed involuntarily a path from those horns on to the broad, dark-haired forehead, the hair separated there as if it had a natural parting, strong black hair. It was all buffalo, down the long snout where the hair became black skin, Jack could even feel the breath. The tongue came out a little and Jack took in that brawny muscle. He also noticed the teeth but pushed the vivid thought of their capabilities away. It snorted and sniffed and panic mounted as the beast again made fearful bovine sounds. It advanced on Jack who backed into the space with the very large cooking pots.

Jack noticed Kate who had her eyes closed and knew she was trying to access the Danavas. There was no time for her to go into to her etheric form and he knew she would try to channel them with her higher sensory perception; he was also aware of how it went wrong the last time she tried channelling. Those thoughts flashed instantly in and out of Jack's terrified mind for he knew he was in a place of sacrifice and this time he was the offering. The temple altar to this beast's mother Jyestha had been disturbed and now the son wanted the blood of retaliation and the restoration of her presence. When the beast turned on Kate who had appeared deeper into the corridor carrying one of Grandmother's silver prayer lamps, strength came from somewhere deep within and Jack leaped on to its back and grabbed its horns and pulled its head backwards. But the beast simply shook him off as if he was little more than a cloth tangled in the horns and Jack was slapped hard against the tiled floor. He tried to pull himself up but his head spun, he heard Girija's loud cry from just behind the beast.

'Ailill…' she wailed desperately. Jack could just distinguish her, she too carried a prayer lamp and like Kate, she too poked the beast using its pointed tip.

Jack saw two of everything, they were fuzzy but he could make out the space; the beast turned and gave its loudest roar yet and the girls withdrew into the corridor out of Jack's line of disturbed vision. Jack took this opportunity to leap once more on its back but with his uncorrected sight he missed one of the horns and scrabbled on by grabbing the other horn with both hands which caused the head to bend in his direction and thus made it easier for the human-like hands to grip him round the throat. At this point Jack became aware of how long the hair was on the human chest: strong black hair, caveman-like on the neck and shoulders.

The girls continued their offensive. Jack could just see them poking the sharp parts of the ornate lamp tops as hard as they could into the side of the beast which caused him to flail at them with one of his arms taking the pressure off Jack's airway, just as the breath had left him. Jack kicked and punched and freed himself momentarily; he tried to get past the beast to join the girls and corner the buffalo in the space, but he failed. As he approached the man-buffalo bent his head low and came at Jack, horn spikes first. Jack leaped backwards, hit himself hard on the shoulders against one of the giant cooking pots but by stumbling bottom first into it he probably saved his life. His hand automatically went to the stinging pain he felt across his chest and as he felt the wetness of blood the beast loomed above him, ready to gore.

The girls advanced and one after another they actually flung their heavy prayer lamps at the beast. Kate's was silver and had no impact other than distraction but Girija's was brass and she flung it with all her might as she had advanced almost to where Jack's legs protruded from the cooking pot. The heavy brass hit the beast on the right shoulder and momentarily he had to step backwards due to the weight of the blow. Girija began pulling at Jack but his wound caused him to cry out; it was impossible to lever himself up with just one hand from his awkward position. The beast threw back his head and gave a horrendous bellow and then bent forward once again. The girls were unarmed and thus their situation dire.

'Get out,' Jack shouted impatiently to Girija and as he turned to face his executioner he became aware of the barefoot Tuatha warrior at his other side. Looking up a little he noted that the warrior wore a Katcha, not a kilt and knew he meant to kill this time. The De Danann bowed to Jack's aggressor and the beast bowed to him and as the battle was about to begin Kate stepped over Jack's legs, slipped her arm under Jack's good one, levered him up with his help and both Girija and Kate hauled him out into the corridor, Girija having grabbed him by the waist of his shorts.

INTERCESSION

 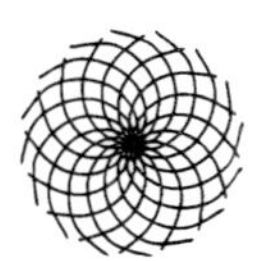

ONCE IN THE corridor Girija examined the wound which was about one foot long over Jack's lower right ribs. It was still bleeding profusely but Girija left in the direction of the dining room.

'As far as I can see the muscle is not torn,' she called back to Kate and Jack.

'Better sit down,' Kate urged.

'I'm alright, I just have to stop the bleeding,' replied Jack impatiently.

Girija brought back a hand towel almost immediately.

'Press it firmly against the wound,' she instructed Kate and then disappeared into the corridor leading to the battle.

'We have to go with her,' said Jack. 'I can look after this,' and he moved in after Girija away from the pressure of Kate's hand. Kate and Jack pressed in behind Girija. The fighters were still circling round the small space; they had kicked the lamp missiles to the sides of the room. When the buffalo came near the passage the De Danann shouted something to Girija in Sanskrit and she ordered the other two to back away out of sight which she did too. But within seconds all three rushed back into the darkness, summoned by what sounded like an agonising bawl from the buffalo man.

The De Danann warrior stood with his blade sheathed and the beast appeared to be restrained by something invisible.

'Is it the Danavas?' Jack asked Kate.

'There are loads of them… they have ropes made out of some sort of vines… two around his neck which are held by two men to the right and two to the left behind the beast, others are feathering his legs and four more are trying to tie his hands behind his back,' she explained excitedly.

'I wonder what will happen to him, what they will do with him?' wondered Girija out loud and then proceeded to apparently ask the same question of the De Danann warrior. He gave a quick glance in her direction but kept all his concentration on the buffalo and gave her a short answer which she translated.

'Ailill says, once the restraints are secure the beast should re-enter its realm aware that he is defeated but spared,' said Girija, who moved and stood next to her other-worldly friend.

'Did you notice that Nisha is nowhere to be seen?' Jack whispered to Kate. He had begun to feel himself become normal but he never took his eyes off the man buffalo who was frothing at the mouth much more than before; it flinched and recoiled against his invisible restraints and Jack could feel the piercing look he gave him, the eyes never straying from him. Jack didn't have the stomach to stare the beast down; he was overwhelmed by the very sight of it and as he moved his frightened eyes away from the expressionless huge dark globes he couldn't help notice the tip of one of his horns was stained with his own blood.

'They've got him under control now', informed Kate and with that the beast disappeared.

'I can't see him…' Jack said anxiously.

'I can, they are marching him off through the walls, through the kennels, through the outer wall and, no… they have left,' explained Kate.

Her reassurance did not convince Jack who stole along the corridor past the dark room and out into the light. The others followed him, Girija in deep conversation with the warrior.

'Ailill advises strongly that you should apply certain herbs to your wound Jack. You did not get it from a mortal being so it must be treated in a different way. The herbs grow in the garden and Ailill will show them to Kate,' Girija instructed.

Kate took the short-cut to the front door, between the library and the closed wing, through the little sitting room and into the front hall. Girija and Jack followed into the front hall and watched Kate speak and indicate to what seemed to them thin air, the warrior having disappeared for those who were normally sighted.

'He saved us again,' said Jack; it was his way of saying thanks to someone who was going to take away his cousin. Girija just smiled.

'Why can't you be happy with this much of him?' continued Jack.

'Oh Jack… I just want to be with him all the time and…' she trailed off, happy not to discuss it as Kate came in with a handful of leaves and locked the front door.

'We have to find Matt.' Suddenly Jack was panicked.

'I know where he is,' said Kate. 'But where is Nisha?' she asked, looking at Girija.

'Probably hiding in the bathroom,' replied Girija with a twinkle in her eyes. 'I'll take her out of her misery.'

'Where's the first aid box?' enquired Kate.

'It doesn't exist,' replied Girija who went to the nearby linen cupboard, took out a crumpled up mundu and tore long strips off it. She then went to the little study at the front of the house and procured a pin from the drawer in Grandmother's sewing machine, placed them in Kate's other hand and told her to soak the bloodied towel in a bucket of water and leave it in one of the girls' bathrooms for the dhobi to collect and there would be no more questions. Knowing looks were exchanged all round and Jack began to climb the stairs; he was more worried about Matty's state of mind than anything else.

HIDE HOLE

 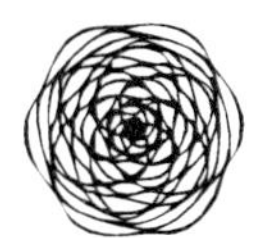

ONCE INSIDE THE big bedroom Kate tossed the herbs and bandages on the bed and marched purposely into the dressing room. Jack followed bemused, hand still clutching the towel to the soreness in his side. Although the flow had been staunched it still bled a little when he took away the bloody towel. He prided himself at knowing every nook and cranny of Nani Bhavan and this mystified him. Kate removed the top section of the built-in shelves and knocked on the wall behind them. That was nothing new to Jack: he had discovered those came out ages ago and there was no room behind them except to hide something like papers.

Jack felt tiredness wash over him; he realised he was still shaken and had to slump against the wall separating the dressing room from the bathroom to hold himself together and eventually just slid on to the floor and waited while Kate knocked on various shelves on the lower part of the bookcase and waited. It became obvious to Jack that Kate herself did not know precisely where Matty had hid himself; he must have told her about the hide hole. Matty never ceased to amaze Jack in pleasant ways but with Kate failing to find him Jack became even more edgy and the soreness in his side seemed to sting.

Kate had been on her knees knocking and listening for some minutes, she then sat back on her heels giving Jack a worried look. Then:

'Aoife,' she said, quite loud, and after waiting for a little while repeated it.

There came three regular muffled taps from deep inside the wall behind the lower bookcase. Kate repeated the taps and called out the name again and with that the entire lower section of the bookshelves swung open to reveal Matty, head on his knees absolutely and completely taking up the entire space within.

'I don't think I can get out of here,' he said, sounding choked, 'I'm completely numb.'

'Don't worry Matt.' Kate had landed on her behind to avoid the bookshelves as they swung free.

'Move the foot nearest me, bit by bit,' she instructed as she knelt and assisted the numb foot within her reach.

Within a minute or two the cobweb- and concrete dust-covered Matty had been extricated from the hide hole.

'You didn't know where the hole was, did you?' asked Jack.

'Nope, but I do now,' said Kate, gleefully beaming at Matty.

'What's all that blood…?' asked Matty, fright making its reappearance. 'Did it get you?'

No, no, nothing got me… I cut myself with one of Grandmother's prayer lamps, or rather Kate did,' said Jack, looking at Kate who was examining the hinged bookshelves. She opened and closed them and then failed to open them again.

'I did?' she asked.

'Remember, in the place beyond the dark room… where we had a sword fight with the two lamps…' Jack struggled to invent credible lies and more lies.

'Oh yeah, we'd better get you fixed up; remember, Matty not a word to your mother,' Kate reminded Matty, 'Jack will be in trouble again, remember the monkey bite and all the fuss…'

'Lie down on the bed Jack,' instructed Kate and she began to undo Jack's shirt.

'I can do that…' he brushed her hands away.

'Ouch, ouch… you're not telling me the truth are you?' demanded Matty.

'We are Matt, I think what you saw was the shadow of one of the cows… one of them got out of the cow shed this afternoon,' lied Jack, again.

While Jack was lying Kate was busy placing the leaves all along Jack's wound which had clotted; there was oozing here and there when Jack twisted himself upright so that she could secure the bandage around his chest.

'You have to put Dettol,' insist Matty.

'Not on this wound,' said Kate firmly.

'Why not? Mum always cleans the bugs away with Dettol first,' persisted Matty.

'Matt if you will stop talking for a little while I will tell you a story about an elderly couple called Macha and Magh who live only a mile away from me at home, I'll take you there next time you come to Ireland,' said Kate as she wrapped the cloth on top of the leaves, instructing Jack to keep his hand on the wound. With the leaves in place, she wound the strips of fine cotton all around his chest.

'I'm not a child, you know…' stated Matty confrontationally.

'So… I never said you were, did I?' replied Kate defensively.

'Why are you not doing Jack's cut properly then…. and what's it got to do with your story anyway?' demanded Matty, unable to resist a story under any circumstances.

'The strange thing about Macha and Magh is that they have been old for hundreds of years, they still live in a thatched, tiny cottage, actually they are quite tiny themselves, shorter than me even though they are grown-ups,' she said, placing the pin in the bandage.

'Tell him Jack, you've seen them, you know the Rhubarb People,' she said to Jack.

'Oh yeah, they really exist Matt, it's where we get the rhubarb for Mum,' reminded Jack.

'Uch, I hate rhubarb,' replied Matty, but he was hooked.

'You'll have to get a clean shirt and wash the blood off your hand… give me the soiled one and I'll soak it with the towel,' Kate said to Jack.

'Jack's cut and the old couple… I'm waiting for the connection, Kate,' Matty tapped one dusty foot on the floor, arms folded across his chest and with an expression which accused Kate of prevaricating, and of course she was but not on the subject of Macha and Magh and the healing of a wound but of how the wound had been inflicted in the first place.

'Oh yes Matt I'm sorry… Macha and Magh are actually faerie folk,' she continued.

'Leprechauns?' asked Matty.

'No, a different type, you'd really have to see them to understand. Magh has pointed ears, she keeps the tips hidden by her long hair which she wears in a bun and Mach has the strangest green eyes you'd ever seen. I got to know them when I had to buy rhubarb for Gran, they grow the very best rhubarb every spring. Now I visit them all the time and that's how I learned about herbal remedies. The leaves which I put on Jack's cut will give off juices which will not only kill bugs but heal the skin as well.'

ALTAR FOR A GODDESS

EVERYONE STAYED IN their rooms for the rest of that afternoon. Jack actually slept for a while and when he woke Matty was no longer with him. His wound hardly hurt when he bent to get up; he checked his shirt in the tall mirror of the dressing table and there was no sign of oozing.

Downstairs was a hive of activity. His mother had on a sari, a habit she had begun since moving into Nani Bhavan. At visiting time most evenings some of the relatives and Grandfather's acquaintances came to enquire about Grandmother. She had been given the official line which was not a problem with relatives who could speak English but she didn't even try out her Malayalam on people who didn't. Once when Jack's mother tried to stop the sweeper causing the dust to fly all about she called out 'Dust, dust' in Malayalam but it sounded like 'Go, go' and the cleaner duly left. Only one of the drivers and the people who worked with her for a while understood her and so she lost confidence and had been relying on Jack since he was five years old. This in turn caused everyone concerned to become distracted from the point of conversation as they smiled and oohed over the small boy translating for his mother and they would continue to ask him personal questions, not only to test his Malayalam but to find out how the strange mixed family actually functioned. Jack felt it was his mother's pronunciation that was the problem because she did have a fairly good vocabulary. Girija or he needed to be at hand to translate and make everyone feel comfortable during the time they spent at Nani Bhavan.

That evening, however, his mother was standing in the long corridor directing Babu, who had high school English, to replace all the steel and silver. Jack crept cautiously towards the dining room door in an effort to make contact with the girls who he could hear chatting in the dining room so that their stories of the scattered steel would tally. Once in, he noticed that Matty was having milk while the others sipped their teas and to his relief the atmosphere was light and cheerful.

Nisha was in a good mood too, she was very slowly eating a bread-type bun stuffed with a creamy mixture as if it was forbidden; all the while checking to see who was watching her despite the fact that there were plenty of buns.

'I see the books are still in the middle hall,' announced Jack's mother, appearing in the doorway. 'Can you all try to do a little more this evening and Kate and Girija will finish tomorrow while you three are at school?'

'I've finished the comics and that's all someone my age should be asked to do,' announced Matty. This was followed by loads of teasing from the girls; their giggles and questions annoyed Matty who left, narrowly avoiding a collision with Babu and another bearer who passed by with a mattress heading in the direction of the closed wing.

'I'm locking up now. Matty, have you left anything in the dark room? Your bag is just thrown on the floor here,' their mother said as she pointed towards the end of the long corridor.

'And Matty, will you take your bath early, you're covered in dust, were you poking around in the outhouses again? You don't need me to remind you about snakes...' his mother continued on.

'I only fell over the steel things...' said Matty as he doubled back to fetch his bag, skirting by his mother sheepishly.

'Well you didn't get all that dust from this floor...' and she gave up as Jack identified with her; she knew it was fruitless to pursue Matty for something he didn't want to reveal.

With both of them out of the way Jack quietly addressed Nisha.

'Nisha, replace the pooja things in the room beyond the dark room,' said Jack, mandatory was how he wanted the words to emerge but the statement was not nearly as firm as he had intended.

'I don't know what you are talking about,' she said curtly in Malayalam and stood up to wash her hands.

'Nisha, we know you've hidden Mummy's... things... somewhere, please put them back, Jack could have been killed this afternoon,' Girija too stood up and approached Nisha who had rinsed her hand and began to leave.

'You're a murderess... a destroyer...' Jack had stood up and blocked Nisha's path out of the room. He was so angry with her he didn't realise he had actually left his seat.

'Move,' was all she said to him in Malayalam, her eyes dark orbs of steel.

'Fine Nisha, you live with the consequences then...' said Girija.

'By protecting her you are just as responsible for killing Grandmother as she is,' accused Jack with as much venom as he could muster, hoping the words came out poisonous.

'Grandmother is dying of cancer,' said Nisha defiantly as she turned her head and looked out the window.

'She's being helped and you know it,' he accused her.

'Did you know that you are another one of my mother's misfortunes?' She spoke quietly, looking Jack straight in the eyes after a short pause. 'And you too, Chechi, another one of her misfortunes.' She turned to face Girija,

'Mummy asks the Goddess of Misfortune to remove all her misfortunes…' she turned to face Jack again. 'One by one,' she paused. 'There is no murderer, Jyestha is the sister of the beautiful Goddess Laxmi who you are so fond of Jack, but when the older sister acts the younger one will do as she is told so forget about your yantras to Laxmi, she will do what she is told by her big sister Jyestha and it is the same with my mother and your father, my mother is the eldest and his time here is finished, we are homeless and she needs her home back. So get out or your mother will go the same way as Grandmother.'

'So you admit your mother is the cause of Grandmother's cancer,' Jack whispered, half-spat as he pressed her while she was in the dizzy display of her power.

'Replacing Jyestha's idol will not save you or your family, stupid,' she fought back.

'No, oh no, she uses the village Goddess for that, doesn't she?' Jack and Nisha were nose to nose.

'That's a lie,' whispered Nisha and withdrew a little from her proximity with Jack.

'I have proof,' said Jack, almost carried away with anger.

'You spend too much time hanging around with the drivers,' Nisha half-sneered.

'I don't depend on drivers for gossip like you and your mother does…' Jack was desperate to protect Vishu.

'Ask her which temple she visits… if you don't get an answer ask Aunt Abja, she takes her along as a decoy and probably for advice too. After all, she had her brother killed so that she could take over her father's business,' Jack said, the electricity frantically circulating in his brain in an effort to convince Nisha without implicating too many people.

'Liar, that's a rumour started by your father because he doesn't like Abja,' she accused and tried to get past Jack who stood firmly in her path.

'Well why did Uncle die then and where are his wife and son? Gone, banished without a rupee and, worse still, filthy rumours about Aunty's morals…' shot back Jack.

'Shut up, shut up,' spat Nisha, putting her hands on her ears.

'You've seen your mother's strength… that night in the garden, she almost killed your sister, she had a blade at her throat more than once…' Jack said, reaching out and grabbing Nisha's arms and pulling them away from her ears but she cut him off mid-sentence.

'That sister had a gun to my mother's head only weeks before and she pulled the trigger, my mother spared Girija,' replied Nisha triumphantly.

'She didn't spare her... she was a mad thing, intoxicated with a supremacy, she felt she could do what she liked, including taking life... think, Nisha... just think, can't you...? Praying to the statue of Jyestha didn't get her those powers... no she has been busying herself with blood sacrifice and if you don't believe me go to the village temple with her when she gets back from Madras, go on... see if she will take you... I can guarantee she will not.' Jack was stopped again.

'Hey, what's going on here?' It was Jack's mother.

'Nisha refused to help stack the books in the library,' said Jack, quickly taking a deep breath and managing to get some control. He was shaking but no longer fazed when his mother popped up where she was unwanted; he had had more alarming intrusions to cope with.

'Maybe you could take charge of the Hindi books Nisha... and everyone else can take a subject...' said Jack's mother who trailed off as Nisha strode out of the dining room, ignoring her.

'Jack I hope you have not been bossing her around too much, have you?' she questioned Jack who had sat down again.

'No, and I have witnesses,' Jack replied, exasperated at Nisha, indicating his hand towards Girija and Kate, trying to control his breathlessness.

'She is difficult,' Girija said.

'She seemed in good form in Madras,' remarked Jack's mother as she poured herself a beaker of tea from the flask.

'She hasn't bathed for days, doesn't listen to a word I say,' said Girija. 'My new strategy is to not say anything about a bath and maybe she'll just have one.'

'She keeps apologising for the armpit smell, "Oh don't come near me I haven't taken my bath," she says,' said Kate. 'Wouldn't it be easier to just take a shower and not have to apologise about the smell all the time?'

'It's hard on her having to adjust to life here, I suppose,' remarked Jack's mother, pulling out a chair and sitting down.

'Kate why don't you and I do a bit in the library?' suggested Girija, and with that the girls left.

'All ready for school tomorrow, any study to do?' asked Jack's mother.

Study was the furthest thing from Jack's mind.

NOCTURNAL NOISE

MATTY WAS A sleepwalker. Jack never got used to being woken by another presence at his bedside. The sleeping Matty always stood in the same spot beside Jack's bed at all hours of the night but mostly when it was darkest; and he always sought Jack out in his sleep and nobody else.

That night when everyone was getting ready for bed Jack found his younger brother standing in front of one of the large windows of their bedroom. His mother had warned that Matty was not to be woken but guided back to bed, but that particular night it was impossible to guide Matty anywhere. He was asleep but his eyes stared wide open, not seeing the mango leaves through the bedroom window. Jack thought it better to inform his mother and she took Matty by the hand and slowly coaxed him to move a little and finally got him into bed in the air-conditioned room where she could keep an eye on him.

'Where was he today?' she whispered to Jack. 'He was covered in dust.'

'I've no idea,' Jack lied. 'You know how he likes exploring on his own… you better take his bag…' Jack urged and handed her Matty's bag which he had brought with him from the big bedroom.

Jack didn't need to read, he was exhausted emotionally and physically and fell asleep almost immediately. Sometime later he was disturbed by faint noises of movement on the stairs and the opening and closing of doors. When he opened his bedroom door the light from the room at the bottom of the stairs illuminated the lower part of it and exaggerated the darkness above. Jack quickly crept down to find his mother, torch in hand, who had her back to him standing in the doorway leading to the long corridor. Kate was at her side.

'It's probably haunted,' Kate was saying quietly.

'Don't say that Kate, you'll frighten the younger ones,' said Jack's mother.

'Mum, what are you doing down here?' whispered Jack when he joined aunt and niece.

'I came to get Matty some cocoa, he's having a terrible night, nightmares one after another, all about a Minotaur. I think he's delving too deeply into history for his age… I will censor what he reads in future,' she said, more to herself than to the others.

'Minotaur,' repeated Jack.

'Yes, watch out for the Minotaur or mind the Minotaur, all while he's fast asleep. Like I said, I'm thinking of waking him and giving him something to drink…' She trailed off and started towards the dining room.

There followed two loud bangs on the black door leading into the closed wing at the end of the corridor.

'There it is again,' said Jack's mother and she came out into the corridor. 'Do you think there is someone locked in there? Perhaps someone got in while we had it open…' She stopped talking as there was another wallop of something so hard on the door it made it vibrate.

'If there is, Mum, it's better they stay in there till morning,' Jack quickly offered and glanced at Kate.

'He's right, Aunt Elizabeth, the two watchmen are too old to actually restrain that intruder,' added Kate.

'He will break down the door if this goes on much longer,' said Jack's mother. She switched on the light in the corridor and stood watching the black door ,waiting for another thump.

'Maybe I should phone Inspector Arun,' said Jack's mother to herself and went to the desk in the large sitting room in search of the phone directory, switching lights on as she went. At that point Girija and Nisha appeared sleepy-eyed from their room.

'What's the matter?' asked Girija.

'Mum heard noises… well we heard noise from the dark room,' Jack explained, keeping his eyes steady on Girija's to convey the real meaning he hoped to convey. There was a loud bovine bawl followed by several hammering sounds on the door, again followed by screams from the lower part of the letter E which made up Nani Bhavan. Jack's mother joined the little group again, phone directory in hand.

'That'll be the kitchen girls, they'll be terrified,' she said. 'Girija, take the keys and let them into the main house, tell them to bring the straw mats with them, they can sleep upstairs,' and then, 'is one of the cows loose, did anyone hear that awful bawl?'

Girija looked at Kate, Kate looked at Jack and both girls disappeared in the direction of the kitchen.

'Did I hear a cow bawl from inside the house?' Jack's mother asked, perplexed.

'No, did you hear a cow, Nisha?' asked Jack.

Nisha did not answer, instead shrunk back against the wall.

'Nisha, can you find Inspector Arun's phone number in here for me? Some of it is in Malayalam,' Jack's mother said to Nisha who was shaking so visibly that she was unable to turn the pages properly. 'Come with me Nisha, we can sit down to do it.'

While they were bent over the little black phone directory in the sitting room Jack began to make plans for a barricade if the black door gave. He thought he would bolt the double doors leading to the long corridor but even though they were solid panelled doors they were not as strong as the black door which was being pounded. He thought he would place the great-grandfather's bed in front of the door and maybe pull the heavy wooden desk with the TV on it in front of that, all the while hoping that Girija and Kate were calling in the Danavas. The two girls from the kitchen passed him quietly and quickly disappearing upstairs, straw mats rolled around their pillows and sheets which were hastily enclosed hanging out of the rolls. He was somewhat assured when Girija and Kate did not return immediately.

He turned around to find Nisha peering at him from the sitting room; his mother was already dialling.

'Why couldn't you have just replaced the altar?' he rebuked in a hissed whisper.

She said nothing, only retreated into the sitting room again where Jack's mother had managed to wake up the policeman and was apologising and repeating her story of the noise for the third time in very slow simple English, minimising her Irish accent as much as she could, her voice growing louder with each repetition.

'Nisha, get the front door key and call the watchmen and tell them to let Inspector Arun's car in when he comes,' she said to Nisha finally.

'Where are the girls?' Jack's mother asked when she joined him.

'They are probably having a look round down there. I'll go and fetch them, you stay here,' he said.

RED HERRING

JACK FOLLOWED THE corridor down by the dining room towards the one leading to the kitchen. In the big kitchen he found Kate and Girija and the De Danann warrior.

'Will he be able to subdue the buffalo?' Jack launched into the conversation taking place in pigeon Sanskrit and Gaelic.

'Not on his own, it will take a little time to get help,' replied Girija urgently and tried to continue her conversation.

'Mum has called inspector Arun,' Jack said interrupting again.

'That peacock,' said Girija, shaking her head. A look of worry took hold of her face.

'It's alright,' said Kate. 'When he comes hopefully we'll be rid of the Buffalo man.'

'How will we explain the noise?' asked Jack who jolted a little, still not used to the De Danann dematerialising in front of his eyes.

'Would you rather explain the beast?' asked Kate, alarmed at Jack and then as if she wanted to mitigate her explosive reaction she added with a wry smile, 'I've already told your Mum the place is haunted.'

'We had better go back,' urged Jack who did not see any comedy in the situation they were in; instinct kept him on high alert. 'Mum is worried about you two poking around down here in the dark, she still thinks a thief may have got locked in the house and has reminded me that thieves usually work in gangs.'

'Let's go,' said Girija.

'Why is the warrior dressed as a Danava?' asked Jack.

'He's been accepted by them and is staying to protect us,' replied Kate.

'Protecting his girlfriend, more like,' said Jack sarcastically, looking at Girija.

'Protecting all of us Jack,' said Girija sharply. 'Remember you are a child of the Goddess Dana too. Kate has the Tuatha dé Danann, I have the Danavas, but you… your situation is unique: you have the beings of two cultures watching over you,' and with that she swept past him in the direction of the corridor.

'You asked for that,' whispered Kate as she followed Girija.

All was quiet when they entered the long corridor again. Nisha and Jack's mother were in the big sitting room having a quiet conversation: mostly disjointed sentences came from Jack's mother with what sounded like monosyllabic barely audible sounds from Nisha which emanated through the open architecture of the walls.

'Will I check on Matty?' asked Jack who stepped into the room below stairs partly to let his mother know they were back and partly to see if Matty was asleep and that nothing from the underworld had materialised elsewhere in the house.

'No, we've just been up and he seems more settled, we're waiting here for Inspector Arun' she said.

'Ailill is in there,' whispered Girija as she moved further along the corridor in the direction of the dark door.

'Chechi, don't go too near, what if it starts head butting the door again?' warned Jack.

Scuffle sounds were perceptible in the quiet hallway, not unlike those Jack remembered hearing from outside another door, the bathroom door in the Little Pink House when his father tried to kill a snake. These were audible halfway along the corridor and Jack found himself advancing on the black door together with Kate and Girija.

'Can you see anything Kate?' asked Girija.

Kate stood still and Jack watched her adjust her sight; Swami had explained that she used the rods rather than the cones in her eyes after he watched her scan the garden at the Little Pink House. Kate took a little while to do that while Girija scraped the nail of her left thumb across her bottom front teeth, her face tense and anxious.

'Ailill is in there… still alone, he has his blade unsheathed and his buckler in a protective position but the beast is just snorting while Ailill seems to be trying to communicate with it,' replied Kate.

There were sounds from the front, the sound of the large bolt on the gates being drawn back.

'Arun is here,' said Girija, alarmed.

'I'll try to delay him… you two be careful…' ordered Jack and he left the girls and began running.

In the few seconds it took for him to reach the front hall he noticed that not only one set of headlights beamed around the drive but a second set, slightly higher, followed. His mother had unlocked the front door and Inspector Arun emerged from his car in uniform and placed his khaki police cap on his head. The vehicle behind was a police Jeep with four uniformed police men in it: they dismounted, saluted and followed him up the steps and into the hallway.

Jack's mother began a description of the night's events but was ignored while the inspector sweet-talked Nisha in Malayalam, holding her chin in his hand. Jack knew his mother didn't understand a word of this and anyway it was all a lot of silliness about Nisha being naughty, more appropriate for a four-year-old but Jack let it go on as a delaying tactic. Nisha, who had to play along in any situation for her entire life as she never could be sure of an outcome, didn't try to escape either; she just smiled when appropriate and she pulled herself together sufficiently and responded economically with a word here and there, head down, dark eyes rolling from side to side.

'Why so down… no smile…?' the Inspector went on in Malayalam.

When Inspector Arun felt he had sufficiently taken control not only of his uncle's front hall but of the entire household, he turned to his men for their diligent grins and endorsements.

'I'm beginning to wonder why I called this fellow,' said Jack's mother quietly as she made her way past the throng of policemen towards the sitting room.

'He's an idiot Mum, ignore him, he's just showing off as usual,' Jack whispered quickly and very quietly.

'You have a problem?' Inspector Arun finally addressed Jack's mother as she was about to leave.

'I wouldn't say it's a problem,' she replied. Jack knew she was in a contrary mood; the Inspector had earned it.

'But you telephoned me, no?' Inspector Arun was becoming a little uneasy as he glanced over his shoulder for reassurance again from his men, Jack thought, perhaps to show he had troubled himself to not only come but brought a strong backup.

'Yes, yes I did,' she paused. Jack enjoyed this so much he forgot about the buffalo man for a short while. He was often a victim of her persistent mood when he was being evasive in order to cover up his own frequent misdemeanours.

'Why did you telephone me?' he asked again, a look of puzzlement descending over his face and Jack could see his mother had regained control.

'As I told you… many times… and I shall repeat it once again, for you… we heard a noise from one of the bathrooms.' All this was spoken in calm and very slow English so that even if the other officers had high school English they would be able to understand.

'Show me, show me,' instructed the busy, important Inspector Arun who had raised his hand in the direction of the sitting room; but, Jack noted, he was duly flustered. Just as Jack needed another delaying tactic, Girija and Kate appeared at the far door of the sitting room.

'You girls afraid of the noises too?' the Inspector greeted and questioned them, having regained some control. The girls did not answer but stood aside so they would not impede his march and let him through into the room with the ornate great-grandfather's bed.

Once the throng had passed, Kate and Girija smiled at Jack and he knew all was clear, but by that time the inspector had disappeared into the bedroom Girija shared with Nisha. Everyone else stood still in the room below stairs and waited with looks of bewilderment. Jack exchanged a glance with his mother who was still enjoying herself.

'There is no one in that bathroom,' announced the Inspector triumphantly.

'I should hope not,' replied Jack's mother, purposely looking puzzled.

'But why do you call me?' he asked.

'Because of the pounding on the door… Sorry, the noise on the door,' she replied.

Jack watched Girija and Kate elbow each other and grin.

The Inspector took a look back into the bedroom in the direction of the toilet door.

'Noise, on that door?' he asked, confused.

'No, noise on *that* door,' replied Jack's mother and pointed in the direction of the door leading into the closed wing.

The Inspector and his men strode down the corridor towards the black door. Jack's mother collected a bunch of keys from the cupboard and followed them.

'It is locked,' he said.

'Here is the key,' she said singling out the small key which opened the old door.

'There is another way in?' he asked.

'Yes. Jack, will you bring the other key ring and open the bedroom door?' she asked.

Jack, now light-hearted with the thought of the beast well and truly out of the dark room, opened the door leading into the passage between the library and the closed bedroom. He switched on the lights, opened the bedroom for two of the policemen and let them in, explaining in Malayalam that the lights did not work well and offered them the torch which he had collected with the keys.

After a minute or two while the three girls, Jack and his mother waited in the long hallway watching the beams of light from the torches flash in all directions in the closed wing, the heroic Inspector emerged from the black door followed by his men who had caught up with him through the warren of passageways that made up the top part of the capital letter E of the building.

'There is nobody in there,' he announced and then, 'only you heard the noise?' it was a question and the Inspector directed it at Jack's mother. A knowing smile had formed beneath his whiskers.

'We all heard the noise,' replied Jack resolutely, for he knew this man did not like his father's return from Europe and his control of favours for the free-loaders of the family, and his dislike included his mother and himself. Jack turned to the girls and both Girija and Kate nodded their heads. Nisha just stood stunted behind them.

'There is no way in and no way out,' said the Inspector, striving to convince everyone that nothing could have happened.

'There was also a sound of bawling, like a bull, much stronger than the cows… and it came from in there…' continued Jack's mother.

'That's the solution… you heard the cows… open this door,' commanded the Inspector.

'It's on the ring you have, Jack,' said his mother.

Jack found the right key on the third attempt.

'You don't know which key…' said the Inspector, smiling and nodding. Jack felt he was jeering and ignored the slight, glad his mother let it pass too.

When the doors to the backyard had been opened wide the Inspector, shoulders high, strode out into the space between the dining room and the closed wing followed by his men, all following his gaze, looking right and left into the shadows cast by the veranda and the house in the starlight and further into the clear spaces where the coconut trees cast their shadows.

All the teenagers exchanged relieved glances while Jack's mother busied herself locking up the unused wing again. She did all that without going in to have a look around, Jack noted.

'I think you might be right,' she whispered to Kate when she was finished.

'That's the only explanation I can make for it,' Kate replied.

The cows were found to be in the cow shed, tied with no evidence of having had a walkabout; all this was reported when the police returned after six or seven minutes. The Inspector was sincerely thanked and left quickly, the entourage departing at speed around the drive, underneath the car porch protruding from the bungalow and finally headlamps beaming as the vehicles dramatically sped through the open gates.

Jack began to switch off the lights and one by one everyone left on their way to bed for a second time that night. Last of all he bolted the door leading to the long corridor. He was surprised to find Nisha had not joined Girija in their room; he gave her a baleful look.

'The altar will be replaced tomorrow morning,' she said in Malayalam and with that she slipped into the bedroom.

REALISATION

THE FOLLOWING FEW weeks were the worst Jack could remember ever experiencing in his life. Grandmother was brought home; she was weak after the operation which his mother referred to an 'open and close', meaning the diagnosis was confirmed and there was nothing that could be done. But there was something more: Grandmother was somehow not herself, she was as if she was far away in her mind, detached but she seemed happy and smiled and didn't appear to remember any of the visitors she had, once they had left. She got up for short periods to sit in the big sitting room but needed help from Nisha and Aunt Saroj to walk and she had lost her appetite completely.

Jack went over the difference he found in her character with his mother who said it was probably due to the medication the oncologist had given her, addictive-type medicines which would help her cope physically and mentally as she neared the end. Memories of exchanges Jack had with her over his childhood flashed off and on in his mind as he looked at the placid weak woman who was no longer Grandmother to him. He was so sorry for all the 'naughtiness' which so upset her, sorry for making her the victim of the teasing which made Grandfather laugh, sorry for breaking her beloved cuckoo clock when he was five and most of all he missed her calling him '*mone*'; her affectionate tone still rung in his ears.

At the same time he barely tolerated that anguish; Kate, he realised after about a week or so, had been drip-feeding him information which Girija wanted him to know. The drip-feed technique he considered afterwards was not to add to his torment, not too much at a time anyway. So one Saturday night after dinner at the Little Pink House, when he finally felt like a fool for not piecing all the information together earlier, he said to Kate in imperative tones, 'Meeting tonight in the little sitting room.'

Kate, who was curled up in one of the armchairs at the end of the dining room absorbed in Swami's ancient book, was economical in her reaction: she tilted her head slightly in his direction and allowed her eyes to communicate the fact that she was not to be ordered about but said 'Fine' after a short thoughtful pause in which she seemed to assess him.

Jack chose the little sitting room because it was a passageway between the hall and the large sitting room. One of its doors led into the big sitting room which had a doorway leading into Jack's parents' bedroom; the other door opened into the front hall of the Little Pink House which meant if Jack's mother went walkabout they could make their escape back to their rooms or hide behind the sofas in the big sitting room. It didn't matter which path she took even though she was more inclined to head out on to the back veranda and sit there. Jack covered all options to avoid a lecture on the importance of sleep and, more important than discovery, they could not be overheard in that location without first being alerted.

'So what's the plan?' Jack had decided on a direct approach to pre-empt any psychological niceties that Kate might introduce to make Girija's planned departure less devastating.

'The Residency Lake,' she replied after seating herself on the sofa beside him opposite the bay window with its open shutters.

Even though this shocked Jack to the very core he tried to bury any outward sign it had and looked away from her out through the metal decorations which made up the security of the bay window. It was as if something invisible but loaded with energy had just slammed into his chest.

'When?' Jack asked the darkness as his eyes became blind to his vision of the window.

'Next Friday night,' she whispered the reply.

'Why Friday?' was all that Jack could say as another terrible lump walloped into his chest and stayed there, heavy and debilitating.

Kate got up and sat in one of the armchairs opposite Jack, for he knew he had cut himself off from her. If he was really honest with himself he also knew she found their conversation as astounding as he did and she wanted to make contact: she seemed desperate to make contact with him.

'Oh I don't know.' She got up and paced in the small space of the little sitting room. 'Something to do with the moon and tides.' She sat down again opposite to his bent frame and looked him straight in the eyes.

'Don't you see Jack… she's trying to protect us by involving us…? Well, actually she wants us with her as well as the practicalities of working out alibis,' Kate explained.

'Why now… when Grandmother is so low…?' Jack said, ignoring the opening Kate had made to further their discussion on Girija's actual departure.

'She thinks she can help Grandmother pass over,' Kate said.

'How…? They are in two different dimensions,' asked Jack. All the while he wanted to say to himself: *Listen to what you are saying, do I really believe in these other invisible worlds? Kate can see them, even pass in and out of one of them and I can't believe that Grandmother will end up as nothing either, not every bit of her, her energy has to go somewhere…*

Kate had not bothered to answer him, seemingly prepared for his protestations and let him go on.

'It's easier for you Kate,' he said at last making eye contact. 'You can actually see other beings… it takes a lot of trust for me to even admit these other worlds exist.'

'Yeah, I know that,' she replied very quietly.

'I know you're struggling with it and it must be downright frightening at times but to be able to see Kate, actually see them, these beings… it is incredible,' Jack went on.

'It's a bit like seeing a ghost or a spirit, remember you almost saw your great-grandmother in the corridor, it's just that the light levels were right that night. A lot of people can do what I do and it's a pity everyone can't do it,' she said, looking down at her fingers as she wove them between each other. 'Maybe then the people would have a lot more respect for each other… I mean if they possessed their level of intelligence as well.'

'Or not; what about those who have base instincts? They would just hook up with the underworld and create anarchy,' countered Jack, the heaviness in his chest easing slightly.

'You have experienced for yourself the balance, the protection you had from the other world before we even asked for it… No, there is more good than bad, Jack,' she said very convincingly.

'I hope you are right for Girija's sake,' he said, giving her the opening she was so anxious to talk about.

'We had better talk about it Jack, make plans, protect ourselves for the police enquiry… there will be her body.' She looked again at the unwoven fingers which were tense and unyielding.

'Alright then, tell me what she wants us to do,' he said with a sigh.

'She asked for Swami to attend too, she felt we should have an adult witness in case something goes wrong,' explained Kate.

'She's thought of everything,' replied Jack morosely.

'You and I will have to go in disguise even though it will be midnight. We would attract too much attention as we are; someone might remember seeing us,' Kate continued, no longer trying to weave her fingers but thinking systematically.

'So I dress up in Ramesh's dhoti again…' said Jack heavily.

'No, a dark pair of trousers and a long sleeved shirt, then I don't have to mix too much of the tea dye, just feet, ankles, hands and wrists, neck and face. You will have to ride the watchman's bicycle, though,' she explained.

'Can't we walk?' he asked.

'Girija says no, a bicycle is much faster, anyone out and about would not have time to take much notice of us as we slip by into the darkness... By the way, do you think you can balance and ride with me sitting side-saddle?' she asked.

'Will the watchman's bicycle take both our weights? Mine is better...' Jack wondered.

'No, we can't take yours, it's too nice, too shiny... we're supposed to look like... the dhobi and his wife...' Kate interjected, frustration appearing.

'OK, OK... what about your hair, how are you going to disguise that?' Jack asked, realising he was involving himself actually committing himself to be part of this awful event.

'I'll wear my scarf over my head and shoulders and like you I'll just have to colour my feet, ankles, hands, wrists and face,' she said, touching her wrists without emotion and Jack realised she had heard the plan many times before.

'And Swami, where does he come in?' Jack asked.

'He will walk there and back, we meet him near the jetty,' Kate said quietly as Jack had once again slipped back into his former reservation.

'Whoever arrives first finds a hiding spot and must not show themselves until after some time when the next person arrives so that no one of us has been followed,' Kate went on.

'What actually happens to Girija... how will she pass over?' he asked after a while in silent night.

'Apparently she just lies down, concentrates her mind, her heart is supposed to stop and her breathing and Ailill will carry the body into the water; only then can she manifest in the other world.' Kate said all this slowly and quietly as if she wished she didn't have to express it.

'This is madness, how can you will your heart to stop...? It takes rishis years and years of meditation and training to even slow down their heart rate, how can Girija actually stop hers at will?' Jack was frustrated and annoyed and kept changing his position on the sofa.

'Don't ask me, I told you I've heard stories of bodies beside faerie mounds in Ireland, that's all I know,' Kate said defensively and later, with more composure, 'She gets her information from Ailill.'

'You see Kate, this is what really worries me. How do we know he has not hurried her decision by telling her she can help Grandmother?' asked Jack, intolerant. 'Well, how?'

'I really don't know Jack… to be very honest I wish she hadn't asked me to accompany her. Like you, I too have reservations about the whole theory, actually,' said Kate, head down as she tried to weave and unweave her tense fingers.

'Then let's tell her neither of us will help her,' Jack grasped at the only bit of weakness she had so far let him witness.

'She will do it anyway. She doesn't need us, she would like us to accompany her… I suppose it is like going to a funeral of a loved one… oh I really don't know, it's asking too much of us; sometimes, like you, I feel it is aiding and abetting suicide…' Kate got up with one hand on her forehead and such a sorrowful look on her face. 'I hate this.'

'It's just that I don't know where she is going exactly. You know what I mean, I can get back, have a normal life, only choose to switch it on and off that… that other world… Girija doesn't know where she is going, even if she will be accepted. They are dying out, you know.' She looked at Jack. 'The Tuatha dé Danann… Magh told me… maybe that is why he is so keen to take her… and who knows if she will even be accepted there, she's not a faerie, she's human, she'll always have those characteristics… Maybe when she has a baby she will be safe there…' Kate just stood there in the middle of a rug bathed in the gloom ,with the only light coming from a garden lamp; she too was lost.

'You are at last admitting what I always felt about this whole thing,' said Jack without recrimination. 'How do we know he has not cast a spell on Girija?' After a little while Jack asked, 'What's your role in this, will you be with the Tuatha dé Danann?'

'No, it's not possible for me to connect with them for now… I don't know how to and I don't want to… remember I inadvertently channelled him in the first place… and that's another thing Jack… I feel an enormous guilt… and responsibility for all of what is happening to Girija,' she said, sitting opposite him again, a look of absolute desperation on her face.

'Maybe he chose to come… like Girija said… we are all children of the Goddess Dana if you go back in our histories, however far removed we are now… maybe the disturbance my aunt created in the underworld inadvertently alerted the Danavas and the Tuatha dé Danann and when you asked for help he felt a compunction to maintain balance as Swami has pointed out.' Jack tried to provide rational comfort to his deeply troubled cousin.

'All I know is that Swami was right to caution us: look what happened when I tried to channel the Danavas… this De Danann warrior materialised… I'm really scared, Jack,' she said, head down.

'You'll have to consul Magh when you get home,' he said; 'be guided by her.'

'Yeah I know, I was thinking the same, Swami has been wonderful but his knowledge is limited by his very being,' she said, looking up.

She had been crying; large tears ran down her cheeks as she raised her head. He found himself continuing to console, implicating himself in a situation he knew nothing about and defying all practical knowledge.

'You mean, being human,' Jack confirmed.

'Yes,' she replied, still heavy with worry. She wiped her nose with the tail of her shirt and drew the back of her hand across her eyes to collect the moisture.

'Will the warrior take Girija to Ireland to a Sidhe?' asked Jack.

'No, they are celebrating with the Danavas where Girija will stay for a while… their customs are similar to the Tuatha dé Danann. Once out of this world they will follow linear ceremonial paths, supernatural highways if you like,' said Kate, 'You know he's wearing their clothes.'

'Tell me more about the paths,' said Jack inquisitively.

'From what I understand from Girija is that she must travel in a straight line as the Tuatha dé Danann do in Ireland when they travel from one Sidhe to another or one Rath to another, here it will be a fort and her first journey will be a ceremonial one… I asked Swami about these paths and he knew of earth stars here, grid-like geometry and he referred to them as earth star chakras,' explained Kate.

'There's so much more…' added Jack, but having little energy for the subject he stopped.

'I believe I will travel with her in a chariot to the Danava fort where I was taken that first night. Ailill has worked out how long it will take in human time for me to leave her and return as I must be back before sunrise,' Kate told him with similar emotional exhaustion, more as if she felt that he should know the procedure than anything else. She took a deep breath and let out an audible sigh.

'Will you eventually be able to contact her when you go back to Ireland?' Jack asked, not wanting to think that far ahead but needing to help Kate come to terms with what Girija wanted to do.

'I don't know; I will just wait and see what materialises for me when I get there,' she replied, still very unhappy.

'None of us know or can be sure of anything, even in this world,' replied Jack deep in thought, as he remembered Swami's prediction about himself and his family leaving. *That very feeling had been growing stronger and stronger of late and he couldn't say why. Was it because of everything that had happened since the Onam holidays last year? Maybe, like Grandmother and even Girija, he too had a journey to make. All of them on different paths with unknown destinations. Somehow it was beginning to feel right that he should accept the break from his past, from who he thought he was.*

'Why drowning?' asked Jack

'Well, it will not be a drowning… theoretically, she will have stopped breathing on the jetty… I gather,' came her bewildered answer.

'What if she just stays in Nani Bhavan… as she is… maybe we can ask her to postpone the… the… crossing over, does she have to die?' asked Jack.

'He can bring her with him, I think. Magh has spoken about this sort of thing… thinking back, I now feel she was warning me, perhaps she thought I would be taken by the faeries. I gather the body of the person disappears and occasionally when they want to re-emerge in our reality, this world, they appear weak like someone suffering from anorexia, thin and dying, until the body deteriorates and the heart stops. Jack, that sort of lingering thing is even worse…' Her voice sounded as if she was strangled inside.

'You know Kate,' Jack said, more at ease, 'about Girija, I think we should leave it, we have a week, let the whole thing of whether we attend or not just sink into our minds, let's not make a decision now, we'll wait till Wednesday or Thursday.'

'Yeah, OK,' replied Kate who got up and left the room slowly.

'Night,' she whispered softly as she turned into the middle hallway.

'Night,' replied Jack, still seated on the sofa looking blindly out the bay window.

FUNERAL ESCORT

THAT SAME WEEK Grandmother's ankles swelled and she became breathless; she could hardly talk and needed oxygen most of the time. Jack returned to the Little Pink House raging one evening after his regular visit which was the first thing he did after school. He paced up and down the dining room and accused his aunt of poison. It took a lot of quiet patience between his mother and Kate to explain to him that, yes, his aunt no longer gave his grandmother the medicine ordered by the oncologist and instead had a homoeopath who was trying to cure her.

'There is no explaining to them that this will not work at this stage,' Jack's mother repeated a second time.

'Well… why can't they give her the medicine she was given by the doctor in Madras…? She was happy, she wasn't aware of what was happening to her and now she… she's just suffering…' he finished quietly and flopped down defeated in one of the two armchairs.

'You know what has happened, Aunt Saroj has convinced Grandfather that Grandmother can be cured,' he continued, still frustrated. 'But instead she is just making her suffer and suffer…'

'Let's be fair Jack, what if she really believes that the homoeopath and his medicine can cure Grandmother?' said his mother.

'She doesn't want her cured Mum, she wants her out of the way, don't you see…?' and Jack stopped himself mid-outburst; he knew his mother couldn't see, she didn't know what Kate and he knew.

'Even with the oncologist's medicines your grandmother will still have the breathlessness, Jack,' Kate said, turning the conversation back to Grandmother; obviously she had realised that Jack had almost gone too far.

'But she would sleep most of the time and not feel the pain…' Jack just shook his head, defeated and frustrated by his powerlessness.

'Can you imagine how aggravated your father is?' asked Jack's mother and then continued: 'Jack, you have to learn to… to somehow… detach yourself, Grandfather is the only one who can make decisions for your grandmother. Yes, yes I know what you are going to say,' continued his mother as Jack opened his mouth to protest. 'I know how you want to protect her, relieve her suffering but there is nothing we can do, so try not to upset yourself so much.'

That visit was the catalyst that finally made Jack's mind up to accompany Girija. She would do what she wanted to do anyway; the fact that she brought the date forward so that she could help Grandmother made no difference to whether he disapproved or not.

So he began to plan the deed with Kate as meticulously as they had planned that first trip to the village temple in the car boot, except this time Kate would do the journey with Jack as far as the lake and the rest of the way she would go with Girija.

The watchman's bicycle was checked out for roadworthiness for two heavier passengers than its elderly owner. This was done while Ramesh was watering the plants elsewhere in the garden. Kate made sure she made her decoction of tea dye in the afternoons, before Matty returned from school, while his mother was sleeping and when the ayah had her shower. She checked Jack's cupboard for an old school shirt which was a bit yellowed and had the fold wrinkles in it. The only dark trousers he had were corduroys which he used in Ireland; they were too warm but they'd have to do. These she stored with a shirt and shalwar; she had chosen one she had used the most as it had faded a little in the wash over three months. All these she hid in her room ready for their funeral night – or rebirth, as Girija preferred to call it.

On Friday night they met in Kate's room at midnight, those two cousins with minds weighty and stomachs sickened with the task ahead. Jack changed in the bathroom and then they painted their hands and feet with the tea dye quickly and silently, all the while the revolting deed pressing down on their minds; and Jack could feel it across his shoulders too. Kate inspected the back of Jack's neck and his ears to make sure his colour was even. Once she had finished her own she secured a long scarf to her shoulders of her shirt with two pins, draping an inch of fabric over her forehead. From then on they would move silently until they reached the lake. Kate closed her bedroom door, glancing back at the body-shaped mound under the sheet and Jack nodded to indicate he had done the same in Matty's room.

It bothered Jack once again that he had to leave the kitchen door unlocked but Kate had assured him that the Danava watchers would prevent a thief from getting into the house and by the time night arrived he became reassured, remembering the tormented old man who tried to follow him from the village temple. They slipped out on to the veranda one at a time and one by one headed to the garage where the watchman was snoring loudly. Once there Jack took command of the bicycle and Kate took the keys from near the watchman's unconscious hand. She had a quick look at where she had placed the crystal; satisfied, she joined Jack as he quietly rolled the bicycle towards the gate. Jack noted that the dog was not to be seen; obviously she was at the back of the house inspecting the Danavas.

As they slipped out the gate having checked the street Jack glanced at the gates of his grandfather's house for any sign of Girija and Ailill but all was still. He waited in the little lane which separated the Little Pink House from its neighbour Kumari's where Matty and he had tuition while Kate locked the gate.

That little lane was a short-cut for the *maidan*, the open green square where they would be at their most vulnerable; it avoided the tea stall and the hospital on the main road which were always busy. The *maidan* was surrounded by houses which sat back from the roads on three sides and the residency wall was on the fourth.

Their first attempts to maintain two on the bicycle in the lane had little success; Kate had to keep jumping off the carrier as Jack wobbled, but that was a road without a surface and it was uneven with a raised area in the centre and two uneven tracks each side of it which were full of pot holes. So they decided to walk and were lucky: they met no one.

As the *maidan* came into view Jack half-whispered, half-signalled that Kate should try to jump on as he began to pedal. This they did once they got the bicycle onto an even surface. There was a lot of quivering and Kate later told Jack she hung on to the springs in the saddle with her fingers and just about stayed on the carrier on one hip.

There were several moments of anxiety when the headlights of a car came along the main road facing them; it was then that Jack realised he did not have a light and kept well to the side of the road, almost ejecting Kate off her insecure perch as the cycle tyres hit the tufts of dried grass and pebbles of the verge. He quickly compensated and veered into the centre of the road and increased speed once the car had passed. He was used to the drag made by the extra weight on the back by the time the Residency Wall loomed up in front of them.

They found themselves inside the grounds within minutes after that and dismounted as they were back on an unsurfaced drive. They continued to walk in silence quickly favouring the shaded side which skirted the lake. As the building came into sight round the drive Jack looked for a suitable place to hide the bicycle in the undergrowth. While he did this Kate stepped into the bushes out of sight but then Jack realised she was not used to snakes and hissed: 'Snakes.' She whispered loudly, 'Danavas.' So he understood they had company and the snakes would have left the neighbourhood.

From then on Jack followed Kate's lead as she appeared to be following someone or something; she half-turned in his direction and beckoned to him. Jack was still scanning the darkness near the Residency which was used as a government guest house for a watchman or even some of the bearers who may sleep on the veranda but then he considered that the other-worldly beings would have taken care of all that. This was a big night for them too.

When they arrived at the top of the steps leading down to the lake Jack saw Girija and Ailill standing together like young lovers in the moonlight. They stood as one, talking to Swami like a minister performing a marriage ceremony, Jack thought. The full moon was enormous that night, its light more gold than silvery and the glow from it was reflected in the water and caught some of the Zarry on Girija's sari. She sparkled and shimmered as she moved towards the bottom of the steps to greet him. The Danava warrior disappeared and Jack could see this had the same effect on Swami as it had on him.

As Jack began to descend the broad steps he had no idea what to say to her for he could tell she was radiating happiness. She waited at the bottom of the steps and Kate moved along the jetty to be with Swami. Girija held Jack's hand at first and then embraced him and said, 'Thank you little brother.' Jack felt this absolved him of any responsibility for her decision. As she released him she kept hold of his right hand and into the palm she placed a ring and whispered quietly, 'For your protection.' Jack dropped the ring into the pocket of his shirt without thought and followed her to where Swami and Kate stood by the edge of the jetty.

'I need to lie flat to be in my etheric me,' explained Kate and looked at Swami and Jack in turn.

Girija turned and bid Swami a goodbye nod and lay down beside Kate, much to Jack's astonishment: he really had no idea what to expect and Kate had omitted any explanations other than what they discussed the night they met in the little sitting room at the Little Pink House.

There they lay as the moon moved away on its nightly orbit. Jack couldn't remember which direction it went; it just seemed to disappear and they were left under the brightness of the stars, Swami and him seemingly alone which he knew was not true. Jack had no idea how long he stood looking down at Kate and Girija: it never dawned on him to see if they were breathing, he stood there half-stunned, waiting, but for what he did not know. Then the De Danann warrior came and as earlier he carried no armour and somehow Jack knew he was going to take her into the lake. His own reaction was quick and violent: it shocked him and it shocked Swami.

'No way!' Jack's words sounded as if they were annoyingly spat out.

Jack sat cross-legged beside the still Girija and Swami settled himself down on the jetty sitting on one hip beside Kate. A long time had passed and Jack began to feel cold and immediately Ailill appeared again. Jack shot up and said rather too firmly, 'No.'

After this Swami began to reason with Jack in his gentle, wise way. Jack couldn't respond to any of what he had to say. It just was not right and he had been over and over the arguments before.

VOTIVE OFFERING

THEY STOOD IN the semi-darkness with a luminescence in the eastern sky creeping in above the trees on the distant side of the lake: just Jack, a youth, and the old man in the still hour that was quickly giving way to dawn. Both heads were bent in silence as they stood there on the jetty, one at each side of the two bodies which lay motionless on the wooden planks. The water continued to lap against the supporting structure of the jetty, apparently ignorant of what was about to taken place.

Jack wanted to shout; he felt he would burst if everything just went back to being normal. How could the water come and go and the light come back after this night? How dare the water carry on ignoring the decision she had to make? It was as if nature pretended it didn't happen; carry on as if it didn't matter. He should have been able to prevent it. His cousin had decided to give up on mortal life. She should not have had to make that decision. He was sure she would not have if her circumstances were different.

'Let her go, son,' Swami quietly urged in softest Malayalam.

'It's not right, Swami,' Jack's reply was whispered and his eyes were full of tears.

'Son, she was nineteen, old enough to make the decision, you did your best to dissuade her... son, we have been over this and over it,' Swami's hands were open, again offering the same explanation.

'Is she a rose or a jasmine? Are we to offer her to the water? Float her out there on a leaf. How do we know for sure that she is not just that... Swami... a votive offering?' Jack had raised his voice and stared straight at Swami.

'She has only his word for that... and you know that they make water offerings, especially to lakes...' Jack continued, his troubled thoughts vocalised.

'Kate has confirmed a form of life in the other-world,' Swami offered quietly.

'But Chechi is going before her time... long before her time,' Jack protested, quieter now, eyes fixed on the still Girija and how he wanted her to wake up, just to have one more discussion with her about this.

'We don't know that son, I haven't been able to ascertain the time of her birth to calculate her horoscope…' Swami continued his composed rhetoric, even though Jack felt he was anything but: how could anyone accept what the young woman had done?

'Forget all that Swami… what does it matter whether she had a long or short life…? This is wrong…' He pointed down at Girija's body.

'Right or wrong, she has done it and you are left with the consequences….' Swami said firmly, looking straight at the distraught Jack and continued with firmer tactics:

'We can't reliably make judgments on things we do not know about or understand… this now, this minute, is our only real truth… our beliefs become mere philosophy if we lose our relationship with a divine… or in physics terms the orgone, the superluminal connectedness… the very thing we are trying to measure. Son, they are not of our time or our intelligence… I honestly think theirs is greater. We can only trust what she has done is right for her.' With this Swami turned his back and faced out to the lake. It appeared to Jack that he was also trying to make sense out of what Girija had chosen.

After some more minutes in the darkness he began to speak again in a hushed voice.

'What I advise is, next time he appears in mortal form let him take her, it is what she wanted,' Swami continued with his back to Jack and then he turned to face him.

'Bend down, son, and touch her and then compare the body with your other cousin's.'

Jack knelt down on the jetty and slowly reached to touch Girija's arm nearest to him. It was very cold and he looked at her face and realised it had lost its colour: she was so still and lifeless, no breath.

'She is very cold,' was all he could say.

'Now come over here son and feel Kate's skin,' instructed Swami with empathy.

Jack raised himself and walked slowly round to where Swami stood and slowly bent down again and reached out to touch Kate's hand, checking her face at the same time.

'She feels warm and her face is… not so… fixed…' he replied.

Jack walked around and stood by Girija again, feeling he should stand by her decision and stand sentry by her dead body.

'It's time to let her soul go free,' Swami joined Jack and reached up and placed a hand on Jack's shoulder.

Jack began to realise that the beings of the universal consciousness must have been witness to his misery as he tried desperately to come to terms with the two worlds.

'Fine,' was all he could reply to Swami.

Shortly there was the sound of a foot touching the wood of the jetty. They both looked up to find Ailill once again without his armour, waiting to collect his dead bride with an anxious look on his face, for Jack knew she would be trapped elsewhere if he did not allow her to be consigned to the lake. They acknowledged each other with an almost imperceptible bow, the bereft cousin and the bridegroom both identified with each other: a life-form who could be mortal, and Jack. Swami touched Jack's arm and stepped back away from Girija, giving Ailill room to move in close to the body. He knelt down and scooped up her corpse. Jack took a place beside Swami and once again made eye contact with the other-worldly being, which verified his decision to let Girija go.

They both watched as the solemn being walked along the jetty and onto the bank of the lake; the golden threads of Zarry on the fall of their grandmother's wedding sari trailed from underneath the being's right arm caught the early dawn light which caused it to shimmer. Both turned and faced the lake as the solemn being slowly walked into the water and proceeded towards its centre at a slow and steady pace and all the while the water advanced up his body. When Girija was no longer visible and the water had reached Ailill's chin he turned to face them and then slowly sank beneath the mirrored surface.

Jack looked up at the firmament; most of the stars had disappeared. The water lapped. They both sat down without a word of exchange, exhausted physically and mentally. In silence they sat beside Kate and waited for her. Peace reigned. After what seemed to be a long time Jack felt a new energy and found himself telling Swami of the story of his grandfather nearly drowning in the lake when he was a schoolboy. Swami just nodded.

When the sky was almost light and the sounds of music from the temples and the call to prayer from the mosque minarets were audible in the distance, Kate sat upright. She was animated but quickly adjusted to the feeling of loss on the jetty.

'She is with them then?' It was more of a confirmation than a question from Jack.

'Yes,' she replied, head bowed.

'Did I mess it up?' Jack asked.

'No,' was Kate's short, unreadable reply. 'She knows it was because you wanted to protect her…' Kate followed.

Jack was too tired to go into it any more. After sitting for a few more minutes Swami urged the teenagers to hurry home. As all three stepped off the jetty to ascend the steps of the Residency Lake, they turned to have one last look at the still water which had taken on a little ripple here and there out in the depths.

DEATH WATCH

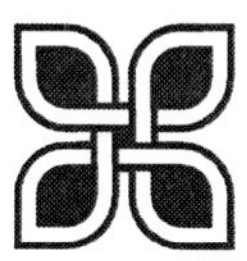
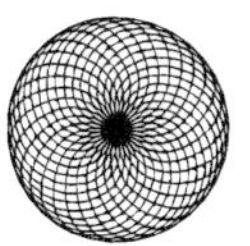

JACK AND KATE'S meticulous planning paid off. Even though they passed and met people walking in the early hours of that morning on the main road and more in the lane, where Jack did not give Kate time to dismount but plunged into the gravelly bits and compacted earth at full speed; even though he wobbled dangerously at first trying to balance by sticking out his knees, first one on the right and then to compensate the left one shot out, nobody had time to look at them. After replacing the bicycle and locking the kitchen door on the inside they both went to their individual rooms after Kate reminded Jack to hand over his shirt with the tea-stained ring around the collar which she thrust into a bucket of soapy water with other clothes, awaiting Radha's cleansing hands in an hour or two.

Neither of the teenagers rose early that day but Matty did and was attending his little herd of rabbits as it was a Saturday and they could spend the whole day on the lawn. Radha, well used to returning small items from Jack's top pocket, mostly well soaked two rupee notes, called Matty and indicated that she had found a ring in Jack's school uniform shirt. 'Thanks Radha,' said Matty and gave what looked like a silver ring a look over and because it was small and possibly valuable he placed it in the hidden compartment in his Crane Bag, namely a torn bit of the lining which gave Matty an extra safe pocket at the bottom of the canvas. It was to stay there for a very long time before it was needed again.

For the last week of Kate's stay in India Jack made the nightly journey between the Little Pink House and Nani Bhavan with his invisible protection. He still paid a visit after school as a red herring for the aunt. He held Grandmother's hand when nobody was looking and stroked it. Grandfather would come into the room; she was nursed in the aunt's room. Grandfather would look at her as she slept against the pillows with a nasal cannula bringing in the oxygen. He would turn and walk out again, hands behind his back, only to reappear five minutes later as if lost in his own world. He'd stand and stare at her as if he was waiting for her to open her eyelids but nothing ever happened. Words were never exchanged but Jack knew he was always looking for a sign that she would get better.

Jack himself could not believe his grandmother would, like Girija, disappear and not be with them. He was used to seeing Kate in her unconscious state laid out on his bed like a dead Ophelia. This pose was a sure indication that she had already left and met up with Girija for the healing and easing session with Grandmother. Jack would head to the kitchen and wait inside the kitchen door for a brief moment to check the garden stretched out before him. He was aware of the neighbour's house with his aunt's lackey who may peer from the shadows, perched on her kitchen table. He'd slip through the door on to the back veranda. He'd crouch low and slide under the chicks. He'd remain low when he passed by his parents' bedroom windows as they were open, reaching out for the cool night air. He'd hug the still warm bathroom wall as he surveyed the car shed in an effort to locate the night watchman. Every night the same schedule and even though he had been doing it forever it seemed he always resisted the temptation of rushing any part of it for fear of being caught and his freedom curtailed. He'd hoped the Devas had done their magic and lulled the elderly man into a deep sleep with their perfumed soporific orgone. Kate had found out how they did it: they skipped past the preparation which took place in their sleep temples. This nightly induced sleep was necessary for a short time only, so no fasting, no chanting, no meditation, just a mere orb of energy dispelled the magic slumber from the crystal in which they dwelled. They were strategically located near where the watchman placed his mat who found himself unable to resist his sleepiness.

Jack was very aware he was at his most exposed against the pink walls with no shadows or vegetation. He'd jump as he felt moist pressure on his fingers. It was always the Great Dane on her way from the back of the house where she would have sensed the activity of the Danavas and was probably more aware of them now than he was. She'd seem to pant at a quicker rate and she whined a bit as if she wanted to tell him something every night. She'd lick in the drool now and then with her tongue which lolled rhythmically with each pant. He'd caress her head and moved forward into the shadow of the fronds of a young coconut tree which were still at ground level. Jack would be able to see Ramesh from his hide, asleep on the plaited coconut mat and could even hear the loud snores from that safe position. He'd quickly cross the sandy space; the dog bounded happily (and thankfully silently) with him, every night as if she knew the drill. It always took him some time to find the ring with the key for the padlock on the gates, as he had to keep one eye on the large dog to discourage her from leaving a deposit of saliva slobber on the watchman's unconscious face as she always stood and looked down at him; she'd voice little whines that seemed more contented as the nightly activities continued.

Jack unlocked the gates and eased himself through a tiny opening as the dog at all times tried to insert herself between the gate and his thigh. He'd lock the gates again and wait in the shadow of one of the pillars before scurrying across the road in the direction of the gates of the main house which he noted were forever bathed entirely in moonlight, with not even a bit of shadow. Before he could bend to see the watchmen the keys jingled above his head and descended into his open palm and despite his nervousness he couldn't help smiling at what must appear to be magic. He visualised Kate in her etheric self – or could it have been Girija? More like one of the Devas, he thought, as he judged how the keys had such a controlled descent. He unlocked and locked the gate; both watchmen were stretched on the tiled walkway buttressed around the bungalow in deep sleep, Kate having placed the clear quartz crystals in the triangular waterlily pond which was built into the corner next to the walkway where the watchmen slept. Jack made a mental note to click the timer on for the length he was in the grounds so that they would not be questioned on missing puncture marks. And then again he considered if the aunt even checked the timer papers. She had become more relaxed as Grandmother sank and she carried out the running of the house. Grandfather, so distracted, never questioned any of the bills, but Jack's father was astounded by them.

There was plenty of cover in the big garden. Jack would skirt along by the boundary walls, pass the room that Girija so briefly used and even though he knew she was happy Kate had visited her only a couple of times, she was gone. It was still risky in the other world, Kate had been told, for she would still have to travel on horseback to the city she was forced to hide in that first night when she accompanied Jack to the village temple with the Danavas. When Kate enquired about the forces of evil, she had been told that the aunt was not calling on the underworld so frequently but the people of the Goddess Dana preferred to play safe and they kept a wary eye. They reluctantly accompanied Girija and her Tuatha dé Danann warrior on the first of their nightly ride across the plains to perform the healing with Usha the commander's daughter who Kate had stayed with. In fact, Girija and her warrior were their guests and Girija was learning about crystal healing. However, thereafter Usha was not permitted to travel with them so Girija and her warrior arrived on a very large strong mare every night, according to Kate, Girija clinging on to her lover as she adjusted to riding. Kate took a little time each night and reported back to Jack on Girija's life in the other world; he was overcome with sadness that she had gone from human contact.

The fact that the next set of rooms was where the sick room was didn't help.

Jack hated seeing his grandmother swollen and breathless, unable to talk, only nod or point. When he'd arrive at her window there was always quiet activity inside; the girls were already ahead of him making her comfortable. What he saw those nights looked like magic but it didn't bring a knowing smile to his lips. He could see the oxygen tubes being removed from her nostrils and hung around the gauge at the top of the cylinder. He watched the bobbing marker descend its graduated tube as the oxygen had been turned off. The pillows seemed to magic themselves from behind his grandmother to an empty armchair. Nearby he checked the two young nurses sleeping soundly on the floor on their straw mats, heads cushioned in the crook of one V-shaped arm. He watched the indents on the sheet and knew that was where Girija stood; and then she moved to another spot and made another indent, she placed the healing crystals which grounded Grandmother in this world to ease her breathing pain which she suffered and more since the oncologist's medicine was no longer being given to her.

As his grandmother was gently rolled on one side she caught his eye from his position outside the window through the netting and she stretched a hand in his direction while he raised his in an everlasting kiss. No bravery or daring could hold back the tears of these nightly embraces so subtly invoked as he became witness to her departure from his world. Every night, no matter which position the girls placed her in, she would search the gloom beyond the mosquito net for him, her mind totally free of the medicines, and some nights she would only be able to raise a finger, their distant hugs before that restful sleep. Every night he wondered, *would that one be their last?*

The first morning after the girls had nursed her and given her ease was a Saturday and he had made his way anxiously to his grandfather's house to check the reaction to his grandmother's sleep without oxygen. Aunt Saroj was in the room and Grandmother was breathlessly propped up as usual on pillows with oxygen attached. He was asked to leave by Aunt Saroj who ordered the nurses to take care of Grandmother's toilet.

Nisha was seated at the table in the room leading upstairs. She had become more diligent towards her mother since Girija had disappeared and even more sullen. Jack sat with her, aware of the enormous distance between them, cousins but strangers; in truth he felt closer to Girija, he sort of knew when she was near and he could smell the incense she used to burn in her room. He knew Nisha's and his own mind could never meet. She would never be what he considered normal. He would never be able to trust her; she was damaged, a childhood ruined; those eyes would always rove suspicious of everyone and of every activity. She trusted nothing to be as it seemed. Nothing could be gained unless deviant tactics were employed. They rose and sat again in silence as their grandfather passed through from the dining room after breakfast. After a short while Jack followed him to his armchair in the front hall and politely enquired how Grandmother was. His grandfather was lost in thought, eyebrows knitted together, fingers tapping the arm of the chair unconsciously.

'What did you say, son?' he said quietly, not taking his eyes away from the window.

'Grandmother is just the same?' repeated Jack.

'She was better earlier,' he replied.

'Really, did she have breakfast?' said Jack encouragingly.

'No, but she slept. When I got up at five she was fast asleep and on her side without the oxygen and only one pillow,' he explained in the same desultory tone.

'That's good, isn't it...? To get a good night's rest...' Jack trailed off as his grandfather didn't even look in his direction, his eyes stayed fixed and blind out of the window somewhere.

'As soon as Saroj went in and woke the nurses the breathlessness came back and the oxygen had to be started again,' he said quietly, more to himself than to Jack.

After waiting a little longer in the quiet, Jack silently left through the front door, realising that nothing mattered to his grandfather anymore. He also realised that Saroj and her green entity caused the Devas to disappear and with them their peaceful energy. But he was thankful for small mercies. The aunt felt in control and therefore off-guard. It was easy to get in and out of the garden at midnight.

LAKE BODY

THAT LAST WEEK brought the anticipated visit from the police. Girija had not been missed for almost twelve hours after she had left Nani Home for the last time as a human. With all the activity that entailed the care of a dying person her father had not been contacted until that evening as everyone had assumed that she had taken the train north again. When it was discovered that she was not at home or with any of her schoolfriends there the police had been notified.

Jack was on alert for any information he could glean on his trips to sit with his grandmother but there was little talk or wonder being expressed; nobody seemed to know how or why and eventually the conversation settled back on Grandmother's declining health.

On arriving home from school Kate informed Jack that Aunt Saroj had been asked for recent photos of Girija and some close-ups of her at the birthday party had been given by Jack's mother. Girija looked beautiful, Kate had said, and Jack thought so too. He remembered her alive and at first didn't want to think about her face in the photos.

Jack was amazed at the lack of concern as the week wore on; even Nisha showed no signs of disquiet when he enquired on one of his visits. However, with Nisha he was not sure if this was all front and perhaps she was really worried inside.

'Why should I be worried?' she asked Jack. 'She's old enough to know what she is doing, isn't she?'

'I suppose she is,' Jack honestly agreed.

'She may be gone to Madras to my aunt,' replied Nisha.

'I didn't know she was in contact with your aunt,' asked Jack.

'Well we're not, but she may have contacted her when we were all in Madras,' explained Nisha.

Jack had nothing to say to this and didn't want to draw undue attention to the missing Girija. It was on the Friday, exactly one week after Girija went on her new path, that Jack met the sombre face of his mother who stood at the front door of the Little Pink House when the car drove them in after school. Matty and Jack dismounted and the car took Nisha into Nani's Home.

'What's up, Mum?' asked Matty.

Jack didn't need to ask.

'Leave your bags here,' his mother indicated a spot in the front hall, 'and come with me.'

They both followed her to the big sitting room where Kate stood waiting for them; the shutters were closed and the air conditioner was on.

'Tell us…' demanded Matty, but before there was time for an answer he asked anxiously, 'Where's Dad?'

'Dad's next door. Let's sit down,' said their mother.

'Girija had an accident,' said their mother and Jack knew she tried to soften the news too late by adding: 'She's gone to heaven.'

'She went home on the train,' said Matty.

'No, she didn't go home Matt, we all thought she went home but she didn't,' replied his mother.

'Where did she go then?' enquired Matty.

'Well she must have gone to the Residency for a walk and slipped and fell into the lake,' his mother lied; her face was very red and her eyes flashed here and there in the effort to whitewash the darkness of the terrible news.

'Why did she go on her own?' enquired Matty.

'Nobody knows Matt, she must have been on her own,' said his mother, thinking.

'Does Dad know?' asked Jack.

'Yes, he's next door with Grandfather and your aunt,' replied his mother.

'Come Matt, let's get changed and have your milk,' said his mother after a little pause while Matty digested the news and seemingly had no more questions.

'When did this all happen?' Jack asked Kate when they had left.

'This morning, a fisherman found her body washed up on the shore when he went to push his canoe out. Apparently the sun glinted off the gold Zarry of her sari as the sun broke the horizon and alerted his attention,' said Kate quietly.

'Have the police questioned you yet?' Jack asked.

'No,' she replied.

'How did Mum react?' Jack asked.

'They told your father at the office first as the inspector was concerned about your grandfather with Grandmother sinking. Your father came here on his way next door… I think your parents are blaming themselves for not paying more attention to Girija, they think it was a suicide,' Kate explained.

'You remember your alibi,' reminded Jack. 'The last time you saw Girija was Friday morning when you visited Grandmother with my mother.'

'And the last time you saw her was Friday evening when you went to visit your grandmother,' said Kate.

But later that evening Kate was questioned a second time alone: what did she and Girija talk about all the time they spent together, had Girija said anything about her plans for the future, did she have a boyfriend? Although Jack was worried about this he need not have been: Kate had a loyalty to her friend and cousin that could not be shaken. She convinced Jack that she was so focused on each and every word that was used to question her she was sure she missed nothing and was careful not to lead the Inspector in any direction for fear of letting some little bit of information slip.

The next morning they heard there was a post mortem and Jack became protective of Girija's body: he did not want a post mortem, he couldn't stand the thought of the body being cut open and all the organs examined. He pleaded with his parents to make contact with the coroner.

That was the last time Kate was there to console him.

'Jack she knew what would happen to her body, she had researched everything about suicide. It's not enough just to take fluid samples, it's a suspicious death, they have to check for poisoning and all sorts of things that we don't know anything about,' Kate said quietly as they swung back and forth on the swings at the end of the lawn near the nosey neighbour's house and far away from the Little Pink House.

'Nobody knows what you and I know, to everyone else this is a real mystery, so they have to know, your parents, her father…' she continued.

'Yeah I know all that… but it feels that it's getting worse, it was bad enough to let her go at the lake but… now it's like having to let her go all over again,' he muttered, head lowered.

'I know, it's just devastating,' replied Kate. 'By the way the gold chain she wore was still on the body…'

'And the crystal?' asked Jack.

'She wears it all the time and she feels that Grandmother has glimpses of her as she is now. Your grandmother is partially out of this life some of the time and when she is she can see Girija. I can see your grandmother in spirit some nights before we place the crystals around her to ground her to relieve the pain. Last night she gave us both a hug,' said Kate, her eyes welling up with tears which she wiped away with the back of her hand.

'Are they happy, Kate?' Jack asked after a moment or two.

'Yes, I don't know how to express it…' she sobbed, 'it is as if their deaths are birthdays for them, the birthday into their new lives but it's not like this life, it's as if you or anyone goes back home... and you are wiser. I really don't know how to say it to make you understand. But please don't be sad for them; they will feel it and it will upset them to see you suffer.' Kate had stopped swinging and looked directly at Jack who had been motionless for some time.

'The cremation is this evening, I hate going but in another way I feel I'm accompanying her again, this time for the very last time,' he said with slightly more hope. 'Your Mum explained that women don't go,' added Kate.

'Her dad will light the pyre,' said Jack quietly.

'I can't imagine it,' said Kate.

'Neither can I, I've never been to the cremation grounds before... never actually seen a cremation before... it would be like the end if I didn't know what I know about Girija, actually seeing the indents where she places the crystals every night for Grandmother.' He took a deep breath and went on, 'Although the sight of the flames must be terrible; there is no smell as they use perfumed wood like sandalwood. Somebody from the factory is helping Dad organise it all, he had to light his grandmother's pyre,' he explained.

Kate just listened. Nobody disturbed them; the dhobi came and went, there was no food bought that day and the cook was told not to come. It was customary to fast or take vegetarian food which Kate and Jack found easy, they had no appetite and more importantly because they wanted to pay tribute to the truly beautiful human being that Girija was.

LAST JOURNEY

JACK ACCOMPANIED KATE to the airport just as he had collected her there three months earlier. Although she stared out of the window actively, an enormous change had taken place for both of them. Jack considered this and it felt as if it was alive and living with them. India and all that had happened had given Kate confidence to live with her 'gift', as she called it. It took the terror out of what was incomprehensible to her mind and she seemed to be more self-assured about what she could do with her body, especially the frequency with which she had to enter and exit her body during the last week of her stay.

Jack had no doubt that he too was on a journey. The frustration his father had been experiencing within the companies during the last year, thwarted and curtailed by Jack's grandfather at board level had left his father little choice but to make his own way in life. Jack overheard his parents discuss the pros and cons of his father's idea to start up an abattoir. This was their topic of debate almost every night when they sat alone under the stars, in the cool on the lawn when everyone else was in bed. The Irish meat exporter and his accountant who had visited before Kate had arrived, the visits from English men with expertise in sanitising and food flavourings: Jack connected the trail which was carefully laid to lead both him and his father away from where they considered home.

Jack had gone with Kate to Swami's house the previous evening after school and his visit with Grandmother. She returned his book on yantras and placed it in his hands reverently. She considered him her guru and they promised they would keep in touch. He advised her to keep on seeking the knowledge she needed to understand herself and her path in life. Jack desired his life to be simple too, but like Kate he did not know where his life would take him either. It wasn't just the geographic change, which he did not want, it affected his mindset too. He felt Kate was going home and even though she would stay in her familiar places that too would no longer have the relaxed aura of child-hood. He hated the thought that his comfortable world had gone for good and although outwardly everything looked the same, it felt like he no longer had possession of it. So even then, on the drive to the airport, like grown-ups they sat silently in this new atmosphere, with no need to indulge in frivolous conversation anymore.

They checked in the suitcase in the same silence, Jack taking command in Malayalam when the check-in man started unnecessarily to question Kate. They spent half an hour browsing in the little shop separately, not talking at all because it was too much of an effort to keep a sunny façade. When they were tired of that they sat down and waited for the flight to be called.

'I sometimes cannot believe what has happened to us, Kate.' He looked at her as if it was a question.

'I know what you mean. It feels like we're on our own, from now on we don't consult parents for reassurances, we must make our own decisions… and they have to be the right ones. That's what's scary,' she replied.

'I've always made my decisions on my own, purposely rejecting advice, particularly from my parents. Maybe I'll try to listen for the deeper meaning from now on,' he said pensively.

'Your mother said that your dad is going to set up an abattoir, maybe in Karnataka,' Kate said hopefully.

'Yeah I know they told me, Grandfather is disgusted… from a religious aspect,' Jack said.

'But from what your mother said he will buy only the male calves and the old, worn out buffalo which would be culled anyway,' said Kate defensively.

'But Grandfather is not trying to stop him leaving, is he?' asked Jack.

'No, that's true, your mum thought there would be objections to the move; nothing but silence except for what your Dad plans to do with the abattoir,' she agreed.

When it came time for her to pass through security they hugged openly and sincerely and made good their promises to write to each other. That part over with had not helped Jack feel any better. He somehow felt that if painful events came and passed the hurt would leave him alone, but it didn't; it just stayed pushing him down into the earth, almost.

The two-hour drive back seemed endless: the driver was not Vishu and he did not intrude on Jack's silence all the way back to Adoor. When the car reached the gates were flung wide open; Jack realised that yet another had left. Jack got out, witnessing a marquee being erected around the front of his grandfather's house. The garden was full of workers quietly thatching the roof of coconut leaves in place and others had begun lining the inside with metres and metres of white cotton cloth. His father stood to one side near the bungalow with the tin factory foreman. They seemed to be discussing the construction and as he turned Jack saw his face and he knew what his father had to tell him long before he reached him at the gates... Grandmother had left too.

Grandmother was buried early in the afternoon the following day. Her body had been adorned with one of her wedding saris and surrounded with flowers. The gold from her wedding garland was pinned to the sari. Ice had been placed, hidden from sight by experienced women who knew how to pack it and collect the melt. Her body remained like that for the first night after her death and all the next morning. People filed past, momentarily pausing, and as they left they gave their condolences to the senior family members. Rituals were performed and the body which was removed from its enormous bed of flowers; it was placed in a coffin instead of a funeral pyre. It would have been Jack's duty to light the funeral pyre and his parents had prepared him for it. Jack's father requested that Jack's mother accompany Grandmother's body to the cremation grounds even though only men attended the last rites but he too, Jack felt, couldn't take in the fact that she was no more. However, to everyone's surprise Grandfather decided that he couldn't possibly cremate her body either and decided on a burial near his ancestral home, not far from their temple. This seemed less final and it was a procedure everyone at the Little Pink House could actually accept.

And so as the heat of the Kerala sun began abating, the closed coffin was borne on shoulders. Jack's father, his uncle, Nisha and Girija's father and four other cousins bore the coffin to a little field with sunburnt grass the colour of straw to the grave which was already lined with concrete. Very soon the place was full of people pushing so hard to get a glimpse of the grave that Jack had to physically resist the pushing to avoid being hurled forward and into the open grave. Once placed in the grave the lid was removed one last time; there was another ritual and something akin to sandalwood was sprinkled on Grandmother, occluding her glasses. This last image of Grandmother stayed with Jack forever.

EPILOGUE

JUST A SHORT couple of months after Grandmother had passed away Jack, with his back against the white, cool tiles of his bathroom wall and his seat on the chilly mosaic, resented the generous warm tears which cascaded down his cheeks. As quickly as he wiped them away with the sleeve of his shirt, more rolled down and soon he had to use the other sleeve to wipe away the sadness. Loud sighs literally burst out of him. Grief, humiliation and the terrible feeling of defeat were all in abundance and he missed not having Kate to confide in. At the same time he was glad she couldn't see him in such a state.

He felt life had no meaning. He knew it was love his grandfather had for him all his life and to a certain extent he knew he was taking it for granted, but the fact that he did expect it didn't make it any less precious. Was it all for nothing? It had to mean something. He pondered on this intangible love that was no less real even though it could not be quantified. Obviously a father's love is stronger than a grandfather's. And then he considered his father and thought again about the love of a father for his children. There must be degrees of love for a grandfather to choose between his children. For whatever reason Grandfather had made his choice: his father had been stealthily nudged out of the family business and Grandfather let it happen. There were definitely degrees of love and he hoped that the tight little unit of four, his parents, Matty and himself, would never let go of their love.

And then there was his own private battle for survival… lost. *Karma!* Swami had said, some other life loomed, he said. Jack felt this was the Indian resilience: millions of people somehow coped with adversity right down to starvation every minute of every day in India. Karma was the perfect solution for helping him cope with wrongs done in previous lives. How much of this misery did he have to endure to right his previous wrongs? He cast the cynical thoughts aside and rose from the bathroom floor, wiped his eyes again and unbolted the door.

His mother was sitting on a mattress on the floor of his bedroom, cradling

Matty's head. They looked as miserable as he felt. He joined them, easing himself down on to the other mattress. He expected his mother to ask if he was alright but she didn't and he reckoned she knew the answer by looking at his swollen, red eyes. She had bolted the door, scared she may be taken in the night. She had not eaten any of the food which had been sent from Grandfather's house. She had not been invited to dinner with his father or supper with himself and Matty; instead a tiffin container had been sent over. She was being furtively blamed for their departure and boycotted. Another quirky self-deluding excuse hiding the real reason for their departure and, worst of all, Grandfather seemed to believe it. This last bit of publicity Jack felt was ingenious. However, he knew his aunt and it wasn't that she was particularly intelligent, it was her negative instincts of lying and cheating that made her so very convincing. The ayah had heard rumours of possible incarceration into a psychiatric home as a way of ridding the family of his mother but Jack suspected that these were the result of promptings Aunt Saroj had whispered in Grandfather's ear and being mendacious and not always specific, trusting that Grandfather would come up with the solutions himself it was only half a plan, as Aunt Saroj's real aim was to rid the family of his father.

Before the ayah left, which was at the same time as the lorry left that morning with their furniture and belongings, she told his mother of more 'rumours' she had heard from next door's servants that she may be poisoned. Whether all those rumours were put about to ensure their speedy departure or if there was truth in them Jack really never knew. All he did know was that his mother was playing safe. The rumour strategy was unfair but effective. Jack's mother was frightened. But Jack felt there was one good thing about it: if the aunt was satisfied that it was having the desired effect at least she was not calling on the underworld and so he left them unchallenged, accepting the lesser of two evils.

They had hung about the Little Pink House all day, just the three of them, sitting on the floor, backs against the walls. When Jack's father came from the office at one-thirty as usual, they all went next door for lunch except his mother. Jack automatically stopped while the gates were opened, he passed blindly through. Kate had prompted him to think of his mother's life within the family, fascinated that he had never thought of it before. He remembered arguments between his parents and would hear his father defending Nisha and Aunt Saroj. None of this he even bothered to consider as they subsided but of course it made perfect sense: his mother was his father's weakest link. Harass her with their malicious mischief and the whole house became unhappy.

And so he went and sat gloomily among the ominous remains of a family, Grandmother absent, her successor, his mother on the run. Even Grandfather had disassociated himself from Jack, he could feel it.

He rolled on his back as his mother eased Matty into a sleeping position on half the mattress they shared. At lunch Jack remembered his father had asked if they could have beds. One single bed arrived in the afternoon and two mattresses. Jack's mother had directed the servants to place the single bed in his parents' bedroom for his father and the two mattresses in the nursery, Jack's room. No bed or mattress had been sent for her, despite all the empty beds in Grandfather's eight-bedroom house. Jack quelled his aggravation and kept on repeating Swami's mantra to himself, *the lesser of two evils.*

As his mother settled down to sleep beside Matty, Jack suddenly remembered the snake and whispered that they should close the shutters just to be safe. She didn't argue despite how hot she knew it would become. He quietly got up, increased the speed of the ceiling fan and hooked the shutters of his bedroom windows in the Little Pink House for the last time.

Book Two

THE TALL MAGNOLIA HOUSE

TO UNDERSTAND MATTY we must very briefly go back two years to when he was eight years old. That was before the move when he lived at his childhood home, the family seat, the dynasty of a grandfather, his son – Matty's father – and Jack his big brother and of course Matty. It was towards the end of that year that the dynasty was shattered and some members were scattered into cosmic energy but Matty survived. He and his family felt as though they had been thrown to the four winds. We catch up with Matty in Madras, as it was known then – now Chennai, the capital of Tamil Nadu State – still in India, aged ten.

WHITE STATION WAGON

MATTY JOINED THE throng of schoolchildren on the large, wide veranda of Sherrington House School. Although he was at the back and unable to move forward, he scanned right and left at head level in search of Jack, who would be head and shoulders above the other pupils. As usual there was no sign of him.

As the mass of pupils on the veranda began to thin out and neither Jack nor their old cream-coloured Ambassador car with its sun visor had arrived, a certain unease added itself to Matty's aggravation. Matty tried to quell his annoyance; he really didn't want to hold up the queue of cars again, waiting for Jack to make an appearance on the veranda while all the other pupils goaded Matty to make his driver move on to allow the next car to come forward and take its passenger. Matty had spoken to Jack about this embarrassment but Jack only laughed it off. Matty felt he just did not take things seriously, especially things which affected Matty. It felt as if Jack treated them as if they were inconsequential.

When there were just one or two others waiting for their cars and the horseshoe-shaped drive was empty, Matty decided to walk out on to the street to see if Jack and Shaker, their young driver, were parked out there. It had happened on a couple of occasions previously that Jack, being on the veranda unusually early, had taken the car out on to the road, more or less ordering Shaker to allow him to change gears and steer the vehicle. Matty had found them then, the car carefully parked and both of them laughing together at a joke, probably, as Jack had a pigeon grasp of Tamil. The last time, a bidi had been quickly passed to Shaker and extinguished and placed in his pocket for later, obviously; Matty pretended he hadn't seen it.

Matty, with his heavy school bag sitting squarely on his back, stayed to the side of the drive where the cars drove in but when he reached the gate he could not see their car. Looking back at the old colonial building and following the columns to the first floor windows, there was no sign of Jack or any of his friends either. After a short hesitation, Matty decided he would venture up the street a little way in case Shaker had to park nearer to the main road. He had only gone a few steps along the pavement when a young man approached him.

'Your brother, your brother is here,' said the man, who had a moustache and a plaid shirt.

'Where is Shaker?' asked Matty and wondered why he asked that as he followed the man another few feet along the pavement, feeling distrustful. The man stopped and stood beside a white Tata station wagon.

'See... see your brother...' The man anxiously beckoned Matty to look into the car as he held open the back door.

Matty heard a muffled sound and a lot of shuffling but before he could run, the moustachioed man caught him by the collar of his shirt. Although he struggled to free himself, he was powerless against the firm muscles of arms and thighs which blocked his legs as he was hurled vigorously onto the remaining space on the back seat of the car where to his horror Jack was pinned tight between two other men. Jack's face was a disfigured red jelly due to a swollen mass around his right eye. It was bloodied, grotesquely engorged, liver-red and bright and even black in places. He let out a howl when the car took off at speed and one of the men was propelled backwards pushed against his shoulder. Matty felt that the facial wound was not the only one Jack had sustained.

Matty stayed perfectly still, intending to obey everything those men asked him to do. They were dangerous and violent and obviously his brother had put up quite a fight. As the car slowed at the T junction which led on to the Mount Road, Matty noticed their own car. The driver was inside, his face pushed up against the driver's window and a man held what looked like a truncheon just in front of it.

Matty stole a sideways look at his brother. Jack was quiet, obviously in pain but Matty didn't see any of the terror he felt himself in Jack's good eye. The muscle-moustache who had forced him into the back was now seated beside the driver and turned around to see Matty look at his brother and asked Matty if he would like a bloodied eye too. Matty ignored him. The driver said that Matty probably did not speak Malayalam, so the excited grinning moustache tried intimidation again the second time in English.

'You like to have a big eye too?' he jeered.

Matty continued to ignore the rough man and was glad that Jack did not react either.

The muscle-man who sat between Matty and Jack placed an arm across Matty's chest while the car threaded its way hesitantly along the Mount Road through the heavy traffic. Once clear of the main road, they drove recklessly and at great speed for about five minutes. Matty could feel the cold from the air conditioner change the feel of his sticky, sweaty shirt. The muscle beside Matty fidgeted in his back trouser pocket and produced a couple of pieces of cloth, one of which he looped over Matty's head, so suddenly that Matty's hands went up in a defensive move. The slap came without warning and shook Matty to the core; he became puppet-like as he had the cloth tied tightly at the back of his head, his eyes sightless and the side of his face nearest the window hot and scalding from the clout.

Once Matty's blindfold was secure Jack began to roar and Matty in his pain and terror forced yells up his palpitating chest and through his constricting throat:

'Stop it, stop it, leave him alone, he can't see with that eye… it was too swollen to tie on a blindfold…' and Matty began kicking the back of the seat in front of him and at the legs of the man beside him. He then walloped the back of the front seat and twisted and then pounded the man beside him with his fists as hard as he could blindly raging inside.

'Addy, addy…' shouted the moustache from the passenger seat and with that Matty felt his hair gripped very tightly and his head pulled forward. He prepared himself for another smack, he knew *addy* meant 'beat' in English, but it didn't come, perhaps because he had stopped kicking and shouting.

Shortly his hair was let go and he could only hear Jack wincing. He was too scared to ask Jack if he was alright in case the men pinning Jack to the back seat might hurt him even more, as they seemed to have had little grasp of English.

As the car sped and slowed and the driver pressed the horn almost continuously, a thought about Enid Blyton's 'Famous Five' came to Matty. He immediately knew he should be using his mind to pick up clues as to where they were going: was the road even or were they driving on a rough surface, how long had they been in the car? Matty could no longer check his watch and he had no idea of how many minutes had passed. The stress and physical violence had exhausted him and it felt like hours and he had no idea of how long he had waited on the school porch before going out into the road.

Although Matty was frightened, almost terrified, he was also angry. He decided he would count distance in time. He had ten fingers, one for each minute. So he counted to 60, little finger on the right hand; another 60, ring finger on the right hand; another 60, middle finger on the right hand; and so on and on. When Matty had counted to 60 nine times, the cars slowed almost to a stop and seemed to ease itself on to an entirely different surface. Matty began counting again as the car bounced more and slowed, at times almost to a stop. He had counted to 60 fourteen times when the car halted. He reckoned that this place was just over half an hour from Madras city centre and that they headed north after they turned off the Mount Road.

Matty felt the door open and the man who had sat between himself and Jack pushed at him and ordered him, in Malayalam, to get out. Matty scrambled to find his footing which when his feet found ground he noted was uneven. It felt like a mixture of compacted clay and pebbles. He was glad they hadn't tied his hands.

He listened for sounds that Jack was near and heard only footsteps shuffling, so he concentrated on the language and tried to find out about Jack from that. All four rogues were talking very quietly. A door opened: it didn't sound like a door made out of wood, more like a metal sound, Matty thought. A new voice joined the others but the language was Malayalam: all these men were from Kerala State, not Tamil Nadu.

Suddenly Matty's arm was caught in a grip above his right elbow and he was hauled along. He didn't resist, ears straining for sounds from Jack or any clue in the conversation among the blackguards as to where he was. And then just as suddenly he was let go and then there was the sound of a door closing, this time like a sound of a bolt in wood.

BLINDFOLD

THE SOUNDS OF the footsteps and the conversation died away and Matty whispered: 'Jack...'

'I'm here Matt... I need to lie down...' came Jack's voice intermittently as if it hurt to talk.

'If I can find you I can take off the blindfold...' replied Matty as he tore at the knot at the back of his own head and eventually had to pull the tight band down over his nose and finally down over his mouth, leaving it hanging around his neck. It smelt awful.

'I've taken it off Matt, I just need to find a wall and rest a bit... I can't see a thing...' replied Jack.

'Don't move Jack... just sit down where you are... you shouldn't try to move just yet,' instructed Matty.

'Why not?' demanded Jack's weary, weak voice.

'Jack, remember the boy in the book *Kidnapped*?' Matty tried to explain.

'Oh come on, Matt...' came Jack's cantankerous sound.

'Listen, just listen to me for once.' Matty was angry and let rip.

'Do you want to fall down into a pit or something? We can't see a thing in here; all we know is that it has a roof, because I can't see light. It has no windows and a door... so let me explore on my hands and knees... just lie down... I'll get my school bag as a pillow... let me have a feel around.' Matty was irascible: why should he have to explain caution to Jack as well as cope with his injuries and make both of them safe? He released the heavy bag from his back and let it flop on to the floor. It was obvious Jack's strength was ebbing but Matty didn't want to think too much about that.

'Did you hear the thud?' asked Matty.

'Yes, you are to my right,' replied a voice, so tired that Matty's heart literally gave a little jolt.

'Your voice has been coming from my left, so stay put, I'll find my way to you,' instructed Matty. He got down on his hands and knees and padded past his big school bag. He continued padding; he wanted to ask Jack to keep talking but he trusted his instinct and said nothing. He reached back every so often to drag the bag behind him. Very shortly his chin came into contact with Jack's right knee. Jack had done as Matty urged and lay down on the earth floor. Matty felt around him and placed the bag at his back and asked him to lay his head on the bag. Jack was so ill he needed to prop himself up with his arms which were jutting out behind his back. He could feel Jack sinking onto the bag.

Matty sat down beside his big brother and tucked his legs underneath and waited in strange silence and then waited some more. He didn't want to dwell on Jack and his injuries but he was aware that Jack may fall unconscious. He had witnessed that before but he had his parents to call on then. That led to another thought: Shaker and his parents. Had the man released Shaker? If so, the driver should have reported back to their parents, who would call the police and Shaker had descriptions of these men and maybe even the number plate of the white station wagon. What if they had not released Shaker? Either way his parents would have contacted the police by now.

'My head is throbbing Matt… it doesn't hurt so much if I sit up… but my back is too weak… we'll have to try and find a wall that I can lie against…' came Jack's agonising voice out of the blackness.

Matty could hear him get up; even feel him as he drew up his knees.

'I'll go exploring again, don't worry…' reassured Matty, feeling anything but safe.

'I'm sorry I'm no help Matt…' began Jack.

'Forget it, you're really badly hurt. Did they hurt your shoulder much?' asked Matt.

'No that doesn't hurt much, only when I move… my head got it the worst… we could do with your Crane Bag…' Jack went on after another little pause.

'But I have my Crane Bag,' replied Matty.

'You have your *school* bag,' reminded the weak voice.

'Inside is my Crane Bag,' confirmed Matty, rooting around Jack in search of the school bag.

'Why… why bring the Crane Bag to school?' moaned Jack between breaths.

'If I leave it at home Mum will try to wash it and throw away half of my stuff. That happened before so I can't risk leaving it at home. I roll it up tight and put it at the bottom of my bag,' Matty explained while he felt for the buckles and undid them.

'Don't tell me you bring your Swiss Army Knife to school?' asked the feeble voice; 'but I'd be really glad if you did today,' he added, hope in his voice.

'Sorry Jack, can't risk that either, then I'd be in real trouble… but I see your point, we could unscrew the door from its hinges… or… well there are loads of possibilities… if we had it but… I haven't… but I do have this,' and with that Matty saw Jack's spoiled face again as he flashed the weak light from his pen torch on him. It looked no better; in fact it seemed worse, like an afterbirth that had come away from one of the cows who had given birth at his grandfather's when he was very young. It was so raw and bloody it nearly made him sick.

'We'll find a wall now…' Matty didn't finish, instead he scanned the floor behind them and then searched for the nearest wall. There was no door step so he couldn't tell how far into this shed or room they had walked. He wanted to find the nearest wall so that Jack would not have far to move.

'No pits in this direction,' came Matty's voice. 'Jack, there is a wall only six feet behind where you are now…' Matty returned but Jack had hauled himself upright without help and Matty shone the torch on the floor as Jack moved slowly in the direction of the wall. Once seated and slumped against the wall Matty retrieved his bags. He sat with his back against the wall beside his brother who was very quiet.

'Don't suppose you have your water bottle with you?' came the frail enquiry. Matty felt Jack sounded sleepy and wondered if it was good or bad.

'I do but I had finished all the water at school,' replied Matty.

Another long silence followed. Matty thought of counting minutes again to take his mind off Jack. *It was a pity he didn't have his Swiss Army knife. He could have dug the earth floor, checked out the hinges of the door… even used the corkscrew to bore a hole in the wooden door so he could check out where they were.* Instead he checked his watch with the torch light: almost six-thirty. It would soon be pitch dark outside.

Those were the kinds of thought going through Matty's brain when he felt a movement at his other side. He switched on his torch, mindful not to waste the battery, to see the fat little fellow with his swinging trunk, skipping and pointing further along the wall. Matty got up.

'What you doing?' came Jack's lethargic voice.

'Nothing… just going to check out the door,' replied Matty. He avoided being too evasive so that Jack would relax back into his exhaustion and not bother him.

Matty used the wall as a guide and when Ganesh stood still, blocking his path, he stopped. He pointed his right index finger towards the floor in an exaggerated gesture.

'What?' asked Matty, having used his torch to search the clay near their feet.

'What?' asked Jack.

'Nothing… I'm talking to myself,' replied Matty.

The chubby little boy with the elephant trunk sank low and squatted and pointed in the same direction as before. Matty followed him and as he saw the lines and dots arranging themselves in the clay he whispered:

'Are you doing that?'

The elephant head moved from side to side slowly, indicating no.

'Doing what?' asked Jack.

'Nothing, I thought I heard a noise,' lied Matty but he was too intent on the marks.

A long vertical line had been drawn. It was crossed by five short lines which slanted. There were five dots being made on the vertical line above the slanted ones. Matty smiled to himself: a space was left to denote the individual alphabets. Like magic another space and then three slanted lines were added above the dots. The little elephant boy smiled. Matty returned his smile but then confusion took hold. He sat down and switched off the torch to save the battery. The language was Ogham and only one other person in the whole world knew he knew Ogham and that was Kate. Matty's cousin Kate had taught him the Ogham alphabet two years ago during the monotonously long monsoon days when she spent three months with them in Kerala. Matty was trying to understand how the alphabets were forming themselves in the clay of the floor when he felt a light tap on his knee. He immediately switched on the torch again to find Ganesh peering down. Matty followed his gaze to see the vertical line being drawn again. Then the same first letter which was an 'R'. Again an 'I' but instead of the markings slanting through the vertical line as before this time five horizontal lines emerged to the right side followed by a space and two more slanting lines dissecting the vertical one. 'N' and 'G', thought Matty: 'R-I-N-G'.

'But what does it mean?' he asked the elephant boy.

'What does what mean?' queried the weak voice.

'Ring Jack, the word ring,' called back Matty.

'Telephone rings, doorbells ring, ring a bell… Ganesh must be deaf with all the ringing you do at the temple… Matty, what exactly do you mean?' asked Jack and Matty could tell from his voice that he was stronger.

'Jack can you come over here…? I want to show you something,' said Matty, flashing his tiny beam at Jack's legs.

Jack crawled along the floor until he reached Matty. He sat with his back against the wall again and Matty moved to reveal the marks on the floor with his torch.

'You see this one Jack, this was the first to appear but I couldn't understand that letter,' explained Matty as he pointed out the alphabets to Jack.

'What is it Matt?' asked Jack bewildered.

'It's Ogham. Kate taught it to me,' explained Matty.

'Ogham?' repeated Jack.

'The Irish language was first written in Ogham,' continued Matty. 'Look Jack… see, the second time the marks appeared it had four letters which make the word ring,' said Matty, still puzzled.

'Why are you not surprised about this, why are you so calm?' asked Matty, watching Jack's brutalised face intensely.

'Did you actually see the marks being made, Matt?' asked Jack.

'Yes… I just told you… they were not there before…' Matty did not know how to convince Jack.

'It's alright… I believe you… listen Matt, it's Kate,' said Jack quietly and cautiously.

'I know its Kate but… how can she do it now…? She's in Ireland… and… and this is just appearing…' said Matty, switching off his torch again. His friend the elephant boy god had been standing watching the boys but Matty was relaxed about that as he knew Jack could not see him.

'Kate can live in two dimensions… no that's not right, well it is right… she can travel inter-dimensionally, I really don't know how she does it… *she* doesn't know how she does it… but she can… and distance doesn't matter, she can be here in seconds,' Jack tried to explain.

'What exactly do you mean?' persisted Matty, despite the weakness which had overtaken Jack once again.

'Jack?' asked Matty again when he didn't or couldn't answer.

'You know ghosts and spirits, well spirits more than ghosts, well Kate is sort of like a spirit… you remember when we couldn't wake her up when she stayed with us in Kerala…? Well she got trapped with the Danavas, or part of her did,' explained Jack with what sounded like great effort, judging from the obvious and frequent intake of breath.

'Who?' asked Matt.

'They are like the Tuatha dé Danann in Ireland,' said Jack.

'Leprechauns?' came back Matty's astonished voice.

'Yeah… she is able to talk to them… get into their world… I wonder how she knew we were in trouble,' said Jack, so quietly that Matty felt he was talking almost to himself.

'The word has to mean something… that has to be a clue… she is trying to tell us something… isn't she, Jack?' said Matty, excitement taking hold.

'The only ring I can think of is the ring Girija gave me,' said Jack quietly after a pause.

'Girija gave you a ring?' asked Matty. 'When?'

'Before she went away,' said Jack as if he wasn't thinking.

'Before she died, you mean,' said Matty, hoping that the head injury hand not affected Jack's reasoning.

'Well, where is it?' asked Matty.

'I lost it,' said Jack.

'Lost it, how could you lose it?' asked Matty, annoyed with his brother.

'I put it in my pocket and forgot about it... there was a lot going on in those days Matty... Grandmother was dying...' continued Jack.

'Wait... wait a minute... just one minute...' Matty was excited and thinking and remembering.

'Radha gave me a ring...' continued Matty, remembering.

'Who?' asked Jack?

'The dhobi's wife... remember...' Matty was impatient with Jack.

'When, what ring? Was it Girija's ring...? When did she find it...? I remember now, I put it in my shirt pocket,' asked Jack.

'Yes... it was ages ago when Kate stayed,' said Matty.

'What did you do with the ring Matt?' asked Jack anxiously.

'Put it in the Crane Bag of course... where else...' said Matty as he crawled along the floor with his torch in his mouth, searching his way back to where he had left the bags.

Matty held the torch between his teeth for a while longer as he felt his way down the inside of his almost empty rucksack. He was anxious for he too had forgotten about the ring but he remembered where he had put it or he hoped he had put it. Sure enough, he felt the hardness of the tiny shape before he squeezed his fingers into the torn lining at the bottom of the bag which served as a secret pocket.

'Did you find it?' asked Jack.

'Yep,' answered Matty and stood up, walking back to Jack with the weakening beam still on.

'Can I have it?' Jack asked as Matty took his time examining the ring in the torch light.

'Is it the ring?' said Matty as he handed it to Jack.

Jack took a little time examining it with his one functioning eye, commanding Matty to point the weak beam of light where he could use it to his best advantage.

Then he said, 'Watch me... don't be afraid, I'll come back...' and instantly on that instruction Jack disappeared.

Matty flashed the torch all around where Jack had been. The beam was really quite faint, too faint to see if Jack was elsewhere in the darkness. Matty pointed the torch to his right side and he could see Ganesh but not Jack. As the apprehension began to mount Jack reappeared sitting cross-legged just where he was before and inch or two away from Matty.

'Where did you go?' Matty was truly astonished for the second time despite their fragile existence.

'Nowhere,' answered Jack.

'But I couldn't see you,' asked Matty.

'Exactly… listen Matt, I've got an idea. The next time they come for us we can try to escape using this,' said Jack.

'But how?' asked Matty.

'Have you found the door yet?' asked Jack.

'No and my torch light is getting weaker and weaker,' replied Matty.

'Let's find it then,' urged Jack who pulled himself unsteadily into a standing position.

Ganesh tugged at Matty's trouser pocket and instinctively Matty trained his torch on the little elephant-headed boy. He led them along by the wall and almost immediately they found the door. Matty turned off the feeble light.

'Switch on the torch Matt, I want to have a look at the door,' instructed Jack.

'They may see the beam of the torch if they are standing guard outside,' whispered Matty.

'Matty we can't see any light coming in so they will not see any light from in here, especially that torch, it's dying,' explained Jack in a whisper.

'It's dark outside Jack, I checked my watch, it's almost seven,' explained Matty.

'They will not see a beam this weak Matt, believe me,' Jack repeated assuredly.

'Matt you wouldn't have any string or twine in the crane would you?' asked Jack after feeling the wooden planks of the door.

'I've got the kite twine,' whispered Matty.

'Great, get it will you?' ordered Jack.

'What are you thinking, Jack?' asked Matty after he got back and switched of the fading beam.

'Did you notice the door has vertical boards of wood held together with two cross boards?' asked Jack in the darkness. 'If we could loop some of the kite twine between the vertical planks, just enough for you to get your hands through, then you could grip onto the cross board with your fingers and loop the string around your wrists for an extra bit of support. If you place your feet sideways on the lower cross plank I think you could cling on to the door. When they open it I hope it will swing as you are not heavy… and they will think we have gone… because I will use the ring and hopefully they will leave the door open…' Jack could not finish his sentence.

'And they would go out again and then we can break out,' finished Matty.

ESCAPE

 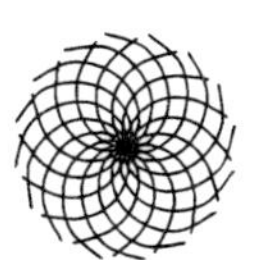

IT TOOK A long time for Jack to force two loops of kite twine between the tight vertical wooden boards at the very top of the door. Matty couldn't help him because he was not tall enough. Jack's arms ached just from the effort of reaching up. He used a sawing motion once he managed to slip the twine between the tightly placed timber panels. This he did by touch as there was little or no light left in the pen torch. Matty, unable to listen to the sound of his fumbling efforts any longer, went in search of the Crane Bag. He returned to the door, switched off the weak light and sat down to do some fumbling of his own.

'Jack, try this,' encouraged Matty after a good rummage in the bag.

Matty stood up and felt his way towards the sound of rubbing thread on wood and eventually his outstretched hand met the back of Jack's uniform shirt.

'What is it?' asked Jack.

'Flint,' replied Matty.

'Where did you get it?' asked Jack as he found his brother's hand and carefully took hold of the piece of stone.

'The Keeragh Islands,' replied Matty and if they had been in the light Jack would have seen the supremely confident look on Matty's face.

'But it's years since we went there,' came Jack's astonished voice.

'I know… and Mum didn't want me to go in the boat… she thought I was too small,' remembered Matty aloud.

'You were only five or six Matt,' reminded Jack.

'I was seven,' replied Matty indignantly.

'Whatever age you were, I'll never criticise your magpie instincts again Matt,' came Jack's grateful voice.

Jack was able to work more efficiently and effectively with the flint and after many rests when Jack allowed his arms to hang down heavily, Matty noticed a faint incision of light appear between the panels. It wasn't really light, more a luminous black surrounded by a dense blackness. The flint was used to cut the kite twine into sections. Finally, it was time to put Jack's idea into practice.

'I'll prop you up while you get your footing on the cross beam and find the loops with your hands,' explained Jack.

'I can manage,' Matty assured him but found it impossible to cling on to the narrow cross plank with his fingers while extending his arms and placing his feet sideways on the lower cross plank.

'I will need you to prop me up,' he said to Jack after some clawing and having to jump back away from the door to prevent himself from falling.

'I told you… it isn't easy,' repeated Jack.

And so a thought became a manifestation as Matty hung like a young monkey yet to find his strength to the door of their prison. He undid himself from the twine loops, learned to jump clear of the door and practised hanging so that he would be confident when the time would arrive to escape. Finally when he was sure of himself and the door trap he joined Jack on the floor. They talked about their distraction plan, once the kidnappers came in, Matty decided that he would put on his school bag and be ready even though they whispered and listened intently for any sound from outside.

'Matt, forget about the school bag. It's too heavy, you may have to run a long way,' explained Jack.

'Mum will be mad if I lose my books,' said Matty. 'Remember all the fuss about your science book.'

'She'll be in a much worse state if we don't get home,' said Jack. 'Anyway, the door needs to swing freely, if you have all that extra weight on your back the door may bounce off the wall and the kidnappers may see you.'

'Yeah, you're right… I'm not leaving the Crane Bag though,' insisted Matty and looped his arms through the straps after checking the buckle was fastened.

'That's OK, it's almost empty,' agreed Jack.

They sat and waited. Matty checked his watch: it was nine-thirty and his stomach was rumbling with hunger. He wondered what he would do when the torch spark eventually died; how would he be able to tell the time? He could use the narrow slits between the boards at the top of the door, but that would only distinguish day from night.

Jack was quieter than usual but Matty was glad he was able to get up and move when necessary.

'What happened to your school bag?' Matty enquired.

'It's in our car,' replied Jack.

'Were you out of school early this evening?' asked Matty.

'Yeah, I took the car outside with Shaker and parked it near the school gate but those men ganged up on us and roughed us up while we were waiting for you,' explained Jack. 'After the one who caught you in the street punched me, the others pushed me into the back of their car and I could no longer see Shaker.'

'But our car was near the Mount Road when they took us away,' said Matty.

'Did you see it?' asked Jack.

'Yes, Shaker was in it and some bad man had pushed him up against the window,' said Matty.

'I hope they haven't hurt him,' replied Jack. 'I hope he has gone for help.'

'Whether they have or have not let him go, Mum and Dad will know something is wrong now,' Matty repeated what was in his mind.

Jack remained quiet.

'Why did they kidnap us Jack?' asked Matty after a little while.

'I'm not sure,' replied Jack hesitatingly.

'You know more that you are telling me,' remarked Matty and he hoped it was a question with an answer. But after he waited a while he knew there was no answer forthcoming.

'Is it for money… or maybe body parts…? We are half European.' Matty could not hide the tremor in his voice.

'What's that got to do with it?' came back Jack's agitated voice.

'Genetic compatibility… maybe… I don't know,' replied a frustrated Matty. 'We're doing genes at school… it occurred to me… maybe not…'

'No Matt… I don't think it is either of those,' replied Jack quietly.

'Why then?' persisted Matty, surprised at his own words, words he could barely utter, they shook him so much.

'Did you notice they were from Kerala?' asked Jack.

'Yes… but that does not mean they wouldn't sell body parts,' exclaimed Matty, unable to control his trembling.

'Do you know the real reason why we left Kerala?' asked Jack.

'What does that have to do with this?' replied Matty, frustrated.

'I think it has everything to do with it,' said Jack and Matty noticed how determined his voice had become again.

'Jack, you have to start explaining things to me. I have just asked you questions to which you have given me nothing… but more questions… and worst of all you will not even share with me what you think is going on…' Matty felt exasperated with fear, thirst and hunger and he felt he was in the darkest place he had ever experienced both mentally and physically in the ten years of his life. He was even beginning to think of the things and people he may never see again.

'Listen Matt, don't panic. If I'm right, these thugs will do nothing more than just keep us for a while in order to scare Dad and especially Mum, who they think will run to Ireland with us,' said Jack who had moved closer to Matty on the floor, Matty could smell his clothes: *they smelt of sweat and dried clay from the ground and sticky blood, was it possible to smell blood or was he imagining it?*

'All I can say to that is why?' Matty could not release the knot in his throat and for once he was glad they were in the dark as two big tears sat on the edges of his eyelids. He placed his knees near to his chin and hugged his legs with his arms.

'Aunt Saroj somehow or other turned Grandfather against Dad,' Jack began.

'But they are very friendly; remember last month when he visited... we all went out to dinner at the Coconut Grove...' Matty stopped talking to let Jack carry on.

'Well it's all very subtle and mainly to do with the businesses. Dad's plans would be blocked at board level by Grandfather's cronies and in the end Dad was just sitting around in the office all day with nothing to do.'

'But couldn't he talk to Grandfather?' asked Matty.

'You see Matt, our grandfather is the best in the world... but a bit fickle. Five minutes with Aunt Saroj and he has his mind changed back again, Dad knew this and recognised there was no point in trying... it had been going on since she came to live again in Nani Bhavan,' explained Jack.

'But why doesn't she like us?' asked Matty bewildered.

'She doesn't want to share, she wants everything for herself and is very good at manipulating people and has managed to keep Grandfather all to herself, completely brainwashing him... Dad said Grandfather can hardly think straight, such are her daily sermons...' explained Jack.

'But that's ridiculous,' exclaimed Matty.

'She and Nisha were harassing Mum as well,' said Jack.

'How?' asked Matty.

'They stopped the bearer who did the shopping and delivering our lunches at school from coming to the house, told lies, said bad things about Mary: she really hated going to Nani Bhavan for lunch on Sundays, the kitchen girls there were set against her,' Jack explained.

'And our kidnapping has something to do with Aunt Saroj? Matty asked, 'But why...? We are no longer in Kerala, Dad has his own business here, hundreds of miles away.'

'Grandfather probably went back after his visit with us and talked too much about us and she resents the closeness he has with us... or rather did have,' explained Jack. 'She wants us out of India.'

'How can she know a gang like these men, though?' asked Matty.

'Believe me Matt, she only knows bad people. Uncle Rajan probably organised this for her,' Jack's voice came quieter as if he was thinking.

'But they are divorced, why would he help her?' asked Matty.

'Money,' replied Jack. 'He has none and she has access to a lot of it and he has been living here in Madras for some years now.'

'They beat you up for money,' repeated Matty to himself.

'They possibly didn't plan that part… but yeah… she had us kidnapped, I'm sure of it,' he replied.

There was silence for a long while and Matty checked his watch again with the spark from the torch. It was midnight.

'Are you OK, Jack, is your head hurting?' asked Matty.

'It feels heavy and sore, it hurts more than it pains,' replied Jack.

'How did Kate know?' Matty ventured after a quiet time; he was anxious not to tax Jack too much with the discomfort he was suffering from his head wound. He knew too that Jack was probably not telling him the truth as to how painful his face really was.

'That's a really long story Matt… I'm not sure I have the energy to go into it all right now… have you got enough light to find your school bag? I think I'll try to lie down again and I need it to rest my head on,' asked Jack.

'No,' Matty replied when the torch did not respond to the forward pressure he placed on the little slide along the barrel. Despite his exhaustion Matty decided he should crawl along on hands and knees to try to locate his bag. It was not very far away, it was just very difficult to discern direction in the blackness. He pulled his arms out of the straps of the Crane Bag, felt for the buckle, undid the leather and carefully placed the torch inside.

'What are you doing?' asked Jack.

'I'm going to have a feel around for my school bag, it can't be far from us,' replied Matty and almost immediately he felt warm breath on his right hand. Matty knew it had come from the nostrils of a small trunk. Matty reached out and felt an almost imperceptible pressure of an arm and then inside his palm. He stood upright looping one of the straps of the Crane Bag over his left shoulder so as not to lose it. He allowed himself to be led blindly and slowly into the darkness and after only ten steps his right foot came in contact with the bag and the pressure left his hand.

'Found it,' Matty called into the darkness after looping his right arm through the straps of his Crane Bag, he picked up the heavy school bag and cradled it with both arms. He turned three hundred and sixty degrees.

'Jack, can you talk so that I know I'm coming back to you?' asked Matty, standing still with his load.

'I'm over here,' came Jack's voice.

Matty counted ten feet in the direction of the voice but didn't collide with Jack.

'Where are you?' he asked.

'Right beside you I think,' said Jack and Matty put down the school bag.

He heard Jack drag it and knew he had settled himself down. Matty stayed quiet; he knew Jack was not being evasive; he was probably exhausted like himself. Matty decided to lie down too but did not want to take off the Crane Bag. Because it was almost empty Matty was able to pull it up behind his head and keep it there while he stretched out flat on the clay floor. Matty was aware of Jack's regular breathing and knew he must have fallen asleep. He felt his own eyelids grow heavy, and just as they began to close Matty heard a voice. He sat bolt upright. It was as if someone outside was taking instructions from a voice which sounded very faint and further away.

'Wake up,' Matty whispered. The heavy sleepy breathing continued.

'Wake up,' Matty repeated in a harsher whisper, feeling around in the darkness; he recognised that he had found Jack's leg. He shook it as hard as he could, then pawed about further along to find an arm and shook them both together.

'What… what…?' Jack was awake.

'They're coming…' said Matty and padded his way to the door on all fours.

'Are you up Jack?' Matty projected his voice in as loud a whisper as he could while clinging to the cross boards on the back of the door and desperately groping for the loops of kite threat.

'Ready,' replied Jack in a quiet voice as the sound of the bolt in the door was scraped loose.

Matty did not have time to reply; he had one hand through the loop and was still manipulating his fingers through the second loop when the door swung open. There must have been a light outside as Matty could see his school bag lying on the clay floor in the rectangle of yellow light the open door shone in before the door ended its motion just short of the wall. Matty secretly smiled: there was no Jack and the man left after a quick search with a large torch beam. Matty knew he had to be ready to run and quickly undid his hands from the loops, then clung momentarily to the upper cross beam before jumping off the bottom beam. The door swung forward slightly. At that same second Jack appeared. They both ran outside and instantaneously Jack made a decision.

'Matty, see that building over there… it must be some sort of a factory, the large building, the one with the lights… and machinery, hear the noise… head to there… find somewhere to hide… I'll distract them with the ring…' Jack said all this hurriedly, anxiously looking around.

Several voices came from the building in front of them which looked like an industrial estate-type building, smaller than the one Matty was destined for.

'Quick, go…' ordered Jack, '… and wait for me… no matter how long it takes… remember the SAS manual…'

Matty ran on uneven ground in the semi-darkness, away from the light which was attached to the roof of the building in front of them and to his left. He could not help but slow down and turn when he heard the voices of the men who had kidnapped them become raucous. All four of them were outside and Jack was walking right up to them. Matty had to stop and watch; his brother could not take another beating. Just as the men converged on Jack he disappeared. They shot back a pace or two, all of them together. Matty continued on his way, reassured. He decided to keep to the shadows and wide of the arch of light coming from the top of the designated meeting place. As he slunk into the half-light he could make out one of the men saying he had seen Matty go in the direction of the nearby building. Matty slunk further into the darkness. It wasn't as bad as the shed they had been in; he could at least see the lights of nearby buildings and there was starlight. What bothered him was that he could not see where his feet were and there was the possibility of snakes always. Two years before his pet rabbit had been devoured by a python.

In a short time Matty was opposite the back door of the building where he was to meet Jack. He stopped resting his hands on his knees to catch his breath as he checked the building. He was facing the gable end; it had a door with lots of wood and barrels and bits of galvanised metal propped up against the wall. *A perfect hiding spot*, thought Matty. *Not large enough for Jack but there are several places I can squeeze into.* To his right, in the direction he had just come from, came the beam of a powerful torch and voices. Matty's heart sank: he had to think quickly. He was reluctant to slink further into the darkness behind him because there may not be any cover there but at the same time he could not run for the building because he would be terribly exposed by the outside light. He ran, continuing to his left and keeping short of the arc of light, and headed for the far side of the building which was mostly in shadow. While panting in the shadow of the factory he decided he would circle the building when the two with the torch would come – he would follow them. And come they did. He could hear them talk and move the metal pieces at the back door and he knew from their conversation they were looking for him.

When Matty realised he had to expose himself in the light at the other side of the factory building he comprehended his plan would not work. He would be completely exposed to the two his brother was still playing hide and seek with. He ventured into the darkness on the shadow side of the building just in time; the torch light flashed here and there, where he had been lurking just seconds earlier. He had no choice but delve into the blackness once again. He crouched down and scurried in a zig-zag path he hoped he could avoid the torch beam. Shortly he crashed into and almost fell into what felt like a sawn-off barrel full of water. He recovered quickly, panting in fright at the unexpected obstacle and felt it all over. It was hardly enough to cover him, so he lay down on the ground, drawing up his knees and lay at the back of the barrel in a foetal position and prayed. What saved him turned out to be information on his brother's progress. The two men with the torch seemed to stand still and watch as their companions continuously pounced on Jack to find he had evaded them. Matty listened as the two who were searching for him decided between themselves that they should help the others catch Jack and he would lead them to Matty. As their footsteps died away Matty uncurled himself and knelt behind the half-barrel. The ground stank: he figured the factory workers were using it as a urinal and the water may be for washing; he'd check his clothes for excrement when he got into the light again.

Jack had progressed to the cross roads which lead to their place of detention. The men appeared to be wising up to his limitations. Instead of moving away each time he disappeared they stayed put so that when Jack reappeared he had to run very fast to get away and the two who had abandoned the search for Matty were closing in.

Matty became desperate again, racking his brain for a distraction and came up with nothing. He calmed himself as best he could, knowing that as long as he panicked his mind would not come up with a solution. He decided to do what they had already determined would be the meeting place, the gable end of the building with the back door and all the scrap. However, when he got to the shadow side of the building he realised there was a man smoking and watching the four men on the road. Matty did not know what to do. If he appeared and asked for help the man may raise the alarm so he stayed hidden until he felt a tugging on the pocket of his uniform trousers. Ganesh was with him: he nodded his head. Matty hoped he had interpreted the sign correctly and with a deep breath he advanced around the corner.

'Can you help me,' Matty said in Malayalam. The man in the dhoti and shirt, who was by this time stubbing out his cigarette, literally appeared startled and replied in what Matty felt must be Tamil. The relief relaxed Matty and he continued in English.

'My brother and I were kidnapped earlier today, after school, by the people who own that building,' Matty pointed to the building, straining his body just a little further to see if Jack was captured. To his relief the four men seemed to be circling something or somebody but Jack was not visible.

'What have you and your brother done?' asked the man, in control of himself again. 'Did you steal from them?'

'No, no… they took us from school… our parents will be very worried… have you got a telephone?' Matty found himself wittering on, not expecting to have to validate himself to this stranger. And then he realised that his uniform must be so dirty and himself smelling of a latrine, that it was no wonder that this man questioned him.

'Which school? Where do you and your brother live?' the man came closer and seemed to examine Matty with more scrutiny.

'We go to Sherrington House School, near the Mount Road and we live on Nungambaccam High Road… my father's name is Ram… may I please use your phone to call him…?' Matty pleaded, looking the stranger straight in the eye. 'We are not thieves.' And Matty strained once again to see if he could see his brother but neither Jack nor the men were visible. Just as panic crept once again into Matty's chest the sound of voices almost beside them rang into his terrified ears. He quickly shot under the rusty galvanised sheet which was propped up against the gable end of the building.

'We're looking for two rag pickers who have run off with some cloth from our textile factory, have you seen two boys… one tall and one short, fair… ?'asked one of the men in Malayalam while Matty closed his eyes. He felt that if he stared at their legs and feet it might in some way draw their attention to him and his hiding place behind the galvanised sheet.

'I didn't know you had a factory over there,' came back the stranger's voice in English. Matty hoped he was distracting the others.

'No, no… factory… the Ambatoor Estate… we teach… the thieves a lesson… locking them… here…' replied one of the kidnappers in broken English.

Matty had to hold himself tightly; his father's cold store was in the Ambatoor Industrial Estate.

'Give me your telephone number and I will ring you if I see them,' said the stranger.

'No, no telephone…' replied the talkative Malayali.

The stranger went back inside the building and the two kidnappers went back in the direction of the building where Jack and Matty had been kept. Matty stayed still and waited in the darkness and absorbed the conversation and the two men.

Shortly and very slowly the back door opened and the stranger beckoned to Matty to come inside the building. Matty expected to see a factory in operation as there was a noise similar to the sounds he was familiar with when he lived in Kerala and visited his grandfather's tin factory: the sound of dyes clamping down noisily on tin sheets, cutting and making lids, and other heavy machines joining the seams forming tins. Instead Matty found himself in a tiny office without a ceiling and knew he was in a factory of some kind. His eyes went straight to the heavy black telephone on the wooden desk and then to the clay water container.

'Drink,' ordered the man.

'Thank you,' replied Matty and knew he was taking a chance, not knowing the source of the water or if it had been boiled, which he doubted, but his tongue felt swollen and his lips had already cracked with the thirst.

'My brother may come soon… we saw your factory from the building where they kept us… he told me to wait here for him…' Matty went on, now more grateful after two steel tumblers of water which tasted of clay.

'Can I telephone my father please?' he asked.

'Go, go,' said the man.

'Dad,' Matty said into the receiver after dialling looking straight at the man who was still eyeing him.

'I'm not sure… wait a minute…where is this?' he asked the man and to his embarrassment tears coursed down his cheeks on hearing his father's voice.

'Wallywackam Industrial Estate, plot eight hundred and eighty-eight,' instructed the man.

'We were kidnapped Dad… we escaped… this man has helped me…' said Matty between wiping the wet from his cheeks and checking his uncontrollable heaving chest.

'Jack is still hiding from them… he said to wait at this factory for him… I'm waiting…' but before Matty could elaborate the stranger curled the fingers of his right hand repeatedly at Matty and he handed over the receiver and spoke in Tamil to his father at some length. Matty was oblivious of what transpired between them, the relief of hearing his father's voice had overwhelmed him. Finally the man handed the receiver back to Matty.

'Yes Dad, yes I will do whatever he says,' said Matty into the phone and replaced the receiver. 'Dad says that he will come with the police and go to the shed where we were put and when they are there my brother and I will come out of the darkness pretending that we hid out there all the time, so that you will not be in trouble with our kidnappers.' Matty felt he was reassuring the man by repeating what had obviously been agreed on. The man just nodded, sat down and began shuffling papers on his desk. Matty sat cross-legged in what was the middle of the floor as there was no space around the sides. Slowly his head tipped forward as sleep took over, exhaustion preventing his brain from the mental activity of worry about his brother… he did have the ring after all. He was jolted alert by three quiet taps on the door. The man stood up and motioned Matty to crawl under the desk. He glanced back to check that Matty was tucked away and gradually opened the door.

'Your brother is here,' came the man's reply in English to Jack's whispered pigeon Tamil.

Jack had been offered water from the clay pitcher which had a cow's head as a spout: when the tap was turned water ran out of the cow's mouth. Jack drank nearly a litre before he felt sated.

There was a clock on the wall; the hands pointed to two-forty-five. When they rotated to three and five minutes past the hour the boys were curled up on the floor asleep. They moved when the factory owner returned from another cigarette but were unable to wake up.

Sometime later, Matty woke as the man kept shaking them both, saying it was time to go into the darkness as there was a police Jeep and a cream-coloured Ambassador car parked outside the building nearby. Through the haze of restful sleep recognition returned and Matty, once again that night, shook his brother hard and helped haul Jack up.

The arrangement went as planned. Matty led Jack beyond the arc of light into the darkness in the direction of the place of their incarceration and eventually Matty buried his head in the soft laundry smell of his father's shirt. He was home.

KATE

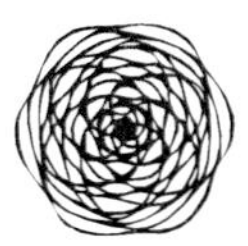

FOUR WEEKS LATER, Kate arrived from Ireland for her school summer holidays. Jack picked her up as before but from Madras airport with Shaker. It took Matty a little while to get used to her. She looked adult; there was something of a woman about her. Even though they had grown close on her last visit, this physically altered Kate created a barely perceptible barrier between them. Matty considered all of this during the first week of her stay at the Tall Magnolia House. Inside she seemed to be the same Kate; Jack and his mother's rapport took off from where it had left off two years earlier but Matty could not get beyond the change in her physical appearance. Her hair had darkened a little: although the sun still caught golden strands, some of the blond just wasn't so light anymore. She had grown almost as tall as his mother and she had breasts and a woman's shape moved inside her old, too-short shirt and shalvar. There was also the fact that Matty had finally learned of her psychic abilities which disconcerted him even more in her presence. He tried to relate to the Kate of old but her strange abilities and everything he had not understood two years ago felt like resentment.

She had knocked quietly on his bedroom door one afternoon when Jack had gone for his tennis lesson. He understood that she was trying to continue their relationship but he just couldn't raise the effort to really get very much involved, regardless of his new knowledge and the altered Kate.

The next afternoon, after school when Jack had left for tennis, she quietly knocked again. Matty, whose bed stuck out into the middle of the room, was sat cross-legged as usual with some of his belongings strewn about on the bed. Kate sat on the bed which was alongside the wall at a diagonal from Matty's that evening. She had chosen the one which ran along the wall opposite the end of Matty's bed the previous evening. But that particular evening after a few minutes of meaningless conversation she came out with what Matty least expected.

'Why does he always sit in that corner beside the cupboard?' she asked.

'Who?' asked Matty.

'Oh come on Matt, you know exactly who I mean,' she said quietly, friendly and knowingly.

'If he moves about when the others are with me I look a bit... distracted... Mum, especially, worries,' said Matty with a sigh, concentrating on the objects on the bed and at the same time knowing full well it was pointless to deny Ganesh's presence, faced with extrasensory abilities like Kate's.

'When did you start seeing him?' Kate asked.

'When we went to live in Bangalore and I nearly choked,' Matty answered. He had a suspicion that she was helping him become more open and he resented that: he did not want to talk about what had happened to him. However, if he was to share anything with anyone, Kate would understand more than any other human being he knew... he was sure he could trust her. More than that, he could feel himself gravitating to the Kate inside the new grown-up body; the real Kate was still the same. All this he considered in the silence between them. He needed to swallow, to get rid of the pain that nearly made him cry at times so rummaged in the Crane Bag and produced a biscuit for Ganesh.

'How does he communicate with you?' she asked, turning and giving Ganesh a reverential *Namaste* as he moved onto his little feet, eyeing the biscuit. Matty watched as the boy God stood up and began to move towards his bed. The portly body of a youngster just short of Matty's height always amazed Matty as it moved deftly and with speed as it did then across the bedroom floor. The little mouse who had been sleeping curled up partially visible underneath Ganesh's yellow lungi roused himself and followed Ganesh across the floor in the scampering way that mice did.

'He puts the thoughts into my head… and sometimes… I feel his touch… even when I can't always see him… like when we were kidnapped…'

'It must have been great for you to have him with you then…' Kate said, leaving the sentence in mid-air as if she was waiting for a reply or confirmation.

'He showed me the Ogham,' Matty found himself willingly giving up his remembrance of that awful night, finding that he could at last talk about what had happened to somebody who would actually understand. It was as if he could let it out of the greyness. Some of the numbness he had been feeling for what seemed years and which had been compounded by the kidnapping seemed to ease away, from his very shoulders and from down his back. He felt safe to question her, half-assured that her answers would not plunge him into confusion and loss again.

'How did you know Kate, how did you know Jack and me were in trouble?' he asked, head down, still fingering the tattered biscuit wrapper which had a couple of biscuits still wedged into the bottom of it, their corners disintegrating into sweet crumbs. Ganesh's mouse appeared on top of the bed, sniffing the biscuit wrapper. Matty emptied the crumbs on to the bed sheet, reserving the biscuits. The mouse busied himself, nibbling the sweet crumbs greedily.

'Just like you can see Ganesh… I can see the people of the Goddess Dana… here and at home in Ireland… they appear to me sometimes… By the way, is Ganesh with you all the time?' she asked, breaking away from answering Matty's question. She had been watching Ganesh feed the little rat the remainder of his biscuit crumbs. He knew she was being open and genuinely curious about Ganesh and not evasive.

'He comes and goes… but he was with me the night of the kidnapping,' replied Matty, looking up at her as Ganesh's trunk sniffed the biscuit paper.

'It's the same with me, they come and go and thankfully they appeared the night you and Jack got into trouble,' Kate eventually answered.

'What are they like?' asked Matty, giving Ganesh the second last biscuit. He took that one with his right hand and popped it into his mouth, the whole biscuit at once.

'The people of the Goddess Dana are a little different here from those in Ireland but only in appearance… and language of course… but I can understand the Danavas here – that's who they are, Danavas, which means people of the Goddess Dana. In Ireland they are called Tuatha dé Danann, which means again people of the Goddess Dana. Both races are ancient and live underground, the

Danavas because they were punished and the Tuatha dé Danann because they were defeated by the Gales and conceded the part of Ireland above the ground to the invaders and they took the bit below for themselves,' Kate explained.

'I can't understand it, Kate: if they are ancient... how and why are they still around?' Matty looked straight at Kate while breaking the last biscuit in half and giving it to Ganesh who was leaning against the side of Matty's bed munching on the previous biscuit. Occasionally, for those who could see, he crumbled a little bit for the rat, who nibbled every bit off the floor, he had consumed every crumb on the bed sheet.

'In Irish mythology there is a place called Tir na Og which means the land of youth. Anyone who goes there, any human even, will live forever. There is no disease, no ageing and no hunger. I suspect the realm where the Danavas live is similar,' said Kate.

'But how can they move between... our life, our space on earth and theirs... and why?' Matty went on questioning with a look of bewilderment.

'Our space and their space is this close,' she pointed at his Crane Bag, 'lift it up Matt. Look at the outside of the bag, it's green; look at the inside, its colour is just lighter, but you cannot separate the outside from the inside of the bag, without both sides the canvas could not be woven, we are that closely intermingled with other worlds but our senses are too rudimentary to sense them...' she went on as Matty continued to look puzzled. 'You remember your grandmother, don't you?' she asked.

Matty nodded.

'I'm sure you don't feel she is really gone,' she asked.

'No, she feels like you just said, close but I can't see her... but Jack dreams about her all the time,' Matty said.

'Exactly, she can only make herself felt in his dreams because of the form she is in now,' explained Kate.

'Then she hasn't really left us?' asked Matty.

'No, and she will be near because of the trouble in the family, I guess...' Kate trailed off.

'I heard Jack tell Mum and Dad about a horrible dream he had... Grandmother came out of a forest covered in blood... it really scared him... otherwise he wouldn't have told our parents,' continued Matty.

'How long ago was that?' asked Kate, alert again.

'A while back, I don't remember,' replied Matty.

'Before the kidnapping?' she asked.

'Oh yes,' said Matty.

'It might have been a warning, then...' she trailed off, again thoughtful.

'Are you saying Grandmother knows everything and is trying to help?' asked Matty.

'Sure she is, naturally she would...' Kate answered, still thoughtful. 'I just wish...'

'What?' asked Matty.

'I wish that Jack would tell me these things... then I could maybe... interpret them for him... and keep him out of trouble...' She trailed off again.

'You think she was warning him... in the dream, because she carried a knife?' Matty continued.

'I'm sure she was... the blood could mean Jack's injury; a knife was held at Shaker's throat...'

They watched as Ganesh chased his mouse across the room, fed him the last of the biscuit crumbs and after some time settled down in the opposite corner.

'But you helped us; how did you know, Kate?' asked Matty quietly.

'I was at school, as usual, and I normally go down town at lunchtime, we have an hour... that day I was so uneasy... not able to concentrate from about half-eleven, which was roughly the time you had been kidnapped, in your time. Instead of going to the shops with my friends I went into the Friary near my school and hung around near the garden which has a railing around it. If it has anything to do with the other-world it is better to be alone, otherwise you can appear flaky, as you rightly said. Anyway, Ailill appeared from behind one of the shrubs and we managed to have a conversation unseen through the railing,' Kate explained.

'Who is Ailill?' asked Matty.

'He's actually a Tuatha... he's a bit like a spirit guide, have you heard of spirit guides... guardian angels?' Kate proffered to Matty's blank look.

'Yes, I have heard of angels, Mum taught us to say the Guardian Angel Prayer when we were little,' said Matty.

'Well you get the idea then, Ailill is sort of like a personal angel but he is actually my spirit guide, I think,' replied Kate.

'What does a spirit guide do?' asked Matty, much more attentive.

'Much the same as a guardian angel... actually sort of like how Ganesh is with you... He's gone again,' she said, looking around the room.

'What does Ailill look like?' asked Matty, nodding to affirm Ganesh's absence.

'Well, much larger than Ganesh. He is a warrior, part of the Fianna which is a famous army going back to before the pyramids... he has red hair and he carries a buckler and short sword, more like a long knife. He wears a kilt and leather sandal-like boots... like Roman soldiers wore. He is ageless and has lived through many lives in Irish history and his job with me is to protect me and Jack and yourself too,' she said all this and then took an obvious breath.

'So what did he say to you in the Friary garden… and how did he know we were in trouble?' asked Matty.

'He has a connection with the Goddess Dana's people here in India through Girija,' Kate began to explain. She moved into a sitting position on the bed with her feet touching the floor and hands active as if preparing to explain something complicated.

'Girija, but Girija is dead,' Matty said and he moved into a similar position on his bed, now facing Kate, almost.

'This is a really long story Matt… you probably don't know about the trouble Jack had with your aunt, the last time I stayed with you in Kerala,' she began.

'He told me that Aunt Saroj wanted Dad out of the business,' explained Matty, 'and you helped him when he went spying on her at a temple, because you can be invisible.'

'Well Jack actually caught your aunt doing black prayers… and… and I could see the black cloud around her too, and when Girija was going to use the gun… remember that day… I called on the Danavas for help but because I was new to all my psychic… well the things I can see and do… Ailill appeared instead,' she said, looking intently to see if Matty understood.

'I understand that… but why were you calling the Danavas for help?' he asked, puzzled.

'They appeared outside the nursery window when I stayed at the Little Pink House warning me that Jack was in danger, remember the snake…?' she asked.

'The one that ate Dodo?' asked Matty.

'Yes, well it was sent by your aunt for Jack, we think or maybe your mum… we're not sure because of my translations and interpretations from the Danava language are not accurate,' revealed Kate.

'But why? Why would Aunt Saroj harm Mum or Jack?' asked Matty, incredulous.

'To scare you all off, get rid of you… and the aunt knew that Jack had spied on her…' Kate stopped. 'Look Matt, I hope this is not too much for you to take in… you know your Mum doesn't know all of this; she suspects it but just doesn't have the proof that we have because she doesn't know about me being psychic… and all that…'

'I didn't tell her about Ganesh either,' admitted Matty.

'I know how you feel, before long they would be bringing us to see psychiatric doctors…' laughed Kate.

'Tell me about Girija, how can she be involved… she's dead?' asked Matty.

'Well Ailill can be mortal for short periods and when he is Jack can see him and so could Girija. The Sunday that Girija brought the shotgun I evoked him and he did not appear in his mortal form till much later that day in Girija's bedroom,' explained Kate. 'I didn't know I had a guide then and I didn't know it was him till I went back to Ireland and Magh told me, you remember the lady I told you about who is the herbalist?' Kate asked Matty.

'I thought you were making that up,' said Matty.

'No I was not but it was Ailill who told me which herbs to use on Jack's wound that day he was injured,' she replied.

'That was later though, the Minotaur,' Matty said making a real effort to acknowledge old terrors.

'Yes and I will tell you about that too but for now I will tell you about Girija,' said Kate. 'Girija fell in love with Ailill and against our wishes decided she wanted to live in Tir na Og.'

'But how? So she didn't slip and drown in the lake...' Matty said to himself, remembering and trying to distinguish between stories and reality. 'Do Mum and Dad think she has drowned?'

'Yes, everyone does,' replied Kate, 'Oh, except Swami.'

'Swami, what...' but before Matty could put the conundrum into words Kate went on.

'He knew everything, he was our advisor, he gave me books to read and advised us on how to protect ourselves and the people in the Little Pink House,' she finished off for him and added, 'You remember the yantras?'

'So... so how did Girija get to Tir na Og?' asked Matty, ignoring her. He felt that that question should be answered as it seemed even more weird than the protection and he wanted to know for himself, he wanted to know of a safe place... if there was such a thing.

'She had to follow Ailill's advice on that. Jack and I were very upset as unlike me there was no way back for her. See, Matt, I don't have to change my consciousness, my brain is tuned to pick up dimensions and the entities that live in them but Girija like most human beings cannot. I would guess that your consciousness is slightly changed because you can see Ganesh.'

'What did Ailill tell her to do?' asked Matt.

'She never told me,' she said and after a pause she went on, 'but she went ahead with it anyway after spending all the school holidays thinking about it. When the time came we all met up at the Residency lake, Swami, Jack and I on a particular night, all according to the traditions of the Danavas and the Tuatha dé Danann. Ailill was accepted by the Danavas at that time and I accompanied Girija on her journey to the other-world... even though I didn't want to...' she stopped... she looked like Matty felt, sad, displaced... sort of just hanging in, but it was just for a moment.

'How did she go there... her body washed up on the lake... remember?' asked Matty.

'We both lay down on the jetty, like I do when I want to be in the otherworld. I waited and waited there with the Danavas and Ailill in their frequency. Ailill would be his mortal self sometimes and go to take Girija as somehow or other her heart had stopped beating and her lungs stopped breathing but Jack would not let her go… he was very upset…'

'Did she commit suicide?' asked Matty.

'No, she just wanted to be with Ailill. I don't know how they do it, but Ailill took her out into the lake eventually, after Swami had persuaded Jack that she was no longer alive. They both disappeared beneath the water, way out in the lake.' Kate had tears in her eyes.

'Do you see her, can you see her now?' asked Matty quietly.

'Yes, she lives with the Tuatha, she lived here with the Danavas at first and had a really hard time, they didn't accept her very well being human and all of that but she is one of them now and has a little boy… a baby,' Kate said, smiling through the tears. 'The Tuatha liked that… the race is dwindling and now she is a sort of hero.'

'Is she helping us too?' asked Matty.

'Yes, very much so… and I don't know why I'm still sad about her. I have visions of her with her baby son in my dreams.' Kate wiped her tears on the tail of her shirt.

'It's like me and Jack and Grandmother,' Matty proffered.

'Yes, there really are heart strings that bind us to the ones we love… I guess,' she said.

'Can we get back to the Friary Garden now, how did Ailill know about us if he is in Ireland?' asked Matty mechanically. It was his turn to pull Kate out of her mire of misery and the fact that he was not suffering alone gave him strength, he could actually feel.

'The Danavas sent word, they are telepathic,' she replied and let Matty digest that piece of information. After a little while she added, 'I don't know if you know, Matty, but if you remember how they came to the Nursery window to warn me… that Jack was in danger all that time ago… well they have been protecting you all for a long time,' Kate said, curling her legs up on the bed again.

'But… why?' asked Matty.

'Jack used to ask the same question and I really think he has forgotten he has their protection, he is still sceptical I guess and he just… battles on in his physical world alone all the time. Because you are still much younger and can see Ganesh, it is easier for you to understand. Your grandfather was a philanthropist, he spread his money around, helped everyone who came in contact with him, that was his philosophy to be continued by your Dad and eventually yourself and Jack. However, your aunt thinks differently, she is a being of... her ego.... her dark subconscious... and strangely enough Ganesh also holds the answers to her misery,' she said thoughtfully.

'How do you know all this?' asked Matty.

'Swami's books,' replied Kate. 'You should check it out, Matt. As far as I'm concerned all the answers are in Hinduism. In some pictures of Ganesh he holds a noose which means bondage of a person's desires and in another hand he holds an axe to cut these ties... what a philosophy you have inherited,' her eyes sparkled and her cheeks were flushed. 'So many symbols.'

'But it's hard not to want things,' countered Matty.

'You don't have to do without things, you have to go back to moderation... listen, what's your favourite food?' she asked.

'Noodles,' Matty immediately replied.

'Well, they wouldn't be if you had them for breakfast, lunch and dinner,' she said with raised eyebrows and her practical look.

'OK, OK.' Matty wasn't too sure but he got the idea. 'So we shouldn't be greedy.'

'Now you've got the idea,' she said, animated again.

'But how do we protect ourselves from our aunt and cousin?' Matty asked, perplexed.

'You already have help...' Kate looked at Matty and waited.

'You mean you,' he said.

'And the Danavas and the Tuatha dé Danann and Ganesh... that's what I'm trying to explain... how this help comes about,' she continued on, explaining what she had learned from Swami two years earlier. 'We are not just living here, Matty, where we do things and things happen to us because someone else has caused them to happen; we are part of a greater place that actually sustains this world.'

'Sustains...?' asked Matty.

'The supernatural, Matt: it exists, the world we live in is a small part only,' Kate was triumphant.

'Were you in that shed with us? Could you see Jack's injured face? And the kidnappers, could you see them too?' he asked, unable to take much more Hinduism or science or both as Kate went on about how the God Krishna revealed other universes to his mother Yashoda.

'No Matt, not till just before you found the Ogham. I had to wait till evening, when I was at home, after school, pretend I was tired so that I could go to my room for an invented sleep, then contact Magh and travel with her. She had not used these particular ley lines before, so that took some working out but eventually we found Ailill,' she assured him.

'You remembered the ring,' he said, putting the rescue back together in his mind.

'Ailill remembered the ring,' she corrected. 'He tormented the kidnappers and frightened them and helped Jack eventually make his escape. But what it means, Matt, is it all comes down to cosmic balance.'

'Balance… what balance… violence and kidnapping and having to uproot…?' Matty was near tears with the frustration of what seemed mere philosophy.

'Challenges Matt… OK, tough ones I agree… but what I'm trying to get across is that you are not alone… and I only wish Jack would get that,' she trailed off as there was a knock on the door.

'Laundry,' came Matty's mother's voice as her nose and the mid-section of her face appeared in the small slit of the barely opened door.

'I'll just put these in the cupboard and then I'll be out of your way,' she said as she opened the cupboard doors and began offloading folded school shirts, trousers, white socks squeezed into balls, T-shirts, etc.

'No problem,' Kate replied, appearing as uneasy as Matty felt.

'Actually… can I suggest something?' his mother went on, continuing to add to the neat piles on the shelves of the cupboard.

'Yeah,' Matty shot in, wondering how long she had been outside the bedroom door.

'Unlike Kerala, Kate, we get a breeze here in Madras around sundown… well a warm breeze, but it's pleasant… would you two like to go for a walk before supper? Only halfway up the lane, don't go all the way to Nungambaccam High Road. Then I can air out this room,' she suggested while closing the cupboard doors and facing them for the first time in the exchange.

'Yeah, let's go Matt,' said Kate.

'Be careful, only go halfway up the lane,' Matty's mother called after them as she followed them out of the bedroom and into the large upstairs sitting room which had the furniture from the big sitting room in the Little Pink House. The furniture from the little sitting room was downstairs in the dining room cum living room which the boys' father used as an office. The dining table was his desk and various people, from the factory workers to jobbers selling buffalo, were seen down there.

There were two entrance doors on the Tall Magnolia House, they were at right angles to each other. Kate and Matty skipped down the stairs and out the door that was used by the family. It was easy to slip into the hallway and up the stairs or go to the kitchen without being seen by their father's visitors or disrupt the proceedings there. Matty wondered why anyone would make two front doors – even though they were ideal for them. He had been told by the owners who lived in the same compound but to the back of the Tall Magnolia

House that it was all to do with Vastu, a sort of Indian Feng Shui, which he was familiar with as his mother had book on both philosophies.

Matty and Kate waved to Emma, Aunt Rose and her mother, Mrs Jaya-Raman's cook. Kate had not yet met the landlady and her beautiful daughter who worked in administration in a construction company. She had met Emma, though, and they communicated in the same way Matty and his mother communicated with her, a Malayalam word here and there from them as they had no Tamil and an odd English word from Emma, accompanied by a huge amount of gesturing. Despite the regular and sometimes good-natured frustrations this caused they had one common cause, the care of the dog.

Matty's father had bought a dog from Bangalore for him shortly after they settled in Madras. A Pomeranian had been advertised and ordered but what arrived was a white ball of fur and when he finally grew up a little he looked more fox than Pomeranian except for the fur and the curled tail. Emma took great pleasure in grooming him and made Wellington boots out of plastic which was secured with rubber bands for him when both yards flooded in the monsoon. He was named Fluffy but Emma had her own name for him.

Their landlady Mrs JayaRaman's watchman was from Nepal; he was educated and spoke fairly good English. He always sat on the porch of Matty's house to be near the gate which let in traffic for both houses. The children skipped past him on their way out; he was busy sticking stamps on rolled up newsletters for Matty's mother who typed and sent out the monthly Overseas Women's Club newsletter. Matty's father had enquired at the British Consulate if there were any clubs for foreigners and this was the one that came up. After the isolation of her life in Kerala the boys' mother was out a couple of days a week, on charity work mainly as that was the ethos of the club as well as providing company for expatriates. Matty was glad to see his mother go out frequently and knew that Jack felt the same.

Matty relayed all this to Kate as they made their way out the gate and up the lane. When he eventually had to draw breath he realised he had not spoken so much for ages, possibly years, and fell silent again.

HISTORY

THERE WAS A very small lane which branched off the end of the residential cul-de-sac that made up Fifth Lane the rented Tall Magnolia House shared this with about eight other houses. Matty decided to introduce Kate to the neighbourhood kids with whom he and Jack played cricket on the road outside their houses for a short while most evenings, but that particular evening nobody was about: *probably at tuition*, Matty thought. When they rounded the bend, into the long part of the lane that led straight up to Nungambaccam High Road, there was no sign of Ackshae either. He was a frequent visitor to the boys' home. He was an only child and his mother and Matty's mother visited each other for tea and exchanged gifts of sweets at festival times.

Kate and Matty strolled along in the heat and the descending twilight. Further along, they noticed Laxmi's children, a boy of about eight and his younger sister, sitting on the kerb with school textbooks, notebooks and pencils underneath a street light, talking in Tamil. Laxmi was a full-time employee at that particular neighbour's house but came to clean the floors and bathrooms in Matty's house too.

'Why are they doing their homework out here?' asked Kate.

'They need the street light to see their books,' explained Matty 'They don't have a room of their own; they probably sleep inside the main house, on the kitchen floor, when dinner is over.'

'Couldn't they sit on the veranda?' asked Kate.

'Servants are expected to be invisible; BuddiaRam sits on our veranda because he is a watchman,' explained Matty.

'We're nearly halfway up the lane,' reminded Kate. 'I don't feel like going back in yet.'

'We don't have to, but this is far enough,' said Matty, looking around. It was quiet in Fifth Lane. There were mostly larger houses hidden behind high walls and watchmen in uniform at the gates on one side of the road and a park on the other which was behind a high wire fence.

'Why don't we sit down on this kerb?' suggested Kate. 'The mosquitoes are not much of a problem yet.'

'OK,' agreed Matty, checking that an approaching car was slowing to go into one of the houses. He couldn't help but be alert and suspicious after the kidnapping.

'Tell me everything that happened since you left Kerala,' said Kate.

'Don't you know?' asked Matty.

'Only the basics: we got a Christmas card from Bangalore the first year and then from Madras the following year, otherwise the telephone calls are few and far between and are amongst our parents. Jack as you know is hopeless, not one letter did I get from him… maybe you'll be better,' she said, smiling mischievously at him.

'It's a long story… and I haven't really thought about it much… I mean in a chronological way… I wouldn't know where to begin,' he said.

'As they say in Alice in Wonderland, "Let's begin at the beginning",' she said, still smiling at him.

Matty was quiet for a while and the light of day had gone by the time he began. Both of them sat on the kerb, the street lights forming golden halos at regular intervals high up in the enclosing darkness. They were just a little bit further along from where Laxmi the cleaner had joined her children and was coaxing them to continue their homework; they were avidly watching Kate and Matty. Matty felt safe physically and secure enough to let go some of his anguish.

'Our first move was to the State of Karnataka. Dad rented a house just outside of Bangalore – it is a plateau city, you know.' Matty turned to look at Kate who was looking through the wire fence into the park. She didn't react so Matty continued as if talking in his head, 'I think Dad thought the climate would be good for Mum's health, the weather was cool and we even needed heaters and hot water bottles in winter.' Matty paused and began again as if thinking back and piecing the bits of his life back together.

'Was your Mum sick?' Kate asked, quietly but surprised.

'She was having problems with her kidneys I think… she had to drink four litres of water a day… which was impossible…and… she was in and out of hospital having tests and sometimes bleeding,' explained Matty, slowly surprised at himself: he had actually forgotten all of that.

'I didn't know that, Mammy didn't say anything to me,' replied Kate.

'Maybe she didn't tell them… your parents or Gran, anyway she's alright now… and all that was ages ago,' explained Matty.

'What I don't understand is, why your Dad was here and you three were in Bangalore,' asked Kate.

'The Karnataka State Government would not grant Dad a licence for an abattoir,' Matty elucidated, 'so he tried here in Tamil Nadu and finally got a license in the State of Andhra Pradesh. He bought land there and it took two years to build an abattoir… he did it as per European guidelines. He hired the butchers from Bombay so Madras was the nearest city for him… the cold store for the meat is here in Madras and there is a port for shipping the meat to the Middle East.'

Then he continued enthusiastically: 'After six months Jack and I and Mum moved into an apartment here with Dad; he had rented it as an office but he lived there too. Mum said she could no longer be separated from Dad and even if we had to move again, so be it, we would pack up yet another time. We would have to start at other schools until we found the place we could call home,' Matty said, not looking at Kate but, like her, looking through the fence as if he was talking to himself. The story had been said slowly and thoughtfully as if Matty really understood it for the first time.

'That sounds very romantic… but I know it must have been anything but,' said Kate. 'What happened to you, how did all this affect you… moving again?' Kate asked.

'All that time I felt I was in no man's land.' Matty stopped talking for a while and then continued.

'Madras did become home, not the apartment but later on through a chain of what Mum calls Earth Angels the parents found the Tall Magnolia House,' said Matt, feeling better than he had in ages.

'Did your parents know the landlady?' asked Kate.

'No,' answered Matty. 'It started with Father Tom who is a really good friend of Dad's from way back to their university days in Dublin. He used to visit us in Bangalore and we would go to his small room at the Seminary near our house. Mum says Father Tom was always at the end of a telephone line whenever anything went wrong, especially when Jack or I got sick as he is a psychologist at St John's Hospital in Bangalore and got us help from any speciality that we needed. In the short six months while we lived in Bangalore I in… what's that word you use when you want to say "by mistake"? It begins with in…' he asked, still lost in his retelling.

'Inadvertently,' she proffered.

'That's it, I swallowed a double dose of de-worming tablets left on the dining room table for Jack and myself, while Mum was on her nightly call to Dad over here. When she later asked us had we taken our medicine Jack said he hadn't taken his and I realised I had overdosed. Within an hour we were all told everything was fine by Father Tom who had spoken to a paediatrician, from St John's Hospital,' Matty said half-laughing.

'How many pills did you eat?' asked Kate.

'Four,' replied Matty.

'Four, that's a lot of tablets... didn't you think it was a little much?' she asked.

'When Grandmother gave us homoeopathy pills we always had to eat several in one go... so I just didn't think...' explained Matty.

'The house you are in now is really a lovely house. I'm not sure which one I like the best, this one or the Little Pink House,' Kate said thoughtfully after another pause as they both stared at the wire fence across the road which was lit by an overhead street light.

'Otherwise, Matt... what was it really like in Bangalore?' asked Kate, seriously.

'I don't miss the time we spent there. For most of the time I felt as if my heart was pinned on a wire outside my chest, it hurt so much. I missed my dog – you remember Daisy; I still have a little bit of her fur in an old match box.' Matt stopped for a while; his head hung down, looking at the weeds growing between the road surface and the concrete kerb. He pulled at them with one hand between his legs in an effort to stop the tears falling from his eyes; he didn't want Kate to know he was upset.

'I couldn't bear to think about the rabbits and although I was allowed to bring all of my toys both Jack and the parents felt we should donate our books to the Atoor Municipal Library as they had no books for small children there and Mum said I had outgrown most of them anyway. It was alright for Jack, he doesn't attach himself to things or pets and he likes adventure and discovering new things and experiences and seemed to have no time whatsoever for how I felt,' Matty continued, to explain the glumness.

'Maybe he does care but can't show it, or doesn't know how to show it... or maybe it was his way of helping you... and helping himself cope with everything that happened to you,' Kate said very quietly. It seemed to Matty she didn't want to intrude on his miserable monologue and at the same time wanted to be part of the experience, so he continued.

'I hated the change, the Bangalore house was so small compared to the Little Pink House that I felt as uncomfortable as Alice in Lewis Carroll's *Alice in Wonderland* as you just said Kate, when we started talking about all... all of this,' he looked up at her. She put her hand on his shoulder ever so lightly and he was able to go on; it was as if it was all spilling out of him.

'We had too much furniture and not only that, the dining table and armchairs were far too big for the rooms. The bedrooms looked normal but they had hidden dangers too. One weekend when Dad was visiting from Madras he actually saved my life. I got my head stuck between the security metal on the window of the tiny bedroom I shared with Jack, lost my footing on the bed and was hanging by my neck from the high window, only able to make squeaking noises. Fortunately Dad thought he heard a whimper and luckily followed his instinct and ran upstairs in time to rescue me… my face had actually turned purple,' Matty said, touching his throat.

'What made you stick your head in the security bars?' asked Kate.

'There was a small garden, well hardly a garden, at the back of the house; it had a small tree, I don't really know what the tree was but I thought I heard a noise and wondered what Jack was up to so I opened the window and couldn't see much and then pushed my head through the bars… really because I could do it to have a better view and…'

'Got stuck… and nearly hung yourself…' finished off Kate.

'Yeah,' said Matty but didn't feel it was very funny thinking about it again.

'When Dad was in Madras, which was most of the time, he hired a watchman. The watchman came at seven at night and left at seven in the morning. He wore a khaki uniform not like the watchman at the Little Pink House who wore a lungi and shirt, who was friendly and helped me with the rabbits and dogs and Mum with the garden. This very thin man spoke a language that made talking impossible, not that I saw much of him anyway. More upsetting for me was the driver who took us to school and took Mum shopping for the groceries and to visit Irish nuns Father Tom had introduced her to. Several times the car ran out of petrol on the lonely highway between the city and our house which was in a residential area five mile outside the city. Apparently the driver had been siphoning off the petrol and would arrange for the car to run dry at certain times, especially when Mum was in the car and had money to give him to buy more to get us home. Added to this despair… at not being able to do anything except watch her pay up was this tense atmosphere, which I picked up from Mum as we sat waiting in the dark on a motorway with nothing but open countryside all around us… waiting for the driver who never took that long as the car always ran out of petrol not too far from a petrol station. Sometimes he would ask for money to pay for an auto rickshaw to get to the garage. It was awful; that part of the countryside was full of bandits known as Dacoits.

'And then there were the snakes. The first one was a Russell Viper which came within two feet of Dad's head when we visited a park on our very first week in Bangalore. Dad drove us around the city and we found a large park. The parents had stretched out on an area of rock enjoying the mild climate while I followed Jack as he explored the park. Fortunately Mum heard a rustling sound; she felt it was dried leaves at first and ignored it but when she lifted her head to check and saw the snake with the killer venom,' Matty said, reliving the alarm he had felt back then.

'What a shock, Matt,' Kate said.

'That's not all Kate. There was a hedge separating our house from the next one, we found out it was full of snakes. Halfway into our stay in Bangalore the Snake Catchers had to be called again, different ones although they were much like the ones who came to the Little Pink House; but I hadn't the heart for it, I just couldn't care about things too much then. Jack was angry and I couldn't understand why… but after what you told me about the snake in the bathroom in the Little Pink House I think I know why he was so annoyed,' said Matty, looking at Kate for an answer.

'There is no proof… but it makes you wonder… and lately the kidnapping…' she trailed off, deep in thought.

'Should we be forever on our guard Kate…? This is not a life…' he trailed off and stared through the wire fence; he had his lower lip trapped between his teeth.

'I don't think she'll try kidnapping again,' Kate said at length.

'Why, how do you know?' asked Matty.

'I talked to Jack. You know how my bedroom downstairs is right beside the living room? Well, Jack apparently overheard a conversation your Dad had with someone in Malayalam on the phone just after the kidnapping. From that he could glean your grandfather was very angry with your aunt as it turned out her ex-husband had something to do with hiring the ruffians who grabbed Jack and you,' explained Kate.

'Nobody told me this,' said Matty.

'I don't think they know how to handle you Matt, they are afraid to tell you anything in case they upset you more than you have been already because you're only ten,' she said. After a little while she added, 'Your Dad and Jack don't know about Ganesh, do they?'

'No,' and then annoyance metamorphosed into frustration. 'I've survived a kidnapping and two moves and this is my third school… you would think they would talk about things… Mum tries but the way she comes about it really makes me want to… well, close up and not talk at all, and as for Dad, well…' Matty stopped.

'What?' asked Kate.

'Well he says,' and Matty did his best to put on his father's accent, 'You must be ready to move anywhere in the world in ten minutes.'

'You are funny, Matt,' said Kate, giggling.

At that moment at the end of the lane Matty's mother appeared. They both noticed her at once. She waved and then beckoned to them to come home. They both stood up and she disappeared around the bend.

'Tell me about Ganesh,' said Kate as they began sauntering along the lane towards home.

'Why?' asked Matty.

'To be honest Matt I'm trying to… ascertain,' she had her fingers interlaced and opened her palms as if trying to express herself, 'if you are psychic or if Ganesh made himself visible to help you through your bad time,' Kate said and stopped and looked straight at Matty.

'I think he's helping me Kate, like a guardian angel. I don't think I'm psychic,' Matty said honestly.

'You're a very mature young man Matt, but tell me how he came about anyway,' she said, starting to stroll along again.

'In the midst of all of the uncertainty and… well, my unhappiness I just… spent a lot of time in the little bedroom in the house in Bangalore. The weather was cool enough to wear socks and a sweater and the smallness of the room somehow made it cosy. Jack often nagged me to come to the neighbour's house to meet the children there, a boy and a girl. Sometimes I went but mostly I preferred to be on my own with my things. Jack spent a lot of time there; the kids' parents rented out videos so Jack spent ages watching videos with the boy. Mum did not have help so she spent her time doing the cooking and cleaning, so I was on my own a lot of the time. It was during that time that I saw him for the first time,' Matty said, slightly embarrassed, as he moved slowly along at Kate's snail's pace.

'I had my own other-worldly encounter when I was a little older than you. Well, I could always see orbs and I could feel presences but didn't know what they were… or if I needed an eye test,' Kate had stopped walking as if thinking back, she giggled and went on. 'Two years ago, a little while before I came to stay with you in Kerala, I started seeing the beings. Sometimes they are so real, like Ganesh, when he appears. I can't tell if they are physical or not… mostly with the Tuatha I know due to their clothing but here it is impossible as people have been wearing the same clothes for thousands of years. Now I know for sure as the other-worldly people are very big.'

'Is it a problem, Kate,' asked Matty, 'having them suddenly appear and then disappear?'

'I'm getting used to it. Magh has explained a lot to me and it is easier and less frightening… and of course I'm able to switch off partially and on again when I need their help… I must say I am a bit afraid of meeting them in case there may be bad ones out there who might want to hurt me, just like here with you and the kidnappers.'

INCUBUS

JUST AS THEY were about round the bend into the last of the cul-de-sac the sound of a diesel Ambassador ended their conversation as they moved out of the road and onto the pavement. It stopped and Jack jumped out of the passenger seat, leaving the driver to deliver the car home.

'What are you two doing out here?' he asked.

'We're out for a stroll and a catch up,' explained Kate.

'Catch up on what?' asked Jack.

'On what has been happening to you all since I last saw you,' explained Kate with a hint of sarcasm.

'I thought we went through that,' said Jack seriously.

'Jack you don't have to be so… furtive, Kate told me all about what happened with the aunt in Kerala,' said Matty with more than a hint of scorn in his voice.

Jack stopped in the middle of the road and so did Kate and faced him.

'Like he said, Jack, he has been kidnapped, moved from pillar to post… he has a right to know exactly why,' said Kate defensively.

Matty stopped walking too and stayed a little distance from the two conspirators, watching them, waiting for possible arguments as to what might be disclosed.

'For God's sake Jack, he's just two years younger than you and I were when all this happened… no, no… just one year younger than you were when you first suspected the aunt.' Kate was fiery, defensive, justifying her disclosure to Matty.

'OK,' was all Jack said and began walking ahead of the other two until he reached the porch and the downstairs sitting room where he flung himself on to one of the armchairs. It was night and work in the office had finished for the day. They could hear their parents talking to each other upstairs. Usually they lay on the bed under the fan cooling off after their work. Kate and Matty sat down on the sofa at right angles to Jack and looked at him and waited. He was agitated. They heard the gate scrape as the watchman let the driver walk his bicycle out on to the road. Kate got up and put the fan on full speed; it was still hot inside the house. She shut the door, stood briefly on her toes to look out through the little window at the top of the door and sat down in the other armchair extending her arms out on the arms of the chair, keeping them far away from the heat of her body.

'If the parents know you know everything Matt, Kate and I will be in trouble,' said Jack, looking straight at Matty.

'Is that all you are worried about… how to save your own skin?' countered Matty.

'No, they will worry more about you worrying –' Jack was cut short by Matty.

'Remember what Father Tom said, I have a mind like an oyster, whereas you just spill the beans,' said Matty.

Jack could not help laughing. 'That was ages ago Matt.'

'What's with the metaphors?' asked Kate.

'He's right, he's better at keeping secrets than I am,' explained Jack, unable to hold a dour mood for very long. 'Father Tom used to practise psychoanalysing us when we were younger.'

Matty sat and watched them, he was sure there was something they were not telling him. Finally he said 'What?', and looked at them both.

'The parents are thinking of sending you to Ireland with Kate when she goes back in September,' said Jack, half-whispering and listening intently to see if his parents were still talking upstairs.

'Why… it's because of the kidnapping, isn't it?' asked Matty.

'Yeah, it's spooked Mum big time,' replied Jack.

'What about you, why should I be the one to be… to be dispatched?' Matty asked petulantly.

'Jack needs to be here to keep an eye on your father,' Kate said.

'What's wrong with Dad?' asked Matty.

'I can see a dark energy… which follows him… once he goes out the gate,' said Kate hesitatingly, looking both at Jack and Matty. She spoke quietly and carefully.

'Outside, you mean out on the road?' Matty asked.

'Yes Matt, it will not come into the yard, it will not pass the gate, it waits out there and attaches itself to him when he leaves,' she explained and listened again to hear the conversation upstairs continuing.

Is it harmful?' asked Matty, trying not to show fear as he needed to be part of them and their strategies.

'We think it probably… is negative for him…' for a short second or two Kate appeared as if she was prevaricating, then she said, 'but we also think he is aware of it. Jack says the Hindu priest who does pooja every evening at sundown was arranged by your Dad, so we think he is taking measures to counteract this thing.'

Matty looked at Jack.

'If you go to Ireland for a month or so, Matt, I will have less to worry about. The focus seems to be on Dad at the moment. Mum is not showing any signs of psychic attack and they will not try to kidnap me again,' Jack explained.

'What good are you? You cannot see this thing like Kate can, you won't know if it is still following him or not,' argued Matty.

'No, but I can keep an eye on him, go to the factory with him – and the cold store especially, he generally goes there after his work, at night,' explained Jack.

'What about Ailill, can he help Jack when you are not here?' Matty directed the question at Kate.

'Wow,' Jack shot upright, 'you really have told him everything,' he accused Kate.

'I had to explain how I was in that shed where you were locked up,' she replied indignantly, 'and yes Matt, he will be the go-between. Jack,' she said, looking at Jack, 'you have got to get a grip on Ogham, it's a must… what's the point of him being mortal and you not able to communicate?'

'But why doesn't it come inside?' asked Matty.

'What, Matty?' asked Kate.

'The thing, that dark energy, surrounding Dad,' Matty asked.

'Jack and I think it's repelled by the prayers. Your landlady, Jack tells me, prays all day, rosary after rosary and then there are the prayers your father is conducting here; anything negative would not be able to stand cleanliness or holiness,' she said.

'So how can we… detach it from Dad?' Matty asked.

'I'm working on that and he is working on it too except we don't think he has told your Mum about it, so don't say a word to her, Matt,' warned Kate.

'I think she knows, I wondered why she was on about culture and finding my Irish roots lately,' mused Matty.

'Who's talking about Irish roots?' asked the boys' father as he stepped into the room.

'We were,' Kate said quickly. Jack had a startled look and there was so much going on in Matty's head his normally quick brain was immobilised with what he had found out that night; the sudden appearance of his father dressed in a suit rather than the dhoti he wore around the house indicated that he was going to the cold store.

'Where are you going, Dad?' asked Matty, the suit bringing him back to reality.

'To the cold store, the lorry is on its way from Andhra,' he explained.

'Can I come, Dad?' asked Jack.

'Why, it's a school night…?' their father began.

'I'd really like to see it, Uncle Ram,' Kate quickly pleaded.

'Maybe some other time, Kate. I'll be there a long time, we're unloading a lorry load of meat…' he was cut short once again, this time by their mother.

'Who's going to the cold store on a school night?'

'I haven't been yet,' said Kate quietly and Matty watched her 'poor little thing' act; 'and I don't have school, my yoga classes don't start till Monday.'

'I've done my homework,' Jack added. Matty knew Jack was lying: he had spent the evening with his friends after tennis.

'Jack, who do you think you are fooling?' asked his mother harshly. Matty knew Jack managed to fool her most of the time but this was not one of them.

'Projects Mum, haven't you heard of team work?' Jack shot back at her as harshly as she had accused him of the hidden lie in the tone of her voice; he tried to undermine her with his.

'Stop this,' interjected their father who like Matty recognised the underlying warfare that had been ongoing between Jack and his mother about lying.

Matty watched the parents look into each other's face.

'You had better catch up on your studies tomorrow evening, Jack,' their mother said threateningly.

'Thanks, Aunt Elizabeth,' said Kate who disappeared into her room.

'There's no point in even asking, is there?' said Matty.

'As always you're right Matt,' said his father sitting on the sofa and putting an arm around Matty's shoulder, pulling Matty towards him. Matty leaned into his father's soft chest, searching for the reassuring comfort of the laundry smell and Old Spice aftershave. This was never put where it was meant to go: it was splashed on the under arms of his shirt instead and when he and Jack were little he would splash some on the under arms of their shirts too, both he and Jack holding up their arms in unison for the careless splashes after dressing to go out. Their father made this more exciting by keeping a watch out for the mother and they would all three process out of the dressing room with benign smiles in her direction as she pinned in the pleats in her sari or merged lipstick onto her lips.

That night Matty was not really upset that he couldn't go to the cold store. He had a lot to digest and felt a lot more in control after his talk with Kate, despite the revelations. He sensed that if Jack was with his father his place was to keep an eye on things in the house. He had his supper and did his homework at the desk in Jack's room which Kate now used. The mosquitoes had bothered him under the kitchen table; despite the fact that the doors were closed at twilight and the windows netted, the odd mosquito got in. He didn't put on the air conditioner, preferring to look out into the yard through the open windows.

That part of the compound was for their landlady; a wall separated it from the front entrance. It was erected between their sitting room and bedroom windows and was very much part of the garden with a tree growing on the landlady's side and shrubs growing on their side. Emma was in her kitchen cooking dinner. He could hear the clang of metal ladle on aluminium as she stir-fried, while Fluffy lay dozing on the doorstep.

Even though they lived in the middle of a very large city the Tall Magnolia House and its grounds were always peaceful. It was set in a hollow, not apparent from the road but at the back of the compound the roof tops of huts were visible above a thirty-foot-high wall that ran along behind all the houses in the very end bit of the cul-de-sac. Nobody ever shimmied down the wall to rob or prowl. The only things which came over and down from that high wall were kittens – lots of them – two and three at a time, for many evenings in succession. They had to be hidden from Matty's father as he didn't like cats at all. Matty's mother was fine with them and Emma agreed to hide them in Mrs JayaRaman's unused downstairs sitting room. Mrs JayaRaman preferred to stay upstairs in her bedroom where she had a very large, elaborately carved altar in a dark wood: *probably teak*, Matty believed. The kittens were taken out to the back of the Tall Magnolia House every evening to be touched, admired and fed more milk. One evening they were caught and Matty's father ordered Emma, in Tamil and in no uncertain terms, to get rid of them. She quickly gathered them up, helped by Matty, while his mother pleaded with his father. He eventually agreed to have one, as long as it was kept outside. The others were packed into a gunny bag and after a lot of incomprehensible shouting upwards from Emma, with her head tilted backwards, the faces of children appeared, looking down, and conversed. After a little while a youth above suspended a rope to which Emma attached the bag and the kittens were hoisted upwards, never to be seen again. Matty remembered he didn't have much choice but Emma was allowed to keep her favourite, whom she named Kavatia; after all, she looked after the kitten and would have to take care of her as it was not allowed into the Tall Magnolia House. That didn't bother Matty too much as he spent a lot of time in Mrs JayaRaman's kitchen with Emma and Fluffy anyway. Matty smiled to himself as he picked up his fountain pen: Emma's kitten turned out to be a boy but she kept the girl's name she had given it.

FAMILY

BOTH JACK AND Matty were woken by their mother at the usual time. Matty crept sleepily to the bathroom as it took Jack longer to wake up and it was easier to just get on with things and avoid the row that would break out between Jack and his mother otherwise. Shaker had been kept waiting several mornings during the last year as Jack staggered out of his room downstairs and had to leave for school without breakfast. He had become nocturnal, playing computer games and watching cable TV into the small hours. The television had been removed from his room and was placed in the upstairs sitting room where the sound of it would wake their mother, if he was tempted in the night. The reason it had been in the downstairs bedroom was because it was easier to cool, being a smaller room than the upstairs sitting room; but Jack's night viewing put an end to all of that. Matty suspected that the computer would be the next thing to be carted upstairs. Although he figured that, because Jack had been made to sleep upstairs in Matty's room since the kidnapping and his mother padlocked the door leading from the stairs into the upstairs sitting room, the computer may well stay in place; his mother used it for typing the Overseas Women's Club newsletters.

When Matty finished with the bathroom, remembering to go over the difficult bits of Hindi pasted around the mirror while he brushed his teeth, he called Jack again and began dressing. Jack was laconic in the mornings and Matty knew it was pointless to ask questions about the 'leviathan'. He wanted to know what Kate had seen on the trip to the cold store. He didn't have to wait long for news. Shoelaces tied and his school bag slung over one shoulder, he slipped downstairs to find Kate helping herself to Scotch pancakes with honey and a mug of tea at the kitchen table.

'First one down as usual,' she said cheerfully.

'Where's Mum?' he asked.

'Gone upstairs to change, here, have a Moon Rock, she's just made them,'

Kate urged as she took the lid off the warm container, holding it in Matty's direction.

'How do you know they are called Moon Rocks?' he asked smiling, stretching out for two from behind one of the two glasses of milk his mother had set in place for Jack and himself.

'I have had the pleasure of living with you people before,' she formulated feigning a questioning look.

'Oh yes, sorry… I forgot,' replied Matty, momentarily a little disconcerted.

'No problem, you are just not used to seeing me at this dining table… Well, same table… different house,' said Kate mitigatingly.

'How did things go last night?' Matty asked, keeping his voice low and pouring honey liberally over one of the pancakes, then pushing his plate slightly to the side. Ganesh appeared, heaved himself up on to the chair next to Matty's and began breaking off bits of the gooey pancake and sniffing the plate with the tip of his trunk. As he brought those pieces to his mouth Kate watched him eating.

'You meant the incubus?' asked Kate, eyes on the little God.

'Yes, did it go with you to the cold store?' Matty asked, slowly eating the other pancake, wiping the little portions on the end of his fork in the excess honey from the one Ganesh had almost finished.

'Oh yes, it put itself in the car between your Dad and Jack. It was a good opportunity for me to get close to it…' She didn't finish.

Ganesh's mouse leaped from a vacant chair on to the table, startling the two momentarily.

'Well… how bad is it?' he asked after watching the mouse approach Ganesh's plate, hoping he appeared courageous, afraid she may become reticent.

'I still feel an acrid taste in my mouth this morning; it is horrible, Matt. You see, I'm able to see it, smell it, feel it and I think even taste it. There is actually a smell of sulphur off it. It's angry,' she whispered. 'I think it knows your father is trying to get rid of it… so it's as if it's clinging more… and the change it makes in him: he was cross and short-tempered at the cold store.'

'I know; he and Mum had a row at the beach one evening just before you came. Mum ran off into the darkness towards the sea… I was really scared, Kate,' Matty admitted, looking but not seeing his untouched Moon Rock.

'Better get another one Matt, he's already finished,' urged Kate. By this time the little mouse was standing on his hind legs sniffing the air.

Matty took up the lid off the hot dish and placed another pancake on the plate, again dribbling a tablespoon or more of honey over the butter he had spread on the Scotch pancake, and they both watched the little elephant God help himself. The mouse nibbled at the non-buttered edges; Ganesh appeared happy to share.

'Is there anything else that can be done… other than the prayers Dad is doing?' Matty asked as he cut a triangle out of the spongy pancake that he brought towards his mouth.

'I'm going to work on that today,' Kate said, smiling and added, 'I will be having a very long nap to get over my jet lag.'

'But you're over it,' said Matty, surprised, after swallowing the well-chewed triangle of pancake.

'I know that, you know that, but your parents do not know that and I need a couple of hours with the Danavas and maybe even the Tuatha,' she said, winking.

'So you're going into your other self,' Matty said, understanding. 'Have you seen the Danavas yet?' he asked, cutting into the pancake again.

'No… I sort of expected them… but… nothing or no one…' She was cut off by Jack's arrival.

'Moon Rocks,' he said, 'lovely.' *More sociable than usual because of Kate*, thought Matty. The others did not respond. They were watching Ganesh and the little mouse slide off Jack's chair and disappear under the table.

'Did you tell Jack?' asked Matty once he was sure his brother had not squashed Ganesh.

'Yes, at the cold store,' she nodded.

Matty's eyes widened as he watched the last morsel of a Moon Rock being snatched from the plate in front of Jack's chair. It disappeared in speedy nibbles before the normally sighted Jack could see it.

'Hey,' said Jack, 'whose plate is this?' He realised there was honey on it just as he was about to place a pancake on it.

'Oh… I think your mother may have had a pancake before she went upstairs,' Kate quickly interjected. Jack rose and got himself a clean plate from the cupboard.

There was a knock on the kitchen door at that moment and Kate unbolted it to let Laxmi in to clean the floors. Kate gave her a *Namaste* and Laxmi gave her a half-hearted one in return.

'She gives such a harmless *Namaste*,' remarked Kate when Laxmi had taken the broom and disappeared into the sitting room.

'Mum says the same,' said Jack; he was already on his second Moon Rock.

'She gives Grandfather one that is right above her head,' remarked Matty as he cupped his hands around the glass of milk in order to hide the fact that the milk was disappearing. Kate winked an approval at his technique as she watched the little trunk lift itself from the glass, a drop or two of milk dripping off its tip as it disappeared under the table.

'Mum thought it was because she was Christian and Grandfather and Dad are Hindu, but Dad says that Grandfather tips a lot better than Mum and religion doesn't come into it,' laughed Jack between mouthfuls.

'Well… what sort of a *Namaste* does she greet your father with?' asked Kate, quizzically bending and looking at Ganesh pour the milk so expertly into his mouth with his trunk.

'Better than the one she gives Mum, but not as good as the one she gives Grandfather,' replied Jack. 'But then she knows who pays her wages,' he added after swallowing another wedge of pancake. Kate resumed her upright position at the table and began eating again. Matty noted that Jack look at her strangely but was so involved in his breakfast that he obviously did not give her duck and dive another thought.

Shortly Meena the cook arrived. She spoke English. She greeted all three by standing formally at the end of the table leading into the little kitchen, a type of scullery attached to one side of the main kitchen. There was one at Matty's grandmother's house in Ireland too; that was known as the back kitchen.

'Good morning,' she said smiling.

'Good morning Meena,' chorused all three as Fluffy rushed in through the open door and immediately began sniffing the floor underneath the table, white tail curled over his back.

There was rustling of fabric as Meena changed her sari in the part of the little kitchen which was hidden from view, as it didn't have a door. By the time breakfast was finished and Meena had on her work sari the boys' mother appeared.

'Good Morning Madam,' said Meena with a smile as Kate and the boys watched their mother take raw meat from the fridge. It was veal fresh from the abattoir and as she discussed the menu with Meena, the boys rose to leave for school. Fluffy began to growl and Ganesh's mouse ran right across the kitchen table, causing Kate and Matty to shoot glances at each other. *Where had he come from? There was no sign of Ganesh.*

Matty called Fluffy to his side and went into the other room on his way to the car. The dog stood on his back legs and pawed Matty's trousers and ran alongside him towards the front door, some of the time on four legs and the rest of the time on two, enjoying the attention. Matty rubbed Fluffy's tummy reassuringly before getting into the back seat.

MAGH

MATTY WAS DISTRACTED all day in school. His friend Nikil got into a bad mood with him; he was so inattentive to his conversation, apparently.

'Well, are you coming or not?' asked Nikil for a second time and not a little tersely.

'When?' asked Matty.

'This evening,' repeated Nikil; he stood akimbo.

'I think I have Karate,' replied Matty, desperate for an excuse.

'You do Karate tomorrow evening,' said Nikil and walked away fuming.

'Nikil, Nikil,' called Matty as he threaded his way among the throng on the school veranda. 'Your mum is here,' and then he followed on with: 'Saturday, will you come to my house on Saturday? My cousin is staying with us, she is from Ireland, you can meet her,' said Matty pleadingly as Nikil opened the front door of his mum's Maruti.

'OK, what time?' asked Nikil; having closed the door he was winding down the window.

'Around ten, stay for lunch,' shouted Matty as the car pulled away from the veranda and the car behind moved forward in the queue and came to a halt.

On arriving back home Matty found Kate was nowhere to be seen. He peered from the kitchen door. Radha the secretary was typing in the little room off the sitting room. His father was in conversation at the dining table-desk with Suresh, the young man who ran the company with him.

'What are you looking for, Matty?' asked his mother, laying out their milk and biscuits.

'Nothing,' Matty thoughtlessly answered.

'Remember you have Hindi tuition at seven,' she reminded him.

'I know,' replied Matty, pulling out a chair.

It was an hour later that Kate appeared in the upstairs sitting room as the boys watched *Drop the Dead Donkey* on cable.

'Were you... somewhere...?' asked Jack without turning down the volume on the television.

'Yeah,' said Kate wearily and Matty thought she looked very tired.

'Well, is there anything, any help, anything that can be done to help?' asked Jack.

Matty sat and listened intently.

'I got hold of the Danavas...' she took a breath. 'It was hard going, I had to search for ages along the paths I used two years ago and then I only got hold of a few of them. Apparently... from what I can gather, the man, the commander we knew, remember,' she said, looking at Jack, 'well, he is no longer about... and I don't understand why, has he moved or what... I'm just not fluent enough with their language to understand what they say about him. They seem to recognise him, though... No, so I don't think we can count on them for much help, especially with the incubus. The very mention of it frightens them and they just didn't seem to want to know me.'

'So we have no protection at all,' Jack said.

'I have the feeling that they are pretty powerless against the incubus... but they seem to know you are under psychic attack, they are aware of that, that there is something bad going on. That doesn't mean they cannot help you in small ways, so I made a specific request to them for help... all these otherworldly beings are the same, they will not interfere, so as I said, I have now made a formal request for their help,' she explained with a sigh.

The room was quiet; the applause and witty remarks from *Drop the Dead Donkey*, although loud, seemed far away. After a little while Kate seemed to light up. 'I did find out something useful from them, though: the incubus has been invoked by a very powerful pooja, a combination of three of the vilest parts of Christianity, Islam and Hinduism.'

'Religion is supposed to be good,' Matty said slowly and thoughtfully in low tones, disheartened.

'I don't know anything about Islam and only a little about the darker side of Hinduism but in Christianity it would mean the Antichrist,' Kate said gravely.

'You mean the Satan?' asked Matty.

'Yes,' was all Kate answered and then added, 'that, I think, explains the power of the thing.'

'So what should we do?' asked Jack and looked blankly at Kate.

'Were you able to contact Ailill?' asked Matty before Kate could answer.

'Yes, but first I thought I should have a word with Magh – you remember Macha and Magh, the rhubarb people?' she asked, looking at both of them in succession.

'But, how...?' Matty began.

'Matt, I can travel back and forth between the worlds, as can the beings that are not living in linear time, like Ailill. Magh taught me reliable travel paths, especially for my visit since we knew you were in trouble again,' explained Kate.

'So… it's much easier for you now, to travel I mean,' began Jack, 'no more fear of the unknown?'

'Yes, it is always scary, but my path to Magh has been studied and rehearsed. The trip to find the Danavas was something else, though. Magh has advised me not to go out again searching for them. Oh, and by the way, she told me the exact term for the dark energy following your father is known as a succubus not an incubus, but it's the same thing really,' she added.

'Has she ever dealt with a suc… how you say it, incubus?' asked Jack.

'Yes, incubus is easier. She suggested I meet the faerie woman from Cruachain when she heard about the succubus,' Kate went on to explain.

'By faerie woman…?' Jack began.

'Yes Tuatha de Danann, but a dangerous type… sort of a witch, but I don't have to meet her in person, Magh knows someone who can be an intermediary,' said Kate, unusually uneasy.

'Dangerous how?' asked Matty anxiously.

'Normally when black magic is used here or elsewhere a payment has been given… well it's the same to have the magic undone… and it's going to be tough to get rid of the succubus,' explained Kate, looking at her interlocking fingers.

'What are they asking for?' asked Jack.

'Too much… it's not something that we can give…' Kate seemed evasive, disturbed almost.

'What do you think it might be?' persisted Jack, poised and piercing.

'That's the trouble, they decide the payment,' said Kate; 'usually the price is high and we have no way of knowing what they might ask me for.'

'I think you do Kate… what did Magh say the witch would ask for?' Jack sat even more upright and stared right at her.

'Matty… she may ask for Matty,' whispered Kate.

'Where is Cruachain?' asked Matty.

'It's a gateway linking our world and the dark other-world,' said Kate. 'Geographically it is in Connacht in Ireland, used to be the old Tuatha capital,' she answered a little lighter and then added, 'I can get there from here. Magh said she would give me some protection but…'

'It sounds too dangerous,' said Matty, standing up. 'And what good am I to a witch?'

He felt so restless. He had a quick look down the stairs and could hear his mother greeting her yoga instructor in the kitchen. He walked back to the sofa, sat again beside Jack and looked at Kate.

'You remember the changeling game we made last time I came to India?' She waited for their acknowledgements and then continued, 'Probably to enslave you. Cruachain has a lot of burial mounds; some of the skeletons belong to children.'

'So it's real, they're mining for gold?' asked Matty.

'They are mad about anything shiny and especially gold,' Kate confirmed with conviction, 'but they are not all like Cruachain. She is a dark one; according to Magh, the only one who snatches children still.'

'This is madness,' exclaimed Jack. 'Why are you even telling him… any of this?'

'I need to know,' insisted Matty passionately, turning to face Jack.

'There is another option… it may not be as powerful though…' Kate said placatingly.

'Is it dangerous?' asked Matty.

'Magh doesn't think it is as dangerous as asking the witch directly, mainly because she doesn't feel she can trust the witch of Cruachain,' answered Kate.

'What is it?' asked Matty.

'Magh knows a woman… she is not of the Sidhe but she is Tuatha dé Danann. This is the person who she will ask to intercede for us with the witch,' Kate began to explain.

'How can that be?' asked Jack. 'Surely she is a faerie or she isn't!'

'No Jack, it can happen; look at me, for example,' Kate attempted an explanation.

'Like Girija,' Matty's input clarified everything, instantly permitting the plan to unfold.

'Well I don't know how she came about… Magh says she came from the shining Brugh in the east. Don't ask me what that means, I didn't have time to go into that; I was more interested in Magh's idea. But she is the granddaughter of the Dagda,' Kate began again.

'The Dagda, who is that?' asked Jack sarcastically.

'He was a Father-God of the first generation of the Tuatha dé Danann, the ones who settled in Ireland. He no longer lives in the other-world, in fact he is buried at Newgrange – remember, I told you about the tombs at Newgrange,' she said, looking from one to the other. Matty nodded his head. Jack wore an expression of impatience and disbelief and shook his head from side to side in disbelief at Kate's explanations.

'This woman is a famous shape shifter and her name is Aillien,' Kate said, appearing more confident. 'Magh thinks she may intervene for us with the witch… it would be a lot safer for us that way.'

'Will she not ask for fees…?' warned Jack, cynically.

'According to Magh, no; maybe a visit,' she said very quietly.

'Visit, who will she want to visit?' demanded Jack.

'Magh hopes that if Matty just appears… as a sort of thank you… and acknowledgement for Aillien's help.' She no longer could look at Jack.

'I actually suggested Matty… your parents are sending him to Ireland anyway,' she added defensively.

'Like Girija, remember Ailill and Girija?' Jack's anger came spitting out with the words.

'What do you mean? Was Girija given to the Tuatha dé Danann as payment for our escape…?' asked Matty, perturbed with sudden realisation.

'Girija went of her own free will, just like I told you,' replied Kate firmly.

'Can you prove she wasn't brainwashed in her vulnerable position?' Jack shot back.

'We will never know for real, Jack,' said Kate quietly; 'I only have her word for it,' she added with a little hint of ridicule.

'Did Magh really tell you what payment would be expected for this… this ban-sidhe?' demanded Jack with not a little arrogance and unease. Matty felt Jack resented having to deal with the other-world, having to obey rules that he couldn't quantify scientifically.

'I told you she is not from the Sidhe… she has her own body which… has not aged or wasted despite her age…' Kate trailed off, lost for proof she needed to persuade Jack, who was seemingly more convinced of the opposite.

'She's a faerie woman and will need paying,' Jack spat back, getting up and looking out the window.

'As I said earlier, Magh thinks she may want to meet Matty and that is all,' Kate said to Jack's back and then to Matty.

'Forget it,' said Jack, swinging round to face them both; 'see, he's already brainwashed; feels he has to sacrifice himself… like Girija.'

'Wait a minute, don't I have a say in this?' asked Matty, hands outstretched.

'Are you mad…? It's too dangerous,' Jack raised his voice, 'and anyway how do you propose getting him to Tir na Og?' he asked Kate accusingly, laced again with cynicism. 'The whole plan is the craziest thing I have ever heard of.'

'As crazy as battling a buffalo man?' Kate shot back with raised eyebrow and stood up to face Jack.

'Wait, wait you two, you are talking about the Minotaur, aren't you?' Matty too stood up and placed himself between the taller warring cousins. He needed to know that the shadow he had seen two years ago was the Minotaur. He had pushed them an arm's length apart and was looking up from one to the other when his mother and the yoga teacher walked into the room.

'Heavens, what a racket,' exclaimed their mother, taking up a position in the middle of the room while the yoga teacher Shana, who was Scottish and always wore her blond hair in a long plait down her back and dressed in a shirt and shavar stood in the doorway with an uneasy smile and an uncertain look about her.

'What is going on?' the mother demanded and when she didn't get a reply from the three who had placed themselves in a row, lost for words because they had been taken unawares, she continued: 'Why have the television on too?' She looked accusingly at Jack mainly, Matty thought. Matty also felt he should have tried to warn the others when he had heard his mother speak with the yoga teacher; they always worked out in the sitting room upstairs.

'Go for a walk… play cricket… anything to let off steam…' The children scattered and ran for the stairway. 'Come on in Shana,' Matty heard his mother say as the click sound from the TV reduced the room to silence.

They all skipped down the stairs in a bundle, almost tumbling into each other at the bottom where they came to a halt; the boys' father was sitting in an armchair still talking to Suresh.

'The roof,' ordered Matty and was amazed that the two turned at once, their energy heightened but quieter. It stopped at the door leading into the sitting room where Shana was arranging the yoga mats on the floor. The teenagers slid past, leaving Matty to slide the key out of the padlock, thus freeing the bunch with the key to the door for the roof. It was hot at the top of the house; it consisted of a landing with only a door which led onto the roof. From outside it was as if the Tall Magnolia House had a little top hat on top and to one side of the first floor.

Matty quietly undid the padlock and felt the breeze once he opened the door.

'It's lovely up here,' remarked Kate. 'Why do you not use it more?' she asked as she explored the wide, red-tiled roof space.

'It's the parapet,' explained Jack, 'it's only half a metre in height. Mum is afraid we might fall over it,' he said as he strolled around the peripheries. 'She loved it when we first came but we hardly ever have time to come up.'

Matty had carefully closed the door and beckoned them into the shade made by the tiny second floor.

'To get back to the Minotaur,' he said, using his new found sense of command. He looked straight at Kate who had sat cross-legged in front of him with Jack making up the triangle to his side. It was not possible for Kate to tell a lie, especially about something serious.

She glanced at Jack, Matty glanced at Jack, who then gave her a most piercing look, his dark eyes set in an accusing stare. Matty surprised himself: she had to look down at her lap where she had begun lacing her fingers through each other again.

'It wasn't the Minotaur, Matt,' she said quietly looking up at him.

'Then what was it?' he asked after considering her for a moment; he knew she wasn't lying.

'It was the son of a Goddess Aunt Saroj brought into Nani Bhavan,' said Jack who had calmed down.

'The shadow was definitely a man's body and it did have a buffalo head with horns,' Matty stated; he said it quietly and with conviction. 'And it had a tail.'

'You are right Matt,' replied Kate. 'I didn't make the connection until you said it that afternoon, I had never heard or seen anything like it before and I don't know why I didn't... I didn't think of the Greek Minotaur... it seems ages ago,' she trailed off and then added: 'that afternoon; it feels as if it all happened a very long time ago.' She looked at Jack.

'Which Goddess?' asked Matty. He needed to keep them focused.

'What?' asked Kate. The definitive way in which Matty spoke seemed to shake her out of her reverie.

'She is called Jyestha,' replied Jack.

'I never heard of her,' said Matty, looking at his brother.

'Neither did Grandmother,' said Jack.

'Did Grandmother see him?' asked Matty, alarmed.

'Yes,' was all Jack said.

'When?' Matty was pushy: he had found out amazing things, frightening things.

'It attacked Girija and me in the Nani Bhavan garden one night... you know how Grandmother didn't sleep very well,' he asked, looking at Matty and then went on, 'well, Grandmother appeared at the front door when... when it was all going on…' Jack trailed off, somewhat upset at the memory of it, just as Kate had been. Matty considered: *he didn't know half of what had gone on before they left Kerala… or was this what caused them to leave Kerala?*

'What happened?' he asked urgently, still with the imperative tone.

'Ailill helped us… and maybe the Danavas…' Jack replied quietly.

'What do you mean?' asked Matty. 'Maybe the Danavas helped, we're not sure. Tell me exactly what happened.'

'The fountain erupted, I don't know if you remember but there was a problem with the water supply to Nani Bhavan before Grandmother died. The well water was full of clay and the fountain had stopped working. Well, that night it just erupted and jettisoned what seemed like a lake of water over the Goddess who was in front of the front door…' Jack explained, looking at Kate. 'The Goddess just collected up her two offspring and disappeared.'

'*Two* offspring?' asked Matty.

'Yeah, the buffalo-headed man and a woman,' replied Jack and then explained, 'the sister, the woman, she was just dancing a crazy dance with Aunt Saroj; the man was attacking us.'

'That's how it happened, Matty,' said Kate truthfully.

'What does she look like, the Goddess? And why was Aunt Saroj dancing?' asked Matty.

'Big, fat and ugly, just like a troll, and Aunt Saroj was like a mad woman, dead flowers around her neck, no sari, just a blouse and mundu and her hair flying loose like Kali,' answered Jack.

'But why would Aunt Saroj bring a thing like that into the house?' asked Matty.

'To get control, she was jealous and insecure,' answered Kate.

'Jealous of who? Us?' Matty asked astonished and looked from his brother to his cousin.

'Mainly of your dad and mum,' replied Kate.

'Why?' asked Matty.

'Well, your parents were a sort of fascinating couple in that society and then there were the two of you… and she… well, she was separated from her husband and nobody gave her a second look… and your grandparents would not permit her to marry again. So she probably… didn't want a sort of widow lifestyle, she liked lots of money, was always used to getting plenty from your grandfather and so she decided to just take it all… really…' Kate looked at Jack.

'That's about it, Matt,' confirmed Jack.

'And what, she prays to this Troll Goddess for help to destroy the family?' asked Matty.

'Yep, that's it in a nutshell,' said Kate.

Matty looked from one to the other; astounded that he had been ejected from his home by an aunt, he held up both his hands.

'I know it sounds simple Matt,' Jack began to explain, 'but the aunt was really serious, *is* really serious – do I need to remind you of the kidnapping?'

'The Goddess is known as the Goddess of misfortune,' Kate began to elaborate, 'Nisha said they worshipped her at a temple near where they used to live in north Kerala. Nisha also admitted one evening when Jack challenged her... actually the day you saw the buffalo man... well, Nisha said her mother was using the Goddess to rid herself of everyone except your grandfather.' She looked at Jack and said, 'and like you we just couldn't believe it either.'

'You know the Goddess Laxhmi, Matt?' put in Jack.

Matty nodded.

'This Goddess Jyestha is Laxhmi's sister, but she is opposite to Laxhmi in every way. Laxhmi is the Goddess of good fortune and everything that is beautiful...'

'And Jyestha is filthy and awful,' added Kate.

'Is she as powerful as Kali?' asked Matty, thinking about the dangerous, dark Goddess.

'No, but bad enough to scatter you all to the four winds,' said Kate.

'Are you saying she caused the death of Grandmother and Girija?' Matty asked uneasily after a period of silence when all three were deep in thought.

'We can't say for sure, Matt,' answered Kate.

'Well... who is in Nani Bhavan now?' asked Jack. 'Just the aunt and Grandfather, there's your answer.'

'There's Nisha,' put in Kate.

'Nisha knows how to play her mother's game; no harm will come to her from her mother,' answered Jack.

'This isn't right, it isn't fair...' Matty started.

'In the beginning I felt the same, Matt... and for a couple of years we were alright... but lately she must be feeling threatened again...' said Jack.

'You mean the kidnapping and Dad's incubus or whatever its name is?' asked Matty.

'Yes,' was all Jack said.

'But how can she... make unnatural beings appear and cause destruction? Remember the wound you had, Jack... the day of the Minotaur or buffalo-headed man, did his horns cause that?'

The two teenagers exchanged looks and then Jack answered, 'Yes, Matt.'

'But how, how can this come about, Kate?' Matty asked, bewildered.

'Matt, remember we just talked about other realities that exist, that can actually affect each other, Magh says even sustain our world. This reality... look at me Matt, I can be in the world of the Danavas or Tuatha dé Danann at will, ask them for help… remember what we talked about in your room… beneath us, above us, all around us are other worlds, the spirit world, remember your grandmother, the underworld… well the aunt has a way of accessing… particularly the underworld and the very powerful entities… maybe she uses drugs to do this, in fact she must do,' explained Kate as if speaking to herself. She went on: 'She was dancing a trance dance, getting into their dimension. These beings can influence our reality, like Ailill helping us, but she uses their power for her selfish plans.'

'She was definitely on something that night in the garden,' added Jack, as he realised too late and wanted to stop the following discussion which he knew he had inadvertently set in motion.

'I'm going to have to meet with Aillien, Kate,' said Matty, thoughtfully determined, after sitting quietly for a little while.

'Forget it Matt, it's madness, there are just as many evil elementals among the Tuatha, tell him Kate…' demanded Jack.

'You've been fighting this for too long alone, both of you… taking terrible risks. I want to help Dad; whatever he is doing it's not powerful enough to get rid of the incu-… succubus. What did Magh say I had to do, Kate?' Matty asked.

'We have to get to Connacht, Matty… but if you come back with me to Ireland, like your mother wants you to do, then it will be easier. I am booked to go to the Gaeltacht with my school to brush up my Irish before my exam next June. I was thinking of asking if you could join the group in September for two weeks, it's a bit of a long shot but if Magh does a little magic I might persuade the Reverend Mother…' said Kate, perking up for the first time that evening. 'The Irish school is very near Cruachain; it would be easy for us to creep out at night.'

'For heaven's sake Kate, what are you talking about, what are you doing…?' Jack jumped up, exasperated by what Kate had said, irritated by the biting mosquitoes which he smacked off his arms and feet.

Matty rose gradually: it was dusk, time for his Hindi tuition and the forbidden coffee that went along with it. He descended the stairs, slowly, thoughtfully, winding all the way down with one hand on the banister. He couldn't hear the argument on the roof; he had shut the door to prevent the mosquitoes getting into the house but knew it must be raging. His brother was protective and asserting this passionately; his cousin surer of the other-world and motivated to help them with all her will. Matty had made up his mind: he was going to Ireland, but not to the safe haven his mother had planned for him. No, he was entering into a world his mother hardly knew existed, fraught with dangers she could never ever envisage.

BLOOD

NIKIL ARRIVED AT ten on Saturday morning as planned. His mum dropped him off and the two mothers exchanged arrangements for his pickup in the downstairs sitting room. After she left Matty brought Nikil upstairs and for a while they rummaged around in the disarray of the little play room, Nikil was interested in Lego and other toys Matty had brought back from his Irish holidays over many years. They watched Star Plus television for a while before lunch and Matty began to relax a bit. He did not see Jack or Kate until lunch time. He had been anxious about lunch due to a grunt which Nikil emitted on swallowing his food. Jack usually made a silent issue of it at the table, choosing to sit beside Nikil and make faces across the table at Matty, rolling his eyes and feigning a choke; one hand flew to his own throat every time Nikil grunted. Matty dreaded the time for the call but it came and he watched, waited and grabbed the chair beside Nikil. *Surely Jack would not embarrass Nikil by miming directly in front of him?* Matty could never be sure with Jack but this was the only option he had.

The boys' father was back from the cold store and the table was full: parents at each end, Jack directly opposite Nikil and Kate opposite Matty.

'Hi Nikil, I'm Kate,' said Kate, smiling at him as she seated herself.

'Hello,' replied Nikil quietly; shy, he hardly looked at Kate.

'Hi man,' said Jack, flopping on to the chair next to Kate.

'How are you Nikil?' asked Ram as he sat between Jack and Nikil.

'I'm well, thank you,' said Nikil, so very obviously diminished by all the big personalities who surrounded him.

The boys' mother made the usual fuss over Nikil, explaining every dish, emphasising the vegetarian ones as Nikil's family did not eat meat or fish. It got on Matty's nerves a bit as Nikil was used to the food at the Tall Magnolia House – and anyway, if his parents were that pure they would have declined lunch.

'Beth, why don't you sit down? Let's eat,' urged Ram, much to Matty's relief.

Matty waited and sure enough Nikil still gulped loudly and grunted afterwards. Matty looked at Jack, whose eyes were alight with laughter.

'Eat up Matt,' encouraged his mother.

Matty began picking up rice and broke off a little of the egg from the egg curry and put it in his mouth. He was not as good as Nikil at making little balls out of the food to pop into his mouth. Nikil continued to eat slowly and chew for a long time. This made the anticipation of the grunt even tenser. Matty could not look at Jack; instead he looked directly at Kate who seemed to be checking out the others' reaction to the swallow-grunt. Matty noticed too that his mother had begun instigating conversation just as Nikil dropped the perfectly made ball of food into his mouth. To made matters even more uncomfortable nobody answered her.

Matty didn't dare look in his father's direction, he knew his opinion on Nikil's grunts. 'It's just a bad habit, he should be told to stop it, what is his mother thinking?' his father had said after Nikil's first lunch at the Tall Magnolia House. 'Maybe they all grunt,' Jack had replied, laughing.

Eventually Kate began to add comments to the neglected words issued from the boys' mother and most of the swallow-grunts were forgotten until a scuffle became apparent underneath the table. Jack and Kate's feet had been kicking one another.

'What is wrong with the two of you?' asked the boys' mother, obviously annoyed. 'You two got on so well the last time Kate visited, I don't know what has got into you both.'

Matty knew exactly what was going on: Jack was trying to draw Kate into Nikil's gulp grunt habit. Matty was infuriated with him.

'Sorry, Aunt Elizabeth,' said Kate.

'Kate, would you exchange places with Matty?' the boys' mother asked.

'Matty, sit over here, beside me please.'

Matty wanted to wear a triumphant look as he stood up and looked directly at Jack but he knew Jack would not be able to resist. So he put on his 'not fair look' as he walked around his mother's chair to sit beside his brother.

The remainder of the lunch went off without incident. Nikil's swallow-grunts became almost inaudible like the whirling of the overhead fan. Matty relaxed completely and began to enjoy his friend's company.

They went into the little road off the cul-de-sac in the evening for the usual sweaty game of cricket and only returned after dark when Nikil's mother's Maruti appeared.

'Get washed Matt, we're going to the beach,' said his mother as he arrived in the front door.

Jack and Kate were in the upstairs sitting room, damp hair and clean clothes with Star Plus on. Matty wondered what conversation he had missed out on. He knew only too well what the topic would have been.

'Hurry up Matt, we're going to the beach,' said Kate cheerfully.

Matty thoroughly enjoyed their stroll along the beachfront; he felt he was back to normal inside. Nikil's visit had gone better than anticipated. He felt looser, able to let go and feel safe; part of it was having Kate in the family again. He was able to find courage again too, even to take on the unknown.

'It's so wide,' Kate was saying to their mother.

'I know,' replied his mother.

'What is?' asked Matty, leaving his thoughts behind.

'The beach, Matt. I don't think we have anything like this in Ireland,' she said.

'Where's the tide mark?' she asked.

'Way out there, in the darkness, we can't see it in this light,' replied Matty's mother.

Jack and his father were already approaching the smell of deep fried food.

'What's that smell, it's gorgeous?' remarked Kate.

'I'm not too sure you should eat the food cooked here,' advised Matty's mother.

'You may get worms or amoebiasis,' she warned.

As they caught up with Jack and his father the cool breeze mingled with the delicious cooking air and little eddies of smoke and air blew over them. They surveyed the various barrows offering cooked food. Corn on the cob was being roasted on hot coals on one; on another, peanuts coated in a crispy batter were being hauled from a metal container full of hot oil on a gas stove with a huge ladle and left to cool before being wrapped in cone-shaped newspaper. Kate stopped and watched sugar-cane being juiced, fascinated as always.

'Our sugar comes from beet,' she said, turning to Matty.

'What do they look like?' he asked.

'They are roots, they grow underground like potatoes but they look like fat parsnips,' she explained.

All the while, a debate was going on between the adults; Matty's ears homed in on it.

'Look Beth, anything deep fried should be alright, what bug could withstand the temperature of hot oil, even for a couple of minutes?' his father was saying while rooting in his shirt pocket for rupees to pay for a newspaper cone of peanuts.

'Not the corns, then,' his mother replied, moving away and surveying the other food barrows under the fluorescent tube lights lining the pavement bordering the sand.

They ended up eating pakoras of onion, aubergine and potatoes; Jack and Ram had batter-coated capsicums, which they took further down the beach towards the waterline. They sat on the sand and ate out of the newspaper wrapping. Kate ate something hot and asked for ice cream but even the boys' father said no to that. He told her the best cure for chilli was sweets and that's where they went before going home. He loved undas – golf ball-like sweets, coloured yellow – and tried to persuade Kate to eat one of those.

'I remember them from last time Uncle Ram, they are just too sweet for me,' she protested in the sweet shop. Instead she examined the vast array of shapes and colours through the glass counter.

Matty noticed his mother was ordering carrot halva as usual; she warmed it and had it with vanilla ice cream.

'Will I get some Mysore pak for you, Matt?' she asked.

'Get a mixed one kilo box,' ordered his father.

'A kilo, isn't that too much?' protested his mother as usual.

Matty went to the shop door and waited, looking out into the street but not seeing the traffic; he was impressed at how content he felt for the first time in ages. He was half-aware of the commotion that Kate was causing in the shop behind him: the counter assistant kept giving her samples to taste. Jack was in on it too but Matty didn't care; life was normal again.

He sat in between the cousins again, in the back seat on the journey home. Kate sat with her face up against the window as always, delighted that the boys' father gave money to the throng of partially limbed beggars when the car was halted at the traffic lights.

'They are so thin,' she said quietly, looking at a toddler with really scraggy hair and a runny nose.

Inside the car there was silence, faces turned from the hungry, as they made their way to the next car.

'How can you bear it, Uncle Ram?' Kate asked.

'We grow up with it,' he replied quietly.

'You know Kate, I asked the boys' grandfather much the same question when I first came to live here and his advice was that you should try to help everyone you come into contact with, like the people who help us at the house and in the business.'

'It is a way of managing it, I suppose; it's impossible to help everyone,' Kate said quietly and thoughtfully to herself, almost, as the lights changed and the car moved forward on Nungambaccam High Road before turning into Fifth Lane and the Tall Magnolia House.

'Dinner before sweets,' proclaimed their mother as she went to the fridge and peered into steel and plastic containers inside.

'Sweets are for dessert.' She made another statement as she placed leftover fish and chicken curry on the table as the hands withdrew from the cardboard box of sweets.

'No more Mysore pak, Matty, until you have eaten,' she declared.

'I'm not very hungry,' Kate said.

'Not after all that food on the beach,' she added.

'I'll have something light too,' said the boys' father.

'Jack?' The mother looked directly at Jack

'Is there any chicken curry and rice or bread?' he asked.

It was much later, when everyone had almost finished the imposed food, that Matty went to answer the doorbell. He had eaten some warmed up pancakes and had been sent upstairs to brush his teeth and change for bed. Feeling left out, he came back down to the kitchen for the ubiquitous drink of water.

'Get the door, Matty,' his father said as he went to wash his hands and mouth.

'Check through the window first, I wonder who could that be, it's very late,' said his mother.

Matty wasn't tall enough to peer out through the little window in the double doors so he went to the large window near the door and called to BuddiaRam the watchman.

What came into focus outside in the yard was not at all what Matty expected to see. He withdrew and walked slowly to the kitchen where his father was helping himself to the sweets again. Matty's face was so pale that the conversation ceased and his father went into the sitting room in the direction of the front door.

'What's up, Matt?' asked Kate, rising from the table.

'There are two men… covered in blood,' he was able to reply.

'Blood,' repeated his mother turning away from arranging the dirty plates in the sink.

Jack jumped up, rinsed his hands under the tap at the sink and disappeared in the direction of his father.

'Sit down, Matty,' urged his mother.

'Do you know the men?' she asked, putting her hand on Matty's shoulder.

'I think it's Joseph from the cold store,' he replied.

Kate went after Jack.

'I'll go and see if they need help,' said his mother.

The violence associated with the kidnapping had refreshed itself in Matty's mind once again. He felt sure earlier that he had conquered it but here it was. It took him a little while to separate Jack's swollen and bloodied face from the present and when he did he wandered into the sitting room where the two men had been seated.

'I'll get some Dettol and cotton and clean the blood,' his mother was saying to his father.

'Then we can see how deep the cuts are and if they need suturing,' she added, turning to go to the kitchen.

'No Beth, I'll take them to a hospital,' the boys' father said, checking his shirt pocket to see if he had adequate money to pay for the treatment.

Everyone followed the two injured men out on to the porch and watched as they climbed slowly into the back seat of the car except Matty who sat himself on one of the chairs at the dining table.

'Their bodies ache, I think they have been beaten all over,' he heard his mother say to the others.

The three returned quietly and thoughtfully and Matty watched as his mother locked the front door.

'It's Aunt Saroj again, isn't it?' asked Matty.

'We don't know that for sure,' his mother said coming towards him.

'It's not fair,' he said, feeling the anger rising.

'No it's not fair that those poor men should suffer because they work for your father,' she said, pulling out a chair next to him.

'Was it four men in a white station wagon car?' asked Matty, anger in his voice.

'We didn't ask for descriptions,' explained his mother.

'Well, Jack and I can give detailed descriptions, and and… I think we should.' He was so angry then.

'First of all they have to be seen by a doctor and treated, maybe hospitalised for a while. Then your father will report it to the police, just as we did when you were kidnapped,' she said, placating the anger.

'Why…?' he asked looking up at Jack and Kate, who stood behind his mother.

'Why can't she leave Dad alone, what harm are we doing to her?' he hung his head over his hands and stared at the stripes on his pyjama legs.

'There are ways of dealing with her, Matt.' Jack stared hard at Matty when he made the statement.

Matty looked up: he knew his brother was afraid he would say too much.

'Jack is right, Matty, we will do things properly, go to the police,' his mother said holding his hand.

'The police are corrupt,' snapped Matty. He withdrew his hand and fled up the stairs. He held back the tears and part of his anger was at himself for not containing his emotions. Would the other two trust him again, would they confide in him?

'Matty,' called his mother after him.

'I'll go talk to him,' said Kate.

'Would you?' he heard his mother say.

Matty sat cross-legged on his bed waiting for Kate to appear. Instead, when the door opened slowly, just a little, two heads appeared, Jack's on top and Kate's below his. They were smiling at him and he couldn't help but smile back. Kate had a sort of nice, safe madness that he noticed his mother had. She did the strangest, unexpected things at times.

'I know, I lost it, so what?' he said as they came into the room and closed the door.

Jack seated himself on his bed and Kate took the one underneath the air conditioner.

'It was a bit of a shock for us all,' said Kate.

'They are cowards, to take it out on defenceless employees,' added Jack.

'I'm going to Ireland, Kate,' Matty said.

'I'll even meet Cruachain if I have to – anything to stop this,' he added.

'The witch of Cruachain is for the incubus, I don't know how we'll stop this,' said Jack.

'Well, he's out there now with that stuff all around him,' said Matty, getting angry again.

'I should have gone with him,' said Jack dismayed.

'It all happened so quickly, none of us had time to think except your dad,' said Kate.

'We've let our guard down lately anyway,' said Jack.

'We'll have to be alert all the time and not just for psychic attack,' he reiterated.

After that there was a subdued air about the house. Ram increased the security on the cold store. The incident was reported to the police and Joseph gave evidence after a two day stay in hospital. He had two fractured ribs; the other man was discharged that night.

It turned out that his descriptions of the attackers partially matched that of the boys, but not enough to be conclusive. The attackers spoke Malayalam, so they were from Kerala. Most of them wore moustaches, but that was not unusual, Ram said: most Malayali men wore moustaches.

Kate took to watching the incubus from the rooftop in the evenings after her class, when Ram was at home and she could see it. As soon as the sun went down she stood by the parapet, like a statue, examining it, trying to understand it and its negative powerful energy. Matty would wave to her on his way out to Hindi tuition and barely get a movement of a hand, she was so intent. Often she would be still there on his way back after dark, only her shirt moving ever so slightly in the light breeze.

Kate was focused and on guard. They were all on guard again. BuddiaRam was sent ahead of Matty to check the cul-de-sac for strange cars; the boys had already been instructed by their mother to get to know the neighbours' cars and their visitors if possible after the kidnapping, so as not to venture out for cricket if an unknown car was parked nearby.

CRASH

THE FOLLOWING WEEK the boys had Friday off school so their father planned to go to the abattoir in Andhra Pradesh as the car was free. Jack was to chaperone Kate to and from the Yoga Mandir which he did, leaving by auto rickshaw at school time. It was a quiet day; Matty watched TV with Jack, read a bit and thought a lot about his trip to Ireland.

Matty was allowed up late that Friday night because there was no school the following day either, it being Saturday. Everyone had dinner together in the kitchen and later they all went upstairs to watch Star Plus, the cable station on TV. Much later when Kate went downstairs to sleep, Matty overheard her talking to his mother whom he imagined had been in her room.

'What is it, Aunt Elizabeth?' asked Kate quietly.

'It's your uncle, he should have been home long ago,' answered Matty's mother.

'How long does it normally take… the trip?' asked Kate.

'Not this long… sometimes he goes to the cold store on the way back…' the voice trailed off as Matty who had been leaning over the banister realised his father was away and the incubus was with him. He waited inside his room until his mother went up to her room. Then he changed into his pyjama because he knew his mother wouldn't sleep and just in case she found him downstairs he could say he needed a drink of water. He slipped past Jack still engrossed in *MASH* on the TV and crept downstairs and knocked very lightly on Kate's bedroom door.

'What's up?' she asked, still dressed.

'Dad. He's really late… and… he hasn't even called,' he said anxiously.

'I know,' she said, opening the door a bit wider and gesturing him in with a turn of her head.

'Can you do anything Kate? Can you search for him on the planes you go to or the ley lines you follow, anything?' Matty asked.

'He wouldn't be there Matty, no un-...' she stopped abruptly.

'No, unless he was dead. Right? That's what you were going to say, wasn't it?' Matty's tone was accusatory.

'I can only see spirits, elementals and fairies Matt,' she said and then: 'When I found you were both locked in the shed, that was different; I came with Magh and Ailill, he knew where and how to find you. I have no idea how to search for your father in this reality,' she explained calmly, and then added:

'Maybe we should be quiet, Matt, my windows are open and sound travels up. Your mother will hear us.'

'Her air conditioner is on,' replied Matty defensively but quieter.

The telephone rang loudly on the dining room table. They could hear the boys' mother jump on to the bedroom floor above their heads, the bedroom door flung open and the sound of the slap of her bare feet on the mosaic on the stairs. Kate opened her bedroom door. Matty slipped into the shadow beside a steel cupboard in Kate's room and listened.

'Where are you Che?' came the anxious question. She called him Che which she had shortened for *Chettan* which means 'elder brother' in Malayalam. Wives did not use their husband's given name but referred to and addressed them in this way as a sign of respect.

Then after a period of silence: 'Are you hurt?' came the anxious question.

'And Shaker?' *Asking about the driver too*, thought Matty: *there was a problem.*

'When will the car be repaired?' Matty gathered that there had been an accident but both were not badly injured. All of this he heard again as his mother explained to Kate that the car had gone off the road for no apparent reason on their way to Andhra Pradesh that morning.

'We'll all sleep now, thank God they are safe,' Matty heard her say as Kate came into the room again.

'You heard that, I expect,' Kate said to him and sat heavily down on the end of the bed.

'But they are OK?' asked Matty.

'Yes... they're OK... the car was badly damaged, the left front wheel and the chassis I think your Mum said...' she trailed off.

'What's up Kate?' asked Matty 'You look worried.'

'I'm going to have to do something Matt... and now, right now,' she replied.

'Why now, what's the urgency, they are safe, are they not?' asked Matty. 'Is there something you're not telling me?'

'Matt, he didn't even get as far as the state border, the accident happened in Tamil Nadu... and he still plans to go on to the abattoir tomorrow when the car is repaired.' She stood up and began to pace.

There was a quiet knock on the door and Kate and Matty warily watched the handle turn. They relaxed when Jack's head slowly poked its way into the room.

'Mum says Dad's had an accident,' Jack stood and looked to both of them, unable to hide the anxiety in his voice.

'I've decided,' Kate stood up. 'I'm going now. First I'll talk to Magh… see how easy it will be to see Aillien… what time is it there?'

'Five hours, which would make it about six in the evening,' said Jack, obviously calculating.

'Perfect, I've got the whole of the Irish night to contact the Tuatha; all this takes place under the cover of darkness,' said Kate.

'We didn't decide on this… we never agreed, remember,' Jack looked from one to the other.

'We have no choice Jack. You heard what happened today: we have to rid your father of the incubus as quickly as possible.' Kate had a certainty about her that overrode any doubt.

'Payment, Kate, have you forgotten about the payment?' reminded Jack. 'And besides, how do we know it wasn't a real accident, nothing to do with… with…the negative energy… thing?'

'Have you forgotten what happened last week… Joseph… the beatings?' reminded Matty.

'It feels like she is escalating her activities again,' agreed Kate.

'Maybe if I can speak to grandfather…' Jack began.

'You said yourself Jack, five minutes listening to her and he will forget all about you,' said Kate.

'Anyway, I'm the payment, remember that, and I have a say in this,' put in Matty as firmly as his brother's words.

'I promise you I will not allow him to be taken away by the Tuatha dé Danann,' said Kate. 'We have no choice, Jack… we have to do something right this minute… otherwise you'll…'

'We will have no father, is what she was going to say,' said Matty quietly. 'We will figure out how to make the payment later on. Magh will help us… she's very wise Jack, trust her a little.'

She looked from the younger brother to the older one who threw up his arms, turned away and said nothing. She waited till he turned to face her, still silent.

'Leave me alone you two,' ordered Kate and lay herself on the bed in what Jack called her 'Ophelia pose'.

The two brothers left reluctantly. 'Should we watch her through the bedroom windows?' Matty asked.

'Better not,' replied Jack, 'we'll check in on her after a few hours.'

And so the long night began. The boys went to their room and read but failed to live vicariously in the different worlds they tried so hard to immerse themselves in. After an hour Matty suggested checking on Kate but Jack replied that it was too soon. Matty ignored him and went downstairs anyway. Not wanting to open Kate's bedroom door because it crackled and squeaked a bit he went to one of the front doors and undid the bolt which did not have a padlock on it. BuddiaRam was seated, sleeping upright against the wall of the porch, his legs stretched out from his erect upper half on the mosaic. He had Matty's mother's moth-eaten winter coat on him back to front for warmth. He woke as soon as the wood in the double door squeaked when Matty opened it.

'I'm going to see Kate,' he whispered in English; the watchman spoke pidgin English.

'Sleeping,' replied BuddiaRam.

'I want to see,' replied Matty who began descending the three steps on to the compacted earth of the garden. BuddiaRam threw off the coat and followed him quietly. They both entered Mrs JayaRaman's part of the property and crept between the large potted shrubs and up a step onto the little tiled veranda where Matty could hear the sound of the swirling fan in Kate's room before he got to the netted windows. *Jack was right: she was still there in her Ophelia pose.* Matty turned away from the window and went back inside the house, leaving BuddiaRam totally puzzled.

When Matty got back up to his bedroom he found Jack fast asleep. His brother had a thumb still inside the pages of his book which lay partly on the bed and partly overhanging the mattress. Matty was unable to settle. He switched off the light and used his torch to read a bit more before eventually falling asleep himself.

There was a greyness illuminating the bedroom window when he awoke. The air conditioner had been switched off; so too had his torch been switched off. His mother must have been in; she generally turned off the air conditioner about two in the morning and put the fan on. He checked his watch. It was five a.m. He flung his legs over the side of his bed and headed for the bedroom door. He used the front door again to check on Kate; fortunately BuddiaRam was about his morning chores. Emma was up – he could hear the banging of woks in Mrs JayaRaman's kitchen – but there again he was in luck; she had not yet opened the kitchen door and Fluffy had not been let out. To his dismay Kate was still in her unconscious pose: he had hoped he would find her curled up on one side or even in the kitchen, but she was lost to his world. He slowly ascended the stairs and slipped back to his room again and waited, unable to concentrate on his book. There was no sign of Ganesh either. He would be glad of any thought, of any vision even at that moment, but nothing came. An hour passed. Matty heard his mother go downstairs. His room was bathed in light but Jack did not wake. *Should he wake him? What could they do? Nothing. Absolutely nothing.* Matty began biting his fingernails.

When Kate did not arrive for breakfast Matty's mother apparently thought nothing of it. 'It's the end of her first week and she is bound to be tired. I suppose Jack is still asleep too?' she asked when Matty appeared in the kitchen at about seven.

Just before noon Kate's door opened uncertainly. Matty had spent three hours sitting on the steps of the stair opposite her bedroom door waiting and waiting. She looked terrible when she emerged from behind the slowly opening door.

'It's OK Matt, it's done,' she said quietly as if her head had an awful ache in it.

'What's the matter Kate, what's wrong with you?' asked Matty as he guided her to a chair at the office dining table, barely covering up the alarm he felt. She sat down heavily.

'I've seen terrible things Matt…' and after a pause, 'I'm just very, very tired.' She lay her head down on her arms on the table top.

'Will I get Mum?' asked Matty anxiously.

'No… too much explaining… lying,' she said resting her head on her arms and half-closing her eyes.

'Will you get me a cup of tea Matt?' she asked when Matty moved into her line of vision at the table.

Matty ran to the little kitchen and asked Meena to make tea for Kate and then raced back the short curving path to the dining room. 'I think I'll lie down again Matt,' she said and staggered towards the bedroom door. Matty caught hold of one arm while Kate stretched out the other even though they were many feet from the door.

'What's the matter?' came Jack's voice from behind them.

'She's really weak, Jack,' explained Matty, half-turning his head. Jack went ahead of them and opened the bedroom door wide and as they passed through Kate grabbed his arm for support. When they got her to the bed she collapsed onto it. Jack closed the bedroom door and Matty felt he was evaluating Kate and whether he should call his mother or not. Before any action was taken or words exchanged there was a quiet knock on the door. Jack looked startled. 'It's Meena,' explained Matty and opened the door.

'Thanks Meena,' said Kate as she bent her knees and tried hauling herself up on the pillows.

'What's the matter?' asked Meena, smiling uneasily. 'Is it tummy?' and she made a circular motion in the area of her own belly button.

'No, nothing like that, Meena,' replied Kate, reaching out for the mug of tea, 'just very tired. Thanks.'

Meena left closing the door behind her. Both the boys sat themselves down on the leather sofa opposite Kate's bed and the open windows and waited.

Kate drank half of the tea thirstily and then laid her head back against the pillows cradling the tea in her hands, knees still bent as if they were supporting her upright. She looked at them both and smiled.

'You've been here before Jack, stop worrying… and you too Matt, although you didn't know exactly what had happened in the Little Pink House that night.' She seemed to be reassuring them, or trying to, unsuccessfully.

'You were not this tired before,' countered Jack in a quiet voice. Matty felt he did not want to cause her any more stress, particularly the stress of an argument.

'I'll be alright… just have to build up my strength again,' she said as she started sipping the tea once more. Then after a little while she said, 'Is there any cake or biscuits around? I need sugar,' she explained.

'My milk biscuits,' said Matty and shot upright.

'No Matt, I feel like… something with… loads of cream, chocolate cake or something substantial like that…' she said.

Maybe it was her need for food; whatever it was, the boys became electric with life as opposed to the moments before, when they were considering the intervention of their mother.

'You need meat or fish, Kate,' suggested Jack. 'Mum always has to have really heavy food after an amoebiasis attack… Believe me, you will feel much better after something solid,' and with that he disappeared out the bedroom door. He returned five minutes later with his massive elbowing movement through the bedroom door, with a plate on which two of Meena's cutlets from the fridge barely clung and in his other hand a bottle of tomato ketchup gripped tightly by its neck. Meena's cutlets took ages to make but were delicious. There was a ball of spicy mince lamb in the centre surrounded by mashed potatoes, coated with egg and breadcrumbs and deep fried.

'I'm really grateful Jack… but I'm not sure,' faltered Kate.

'Trust me, I've seen Dad do this for Mum so many time over the years… come on… it always works,' and he laid the plate between her bent knees and stomach, holding his hand out for her mug. 'Go easy, they may be too hot; I've microwaved them.'

As Kate broke into the second cutlet, dipping it sparingly into the tomato ketchup, Matty fetched a glass of ice milk from the fridge for her. 'Just the ticket Matt,' she said as she handed him the empty plate and started drinking the milk. When the glass was half-empty she left it on the bedside table and lay back on the pillows and within a minute or two she had fallen asleep again. The boys exchanged glances and eased themselves through as small an opening as they could to avoid the crack and squeak of the wood in her bedroom door.

'Meena said Kate is ill,' said their mother as she pushed them aside to enter.

'Don't go in Mum, she's just fallen asleep again… we have fed her, she is just really tired,' Jack quickly put in.

'Where is all this tiredness coming from?' said their mother out loud. 'Must be delayed jet lag… I wonder, is she pushing herself too much at yoga… you know how she is, no half measures with anything.'

'That's for sure,' replied Jack.

'We'll let her sleep a bit longer then,' agreed their mother.

AILLIEN

 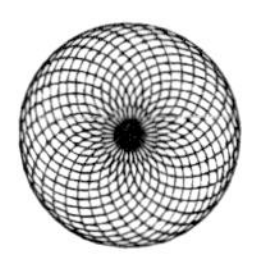

KATE SLEPT THROUGH lunch and on into adult siesta time. Matty took up residence with enforced homework in the downstairs sitting room cum office; he felt anxious and when they both were given a choice by their mother, he choose the room nearest to Kate; his voice sprung out the word 'Downstairs' automatically. Jack lounged on one of the beds in Matty's room with school paraphernalia strewn all around him on the bed and on the floor. That was how they spent most of the quiet hours in the sultry Madras afternoons, waiting for the less intense heat of the evening when they played cricket with their friends in the little extension off the cul-de-sac.

When Kate finally emerged she was walking steadily and looking much more herself. She went to the kitchen and drank copious amounts of water from the electronic wall filter.

'Would you like some tea, Kate? Mum has just had hers and there is more in the flask… and she has made upside-down pudding… would you like some?' asked Matty anxiously after following her to the kitchen where he had taken up a position next to the table, watching her while he talked, assessing her health.

'I'll get myself a glass of milk… oh will there be enough?' she asked, talking into the large cavity of the American fridge.

'It's just arrived, it's still in the sink,' explained Matty.

Kate went to the sink and touched the plastic bags the milk was delivered in. She then went to the drawer and got a pair of scissors.

'Where's the jug, Matt?' she asked as she held the floppy plastic in one hand and by one of its corners, between thumb and forefinger, of the other. It had condensation on the outside of the plastic as it warmed up in the heat of the house.

'It has to be boiled first, Kate…' Matty prepared himself to explain why but didn't have to.

'Oh yes, I forgot… get me a saucepan Matt,' she said, and then added, almost to herself, 'I hate the taste of hot milk.'

Matty placed the stainless steel saucepan underneath the badly controlled plastic bag while Kate cut off a small triangle of plastic at one of its corners and successfully got almost all the milk into the saucepan placed on the draining board.

'That's not easy, is it?' she asked and then said, 'I think I'll leave the others for your Mum. I'll help myself to a beaker of tea… even though it's going to make me feel more sticky and sweaty than I already am.' This last bit she seemed to be saying to herself, and then:

'Will we take a few slices of pudding up to the roof where we can talk?' she asked.

'I'll get Jack… he's playing cricket,' called Matty and he leaped onto the step that led into the hall at the foot of the stairs and sped out the front door that was nearest in the Tall Magnolia House.

When Matty got to the roof a few paces behind Jack, Kate was already settled in the shade of the little top hat. She offered slices of pudding to the boys.

'Oh you're all dusty and sweaty,' she exclaimed as Jack took his piece of pudding with a hand covered in wet sweat and red clay dust. There were rivulets of perspiration running through the dust down the sides of his face.

'What happened to you?' asked Jack, ignoring her remark.

'There were problems…' she began.

'Did you get stuck, like before? You were so long, more than fourteen hours,' asked Jack.

'Not stuck, time is different from linear time here; I was there almost two months their time… and I had to stay until it was finished… the incubus has been bound and sent away from your father… where it is, I'm not sure… but Magh feels it is still powerful enough to find a target, though,' she finished off quietly.

'Is that good or bad?' asked Jack. 'I don't really understand… I just… well… assumed it could be destroyed.'

'But it wasn't,' Kate added pensively.

'Maybe…' she continued and then stopped talking, closed her eyes and using one of her arms which seemed to sweep in front of her face.

'It's difficult to explain… I think the best way to convey the implications is to explain what exactly happened.'

'Whatever is easier for you, Kate,' Matty put in quietly, seeing her overwhelmed mentally and he remembered how weak she had been earlier.

'Magh and I journeyed to Aillien's castle in the west of Ireland; she is the second wife of a very old King. Magh uses the servants to get to Aillien so she went into the kitchens. By the way we dress like country-dwellers. Magh says it draws less attention from the other-worldly people than if we wore nicely made clothes; people may ask who we were. She asked for one of the servants to fetch one of Aillien's handmaids, who appeared after a little wait in the castle bailey. Magh explained she needed to see Aillien urgently.' Kate took a deep breath as if reliving it and continued:

'We were then directed to an orchard and told to wait again. Aillien appeared in the form of a snake – she shape shifts, by the way; it really threw me, I wasn't expecting it, but Magh was, she had no problem at all with it,' Kate had placed a palm on her heart, remembering the obvious fright she had experienced.

'I had to meet with a snake, Aillien... to make the request for her help formally, Magh said... but it wasn't as straightforward as that,' said Kate, who had been sitting cross-legged. She undid her legs and placed the soles of her feet on the warm tiles of the roof and hugged her knees close to her chest as she continued her story.

'Magh and I then journeyed to a lake which was also in the west of Ireland; Magh knows all the Dragon Lines. It was the lake of Cruachain.'

'But... isn't that the same name as the witch?' interrupted Matty.

'Yes Matt, same name and same place, but she didn't put in an appearance. The location had been designated by Aillien, who had agreed to intercede on our behalf with Irnan, the witch of Cruachain.' She looked at them both directly and in turn, as if checking they were following her journey.

Jack was uncustomarily quiet. Matty sensed his reluctance to involve himself once again with the other-world.

'As we waited in the darkness of the Irish nights, by the side of the lake camped in a nearby wood, Magh explained how the witch worked. Apparently she spins yarn widdershins, which means opposite to how the sun revolves around the earth. In this spinning she ensnares whatever has to be bound and so the incubus would be made powerless.' Another checking look along the wall of the building where the boys' legs were stretched out in the shade on the roof tiles, their backs against the magnolia wall of the top hat in a row, shielding them from the evening sun. Satisfied that her cousins were attentive, Kate continued.

'We had made a camp in the woods near the lake as your night turned to morning. Magh made a circle of protection and we rested within it and waited for a message or some news, but nothing came. Day after day the same routine: gathering wood for a fire and Magh gathering food to cook to nourish us, leaving me in the protection of the circle. Then slowly one twilight, Aillien's long boat emerged out of the mist on the lake. She had one hundred and fifty hand maidens with her. They were various ages; the older ones stood next to her. The boat just glided across the lake, none of the women used an oar. I felt really nervous but as soon as I was close to her all that left me... probably the Tuatha magic... anyway, she is the most beautiful woman I have ever seen... nothing of the snake about her, she looked about twenty or... younger and there was an aura about her... like how you would imagine a goddess. Magh bowed to her on this second meeting and I did the same as soon as she alighted from the boat and stood in front of us on the shore. She began speaking and I could not follow the Gaelic-Ogham but I noticed Magh did. What we found out was that the witch's distaff broke as she enmeshed the incubus which not only made the witch very angry but it is not good news for us: it means the dark material will find another target, as I said.'

'It broke due to the strength of the incubus,' Jack concluded.

'Precisely,' Kate agreed with him.

'So why were you delayed... how did this affect you?' asked Jack.

'The wait in the woods for Aillien, it took ages even in their time. She had to contact Irnan and I imagine negotiate with her. When she eventually arrived she was uneasy. As she spoke with Magh I sensed something was not right; some of the goddess aura left her as their conversation went on. I could pick out words here and there. Apparently the witch threatened Aillien with the twelve horned witches of Slievenamon and although they are not as powerful as the Cruachain witch they are frightful-looking, apparently, and have to power to kill humans, and I gather that Aillien does not have the type of magic that she can protect herself with so the witch of Cruachain has ordered Aillien to get her a new distaff. And this is where we come in...' Kate had been looking at the tiles and from one of the boys to the other while she spoke but then she stared straight at Jack.

'Aillien has asked… demanded actually…' and here Kate stared straight at Matty. 'That we… meaning one of you and I bring a distaff from our world and time which she can present to the witch of Cruachain.'

'So, your plan for Matty is no longer a courtesy meeting?' Jack asked.

'No but if we can locate the distaff I really don't see danger in it… and and… neither does Magh,' she finished defensively.

'Have you any idea or does Magh know where we will find such a thing?' asked Matty.

'No; and not only that, there are specifications,' said Kate, looking from one brother to the other earnestly. 'It has to be made of twisted holly, the distaff has to have twists, natural curves and grooves formed as another shrub grew around it.'

'Why holly?' asked Jack.

'Apparently it has magical properties,' replied Kate.

There was a long silence on the roof as the sun dipped and a cool breeze arose but made itself barely perceptible.

'Do you know anywhere in Ireland where holly grows?' asked Jack at length.

'I know Gran's sister has really old holly bushes in one side of her orchard, but they do not even have berries and I've never see ivy climb on it anyway, the bushes grow upright… they are as big as trees… I could check for deformed branches I guess,' replied Kate thoughtfully.

'It's impossible,' said Jack, clearly irritated; he pulled up his legs out of their splayed position on the roof tiles. 'Why are we even talking about holly trees or bushes… which of you are going to carve a distaff? Like I said before, all this is madness.'

'Say that again when your father gets home safely,' shot Kate defensively.

'He is right though, Kate,' said Matty quietly after a period of tense silence.

'Do you two not think I have not said all this to Magh?' she asked, somewhat frustrated herself.

'We heard… Magh isn't worried too much either,' replied Jack sarcastically.

'What exactly did Magh say?' asked Matty, consciously using a conciliatory tone.

'She told me not to get too caught up in details, that the new distaff would appear when we needed it,' said Kate, sounding as if she was not even convincing herself.

'Lying on the floor of an orchard or wood somewhere in Ireland,' Jack put in sarcastically as he raised himself from the roof. 'I'm not letting Matty go to Ireland alone with you, I'm coming too,' he said authoritatively.

'That won't happen, Jack. Gran will not agree to mind the two of you and anyway your parents will not allow you to miss so much school.' Kate had stood up too and they began pacing in different directions in the long shadows on the flat roof.

As Matty began to feel that there was no solution either to the difference of opinions between the cousins or the dilemma in the faerie world, his mother appeared at the door.

'Jack,' she called on seeing him first, 'tuition time,' and then finding Matty still in the shadow of the building, 'you too Matty.'

As Matty rose up he heard the beginning of a suggestion his mother made to Kate.

'You're sleeping a lot Kate, do you think you should take a few days off the yoga asanas and the chakra study… just to rest your body and… your brain,' his mother began. Matty felt she must have picked up on the tension between Kate and Jack too. He left them in the warm, descending dusk and made his way down into the house which was still stiflingly hot.

BREEZE HOTEL

THEY WAITED AND waited; showers, tuition and dinner came and went and no sound of a diesel Ambassador approached. At one time they heard the gate scrape open but it was Auntie Rose's car that went directly through the yard on into the landlady's house. Bedtime came and the house settled down; silence, but lights stayed on in all the bedrooms with one standard lamp lit in the downstairs sitting room near the front door.

Finally, close to midnight when everyone except the boys' mother had dozed off, the sound of the heavy door of a diesel Ambassador woke Matty as it shut.

'Jack, Jack,' he said in loud whispers but Jack did not stir.

Matty jumped out of bed and shook Jack's leg.

'Jack, Dad's home,' he said.

Jack cried out and almost attacked Matty.

'Jack, you're at home… wake up,' Matty realised that Jack was back in the shed in his dreams. He stood back and waited for the light in the room to bring him back to reality. Matty understood this terror so well; he hated waking up in the dark for he too reacted like Jack.

'What…?' said Jack who had hauled himself upright.

'I heard the car, I think Dad is back,' said Matty again.

They both went downstairs together; Matty noticed his mother's bedroom door was open. Kate was emerging from her room downstairs and their mother stood and watched Shaker leave the overnight bag on the sitting room floor. He noticed the special look his parents exchanged sometimes, like a secret caress.

'What's this, a reception committee?' asked Ram smiling.

'Why isn't everyone in bed?' he continued.

'Are you alright Dad?' asked Jack.

'What part was hit when you crashed?' asked the boys' mother.

'I wasn't, hold on a minute, let me send Shaker home,' he said as he went out on to the veranda, his hand foraging in his right shirt pocket for a wad of rupee notes.

'Do you want anything to eat?' asked the boys' mother.

'No, Shaker and I had something on the way,' he replied.

Matty went closer to his father as he picked up the overnight bag. His father placed a hand on Matty's shoulder.

'Shouldn't you be in bed?' he said gently.

'We were worried about you Dad,' Matty said, thinking again about the risks Kate had taken and his own part yet to come to keep his father safe. Parents who were oblivious to the intervention of children.

'I'll take that,' said Jack, reaching out for the bag as Kate joined him on his way upstairs.

Matty and his father followed and his mother locked the front door and switched off the lights. Halfway up the stairs she realised that Kate had joined the others.

'I hope you two are not settling in for a late night,' she called up after the others.

'Just want a quick word with the boys about what we'll do tomorrow,' replied the quick-thinking Kate.

'Whatever you plan for the day make sure you are ready for supper at the Breeze Hotel,' said Ram.

'The Breeze Hotel, I remember that from last time,' said Kate.

'I love the Breeze Hotel,' added their mother and disappeared into the bedroom with their father.

'Are you thinking what I'm thinking?' asked Jack.

'You bet I am,' replied Kate.

They both went to the door which led out on to a balcony off the sitting room. Matty realised what they were going to look for. The relief of seeing his father safe had wiped away the underlying cause.

The key to that door was always in the lock as access to the upstairs sitting room was impossible through that door. The two teenagers once again were happy co-workers. Jack turned the key slowly, looking back into the dimly-lit room for signs from the parents' bedroom door. Kate took a quick look round at the same time as they both squeezed through the small opening they allowed to prevent wood squeaking or scraping. Matty followed out onto the small balcony which had the wicker chair and table which used to be on the back veranda of the Little Pink House. This space was indented, incorporated into the side of the Tall Magnolia House as opposed to jutting out like a balcony. It was a nice place to sit in the evenings as it got the early morning sun. Matty closed the door as quietly as he could to keep mosquitoes out of the house. Kate stood still, holding on to the railings which were at waist level for her. Jack stood silently beside her and Matty stood beside his brother and waited. They waited several minutes, both of them staring in the same direction as Kate, at the gate.

'Nothing,' she said at length. 'Nothing, it's gone, it's really gone.' She grabbed Jack and hugged him, drawing Matty into the hug.

'It worked, it's over,' she said as she pulled away from them, taking a deep breath, a pleasant and serene smile on her face.

'I can't believe it,' said Matty, 'you did it.'

Jack sat heavily on the wicker chair, his silence and lack of excitement was obvious.

'I know what you're thinking Jack, but let's not spoil this moment,' she urged, speaking quietly and leaning against the railings.

'Payback time next,' was all Jack said.

Matty perched himself cross-legged on the little wicker table to listen to the two experienced ones; next it would be his turn to deal with the other-world and like Jack the thought of the unknown somehow cast a heaviness over his father's safe return.

Kate's summer holidays passed in much the same atmosphere and she spent time more in this world, there being no need to visit the other-world, with the exception of a few trips to catch up with Magh. The fun had somehow *gone out* of Jack, which was how Kate put it to Matty once. But even though Matty had dealt with the kidnapping and was relieved that the incubus stayed away from his father, the thoughts of what was to come, the other-world, were weighty.

Kate had been relaxed and enthusiastic and continued the yoga practices and teaching in depth. Matty had found her copying the Bharatanatyam Dancing Class one evening after his martial arts class at the Yoga Mandir.

'Oh there you are Matt, are you in a hurry, can we stay here for a bit and watch?' The jet of words accosted Matty as he arrived in his white martial arts outfit.

'Yeah, sure, Dad doesn't need the car till later, after supper,' he replied.

'I'd really love to learn to dance,' she said, staring at the dancers and their teacher and moving the palms of her hands together with the rhythmic sounds the dance master was making, her head nodding up, down, pause, *Da Da Di Di Da Da.*

'Mum will freak, she thinks you are overdoing it already, in the heat and all that,' he reminded her.

'You know it's not due to yoga or the heat. Anyway I haven't been as tired lately, everything has been quiet, I haven't been in touch with Magh for ages,' she replied, still concentrating on the dance class.

'*I* know that, but *she* doesn't,' said Matty.

'Don't worry Matt, I'm not planning on it this trip but maybe next summer,' she said, mostly to herself.

It happened on an evening such as this, that once again the front door of the Tall Magnolia House was answered after supper by Matty. He had an earlier bedtime than Jack and Kate and generally had supper rather than the later dinner. Jack was still at Hindi tuition, his father was out at a meeting – something to do with testing the species of meat – and Kate was practising yoga in the upstairs sitting room. Every time he walked in on Kate lately she was either on the palms of her hands and crown of her head upside down or doing a shoulder stand, she was very rarely right side up. His mother was preparing the food for dinner and so Matty answered the doorbell.

It was Joseph and the other man from the cold store again, looking very uneasy and asking for his father. Joseph was shivering and clasped his arms around his chest while the other man looked wide-eyed into the sitting room. Matty called his mother and while she spoke he went upstairs to alert Kate as he felt something was wrong.

'What's up?' she asked her aunt on her way down the stairs with Matty.

'I don't know, they will not tell me,' she replied.

'Matty says they are shivering,' Kate pursued the issue.

'They are in an awful state, they keep looking around, into the house and out into the darkness,' she explained.

'I'll make them some tea with plenty of sugar,' Matty's mother said aloud to herself.

'Can I take it out to them?' asked Kate.

When Kate returned ten minutes later with the empty tray Matty's mother had finished in the kitchen and had disappeared upstairs to watch *The Bold and The Beautiful* on TV. Jack arrived back from tuition as Kate sat with Matty while he finished his pizza and milk.

'Why is Joseph here?' asked Jack.

'Something's wrong again, they are really scared,' replied Matty.

'Do you think they have been threatened again?' asked Jack.

'They don't threaten, they just beat people up, if you are thinking about the same ruffians who took us and beat them up before,' replied Matty, a half-eaten triangle of pizza in hand. They ate pizza the New York way, something their father picked up when he studied in America.

'Could you detect anything about them, Kate?' Matty looked across the table at Kate as she helped herself to a wedge of freshly peeled mango.

'No, but I couldn't just stare at them for long; but nothing obvious. They are definitely frightened, though,' she replied, looking from one brother to the other.

'They didn't even reply to me when I said hello,' added Jack. 'What's going on?'

'She must know that the bad energy she sent to your father has been lifted, it's been almost two months now,' said Kate thoughtfully.

'The aunt, yes, she would have consulted her evil associates, it's been disaster-less for several weeks,' agreed Jack.

'You think whatever is going on with Joseph has something to do with her?' asked Matty as he finished another triangle of the pizza his mother had made.

'I would bet on it,' she replied.

'By the way, do you think she knows your father had a car accident?' she asked.

'I don't know, why, what difference does that make?' asked Jack.

'Well if she knew, she may consider that the dark energy had done its work and maybe leave him alone,' she remarked unconvincingly.

'Kate that stuff was so powerful even Cruachain couldn't deal with it. No, she knows it hasn't worked properly and is probably up to something else,' replied Jack.

'Bedtime, Matt,' came his mother's voice down the stairs from the landing.

'Coming,' he shouted back up through the kitchen door and swallowed the last of his milk.

'Can I have that?' Jack asked, pointing to the last triangle of pizza.

Matty placed his glass and plate in the sink and at the kitchen door he turned and said:

'Let me know what you find out, I won't sleep for ages.'

DEMONS

WHAT MATTY NOTICED next was a shard of daylight coming in between the curtains. The air conditioner was off and the fan was on. Jack was fast asleep, in a beached whale position on the bed opposite. Matty jumped out of bed and spent the minimum time possible in the bathroom. His intention was to get to Kate and find out if there was malignancy afoot. Jack had been roused when he got back to the bedroom. Matty dressed; his mother would be in the kitchen. Sure enough, he could hear the musical Irish accents interspersed with little laughs as he got halfway down the stairs. He noticed that his mother's brogue returned once she spoke to Ireland on the phone or had the company of Irish nuns: 'tribal' was how Jack referred to it, *Mum goes tribal.* It wasn't just the accent, it was how they formed their sentences; they put words together that didn't always make sense to someone who spoke English, especially people here in India who had learned it as a second language. His mother told him that some of the Irish English is spoken as it is in the Irish language.

'You're up early, Matt,' said Kate.

'Is Jack up?' came his mother's voice from the little kitchen.

Matty took the chair opposite to Kate in front of one of the glasses of milk and near the honey jar. He turned his head in the direction of the little kitchen where his mother was stirring porridge on one of the two gas hobs.

'He is awake,' replied Matty.

His mother finished quiet soon and dispensed the porridge into three bowls.

'Wait till it cools down, it's too hot to eat now,' she warned before disappearing upstairs.

'I fell asleep… last night,' Matty said to Kate.

'I know, I did look in on you but it was very late anyway,' she replied.

'Is it trouble again?' asked Matty.

'Afraid so,' said Kate as she stirred cold milk into the fast thickening and sticky porridge.

'I had a word with Magh, I think it's the tail-end of the one that was clinging to your father,' she began to explain.

Jack staggered into the kitchen, he had his *Don't talk to me, don't even look at me* face on.

'Just what I need today… I hate porridge,' he moaned, almost throwing himself on one of the chairs.

'What? I mean, is it doing something to Joseph?' asked Matty, still stirring honey and milk into the porridge.

'Well… that's really something else, don't you think Jack… some other type of creature… maybe accompanying it, the dark matter,' explained Kate.

'Kate, please start from the beginning, I don't understand a word you are saying,' Matty snapped just as there was a knock on the back door.

Kate rose and that particular morning Laxmi received in return a half-hearted *Namaste*, such was Kate's preoccupation. The young people waited until she had collected her broom, starting slowly to eat the breakfast, before resuming.

'Now listen, I think there are two different things going on here,' Kate began, lowering not only her voice but her shoulders and head.

'She doesn't understand English,' said Jack, watching Laxmi sweep the dining room floor.

'She'll pick up words here and there; that's enough. We have to be careful: nobody must know that we are involved, it could find its way back to your aunt. She is one of only a couple of people who has access to this family; think about it and keep in mind how resourceful your aunt is,' said Kate, touching the table with her index finger to emphasise each point as she spoke.

'Fine, OK, now get on with what you found out,' ordered Matty impatiently.

'Number one, there was a buffalo killed in the grounds, right in front of the cold store, Matt. Number two, the workers are being haunted by some sort of demon, a Rakshasa according to Magh,' Kate explained in lowered tones as even Jack ate his porridge slowly.

'What buffalo?' asked Matty, dipping in to his now correctly prepared porridge, not because he was hungry but because he was expected to eat it or make a good attempt.

'Apparently a milk seller had this enormous buffalo who gave a really good yield of milk. He not only sold it to the workers in all the units around the industrial estate but to shops as well,' Kate explained.

'Well yesterday morning when the owner turned up to milk it, it was found dead in front of the cold store,' she continued.

'And Joseph?' Matty asked, unable to savour his porridge at all, with the thought of the dead beast in his mind.

'It seems that they were being haunted by something, the Rakshasa, Kate says Magh thinks it is,' said Jack, who was almost finished breakfast.

'Joseph wants to go home, take leave, he's so scared,' said Kate.

'Can you blame him? Nearly two months ago he was beaten up,' put in Jack.

'Wait, wait, hold on a minute, how can a dead buffalo have such an effect on Joseph? It might have been ill or old.' Matty felt the two may be jumping to the wrong conclusion, part of him hoped they were.

'Magh doesn't think so Matt, the dark energy got the buffalo,' Kate almost whispered.

'It had to make a killing, hopefully that is it now,' she added unconvincingly.

'And the Rakshasas Matt, that sounds too familiar, very like the type of beings the aunt deals with,' Jack added in low tones.

'What are they? I have never heard of them,' asked Matty.

'Neither had we, not until last night. Ailill and Magh had a look. They are all over the cold store, like ants on a sugar cube,' Jack explained.

'What?' asked Matty, annoyed.

'Forget it,' snapped Jack.

'Were you in danger, Kate?' Matty asked, more composed and focused.

'No Matt, Magh didn't actually go, she can view distantly, there was no danger,' Kate explained.

'What exactly are they?' asked Matty.

'They are dwarfs with deformed legs, sort of crocked, as if they had rickets. They are really ugly and have a fang each side of their mouth, Magh said,' Kate explained.

'Like vampires,' Matty interjected.

'These teeth are longer according to Magh, but yes, they will suck blood from humans,' she said.

'They didn't touch Joseph or the watchman,' Jack assured him.

'How do they know who they are there then, can they see the demons?' Matty asked.

'No, they can hear them. For nearly two weeks now they have been hearing noise at night, the sound of footsteps, running and pebbles being thrown down on them when they step outside the building, sometimes worse,' said Jack.

'What?' asked Matty.

'Faeces,' Jack whispered.

'Uch, not at breakfast,' said Kate who had almost finished her porridge.

'He wanted to know,' Jack said, his eyebrows rising.

'Wanted to know what?' asked their mother as she stepped down into the kitchen from the stairs but before anyone could answer: 'Matt, look at the time and you have hardly touched your breakfast, hurry now.'

Matty and Kate sat in the back of the diesel Ambassador car for the school and Yoga Mandir drop-off and continued the conversation.

'Anyway Matt, we plan to go to the cold store tonight with your father so that I can have a look around, see what I can see,' explained Kate, speaking in low tones and quickly. It was something she practised with her aunt when they went shopping, slipping into Irish lingo so pushy sales assistants who understood English would not know whether they were really interested or not when pricing fabric for making clothes.

'I'll come too,' Matty affirmed.

'You are supposed to guard the home, Matt.' Jack turned round from the front as Shaker waited to slip into the heavy traffic on Nungambaccam High Road.

'That was agreed when Dad was being pursued, now he's not. I want to see if I can hear the footsteps. I heard Dad saying to Mum that Joseph may be going a bit mad and that he is getting counselling for him,' argued Matty.

'Thambi heard the sound too, Joseph is not mad,' Jack said heatedly.

'Dad didn't say Joseph was mad exactly but he is upset enough to have to have counselling before he goes home to Kerala,' defended Matty,

'It's Friday night, we'll all go, it will be easy to get away with no school,' Kate settled the argument just as the car joined a queue of three cars in the drive at Sherrington House School.

RAKSHASAS

KATE HAD BEEN right; there was no argument about accompanying their father to the cold store that evening. They had waited around the kitchen table as night began to fall at six, waiting for their father to finish his tea in the next room, partly listening to the conversation he was having with their mother. Apparently the new engineer was not as experienced as Joseph; their father would have to check very frequently as the cooling unit had its own foibles and Joseph could handle it in his sleep apparently, he just had a way with electrics.

'Jack, you will have to be on alert then,' Kate whispered.

'You'll have to travel with him, report back to me,' she instructed.

'Why?' asked Matty.

'The attention seems to be on the cold store now, but he is going to be there more frequently… aren't you listening?' she explained and asked frowning at them all at once.

'How am I supposed to report back to you…? Think about it…' Jack cut off mid-question, he was seated facing the kitchen door.

'Everybody ready?' asked their mother as she placed two tea beakers in the sink.

'Dad's just changing his clothes.'

The drive took between thirty and forty-five minutes, depending on traffic in the city. Ram had been quiet throughout, none of the usual teasing. That set the atmosphere for the others: this was serious business. Matty could tell, looking at Kate's face, set, deep in thought. They had such a carefree two months and then, the danger loomed once more.

Matty had developed an aversion to industrial estates, especially during the dark hours. As he climbed down from the back seat and his sandals touched the impacted earth he could not prevent the images and the heart-pounding feelings re-emerge, even the smell of urine on his school uniform surfaced; everything was so vivid. The loud bang of the three heavy doors of the Ambassador car quickly drew him back to reality. He pushed his door shut too; the lock barely clicked into place. Kate emerged slowly from her side of the car, her eyes focused on the roof of the unit. He noticed that Jack held back as their father went into the building.

'I think it's better the three of you stay inside with me… until I'm ready to leave,' he called back at them.

'OK, Dad,' shouted Matty as the other two were preoccupied; Jack with Kate and Kate with… what?

'You can see something, can't you?' asked Jack.

'Yes, on the roof… little beings, lots of them, running this way and that and every so often they stop and watch us,' she said, looking up, using her right palm to block out the large outside light.

'Are they like what Magh described?' asked Matty.

'I can't see Matt, because the light is blinding both my sights,' she said.

'Let's go inside… see if you can see anything in there,' urged Jack.

The large space inside the unit was empty; the floor had wooden pallets laid out in rows, ready to take on the loads of meat from Andhra Pradesh. They held nothing as there obviously had not been a shipment that day. Kate stopped when they were halfway across this space. The boys watched her as she adjusted her sight, her head moving slowly; she could see something, she appeared to be examining it, intently.

'They're inside too,' she said.

'Oh my God, they are terrible looking and they are coming towards us,' she said, so very obviously perturbed.

She looked horrified and began panting, one hand on her heart. Jack stood in front of her and grabbed her with both his hands one on each of her arms and shook her a little.

'Listen to me Kate… look at me… focus on me with your ordinary sight, Matty and I cannot see them,' he spoke vehemently.

She remained stricken and Jack shook her gently again and repeated what he had said.

Matty looked about and he could see nothing moving, no shadows and no sounds. Kate began to focus on Jack's face.

'Are you with me Kate?' he asked.

'Yee-ees,' she replied, looking over his shoulders in the direction of what horrified her.

'Look with your ordinary sight Kate. Are you listening to me? Look with your ordinary sight,' he said again.

'I can't just turn it off and on Jack,' she snapped impatiently.

'Some beings break through and these... are coming through,' she said and shut her eyes and turned her head towards the exit.

'What's the matter?' asked their father who had obviously been watching.

'It's very stuffy in here, she is feeling dizzy, I'll take her outside,' replied Jack, releasing his grasp and catching hold of one of Kate's elbows, leading her to the big double doors of the unit.

'Stay in the car and lock yourselves in until I come,' their father commanded.

'No wandering around in the dark, did you hear me?' he emphasised.

'Yes, Dad,' replied Matty as he left the unit with the others.

'Can you not shut them off at all, Kate?' asked Jack as he pushed the handle of the door forward on both front doors once he had seated Kate in the back. Matty did the same, having to lean over Kate to secure the back doors.

'No,' she snapped.

'Worse than Jyestha's son?' asked Jack.

'There's so many of them Jack... coming from all directions, I just don't know how to fight them,' she said.

'We'll get help, help will come... from somewhere,' said Jack – mostly to himself, it seemed to Matty as he watched him turn around on the front seat to look out the windscreen.

'I can see the Danavas, they are just standing around the perimeter of the factory... just doing nothing,' she said in exasperation after a moment or so.

They sat in silence. Nobody answered her in the dark in the locked car; they had no solution. Matty used this time to listen as the industrial estate was quiet that time of the night. He heard nothing. He imagined that the demons were climbing all over the roof and bonnet of the car and wanted so badly to ask Kate could she see them but when he turned to her he found she had her eyes closed. That increased his concern to almost anxiety: Kate had always been a rock of common sense and now... well, Matty had never seen her like she was that night.

After what seemed like ages, during which time Matty could still feel Jack's desperation and sense Kate's fear, he noticed her roll down the window very slowly.

'What are you doing?' Jack spun around on the front seat.

Kate nodded her head in the direction of two beggars, one very tall man and an old woman. Both had their heads covered with shawls because of the dewy night air; they just stood motionless in the darkness, watching the car.

'We've nothing to give them,' said Jack.

'It's Ailill and Magh,' said Kate.

'What?' both brothers said at once.

Kate spoke in Irish, for Ailill's comfort Matty supposed. While this was in progress Matty strained to see more of the tall man but both he and Magh, whom he had met only once or twice in Ireland, were well disguised as beggars.

'What's going on?' Jack asked after a lull in the conversation.

'Ailill says he can frighten them off tonight but he doesn't know if it will stop them coming back,' Kate explained.

'All of them?' asked Jack.

'He's going to ask the Danavas to intervene... for help,' Kate explained, slightly distracted by carrying on two conversations at once.

'Does he know why they came here?' asked Jack and from the tone of his voice Matty knew it was a futile question for which they already knew the answer.

'The same source as before,' Kate replied and Matty noticed she was once again in control of herself.

'Your father is going to have to perform a Siva pooja,' she added.

'These are Kali's creatures... and also originate from Siva. He will need to petition Lord Siva,' Kate went on.

'How are we going to make him do that?' asked Jack.

'We'll worry about that later, let's get rid of them tonight,' she said and resumed the guttural language with the two beggars.

After some time Kate rolled up her window and ordered the cousins to sit quietly and not move. She explained that Magh would make a circle of protection around the car.

'Dad, what about Dad… and the two workers inside?' Matty reminded her.

'Magh has thought about that. He is in the cold store or working at the electrics; the Rakshasas are not anywhere near the electricity, it interferes with them. The reason why your father has to spend so much time repairing it is because they have disrupted it. Magh can focus the protection in that part of the building,' she explained patiently to Matty.

Matty sank back against the seat, allowing himself to relax. Jack half-turned and watched through the side window as the old woman made a circle on the hard earth around the car with a piece of a branch. Kate sat upright and explained what she could see, no longer afraid. Matty noted the tall beggar had disappeared but Kate confirmed he was in battle gear and speaking with the Danavas who had advanced inside the grounds of the unit. They were armed too, she said.

She narrated a battle, describing how the demons sprang from the rooftop on to the shoulders of the Danavas, some managing to sink the fangs deep into the necks of the unfortunate ones, who then fell instantly to the ground. The description was of a Kalaripayattu style of fighting which the boys had heard of but never witnessed. The fanged demons appeared at first to have the upper hand. Matty became animated explaining to Kate how they had the advantage, attacking from above.

'What are their numbers Kate, the Danavas; are they outnumbered?' he broke into her narrative.

'Matt, the Danavas are holding their own, I don't think they were prepared for the fangs but they are now holding the Rakshasas back. The warriors have employed their whip swords,' she said, a smile spreading all over her face.

'They don't stand a chance now,' she said.

'What's happening?' asked Jack.

'They are actually pulling them off the roof with those coiled swords… I must find out what they are called… the sword is actually cutting into the demons' flesh as it ensnares them.'

She was seated on the edge of her seat, back straight, sometimes straining forward and downwards watching the roof of the building and staring intently at a battle taking place in another world, among primeval beings and ancient warriors, centimetres from reality.

'I don't see Magh,' said Jack when Kate stayed silent for a while.

'If you don't see her she must have gone home,' replied Kate involuntarily, still engrossed in the activity outside the car. Her eyes swivelled this way and that.

'That's a good thing by the way, if she's gone, I mean, it's coming to an end anyway,' she said, peering through the back window, still in automatic speech.

She eventually sat back against the seat.

'It's over,' she said.

'There's nothing out there,' she said quietly.

'What a night,' said Jack.

'Did you call up Magh and Ailill?' Jack asked after a little while.

'I had to,' she replied quietly.

'No, I'm not saying… I just wondered how they appeared so quickly,' he explained.

They were all so engrossed in what has transpired that they all three jumped when their father tried to open the driver's door.

'Sorry Dad, didn't notice you coming,' said Jack, releasing the handle.

'Everybody alright?' he asked, turning towards Kate on the back seat.

'Fine, Uncle Ram,' she said.

'I suppose you are all bored,' he went on as he turned the key in the ignition and pushed the gear stick into position on the steering wheel.

'Not really, just winding down after the week,' Jack said, as cool as if it really was.

'We were just checking out the stars; Kate said we hardly ever had a clear sky in Ireland,' he added convincingly.

Matty glanced back at the unit as his father reversed into the compound where the magnificent buffalo had lain slain hardly twenty-four hours earlier. Would a family starve with its loss? He had real difficulty understanding why some people needed to be so destructive, jealous and greedy. He wanted to cry at the wantonness of it all. He wanted to be left alone, his family left to live their lives. As the car moved forward on the road he felt the warm breath of a small trunk on the back his right hand. He looked down but couldn't see him but he knew he was there. It had been ages since he needed the other-worldly comfort. In fact, Matty thought, it had been ages since he could even see him. He must be growing strong again although it didn't feel like it, or maybe he was growing up. This last incident firmed his resolve to go to Ireland and do the needful. Revenge flashed across his mind again briefly. He had discussed this with Kate who had dismissed the idea outright, despite Jack defending it. She understood but ruled it out completely, qualifying it with a statement that provoked another thought in Matty's mind: *Both sides of their families have survived hardship for higher principles time and time again and yet survived.* What history was there on the Irish side of the family?

Once home everyone went to their bedrooms, even Jack. Matty wondered why: he was always asleep when Jack came to bed, finding him in the mornings in the beached whale position. As Matty emerged from the bathroom, a foam of toothpaste all around his lips he was surprised to find Jack flung across his bed, shoulders and head supported by the wall, his long legs sticking out across the floor.

'What's up Jack?' enquired Matty as he climbed on to his bed, book in hand.

'Matt, didn't you find it strange that we could see Magh tonight?' he asked quietly.

'And Ailill,' replied Matty.

'No, I have seen him before, he can be mortal for short periods,' explained Jack.

'When did you see him?' asked Matty.

'Keep your voice down… in the garden at Nani Bhavan, you know the night Grandmother saw everything, the night the fountain burst, remember?' said Jack sitting upright, his voice almost a whisper.

'Yeah, yeah, I remember,' whispered Matty.

'You having an early night?' enquired their mother as she came into the room.

'I'm tired,' replied Jack.

She bent and kissed Matty on the forehead.

'Nighty night,' she said and then went over to Jack and kissed him on the top of his head.

They waited a few minutes before resuming the half-whispered conundrum.

'If Magh was in her etheric form, we would not be able to see her,' explained Jack, mostly to himself.

'Let's ask Kate,' suggested Matty.

'Wait about five minutes, until the parents have settled down, then we'll go downstairs,' instructed Jack.

'No Jack, it will be too quiet then. I know Dad falls asleep quickly, but Mum doesn't. Let's make a move now, while they have the taps running in their bathroom and they are still talking,' said Matty convincingly.

They both rose and slipped through the bedroom door. Down through the darkness of the staircase and once at Kate's door Jack knocked, three little knocks.

'What's up?' she asked, peering out.

'We need an explanation for Magh tonight,' whispered Jack.

'Let us in, will you?' he said as Kate had opened the door just a smidgen.

'Careful,' she instructed them as Jack narrowly avoided sheets of paper placed all over the floor.

'Can you test me on the chakras first, though?' she asked in an appealing way.

'What do you want?' asked Jack as both brothers sat themselves on the sofa well clear of the littered floor.

'I want you to examine me on all the properties of all of the major chakras,' she said, picking up sheets of papers from what seemed to Matty to be different groups.

When Jack had about six sheets of paper in his hand he began.

'Crown Chakra, Sanskrit name?' he asked.

'Sahasrara Chakra,' replied Kate and went on to spell it, define it and describe the word and its origins and finally its location.

'Next page,' she instructed.

'Third Eye Chakra,' Jack said.

'Wait, wait Jack, you've missed something,' she said, getting off the bed and looking at the sheets of paper she had handed Jack.

'My fault,' she said and began rummaging through her scattered piles on the floor.

'Here they are, we should have started with a proper introduction,' she said as she handed Jack several sheets of paper.

'Look at the headings, starting with energy centres, then move on to prana and then nadis, oh and don't forget the kundalini,' instructions which she delivered while seating herself cross-legged on the bed again.

'Listen Kate,' Jack began.

'Oh and Mudras, I'm really proud of myself Matt, you know the dance class at the Yoga Mandir, will they use Mudras too and I've just learned the ones that go with each chakra,' she explained, beaming at Matty.

'Kate, my mind is just not on this right now, can't we do it tomorrow some time?' asked Jack.

'Oh come on Jack, when do I ask you to do a favour for me? This is just not fair,' she pleaded.

Matty was sure an argument would ensue so he intervened.

'We just can't stop thinking about tonight, Kate; you know, what happened at the cold store,' he said as gently as he could.

'You can't stop thinking about it and you only saw two beings who were non-threatening, what about me…? I had to look at those terrible creatures,' she said, hesitating at the thought of them.

'Why do you think I'm not sleeping… I'm afraid they will come back in my dreams…' She was looking down at her palms, fidgeting with her fingers.

'I'm sorry Kate, I didn't think, we didn't think…' Matty said in mitigation, looking at Jack.

'Would it help to talk about it?' asked Jack, a lot quieter.

'Get your cover and come up and sleep with us on the spare bed,' Matty suggested.

'I think I might,' she said, rising up and turning off the air conditioner above the bed.

In Matty's room Kate and Jack didn't bother to undress, they lay on their separate beds and Kate pulled the cotton bed cover up to her waist and turned on her side to face her cousins.

'I think I'll turn off the light in case Mum is prowling,' said Matty, jumping off his bed with his torch already switched on.

'Good idea, Matt,' whispered Kate.

'What are you guys agonising over anyway?' she asked, sounding much less tense.

'It's Magh,' said Jack quietly, drawing up his legs and sitting cross-legged in the torch light.

'How come we could see her, Matt and me? If she wasn't in etheric form, how did she get here so quickly?' he asked.

'You are right, she wasn't. It was all Magh, the whole Magh as you see her in Ireland,' said Kate, partially rising off the pillow and supporting her head forming a buttress with one arm.

'She uses the giant's shoe… when she has to be somewhere in a hurry,' she replied.

'Are you mad, a giant's shoe, which giant?' asked Jack scornfully.

'It's true, although you wouldn't think anything of it, if you saw it, it's like an old piece of worn out leather that would fit… say… a Neanderthal foot, yeah, think of something that size, which just pulls on over the foot like a bootie,' she said, no longer prone but upright, cross-legged like Jack and Matty.

'You have got to be joking,' said Jack, some of the scorn draining away.

'But you are not… are you?' he added.

'No I'm not, and yes it works… she showed me once,' Kate said.

'You actually travelled in it?' asked Matty

'Well… I didn't put it on, Magh… sort of held on to me,' she explained.

'What did it feel like?' asked Matty.

'Like nothing strange really, one second I was on the Big Borough and the next I was in Magh's cottage,' she said.

'Really? You are not just making this up?' asked Jack.

'No-o, I'm not,' she said defensively.

'I was having a lesson, sort of hedge school like, Magh and I arrange to meet there often, especially if the tide is right… and she teaches me… how to live with my second sight… and things like that…' she trailed off.

'And she just happened to hold a flight by slipper lesson,' said Jack, still a hint of mockery in his voice.

'No, she used the slipper to get to the Borough, she's old now and runs low on energy often, so... she uses the slipper to go places, especially remote, where others cannot see... her arrival,' Kate explained in the only way she knew how in an effort to convince her cousins.

'And she couldn't carry the book,' Jack put in, sarcasm obvious.

'She doesn't need the book of shadows for our lessons, she's old-school, like Druids, very little is written, all must be learned... and it is the same for me...' she trailed off, easing herself back into a prone position.

'What is the book of shadows?' enquired Matty out of interest and he felt Jack's questioning – more importantly, the attitude he used – had to be stopped.

'It is where she has written all her spells and remedies, that day she felt she needed a particular spell to protect me and she wasn't sure of some of the herbs,' replied Kate.

'What about all the knowledge being memorised?' continued Jack with the attitude, although less aggressive.

'There are two aspects to Magh, Jack: one is her other-worldly self, half in this world and half in the other world, if you could see her as I sometimes can, half of her body is like ours and the other half is like Ailill's, faerie. All the knowledge to do with that world is learned and never written. In our reality she is an old woman who ordinary folk come to during the winter months for cough remedies and sometimes for cures for tumours, all to do with that aspect is written,' explained Kate, sounding sleepier and sleepier.

Both brothers stretched out on their beds; peace had permeated the room. The extraordinary had somehow become the ordinary. They were soon asleep, reassured that they were safe in an uncertain world. Lulled by beliefs that only they had proof of, occurrences that could not be explained, not even to their parents.

CLOUD

A FORTNIGHT LATER, Matty was on the other side of the world. The coastline was not visible from the Aer Lingus 737 as Matty twisted his neck in search of a break in the clouds. He was reliving the same night and his body felt strange; not tired in the usual sense, sort of strung out. The flight was full; it was the first one out of Heathrow for Dublin. Kate sat in the middle seat, between Matty and a dark-suited man. The flight seemed to be full of them with the odd, weary faces, pale and drained like theirs. Kate and he had been escorted between terminals in the middle of the night by a British Airways air hostess; they were labelled as unaccompanied children. He had forgotten to adjust his watch and for a little while he was without time, consciously relying on the light to tell him where the sun might be. But the darkness remained outside the walls of glass. They had sat and waited, Matty for the shops to open, Kate buried in a book on Eastern Philosophy she had bought at the Madras Airport shop. It was still night, it was night when they left Madras and so he had given up and after a sleep, stretched out on three seats he asked Kate the local time and adjusted his watch too.

The light did eventually emerge, slowly on the horizon: he noted it as they boarded the flight. He dozed again for a short while on board and missed the take-off, which was the best part for him. Then came an announcement to remain seated and buckle seat-belts, followed by a huge roller coaster dip that was felt in the stomach; he looked at Kate who had lifted her head from her book as the aircraft seemed to be correcting itself.

'We're arriving in Ireland like the Tuatha dé Danann, Matt, on a cloud,' she said with a twinkle in her eyes.

Matty wondered if she was serious but his brain was too tired to question her. He considered it may be the lack of sleep or the altitude, or maybe both combined that made her sound a bit mad. Jack had looked into the effects of altitude on the brain after witnessing their mother continuously giggling after having wine with a meal on a flight from India once. He wanted to try it out but was not allowed.

When they emerged from the flight in Dublin the fog was even denser. It amazed Matty how the flights found their way into this cloudy island. Jack would have hit him with a barrage of technology had he asked the question but Matty's brain was satisfied just to wonder at it all that particular morning. After another long walk they were finally delivered to Kate's mother by an Aer Lingus flight attendant along with their passports and luggage. The walk to the car park was cold, which seemed to penetrate right into his very bones. It seemed to Matty that one of the clouds just sat on the earth: it cloaked everything, even cars and buses had their little red lights lit. Matty stretched out on the back seat of the car as soon as his aunt had heaved the two heavy cases into the boot. He quickly fell asleep as mother and daughter conversed in their quiet, lilting accents from the front on the final part of the long journey, the three-hour drive to Wexford.

When he awoke he was at his grandmother's house. He had a silent sign before pulling himself upright; he would have preferred to stay at Kate's house. More toys, more electronics, plenty of television stations, unlike his grandmother's – she stuck to one or two and seemed to watch a lot of news and weather forecasts. He reminded himself that he was here for a purpose and anyway best not be distracted and too comfortable: it would only blunt his focus. Then there was the call to India. Several attempts were necessary; they eventually got through only to be cut off after the receiver had been passed to him. He wanted to reassure his mother that everything had gone well. He calculated the time: darkness would be just descending again in India. His grandmother had a meal ready for all of them and they sat and ate. It was decided that he should try to stay awake till seven or eight to realign his body clock and so he accompanied Kate to see Finn after dessert. He was in a field at the back of the farm's haggard, where he and the other animals were housed. After a while petting him and talking to Finn, Kate motioned Matty over towards the gate leading into the lower meadow.

'Where are we going?' he asked.

'Just want to let Magh know we're home,' she explained.

The cloud on the ground was turning to drizzle.

'Take cover under the fir trees,' Kate said, pointing across the track to where the apple trees grew, bordered by a line of fir trees.

They lifted the barbed wire and carefully eased themselves through between the upper strands, Kate holding the topmost wire as high as she could to allow Matty through and he in return doing the same for her; although he had to pull with all his might, she barely got through without snagging her anorak. They stood in the shelter of the large canopy of one of the trees. Kate closed her eyes for a little while and seemed to be concentrating. Matty just waited.

'You tired, Matt?' she asked.

'Just the usual flight thing,' he answered.

'What about you, are you relieved to be free of demons and dark energy?' he asked.

'I am, actually,' she replied.

'Tired like you and I'm going to try not to sleep till about eight or nine,' she added.

'I have to say Matt this is a safe haven... compared to what's going on in India: I haven't yet seen anything here like what I saw there,' she said as if thinking aloud.

'That's only because you haven't encountered the dark side here,' came a woman's voice.

Matty spun around. It was Magh, dressed in a raincoat and holding a navy blue floral umbrella above her head.

'Magh,' said Kate and jumped down from the bank where the trees grew to embrace the old woman, who stood by the stone wall bank in the little lane leading up to the haggard.

'Welcome young man,' she said to Matty when he had jumped down into the lane to join them.

'Thanks,' was all that Matty could say, suddenly tongue-tied.

'You can speak freely, Matty knows everything,' Kate said.

'How are things, any news from the west?' she asked.

'Nothing strange here, the meeting with Aillien is on schedule, it's set for a few days after you both arrive at the Abbey,' Magh replied.

'And the distaff?' enquired Kate.

'Still don't know of its whereabouts, other that it will be drawn to you and you will find it when you need it; don't worry too much about that now,' she said.

'Thanks for your help at the factory,' Kate said.

'Let's stand under the trees, you two are getting wet,' remarked Magh.

'I don't know what happened to me, there were just so many of them, the demons...' Kate just stopped.

'Look, you are new to this, you'll get used to the dark ones and learn how to deal with them. You're tired now, don't think about any of this till you have had rest,' Magh said, placing a hand on Kate's elbow.

'Have you eaten?' she added.

'Yes, a mighty feed and apple tart with ice cream for dessert,' Kate replied, puzzled.

'Good, good, that's very important,' Magh said.

'I'm back at school the day after tomorrow and we leave two days after that, we need to talk, organise…' Kate said.

'Not today, you're both exhausted. I need you both to have clear heads, to plan the meeting. Finn needs to be exercised. After you have galloped some of the fat off him come to Hedge Cottage after your dinner. Cormac and himself can have a catch up while we plot and plan,' she said assuringly, giving Matty a wink.

ABBEY

THEY ARRIVED ON a Wednesday. According to his watch they had been travelling for over an hour since their last stop in Athlone. When everyone got back on the coach then Matty found himself on the back seat alone and stretched out as he felt tired and unintentionally fell asleep. It was sunny and warm inside and he had been up very early for the journey to Kate's school in Wexford. He awoke to the sound of an indistinguishable radio discussion which only the driver was listening to: indistinguishable because nobody else was interested in it, but he became aware of it because he could hear it for the first time. The animation and the excited melding of expressions and chat from the teenage girls for the first half of the journey had subsided and by that time had dissolved into quiet conversation and whispered giggles.

As Matty hauled himself into an upright position he realised the landscape had completely altered. They were on a very narrow road and the sky had become heavy, overhung with ash-white and cobalt-blue clouds which cast an eerie greyness over everything despite the fact that they moved briskly across the sky. There was no shrubbery outside the windows; instead, they seemed to be on a very uneven road with mountains on all sides but a good distance away. There was no traffic and he wondered how long they had been in this new landscape.

The first sighting of the school itself was an awesome vision. It was dwarfed by the mountain that stood at its back and it seemed to Matty to appear out of nowhere. As soon as the Abbey came into sight the clouds left and the light made its very position wondrous. It looked like a medieval castle complete with turrets and all of it was reflected in the lake that extended out at its front. Matty slid over to the window and didn't take his eyes away from the beauty of it even when Kate called from the seat in front, 'Matty, we're here.'

Watching the Abbey from across the lake as the coach bumped, swayed and wove its way closer and closer, Matty's mind flitted from what it must have been like to be one of the eleven children whose father had constructed the castle for them to live in, to why he had chosen the wilderness, however beautiful, in a century when the only transport was horse and carriage.

By the time the coach parked Matty was still at the window staring up and checking out the building. It was a portent, he had resolved: meeting a faerie queen in such a setting could not be bad. He was so impressed, he made plans for spending two weeks in such a place; the exploring he would do and not just the Abbey, there was a small rowing boat on the lake and the woods stretching along by the side of the massive grey mountain... and he could just make out the spire of what must be an oratory. An enthusiasm for even the study of Irish was birthed, but that, he had to realistically admit, was still somewhat tentative.

'Matt, get your coat on,' Kate shouted from the back of the queue halfway up the coach.

'Oh Kate, it's a beautiful place,' said Matty as she waited for him to shove his arms down the sleeves of his anorak.

'It is lovely and remember it's a mock castle Matt, medieval at that,' she said, her head nodding ever so slightly, confirming that she understood his mindset entirely.

'I'm no longer worried about Aillien,' whispered Matty when he joined her at the end of the queue.

'Good, worrying never got anybody anywhere,' replied Kate in her mother mode.

When everyone had dismounted and lined up near the front door, the two head girls from each of the classes, Junior Certificate and Leaving Certificate, precipitously checked their charges and stepped towards three nuns who had come out to greet them. Kate and Matty were the first to be asked to come forward and Kate's prefect introduced them.

'*Céad Míle Fáilte.*' Matty knew that this meant a hundred thousand welcomes. 'We will put you two in the retreat rooms; your cousin has requested to be near you since you are here all on your own and so young and you have come to us all the way from India to learn Irish,' said a very sweet, numinous, incredibly white and softly wrinkled nun with glasses which had round lenses which made her eyes appear very large. She was not much taller than Matty.

'Thank you, Sister,' said Kate.

Matty closed his opening mouth ambiguously and made it smile instead.

'I see she has already appointed herself as tutelary,' continued the nun, winking at Matty smiling.

Matty smiled again, the meaning of the statement lost on him.

'I'm Sister Perpetual,' said the kindly nun louder and addressed everyone, 'I am the home sister in charge of dormitories, meals, timings et cetera,' and then, looking at Kate and Matty, 'and rooms, we can't have little boys in with the girls, can we?' with another of her numinous smiles to Matty.

A taller, very erect nun who wore glasses too began to speak and as she did, Matty had a chance to check out the black robes. He was used to nuns in infant school in India, but they wore white and most of them had the veil on the back of their heads with their hair visible in the front. These nuns were completely enclosed with their faces only partially showing along with their hands. There was a white band of fabric across the forehead which was overlapped with more white fabric that covered part of the cheek, neck, ears and shoulders. He found out later that it was called a wimple. This was covered by a black veil which dipped over the forehead, almost obscuring the white fabric underneath. The sleeves were dolman and when Sister Perpetual had finished speaking she placed her tiny white hands inside the wide cuffs. There was an apron-like layer of black fabric over a long dress-like garment held in at the waist by a giant rosary beads; this lay over their shoulders stretching all the way over their backs as well as their fronts. Both sides reached the ground. Matty focused on the round toes of little Sister Perpetual's shoes which were just visible underneath the hanging layers of black fabric, like someone hiding behind floor-length curtains with just the toes of the shoes jutting out.

'I'm Sister Oliver and I am one of teaching sisters,' said the tall nun to everyone and then to Matty, 'you will be on your own a lot, we have very few juniors this month. They will come for class during the day so you will have to amuse yourself in the evenings,' and then she continued, looking at the other nuns, 'Prefatory work, the child doesn't have a word of Irish.'

'He likes being on his own,' said Kate and Matty could feel the edge in her voice.

'I hope so,' said the surly nun before Kate had any more words out of her mouth. Matty felt it was time to put on his innocent angel look. He also felt that this pejorative nun would be difficult to deal with. How Kate and Magh had managed to get rooms apart from the other pupils seemed to have been quite a feat but Matty felt if he was the reason to achieve it he did not mind being a burden on Sister Oliver's shoulders. They had their objective and that was to get complete privacy for Kate which would not be possible if she was to share the dormitory.

'Come Sister Oliver, perhaps we should use euphemisms, little ears and all of that,' put in the kindly nun in words barely audible; she had tilted her head in the tall sister's direction as she said this.

'We should give you a title, Sister,' replied the tall nun sarcastically, 'children's paeaner.'

And so Matty and Kate were taken by the third nun, who introduced herself as Sister Patrick, to their rooms which were beside each other. There was a single bed, a sink and a narrow desk with a chair in front of it at the only tall narrow window. Matty flung his rucksack on the bed in which he had the Crane Bag and followed the nun and Kate into the next room which was an exact copy of the one he had been shown into. She referred to Matty as Matthew and Kate as Catherine. She was trite but not quite as formidable as Sister Oliver.

Thursday was the first day of class; after breakfast Matty realised Kate appeared to know which classroom he should be in and delivered him to the teacher in a large room with about ten pupils his own age, all seated two at a desk. The brief exchanges between Kate and the young teacher, who was not a nun, were in Irish. Matty noted there were four rows of desks. The teacher welcomed him in English and placed him at the front desk in the row next to the one which was partially full, very much like how desks were placed in an Indian class room. Matty was surprised at this; he expected to be in a room with lots of tables with chairs all around them like he had seen in Nicky's school.

After a brief few words in Irish directed at a boy occupying a desk on his own in the partially full row, the teacher appeared to change to English:

'Sean would you please sit beside Matthew, over here in this row,' she indicated with one arm outstretched. The boy, who was a little overweight and shy too, Matty considered, sat next to him.

The teacher next gave them both books, like the first Hindi books Matty had started with in India. There were two pictures on each page with text underneath: a house, a tree, a dog and so on and on for most of the book. It ended with what seemed to be a sentence beneath the pictures. Matty felt relieved that the text was in English letters although when he put them together he felt he couldn't pronounce them. He looked at the boy next to him who smiled and said 'Madra,' pointing at the dog in the picture.

The teacher who had been busy pointing to the blackboard and speaking mainly in Irish, although Matty caught the phrase *no indefinite article*, advanced on Sean and encouraged him to pronounce all the text on the first few pages. Contented, she then advised he should repeat the words to and with Matty.

After an hour Matty remembered a lot of the nouns and tried to remember their spellings. The teacher once more broke away from the others and opened a large double door cupboard revealing what looked like a shop set up on the shelves inside. Familiar empty cartons of cheese, milk, matches and cereals and lots more, mostly food, Matty noted.

'*Tabhair dom an cais*,' she said after placing both boys in front of the cupboard.

The others were busy writing and alternately checking the blackboard. Matty remembered there was a picture of a wedge of yellow cheese in the picture book and worked out that *cais* was the word for cheese. He waited to see if Sean understood and he did and advanced on the cupboard and took the empty box of Philadelphia from the shelf.

'*Buiochas*,' she said and made them repeat it.

'*Maitiu tabhair dom briosca*,' she said.

Briosca he understood and she had used *tabhair dom* before but *Maitiu*…

'I'm sorry I think I know everything except Maitiu,' he said uncertainly in English after what felt like too long.

'*Maitiu is anim dith*,' she said smiling broadly.

Matty moved his head from side to side, still lost.

'*Sean is anim dom*,' said Sean turning to face him and smiled as Matty realised 'Maitiu' was his name.

Matty couldn't believe his luck; the rest was easy. *Briosca*: the picture in the book looked like the arrowroot biscuits Gran had with her three o'clock tea, he needed to search the cupboard as Gran's biscuits came in a paper packet like his milk biscuits. It would not be possible to preserve the paper as it tore easily. After searching along the shelves and through many boxed, plastic and cardboard he finally found a packet belonging to oat biscuits with a tartan design and presented it to the young teacher who smiled encouragingly.

'*Go raibh matith agat Maitiu*,' she said, adding emphasis to his name.

And so the day progressed, Matty relaxed a good deal and an hour later after a lunch of ham, cabbage and mashed potatoes with a white sauce, he found himself suggesting to Sean that they explore the school grounds. Sean was a wonderful companion: he went along with all Matty's suggestions which were self-serving. Matty decided to explore the little chapel which was in a thicket further along the lake and to the right of the castle.

'We must not miss our lessons,' Sean reminded as they ran along the drive.

Matty reassured him by pointing to his watch, 'We have half an hour Sean, I will not forget.'

Sean smiled as he ran with effort several metres behind Matty with a very red face.

Matty reached the door first and was busy admiring the handle when Sean caught up with him. It was black metal with rivets so ancient and weathered that it seemed part of the wood. Matty put his fingers through the circle of metal and twisted it and it lifted; with a little push the door opened.

'Don't go in there,' warned Sean who stood sweating; 'the nuns will kill us.'

But Matty had already entered the world of the three musketeers in his head, remembering their adventures in past times. He crept into the still church and just stood checking the angels and green men carved into the stone at the end of the timbers high up in the ceiling. Sean joined him and to Matty's relief he stood too, his apprehension quietened by the stillness.

Matty turned and closed the door; the handle fascinated him, it brought all the medieval stories he had read to life.

'Let's explore,' he suggested to Sean as he advanced up the main aisle touching the wooden pews as he did. He noticed they all had little cushion-topped kneelers attached to tiny hooks. He was particularly keen on those: *How comfortable they would be in Gran's Parish Church where the kneelers were so uncomfortable being bare wood.* Sean followed closely behind. When they reached the transept and Matty advanced towards the rails Sean called out to him 'Matthew, wait.'

'Everybody calls me Matty by the way,' he said, turning around, 'what's the matter?'

'Don't go up on to the altar,' Sean said, a little shy.

'I want to see the carving, did you notice the stone carving Sean…?' Before he could finish, Sean blurted out, 'But Jesus is here.'

'How do you know?' Matty asked perplexed.

'The light.' Sean pointed to a tiny flickering light in a red glass holder suspended high above from the right side of the large arch near the altar. Sean immediately genuflected and Matty followed just as he did when he went to Mass with his grandmother and Mother. He remembered what the light meant.

'It's time to go,' he said, checking his watch and aware he was not very sure of how to find their classroom. Sean appeared relieved as they silently walked down the aisle.

DEVIANT DEVILS

 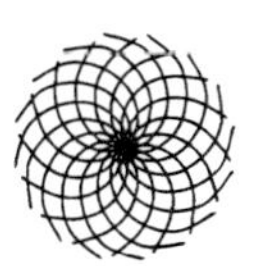

ON FRIDAY AFTERNOON it was announced that a coach had been arranged to take everyone into Galway City the next morning for shopping and sightseeing. So Matty joined the pupils in their moss green uniforms and they began loading onto the coach, which was parked near the inner gate next to the staff quarters to the left of the castle. Kate indicated a seat just a few rows down the coach. Matty slid in by the window and Kate sat beside him in the aisle seat just across from her friends, Sinead and Ciara. Matty was relieved that they were so excited about getting away from the convent that they forgot to tease him. His classmates were not on this trip; they were day pupils and obviously had a different schedule.

The coach bumped and swayed its way slowly through the fern-covered, rocky terrain just as the other one did three days earlier. Mountains were coloured gold in the weak sunlight, with the autumnal cold nights causing the vegetation to change. Pools and ponds of clear water here and there reflected the blue sky with its fast-moving white clouds. Uninterested in the animated conversation and with his eyes unintentionally taking in the scenery, Matty considered how lucky he was to have a brother and not a sister. All this incessant chatter and excited squeals irritated him; it seemed to be out of proportion to what was going on or being said. Who would want to exert themselves and become frenzied over a new colour of nail polish, which was forbidden anyway with the uniform? Kate was fine as a sister especially when she was on her own but when her friends were involved, even though she didn't squeal she did seemed to be extremely interested in fashion and nail polish. Anyway, these were forbidden items, carried about in pencil cases and uniform pockets.

It was not until they had left the mountains behind and were speeding along a road which had two lanes of traffic that Matty realised the driver was watching Kate consistently in his rear-view mirror. Whether it was that Kate was a little more sensitive than a normal girl her age or maybe it was because she was psychic but Matty felt she was aware of the driver too. She would turn her head forward and watch the driver from behind the headrest of the seat in front of her occasionally and then resume the conversation with her friends. At one stage she and Matty exchanged glances and he knew for certain that she knew he knew too.

Kate allowed all the pupils to get out of the bus so that Matty and she were the last to leave. Matty didn't like the driver; somehow or other he made him feel uneasy. He was a thickset man with a full, round face and very short red hair and the translucent pale skin that went with it.

'How do you like Galway?' he drawled as Matty turned to descend the steps.

'We like it just fine,' replied Kate dismissively. Matty stood still on the step and turned to face the driver.

'That's good to hear.' He issued a shadow of a smile. 'I understand you will be staying with us a while then.'

'Two weeks, like all the other students,' replied Kate, moving forward to leave the bus.

'Ah but you're not just a student are you?' he persisted audaciously.

'I have no idea what you're talking about… let's go,' she instructed Matty and he left the bus.

'Course you do, you've come to see our Queen… haven't you now?' and he turned away and allowed his sarcastic smile to spread all over his face. The bus door closed and the driver moved it away from the kerb.

Kate didn't join her friends; instead, she sat down on the bench at the bus stop as the coach pulled away to a parking area across the square. She appeared shaken.

'Who is he? How does he know the other reason why we are here?' asked Matty quietly as he sat down beside her, pondering this new situation.

'I don't think he's a shape shifter…' Kate had both hands dug deep into her blazer pockets, glowering straight ahead of her across the square and watching him park the coach. She seemed to be talking to herself and Matty at the same time.

'A Tuatha you mean? Would they follow us? I thought Magh was to make contact?' All these questions came out of Matty's mouth at once without his usual consideration. He was a little confounded and the complacency that had evolved out of the romanticism which had engulfed him since spotting the Abbey was giving way to discomfort of another reality.

'If he's not a shape shifter then who?' she continued quietly aloud.

'Are you comin'?' came Ciara's voice with her back to a group of girls staring into a chemist's window.

'We'll catch up with you later,' called Kate and the girl threw her arms up in the air.

'Your friends are fed up with me tagging along,' said Matty.

'Never mind them, we have more important things to think about,' she replied, her focus still on the coach driver who had got out of the coach and was staring at them from across the square.

'I need to contact Ailill but I can't do it now, not with him watching us,' she said, scowling.

'I think I've seen him in the grounds of the Abbey,' said Matty looking up at Kate's set face, her eyebrows knitted.

'He's probably their odd job man, jack of all trades and I'd really like to know who he really is,' she said, still spilling hate but pensive. 'Let's go Matt, the longer we sit here the more suspicious he will get. Let's join the girls and try to appear as normal as possible.'

They caught up with the group which was chaperoned by a nun at the head as it snaked up the street in twos. The girls from the Junior Certificate class greeted Kate as she joined them on their way into a store called Dunnes Stores which had clothes in the windows. Matty saw a souvenir shop opposite and beckoned to Kate and, using sign language, tried to let her understand he was going across the street. But she descended on him anyway.

'If you want to go in there that is OK; just don't move till I come and get you, alright?' she ordered. Matty nodded. 'Oh, and Matt, keep clear of the bus driver.'

There was a tall fat man behind the counter when Matty opened the door of the old-fashioned shop. The bell jolted him as he stepped over the threshold and he looked up to see that it was a real bell on a sort of flexible metal. There were no other shoppers. Matty glanced all around self-consciously at what hung on the walls and the table display. He was fascinated with lots of little drawers built into the wall behind the man. Being the only shopper Matty asked if he could have a look around. The silent shopkeeper nodded reproachfully. *Maybe he thinks I'm going to steal something because I'm just a school kid*, thought Matty.

The first thing which drew Matty's attention was an Irish flag. He felt Jack and he should have one and marvelled how like the Indian flag it was – just missing the chakra, the wheel in the centre of the white panel, and of course, the colours were the same but placed vertically; they had the same symbolism, according to Father Tom. Also hanging were woollen jumpers with the Irish design knitted into them, lots of them mainly in cream or green. Matty felt the cuff; he liked the feel of the pure, coarse wool and marvelled at the designs. As his hand stayed on the wool his eyes roved around the little shop. There were socks on the table with leprechauns on them. Not the type of leprechauns Jack and he had become aware of, these were like cartoons. High up on a shelf were bourans, many sizes; even though they did not look like the Indian tabala, somehow the stretched skin reminded him of them and the summer school he and Jack attended for lessons in percussion. Matty asked how much they cost as he was not tall enough to read the little white price tag suspended with some fine twine. The man said thirty five punts. Matty calculated immediately: even the smallest was way out of his budget, but it was then he noticed the maps, maps of Ireland ancient and modern. He asked the unfriendly shopkeeper as politely as he could if he had any maps of Galway and in particular the area where the Abbey was.

'Come to learn Irish have ya?' asked the man. He spoke differently from the people in Wexford, softer like the bus driver and more musical, almost with a rhythm which had higher notes towards the end of the sentences. Matty nodded his head as the man began to rummage in very deep drawers lower down along the wall the little drawers were built into.

'Where have you come from?' persisted the man, who now wore a false half-smile.

'Wexford,' replied Matty.

'I think you must be from somewhere else though,' said the man as he laid several maps on the counter and began arranging them. Matty thought a while before answering. Firstly he thought about what Jack had said to an airline pilot when he was five and a quarter and had been invited into the cockpit of an Aer Lingus plane on the last leg of a trip to Ireland from London and India, when he was asked the same question. Matty knew this because his parents went on about it as the air hostess had described Jack being a poet; he had said, *I come from a land where the sun always shines.* Probably because all Jack could see at that moment were clouds and no sun, as Matty knew Jack did not write nor was he interested in poetry ever. However, Matty was ten and knew an answer like that would probably make this disapproving man even more disgruntled. At the same time a certain instinct made him want to protect himself so he lied and after watching the man in his well-worn grey cardigan which had tan stains all down the front for a time he said, 'Dublin.'

'Dublin, you're no Dubliner,' said the man, with what Matty considered a disproportionate amount of verbal force. So he lied again; *white lies were sometimes necessary,* Kate had said.

'I don't remember before that,' he looked up with his 'pitiful' face which worked on his mother and then added, 'I was very little.'

The burly, worn-out-grey-cardiganed arm pushed a map of Ireland and one of Galway towards Matty's side of the glass counter. His hand was very fat and very wrinkly with pale brown patches all over the grey, not soft and white like little Sister Perpetual's.

'Can I open them… to look?' asked Matty uncertainly.

'I'll do it,' said the man briskly and opened the Galway map.

Matty stretched up and looked 'Can you show me where the school, the Abbey is please?' he asked.

'Am I a cartographer?' the man asked gruffly and began folding the map up brusquely.

Just then the door bell's sharp jangle made Matty jump. The coach driver slid into the shop through the partly opened door. He took up a position against the wall of merchandise opposite to where Matty stood in front of the counter.

'Mornin' Seamus,' said the shopkeeper.

'Ye have a tourist Gerry,' replied the driver with his eyes full of dark mischief, Matty noted as he looked over his shoulder and then forward again at the shopkeeper.

'Aye. From the Abbey… says he's a Dubliner,' replied the irascible shopkeeper snidely.

'Telling ye fibs was he?' asked the driver and he moved nearer Matty.

'I thought he might be,' replied the fat man who had taken on a different tone, quieter, more conspiratorial.

'He's a VIP… are ye not?' the bus driver spoke directly to Matty and his tone had changed to imperative. He had moved right up to the counter and Matty felt he couldn't take his eyes away from this dangerous man. He felt the lithe weight of the Crane Bag on his back and knew the ring was in its secret pocket: all he had to do was get out of the shop and into an alley… somewhere he could become invisible without causing anyone to notice.

The jangle of the doorbell caused both men to turn suddenly in its direction. Kate pushed the glass door with its small panes of glass all the way back against a display cabinet; the sound of it appeared to rock the entire shop. She stood akimbo in the door way with at least ten fourteen-year-olds in school uniform behind her. After staring down the driver she confidently strode into the shop and towards the counter where Matty stood. The driver stepped back as the girls piled in and for the first time Matty was glad of their prattle and extraneous eagerness; they swarmed around the table display, they had spotted the leprechaun socks.

'Buying something, Matt?' asked Kate glaring at the shopkeeper.

'How much is the map of Ireland?' asked Matty.

'One seventy-five,' replied the shopkeeper, eyeing Kate threateningly.

'I want it,' said Matty, suddenly so relieved and confident he intentionally omitted politeness.

The nun who was in charge of the girls entered the shop, clapped her hands and asked the pupils to reassemble on the pavement outside the shop. She was Sister Joseph, a younger version of Sister Perpetual. Matty paid and while he waited for his change he noticed the coach driver had his back to everyone; he was at the very back of the shop feigning an interest in the woollen sweaters.

Outside Sister Joseph eventually made a line of twos, walking up and down in the street checking that everyone was on the pavement and pointing at the feet of those who were not.

'Why are you two not in line?' she demanded of Kate and Matty who were stood, still somewhat in shock, to the side of the shop adjoining the souvenir shop, both observing the nun but not really present. She was irritable because she had lost control of the girls. Kate came to her senses before Matty did.

'May we stay at the very end of the line, Sister?' asked Kate. 'My cousin is a little... homesick, the man in there... was a little rude.'

'All right, just this once... and no straying into shops not on the plan,' the nun reprimanded.

'No Sister, sorry Sister,' said Kate and caught hold of the strap of the Crane Bag and pulled Matty in behind Sinead and Ciara.

The next shop was a sweet shop and they all had ice cream there. Sister Joseph had a cup of tea and seated herself beside Kate and Matty. They had found themselves a seat alone in order to discuss what had gone on in the souvenir shop.

'Is it all too much for you?' Sister Joseph asked Matty in a kindly voice.

'He's alright, Sister,' answered Kate. 'School reminds him of India and his brother,' she lied.

'What are we going to do with you when the big girls are at their classes?' the nun asked Matty.

'He is interested in the Abbey Sister... and in history, we're half Norman and half Celtic... well actually, Matty is quarter Norman, quarter Celtic and half Indian...' Kate hesitated. Matty knew that she needed the Abbey explored and she was fishing for ways of getting it done. Two days had gone by and there had been no word from Magh – and now this mysterious bus driver and a shop-keeper who knew more about their business than there was need to.

'I'll take you round the Abbey, son, and fill you in on all the history you want to know,' replied the nun, now animated. She had yet another accent, defined but more staccato.

'I'm really interested in Celtic history, Sister,' he said in a small voice and then took a chance '... and the ancient Goddesses.'

'Well, we'll see what we can do,' said the nun who turned her eyes in the direction of the chatter.

She stood up. 'Are you all finished? Good, then it's time to go, line up,' she ordered as she surveyed her well folded sheet of paper. 'Listen, listen, one more shop and then back to the coach; follow me.' Before she left the shop she turned to Kate and said, 'You may stay with the little fella, at the back.'

'Thank you, Sister,' beamed Kate and then under her breath to Matty said, 'What's the matter with you, asking her about Goddesses…? She's a nun, Matt, she's going to give you the whole Christian view of Saint Brigit and every other goddess they have turned into Saint this and that.'

'Magh said scratch the surface of any Irish person and you will find the old ways,' replied Matty quietly but indignantly. 'It's worth a try, Kate, everyone is strange around here… even the shopkeeper is one of them.'

'One of what?' asked Kate.

'Well he and the bus driver seem to know each other very well,' whispered Matty as he and Kate tagged themselves in behind Ciara and Sinead.

'How 'ya,' waved the two girls.

'Grand,' replied Kate. 'I just want to talk to Matt for a minute.'

'The shopkeeper asked a lot of questions,' explained Matty almost in a whisper.

'What sort of questions?' asked Kate as they trudged along the pavement slightly short of the others.

'Where I was from and, he didn't believe me when I said I was from Dublin,' whispered Matty.

'I'm not surprised,' giggled Kate.

'Well you said it was alright to lie… especially when I was… in danger,' said Matty defensively.

'Yeah, but the lie must be a little bit credible, Matt,' she smiled.

'What's wrong with Dublin?' asked Matty.

'You've got an Indian accent, Matt.' More smiling and then she was deadly serious again. 'What did the bus driver say?'

'His name is Seamus,' Matty told her, '… and I think he was going to hurt me Kate… he…' Matty stopped walking.

'What did he do?' asked Kate very seriously.

'Well, nothing but he moved very close and said I was a VIP… and Gerry, that's the shopkeeper, seemed to know what he was talking about,' explained Matty.

'The devils,' expostulated Kate.

'Are they real devils?' asked Matty, alarmed.

'No Matt, don't take it literally… they are some kind of deviants though… we'll have to find out who they are… and quickly,' she said pensively. 'Let's keep up, Matt,' and they began walking quickly to catch up on Sinead and Ciara.

'But I haven't told you the best part,' said Matty with an animated look.

'What?' asked Kate, looking ahead; Matty felt she was checking out where the Nun was.

'I found the distaff,' he said.

'What…?' Kate stood still once again while the little queue of schoolgirls snaked its way up the high street, leaving the cousins behind.

'It's at the back of the shop in the container with the Shillelaghs,' Matty continued.

'How do you know it's a distaff?' asked Kate.

'Magh drew it for me, I'm sure,' he said convincingly.

'But –' was all the astounded Kate could reply; she tried once again to catch up with the pupils, deep in thought.

'At least we know where it is now… it's only a matter of getting it,' said Matty, running alongside her.

WARLOCK

 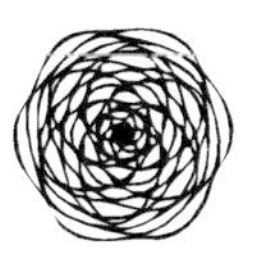

AFTER LUNCH THE pupils were to be taken by Sister Joseph to the garden which was situated about a mile from the Abbey, and as they walked away from the lake and the entrance Seamus was lurking near the minibus. Matty looked up at Kate who was pretending not to notice him despite his open stares. Sister Joseph kept a running commentary as they walked about the type of plants, soil and planting requirements. It seemed to Matty that they were off the curriculum and the young nun enjoyed imparting the knowledge she so obviously found fascinating. They wove their way along a wide, surfaced path among a dense growth of rhododendrons and pines.

'*Eisteacht, eisteacht*,' she announced, halting and turning to face the girls, 'we are going to have a little quiz to see how well you know your surroundings as Gaelige.' She went into the wood a little way and after foraging about on the ground for a short while she held up a nut. She spoke in Irish and pointed to the nut. Where they approached her, the mountain stretched right down to the woodland floor and one of the senior pupils deviated – whether it was opportunistic or not, Matty could not tell, but she pointed out that she had read up on how hydroelectric power was used to supply the Abbey with electricity. This well informed senior asked if it was a natural formation and the Nun, somewhat surprised at the interest, latched on and explained that the original owner had blasted out parts of the mountain to divert the flow of water to make electricity. The senior beamed a smile all around her class: the nun had responded to the question spoken in English and for a moment or two nobody had to remember the name of a chestnut in Irish. Matty had a little more history of the Abbey and continued to be fascinated by the intelligence of the man who built it.

'We will come to that further along the path,' explained the nun hurriedly; perhaps, Matty thought, she too wondered if the question was a distraction.

Kate and Matty were at the back of the group and the nun was less attentive as they were in the grounds of the Abbey. Matty began to push his way forward to listen to what the nun was saying when Kate grabbed him by the arm and inclined her head towards the footpath and the forest behind them.

'What's up? What's the matter?' Matty asked.

'I can't stand this any longer Matt… something is wrong… and now…' she didn't finish.

'And now what?' asked Matty.

'And now… that… Seamus is watching us…' She was uneasy and kept on walking away from the sheer rock of the mountain and the group, deeper into the thicket of lush growth on the opposite side of the footpath.

'Maybe… when we get back you can… get in contact with Magh,' suggested Matty, trying to keep up with her frantic pace.

Finally she stopped near a much smaller rock and leaned against it with her behind.

'What about the nun Kate…? She will miss us,' he said.

'Na, she's much more relaxed now that we're back in the school grounds again… I just had to get away from them for a while… the interference…' she quietly finished, her eyes focusing elsewhere as if she was drifting off in her mind.

Matty, who stood facing Kate and the large boulder, turned his head without moving, looking over his shoulder beyond his Crane Bag. Then he turned back to Kate having seen only the tall pines and the under-planting of the rhododendron bushes, but Kate was nodding even though her eyes were far away. Matty felt it was best not to move and not to speak. After a little while observing her apparently listening, watching something and nodding, she began to focus on him again.

'Matt, Magh is here, she is warning me about Seamus… can you do something for me?' she asked.

'Yes of course; is he following us?' Matty asked.

'Probably. Listen,' she ordered as she approached Matty, 'I need a little time alone… a short time when I don't have to concentrate on the physical world and Seamus. Can you be my look out?'

'Yes, what do you want me to do?' he asked.

'Can you…' and she began to think as she raised her arm to direct him, 'can you watch this area, from the path and back towards the entrance where Seamus was with the minibus, in a sort of arc… just walk the arc back and forward and call out if you see anyone, particularly Seamus,' and she emphasised the last two words.

'What if he creeps up on me and… grabs me… before I can call you?' asked Matty.

'Have you got the ring, Matt?' she asked.

'Yes,' Matty replied as he let the Crane Bag slip from his shoulders. He opened it and rummaged about in the bottom.

When he had retrieved the ring and hoisted the bag on to his back, he noticed that Kate was making a circle with a twig.

'What's that…what are you doing?' he asked.

'I need protection, Matt… you remember the yantra that Jack used, this is similar,' she said and stood in its centre. As well as that…' and she looked up from her task momentarily 'I need a portal… somewhere I can move into the other world, and this is perfect.'

Matty didn't try to enter; instead, he looked at her, showing her the ring and said, 'What if I have to use it… how will you hear me… or find me?'

'I'll be able to see your aura Matt… and you can slip it on and off to find out if you are alone… away from… danger,' she explained, 'just as Jack did, remember,' and saying this she glanced up at him, stood upright and threw away the twig she had made her circle with.

'Ready, wait Kate… how is here perfect?' he asked. 'You said here is perfect.'

'Remember where we stood just now, in the group?' she waited for him to indicate he understood. He nodded.

'The mountain meets the land, I can gain entry here,' she explained.

'Are you going to lie down on the ground?' Matty asked after considering what she had told him. The only time he had seen Kate transition between the world before was in his house in India and she always lay on the bed in her room.

'No Matt. Are you ready?' she said quietly.

Matty nodded again and walked about five feet away from Kate, back towards the path and then walked the arc which Kate had virtually mapped out. He understood that she had allowed for Seamus to follow the group through the woods as well as along the path. At this distance he felt he could still see part of Kate through the shrubbery as well as be a look out.

Every now and again Matty stood at the near side of the Scots pine, chestnut and hazel trees and listened and waited. The falling leaves and particularly the chestnuts made a fairly loud crack and plop sound in this area of the woods in the silence so he could not rely on the quiet to warn him of anyone approaching, but hopefully the twigs may make a different sound, especially if anybody trod on one he hoped he could distinguish the sound from the plop and crack of the falling hazel and chestnuts. He became suddenly aware of movement higher up, above the ground. He turned to find a grey squirrel scurrying down a tall tree trunk; at ground level it sat with its large bushy tail arched over its back. Matty watched the watching animal, noticing its small ear tufts. It was autumn, peak activity time for squirrels. Contented that Matty was no threat, the squirrel began to rove about the tree roots, searching among the abundant nuts. He began to feed on a flower at ground level. Matty was amazed that the little animal didn't take his lunch higher up where Matty considered it may be safer. He envied him. If only *he* could scale one of the Douglas firs and have a squirrel's eye view he would not need to be so nervous. That thought made him wonder: could Magh shape shift? How had she contacted Kate just then? Kate was definitely using her second sight. He almost fell over; he had arched his neck backwards following the trunk of a tree towards the sky.

Matty moved on to the next large tree trunk, he bent and looked and could see Kate's black school shoes and the calves of her legs with her hands in her lap: she had taken up a sort of Padma Asana position. He crouched down to see if he could have a better view of what she was doing. The legs did not move but there was a murmuring: she was communicating with someone or something. *She must be half in and half out of the other world,* he thought. Matty straightened and turned and looked outwards from his designated arc. Instinctively he felt he needed to lengthen the arc to go behind the boulder, maybe even further around Kate's circle. His instincts were right. As he crept closer to the boulder between the ferns he saw Seamus with his back to the boulder, head tilted, listening to what Kate was transacting. Matty panicked. How could he warn her? He slid his right hand into his pocket and slipped the ring into the palm of his hand, ready to loop it on to one of his fingers. Without more deliberation, he hadn't time to deliberate, he should not deliberate more, so he shouted without thinking, 'Deviant Devil!' and slipped the ring on to his left thumb as the ring was too big for any of the other fingers.

He was in black velvet, no light, without sound or shape but his mind worked. He hoped that deviant devil was enough of a clue for Kate to realise who was spying on her; she had called him that when she found out what he was doing to Matty in the shop.

Matty began to count and when he had counted out what he considered to be two long minutes he slipped the ring up his thumb slowly and light penetrated his eyes. He felt that he was looking at the forest for the first time, as if his eyes had been washed with crystal clear water; everything seemed so new and fresh. He immediately squatted to see if he could locate Kate's legs within the circle. What he did see made him feel sick: there were a pair of men's boots and trouser legs in the circle. Matty stood up and approached, keeping a grasp on the ring which lay on the last joint of his thumb next to the nail, ready to be pushed all the way down in an instant. He went round the arc slightly in the direction of the path, with the idea that he could call out to the nun and her group if necessary.

After creeping quietly he squatted once again and peered. This time he was nearer and had a better view. As well as the trouser legs there were scarlet-red stocking legs in old women's walking shoes. The only other person he knew who wore stockings that colour was Magh. His heart gave a little heave. From his hide he could also see Kate's school shoes and legs; she was still seated on the forest floor and from his view Magh's legs were planted directly in front of Kate and pointing towards the trousered legs, with her pale blue plaid, pleated, woollen skirt partially shielding Kate's face. He stood up and moved a branch of waxed rhododendron leaves to get a better view, having to forfeit the ring to his anorak pocket for its safety.

They were speaking in Irish, low snarling words were spat to and fro between Magh and Seamus who stood firmly pointing what Matty considered must be a type of branch – or was it a wand? – at Kate. Kate was frozen with fear: Matty knew her and he had seen her worried and even a little afraid but there was sheer fear on the part of her body in his vision, she was actually shaking. At the same moment Matty became aware of a presence behind him; the only thought which came into his head was Gerard, Seamus's co-conspirator. He let the branch go, it sprang back creating a rustle and suddenly all eyes were in his direction. His hand went instinctively into his pocket in search of the ring but it was too late, whoever was behind him covered his mouth with one hand and dragged him back away from the circle. Matty grabbed the muscled arms but he was helpless to free himself. He tried to make himself heavy by digging his heels into the soft earth and deep layers of scattered leaves but all he left were tiny drills on the forest floor.

If Matty had not been trembling so much he would have been impressed beyond words. He was shaken and unable to confront the man, he whispered the name *Ailill* the moment his mouth was released, not only because he was aware of what was going on nearby but because the shock he was still experiencing chocked his vocal cords. The warrior from another time acknowledged the name with a nod and let go of his body.

'Kate,' Matty managed, pointing in the direction of the confrontation.

The warrior raised his right palm, moving it towards and away from Matty slowly, indicating everything was under control, Matty hoped he had interpreted correctly. He relaxed, letting his shoulders drop, aware that he had been scrunched up inside. His knees still shook. He watched the warrior as he moved closer to the three, careful not to make a sound with his leather shoes which looked like they were made of animal skin. Matty could tell he was on high alert. He was enormous: taller and broader than his Uncle Liam, and he was over six foot high. This was a giant of a man. Matty relaxed enough to take note of the tartan he wore; it was beautiful, he thought.

He had shoulder-length red hair, *which was actually orange*, Matty considered.

This was controlled by a thin leather band which he wore on his forehead and around his head. The hair was wavy and formed curls near its ends. His eyes were large and blue. They seemed powerful but at the same time wary. Matty had a good view of his buckler which was slung on his back to one side, as the warrior strode along an unseen boundary, it seemed to Matty. It had a blue background: the colour lapis lazuli came to his mind. Superimposed on this background were what looked like elongated hounds intertwined with snakes. They were painted gold. This lay on top of the lovely tartan. Matty looked at the coarse weave. These were earthly colours of gold and pale brown, like the autumnal heather Matty had seen that morning from the window of the bus. It wasn't a cape, more a large blanket with two corners pulled over the shoulders and the fabric brought together into a torque at one shoulder. It was flung back: this man was ready for action, the buckler may have been on his back but he kept a hand on the hilt of his sword which was sheathed and hanging from his waist. *Kate never mentioned that the beings she communicated with were enormous, but then Jack and he had never questioned her about them, not in any detail anyway.*

He suddenly sprang in the direction of the conflict, unsheathing his sword in an instant. Matty followed through the undergrowth. For a moment he was blinded with the harsh sting delivered by the whip of an azalea branch. Matty quickly wiped the tears which had protected his eyes. After he had wiped away successive tears from his eyes he could see Ailill's back: he was behind Seamus and had his sword held high with the hilt up in the air and the point lying on the skin at Seamus's neck; his other hand encircled Seamus, pinioning his arms to his sides which forced Seamus to drop what he had been pointing at Kate. Matty noticed that Magh slid what looked like an elongated crystal she had held pointing at Seamus into her raincoat pocket and bent to help Kate stand up. Matty was afraid to move: the tension was palpable in the space all around them and although he wanted to be near Kate he did not want to cause a distraction. Ailill let go of Seamus and moved in front of him, the sword now pointed at his Adams apple, which moved up and down as he swallowed continuously, he seem petrified of the giant from another world. He tried to speak but only gulps and unintelligible sounds emerged. Ailill then spoke to him, guttural words, expectorated with actual specks of saliva, Matty noted. Then he broke the skin to the side of the Adam's apple on Seamus's neck and made what looked like a circle within a circle, like a maze, Matty thought, which became obscured as the blood began to flow from the superficial wound before he had finished. Seamus let out a scream which was ignored until Ailill stood back, sheathing his short sword. Seamus turned and ran, making snapping and whipping sounds as his dark overcoat disappeared through the shrubbery.

'Over here,' came the sound of Sister Joseph's voice followed by, 'Are ye lost? Catherine Garman and Matthew Ram, answer me.'

Ailill and Magh disappeared, just vanished. Matty's mouth fell open and then his heart began to thud loudly in his chest as the tiny little Sister Perpetual stepped calmly and smilingly from behind an azalea shrub. *She has seen everything.* Matty's mind clouded: how would they explain all of what happened? He just couldn't think.

'It's alright, Sister Joseph,' called out the tiny nun, 'Catherine had a bit of a faint; I'm taking her to sick bay with the little fella.'

Sister Joseph appeared in the tiny clearing and the faces of her taller pupils appeared all around her shoulders. The little nun was leading Kate by her elbow towards the foot path but through a different route among the holly and rhododendron bushes. Matty followed and Sister Joseph turned and called out, 'Right girls, back to the footpath and turn left towards the gardens.'

Matty wondered how many, or if any, of the girls had noticed the circle Kate had made on the ground.

MARSHMALLOW

MATTY HAD NO choice but to follow the two women. Kate turned her head as the nun pushed tiny branches aside, allowing free movement through the shrubbery; she looked behind at Matty. From the look on her face he felt the same question had formed in her mind: *what type of explanation would satisfy?* He also knew that Kate realised the tiny little nun had seen everything.

Sister Perpetual said nothing until she had seated them at the end of a long wooden table in the refectory. In imperative tones she said, 'Stay here.' What amazed Matty was how words delivered so gently could have such command: he knew there was no point in creating an excuse to extract themselves from the situation.

'How long was she there, in the bushes?' whispered Kate.

'I have no idea... she certainly was not there when I walked back and forth after leaving you. What are we going to tell her?' he asked, bending closer almost in a whisper.

'We'll see how much she knows first,' replied Kate, looking over her shoulder in the direction the nun went.

'Are you alright?' asked Matty after some time in the anxious quiet.

'She'll feel much better when she eats this,' came the gentle voice of the little nun who suddenly appeared with a small tray, two glasses of milk, one side plate with what looked like a beef sandwich and another one with biscuits. She continued speaking as if what they had encountered was the most normal thing in the world.

'A happenstance with the old world leaves one ungrounded, don't you think?' she directed that statement at Kate. 'So eat up now, let's get your strength back.'

'Was it your first?' she asked Matty as she offered him the plate with the biscuits on.

Matty looked at the kindly eyes and wondered if she was like the stepmother in *Snow White*: there was no cruelty about her – *could he trust her*? He looked at Kate who was devouring the beef sandwich with her eyes on Matty. The nun looked from one to the other and placed a glass of milk in front of Matty.

'Thank you,' was all he could say, hoping to divert her attention; it was pointless to tell a lie.

'Thank you sister,' repeated Kate, a bolus of partially chewed food causing one jaw to balloon on the symmetrical face.

'Aren't you the brave ones,' went on the nun, 'taking on Seamus all on your own?'

'We didn't, we were only trying to protect ourselves,' blurted Matty.

'He is always following us... watching us,' confirmed Kate.

'Why do you think that is?' asked the nun, tilting her head slightly and looking at Kate. She wore a smile. Matty felt there was a knowing expression in her eyes. He watched her for any signs of harshness, but there were none.

There was a loud gulp as Kate swallowed; it was obvious to Matty she was not able to chew the beef entirely, such was her unease. They were caught and he knew he must divulge as little as possible of their real mission. The grinding noise he made as he chewed the biscuit he had taken annoyed himself in the silence as the nun waited and waited.

Matty picked up the glass of milk and drank as quietly as he could. He found his body needed food too; so much energy had been expended, *in shock after shock*.

'You didn't really come here to learn Irish, did you?' the nun asked suddenly, turning her full attention onto him. She still spoke quietly; she still smiled, her eyes were friendly, but she was persistent.

'No,' was all he said and looked at Kate.

The nun turned to look at Kate who had finished half the sandwich and had started sipping the milk. She looked up from her glass, firstly at Matty and then at the nun.

'You can see them, can't you?' enquired the nun.

'Yes,' replied Kate.

'Why here then?' she waited a while and then continued: 'You can see them in Wexford too, why come here?'

Kate did not reply and looked down at her plate for a while and then began watching a squirrel through the large window which was open; the bottom sash slid into place on top of the top part of the multi-pane window.

'It wasn't a happenstance, was it?' asked the nun.

'It was, in a way; we are not here to meet with Seamus or the people he associates with.' Kate looked about the large wood-panelled room and over her shoulder towards the doors leading to the kitchen and lowered her voice even more, 'We are here to meet Aillien.' Kate watched the nun's face as she reflected on the information.

'A faerie queen?' she said with a little inquisitive wonder in her voice which was kept low.

'Do you see them too?' enquired Kate.

'I do,' replied the nun, totally relaxed.

'Then you saw Ailill?' asked Matty.

'I did,' she said.

'He saved us,' Matty said and looked at Kate, feeling he may have said too much.

'From who, dear?' asked the nun.

'You were there, you saw how Seamus threatened Kate,' Matty whispered, annoyed that she continued to be evasive.

'We don't know why Seamus is following us, threatening us,' explained Kate.

'It's must be because of the faerie queen,' whispered the nun, taking a look around the room in an exaggerated way because of the veil obscuring her view.

'Why?' asked Matty. 'We are not going to harm her.'

'She asked us to come here, so why is he causing obstructions…? Or worse,' Kate's whisper disappeared slowly into the ether. The squirrel she kept watching was now on the inside ledge of the open window.

'He is trying to stop us, isn't he?' she asked the nun quietly.

'It looks like it,' said the nun, nodding as she did.

'But why?' asked Kate.

'He must be from Cruachain. He is new here: our driver became seriously ill recently and Seamus was the only person who responded to our advertisement for a temporary driver,' explained the nun. Matty wondered why she divulged so much.

'How very convenient,' remarked Kate. 'Then they must have known we were coming.'

'What puzzles me,' spoke the nun quietly, 'is why is Cruachain trying to stop you from seeing Aillien?' and she looked down at her little marshmallow fingers.

Kate kept her voice low after looking over her shoulder, one eye still on the squirrel.

'Aillien asked the Witch of Cruachain to rid Matty's father of some killing energy; all she asked for was that Matty and I visit her here in return for the favour,' Kate was frank. 'That's why he is here.'

'But Cruachain and Aillien are the antithesis of each other,' repeated the nun, looking puzzled.

'What do you mean?' asked Kate.

'Aillien is the type of queen who tended humans in time of poverty and illness throughout the ages. She still helps those who believe in her. In days of old she would take her barge out at night and visit those in need, laying her hands on the sick and would either cure them or take their souls into heaven. Whereas Cruachain –' she stopped, shaking her head and then continued, 'well, Cruachain is unbelievable… I really don't know how to describe her.' She thought for a little while and then continued, 'Are you Hindu, young man, your surname is Ram?'

'Yes,' Matty answered, accompanied by a nod of his head.

'Well Cruachain is like your goddess Kali, she will do what is requested regardless of the consequences.' She stopped and thought for a moment.

'Who asked Aillien for help?' she asked quietly.

'I have a friend who is of the faerie world and our world,' explained Kate.

'The ban-sidhe in your circle?' asked the nun.

Kate nodded. She fastened her eyes on to the table top – *to avoid looking at the squirrel*, Matty thought, making a quick search of the room himself.

'And she couldn't help?' asked the nun.

'No,' Kate replied.

'And the beings of Kali?' she asked.

'They had been invoked to get rid of my uncle – sorry Matt.' Kate touched the back of Matty's hand and then continued. 'I made contact with the Danavas, the people of the Goddess Dana but they were too afraid, I think they had been intimidated.'

'And Aillien approached Cruachain, but why is Cruachain worried by your visit here?' puzzled the nun.

'The distaff broke as she was ensnaring the evil energy and she has demanded that humans get her a new one… but that doesn't make sense.' Kate looked far away as if she was mystified. 'Why would she try to prevent us from returning the spinning wheel?'

'She may like having power over Aillien,' ventured the nun thoughtfully.

'Have you got the spindle?' she asked, looking at both of them.

'Not exactly, but my friend may be able to help with that,' said Kate sparingly.

'When is your meeting with Aillien?' asked the Nun.

'Friday night,' Kate answered.

Matty felt Kate had become uneasy: she kept looking down the length of the table in a furtive way. He too felt apprehensive but probably for a different reason: they had divulged a huge amount of information to the extracting nun, *and could they trust her?*

'We are all friends here, come and join us,' said the little nun without raising her voice or even looking in the direction Kate had been.

Matty was astonished. He looked in the direction Kate had been trying so hard not to look in and Magh materialised, from the ground up it seemed, complete in her raincoat and plaid skirt, at the end of the table. Magh approached the little group and slid onto the long stool beside Matty. She carried a very old-fashioned handbag with her; Matty had not noticed it in the circle in the woods. Matty looked around to check the whereabouts of the squirrel and it was not to be seen. So Magh really was a shape shifter – *or was she*?

'We have a dilemma, it seems,' the little nun put the question to Magh.

'We do indeed,' replied Magh.

'I'm sorry, I didn't offer you a drink,' said Sister Perpetual to Magh.

'I'd really love a cup of tea… if it's not an inconvenience,' replied Magh.

'Not at all,' said the Nun as she slid off her end of the long bench that faced the open windows.

'Can we trust her?' whispered Kate anxiously.

'We do not have much choice,' replied Magh quietly. 'I get positive vibrations from her. I'm not worried; we need all the help we can get, especially with Cruachain behaving the way she is.'

'What's that all about?' asked Kate.

'I really don't know what she's up to… there is nothing straightforward about Cruachain, she's as slippery and as bad as they get…' Magh trailed off in thought.

'What were the marks Ailill made with his sword on Seamus's neck?' Matty ventured after some quiet time.

'The marks of the triple goddess,' replied the nun. Her silent approach towards the table with a cup and saucer in one hand and a bowl of sugar in the other unnerved Matty for a second time that day.

She placed them on the table in front of Magh.

'Thank you,' said Magh, 'I'm most grateful.'

'I understand,' said the nun, 'you were not expecting today's encounter then?'

'Not at all,' replied Magh, stirring the two heaped spoons of sugar she had added to her steaming tea. This was followed by silence while she sipped appreciatively from the cup.

'Excuse me,' ventured Matty, 'what does the triple Goddess mean… the signs…?'

'I suspect your warrior friend was reminding Seamus that he should align himself with the Goddess Dana, not the old world of Cruachain and the Formorians. What do you think –?' She looked directly at Magh and then said, 'We have not been introduced.'

'I'm sorry,' said Kate anxiously 'This is Magh my friend… she has been helping me…' Kate trailed off as if lost for words.

'Helping you how to live with yourself,' put in the nun.

'Yes,' replied Kate, relieved.

'Well, Seamus will wear the sign of the triple Goddess for evermore; when he heals eventually, he will bear the scars and Cruachain will have nothing to do with him then.' Sister Perpetual continued the monologue while Magh sipped on the sweet tea. She pushed the plate of biscuits in Magh's direction and it was accepted. Magh dunked the biscuit into the tea and swallowed the spongy result silently.

'Finish your sandwich.' The imperative tones did not have an edge, Matty noted as before, when it was directed at Kate; he had never knew a person who could be so gentle in demand.

'Thanks, Sister,' was all Kate replied and took a large bite out of the beef and bread.

She then lifted the plate of biscuits and offered it to Matty.

'Thank you, Sister,' he said and soaked the biscuit in his milk; he let it bathe a little longer than he had seen Magh do as his milk was cold. Eventually he got it to his mouth before it disintegrated and this time his body assimilated the food more comfortably. He noticed the little nun had been watching him with a smile on her lips.

'The meeting should be cancelled for Friday night, don't you think?' Sister Perpetual put forth after a long silence in which Magh almost finished her tea and Matty had helped himself to another soaked biscuit. He was just beginning to enjoy himself, having forgotten briefly the danger of the hour previously.

'No, no we can't do that,' Kate said impatiently, 'we have to leave in a week's time. That may not be time enough to set up another meeting.'

'Aillien is visiting the tower house very briefly, then she will move on with her entourage' Magh confirmed, looking at the nun.

'Obviously Cruachain knows all about this,' the little nun appeared to be thinking out loud 'but how?'

'The witches of Cruachain are very resourceful,' said Magh.

'There is more than one of them?' asked Matty in alarm.

'Oh yes,' replied the little nun deep in thought and then said, 'why don't you hold the meeting the night before...? Pre-empt her?'

'We can't,' replied Kate. 'Aillien stipulated that it should be on a full moon night.'

'The Queen is taking her own precautions,' inserted Magh.

'You are going to have to take a lot more precautions than you have, then,' warned the nun.

'I know,' replied Magh and her hand went to her mouth. The two elderly women exchanged a long look into each other's eyes.

'What do you think Cruachain might do?' asked Kate, looking from one to the other.

The two elder women looked long and hard at each other, troubled and silent; they both seemed to know more than they were sharing with the children.

UNDINES

SUNDAY DRAGGED ON as a Sunday does in every part of the world, Matty felt, but this particular Sunday was heavy, overburdened and, as if to reinforce it, the sky was grey and it rained and rained all day long. He watched the rain drops run down the large window panes of his little bedroom window. Kate was non-communicable and that was to be expected: they were in a difficult and frightening situation. The day was punctuated by meals but she ate hardly any food which was unusual for her. Matty spent the afternoon at his homework but because he found it difficult to concentrate he had to repeat each new word and then the sentences at least three times before his concentration kicked in, then only to lose it again.

From time to time he was aware of murmuring from Kate's room and each time he sneaked into the corridor and listened at her door to voices barely above a whisper. Although he couldn't manage to hear what they were saying he recognised Magh's and the little nun's voices.

The week that followed was much like Sunday: there was more rain and Matty had lost his interest in exploring the woods on his lunch breaks with Sean since the incident with Seamus. When it was wet they played basketball on an indoor court.

When it was dry, he noticed Kate standing by the lake, all alone, on several occasions. The change was not only noted by him but by her friends too. One evening after school her two closest friends descended on him in the front hall and stood watching her with him. 'What's wrong with her, Matty?' asked Ciara.

'I don't know,' he replied, the desperation mounting.

'She's has been like this all week,' put in the other friend.

'I don't know what to do,' he said involuntarily.

'None of us do,' continued the friend, 'she won't talk.'

'It's as if she is cutting herself off from all of us,' said Ciara and then began to leave in the direction of the refectory.

Matty had followed the river which ran along the side of a wood for fifteen minutes, still with no sign of the wooden bridge which crossed it. He had walked it with Kate that evening at dusk but he was listening to her instructions intently and so did not take notice of how long the journey had taken them. The fear that he might have come out of the woods too soon or too late added to his anxiety. The minute he heard the rush and spill of that sparkling water he had turned in its direction as Kate had done earlier. It was Mabon, the Autumn equinox – a time of psychic disturbances – and Kate had spoken with solemnity, looking down at her trainers as they tramped through the remains of last year's leaves and the green, russet and golden new ones that dropped silently here and there as they moved through the forest.

'You might feel depressed Matt… or even afraid due to these disturbances,' she had said to him.

'Desperate,' he answered quietly, feeling the tightness in the centre of his chest.

She stood still and looked at him without a word. He stopped walking too. He knew that, even then, when they were still in the light part of the twenty-four hours of half-light and half-darkness, she felt every bit as fraught as he did. The light was becoming hazy through and above the trees.

'We have to try as hard as we can to use these turbulent energies in a positive way Matt, otherwise… the negative stuff will engulf us… and… we will not be able to think… or react in the right way to save ourselves…' She stopped. It seemed to Matty that she was failing to convince even herself, but she was talking, even though it sounded like what someone else has said to her. Magh, he felt, and maybe the little nun.

'It's you they're after, isn't it?' asked Matty, after a while in which they had stayed still, looking at each other, looking beyond each other into the trees but not seeing them, feeling only the tenseness of apprehension.

She nodded her head once.

'It's nothing to do with payment for getting rid of the incubus?' he asked.

'No,' was all she said.

'The little silver Ganesh will pay for that,' she continued close to tears after a moment or two. She turned her head away, the skin on her neck twisting slightly, personifying the twist that fear caused inside her and which she felt, he felt too.

'It's the Queen… Aillien, isn't it, she wants you because you are like her.' Matty said what he had suspected and probably what Kate never wanted to ever admit.

'Why do you think that, Matt? I feel I can trust her, so does Magh,' Kate replied.

'I don't know, I just have this feeling… like you… that someone is after you,' he let it out, it had to be said; if there was a way of not keeping the meeting tonight he needed to stop it.

'Yes, I think you're right Matt,' she said. She turned away from him and started walking about, stopping here and there and very slowly lifting the dying leaves with the toe of her trainer.

'Kate…' he hesitated; he didn't know how to lessen this new admission. 'Kate, I don't know how I can help tonight…' he said at last. She said nothing during this time, knowing that his fear, his lack of being able to provide an alternative was the same desperation as her own.

'I know it's dangerous Matt… but I don't want to do it alone… I mean if they take me away for good –' She raised one hand and started to rub her brow in an effort, it seemed to him, to hide the glisten of tears in her eyes.

'I don't mean I don't want to come,' he said. 'I just feel so useless, so annoyed with myself… and the reading on strategy from the Greek and Roman wars… and I have come up with nothing.'

'It's hardly a battle Matty,' she replied, 'or at least I hope it will not be…'

'Can Magh do anything? Can we not cancel… postpone maybe?' Matty asked, perplexed.

'She will be there with me in etheric form…' her voice broke and she turned her back to him. 'That's the new strategy,' she said, after taking control of her voice, 'she will be visible as a deterrent for Cruachain,' and she broke down once again.

Matty just stood there hopeless and useless.

After what seem to be quite a while in which there were sniffling sounds she turned towards him, letting the tears run down her cheeks unashamedly.

'I'm hoping that your presence will appeal to their better nature… Aillien is not really the problem… it's Cruachain, Magh is worried about her.' She wiped her eyes on her sleeve and continued more firmly, 'I'm hoping that she will see that I am better living as I am and improving relationships… and communication between humans and faerie, like how it used to be… and… and you would be a reminder of that, and you have the little silver Ganesh?' She finished, still standing squarely in front of him. 'I'll understand if you don't want to do it… it will be frightening… I'm very sure they will try to intimidate both of us and Magh too… if anything bad happens keep telling yourself it is an illusion and firmly ground yourself.'

'How do I do that?' asked Matty.

'Remember your martial arts Matt, your Tan Tien: keep it in your mind and never let it go. What you will be seeing are other-worldly beings not of your space and time.' The fear seemed to have gone out of her as she spoke about what was so very familiar to her and the fight was back in her eyes and, he remembered, her cheeks flushed. Matty began to feel her courage then. He nodded and she looked up at the sky.

'But why do you have to be there? Can't Magh take me to give the silver to the Queen?' he protested even though he would be frightened out of his life, he knew.

'No, for the Queen, we both have to be present… to pay off the debt,' she reminded him.

'It's closing in, we need to hurry,' she commanded and began walking in silence.

After a little while she had stood still and listened. 'Hear that?' she asked, and sure enough the sound of water filtering and splashing permeated the wood and earth of the forest like magic. She turned in the direction of the sounds.

Matty remembered that they had not spoken while they followed the sound of the river and they had walked in single file. When they found the wooden bridge and crossed it there was a grassy field with a bridle path which they took and which doubled back along the path they had taken by the river as they came through the wood. They were on the island. After a very short distance an iron gate just swung open to let them through as soon as Kate pushed it; round the bend, behind a high hedge, the tower house loomed up in front of them.

Matty kept walking, letting all those thoughts filter through his mind, along with the tightness in his stomach and the sick feeling in his throat. He stopped occasionally to peer ahead for sight of the bridge but it was quiet except for rustling sounds which Kate had told him to ignore on their first journey out. She explained it would be birds waking and readjusting themselves in the night as well as little woodland mice scurrying about. She had instructed him about badgers, hedgehogs and foxes: the first two were shy animals and foxes were just curious and not harmful unless he came across an injured one. Luckily he did not encounter any of these; he only heard the far-off cry of an owl, maybe. *It sounds like some sort of bird*, he tried to convince himself. He didn't even need to use his torch; there was a full moon and the stars were bright, which was unusual for the west of Ireland – or anywhere in Ireland, he thought. In India, every night was a starry night. As he walked through the wood at one side and the river busily rushing water by him on the other side he tried to focus on the picture of the Tan Tien. How effective was it? That was entirely another matter which he chose not to explore. He could not concentrate on the reading he did with his martial arts course but he tried to practise some moves while walking to ready himself for anything physical he may have to encounter. It was really not the physical that bothered him; it was more the world of the unseen. However this was known to him, he would soon encounter other-worldly creatures when he finally found the bridge. Earlier that evening they had shot up at them out of the water but Kate didn't even blink an eye.

'Undines,' she called back at him as she strode across the wooden boards while Matty had stood stock still, mouth agape at the tiny human like creatures that began to surround him in what he could only consider an aggressive attitude.

'Naiads, if you are into Greek mythology,' she shouted at Matty, standing still on the far side of the bridge waiting for him, 'remember I told you it is Mabon, psychic unrest and all that, that's why you are able to see them.' She started walking. 'Come on Matt, it's getting late'

Matty had scurried across the bridge before any of the tiny female creatures began grabbing his shoelaces and when he glanced back over his shoulder he saw nothing. There was a memory of the word in the books on Greek and Romans he read, but all his attention was on castles, fortification, armour and strategy; he really wasn't into mythology. He hoped that he would not be able to see the Naiads on his lonely journey. He wished Jack was with him and put his hand in his pocket to feel the reassurance of the ring. *But the ring had not been tested with Other-worldly beings, only on human beings.* He dismissed yet another uncomfortable thought and felt for the gort, which was an extra bit of protection Kate had insisted on, and he felt it may be for both their reassurances. He had a habit of picking up interesting pebbles, unusual leaves and tiny dried bits of wood anyway, so having his pockets stuffed with gort was not something he found difficult to accept. However, like her advice on grounding and the Tan

Tien he tried to believe in it and wondered if it depended on his actual faith and if it did, then he was back to the rawness of the physical, without anything to protect himself or Kate.

So lost was he in the morass in his mind that the wooden bridge was suddenly there just a few feet ahead. He scurried across it and began walking along the bridle path on the far side of the river heading in the direction from which he came. Relieved that there were no Undines, he quickened his pace and in minutes found himself at the Iron Gate, ensconced in its thick hedge of hawthorn. It swung open before his hand reached it but this didn't unnerve him. He took it as a sign that Kate and Magh were with him, walking ahead of him. Kate had insisted he call out Ailill's name if he was frightened and Ailill would appear beside him in mortal form. Matty resisted; even when he felt he may have been lost in the woods, he knew there were certain things he was compelled to do and face alone. He continued on. The tower must be just ahead; one of its outbuildings was being used as a ticket office for tourists and as he rounded this, the tower house loomed high above him. Just as earlier the thing appeared too suddenly, it seemed to materialise, being covered by the woods at the other side of the river. This effect was startling even for a second time.

Matty stood and surveyed the tower house, still in the shadow of the smaller building. All was quiet. He couldn't detect anything other-worldly despite the fact that there were no animal or bird sounds – or *maybe because there were no sounds.* He thought the Tuatha were about. He felt safe in the shadows but imagined Kate waiting for him, perhaps even urging him to come, face her fate with her, get it over with. His nerves prickled his chest inside, frightened for himself and for her again. They had only come this far earlier that evening; he would have to go the rest of the way for the first time on his own. He kept peering out of the shadows. What he was looking for he did not know. He found it difficult to make his feet move in the quietness. He waited again; maybe Kate would give him a signal. But there were only grass lawns all around what he supposed to be the wall of the keep. The tower house seemed so tall. He thought of what it would be like to be thrown from the topmost mullioned windows… and where was Ganesh when he needed him? He had been appearing less and less.

CASTLE KEEP

MATTY FOCUSED HIS attention on the tower house. It looked enormous in the night light; it was six storeys high and looking up it made a giant black form reaching up towards the firmament. From the shadow he counted the windows on each level. As he stepped away from the protection of the smaller building and onto the lawn, he headed towards the inner walls. He discharged the feel of cold fear that began spreading all over his upper back by checking out the defences. The castle, he realised, was built on an island of solid rock. He stopped and looked at what was left of the outer walls and as he slowly walked towards the entrance he wondered at the intelligence of the ancient people who had chosen the site. In the inner yard – *must be the bailey* – he could see the natural bridge of rock; Kate had shown him the smaller entrance which had taken him into the fortifications by the east side of the castle earlier. The bailey area was covered by lawn, too, right up to the main entrance. There was no evidence of steps leading up to it and Matty wondered: had the earth piled up over them or was this how it was meant to be?

At twilight the Tower House had appeared grey, as is the natural colour of rock from which it was built. Matty had felt the stones nearby while listening to Kate's instructions. *Hard as rock*, he thought again. In the moonlight the tower house appeared threatening. It seemed to emerge from above; that didn't make sense, but Matty was compelled to look up at its imposing stature again. There were a pair of arrow slits on each floor on every wall: this was serious defence and it seemed to emanate its own history. The word *impenetrable* came into his mind. He reminded himself that only tourists explored the castle nowadays; the inhabitants of centuries were long dead – *except for the Tuatha dé Danann and they didn't know they were dead.*

He admired the supports for the two turret rooms on the third floor and for an instant forgot his predicament. The main door was right in front of him. It stood open with an arch that was more Roman than Gothic. Matty stopped:

surely it should be protected, no security needed in this lonely place but it would hardly be left unlocked at the end of the day and it was only September, still open tourist season. He stepped over the threshold, the door being at ground level. His mouth still tasted salty; Kate had insisted he drink salt water before he crept out of the convent. The taste that had made him almost retch an hour ago had a reassurance about it in that place.

'It'll keep you grounded,' she had said.

His hand went to his Tan Tien, his feet firmly on the first step of a winding stone staircase that was to the left of the door. There was nothing else in the space at the ground floor, just the winding stair – *inviting him where?* He consciously grounded himself with each step he placed determinedly down on the rock steps. He held the rope which was threaded through metal brackets buried deep in the outer wall as he wound his way to the first floor. There was a doorway and he stepped off the stairs to investigate. Before he actually stepped into this one large room, which seemed to take up most of the space on the first floor, for one instant he witnessed the smell, noise and an enormous amount of culinary activity. Actual people as tall as Ailill, in crude dress, looking nothing like the splendour of Aillien, which Kate had described. It seemed to be some sort of a preparation area or maybe a serving area; there were lots of vessels, food being laden on to platters on very basic tables which had roughly-made long stools at either side. Metal bowls, big ones and little ones, on the table tops. There was a beer-like liquid being poured into metal jugs and all the while the din of the guttural imperative language sent small boys scurrying. Matty waited for more, or waited because he couldn't move. He was frozen in shock. *They were here and they were real.*

After some time he had an urge that he must go to the next floor and almost had to pull himself up with the rope. He waited on the steps without entering the second floor, but there was nothing. He did not have the energy to investigate what lay beyond the single doorway. He continued to the third floor and waited on the steps there. The doorway was in a different position which allowed him to see into the large room which had a huge fireplace. Again he had a split-second vision and the scene was a calmer one. The people were of mixed ages, all enormous. An old woman sat by the fire, possibly a grandmother; a blue fabric cloak was fastened on her left shoulder with a brooch. Matty felt it looked as if it was made of wool. This was thrown back over her shoulders to leave her hands free; she was working some cloth on her lap and she used a type of needle. She seemed to be stitching or embroidering. Matty could clearly see the long dress she wore underneath: this, he felt, looked as if it was made of linen or cotton, not silk. He knew what silk looked like, he was used to silk saris. Children played; they were richly dressed in brocades and a simply dressed teenage girl stood watching them. There were couches covered with furs and animal hides, he recognised these as he had seen them on the floor of a cousin's house. *Cattle hide*, he thought. *This would be the room with the turret windows*, thought Matty but he did not have the stomach to explore it in its apparent serenity; it was disturbing to say the least and the image disappeared as quickly as it appeared, hardly giving him time to take in more detail. He wondered if the castle was actually occupied by a faerie family, *or was this Aillien's retinue*? He decided to continue upwards to the fourth floor; he considered that the scene was domestic and he imagined Kate would be presenting herself in a more formal setting.

Just as he reached the fourth floor an enormous hairy dog shot past him on the stairs. He recognised it: it was as big as a small cow. It was an Irish wolf-hound and he was fairly certain it wasn't real – well, *not in his dimension*, Kate would have said. Matty looked up but the stairs being spiral he would have to advance further to see where the dog had got to. But at the moment Matty saw the dog he also had a glimpse of the faerie realm. The fourth floor was used for sleeping. More fur couches, richly decorated wall hangings and bed covers. As soon as the image passed he knew he should continue on towards the final floor to find out what had happened to Kate.

The entire floor was open. The enormous fireplace stood in the same position as the one in the room where the elderly woman and children had been. It was quiet, the walls were painted white as were all the walls on the all the floors unless the frequencies altered when Matty was able to see. He stood on the final step of the corkscrew stairs and waited. No visions came, no dog either; he had been right about the dog, it wasn't in his element. Matty stood still for a long time. The tower house was very quiet and very cold. Because it was so quiet he got the confidence to walk on to the top floor. He took out his pen torch and in flashing it about he realised there were depictions on the walls. He peered at the pictures and read the text. They explained the history of the castle and who the occupants had been over several centuries. As he peered around with his tiny point of light he came face to face with Kate and Magh in their etheric form. The really strange thing about them was that Kate looked older and Magh looked so young, like someone aged about twenty. The only way he recognised her was by the way she wore her hair, which had not changed, just the colour of it; here it was light brown. They were both smiling at him. Just as quickly they disappeared. Matty ran to the head of the stairs, glancing round again before his planned descent, but the room was empty and quiet. He stopped and waited. He must stay, she may need him; he wasn't sure how he could help her, all he knew was he must stay for her no matter how frightening the experience was. At least he had found her. Mabon, she had said, dimensions that normally inter-penetrated were even more open during the half-day, half-night time of the year. Probably that was the reason he was able to see the beings who were not dead.

He stood once again on the topmost step, poised to flee, one hand on the rope. He replaced his torch in his pocket with the other hand. He would not need it for he could make out the stairs in the gloom. He waited for what seemed ages and nothing happened. He relaxed a little; he needed to move his feet, he was getting stiff. He went over the image of Kate and Magh in his mind, it was so quick, like a flash, an instant; he saw nothing else except their dress. Kate had on a loose baggy garment, it was probably cotton, earthy dye, lighter than the brown in monk's habit and it was pulled into shape by a long narrow strip of fabric in an off-white colour. It had come over her shoulders, crossed at her chest and seemed to go behind again and fall once more to the front where it looped over to make a sort of tie.

SEIZURE

 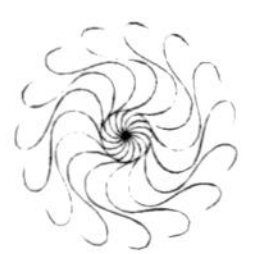

MATTY EVENTUALLY RELAXED enough to sit down; he felt he had been poised to spring into a run for ages. He was aware of all his muscles being taunt and, once he changed his position, he realised they actually ached a little. He took out his pen torch to check the time on his watch: it had been two hours since he left the convent through a basement window aided by the little 'Marshmallow Nun'. Kate had given her that name: she said she was all soft and spongy like a white marshmallow and like him she had learned to depend on her. Magh felt assured that she was of Aillien's people and not Cruachain's. In two more hours it would be midnight – *the bewitching hour*, he thought, and put the thoughts of Cruachain right out of his mind. The steps made out of rock were *stone cold*. It was an expression his Irish grandmother used and it described what Matty felt poignantly as the cold penetrated the seat of his jeans. In India when he sat on the back veranda steps of the Little Pink House, which were made from a granite-like material and absorbed the heat, they felt warm. These steps reminded him of the cold he felt when he touched his grandfather's headstone. He related the cold to death, thinking of his grandfather's body deep below the Irish clay. How could there be life and then no life? What separated living bodies from dead ones and the pain caused by the end of life? He could not reconcile these concepts in his head. His grandmother had been buried in India. His Indian grandfather had made a tomb-like structure of black stone and although he had not seen it yet he was sure it would be warm to touch. He wondered how people of old survived in Ireland: *it was so cold. Poor people in India didn't need a house, really, the nights in the south were warm. Sleeping outdoors must be much more pleasant than inside the concrete buildings which became ovens with the fans just whirling around hot air. But then there were the malaria-carrying mosquitoes… and venomous snakes that were probably fine, unless one rolled over on them in sleep and then they would use the venom to protect themselves. There was no real security in the open air,* his mind supposed.

All the while he pondered he was fingering the little silver Ganesh. As he focused on it he thought of his family in Madras. His mother had given it to him so he would not worry about them. Little did she know he was going to present it to a faerie queen as a thank you for keeping them safe. It was his idea to gift it to the faerie queen and Kate and Magh approved; he was proud of himself for having the generosity.

His seat was becoming uncomfortably cold; he pulled on the rope with his right hand to lever himself upright, slipping the little silver Ganesh into the left pocket of his anorak. He was glad he had worn it and slid the coupling of the zip together and pulled it all the way up to his chin. As he did this he became aware of a light behind him and he turned quickly, alarmed inside. It was Kate again in etheric form and she didn't disappear this time. He never had a vision of her like this before in her three thousand year-old clothing. She beamed and beckoned for him to follow her, which he did, the entire floor coming to life as he did. *It must be a throne room of sorts*, he thought. Because he was the only child present he could not see ahead of himself: it seemed he was behind adults, all as enormously tall as Ailill, in splendidly coloured clothing, richly brocaded. They wore gold brooches inlayed with jewels. Magh came from Kate's left and stood behind her as the tall people parted, making a passage for Kate to pass through. She guided Matty beside her and Magh fell into place behind them. Matty noticed Magh held the distaff he had seen in Gerard's shop; this reassured him and he smiled. However Magh's appearance was so strange that Matty reminded himself to find an explanation for. It was as if she was split down the middle: one side of her was tall like the Tuatha and the other side was human-sized.

Then when they had walked across the full length of the room, Matty saw the faerie queen. She was seated on a chair of wood with a low, circular back and the carved seat was in the shape of a crescent moon. Two sets of sturdy, carved legs, also crescent shaped supported it. Her clothing was magnificent. The dress was purple, fitted to her body, with long, dolman sleeves and a high neck. Over her shoulders she wore a silk cape of the same colour but with much more gold thread worked into designs throughout the fabric. It had a wide border with the eternal knot symbol woven between two heavy lines of gold thread. There were circles precisely placed over the entire cape. Within the circles were other symbols, mainly of wheels and some had a swastika embroidered within. Matty made a second mental note to ask about that as the only other place he had seen that symbol was in temples in India.

To their right sat the King, *an Ri*: Matty for some unknown reason felt the Irish word was more appropriate. He was so much older than Aillien, more like a grandfather, thought Matty. He was a formidable man, large, massive and broad shouldered but very old. Just as Kate had described in India her meeting with Aillien, she was so very beautiful and like Magh, she appeared to move between the split body, half tall and half human. All this Matty noted as they approached the dais. They both wore crowns of gold. To Aillien's left stood all the handmaidens Kate had described seeing on her previous visit to ask for help and again the more senior ones stood next to the Queen. Their faces were serious, even concerned, Matty thought. The younger women stared and smiled at them and whispered among themselves, sometimes giggling. Why were they all so tall? He made a mental note to ask Kate about that too.

Then his attention was drawn to the warriors to the right of the King. *These must be the knights*, he thought. They were richly dressed, particularly the ones nearest the King; others, Ailill among them, had on a layer of waxed cowhide and they wore their swords, Matty noticed. Danger was obviously never far away. In the corner of the room their shields, with edges really sharp, javelins and spears were propped against the walls. *Where were their helmets?* he wondered. They, like the women, stood and all of them appeared enormous. That caused him to search for Girija among the women but they all looked pale-skinned. As they came to a halt he wondered would they curtsy and kept his attention on Kate. She stood still and so did Matty. They were at the edge of the gathering: the people had moved around them, closer to them to watch the proceedings. She bowed her head and he followed. The King spoke and Magh approached with answers and after a quiet discourse she urged Matty to offer his gift. He stepped forward and proffered his silver Ganesh. He sat it upright on the palm of his hand. The faerie queen's hand reached forth and as it came into contact with his human hand it too became less iridescent and more like human flesh. An amazing thing happened: it became human-sized too, just the part close to Matty's hand. He wondered just then if the room would return to its 20th-century state, ending the vision but the moment passed. The queen took the little trinket and examined it and directed her questions to Kate in Irish or Ogham. Kate seemed to understand and moved forward and even though she spoke in Irish Matty could understand, or maybe it was because he knew the meanings himself, he wasn't sure; everything was so unreal that night.

'Actually, Ganesh is a concept…' Kate began, turning to Magh more than slightly anxious and asked for the word *concept* in Irish.

'Concept,' interrupted the Queen, nodding her head, and in Irish said, 'I understand your meaning.'

Kate was in confident mode, Matty noted, no signs of fear or nervousness. This was her subject and she knew everything there was to know about the elephant God. She lapsed into Ogham, slowly explaining all the symbolism depicted on the tiny statue, from the meaning of his broken tusk to the objects he held in his four hands.

'Ganesh is always with a rat,' continued Kate with much more confidence.

The Queen examined the tiny trinket again and found the rat.

'A rat represents the lowest form of life, it roots around in the darkness of houses and streets, gnawing at all types of rotting food and even rags.' She waited for the Queen's agreement and continued, 'Yet a God chooses it as its companion, and the snake, an incongruous animal, yet Ganesh wears it around his waist,' she stopped and waited for her acquiescence.

'What it means is that opposites can live is peaceful existence… the symbol of Ahimsa in Hinduism, which means non-violence, unity in diversity… and people forget it is our duty to maintain this… this boy is the proof of what happens when it is not… upheld,' she turned to Matty and then back to the Queen.

'You are… the help you gave us is the proof of how we can overcome greed and worse. How our worlds can co-operate and achieve peace…' Kate trailed off, suddenly conscious of the quiet of the large room and the attention of the others on her. The Queen began to applaud and every other being there followed, including the King. Kate was determined in her beliefs, sure now they were right despite and at the same time because of the Catholic upbringing. Matty felt as if a dam had broken two years of silence; probably she had nobody to share her new view of the world with in Ireland. How could they understand all the Hindu Gods and the basic truths they stood for? Matty tuned in again to her monologue and like her he felt they were where they should be, conversing with ancient peoples whose concepts were prehistoric but needed reapplication. Kate was certainly making her point about being an interpreter between the worlds, Matty thought, and relaxed as the proceedings seemed to be going really much better than expected.

When Kate had finished, the Queen gave an order and a path was made for bearers to bring in platters of food which were laid on long tables below the mullioned windows. As the Queen stood up Magh passed the distaff to Kate who stretched her arms forward, tendering it to the Queen.

At that very moment silence spread over the large assembly and the iridescence faded from them as an ancient woman, so wrinkled and so very ugly, tramped into the room. She dressed like Magh did in earth reality but not in the bright colours Magh wore. Her clothes were old, worn and had stains on them, Matty noted. She was not huge. Kate pushed Matty behind her as they backed into the assembled beings. The old woman trudged towards Aillien with her staff of knotted wood. A crow flew into the room and landed on the floor between Aillien and the old crone.

Matty glanced at Aillien and felt her brilliance had faded: she looked unsettled and her entire body became human size. Kate exchanged a glance with Magh who nodded her head and then stepped forward and proffered the distaff once again, this time to the witch of Cruachain, Matty supposed. The primeval being turned to Kate and Matty saw the fullness of the horrid face. The toothless mouth grinned a snarl and at that moment Aillien stepped from the dais in Kate's direction just as the crow flew up, cawing, separating Aillien from Kate and the witch.

The witch grabbed Kate's left elbow; she still held the distaff as she was pulled towards the stairs. The Queen shouted what sounded like a command and the knights ran towards their armour. Magh shouted out Irish words, like a threat, Matty thought, or a spell, as she held up her crystal wand. Cruachain stopped, still holding on to Kate and turned and faced Magh. Then she laughed a spiteful laugh and followed it with a curse of her own, and turned, pointing her staff towards the stairs.

Matty felt a firm grip on his left arm and immediately saw only Ailill. The room was empty: he was in his own dimension. Before he could speak he was being hauled down the stairs at such great speed that he slid over some of the cold rock steps and only prevented himself from falling by grabbing onto the rope with his right hand. Once outside he felt the wet grass around his trainers as he was forced to run at a pace he could hardly maintain. The outside was in disarray: again a brief glimpse of chariots and charioteers subduing the horses. He had walked straight through these beings when he entered the tower house.

The Tuatha warrior tugged him by the elbow, along the bridle path, over the wooden bridge and through the woods. Matty was aware of legs, legs running at a fast pace. The Tuatha warrior dragged him through the wet leaves when he couldn't keep up. All the time Matty was aware of Ailill' legs. Strips of leather, bound around the pale ochre horse hide leggings on his calves. That fabric slightly overlapped a leather bootee: *horsehide was weapon proof*, he remembered reading somewhere. By the time they reached the basement window Matty was out of breath, his lungs ready to burst and his heart beating too fast against his breastbone.

The Marshmallow Nun appeared at the window. Ailill spoke rapidly to her in what Matty supposed must be Ogham or ancient Irish.

'Get in son,' she ordered; she wore a worried look.

'Take off your shoes,' she ordered softly as Matty slid through the little window on to the steel draining board, 'they are full of muck.' There was a definite imperativeness in her tone then. The little nun was dressed in a white night dress and shawl with wisps of her grey hair sticking out from underneath a white cap which tied under her chin, like a baby's bonnet.

Matty sat on the cold steel of the draining board unable to catch his breath let alone untie his trainers. The little nun reached behind him and slid the two small bolts into place securing the window. Then, while he was still panting, holding his chest, she yanked him off the steel draining board with a force he didn't expect. He landed on one side on a tiled floor. Looking up he saw, briefly, a deformed animal – or were they contorted human faces? – grimacing in the window pane. The little nun made symbols in the air and raised both hands. There was a flash of white yellow light. She seemed to be waiting. Matty pulled himself up and started towards the kitchen door.

'Wait,' she whispered.

He stood still, staring at the window which was at ground level once outside the convent. He could hear the sound of feet... or was it... hooves, or both? Was Ailill battling some sort of primitive animals?

She turned briefly to him and then all her attention was back on the window pane.

'Look at the floor son, you do not want everyone to know where you have been, take off your shoes,' she commanded in the gentle voice. How could she keep it so even in the midst of... in the midst of battle? He obeyed. He stood in his stockinged feet.

Head still facing the window she said, 'Go to your room, I'll be up shortly.'

He did as he was told.

He stood still in the basement corridor trying to co-ordinate his mind. The panting had eased a little. He realised he was hot and unzipped his anorak. He stole along the tiled corridor; it was the only part of the building that resembled his grandfather's house in India. The tiles were the same, red clay. Once he got to the stairs he slowed and crept up it using the wood where it joined to the banister rather than the middle of the steps where it was likely to creek. He knew his way from the ground floor. Earlier the little Marshmallow Nun had shown them a back stairs that led to the corridor almost opposite to the retreat rooms Kate and he used. Kate was the only thing on his mind. He paused outside her door, muddy trainers in one hand, heart still walloping in his chest but not then from the exertion; it had calmed partly from that. He knew he would find her on the bed in her 'Ophelia pose', as Jack called it. He wanted her body to be alive, not like how she had described Girija's had been two years ago, lying on a jetty beside a lake in another part of the world with no signs of life. He could visualise that so easily.

He opened the door by twisting the knob quietly. It was pitch black dark. No moonlight penetrated the curtains. Then he remembered there was a light drizzle when he left the tower house and all the way through the woods with Ailill. The clouds would have obscured the moon. He knew where to find the light switch, it was near the door in his room. It meant he had to get out of bed every night to turn it off after reading. The switch in Kate's room would be in the same position. At the risk of alerting other nuns he turned it on. He had to see her, see that she was breathing. He closed the door behind him quietly. He went to the bed, muddy trainers still in hand, aware that his hair was dripping rain and sweat wet down his face. He touched her with his free hand. She was warm. Then he consciously steadied himself to watch her breathing. It was so quiet he bent down to look at her profile against the pale blue coloured walls to see if her chest moved. Just then he heard the door open quietly and became alert. Relief when four little Marshmallow fingers grasped the door and almost immediately the little nun appeared.

'She's alive,' he whispered.

The little nun came close to the bed and quietly inspected Kate's body.

'She is,' she replied with a worried look. Matty wanted to stamp out the words *for now* from his mind – *she is alive for now.*

'Cruachain has got her.' He made words come out to stop the bad thoughts.

'I know,' replied the little nun, barely audible.

'What are we going to do, how can we get her back?' he asked in desperation.

'We'll try son, we'll try our very best,' said the little nun, touching the sleeve of his anorak. 'Go to your room and try to get some sleep, I'll sit with Kate.'

'Where is Magh, is she trying to rescue Kate?' he pleaded.

'Magh, Ailill and I'm sure Aillien's warriors are chasing Cruachain, I must stay here in case she comes to claim the rest of her.'

'I won't sleep, Sister.' He couldn't leave Kate.

'Son, I have to protect her, you and myself. If you go to your room and stay there it will be easier for me to concentrate on keeping Cruachain out.' She delivered the words firmly but affectionately, placing a marshmallow palm on his shoulder.

Matty considered what she had said and slowly left the room and entered his own. He noticed it felt stone cold. He slipped off his anorak and left his shoes on the floor and lay on the bed in despair. He suddenly remembered the awful faces he had seen against the basement window but quelled the urge to ask the nun about them. It would be a good excuse to go into the next room to check on Kate too, but if the nun was making some sort of protection that was more important, he should let her concentrate. She had said: *we'll try to get her back.*

Matty lay still for what seemed to be a long time. The cold atmosphere began seeping into his body through his clothing. He couldn't warm up so he pulled the duvet around both sides of his body and they met in the middle and in a little while he began to relax. His mind was another matter. Why had she done it, risked so much for his family? Jack was right, the plan was madness and getting involved with the other-world dangerous. Everything Jack had said was right. But they had no alternative, the alternative was… maybe… without a father. There was no solution. He had been wringing his hands and became aware of it. He pulled the edges of the duvet more snugly around himself, it was difficult to keep warm.

AMBULANCE

MATTY SAT WATCHING the falling leaves through the long bedroom window. He had pulled aside the net curtain to enhance his view. His mind had entered that place without feelings or care again. Like how he had been after the shock of being kidnapped. He looked at the bed once again: no change. *She was so still.* What had they done to her, he and his family in this world? He had no idea what she was enduring in the other world. Where was she, what if she never came back and would she end up like Girija? Girija's body had been cremated. Kate would be buried in the cold wet clay with her grandfather. He imagined it all. His mind was numb to feelings but he noticed with dismay that he was actually considering the consequences. The night had passed and he had fallen asleep. The morning had brought no change in the motionless body. He looked out the window. There was partial sunlight, weak, and gusts of wind. The leaves fell off the trees, sometimes noiselessly and continuously, and sometimes not at all. The pine trees moved as if agitated; they became unruly in the powerful gusts and then the leaves from the deciduous trees were flung high into the air, scattered into the grass and sent flying in all directions and eventually left to drift slowly to the ground as the wind subsided once again. Their rooms were on ground level if approached from the entrance to the castle but one flight up from the basement. Another gust of wind and he could actually hear the wood make a stretching sound as the trees bent further than the point where it was as far as they could possibly go. The door knob turned. He didn't want to converse, he just wanted to be left alone. Sister Perpetual had been in, a doctor had been too: who was it this time?

It was her again but behind her was a green uniformed man and behind him another one dressed the same.

'These men are with the ambulance, son,' she said gently, 'they are taking your cousin to Galway County Hospital.'

He stood up as he noticed a stretcher was being carefully wheeled into the small room. He watched as the two men had an exchange of medical vocabulary. They opened plastic bags and placed tubes and other paraphernalia on the bed. The little nun and he stood in the window and watched as a drip was attached to Kate. They checked her eyes with a small torch and placed a cuff on her upper arm, not the one with the drip needle in it, he noted. They carried out a lot of other medical procedures and continued to exchange medical terminology with each other before heaving her body on to the trolley. Finally an oxygen mask was placed over her nose and mouth and, with a nod at the nun, they began wheeling her out of the room.

Matty followed with the nun, understanding the facts, computing everything he saw but not feeling anything, for if he did he was sure he would cry and wail and shout and kick. At the end of the hallway the ambulance men turned the trolley towards the front door where Sister Oliver stood wearing a supervisory face. He watched the mechanism of the trolley as it was loaded on to the ambulance and marvelled at how different it was in this country compared with India. But Kate lay on top of it, her body was strapped on to it and it jiggled a little with the movement of the trolley. Matty's eyes were drawn to the first floor where the classrooms were and there was Ciara's face at one of the windows looking like how he felt. She must have walked out of the morning's session; she too had been stricken by what had happened to Kate, but unlike him she had not been allowed to see her. One of the men sat inside facing Kate and busied himself hanging up the drip bag and doing other things while the other man closed the back doors and with a nod in the direction of the nuns climbed into the driver's seat and started the engine. Matty stood watching the ambulance disappear down the drive, along by the lake and stood till it minimised itself along the winding roads among the russet gold and the heather and the green, amethyst hills. *Was this the last he would see of her?*

'Young man,' the senior nun spoke to him, 'your aunt and uncle will be here shortly to bring you home. I suggest you go to your room and pack your things.' Looking at the marshmallow she continued, 'Maybe you would see to Catherine's belongings, have them ready for her parents. When they arrive would you show them to my office; they will want an explanation, although I haven't much to tell, have I?' she asked as if to herself, her eyes looking into the distance. 'Catherine went to bed as usual and didn't wake up. What puzzles me though,' she continued after a pause, 'is why she hadn't undressed.' After a moment or two she added, 'Perhaps she was feeing unwell and lay down.' She turned, slipping her hands inside the dolman sleeves of her habit and went inside, striding with intent and purpose as she always did. Matty felt a gentle hand on his shoulder.

'Let's get ready for them,' she urged.

Matty turned once more in the direction the ambulance had gone. Nature was, as it always was, timeless as if it had no memory of her journey out of this strange place or even of their journey into it just nine days ago. He gave a nod and allowed himself to be guided inside. He checked the window again for her friend and the stricken pale face had disappeared, maybe to her class or maybe not, perhaps she was where he was, just wandering about unwillingly inside a numb mind.

As he was guided down the corridor, the soft hand still on his shoulder, he wondered: was the little nun timeless too, like Magh? He hadn't the energy to ask her, it didn't matter anymore, nothing did.

'Where's Magh?' he asked when they reached the rooms. He had no idea where the question came from, it just emerged without thought.

'She's where Kate is,' she replied, positioning herself directly in front of him.

'Captured too?' he asked in alarm.

'No, not captured. She is searching for her,' replied the nun.

'Then Kate is on her own,' he demanded.

'Yes, as far as I know… but Aillien will not let her down. You've seen Ailill, and there are many more like him searching and they'll get her back,' she nodded in reassurance.

'Will they?' he asked near tears; hope had suddenly forsaken him and emotion took over. The bleakness overwhelmed him.

The little nun steered him into Kate's room and sat him on the lone chair.

'You are going to have a story to tell and you must stick to it,' she said and she was so intent he found himself concentrating.

'It would be better if you did not tell anyone you were out in the woods last night,' she said and turned her head in that exaggerated way to check the door.

'Yes,' he heard himself reply, 'I understand.'

'They will never understand,' she emphasised, 'her parents or indeed anyone else who doesn't truly… recognise who she really is, do you understand me, son?'

'Yes,' and as a way of reassuring her, he added 'I do, Sister.'

'I think Sister Oliver has… synopsised it well, don't you?' she asked, waiting for him to respond.

'What?' he asked, not understanding.

'Kate went to bed as usual…' she started.

'…and didn't wake up,' he finished.

'She had been unwell last Saturday afternoon, remember I found you two on the walk to the gardens?' she asked and Matty felt that if her habit had not covered her forehead an eyebrow would have been raised.

'Yes Sister, I understand, I remember… I know… what to say,' he said.

'That's all you need to say: she was a little unwell that afternoon and went to bed for a rest,' she emphasised and then continued after a little while, 'I know it is a lie, son, but we have to protect her parents, they would never comprehend the complexities of their daughter…' she trailed off, eyes looking far outside the window Matty had his back to.

'It's only a white lie, Sister,' Matty said, remembering how Kate had told him they were sometimes necessary.

'Yes, precisely, son,' she said – seemingly relieved, Matty thought.

'Now let's get packing,' she said, turning towards the slim wardrobe.

NEUROLOGY

UNCLE LIAM WAS in an agitated mood. He had said little but Matty was aware of the negative energy emanating from him. Matty had been in the refectory when his uncle and aunt arrived. The little Marshmallow Nun had placed a bowl of porridge in front of him and encouraged him to eat by moving the sugar bowl and a milk jug with cold milk in front of the bowl of steaming paste. Matty was used to porridge; his mother made it at least twice a week in India, but she gave him honey instead of sugar to help get it down.

'If you don't eat you will become ill,' she said.

Matty examined the food but did not see it.

'Your aunt and uncle have enough to worry about without having to stop the car to look after you. You have a long journey ahead of you, now eat a little at least,' she continued.

Matty lifted the heavy jug with the condensation on it and poured a good amount onto the porridge. His brain did work: he figured he needed a lot of milk not only to thin the paste but cool it as well. He then sprinkled sugar liberally on top of that and set about making it edible by mixing the whole lot with a large dessert spoon.

'Could I have a glass of milk please?' he asked the little nun.

'Of course you can,' she said, rising from the bench and setting off in the direction of the door leading down to the kitchens.

'There we are.' She had returned. 'You're doing well,' she continued.

Matty found that when he began to taste the food he actually had an appetite. So he ate. He had considered carefully what the nun had said about not being the cause of more trouble for Kate's parents.

'Thank you, Sister,' he said and gratefully drank half a glass of milk.

He felt vulnerable in the back seat of the car. He had on his safety belt and his belongings were in the boot along with Kate's. As far as his mind had the ability to think rationally, he felt he was not the cause of further problems for his relatives. How he wished he was with his own family. He knew the pain would still be there; the laundry smell of his father's shirt emanated from nowhere and he had to swallow hard to prevent the tears of loneliness emerge. He concentrated on what Jack might do or say if he could at least talk to him, how would he begin?

Aunt Bernie had questioned him again and again about Kate. He was sure he stuck to his story, it wasn't a difficult one but he had a real problem concentrating.

'She was a little tired one afternoon and the nun took them to the refectory and they had a snack,' he had said.

'What did you do yesterday?' his aunt asked.

'I don't know… Kate probably went to her room,' he said.

'Did you have your dinner together?' she asked a third time.

'Yes, she had dinner with everyone,' he truthfully answered.

'And then you all went to bed,' Aunt Bernie said.

'Yes,' Matty repeated.

'No point in talking to him, how would he know anything?' put in Uncle Liam still edgy.

'It's very unusual, she's so healthy normally,' Aunt Bernie replied mitigatingly.

They found the hospital and parked. At reception they were told on enquiry that Kate was in Critical Care Ward in Neurology. A volunteer was offered to help them find the ward, 'Or you can follow the yellow line,' the elderly receptionist said.

'Can you show us the way?' Aunt Bernie said to the volunteer.

Matty half-ran to keep up with Uncle Liam's long strides and Aunt Bernie's fast pace. He watched for the yellow line. It ran alongside blue, green and red lines. The red line branched off at the end of a very long corridor. They all continued through double swinging doors down another corridor and the guide stopped at a lift.

'You can take the stairs or the lift, Neurology is on the first floor, ask at the desk for the Critical Care ward,' he explained.

'Thanks,' was all Aunt Bernie said and she started up the stairs.

At the top the yellow line was on its own; the blue and green lines had disappeared.

More double doors and inside a desk, to the right side and the left there were many doors leading off the very wide corridor.

'Our daughter Kate… Catherine Garman was admitted this morning…' Aunt Bernie began.

'Come this way,' a woman in a white uniform said as she stood up. 'I'm Nurse Phelan. I'm afraid the little fella will have to stay here.'

'Sit down there,' Uncle Liam said as if Matty was some irritant to be dealt with that was not the priority which pressed so much on his mind.

Matty sat down and listened intently to what the white uniform said.

'We have done a CT scan and the doctor is with her now. Perhaps we should wait here until he is finished his examination,' she said.

'Neurology means… that there is something wrong with her brain?' asked Aunt Bernie.

'Well it is the whole nervous system and the consultant is Dr Murphy; he is a specialist in that area, a Neurologist,' explained the nurse.

'Is she awake?' asked Uncle Liam.

'No, she is still unconscious but… I should prepare you, we have had to bind her limbs with foam and bandages, she was hitting out and kicking and there are restraints on the bed, for her own protection,' continued the nurse.

Matty was shocked. *What was Kate having to contend with in the other world that it came through to her physical state? She was fighting someone or something… trying to get back. He hoped it wasn't the demon shapes he saw at the basement window…*

A small, neat man emerged from the doorway in which the nurse, the aunt and uncle stood. He wore a grey suit with a white shirt and tie. He looked immaculate and pedantic. He was introduced as Mr Murphy the Neurologist. Around him were gathered several white-coated younger men and women. He shook hands with Kate's parents and moved a little away from the door, leaving his team and the nurse went into the room. They were much closer and Matty did not have to strain. His relatives were so engrossed in their daughter's health they had completely forgotten about what effect all of these conversations had on him. He tried to appear invisible. He just sat still looking down at his fingers, which he twiddled with, giving the impression he was miles away. But his ears were scanning, in fact he closed his eyes so that he could pick up every single word the doctor said.

'Can you tell me a little about her?' he asked. 'She appears healthy.'

'Yes, she has never been sick in her life,' blurted out Uncle Liam.

'She's active, rides almost every day, eats well, is bright at school…' added Aunt Bernie.

'You say she rides… has she had a recent fall?' asked the doctor with interest.

'Not as far as we know,' the aunt answered, looking at her husband.

'What's the matter with her?' the aunt persisted.

'We have done a CT scan which shows activity in the neocortex. This is not unusual in itself but she is also showing signs of paradoxical sleep…' he said.

'I don't understand anything you are saying,' interjected the aunt, somewhat distressed.

'Her brain activity registers fast waves with high voltage bursts at the same time she has complete muscular atonia... she can't move,' he said.

'So there is something wrong with her brain,' Uncle Liam said.

'Yes, I think the best thing to do would be to transfer her to the Neuro Hospital in Dublin, I know someone there who specialised in sleep disorders. We have examined her thoroughly and cannot find a cause for the lack of response to sensory stimuli,' he explained.

'So she is in a coma?' asked Aunt Bernie, still not having learned anything.

'She is unconscious at the moment; prolonged unconsciousness leads to coma and we want to avoid that. I have booked an ambulance to take her to Dublin this evening,' the doctor explained, 'I'm sorry I cannot tell you more. I have never had a patient presenting with symptoms like these. It's better she is under the care of someone more experienced in this type of consciousness.'

'The nurse says she kicks and moves her arms,' Aunt Bernie put in optimistically, 'how can she do that if she is unconscious?'

'Precisely, this is the reason I need her under the care of Professor Donovan in Dublin. This unconsciousness is not due to a fall or blow to the spine or head,' he explained. 'I have done some blood tests; maybe when we see the neurochemicals we will know more, but I don't want to wait for the results before transferring her.'

'Can we see her?' the aunt seemed finally resigned to the little or no hope which had been proffered.

'Yes, of course,' he said, extending his arm in the direction of the door he and his team had exited from.

His aunt and uncle went towards the door at the same time the team entered another door. Matty took the opportunity to leap up and tiptoed behind his relatives. He only had a glimpse before the door closed. He saw a bed with bars on the side, a white bandaged hand that looked like a boxing glove and a plastic bag hanging from the bed with urine in it.

SOUP

 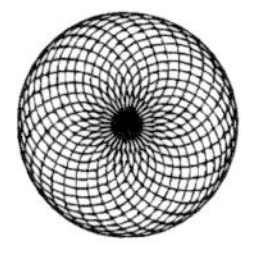

MATTY ACTUALLY EXPERIENCED a feeling that afternoon but it was one of ambivalence. After sitting watching the uniformed people coming and going, conversing outside rooms and sometimes walking along the shiny corridor peeping into the swinging doors that occasionally opened, his relatives emerged. Aunt Bernie dabbed her eyes with a paper tissue. Uncle Liam looked even more agitated and miserable. Matty stood up for fear they may leave without him.

'I'll see you in Dublin tomorrow then,' Uncle Liam said.

'Yeah, yes,' the aunt replied, head still down, tissuing the sides of her eyes.

'Can I see Kate?' Matty managed in his pleading voice.

'No, you have to come home with me now,' replied the uncle mechanically.

Matty looked at the aunt who appeared to have to force herself to focus on him.

'I'm going in the ambulance with Kate to the hospital in Dublin,' she explained. 'I'll see you tomorrow when I get home.'

Matty accepted his lot and dreaded the car journey to Wexford with his tall and heavily built Uncle, especially in the mood he was in.

'You better get something to eat,' the aunt said.

'There must be a canteen here,' replied the uncle. 'Right, we'll go and get some grub.'

'I can't eat, Liam,' the aunt said.

'You'll have to eat before leaving for Dublin,' insisted the uncle, 'it will be night and you may not be able to get food.'

'You go and find the canteen and before you leave you can tell me where it is,' she said.

Matty followed his uncle having to fall into a trot in order to keep pace with him. They found the canteen on the way back to the entrance, near reception. The uncle grabbed a tray and they both moved along with the queue, sliding the tray on the steel track beside the glass covers where the food was kept. Uncle Liam ordered fish and chips from the woman beyond the glass displays.

'Do you eat chips?' he asked Matty.

'I'm not hungry either,' replied Matty.

'You'll have to eat, we have a long drive ahead of us,' insisted the uncle.

Matty remembered what the little nun had said about not causing trouble for his relatives.

'I like soup,' he said.

'We have mushroom and leek and potato soup,' the woman said kindly.

'Leek and potato please,' replied Matty relieved.

He didn't think he ever had it before but he wasn't at all sure about mushrooms, he certainly never had that. His mother never cooked soups in India.

Uncle Liam paid after ordering tea and a currant bun. He bought a Wagon Wheel for Matty. He had had one of those before, *Kate had offered him one after they had been to the sea… Kate.*

The soup was too hot for Matty to drink so he busied himself buttering the roll and taking small bites out of it while the uncle wolfed down his steaming fish, chips and peas. He had already moved on to the currant bun by the time Matty could sip from the hot soup bowl. Finishing his tea Uncle Liam rose and Matty immediately began to get down from his chair.

'You stay there and finish your soup,' he said, 'I'm going to see Bernie and then we'll go home.'

Matty sat back down again; the thought of abandonment slipped into his mind and he dismissed it. *That was not the type of thought one should ever allow.* He had almost finished the soup when the uncle appeared in the canteen again.

'Your Aunt says you might want to go to the toilet,' he said.

'I'm alright,' Matty replied.

Even now Matty has little or no memory of that lone journey back to the ancestral home. He chose the part of the back seat in the car behind the passenger seat rather than the part behind the driver in order to see out but he discovered that, unlike the Ambassador cars, cars in Ireland had headrests, so he busied himself looking out the side window at the city and the traffic before falling asleep.

Once home Matty felt he and everyone were living the expression 'life goes on': he didn't go to Kate's house to play with Nicky as he imagined he would be feeling sad too. Instead he willingly fell into the old routine of life with Gran.

'What have you learned to say in Irish?' his grandmother asked as Matty negotiated the meat and vegetables around the gravy on his dinner plate.

'How to ask what a person's name is,' he replied unhelpfully.

'Do you remember how to say it?' she persisted.

'*Cad is anim dith?*' he stated dutifully in his less obstinate mood.

'*Mairead O'Callaghan is anim dom,*' replied his grandmother. '*Agus tusah?*'

'*Maitiu Ram is anim dom,*' he replied, his spirit lifting slightly.

'That's very good,' she said encouragingly. 'Are you glad you came?'

'Yes,' was all he could say, remembering everything that had happened.

September rolled into October and Matty's daily routine continued, but with the addition of an Irish language text book. This was supervised and taught by his grandmother: they were learning months of the year and he marvelled at how Samhain was the name for November as well as the festival of Halloween.

THIRD EYE

A WEEK AFTER Kate had been discharged from hospital she was still in a dream-like state. Matty visited her every afternoon and some mornings. He would find her lying on her bed in her pyjamas in the mornings in what Jack named her 'Ophelia' state but she was in the present: her eyes were open and they sometimes reacted when Matty pulled out the chair at her desk to sit by the bed but other than that she never responded to him. In the afternoons Auntie Bernie would have dressed and bathed Kate and Matty would sit on one of the armchairs next to the sofa where Kate had been sat by the large sitting room window. She seemed contented to just stare out blindly at the fields stretching away beyond the garden. Matty did consider that she may be seeing through what she called her third eye but on closer observation he knew she was not looking at anything.

Matty was careful to avoid meal times when Uncle Liam was home. He was impatient at Kate's state and gave the impression that by shouting at her she would somehow emerge from where she was in her mind. This upset Auntie Bernie who fed Kate like a baby, waiting patiently while she chewed and reminding her to swallow.

Then one morning Matty got an idea. He had begun talking to her but it felt like he was talking to himself and he hoped that Auntie Bernie couldn't hear him; she kept the bedroom door open. He felt foolish but he was also compelled to carry on. He carefully chose the subjects: the first one was Finn, he commented on how fat he was becoming and how Gran had said it was because nobody was exercising him and how he had asked her for help so that he may exercise the horse but she said no and had explained that Finn was too fresh with all the food and no galloping. The second topic was Jack and India. Again he was careful, aware of a listener; Jack, as was usual for him, had sent no reply to Matty's last three letters and the conversations on the phone were too short. He didn't add that he was lonely as he instinctively felt any negativity should be avoided. When Matty got up to leave Kate's bedroom after the long vigil he said goodbye as usual followed by see you later. As he replaced the chair at her desk he imagined he heard her say 'Bye' and when he looked at her she was staring straight into his eyes. He turned and left. He didn't want to destroy something that might be emerging by probing it more. Neither did he tell his aunt; as he left through the kitchen, he just said:

'I'll be back after dinner, I mean lunch.' He knew Auntie Bernie knew what he meant. Gran had her main meal in the middle of the day.

That afternoon she was as usual in the sitting room. It was a warm autumnal afternoon and the room was very hot; the window was south-facing. Kate had been dressed in a skirt and T-shirt. Matty was somewhat astonished at how thin her legs and arms had become. The normally muscular limbs where shapeless, like his grandmother's, but he accepted the changes of old age in her as Gran was almost eighty years old. He took a little more notice of Kate's face as he started on the series of innocuous stories he had planned in his mind, most of them about his life in Adoor in India, about his pets, school and friends. Her sun-kissed skin was creamy pale: no roses in her cheeks, he had heard one of the great aunts remark to his grandmother.

When an hour chimed on the hall clock he decided to leave, more than disappointed at the consistent withdrawal. As usual he stood at the door and said, 'See you later,' but before he turned to go through into the hallway he could barely believe his ears:

'I love you Matt,' she said so quietly and softly he wasn't sure he had heard it.

He looked into the room. She hadn't moved her head; he felt then that it must be an enormous effort for her to move or talk. He got the confirmation when he stepped into the hall, Aunt Bernie was there with her palms clasped together, tears running down her cheeks. She had heard it too. She held up one thumb to Matt and put the forefinger of the other hand on her lips. He held up his thumb in response and left silently with an unsuppressible smile.

This routine went on for a few more days. Matty did it out of a duty to Kate; it was his responsibility to keep trying but it was becoming so difficult. He persisted, though; he had to. She was like she was because of his family, she hadn't hesitated, she had jumped right in, into the unknown to help them; the least he could do was sit with her.

Then one morning as he lay in bed shortly after waking, he had a brainwave. What if he could bring her for a walk to see Finn? Maybe she would remember something from before. But then the negativity of getting it past his aunt almost caused him to dismiss the idea, until he arrived at Kate's house later that forenoon. He slipped in through the back door which was always unlocked and headed in the direction of Kate's bedroom. However, halfway down the hallway he heard his aunt talking to Kate in the sitting room. On entering he found her lifting Kate's arm and instructing her how to slide it down the sleeve of her anorak.

'Oh Matty, I'm so glad you're here… I'm really late, I have to be somewhere, can you sit with Kate for a couple of hours? I don't think I can take her with me…' and she began loosening the anorak at the back of Kate's neck in an effort to take it off again.

'I'll do that,' he said.

'Good boy… thanks… if I'm going to be late I'll ring you,' she said on her way out through the door.

Matty sat down beside Kate and waited for the sounds of the car to start and to leave. He did not take off her anorak; instead he said, 'Let's go for a walk.' There was no reaction so after a little while he caught hold of Kate's hand closest to him and repeated, 'Let's go.' He stood in front of her and tugged a little on the limp hand but she stood up. He led her out of the house around by the side and out through the gates and into the lane. She walked slowly along beside him; he had to change hands so as to place her on the hedge side of the road, anticipating cars and jockeys on horses. She walked along ever so slowly and he knew not to rush her, those wasted muscles on his mind.

It took a while to reach his grandmother's house and he suspected that their approach may be noted by her through the back kitchen window, which was where she would be cooking potatoes and vegetables and meat for their lunch/dinner. He carried on the next few metres to the stables on the opposite side of the road. Finn was in the high field. Matty opened the iron gate, led Kate through and left her standing as he needed to lift the gate slightly in order to shut it. When he turned around he noticed that she was staring at Finn. He led her a few feet to the gate of the high field opposite the stable. Beside the gate there was a type of concrete structure with metal enmeshed into it and extending above it; everyone used it as a style to gain access into the field rather than open the gate and risking animals getting out. He advanced Kate toward this and watched the house. The net curtain moved: he was certain then that his grandmother was watching from the kitchen window, but he assuaged his unease with the hope that she did not know that his aunt was away and he hoped his grandmother would assume he had permission to bring Kate to Finn.

When he checked Kate again Finn was advancing steadily towards the gate. He snorted as he put his head over the gate and as he did Kate raised up a hand to pat his long nose and brow. Finn whinnied a little and put his head down and then a remarkable thing happened. Kate slipped her hand down his neck and placed her forehead on his. They stayed like that for what seemed a while to Matty only because, due to the urgency of time itself, it seemed to be accelerating for him because of his fear that his grandmother would come out and take Kate back inside. Matty waited. Finn flicked his tail, Kate and her companion stood still, connected, Matty thought, by their third eyes. He began to relax: *if she was going to order them back inside the house she would have come out by that time.*

He gave his grandmother a little silent credit for her intuition. But just as he began to relax, something he had unwittingly put in motion took on an aspect he did not and could not anticipate. Kate let go of Finn, climbed onto the concrete structure and as the horse came alongside of it she placed one leg over the metal bar and then the other. She managed to stay on the narrow piece of concrete until Finn was close enough to mount and as she did she lay forward on his back, resting her head against his mane. She let her hands flop down each side of his flanks and to Matty's astonishment the horse moved slowly out into the centre of the field where he stood still.

Matty did not know what to do. His grandmother said the horse was full of energy: what if he began to gallop? Kate did not have the strength to cling on with either the wasted muscles of her thighs or arms. Just as panic crept up into his throat Matty noticed his grandmother approaching the outer gate from across the road and in a mixture of confused fear he was, he thought, glad she was there. They stood and watched, each from behind a different gate. Shortly, they were distracted by the approach of hoofs: the jockeys were taking race horses out for exercise. Matty often saw Finn run along the inside of the field as it bordered the lane with these horses. He quickly glanced at his grandmother and he could tell she was thinking the same thing; her lower lip was held in by her teeth.

'She's getting out and about again,' came a voice.

Matty turned his vision from Kate and Finn, whom he was willing to stand still, to the owner of the training stables near the sea. He was a man of about Gran's age and they knew each other well. He was driving a horse ahead of him on a very long rope. He stopped beside the grandmother.

'Well... yes,' replied Matty's grandmother uncertainly.

'Best thing for her,' he said with conviction, 'little by little.' He moved off, flicking the rope to urge the horse he was training up the lane after the other jockeys and their mounts.

Just as this remark gave Matty confidence, the look on his grandmother's face was of anxiety and condemnation.

'I don't know how you are going to get her back home, I can't stay out here, I have to watch the dinner,' said the grandmother disapprovingly and left, threading the corner of her apron through her fingers.

Matty climbed up on the style construction and sat on the metal bar, his trainers on the narrow ledge of the concrete, hands supporting his precarious position on the bar. The peaceful scene in the field opposite him prevented him from intruding; at the same time, the uncertainty of how he could lead his cousin back to the safety of her sitting room was uppermost in his mind. He had plenty of time, he knew that, it was just the state of Kate's mind. He checked his watch: they must have been here ten, maybe fifteen minutes already. *Magh would know what to do*, he thought. Matty waited. It was an atmospheric autumnal day. He loved the quietness that came with the mists. It was as if a cloud enveloped the whole area, as if they were inside it and it was at ground level. The sound of hoofs alerted him again: the jockeys and their horses were coming back. He was a little more confident this time. It appeared as if Finn and Kate were locked into something else altogether. They passed by without incident. Shortly after the owner came with his trainee. Matty looked at him as he passed. 'Still out there?' It was rhetorical but Matty nodded his head.

'Give her plenty of time, she'll be alright,' said the trainer and he moved off down the hill.

Just as Matty was scanning the bales of hay inside the barn for somewhere more comfortable than the perch he was on, Kate slid off Finn's back and began walking towards the gate. Matty jumped down to open it for her. Finn walked along by her side. She slid out through the small opening he had made for her. He did not want Finn to get out – then he really would have a problem with his grandmother. Kate seemed happy to leave the animal. A quick thought flashed into Matty's mind that she may want to take the horse home, such was the unity between them. Matty opened the outer gate and Kate walked through. Matty lifted it and sent the bolt home. Kate had waited for him so he took her hand again to lead her. It was frozen cold. He began to worry that she may catch cold and become seriously ill again. When he reached their bungalow he sat her down in the sitting room and searched for the central heating switch. He couldn't find it; he didn't know what it looked like anyway. In his frustration he marched back into the sitting room and without thinking asked, 'Where is the switch for the heating Kate?'

'Soup,' was all she said.

'Soup?' he repeated, baffled.

'In the kitchen,' she said and got up.

'Boil the kettle,' she said when they stood there.

Matty was not used to cooking of any sort, either in India or with his grandmother. She made everything for him, from meals right to his bedtime cocoa. He looked around for an electric kettle, found it and put water from the tap in and replaced it on its electric pad.

'Where's the soup?' he asked.

'Boil the kettle,' she repeated.

Matty looked at the kettle: it was not getting hot, not even warm when he felt it, it was then he noticed the switch, he pressed it down gently and shortly a sound emerged.

Kate went to one of the cupboards and took out a small cardboard box. Matty came and peered into it. There were four or five different coloured little packets inside.

'So tired,' said Kate.

He led her to the table and sat her down. He sat down beside her and arranged the soup packet on the table, calling out the flavours.

'Oxtail, chicken and leek, minestrone and… I think this is Thai or Chinese,' he said aloud but more to himself and to his astonishment he got a response.

'Oxtail,' she said.

'What do I do with it?' he asked.

'Pour water on it… from the kettle,' she said.

Matty rose up from the table with two packets, one in each hand; he had decided on Thai for himself. Privately he was delighted. They were actually having a conversation: a little stilted, granted, but there was an exchange. He opened several cupboards in search of mugs or bowls and eventually found a stack of bowls. He emptied the powders into the bowls and added the water and then one by one he brought them to the table. Then he realised they needed spoons. Several drawers later he had produced one desert spoon and one soup spoon. He dipped in his spoon and tasted the hot concoction. Kate had picked up her spoon and was stirring her soup so he did the same.

They were just finishing the soups when he heard a car. Kate had not spoken throughout but had fed herself, blowing to cool the hot soup in the beginning and then finishing it off.

'Her anorak is still on,' remarked Aunt Bernie the minute she came in the back door. Kate was sitting with an empty bowl in front of her.

'We went for a walk…' began Matty and before the astounded look on the aunt's face turned to anything more sinister he quickly added, 'to see Finn. Gran was there too.'

'I'm tired,' Kate put in.

'Course you are,' replied the aunt and started taking off her anorak.

'I'll go,' said Matty as he stood up from the table, 'Gran will have lunch ready.'

'Thanks Matt,' said Kate.

'See you later,' he said as usual but this time it was an actual reply.

BUSHY MAN

GRAN STILL WORE the censuring look throughout their dinner but did not scold him. When it came time for his visit to Kate that afternoon she enquired where he was going when he began putting on his trainers and anorak. She said she felt it was better he let Kate rest for today and maybe tomorrow too, that she was very frail and any excitement may make her sick again. They would visit for lunch on Sunday as usual. Then he remembered the telephone conversation that had occurred between daughter-in-law and mother-in-law just as they were about to eat and while he was watching TV. He had lowered the volume slightly, keeping both ears on the one-sided telephone conversation. He felt that Gran had been economical with her replies and it didn't take much calculating to know the caller was Auntie Bernie. Matty felt the power of the adults constricting him and his innate feeling about what was best for Kate.

'I'll just go for a ride then,' he said casually.

'Where will you go? Remember it will be dark soon,' asked and warned his grandmother in the same sentence.

'I'll go down to the sea and back,' he said, careful to use her own terminology.

'Alright then, be careful,' her usual farewell, followed with: 'be back in half an hour.'

'OK Gran', he replied as nonchalantly as he could muster, for he was really seething with anger.

Matty had been using Kate's little red and white bicycle. It was the right size for him but he hated it because it was a girl's bike: red frame with white mudguards. It had a cream-coloured basket on the front handlebars which Kate had taken off – 'to take the girl's look off it,' she had said. This all happened before they went to Galway, when he would ride along side of her and Finn down the lane as far as the sea where she would take off along the borough on Finn alone. Sometimes he would wait for her, skimming stones, or trying to, if the tide was in and Kate took the long way round to the borough. Mostly he waited for her when the tide was out and she crossed to the borough through a path in the slime.

This particular day he had to head down there to get away from the oppression. *What did they know? The adults.* For the first time he understood why Jack did not have any regard for rules. Admittedly, Matty did; he actually did see his parents' point of view and also he found going along with regulations he did not actually agree with entirely was easier than downright disobedience. *But this was different.* It also caused him to consider if Jack found adult advice was something in general that he could not agree with, or maybe would not, but for the first time Matty began to understand why Jack appeared to be so defiant at times.

Once out of the barn he even made the supreme effort to close the little gate on the yard even though Brandy, Gran's Jack Russell, did everything in his power to squeeze out while Matty negotiated his bicycle through. Matty was full up of resentment: he really felt like letting the dog out and then closing the gate but common sense set in quickly. He was living alone with this woman without Jack or his mother to defend him and with Kate in the mental state she was in, he considered he had no allies so far away from his own family. He mounted the bike in the yard beside Gran's car and pressed hard on the pedals, making the back wheel spin a splutter of chippings off the surface of the yard. Once out on the lane he kept this pressure on the pedals, rising off the saddle to add more force and by the time he got around the gable end of the house he was speeding, much too fast for the hill but he didn't care, he had to let go of the anger. He was sure if he checked himself in a mirror his face would have been red, he could feel the heat coming off his chest. He barely got round the sharp bend at the bottom of the hill, almost going head-first into the big ditch which at that time of the year was full of water and which ran along the road side in front of the hedge; the only thing that stopped him was the grassy, lumpy bank which he had to direct the bicycle into to prevent himself literally flying over the handlebars. He came to a clumsy stop and had to bail, leaving the bike to fall down in the wet grass and himself to run into the road in an attempt to stay upright. He felt ashamed for being so stupid but realised he had rid himself of the tension. Picking up the bike and getting out of the middle of a blind bend in the road, he walked slowly down the lane.

A little further along and to his right was another much smaller lane which did not have a surface, just car tracks down the middle with grass encroaching either side of these and down the middle between them. He remembered his mother telling him how the adults used to frighten her and Uncle Liam and the neighbouring children with a story, that if they did not come home before dark in the long summer evenings, the Bushy Man would get them and apparently he came out of this lane. His mother had laughed at how all the children believed it and at dusk they would scurry up or down the lane towards their farm houses in absolute fear of this man which none of them expected to look like a living man, more like a darkened cloud of evil with twigs and leaves ominously sticking out of a man shape. None of the children even went down that lane in daytime, except at harvest time, when all the neighbouring farmers came to gather in the hay, wheat and barley. Apparently there was a festive atmosphere as the thresher moved from farm to farm over several days and depending on who was bringing in the sheaves a child might be allowed a ride on the horse and cart halfway up and down the mysterious lane.

Matty checked his watch and decided against parking his bicycle by the side of a hedgerow opposite the lane: *what if there was really something in the story? He may need to make a quick escape and the bike would be faster than running in sticky mud and long very wet grass. He was sure he could keep the bike steady on the car tracks if he needed to ride it… or he could always drop it and run, he was still very near his grandmother's house.*

A few paces in, there was the pond to his left; that he remembered too, his mother showed Jack and himself where Uncle Liam as a boy and his friends collected frog spawns, kept them in jars on the window ledges in the backyard waiting for frogs to materialise and year after year they never did. Beyond that was a tubular gate leading to a big field. Matty checked there were no animals in it, just stubble: *well, it is after harvest time.* The hedgerows were growing wildly, tall and unkept as he moved along down the little lane. It was even quieter than the main lane. Soon Matty came to another gate on his right. He parked his bike and walked in a bit as all the gates were in a recess, off the actual lane. This was a gate made out of wood in two parts. It was tied together with plastic rope and once Matty peered in he knew it was their land. Kate had taken him for a walk to pick blackberries when he first arrived; she loved blackberry and apple tart and Gran had promised to bake a blackberry and apple one in addition to her usual weekend baking if they collected the blackberries. There were sheep grazing in there and Matty realised he knew another way back to the house; he figured this would join the High field with Finn in it, or maybe there was yet another long field in between? It didn't matter, he knew his location. So he continued on, this time without the bicycle. He decided it would be too difficult to wheel it any further as the grass grew longer and the car tracks were barely visible. Instead there were potholes filled with muddy water in line with the tracks. The lane was overgrown and the only break in the hedgerows was a black gate at the very end of it. As he approached it, a very tall man with a flat cap came towards the gate from the field side. He was a mere silhouette in the twilight. Matty turned around at once and began to run back towards his bicycle and once on it he peddled with as much force as he had used in his grandmother's yard but the energy was coming from a completely different source. Despite the effort it was impossible to make the bike go fast; it was an exertion even to stay on. By the time he got to the exit, after great difficulty in balancing on such rough terrain, he calmed himself and looked back. The man was walking slowly but surely up the lane. It must be someone he didn't know yet? It certainly was not a Bushy Man for there were no leaves or branches visible even in the gloom but he decided to go back inside anyway.

'You're back early,' remarked Gran as Matty wheeled his bike into the yard, having to negotiate Brandy's attempts at getting out again.

'I didn't go to the sea, I went down the little lane just around the bend instead,' he replied, finding it was easier to be civil after the outing; he still hated how she had ganged up on his plan to make Kate better.

'Who is the tall man dressed in black?' he asked giving the impression that all thoughts of Kate were far from his mind.

'Where did you meet him?' she asked. *Typical of Gran*, he thought, never spontaneous, always guarded.

'He was way down at the very last gate in the little lane, the black gate across the bottom,' he explained, 'and I didn't meet him, I just saw him in the distance.'

'That's probably Paddy, his land is way down there, he lives in the next farm house, you know the one with the thatch,' she explained.

'The thatched house before the next bend or the one after it?' he asked.

'You know it well, Jack and you used to go see the yellow canary when you were small,' she reminded him.

'Oh, Mrs White,' he said, remembering. 'Does Paddy live there?'

'Yes, he's her cousin,' she replied. 'Do you want to help me feed the horses?'

'No, I'll just go in and do some of the homework from India,' he said, thinking of the homework that had been set for him by his teachers in India. What he really wanted to do was to plot how he would get to see Magh; he badly needed her advice.

He went to the middle room which used to be his uncle's and still had a boy's feel about it even though Gran hung her winter or summer clothes in the wardrobe and at the back of the bedroom door in dust covers. The boy's world was to be found in the drawers of the dressing table and bedside locker which Matty rummaged through and examined and read comic books found there, all about soldiers. This was where Jack usually slept when they came with their mother; he shared the double bed with her then in the far room but that was almost three years ago. He wondered where he would sleep now if everyone came together, probably he would share Nicky's bunk bed at his house.

All these thoughts ran through Matty's mind as he settled himself on the bedside mat and began leafing through a book-like comic named *Commando*. He suddenly stopped, jumped up, ran to the hallway, grabbed his anorak from the wooden coat hanger, slipped into it before pulling and old pair of Wellington boots belonging to Jack in the porch and headed out across the yard towards the barn for the bicycle.

'I thought you were catching up on school work,' his grandmother asked on her way back from feeding hens and horses.

'I think I dropped a glove down the lane,' he replied as he made his escape through the little gate before Brandy got back from the haggard. The little dog accompanied Gran on her feeding duties because he lorded it over the horses, attacking them and barking from various angles in the field while they chewed their hay ignoring him completely.

'It's nearly dark,' called his grandmother.

'I'll be back in a minute,' he shouted as he sped past the gate leading to the lane. He also realised he was becoming a really good liar – *white lies*, he reminded himself, hoping she wouldn't remember it wasn't cold enough for gloves yet.

He negotiated the bend expertly this time and slowed down as he turned into the smaller Bushy Man lane, readying himself to plunge down on the pedals to propel himself through the muddy track as far as the gate where he had left the bicycle last time.

Even though visibility was really bad in the faded light and the bike did not have a lamp, he got to the gate. He dismounted, throwing the bike into a hedgerow of hawthorn and blackberry bushes and searched in his anorak pockets for his torch but remembered it was in the Crane Bag which was at Gran's. He consciously calmed himself and began to examine the grassy area in front of the double gates tied with plastic rope. He walked every centimetre of grass and muddy ground but could not see it despite being bent right over. He knew for sure he had seen it but because he had been in such a rush to get away from Paddy he didn't remember it till he sat quietly on the mat in his bedroom. Even if he couldn't see it, he would have felt it with the toe of his boot for he walked very carefully; but no branch was to be felt or even seen. He walked back up the lane, the way been shown briefly by the headlights of a passing car travelling by the entrance, down the bigger lane. He wheeled the bicycle and walked back up towards the hill, having to stay in the middle of the lane for fear of falling into the ditch which was full of water from stormy rain. Fortunately no car came, but his grandmother did, with a dimly lit torch, full of scolding and reasoning as to why a driver would not see him in the dark. Matty said nothing; his mind was full of the apple branch, covered in blossom. The leaves had been falling and most of the hawthorns were almost bare but the silver branch full of apple blossom lay on the ground, flush with the light green, oval leaves and white-pink blossom of spring, next to the gates just minutes ago. He could even recall the subtle perfume they gave off, it was sort of sweet.

How could that be? he wondered. There were no apple trees growing next to the land and moreover winter was coming; it would be months before any buds appeared, let alone blossoms.

'Did you find it?' asked his grandmother.

'No,' he replied.

'Why do you need to wear you gloves anyway? It's not that cold yet,' she went on.

What Matty was yet to find out was that the silver apple blossom branch was a sign of an other-worldly visitor, the White Goddess.

HEDGE COTTAGE

SATURDAY CAME AND slowly went by and still Matty had not thought of a way to reach Magh. He badly needed to find out what the apple branch meant. He was very careful not to mention Kate. By Saturday night when he was told to have a bath and Gran had left out a clean pair of pyjamas he was totally frustrated with himself. He normally enjoyed a bath and idled for ages deep in bubbles; the remainder of a bottle of bubble bath was, to his pleasure, still among the myriad of shampoos and shower gels belonging to Gran on a shelf at the head of the bath. But that Saturday he had no peace of mind, wondering how long the ban would be enforced. He wondered when his mother was due to arrive and realised he missed his family. He felt no connection here, either with his grandmother or cousins, only Kate – and she had disappeared into her own world, or it felt like that to him. He was sad and so lonely. However, an opportunity awaited Matty and once again experiencing rage he took one of those daring leaps into the forbidden and unknown, just like Jack did.

It came about by Uncle Liam's lack of intelligence – yes, in retrospect Matty had to admit that it was ignorance on the uncle's part, or maybe to be truly fair he was upset and protective of Kate.

On Sundays Gran had lunch with Kate's family and so at about twelve forty-five, a few hours after she and he had driven to Mass in her little Nissan car, grandmother and grandson strolled up the lane towards the bungalow. Grandmother asked perfunctory questions about homework and moving on she made enquiries as to where he went for bicycle rides. He made sure she received muted and economical replies. He didn't want to give any information in case it could be used against him later on.

When they entered from the back door Kate had already been seated at the kitchen table and to Matty's aggravation he knew she had slipped right back into the *cotton wool* world. He sat opposite to her, examining every centimetre of the expressionless face, willing a reaction but nothing and when everyone started to eat as plates of food were passed along his aunt sat down and began to feed her. This was someone who drank her own soup and not only that, instructed him how to make it just days ago. The anger began to rise up in Matty's chest and throat and the roast chicken and roast potatoes just would not go down.

Matty felt that Uncle Liam was in a blustery mood too: his uncle glared at him a lot and at one time actually remarked on the fact that he had not been eating much. Matty said nothing, just kept his attention on his plate, made a cut into the chicken breast and cut again, pushing most of the slice underneath the potatoes and vegetables and gravy and only picked up a tiny morsel on his fork.

Kate took an age to chew, encouraged by Aunt Bernie who took food for herself from her own plate in between feeding Kate. Gran continued to make pointless conversation directed mainly at Uncle Liam whose mood, Matty felt sure, she sensed was dangerous. Nicky too ate quietly, his eyes roving from one of the adults to another. Then Matty had an idea and it just popped out of his mouth as quickly as it popped into his head, it felt so right.

'Can I feed Kate?' he asked Aunt Bernie.

'You?' spluttered Uncle Liam, tiny particles of potato escaping his mouth between the spat words.

'Don't you think you have caused enough trouble here?' His face was red and ugly, with dribbles of gravy and specks of broccoli around the hardened lips.

Matty found himself standing up: he wanted to say exactly what he thought, but the loneliness and frustration enveloped him and he ran out the back door, around the drive, down the lane and finally found himself in tears petting Brandy in the backyard at his grandmother's house.

The tears annoyed him and even Brandy appeared sympathetic, he pawed one knee of Matty's jeans. Matty couldn't understand how the little animal seemed to empathise. But it was not enough. A part of his mind seemed to be working without input from his conscious self: he found himself going to the barn, he grabbed the bicycle and he took off up the lane, pushing on the pedals as hard as he could, seat above the saddle to give him more power. When suddenly he felt the cold wind he remembered he had left his anorak at Kate's house but he was beyond caring what happened to him or his responsibility for the dog. He had swung the gate open so hard it bounced back against the front wheel of the bicycle and with another angry push he had freed himself from the yard. The gate swung open again and Brandy was free to roam like himself.

Matty felt so alone, so hurt and at the same time the feeling of elation caused by breaking rules was unbelievable. It was as if something beyond his conscious control had welled up, invaded his naturally considerate mind and had caused him to do very uncharacteristic things. And when he became aware of it he did not want to stop. When he neared the entrance to Kate's home he slowed a bit, peered in over the wall and as he passed slowly nobody was visible at the front of the house so he decided there and then he was not going back. *He would ask Magh to intercede with Manama Mac Leir, the Sea God, to take him on his chariot over the waves to India.* However, as the rain stung his face and damp soaked deeper and deeper into his jumper, he knew this was irrational but at the same time he could not go back to the disapproving, cold relatives. He had let the dog out, gone into the rain and wind without his anorak... but he was sure that he could not take any more scolding. As he struggled forward against what felt like gales of wind slashing rain into his body he realised he had taken the road that led to Magh's. He had turned right on to the main road at the top of the lane, careful to get on the correct side of the road and peddled quickly so as to disappear around the bend some distance away in case anybody was quick enough to check on his whereabouts. One swift glance back before rounding that second bend in the road and he felt free, except for the cold wind pressing him back as if something was reminding him he was reckless; but it only made him more determined. He pressed harder on the pedals, feeling the chill in his chest and abdomen; he hoped his body would warm up as he kept up the pace against the wind and the rain, but it didn't.

It was an easy journey to Magh's and Macha's normally; he had been with Kate before Galway to make their plans, she on horseback, he on the red and white bicycle. However that emotional, lonely day it felt as if he was living on his nerve endings, every time he heard a car engine approaching from behind his heart gave a little jump: what if it was Uncle Liam? Fortunately for him, each time it happened the car passed him. It did force him to think of the anger the adults would have when they found him missing, the dog gone – how to confront all of that? He pushed it from his mind quickly: he was nearly there, just one long stretch of road and he would be in Magh's front garden. He wiped his dripping fringe across his forehead and it was possible to see clearly even though the rain continued to run down his entire face. There it was: the thatched roof of the tiny cottage from where he was on the elevation of the road.

Matty did not leave his bicycle by the gate of the field where Macha's jennet grazed and where Kate usually tied Finn on a long tether to allow him to pull at the extensive grass surrounding the gate; no, instead he thought he would bring the bicycle into the little garden and round by a tall hedge of hawthorn which was neatly clipped and surrounded an old oak tree which sort of protected the cottage with its ample branches. He leaned the bicycle carefully against the back of another tree which grew next to the oak. Kate had explained the significance of the three plants forming a vortex of energy and what was used as a portal for entry into the other-world but he had forgotten the name; anyway, the bicycle was totally hidden from the road. He turned to face one of the little windows of the cottage and started towards the little green front door.

Before he could knock Magh opened it. She did not show surprise.

'Son… where are you going without a coat on this stormy day…?' Matty felt the question was surreptitious but he was beyond playing games.

'Oh Magh, I hate them, I hate all of them and what they are doing to her…' he blurted out without thinking, the anger had not allowed him to think and he was so intent on escape that he did not plan what and how he would tell Magh of Kate's dilemma. He stood in front of her on the little concrete path which ran all along the front of the cottage, wet through, cold, water dripping from his ear tips, nose and hair and so obviously distressed.

'Come in son, come in out of the cold and the wet.' She placed a hand on his shoulder and drew him into the little hall with its clay tiled floor, had a quick look outside and then closed the door. It was sheet after sheet of heavy rain on each gale of wind: Matty felt the weather was as cold and insensitive as his family.

The little living room was as crammed with furniture, bookshelves and objects that seemed mystical and needed to be explored with all of Matty's senses. He had felt that the first and only time he had been in there with Kate. This, and the warmth, were what his eyes fed on as he was guided towards the inglenook fireplace where Macha was dozing on a high-backed, carved wood long seat that resembled a church pew except for the high back. He stirred and bent his head in Matty's direction and began fumbling in his coat pocket while Magh started removing Matty's sodden clothing layer by layer. What Matty could not take his eyes away from were Macha's ears. They were truly pointed at their tips, long and elf-like. When Magh was down to Matty's trousers she produced a sheet-like, wide red cloth which she wrapped around him at his shoulders and instructed him to remove his shoes and jeans. The cloth was flannel and felt soft to hold and its feel on the skin of his shoulders was barely perceptible, but it gave a subtle heat immediately and, more than that, comfort despite the sight of Macha's ears. How come he hadn't noticed them before?

He was encouraged to take the pew seat opposite to Macha near the flames which were little and had made several logs glow red and orange and which gave off sparks like miniature shooting stars now and then. Magh arranged his wet clothing on a wooden frame which was hinged and opened into three with many rungs and stood it between Macha and himself in front of the hearth. Before he had handed Magh the little striped towel which she had given him to dry his dripping hair Matty watched fascinated as the water evaporated into steam and rose into the air from his woollen jumper. Her gentle urges, he realised, had relieved him from all accountability, even from taking care of his person, which he had done for years. He welcomed it, unknowing to himself, he needed to just be.

The heat from the glowing logs, the sound the wind made around the house was like the sound of the deep ocean, he thought as quiet crept into his mind and comfort into his body. The kettle suspended over the logs began to make a hissing noise, the tinkling sound of Magh stirring metal against ceramic and the heat slowly but surely caused Matty to relax all his muscles, and altogether helped subside the storm inside, except for how he was going to explain himself to his family. *Later*, he thought. He relaxed more and more. He watched Macha pare tiny pieces of tobacco from a *plug of what looked like resin but it was darker and obviously softer*, Matty considered to himself. He noted that, in the few seconds he took his eyes off Macha while he dried his hair, the pixie ears had taken on a human form. He continued to watch as Macha rolled the pared pieces of tobacco between both his palms having put his little knife back in his pocket, firstly replacing it in its leather shield. When the gentle massage was over, Macha stuffed the bowl of his pipe full; he tore off a piece of newspaper, rolled it up and then twisted it tightly and then he bent towards the intense heat emanating from the glowing red-orange logs. The tip of the newspaper became a flame instantly and Macha held it to the bowl of the pipe and sucked air from the shank and threw the quickly diminishing newspaper back on to the logs just as it changed into ash. An aroma of tobacco sublimated Matty's senses. Magh arrived with a steaming mug of something green and smelling of herbs. Matty tied the red sheet around his waist and reached out for the uninviting liquid, unwillingly hoping he managed to hide his ambivalence…

'Go on, taste it,' she urged.

Impossible to hide anything form Magh, she could hear the unspoken, and to his great relief it tasted of honey.

'It's lovely,' he said. 'Thank you.'

'It will stop you from catching a bad chill,' she explained.

Matty needed to sip the liquid as it was far too hot to drink. Magh seated herself on the high-backed seat beside him after she had rearranged his partially dry clothing, which caused more water vapour to be released. Macha sucked tobacco smoke into his mouth from the shank of his pipe and leaned his head heavily against the upright corner of the opposite seat, a satisfied smile on his face and his eyes half closed. *The tobacco must be giving him great pleasure*, Matty thought.

SANCTUARY

MAGH WAITED UNTIL he was halfway through his herbal tea before she broached the subject of his flight.

'They are mad at you because you took her to see Finn?' she asked.

Without looking at her Matty stared down at the green liquid in the mug and said, 'Yes.' And then realised she knew and blurted out the rhetorical question – too late; the words had escaped his lips.

'But how did you know?'

'You did the right thing,' she added quietly, avoiding his futile question and looked up at Macha who seemed half-asleep. Matty followed her gaze and wondered if the faerie in him might appear again, once sleep took hold.

'It felt right,' Matty continued, relieved that he could put his opinion to someone, voice the unmentionable.

'… even the man with the horses said it was the right thing to do…' Matty said defensively.

'Who?' she asked but before he could answer she understood and added, 'He would of course understand, horses are fifth-dimensional beings.'

'Fifth dimension?' Matty queried.

'I'm surprised at your grandmother.' She ignored his question again; she seemed agitated.

'Me too, I wish Mum was here, she would have explained things to me…' he said and annoyingly a lump appeared in his throat.

'That uncle of yours is ignorant, he understands nothing at all,' she said, somewhat disconcerted

'I had him here, you know, warning me off visiting the girl,' she turned towards Matty.

'I suppose I shouldn't really blame him, he believes what the hospital told him that she is suffering from hallucinations.' She was looking at the flagstones again and started nodding her head as if she was conversing with herself.

'I'm sorry if he shouted at you… he hasn't a clue how to help her, he doesn't understand her at all, none of them do… not really. I don't suppose it's possible to make people understand things they cannot see for themselves, and if she tried to explain they would put her in a hospital again.' Matty became aware of how emotional he was and slowed his words and lowered his voice.

'Don't worry about me, son, I can look after myself… ignorance is such a terrible thing,' she went on, nodding a little as if she needed to confirm her own judgement.

Matty made sure he finished the tea; he didn't want to cause more hurt for this wise old woman who taught Kate so much and helped her cope with her strange existence.

For a long time Matty sat in silence with the two elderly beings. He wondered about them: where to categorise them? They were human, certainly, but… also had faerie qualities – shape shifting, appearing and disappearing what seemed like at will. Magh and Kate could move through solid walls and more; and then his mind travelled back to when he was in the tower house on that dreadful night. Magh was half-mortal and half-faerie, tall like them, he remembered.

After quite some time holding and tracing round and round the handle of his empty mug with his right index finger he was amazed at how he could feel completely safe with them, unlike his relatives on both sides of his own family, some of whom actually put his father and brother in real danger. He rose to place the mug on the table but Magh intercepted him.

'I'll take that, son,' she said lovingly.

Matty took advantage of her quiet mind,

'Magh… what exactly is wrong with Kate? Why won't she talk… or even do anything other than sit and stare… I know she can… she talked me through making soup in her kitchen after being with Finn,' asked Matty, almost beseeching an understanding of Kate from the one who understood her most.

'It's simple Matty… she has just turned her perception off,' answered Magh, staring at the layers of very hot, partially steaming clothes.

'But why?' he asked anxiously.

'You see, son… Kate's world is very complicated When Kate's eyes are looking about she sees a lot more than you do,' she started, turning towards Matty who pulled his sheet over his shoulder nearest to the fire as his skin was roasting hot.

'I know, she see the fairies.' He felt he was being helpful, letting her know he knew.

'I don't know how to explain it to you darlin'…' After a small pause she began again. 'All around,' and Magh raised her arm and swept it in an arc, 'is an other-world, actually many worlds… and they… inter-penetrate ours… do you know what I mean?' she asked.

Matty nodded.

She continued, 'Kate sees them all.' She examined him closely; her words were spoken with measure and in confidence.

'I think so. Kate explained it to me in India and I saw the wolfhound in the tower house and the house fully furnished like it was in times past,' he said by way of an explanation.

'Right son, spot on, that's it, you had a brief glimpse into a particular, what is a non-real world to humans and because you were in an altered state of consciousness you could see it, be in it.' Magh became animated and began to elucidate, 'In fact only about two per cent of humans have the ability to see and hear the beings that inhabit these worlds and Kate is one of them. She has to react to them whether she likes it or not. Many types of the non-physical beings, elementals, souls, even ghosts, the Tuatha dé Danann, your Danavas and more she cannot yet understand. She can change her consciousness at will as you know and travel out of her body into non-physical planes which vibrate at a different frequency to yours and where she meets and sees these supernatural intelligent entities. She is supposed to learn about healing and other things but now she has shut herself off entirely. It's a safe place for her, not to communicate at all, well, because you know yourself what happened to you in India, some of these invisible beings can harm you here in the known world, your father's experience for example. However, Kate almost met her death in the other-world, I'm positive Cruachain meant to kill her, if nothing else but to spite me. But then there is the positive aspect: there are good people in that world who help you too, as you know,' Magh took a breath, watching him intently.

'I know, Magh,' he replied assuring her he was not afraid to hear all these things, 'like Ailill. And at the tower house he was helping me instead of helping her, it's all my fault what happened to Kate.' The guilt rose up again, distressing him.

'He did what she had asked him to do, nothing is your fault,' Magh said firmly. 'If anyone is to blame it is Cruachain,' she muttered to herself, 'and me. Kate had to negotiate with them, you know, she had asked for their help. Yes, I allowed her to take the lead, like it was at the tower house, you saw that, son. I trusted Aillien and I still find her blameless. You see, son, in the other-world Kate has to find her own way about, the same as you find out who to trust here in this life. All the worlds are the same; good and evil beings exist everywhere, and struggles are taking place all the time between people like Aillien and the Tuatha who fight to defend us against psychic attack.'

'Like Seamus,' Matty said.

'Not Seamus, he just knows a few spells, he's not capable of travelling between the worlds,' she said, almost uninterested, Matty thought – or perhaps she was just preoccupied.

'Like my aunt,' Matty interjected a second time; it was still difficult for him to understand how the supernatural intermingles with life.

'Not her either son, but she did get a step further than Seamus, if you like.' Magh appeared to come out of her thoughts more. 'Your aunt engaged with shamans who could actually travel between the worlds, I suspect.'

'She is the real cause of all this,' said Matty almost to himself.

'Maybe it was all meant to be, son,' said Magh, leaning back against the wood and looking very tired.

'What do you mean?' Matty asked, a little alarmed.

'Well, it was her experiences in India with you two years ago, or was it more, whenever… that helped her to realise her unique capabilities.' Matty had turned squarely in front of the old woman.

'Before then, she was frightened of the visions she saw… now she has learned how to negotiate her way around with the people of the Goddess Dana, the Tuatha and the Danavas.'

Yes, but her brain is like a vegetable, thought Matty but felt it would be too cruel to say it aloud.

'I know what you are thinking, son: I trusted too much, I did not protect her enough, trusting the Tuatha alone… I should have given her more psychic protection… well…' The old woman repeated and muttered so much to herself that for a moment Matty felt she was losing her mind too.

'That was not enough, she saw terrible things like the therianthropes… half-human, half-beast, like the Minotaur in your grandfather's house.'

'I saw that too,' replied Matty and found himself sitting on the edge of the shiny wooden seat, the memory still so terrifying, 'and the faces at the window at the convent.'

'What faces?' she asked, sitting upright.

'Terrible faces,' Matty said, trying to recall them and at the same time trying not to. They were in his dreams since he returned from the Gaeltacht; he slept with the bedside light on and had asked his grandmother to leave a light on in the hall outside his room, so that when he woke up fighting them he would realise he was in his own time and space,

'One had a mouth like a fish but the rest of the face was like a man; the other had several heads, all different animals.'

'So you can understand, son, she had to cope with all of that and then on top of it all the Cruachain went and called in the Chimera… the poor child must have been so frightened…' she kept shaking her head, her thoughts very deep.

'What are the Ki…?' Matty asked. Kate understood that he was trying to say 'Chimera'.

'They are really the Formorians, long ago defeated by the Tuatha dé Danann and other peoples who invaded Ireland over the ages, but Cruachain can somehow conjure them up to do her bidding,' she replied but not really concentrating on what he had said.

'Do their bodies look like their faces?' asked Matty.

'Yes, terrible looking creatures: half-fish, half-man, like you saw; other creatures who were never meant to have wings, flying around; others with hoofs and fish bodies. Well, I'm amazed her body and spirit are back in one piece… together… her soul could have shattered…' Magh trailed off as if she was talking to herself again, 'and what she is doing now is all wrong, she needs to ground herself. She is in more danger now; in fact she is wide open to psychic attack in the state she is in.' She became agitated.

'Is her soul still in the other world, Magh?' Matty asked solemnly at Magh's mention of her soul, because that might explain to him why Kate was not really the old Kate.

'Oh no, son,' and she touched his hand reassuringly, 'we got her soul back, we got her back, she is back together in all her form, that's why she is partially functioning now.'

'What do you mean? Who got her back?' asked Matty, confused.

'You remember she was in hospital for a long time, unconscious?' she asked.

'Yes, and then she opened her eyes and got better,' Matty added.

'It's because we got her back from Cruachain,' explained Magh.

'You and who?' asked Matty.

'Sister Perpetual,' said Magh.

'The little Marshmallow?' asked Matty.

'Is that what you call her?' asked Magh, a smile on her lips for the first time that afternoon.

'That's what Kate called her, she said she looked like a white marshmallow,' explained Matty.

'That sounds like Kate,' remarked Magh, lost in a sad smile.

'What must she do now, to be safe?' asked Matty, seeing Magh's expression of loss.

'She must eat well and exercise. What you did was the right thing to do, fresh air and she connected with the fifth-dimensional animal which is sort of OK, I think; preferably she should stay in this world, though. That was a good move, son, and you say you made soup afterwards?' she asked.

'Yes and she drank it. She doesn't eat, Magh; Aunt Bernie has to feed her with a teaspoon and then she takes so little, she has become so thin.' Matty explained with all the anxiety pouring out of him.

'Now you see that's the problem, she needs to ground herself in this world and eating is the best way to do that and she's not eating.' She trailed off again deep in thought, looking this way and that and not seeing anything except her thoughts and then:

'This is serious, I have to get to her.'

'She was always hungry when she had been on her psychic travels and weak, but after eating a lot – and my brother knows what to feed her, lots of protein – she got better fast,' Matty confirmed to Magh that her theory was correct.

'Yes, that's very normal, son, and everything you are doing is right, unlike me,' she added.

'Can't you shape shift or something? Ailill was a bird in India: if you could do that then my uncle and aunt would not see you. Kate stares out the living room window all day, you could get through to her that way.' Matty felt he had come up with an outstanding solution.

'Son, if she does not react to humans then she also cuts off her second sight too, she is afraid she will see Cruachain and the Chimera, and that witch could well use this opportunity to attack. This is more serious that I thought.' Magh rose up and began pacing the little room and then sat down again.

'She would use the Kim…?' Matty asked.

'The witch of Cruachain had these ancient of all creatures who inhabited this land and the other world. They were the ones who assisted her in abducting Kate from the tower house,' she shook and bent her head to look but not see the flagged floor, 'but I explained all that to you son, didn't I?' She mumbled, still deep in despair.

'Yes you did, I know you are worried about her,' he whispered, casting a quick glance at Macha who had placed his pipe on the hearth without Matty noticing and was fast asleep again, and this time without faerie ears.

'They are like the Minotaur but worse: if you can imagine an animal, no, parts of other animals all melded together– a giant fish with one human leg – and they would keep changing right in front of her eyes. Massive creatures, monsters, human-like bodies with wolf heads and hoofs, scales, you have no idea how panicked she must have been.' Matty was seriously worried about the state of Magh's mind. She rambled on:

'Yes she took her and no she didn't do anything to her as such. She showed her things that a young girl should not have seen and it frightened the very life out of her. Threatened her with the Formorians,' the old woman said, distraught.

'What was it she showed her? Why did she want Kate to see awful things?' began Matty, a note of frustration in his voice.

'To subdue her, I suppose. It is so rare for a human to have the qualities of the ancient ones, an inter-dimensional traveller. I think she felt she could have an apprentice, someone to pass on the heritage to, the magic… more like evil… imagine involving the Formorians to kidnap a young human. Crazy witch, Cruachain, she must have thought I had used some powerful protection on Kate. How stupid could I have been.' Magh spoke quietly and kept moving her head from side to side. Matty could feel her anguish and perceive her despair.

THE EACH USIGE

THERE WAS A loud crack from an explosion inside a log in the hearth that made Matty jump. He watched as the glowing pile of logs collapsed into shapeless red-orange light. Magh rose slowly as if it was painful, went to a large basket beside the fireplace and arranged three more logs on top of the red glow.

'How did you rescue her, Magh?' he asked, partly to distract her from her guilt and more especially because he really wanted to know.

'There are things a young man such as yourself should not know about...or trouble yourself with, son... leave it alone now,' and she patted his knee as she passed between his seat and the drying clothes.

'I am responsible... my brother and I have put Kate in the place she is in now,' and he was careful to keep his voice even. He had seen Jack make the mistake of impatience with adults and get nowhere. 'I need to know, please.'

She thought for a while and then, shaking her head which was held in her hands bent over her knees, she turned and looked up at him from that strange angle. A face so old and wrinkled with what Matty considered held the misery of ages.

'I suppose you do.'

She straightened her back and began in low tones, throwing an eye in the direction in which Macha was sleeping. Matty followed her look and then went back to watching her speak.

'I don't suppose you have ever heard of an *Each Uisge*,' she said heavily.

'No, what is it?' he asked.

'It's a type of horse, more like Cormac – you know, a jennet,' she explained.

'Half-donkey, half-horse,' Matty confirmed, placing Magh's and Macha's jennet in his mind's eye.

'Yes, son,' she said, her head had turned away from him again and she bent over her knees, propping up her shoulders by resting her elbows on them and spoke as if to herself.

'Well Cormac is one,' she turned her head again from that unusual angle to see if he understood, which gave her an air of being tortured.

'Is he?' he asked, 'What does it mean, did he rescue her?'

'He did actually, good old Cormac,' she said, looking up.

'How?' persisted Matty.

'Cormac is actually an *Each Uisge*... well, was an *Each Uisge*, I should say to be precise. Macha and I tamed him of his violent ways,' she continued.

'Violent?' repeated Matty, trying not to show his shock. 'Cormac was violent?'

'Well they are by nature,' she said, looking at him again but from an upright angle.

'How violent?' he asked.

'Well... this is a bit frightening, son,' she said, looking directly at him

'They generally appear near a stream in the shape of a beautiful pony, friendly enough to entice children to ride on their backs. Once the child is on its back it dives into the stream and drowns it.'

'But why?' asked Matty.

'No reason son, that's how they are,' she said

'But Cormac is fine now, he brought her back,' continued Matty anxious for more information.

'Stupid Cruachain,' she said as if to herself, her head turned to face the floor again 'she must have forgotten about the bridle, I was sure she would cop on to that, that was the one thing I worried might give me away... and I tried, I tried so hard to find a way of disguising it,' she was speaking quietly again as if to herself, reliving the rescue.

'The bridle?' Matty enquired quietly.

'Yes,' she replied without moving, 'once you have its bridle you have possession of the animal, and Macha and I have that.' She turned to face him again. 'You know they have the strength of ten horses?'

'Did you go with Cormac?' Matty asked.

'No, I couldn't risk it, it wasn't necessary, Cormac would do my bidding,' she answered seemingly without thinking, looking at the floor again.

'Did Kate know about *Each*... about Cormac's abilities?' Matty asked.

'No she didn't, that was another part of the plan I worried about,' Magh replied deep in thought.

'What was the plan?' asked Matty.

'Cormac would recognise Kate's entity; the trouble was, would Kate recognise him?' Magh went on.

'It was a couple of days... in our time... probably when the child had been moved to the Dublin hospital,' she explained, having heard his voice but not the actual words.

'Cruachain had relaxed her guard and Kate's spirit was allowed near the barn door.' She turned her head towards him again to check he understood.

'How did you know… could you see?' he asked.

'No, oh no, that was what Cruachain was on the lookout for… me in my various guises, which she would have recognised instantly,' she said, straightening up with a lot more life in her voice and demeanour.

'Then how?' Matty asked.

'Perpetual,' she said.

'The Marshmallow?' asked Matty.

'Yes, the Marshmallow,' repeated Magh with what was a hint of a smile.

'How?' he asked.

'There is more to that woman than I gave her credit for,' explained Magh.

'I thought she had the gift, sort of like Kate,' Matty put in thinking.

'You would never guess who she is?' asked Magh, animated.

'Who she is?' repeated Matty puzzled and then asked again:

'Who is she?'

'Cruachain's sister,' she said, the skin around her eyes stretching and making her eyeballs bulge.

'Crua…, but then she must be a witch,' exclaimed Matty, astonished

'But why did she help us?'

'Cruachain, or I should say Irnan, because Perpetual was originally one of the witches of Cruachain too,' Magh's smile widened as her eyes did.

'Cruachain put a spell on Perpetual, long, long ago. By the time Perpetual discovered how to undo it she found that she was more comfortable worshipping the new God,' explained Magh, still portraying her surprise at the discovery. Matty noticed the life force had arisen in Magh again.

'The new God?' asked Matty, relaxing a little, realising he had been bent tensely in Magh's direction, so intense was his concentration on the rescue.

'Yes, you know, Jesus,' explained Magh.

'Anyway, she undid the spell but never revealed it to anyone except me… and that just recently, and Irnan doesn't know to this day.' Magh was almost ecstatic, as if revealing the burden of a secret.

'But if she is no longer a witch won't she die, like a human?' Matty asked.

'People don't think very deeply except for the occasional one, which is very irritating. You see Mach and me?' she asked, looking straight at him, her shoulders turned towards him.

'Take your uncle for instance. He was brought up here, we were here when your grandfather was a boy like you; it has never occurred to them that we have not died. They say *Magh and Mach must be ninety or a hundred by now* but never think more about it. It's the same with Perpetual; nuns get moved from convent to convent but she has arranged it so that she stays at that particular abbey forever, keeping the balance. As you well know, Cruachain can go to extremes sometimes,' she said as an aside.

'When a new nun is transferred in she may ask how long she has been and Perpetual will literally say *forever* and the nuns will take it to mean a long time and nothing more.'

'But won't Irnan wonder why Perpetual is not dying?' asked Matty.

'She didn't make her mortal, simply imprisoned her in a convent of nuns, so no, she is obviously content to leave Perpetual alone,' explained Magh.

'Tell me about the rescue,' encouraged Matty.

'Perpetual knew exactly where Kate was imprisoned,' Magh explained.

'Where, exactly?' asked Matty.

'In this world, in your reality,' replied Magh, 'in a cottage on the outskirts of a village over there, in the west, next to the lake of Cruachain.'

'The same place you met Aillien when all of this began,' Matty added.

'It's a very large lake, child, we camped at a different part of it, but yes, you are right, it is the same lake,' she explained.

'Is that why she was in modern clothing when she came to the tower house, you and Kate had medieval clothing on but she dressed like Gran except her clothes were filthy?' asked Matty, thinking aloud.

'Yes, she had made her plans, unknown to us. All along she must have pre-arranged to keep Kate in this world as she knew I would find her in the other world,' explained Magh.

'But Kate's body was in a hospital, she must have known she had only part of Kate?' asked Matty, perplexed.

'Oh she knew alright, she was only biding her time… waiting for Kate to come back home and then she would snatch her… you see, that's why I am so worried about Kate's present state of mind, she is very vulnerable,' Magh said and her mind wandered again.

'I see what you mean,' Matty became even more anxious for Kate.

'I must work out stronger protection for her, you can be my go-between,' she said.

'Go-between?' asked Matty

'Yes, you have access to Kate and I have to stop that witch,' replied Magh with purpose.

'But she is three thousand years old… and not only that lives in another dimension, how could Kate live… leave… like Girija…?' Matty trailed off, realising in dismay, not wanting to even think about losing Kate.

'Exactly, I told her, guarding and training Kate was my job, I was to teach her how to get around here, this world, and more importantly how to survive in the other-world, she would learn how to protect herself among other things. Why did she think I have been waiting here so long…? But would she listen…? Never… and now, and now she's damaged the child. Kate has to learn about all these… hidden things, but not the way she did it… and certainly not all at once. Frightening… no, terrifying the poor child… she could have learned so much…' Magh trailed off again, so obviously agitated.

'What sort of things would you have taught her?' asked Matty.

'How to change the weather so the harvests are good and food supply is plenty, cure people who can be cured; her insight and wisdom would have been invaluable moving between the intelligent beings in the other worlds and ours, learning and passing on information to us here… but it's all wasted and a child of the two worlds lost.' Magh became distraught again.

'And to think… when she couldn't have her way with the child,' she paused, tears running down her wrinkled face which Matty felt was like worn leather. 'She was going to sacrifice her… I can't…' Matty witnessed a sob like he never experienced before.

'How did you rescue her Magh… get her away from Cruachain?' Matty was alarmed at the word sacrifice, he hadn't even considered death and it certainly would have killed Kate in the human form. He asked again out of overwhelming curiosity and he felt it was the time for a positive diversion for Magh.

'What?' she asked, turning her upper half, which had been bent over her knees and looking up at him with her head turned towards him as if seeing him for the first time.

'Cruachain, how did you get Kate away from her?' he persisted.

'Oh that,' she replied sitting upright and crossing her knees, 'that's not something you want to be bothered about.'

'Do I have to explain to you again about why?' he asked, keeping his tone even despite his aggravation at what felt like prevarication.

'Alright son, alright, you want it… well here it comes,' she leaned against the high back of the long seat. 'Cormac went all the way to Roscommon, directly to the cottage by the lake,' she explained but her eyes were far away, again reliving the rescue.

'Was he able to see Kate… the form she was in then?' asked Matty.

'Oh yes, no problem there, Cormac has the second sight,' she replied, still deep in thought.

Matty waited patiently for her to carry on.

'He grazed as he was told and waited for Kate to appear… and I don't know how but something in her was drawn to Cormac… she must have recognised him despite the fear she had been living in…' she trailed off, a smile on her lips.

'Did Kate climb on his back?' asked Matty impatiently.

'She did just that,' said Magh, 'eventually,' moving her head slightly from side to side, still smiling, the tracks of wet from the tears still visible on the old skin.

'And through water Kate emerged into our world,' continued Matty.

'Precisely, once Cormac dived deep into the lake there was nothing that mad witch could do,' Magh said quietly, still smiling.

'And that's when Kate became conscious in hospital,' added Matty.

'Exactly, you've got it son, that's it exactly,' she was nodding her head; small nods.

'What an animal. Good old Cormac,' said Matty, relieved.

'It was simple in the end,' she said wistfully.

'But it worked,' added Matty happily, absorbing the old woman's mood.

'Now that we have her back, son, we will have to be on our guard,' she became solemn.

'Cruachain may try to take her back,' Matty confirmed.

'Try to kill her again, more like,' she replied.

'Kill Kate?' Matty asked, the temporary safety vanished.

'If she can't have her she will destroy her,' Magh said.

'What are we going to do?' asked Matty thoughtfully. 'What can *you* do?'

'Like I said before, you will be the go-between… I'll give you protection, and your grandmother's house… and I'll have to renew the protection for Kate and her house, in light of what you have told me, son.' She slowed the last phrase after the frantic pace of the first. She appeared to be alert and purposeful.

'What sort of thing should I watch out for?' Matty asked, 'and how do I contact you? We live a mile apart.'

'I need time to plan… no half measures this time, the child's life depends on it,' she said to herself.

Magh rose and approached the hearth again. She hung a blackened pot, just like one he saw in his grandmother's haggard, and swung the metal arm over the flames which were rising between the newly placed logs. The pot had three short legs and a small lid compared with the circumference of the belly of the pot. His grandmother's no longer had the lid and she used it for chicken feed.

'It's nearly supper time,' she said as she looked out at the approaching darkness.

Matty thought about his relatives and then dismissed the thought. This was more important and anyway Magh would find a way for him to go back.

'Do you like soup?' she asked.

'Very much, please,' replied Matty and his tummy rumbled right on queue. He hadn't eaten since breakfast time.

SAMHAIN

MACHA SLEPT ALL through the warming of Magh's soup. She took a large ceramic bowl from the dresser and tipped the liquid contents – *which were pale green*, Matty noticed – into the warmed pot suspended over the leaping flames, which reached the bottom of the pot. *It was the type of pot seen on advertisements with leprechauns*, Matty thought; he also wondered *if all their food was green?*

'Sit over by the table, son, this will be ready in no time,' she said as she cut slices from brown bread which looked like his grandmother's. Soda bread, his father called it, and he loved it. The cross across it was to symbolise the cross on all donkeys' backs, since the one that carried Mary and the baby Jesus to safety when the Romans slaughtered all the newly-born baby boys: that's what his grandmother told him ages ago when he asked her why she put a cross on the bread before baking it.

This bread tasted even better than his grandmother's did. Magh spread butter on it and passed it to him. *Was she a good cook or was some of her magic in it?* he wondered.

When they were almost finished their soup Macha stirred.

'Supper is ready,' Magh called out to him. She set another bowl down at the table after filling it from the pot which was now suspended from the side of the hearth, away from the flames.

'We'll move back to the fire, son,' she urged.

'Could we get back to our strategy to protect Kate?' asked Matty in battle mode, as he seated himself in the original position he had been in when he was first wrapped in the red blanket. Magh sat opposite, in Macha's spot.

'Well you see the trouble is that it's Samhain and it's a dangerous time, especially for Kate. In fact I'm sure Cruachain will try again.' She lowered her voice, speaking as if talking to herself.

'When does it finish, I mean the dangerous time?' Matty asked, jolting her out of her thoughts.

'We're probably not safe until the winter solstice,' she said, still in automatic speech.

'What makes it easy for Cruachain now…?' asked Matty, who had risen and stood in front of the tattered, smoke-yellowed calendar which hung on a nail over the seat where Macha had snored all afternoon as the storm raged outside.

'It is because the barriers between your world and the supernatural are dissolved for a short period. Humans, spirits and whatever can penetrate each other's space, it's a time of imbalance.' She stopped talking.

'Like Mabon,' Matty said helpfully, seating himself on the seat facing Magh again, a little away from the fire as that side was red-hot.

'Nothing like Mabon, son, much more turbulent,' she said.

'And you think Cruachain will make a move?' he asked, keeping his voice low.

'It would be the easiest time for a snatch,' replied Magh.

'But why would she kill Kate… why not try to snatch her back?' Matty asked.

'She knows that she would never get her back fully because of me, so rather than leave her be she will try to kill her, I'm pretty sure,' Magh said, her eyes looking at the window but far away in thought.

'She's an evil woman,' Matty said.

'Don't be shocked, son, haven't you met evil before?' Magh looked straight at him.

'I forgot for a minute,' he said, memories of the Minotaur surfacing.

'It's easy to forget… fortunately,' she said to herself. 'I hope Kate will forget, in time.'

'What sort of thing should I be on the lookout for, Magh?' he asked earnestly and then stopped.

'I forgot to tell you,' he said, his eyes moved but his head stayed still, as he thought.

'What, what did you forget to tell me?' she asked, brightening a little, as if she was dragging herself out of a desultory mood.

'The branch… I saw an apple branch, full of blossom,' he said.

'You what?' she asked.

'When did you see this?' she was intent and fully focused.

'Yesterday,' he replied and he was reassured that she felt the significance that he felt it had.

'But it wasn't there when I went back, I searched and searched… I'm sure I saw it,' he said, wishing he had a petal to prove it.

'Don't worry, that's how it is with them,' she said.

'You believe me?' he asked.

'It's a message from the White Goddess – why wouldn't I believe you?' she said smiling.

'What does it mean?' he asked.

'Where did you find it?' she pursued.

'Down the Rogeen Lane,' he said.

'Oh yes, that's it, what you saw was real and it means things are getting better... what time of the day was it?' she asked.

'Twilight, I didn't have my torch, but I felt the ground where I had seen it and it was gone,' he replied.

'Twilight, oh yes, it all makes sense, that's when she comes, you know,' she said, nodding her head in assurance, so changed, so animated.

'But why give me the message, you can see her, why did she not come to you,' he asked.

'The sign was for you, son; you were lonely and desperate for Kate, the message was for you,' she explained, smiling, surveying him intensely.

'But... what precisely does it mean...?' he persisted.

'It can only come from Tir na Og, the land of the Tuatha, as you know, and that means they are looking after us first of all. Then the apple means protection and love, it is also a symbol of plenty, but for us it is clear message of protection. I think you better get dressed now son... You'll have to face home, they will be worried about you,' she said encouragingly.

'There will be another row... more scolding... I hate it,' he said.

'The rain has stopped at last, it's a good time to make a move, before it gets very dark,' she urged.

Matty stood up reluctantly. Magh moved over to the table and tended to Macha, slicing more bread for him and offering more soup which he declined. Matty dressed himself behind the clothes horse, starting with clothing below his waist while he still had the cover of the suspended jumper and shirt. However, as he seated himself and had half-pulled on his second sock, Magh, who had been seated at the table, began to giggle and alternately clasp her chest.

'Oh blessed be,' she stood.

'What's up?' asked Macha, soup spoon mid-air.

'I just now looked in on the child...' she explained, looking from Macha to Matty, beaming.

'She's back,' she continued.

'Back?' asked Matty, standing upright, one sock on and one bare foot.

'She's shouting at her father... and her grandmother, accusing them of mistreating you, threatening them... she's so powerful but using up all her energy... get your shoes on, son, we have to go, let her know you are safe,' she commanded as she pulled on her raincoat.

'Apparently they have been as far as the village looking for you, even walked along the river bank searching for you,' she continued as she put on her walking shoes.

Matty quickly tied his laces and as they opened the front door Magh asked him to bring his bicycle indoors.

'But...' he began. 'In here?' he looked at her to confirm. The bicycle was dripping wet.

'Just do it, son,' Macha urged with a pained face; he had accompanied the two to the door.

'We have to get there in a hurry, son; I don't want her to lose so much energy, she is physically very weak already and she will have to protect herself,' Magh continued to explain as she slipped her foot into a giant leather, crude slipper-like cover.

'Hold on to the handlebars, son, you'll feel a bit of a pull, but only for a few seconds, just hang on to it as hard as you can,' she ordered as she placed her arm around his waist.

Matty did what he was told. Immediately he felt the pull of the bicycle; it was so robust that he did not feel he could hold on. Just as he was opening his mouth to say he would have to let go he found himself looking right into Kate's bedroom window. He propped the handlebars against the rough, pebble-dashed surface of the wall and at the same time came eye to eye with Kate. They both smiled and she disappeared from the window.

'She's normal,' he said, turning to Magh.

'I know, son but I must go now,' she said and disappeared.

Kate flung open the back door of the bungalow, ran to Matty and grabbed him and squeezed him so close it hurt. It hurt physically and mentally. He was sure he could feel her relief at being back, free of the horrors she had seen and his too, the anticipated scolding.

'Where the hell have you been... have you any idea what...?' Uncle Liam began.

Kate released Matty, keeping a hand on one shoulder and turned to all the family faces crowded around the back door.

'Remember what I said earlier,' she warned her father.

Matty couldn't believe her attitude. She always had courage to justify herself to her father, the relationship was one of on-and-off war, but this time she had real arrogance. She sounded like the adult. She urged Matty inside and they gathered in the sitting room.

'Where were you in the storm?' asked their grandmother, gently probing, feeling Matty's trousers.

'He was in the barn; were you not Matt?' Kate answered.

'Yes,' he replied relieved, as this part of his return had no time to be planned.

'We searched all the outhouses, and we couldn't find you,' put in Nicky happily.

'Well that shows you are not very clever, doesn't it?' Kate retorted, still full of *don't challenge me* attitude.

'Which barn did you hide in, Matty?' asked Grandmother, seating herself beside him.

'Was it one of the barns here or down at home?'

'Didn't you hear me Gran? He's not going to say, why should he give away a good hiding place…? He may need it again with the way you people… his family… so-called, treat him.' These words she almost spat. They were full of truth; it drew out guilt in the adults like nothing Matty had experienced before. Magh was right: Kate was back and she was powerful.

AN IRISH BREAKFAST

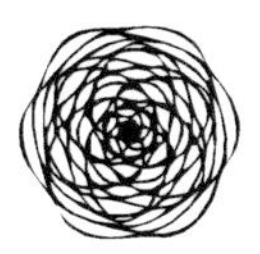

THERE WAS AN uneasy truce between uncle and nephew. Kate continued to be herself after one week and the atmosphere in both houses had what Matty felt was a sparkle. It had been exactly one week since he had seen the apple blossom branch. That particular Saturday Matty rose early as usual and informed his grandmother that he was having breakfast with Kate. There had been no protest all week and so he decided to inform rather than request and it seemed to be working in his favour. He was careful to maintain *a good little boy* attitude throughout.

When he arrived in Kate's kitchen he discovered Uncle Liam busy at the stove.

'Is Kate here?' he asked.

'She's at your house, grooming Finn,' Liam said without turning around.

She had not yet tried to ride as she knew she was not strong enough but since mid-week she groomed him daily.

'How did you know?' asked Uncle Liam as soon as Matty turned to leave the kitchen.

'Know what?' asked Matty shoulders between kitchen and porch.

'That I was making breakfast for you,' he said, half-turning to Matty oil running down the handle of a ladle in the direction of his hand and some dripping on the tiled floor.

'Are you...? I didn't know... I'm not...' Matty began. He was still afraid of the uncle who had an ambiguous way of conversing.

'Sit down there, I'm making my weekly fry up... you'll have one too, once you've tried it you'll have to have one every day, wait and see,' the uncle assured him.

Matty had hardly pulled out one of the bulky, heavy dining chairs and slid onto it when the cooked food landed on the table in front of him with a heavy thud. The fried egg lay glistening, its yellow visible and still liquid beneath the transparent membrane. Matty hated runny eggs. He loved eggs, but the yellow needed to be firm, cooked without this yellow glare. The uncle continued to cook nosily. Matty watched his broad back and large head and stared again at the large oval dinner plate laden with two of everything except for the single egg and worried.

'You had better start eating that up,' said the uncle over his shoulder, pointing the ladle in Matty's direction.

'I'll have another plate for you after you've finished that one,' he added.

Matty wished Kate would come back. Without touching any of the food, he stretched himself from his hips on the chair to the top of his head, without moving and strained himself to see if there was any sign of her in the backyard through the kitchen window. All he saw was the grey curved roof of a horse box.

Uncle Liam joined him at the table, his plate similarly laden. A mug of tea made contact with the table top with such force that Matty wondered how the liquid contents actually stayed within, he could see it rise up and subside again, without spillage.

'What do you eat for your breakfast in India?' Uncle Liam asked, the words finding their way between mouthfuls of toast and sausage.

'Sometimes pancakes, sometimes porridge and maybe idilly or dosa,' Matty began.

'Terrible, terrible things,' the uncle replied seriously, sawing his way through a rasher.

'You should never eat porridge, I'll have to have a word with your mother the next time I see her,' he added, before offloading another fork laden with white of egg and a bit of rasher.

Matty picked up his knife and fork and made a cut into one of the sausages; he liked the taste of the sausages he got in Ireland.

'I have a good friend who makes pancakes,' elucidated the uncle. 'But he only makes them once a fortnight because he lives on a boat.' He took a drink from the steaming mug.

'Why does he live on a boat?' asked Matty. He took the opportunity to encourage this more reflective aspect of this big, larger than life man. And while the uncle was staring at him but not seeing him, resting from feeding himself, Matty considered he was not the only male in the family who was larger than life. Jack was the same, the presence in the room; he would have loved feasting this early in the day and would have had no difficulty at all holding a fun-filled conversation with his uncle.

'He is a fisherman,' replied the uncle, picking up the conversation again with his fork.

'He comes home once a fortnight and cooks pancakes for his two daughters and anyone else who might drop by while he has the frying pan out,' he explained with a nod.

Matty who was still chewing the first portion of sausage had just begun to relax a little when he heard the back door open and close. He could make out Kate's blue anorak and jeans through the stained glass of the kitchen door. When she entered the kitchen she stood at the end of the dining table and unzipped her anorak while watching the diners who sat at right angles to each other. As she removed her anorak she made a declaration, in very definitive language, that Matty was under no obligation to eat the food placed in front of him.

'Leave the boy alone, will you?' the uncle replied indignantly while positioning his two hands in fists at each side of his plate with the knife and fork pointing skyward.

'That's enough food for a man,' Kate argued, returning from the porch where she had hung up her anorak, closing the stained glass door behind her.

'He is a man, well, half a man,' replied the uncle with a little grin.

Matty noted that both hands remained in fists on the table.

'Matty, just take what you want,' insisted Kate.

'What would you like?' she added, taking up a position again at the table.

Matty opened his mouth to reply but another exchange commenced between father and daughter.

'How is he meant to grow up with you fussing about him?' asked the uncle, turning to face Kate.

'Daddy, he is only ten,' she said and stopped slicing through a slice of toast.

'And he will be eleven soon,' the uncle turned to Matty with an impudent grin, his eyes sparkling.

'When I was eleven, I was climbing on roofs, driving diggers into ditches and giving everyone plenty of guff,' he said proudly, digging into the remainder of his fry.

Nicky came sleepily into the kitchen, scraped the huge beechwood chair away from the table and climbed on top.

'What do you want for breakfast, Nick?' asked Kate.

'Cereal please,' replied Nicky.

'Kate take off those boots, they smell of horse sh–' commanded the uncle, swigging the remainder of his tea.

When Kate returned from the porch once again, this time in stockinged feet, Matty asked if he could have what Nicky had; the chocolate rice crispies in Nicky's bowl were irresistible.

'Why does your dad have only one fry-up a week?' asked Matty when the uncle had disappeared.

'Because he had a heart attack,' she said with solemnity, glancing quickly at Nicky.

Matty realised that she had never shared this terrible thing she lived with. He remembered something vague about a phone call in the middle of the night in India a long time ago and asking his mother the meaning of one of the big words he had overheard – 'resuscitated', what did it mean? Both he and Jack were frightened to know Uncle Liam had died in Accident and Emergency and was resuscitated by a young Australian doctor who worked in the Wexford County Hospital.

What upset him then was that neither he nor Jack ever asked her about her own worries. All three ate in silence. Kate had made a sausage sandwich with the remainder of two sausages on Matty's plate. Matty wondered at his strange Irish relations. Kate and her father in particular, they argued and upset each other and yet lived with his terrible diagnosis. Matty felt her father teased her because he didn't know how to show her he loved her. Like Gran, they were not overtly affectionate. Neither was his Indian family; they were reserved, measured, except Grandfather's affection for Jack, but that no longer existed. The Irish side was full of hubris and madness, laughter and nicknames and then calm as if nothing had occurred. While he sank and saturated the rice crispies in the milk before bringing the cocoa-flavoured milk and cereal to his mouth, he considered that the temperament of the Irish side of his family was a little like the Irish weather. Storm fronts moved in suddenly, the slates on the roof of his grandmother's house rattled nearly all the time in the wind, it didn't matter what time of year they visited Ireland, there was always a breeze which sometimes developed into really serious weather fronts, like the one he encountered when he ran away to Magh's cottage. And then, very rarely, there was a brilliantly sunny sunrise, calm, soundless and beautiful, or a quiet dusk when the eeriness became other-worldly.

REVERBERATIONS

THEY SAT IN the kitchen of Magh's cottage, the three of them around the hearth. The elements of log and coal had by that time manifested into glowing clinkers which momentarily held their original shape and were red, yellow and orange instead of green and black and brown. Matty's cheeks reddened like those of his companions from the heat of the fire. He wallowed in the warmth, the physical, tangible heat of the fire and the other, the spiritual and indescribable warmth shared among these three. Kate was back, Magh was free of her agony as was he and the relatives, protective but joyous, but they didn't know the half of it.

'Are you able to talk about it? Tell us what happened, after that night in the tower house,' Magh asked, after some time just sitting within the security. Her tone of voice was soft, not at all probing and she turned her head from the glow in the hearth and looked straight into Kate's eyes.

From the other side of the fireplace Matty's eyes followed those of Magh's and he also looked straight at Kate who sat on a little wooden stool with a padded cushion top which was placed in front of a low table directly in front of the fireplace. The cushion was so fat it reached beyond the wood of the stool and reminded Matty of the thatch on the roof of the house with the yellow canary. That was a long rectangle farmhouse, as was the stool. They both waited. Kate didn't appear upset and in fact Matty had made up his mind as they set out from Blackstone not to bring up the terrible experience of that night or what awful tragedy had occurred. She remained calm, no adverse reaction took place as his eyes flitted from her to Magh, to the fire and back again. After some time, while she looked at her upturned palms which lay limp in her lap she spoke.

'Although it was frightening… no, absolutely terrifying sometimes…' she looked up at Magh, 'I think I can… I think I must… because it keeps coming back…' and she touched the side of her head with the palm of one hand, 'it feels like I should let it out… just to stop it rolling around inside.'

There was silence as she raised her lids and looked into the hearth. There was none of the confidence which Matty had experienced that morning when they set off on two bicycles. Kate told her mother where she was going despite the ban placed on Magh's cottage by her father, and that she would be back for lunch. Aunt Bernie had opened her mouth to protest but Kate halted the delivery of words with one firm question conveyed in a mandatory manner:

'Did you hear what I said, Mammy?'

The protective mother dared not cross this child/woman who, twenty-four hours before, she had fed and bathed like a baby. It must have seemed so sudden, that she had to relinquish all control.

But there in Magh's cottage, where Matty too had felt it safe to confess his misery, Kate became a terrified little girl whose exploits in the other-world had taught her about vulnerability, danger and even death itself.

'I was petrified,' she explained and she wiped away a large tear that escaped one lid. Magh joined Kate on the little stool which was about two and a half feet long. She placed an arm around her shoulder and Kate nestled in closer to the old woman, surrendering the hubris she displayed earlier.

'Once we left the tower house, she dragged me along by the river, I pulled and pulled my arm but her grip was so strong. I even jammed my feet into the soil but she just yanked me forward every time… and with such strength, you would not believe it. I tried hitting her with my other hand but she just ducked and pulled me along, laughing and sniggering, telling me I was a feisty one in Gailge.' Kate used the back of her hand to catch a tear that had crept down by the side of her nose. Magh used the corner of her apron to wipe that remnant and plenty more tears away. Matty noticed that once one tear started more and more followed and Kate spoke as if she had a cold.

'Eventually, after a walk that exhausted me, we came to a cottage on the edge of what seemed like a big forest. She just flung me onto the floor of a small barn-like structure near the cottage and locked the door with what sounded like a chain and a padlock. It was so dark in there… but… I could hear voices, men's voices, talking about me, again in Gailge. They kept saying she has a body, it should only be her head, why has she a body?' With this Kate started sobbing, she took huge intakes of breath and the tears became streams. Magh continued to mop with the corner of her apron and hugged Kate so close that their heads touched and Magh kept rocking her and repeating, 'There, there now.'

Matty's impulse was to grab hold of Kate too but he knew instinctively that he must stay still as Kate would not tell her horrors if she became aware of his feelings. *The best thing to do at that moment was to stay still and hope that she would rid herself of the terror.* So he sat watching the devastation, waiting for more of what he didn't want to hear but knew he must passively experience her petrifying ordeal, ever aware that she involved herself for him and for Jack. Then suddenly the tears stopped and she was off again, she had pulled away from Magh but faced her in a somewhat startled-like attitude, talking.

'At first I thought they were some sort of ghosts I hadn't the ability to see,' she said, continuing to look at Magh directly but not seeing her; it was as if she was there, back in that terrible barn, Matty thought. 'But when light came in the morning it was worse… they were heads… all placed in little alcoves, an alcove for every head.' She stopped briefly as if she needed Magh to explain, waiting for an explanation, but Magh stayed still and began to use the mopping hand to catch hold of one of Kate's hands.

Kate went on, her eyes wild, not really seeing or feeling Magh, 'I must have slept because all the heads were sleeping when the light came in, some still snoring loudly. I got up off the floor to have a better look. Their heads had been severed, there was blood and jagged skin on their necks where… where…' and she started to sob again.

'There, there now,' Magh continued to soothe her, 'these were killed by her, by keeping their heads she has power over their energy, it's a Tuatha custom.' She whispered quietly, 'Cruachain collects them… the mad woman. If the soul had no time to escape its body moments before death… then it is very difficult for the spirit to reassemble itself in the spirit world, so she gathers more energy from the discarnate.'

'I know, you're right… mad… mad and evil… and yes you are right, some of the heads are belonging to warriors, some good but mostly bad ones, they fight and argue all the time as if they are enemies and when they were not arguing they would started on me, telling me it would not be long before my head would be in an alcove too.' Kate sighed deeply, a huge sob escaped and she laid her head on Magh's shoulder.

Magh took hold of both Kate's hands with her free hand, her other arm came across to Kate's shoulder and she continued to lead Kate through her journey in the underworld – yes, the underworld, that was precisely where Kate had been, thought Matty.

'When did Cruachain show up again?' Magh asked gently.

'A long time after the light had come in… she put a bowl of what looked like porridge, terrible looking, grey it was, on the floor for me… and all I could think of was, had I taken in enough salt to counteract her magic…? I was so hungry… starving.' All this Kate said without moving her head from Magh's shoulder almost passively, with her eyes fixed on the glowing embers, sobbing now and again. Matty noticed she was not longer rosy-cheeked but pale and exhausted, with shadows beneath her eyes.

'I begged her not to lock me in with the heads when she started to fix the chain through handgrips on the door but she wouldn't listen… she told me she was not worried about me but about my friends in the other world, that was you, Magh,' Kate said, snuggling her head even further into the crook of Magh's neck and she went on.

'The day was short, just like it is for us at this time of year and I think I actually slept, from exhaustion, I guess.' With this Kate's head shot up and she turned to face Magh again. 'I had the strangest dream: I could see Cormac waiting for me by the river and this puzzled me as there was no river in the forest she had taken me through. But an idea came into my head that it may be a vision… what did you do, Magh?'

'Yes, it was me. You wouldn't have heard of the Tuatha's Dark Schools, it's where students go to study poetry, also diviners. They stay in darkened huts between sunrise and sunset in winter, which, like you just said, is not very long, so that they are always in darkness. While they are inside they concentrate on channelling information by going into trance or doing other things, this is how I managed to get past that ignorant woman and into your head. She must have been expecting an attack from elsewhere, that is why she put you with those warrior heads,' Magh explained very calmly and quietly.

'Well it worked.' Kate had become animated. 'I couldn't believe it.' Kate looked from Magh to the fire as if she was in a trance and continued a long monologue.

'So I sat on the threshold full of hope that I had help. I occupied myself with the vision of Cormac even more… but he had been beside water and there was no river or even the sound of a stream where I was in that hut. All the time the heads kept jeering. They said not long now; when she had enough gold to offer along with my body, I would be like them, murdered and cast into a lake. It was the only subject they agreed on: me, a votive offering. After some time while I covered my ears to block out their distressing conversation and heckling laughs and just when I was about to give up altogether, I had an idea… why not use the nasty men? So I turned and announced that my head would not be joining theirs and that I was there as an apprentice witch. This made them laugh and jeer even more, so I stood up and marched deep into the hut while I could see them as the light was fading and asked where might the lake or river be in which they had been sacrificed? They looked at each other, questions on their faces; some said they had been sacrificed in our world and named the lakes and I said the fact that there was none nearby proved that they were wrong and I was right, and just as I had hoped, the stupid ones burst out laughing and told me to look out the little window opposite to the alcoves. The clever heads immediately began scolding the stupid ones and the arguments went on and on as before. Sure enough, there was a lake and it had long reeds round about it just like in the dream where I saw Cormac. I wondered how I would see him in the dark of night and hoped you would help me somehow. I slept on the floor by the door while the watching heads taunted and argued among themselves. At one point I woke to find Cruachain's dark boots and long skirt just a couple of feet away from my head. I didn't move, pretended I was asleep and listened to the conversation she was having with the heads. I didn't understand every word as the dialect is old or different from modern Irish, I hoped they wouldn't mention the lake as they seemed to be talking about me being an apprentice witch…' Kate placed her head back on Magh's shoulder.

'You have been very brave, if you had not held your mind in check we would not have been able to reach you and help,' said Magh.

'They named me "Blathna",' said Kate and lifted her head and addressed Magh.

'What does that mean?' she added.

'It means little flower in English,' Magh replied.

'I think there was more to it, though; the heads laughed and jeered when they addressed me, it felt like they knew something about this Blathna that I didn't,' Kate said.

'Blathna was the wife of Cu Roi, a king and she kept his castle in the other-world. It was a frightening place where knights went to test their courage, according to myth,' Magh elucidated.

'Was she evil? I don't get their connection,' Kate replied, somewhat at peace.

'Neither do I, probably they may be referring to you belonging to our world. Blathna apparently was stolen from Cuchulain by Cu Roi, maybe they were using that comparison… you were stolen by Cruachain…' Magh said, somewhat perplexed while staring at the chimney breast.

'Wait, wait, before this you said something about help for me, what help?' Kate, although tired, was focused as usual.

'You will never believe who her sister is…' Magh had a twinkle in her eye and she looked at Matty for the first time.

'Who, whose sister?' asked Kate, head up and looking from one to the other again.

'Tell her, Matt,' instructed Magh.

'The Marshmallow,' Matty said and for some reason he could not stop smiling.

'The Marshmallow is Cruachain's sister?' said Kate with a quizzical look on her face and a half-smile appeared.

'I'll let Matt tell you all about it later,' Magh said.

'But why did it take so long?' asked Kate.

'I had to wait till Samhain, until the other-world was free of the space-time barriers which hide it from humans and other beings.' Magh moved her arm down to Kate's waist and seemed to hold her firmly. Her words too had intent. Matty felt she was apologetic for the delay or needed to impress on Kate the importance of the delay.

'I know it was ages and even longer here, over a month. But if it had not been a time of exchange between the worlds she may have noticed Cormac,' Magh used her other hand to tidy strands of hair that had become soaked with Kate's tears.

'Why Magh… I nearly died, the dream of Cormac was the only thing that kept me strong,' wailed Kate and tears began to cascade again.

'Listen darling, at Samhain all sorts of souls are on the move… and…' Magh looked up, 'how can I explain this without causing you more pain?'

'Go on,' said Kate, sniffling and wiping her eyes in the sleeve of her sweat shirt.

'Cruachain adheres to customs, I had this information from Sister Perpetual. I had a strong feeling you were going to be a sacrifice to the Lord as one year ended and New Year began; a lot of the Tuatha still do it at Samhain. There are things about the Tuatha dé Danann that are… difficult to accept, but this is what they do… some of them… human sacrifice…' Magh looked back at Kate who seemed composed, considering that she had just found out why she was being martyred.

'Just as it is normal in our world for the souls of dead ancestors to visit at Halloween it is the same in the other-world. So I had just one opportunity, just a few short hours in our time to whisk you away. I knew Cruachain would leave all the doors and windows open to invite in not just the souls of her ancestors but powerful kings… her power source,' Magh continued in her intensity until Kate interrupted.

'Like the Dagda,' she said without tears.

'No more like Lugh, he's a sun god and this was a solar festival,' reminded Magh.

'And she did,' interjected Kate. 'I didn't know it was Halloween and one night she left the barn doors wide open and warned that if I went outside the heads would call out to her. So I sat on the threshold and as I sat watching the stars the image of Cormac came into my mind again. I stood up and checked the window overlooking the lake and there he was, staring back at me. It was a lovely night, I could see him clearly in the starlight. When I went back to the threshold I sat down just outside the doors. The heads started warning me and I tried playing a game with them. I told them as it was my last night with my head on my body I just wanted to feel the air and enjoy the starlight. Of course this set off an argument between them. The more compassionate ones, which were few, agreed that I should enjoy the night air. So I stayed put and they didn't shout. Slowly I let my head loll to one side as if I was asleep and listened to what they were saying. When they were in the midst of one of their arguments I slipped away and ran as fast as I could and jumped on Cormac's back and that was it… I woke up in a hospital in this world, safe but weak… but still afraid.' Kate began sobbing quietly again.

'You brave, brave girl,' Magh coaxed. 'You have faced and overcome great danger… and… you are safe now… and strength will come back and you will be stronger than ever you were before.'

With that there was a knock on the door and Aunt Bernie emerged slowly into the room.

'I just came to see how she was getting on, it's her first day out…' She had an apologetic approach and hesitated.

'Very wise,' Magh rose to greet the visitor. 'Have you got the car with you? I think she could do with a drive home.'

Kate did not argue, she pulled on her coat wearily and was led outside to the awaiting car. She slid into the front seat exhausted, her head needing all the support of the headrest. Matty collected the little red and white bicycle while Aunt Bernie loaded Kate's into the boot of the car.

'See you in the evening,' Matt said to Kate while zipping up his anorak.

'See you Matt,' she raised her hand behind the closed window.

Matt waved goodbye to Magh and Aunt Bernie and began pedalling uphill in the direction of his grandmother's house. He was shocked at how physically weak Kate was. It reminded him of his mother's tiredness after a bout of diarrhoea and vomiting due to amoebiasis in India: energy-less. But she always recovered, he reassured himself, and he was sure Kate would get her energy back too. He was relieved she had let go of some of the terror and he was sure she would be less remote and afraid from now on. He reflected on Magh's way of life as he pressed down on the pedals in order to get a little more speed out of the bike. It was just another challenge for Magh, having to outwit the hag of the other-world and he, himself a witness to all these things. *Worlds that are conventionally hidden except at the quarterly festivals when the time-space continuum is weak*, he thought. *But who would know such things, incredible for all but a few human beings? He had proof though, proof with his own eyes in the gaeltacht of Connemara and now again, as a spectator of Kate's experience which he knew was real, as real as any experience in this world.*

DEATH MESSENGER

ANOTHER WEEK WENT by and the possibility for him to attend school was being discussed, even though he had been keeping up with homework set for him by his school in India. Gran checked him every day, Monday through to Friday, on all subjects, mostly in the afternoons when she had finished cooking the main meal and they had eaten and she had washed up and swept the kitchen floor. After a little nap while watching a magazine programme on TV and when she had a milky coffee and a biscuit, she would join him at the kitchen table and he too would have his milk biscuits. She was patient and interested in his studies, especially in Social Science; she said children didn't do this in Ireland and she felt it was a good idea. Matty felt she was really good at Maths and English but Hindi she left to him and he really couldn't progress much with it and just practised his alphabets.

Kate seemed stronger too; he was allowed to visit in the evenings before dark and just for an hour or two when Nicky returned from school. They usually sat together in the sitting room all three and watched TV. Matty was keen on a programme called *Bosco* and he would cycle to his grandmother's house afterwards, as it was almost dark by then. Although Kate did not interact much with him or Nicky, she was 'normal', not staring out the window like before. One evening, when Aunt Bernie had to go out, she went to the freezer in the utility room and returned with massive soup bowls piled high with ice cream. Matty began to relax.

Some nights after that he was woken up by the sound of screeching, although he didn't realise it at first. The room was dark. Matty, who was used to street lighting because he had lived either in towns or big cities in India, lay quietly in bed and waited; perhaps he dreamt the sound. He consoled himself with what he remembered his mother had said when he had nightmares in Madras after the kidnapping: day residue, incidences of the day rolling around in his subconscious brain. Then this led to other thoughts: Kate had not screamed, she had cried quietly and sobbed an awful lot at Magh's a week or two ago, but she never screamed.

Then as he felt his limbs sink into the relaxed state just before sleep, he heard it again. There was a screech or a shriek. He was sure he had not dreamt it. He sat bolt upright and waited. How long had it been since the first cry, how many more had there been that he hadn't heard…?

His grandmother's bedroom door opened, the sound of her slippers moved about on the carpet in the hall and then stopped as if waiting. She too had heard it.

The following one was unmistakable. Like the others it seemed to reverberate all around, from near and far away alternatively, a shriek that ended in a type of wail. Matty jumped out of bed and stood in front of his grandmother in the hallway.

'What is that noise Gran?' he demanded. 'It sounds like someone crying…'

'It must be a fox… a vixen,' she said quietly, mechanically. He could see in the light from the hall, which she left on at night so that he could get his bearings, that she was so upset by the sound she did not have the ability to make the reassurances credible.

'Gran, I know about nocturnal habits of cats and dogs. This is not an animal, Brandy is barking as if he wants to attack someone or something.' His conviction was beyond appeasing her and more especially the look on her face contradicted the vixen excuse.

'Whist, shii,' these sounds she made while placing a forefinger on her lips, obviously disturbed but obsessed with the phenomena.

He ran back to his room and pulled the curtains aside and lifting the net curtain he watched Brandy lunging and retreating, barking all the time furiously at the corner of the whitewashed wall surrounding the backyard. He leaned into and towards the window pane which had a very wide sill, trying to get a better view of the road and that side of the wall which induced so much attention from the little Jack Russell. Matty was not tall enough. Then, just as he turned, he was about to drag a chair across the room, he saw it with the corner of one eye: a being, just a little shorter than himself with waist-length grey hair and such a wrinkled old face. It was a woman, the oldest woman he had ever seen. He looked again and she had gone. Had he imagined it? He moved towards and then sat on his bed; he felt ice-cold, especially all down his back.

'What did you see?' demanded his grandmother who had been watching him from the bedroom doorway.

'Nothing… I think I saw something… like a dwarf… I think,' he replied truthfully, shaken.

'A dwarf,' she repeated, 'that's strange,' and after a long pause during which she seemed to be thinking a lot, her hand had touched her chin, she spoke again. 'It must have been a shadow,' she said.

'Try to go back to sleep,' she urged after a little while in the uneasy silence. She put his legs and feet up on the bed and pulled the blankets over him.

'Brandy has settled down now, you know how every little thing upsets him, crows flying over, pigeons… sheep bleating,' she said all this while closing the curtains as if she was trying to convince herself, glancing but not glancing out into the darkness at the same time, as if she was afraid to.

'Goodnight, Gran,' Matty said in the same tone he used every night as a form of assurance, having collected himself.

But he wasn't assured and he knew neither was his grandmother. *Why had the noise upset this confident, feet firmly on the ground person so much… and what had he seen, was it from the other-world and if so why was it screaming outside on the road between the two houses?*

Matty didn't sleep for ages; he lay awake in the still darkness. *The noise, whatever it was could not be ignored, especially his grandmother's reaction to it. And the creature, in the floor-length nighty… was it a nightdress exactly? It was certainly floor-length and white, otherwise his eyes would not have caught it, it was really dark. He managed to see the face though. She had the oldest face he had ever seen and what a strange height.* When the blurred light of dawn began to penetrate the curtain slit, where the edges didn't meet he finally fell into a deep sleep.

When he eventually woke he could hear the sound of pots and Brandy was warning off pigeons as usual. *His bark must have woken me*, Matty considered. Matty reached for his watch in the gloom; the room was a dusky red produced as the light filtered through the curtain fabric, not light enough for him to see the old wind-up clock with the yellowing face on the chest of drawers. It was a quarter to midday, Gran was making dinner. For just one anxious moment the thought appeared in his mind of how he was going to force-feed himself with a main meal without an appetite; he dismissed it. No, he had more important things to do: he must see Magh before anything or anyone else.

When he reached the thatched cottage he dismounted at a trot, flung the bicycle into the hawthorn hedge and burst in through Magh and Macha's front door. He briefly registered Macha in the little barn-like structure to the side of the cottage; he was tying bunches of plants with twine. Matty forgot to acknowledge him. Once inside the front door Magh looked up startled; she was seated on the little stool where Kate had sat on the previous visit. At each side of the stool stood two long candles which were lit.

'Sorry… I'm sorry,' Matty said and turned towards the door.

'Son, son, don't go, I was just divining,' Magh stood up and bent to extinguish the candles.

'I'm a bit worried about something, I thought you were the best person to ask,' Matty blurted out.

'Come in, come in, sit down,' she reassured him. 'What's up?'

'Noise in the night, actual shrieking… and the… the… being, so old… I can't get her out of my mind,' Matty said. He had not given himself enough time to plan how he would describe the incident to Magh. After he dressed, his grandmother, knowing his constitution, offered to keep his dinner warm until supper time; he just took off on the bicycle, telling her he was going to work up an appetite. The whole night crying thing seemed much more frightening with afterthought and daylight carried no reassurances at all.

'Tell me from the beginning, here let me take your anorak, otherwise you'll feel the cold when you go out again,' Magh said.

The mundane act of settling himself in Macha's corner on the bench near the fire relaxed Matty a good deal. He wasn't cold, not after the speed at which he had travelled to the cottage, he just felt safe there.

'I don't know what time it was… I forgot to check my watch,' Matty's mind wandered back to the bedroom. 'I woke up… I was probably woken by the sound of the shriek, sort of a screech that ended like a… a wail, coming from all around the house, outside the house. The dog was really angry and barking at something on the wall around the backyard, at the side near the road,' he said looking at Magh, hoping it made sense.

She appeared puzzled.

'Gran was up too… she said it was a vixen… but I knew she didn't mean it, she was listening… she actually told me to be quiet… she was listening… why was she listening so much?' he asked.

Magh looked a little concerned but said nothing.

'Then I saw it… her.'

'You saw who, who did you see, son? Think very hard…' Magh was intent.

'The old woman, a really, really small old woman,' he replied, 'at first I thought it… she was a little girl sitting on the wall. But then she stood up and turned and looked straight into my bedroom window. I got a fright, she had such an old face and her hair was so thin and wispy.'

Magh gasped and stood up. Matty joined her in the middle of the kitchen floor, near her dining table which was strewn with recently cut herbs; he was aware of the mildly astringent but refreshing smell.

'You know who she is, the tiny old woman, don't you?' he questioned her.

'I think I do… or rather I hope I'm wrong…' she trailed off, one hand across her heart, she turned and began to stare out the little window at the back of the cottage.

Matty followed softly and when he was beside her he said quietly, 'Tell me.'

'Did Kate hear it… the sound… last night,' Magh asked impatiently.

'I don't know, I came straight to tell you… I haven't seen Kate, I slept late because I couldn't sleep last night,' Matty explained. 'It all happened in a second but it was awful.'

'Hopefully she didn't hear it,' Magh said as she pressed her palms down on the top of a chest of drawers underneath the window.

'Why hopefully?' asked Matty.

Magh turned from the window and sat on the long stool in front of the dining table. She turned towards him and caught hold of both his arms just above his elbows.

'Listen son, the being you saw is the *badhb*,' Magh said very earnestly and she began to look beyond him.

'If Kate has not heard it then it is a warning for me,' she whispered almost to herself. 'That will be your next job, son… no wait…' she released his arms and stood up, 'I'll come with you.'

'Magh, I don't understand. First of all what is the *bad*, *badh*… whatever it is, tell me,' he insisted. At that time and particularly because of Magh's reaction he was becoming even more concerned.

'Have you never heard stories of the banshee?' she asked, turning towards him.

'No,' he answered firmly.

'She is a being from the other-world who appears when someone is about to die,' she replied, softening her voice again, encouraging him back into the corner of the bench beside the fire.

'Would my grandmother know that?' he asked as he slid on to the bench.

'Yes, she would,' replied Magh, seating herself opposite.

'Well, why was she listening so much? Does the banshee say something besides wailing?' he asked.

'They usually say the name of the person who is going to die,' she replied, still in her caring voice.

That all made sense to Matty; however uneasy as he was, he had to know, to understand. He needed to know everything and then… maybe he could help Kate.

'I only heard the wailing and the shrieking,' he said.

'Right, we've got work to do,' Magh said and stood up and undid the strings of her apron.

'What are we going to do?' he asked, rising too.

'You must not worry, son, I'm almost sure this is a warning for me, a visit to Kate will prove that,' she patted him on the shoulder 'Get your coat son, we're off.'

'Why do you think it's a warning and who is going to die and how will visiting Kate prove anything?' he asked while struggling with the zip of his anorak. The metal part just would not slide into the coupling for him; it was because his hands were shaking. Retelling, particularly describing the Banshee brought the fear he had felt when the face became visible in the dark the previous night.

'Firstly, son,' she said while pulling on her raincoat, 'the *badhb* visits only old Irish aristocratic families… and your family is composed of a Celtic and Norman mix; your grandmother's family may have the crest of the boar but the royal connection is too far back to have the *badhb* visit. Secondly, I bet you a packet of milk biscuits that Kate had a good night's sleep.' She had finished winding a brightly coloured woollen scarf around her neck and knelt in front of Matty to zip up the anorak, achieving the result he just couldn't manage, causing him annoyance and inadequacy.

'How do you know?' he put those feelings aside and asked her.

'A hunch, son, just a hunch,' she replied, collecting her handbag from a hook inside a cupboard beside the fireplace.

'I meant the milk biscuits,' he said.

'Oh, you just seem like a milk biscuit sort of fella,' she replied, ushering him out the front door.

'We're off,' she waved to Macha, 'on *badhb* business.'

Macha nodded, raised his eyebrows, rolled his eyes and returned to hanging the tied bunches of green. All this horror seemed just routine for them but Matty needed confirmation.

When they reached the little green gate Magh halted.

'I've forgotten the most important thing,' she said, sounding annoyed.

Matty followed her inside again and watched as she went to a little cupboard, hung high on a wall in the darkest corner of the living room. She carefully fingered the tiny dark brown bottles; some were dark indigo, Matty noticed, but Magh rotated the brown ones – *to see the labels*, he figured. Finally she chose one, put it in her handbag, closed the cupboard door and announced again, 'Now we're ready for the road.'

'Who is warning you? You said before that someone was warning you,' he asked, wheeling his bicycle out on to the road.

'Cruachain… but she is trying to frighten us, warning is not the right word,' explained Magh.

'Would the bad banshee be able to grab a human and take them to the otherworld?' Matty asked as they walked in the direction of Blackstone.

'Precisely,' replied Magh, head held high as she maintained a purposeful walk. 'As long as Kate stays together, meaning no astral travel, the *badhb* or Cruachain can do nothing.'

'Well… there's her Great-Uncle Mike, he was her age when he died… and her grandfather… but not often you understand, just sometimes, now and again…' Magh trailed off.

'She never told me,' came the soft and lowered voice of Aunt Bernie.

'Well she wouldn't… teenagers you know, they think they know it all… that's why she comes down to me, she talks, I listen… I give her advice on how to deal with it… when it occurs…' Magh's voice trailed off again.

'So… Galway, what really happened?' Aunt Bernie asked.

'I think she may have seen ghosts… or spirits, maybe both. I'm trying to get it out of her… it's difficult… to get her talking. But she must talk, because… well because…I think she got a terrible fright over there, that old castle, dead nuns. Old buildings carry lots of energy, energy left behind…' Magh again trailed off.

'Yesterday… when I came to collect her… was she… had she been talking…? I only ask because she was so exhausted…' Magh answered before Aunt Bernie could finish.

'Yes, she talked a little… mainly she relived the fear… that's what made her cry, exhausted her,' Magh said.

'Is there a lot… how much more…?' Bernie began.

'Not much, you said she is out and about already today, I think it did her good,' Magh reassured.

'Did she tell you what frightened her?' asked Bernie.

'She described a witch and funny shaped animals, the sort of things a person dreams about in nightmares,' explained Magh, Matty noticed how economical she was with the explanation.

'Do you think she actually saw them?' questioned the aunt.

'I'm not sure,' replied Magh's voice, 'time will tell and talking will help.'

'Well, thank you for helping her,' said the aunt. 'What are the rowan branches for?'

'To keep the *badhb* away,' Magh said.

'So the witch in Galway was real then, not a dream?' questioned Aunt Bernie.

'Maybe… the *badhb* may be around for another person; she was not sitting on the wall of your house, it was the home place she choose… but no harm to take precautions… with the rowans… anyway,' came the economical reminder.

'Is there anything else I can do to protect her?' asked the aunt.

'Holy water, lots of it, sprinkle it all over her bedroom. Get some coal and mark out a ward, preferably all about the edges of the whole compound, if you can't do that just mark the boundary of her room with it, all along the floor. Gort, ivy, use plenty, you may notice she has some in her pockets, leave it there… always, put some along the window sill of her bedroom too… I think that is all, if there is any more I will let you know, oh and this, slip three teaspoons of it into a hot drink at bedtime.' Matty imagined the little brown bottle coming out of Magh's handbag.

'What is this for?' he could hear the puzzled question.

'It's important that she doesn't dream for the next few nights, this sort of paralyses the brain…'

'Paralyse?' protested Aunt Bernie, the words cut across Magh's explanation.

'Not the way she was before… you see, if she dreams they may get hold of her… somehow…'

'I'm not sure…' Aunt Bernie's doubtful voice trailed off.

'It's one of my own, trust me, it's safe, put it in her cocoa and she will snore the house down.'

Matty heard the handle of the door to the utility room rotate and prepared to leave but just had to resist pressing down on the pedal when Magh's voice added:

'Oh, as well as that… make her sleep on the bedroom floor with a circle of salt all around her on the floor.'

'What…?' came the bewildered reply.

'You'll have to go up to the village… no… go to Wexford, a supermarket and buy several kilos of it… people in the village may wonder what you are doing with so much salt.'

'But why?' came the reply.

'She needs grounding, mother earth will keep her safe,' came Magh's voice.

'How am I going to explain all this?' came the astounded voice of the aunt.

'Only Kate needs to know and I'll prepare her, tell her that you know about all her troubles,' explained Magh and added, 'Oh come on, how often does Liam or the little boy go into her room? It'll work, trust me.'

Magh appeared to finish and Matty mounted the little bike and peddled around the gable end of the bungalow out onto the road and turned in the direction of the stable.

THE GROVE

SEVERAL DAYS AND nights passed without other-worldly interference from Matty's perspective; all that time he hoped Magh had control of Kate's protection. Even though his admission to the local primary school had not been discussed, at least not in his presence, there was talk of Kate returning to secondary school at the Sunday lunch that week – and should she travel in by car with her father or catch the school bus? This went on and on and Kate even participated a little. Gran suggested just part-time until her strength was back; she pointed out the days were long, no opportunity for a nap like at home. And that settled it. Matty noticed that Kate's bedroom door remained closed and the children used the sitting room or the kitchen when the adults relaxed after the heavy meal. Often he accompanied Kate to the stable on weekend afternoons if it wasn't raining and watched her put Finn through his paces over horse jumps in the high field and that is where he found himself that particular Sunday. He usually sat on the top rung of the tubular gate shivering as the piercing wind nipped at every nerve ending in his body despite the warmth of Jack's old anorak which was Arctic-proof due to his asthma and the fear of developing a cold on his trips to Ireland. Matty sat, as usual, blowing warm air from his mouth through the woollen gloves on his hands, noting how Kate was almost as strong as before. Her parents would not yet give her permission to go to the borough alone which he felt was no bad thing. He remembered Jack's explanation of her relationship with the people of the Sidhe and that was where she had made her initial contact. He climbed down and stamped about to keep his toes from freezing inside his leather shoes. Life was becoming normal again but deep down Matty had come to expect there would always be undercurrents in Kate's life and those who shared it with her.

The following Saturday Kate arrived at her grandmother's house after lunch and confided in Matty that she was to meet Magh in the village and whispered he should wear waterproofs. Matty pulled on his anorak, grabbed a woollen cap and gloves from its pockets and asked 'What about Gran?' while pulling on Wellington boots. Kate whispered that they were to meet at the grove in Duncormick. Matty didn't know the area and was excited at the change to their usual route, Hedge Cottage. It was not only the prospect of a change of scene that had raised his spirit; Magh had asked him if he would carry her in her squirrel form in his bag. This encounter he had on waking in the early morning over the white-washed walls surrounding the backyard while throwing the little Jack Russell a dog biscuit. Magh was walking down the lane towards the house; she stopped by casually for what was only a moment.

'Ah, is that yourself?' she said and then in almost inaudible words he was instructed to leave the Crane Bag in the porch, on a hook, the porch door always open and unlocked until bedtime. Matty was aware of his grandmother stirring her porridge in the back kitchen on the cooker top and he approached the wall with a question. She would not say why, just thrust the question into the air as she did when she wanted to avoid a straight answer and breezed on down the lane. He accepted this due to the fact that Kate had been having instruction at Hedge Cottage recently on how to protect herself, how to use her own energy and how to deflect others'. The thought that it might be part of a lesson satisfied his curiosity and he ran inside to avoid the chill aware he did not have his coat on.

The grove was situated at the far side of the village along by the river bank. Kate and Matty extracted permission to collect chestnuts. Their grandmother told them that Nicky was too young to be so close to the river and warned them not to tell him they where they were going. She was not too keen on Matty going either but after several reminders on safety she agreed.

'It's too late in the year for chestnuts anyway,' she argued. 'Why now, why this sudden urge?'

'Matty has never played conkers, neither does he know where to find chestnuts,' Kate replied; she was well able to get her way with her grandmother, she had a lifetime of practice. *This was the old Kate*, thought Matty, *she was back.* It had pleased him immensely.

'Well I doubt you will play conkers, even if you do find any, the chestnuts will be soggy by now,' the grandmother went on while Kate slipped out the kitchen door. Kate pointed a curled index finger in Matty's direction while the grandmother kept her attention on kneading dough for soda bread, a once-a-week treat from brown bread and it had sultanas in it.

'Where is she?' Kate asked him impatiently. They had parked their bicycles and were leaning against the bridge in the afternoon winter sun. Matty was amazed there was actually heat in it – a little, but it reached him. The wall of the bridge was only waist-high for Matty and he couldn't help thinking how beautiful it was. The opposite bank was covered with the skeletons of deciduous trees, the ground rose high and it was covered with them. On the opposite side the village spread out: a farmhouse and then a couple of pubs stretched along from their side of the bridge and a garage, followed by a row of cottages on the other side. The road dipped into the village and rose steeply up a long, steep hill leading out of the village.

'Where does that lead?' asked Matty.

'You know the aunt Maura and her brothers?' asked Kate.

'Yes,' replied Matty,

'They live about a mile or two along but there are many turns, don't go without me, you'll get lost,' she instructed him firmly.

After several more minutes Kate began to climb down on the hill side of the bridge. Matty followed.

'Where can she be?' she asked as she loitered, raising soggy leaves with the toes of her boots. This action caused acute discomfort for Matty. He remembered the wood in Galway, when Kate intuited danger when she played then too with the leaves on a forest floor the night she was taken. The fact that Magh had asked him to keep her hidden in his Crane Bag in her squirrel form suddenly set off an alarm. Before he could compute this connection a man emerged out of the woods.

'What are you two doing here so near to the river?' his question was friendly.

'Looking for chestnuts,' Kate answered casually.

'Isn't it a bit late in the year for that?' he asked.

'My cousin hasn't seen them before, he's from India,' she used the same type of persuasion she had used on their grandmother.

'I know who he is and you will not find any chestnuts, the squirrels will have had them all by now,' the man said, smiling to himself as he climbed up the muddy path on to the road.

'Can't you see that the river is swollen and there is fast moving current,' he warned from the bridge and began walking in the direction of the village.

'Come on Matt, let's walk into the woods a bit, the adults feel they have to safeguard us here and Magh will find us,' she explained.

They tramped through the wet leaves. Some part of the ground was slippery and other parts were squelchy; there was very little firm, dry earth.

'Kate, what's going on?' demanded Matty. He was angry with himself for not noticing the signs; the very fact that he had been asked to hide a squirrel in his Crane Bag should have alerted him – and now her mood, one of fear.

'Nothing, Matt,' she replied impatiently.

'I have a really bad feeling, Kate… and you're not telling me everything,' he reached forward in a half-run and pulled firmly on the sleeve of her anorak in an effort to make her turn around and stop plodding away from him on the ground cover of moist, decaying leaves.

She whirled around about to confront him but her eyes were pulled up the slope, among the trees.

'Ah, there's Cormac,' she said and advanced on to a raised bank to get a better view. 'Thank God, I thought something had happened to them.'

'Them… who?' asked Matty joining her and just catching a glimpse of the jennet as he melded with the tree trunks.

'I'm not supposed to say,' she answered softly and began to try lifting damp leaves with the toe of her riding boots again.

'Why the riding boots, Kate?' he demanded. She was always so careful of her riding gear, aware of the expense of it all and she certainly never used the boots for walking other than to the stable.

'Come on, Kate, why are we really here?' He was shouting at her.

'I told you I can't say… I can't even think things…' she was agitated, walked about in circles, half-looking at him, sometimes holding up her arms. 'Matt, don't push me, I'm sorry you have to be here, but like before… I need you.'

'It was your idea to come here today, what's going on…? I have a right to know,' Matty was furious at being kept in the dark.

'Yes, yes you have a right to know, that's true… will you just… just trust me then, please just trust me,' she pleaded.

He turned away from her, into the last orange-red glow of the setting sun. *It will be dark soon*, he thought and then it made sense: the Winter Solstice must be very near. He had forgotten dates, there were lots of Christmas advertisements on TV but there was none of the usual excitement within the family, Gran kept on repeating, *it will be nice to have your Mammy home for Christmas*, that's all, nothing else. *What date was it? It must be the shortest day, sacred to the ancient Celts, that was it, something was going on.* He checked his watch: only just gone three and the sun had already gone. He looked at Kate; she was looking around her, watching through the trees, uneasy, terribly uneasy. Matty began searching for Cormac among the tree trunks but the animal being the same colour and with twilight the light was more difficult to see in than darkness itself. That led to another thought form: was there a moon the night he heard the banshee? He couldn't remember. His grandmother kept an outside light on all night so it was difficult to know as the yard was well-lit. As if picking up on his anxiety he felt the squirrel move on his back, inside his bag.

CORMAC

'MATT, WE MUST go deeper into the grove,' Kate said, looking in the direction of the bridge but turning away from it.

He put on his unwilling face and trudged along behind her, trying to make a plan of action which he was sure would involve the other-world. *What defences had he against that? He had his torch; it would be dark soon and had Kate taken that into account? It was already twilight.* After a very short walk she stopped and allowed her rucksack to slide off her shoulder on to the ground. It looked heavy, something he had not noticed before. She undid the clips; even the snap sound made Matty tense. When she pulled out a plastic pack of salt which must have weighed at least one kilo, his heart sank to depths he didn't know he could feel. He wanted to scream at her, *Are you really ready for this?* but she was in a fearful state like him. He stood frozen while she picked up a stout twig and made a wide circle with it.

'Can I help?' he managed to utter.

'I need your penknife to cut the bag.' She indicated the bag of salt on the ground beside her bag and like him she had hardly any voice.

He slid his bag off his shoulders, careful that it must not land roughly; his only hope – *their only hope* – was the shape shifting squirrel inside. He was careful to open the mouth of the bag away from Kate's line of sight. For a second he wondered how he was going to forage around inside to find the knife, but it appeared as soon as he undid the strings. He handed it to her and she busied herself slitting the bag just so much and began trailing the salt into the superficial channel she had made with the twig. When she had completed the circle she straightened up and put the empty plastic bag inside her rucksack and pulled out a little pot with three legs, a miniature copy of the one Magh suspended in her fireplace. Kate placed tiny pieces of kindling and small pieces of charcoal in it and struck a match from a box she pulled out of her pocket. Matty noted his knife stayed in the circle, blade unsheathed, and something inside him told him not to ask for it. She then pulled a tiny plastic bag from her pocket and threw what looked like dried herbs on to the fire in the little pot. This produced quite a nice smell, Matty felt; for another second it reminded him of the prayer room at his grandparents' house and the temple and the house at sunset when his grandmother lit a joss stick in the hallway.

Kate lifted the pot by its handle and proceeded around the circle in an anticlockwise direction, wafting the smoke from the herbs as she went. She then took out two small bottles of what looked like water and poured it onto the earth inside the circle. This reminded Matty of the tarot card, the Star, he remembered from a pack he liked looking at in Hedge Cottage while Kate and Magh chatted near the fireside. He again had a realisation: *they were not just chatting they were colluding,* while he played with a deck of cards at the table, encouraged by Magh. He felt foolish all over again and then calmed himself: *maybe this was a sacred grove and Kate was just preforming a protection prayer, spell whatever she was doing with the four elements.*

Just as he was comforting himself with that thought he felt an arm slip across his chest from behind. For a second he thought Magh had shape shifted but almost immediately he knew it was not her; the shock on Kate's face made him look down even though he already knew. Yes, that same unkempt cardiganed arm could only belong to Irnan. The nausea rose into his throat; Kate reached for the blade, Irnan laughed like the witch she was. She pulled back Matty's anorak hood and patted his woollen cap with her other hand and spoke softly in Gaelic, Matty only caught one word *buchaill*: boy. He did understand that but felt she was pretending affection with deathly purpose. He only had a glimpse of her in the tower house in Galway; this time she literally had him in her clasp. Matty could feel the strength leave his knees, he willed himself to somehow retain his energy, he screamed for Ganesh in his mind.

Kate stood solidly, knife in hand and shouted to the jennet, 'Cormac!' He came trotting out of the grove and into the circle. The witch continued patting and embracing Matty; he wanted to shrug her off but he felt he must hold onto life if only he could stand the smell of her. Kate shouted at her in Gaelic again and Matty picked two words from the torrent – *fuscailt* let go and again *buchaill* – but didn't understand their meaning of the first word. He continued to reason with his boy God in his mind, pleading with him to find him in the cold, reminding him that his father Siva lived in the cold Himalaya Mountains… However amidst his desperation he noticed that the presence of Cormac in the circle had distracted the witch. She advanced to the edge of it, letting go of him and there followed more exchanges. This time the word *Each Uisge* stood out for Matty and he knew they were talking about Cormac. Kate mounted the jennet. The witch gave a little laugh to which Kate moved her head slightly from side to side, in a little wobble and she wore a smile and a face of triumph. It was then that Matty noticed that Cormac was not wearing his bridle… which meant he had reverted to his natural state, which was savage. *Why would Magh take a chance like this, with Kate on his back, mere feet away from a deep and turbulent river? Magh*, he thought, and looked at the gaping mouth of his Crane Bag. He could see her in the dim light, alert as a squirrel could be, he felt. He had such an urge to run.

TUATHA DÉ DANANN

MEANWHILE THE EXCHANGE continued in Gaelic; the words were electric, challenging, Matty could feel the energy coming from the crone and the maiden. He caught the word *baigh*, which he later found out meant drown; it came from the witch and it was threatening. Kate put on a smug face which appeared to annoy the witch even more. The squirrel leaped forward and placed itself behind Matty. He did not move a muscle, especially the muscles of his eyes. At the same instant Kate dismounted and pointed the tip of the blade she had never let go of directly at the witch, still inside the circle of salt. The *Each Uisge* stayed still. Kate raised her left arm, pointing her hand towards the sky; she closed her eyes momentarily and kept this pose, her right arm, the blade at its end pointed towards the witch, a mere metre away. When she appeared completely composed she began speaking again in Gaelic. Matty caught only a few words, all meaningless to him: *riocht*, kingdom and *cumhach*, force. Much later Kate explained what she had been doing but at the time the unknown just added more fear to his situation. The words were strong and slow, her voice several pitches lower than Kate's normal voice: she was imposing. Matty managed to be impressed for a second when the fear was not overwhelming him. When Kate finished she pulled a tiny bottle of what looked like water from her jeans pocket, having to wiggle to get it free, all the while pointing the knife at the witch with her dominant arm. She put the bottle to her lips and unscrewed the little cap; the witch jumped away from the circle and grabbed Matty again.

'It won't hurt you Matt,' Kate cried.

'I know, do it,' Matty shouted and ran toward the edge of the salt circle. He didn't get far, Irnan had such a strong hold on him, but he hoped Kate would compensate and get the water over her back, which she did from her vantage point. Matty could feel the heat from the flames: some had landed on the cardigan sleeve centimetres from his cheek. He tried to wriggle free; fire burst forth wherever the water had landed. The witch screamed and jerked her body, the more she screamed the tighter her grip became: he was going to burn with her. He could see Kate still inside the circle, stunned, and as the witch twisted and turned in pain he lost sight of her. He noticed his Crane Bag on the leaves: where was Magh…? Then a powerful screech and he was free; he turned to find Kate outside the circle, his penknife handle lolling in the witch's forearm.

'Your cap, Matt, it's on fire!' Kate shouted.

Matty straightened up and reached for his cap but felt a spray of warm water on the back of his hand. The little elephant God stood, trunk pointed at the fire on Matty's head and sprayed. Matty said in his mind, *you heard me* and smiled. He looked at Kate who had seen Ganesh too, but her attention was instantly on Irnan who had dislodged the blade and was placing herself on her back in the damp leaves. Kate jumped into the circle, pulling Matty in with her.

'Get up!' she shouted at Matty.

'Kate, he has no bridle, he'll drown us.' He stayed on the ground with the little elephant God beside him.

'We have to take a chance Matt, it's either Cormac or her,' and she indicated Irnan with her eyes. She leaped onto the *Each Uisge's* back and held down a hand towards Matty. Irnan was up and running towards them with a killing look on her face. Matty did not think, he grabbed Kate's arm and she hauled him up on the jennet behind her. Ganesh jumped up behind him.

'We're going to have to cross the river to free ourselves of her,' she announced with some urgency and Matty felt her riding boots tap Cormac's tummy. He leaped out of the circle of salt just as Irnan fell face down where they stood an instant before. Kate halted the *Each Uisge* at the river's edge and the irate witch picked herself up and followed.

'We may have to go to the other-world for a bit Matt, don't be scared,' she said, urging Cormac again with her boot.

'Kate I can't, I'm like Girija, I will not get back… you know that…' he pleaded, speaking very quickly, words tumbled out urgently.

'Matt it is her or… taking a chance?' she reasoned and stopped Cormac's pacing toward the river.

'Anyway, she'll only follow us and she is much stronger there…' he tried to think of another way.

'Ganesh, help us,' he said in desperation, twisting around.

The witch was heading in their direction at a speed which shocked Matty, her ancient body in total disparity to her energy. A doe leaped into her path. She fell backwards this time and remained on the ground momentarily, obviously stunned by the blow she received running headlong into the deer.

'It's a red deer,' Kate remarked quietly to herself.

The doe meanwhile had turned around and stood over the stunned witch.

'Finally,' Matty exclaimed.

'Don't say it Matt, I know what you are thinking but don't say a word,' she warned.

Matty stopped even the thought of what he knew the doe represented. He remembered something Kate had said a long while ago about the universal intelligence and he also felt he should trust his intuition. *Let the witch think that the battle was between her and the girl.*

'Get off Cormac, Kate,' he demanded and swung his leg over the hind quarters of the animal and let his feet drop to the ground.

'No,' she insisted. 'Why?' she immediately asked, both eyes on the witch.

'Trust me, Kate,' he said quietly but with as much force as he could muster, forcing the words through his teeth.

'Tell me,' she demanded. Both of them kept eyes on the witch and the doe; the witch had levered herself from her back on to her elbows.

'Cormac doesn't have his bridle; you know what that means, get down,' he kept his insistent tone.

'What, what do you mean?' she asked.

'He will revert to form,' he said turning to look up at her for a moment, but only a moment. The snarl caused him to look again in the direction of the witch, who in that moment had vanished or become a dog.

'Get off… now, Kate. Magh has given him his freedom for a reason,' he yelled, not taking an eye off the battle unfolding in front of them.

To his relief she slid off the animal's back. The doe leaped forward as the dog bounded towards it.

'She's going for the throat,' Kate said quietly in trepidation.

'The doe knows that,' Matty replied quickly. 'Look how she moved away from the dog.'

'That's not a dog, Matt, that's a wolf,' Kate replied, eyes fixed on the two animals.

'Wolves are extinct in Ireland,' Matt said without thinking, forgetting that he was witnessing ancient Ireland.

Kate was right: the wolf chased the doe and cornered her. Just as she leaped for the throat the doe disappeared and Matty watched a squirrel dart up a tree trunk, then change and shoot down to earth again, darting and searching for cover.

'She would never revert to her totem form unless she was under pressure,' Kate said quietly.

The wolf chased the squirrel, who took sanctuary in Matty's Crane Bag momentarily before exiting and climbing frantically up the trunk of a nearby conifer. *Not enough cover*, Matty thought; he recognised the Scots pine from Galway. A hawk began circling the tree; Matty checked the grove and there was no wolf close.

'It's a sparrow hawk,' said Kate, 'A big one, it's a female, it can easily take the squirrel.'

'We have to help her, Kate,' Matty said in desperation.

'Have you got your catapult?' she asked urgently.

'In the bag,' and he raced towards where it lay near the circle and Kate with him.

'Give it to me,' she demanded, grabbing wet clay from underneath the soggy leaves. She moulded it and added a little water from the bottle cast into the circle from earlier.

Placing it into the sling and taking aim she pulled and let the missile fly. Matty watched, impressed with her aim and astounded at the flames which emanated from the ball of earth and water. He watched it strike its quarry, momentarily singing the extended wings of the sparrow hawk. It screeched and flapped away from the Scots pine barely visible in the twilight. There was just enough light to see a salmon crash into the river from the great height of the pine. The sparrow hawk recovered and began a dive towards the river. Their eyes followed as Cormac too entered the fast-flowing water.

'What's going on?' Kate said to herself and moved towards the river.

'You must have had a plan,' demanded Matty and began to run, keeping up with her.

'I was to try and entice Irnan on to Cormac's back in the circle and quickly dismount but she grabbed you and things got out of hand,' replied Kate, the words disjointed as she focused most of the time in the direction she was running.

'And then, what was the rest of the plan?' he commanded as they took up a position on the river bank watching the sparrow hawk search the rapidly moving water, flying low down just clear of the current.

'Magh was to take her to the river with Cormac,' she replied her mind on the Hawk.

'She was going to drown the witch,' Matty exclaimed.

'No, not exactly… just deposit her… in a place that… well, a place where she could be controlled in the other-world,' replied Kate, mind still on the hawk.

'What place?' he demanded.

'One of the western islands, Magh said an isolated place for the length of my life here,' she looked at him this time, checking he understood the entire meaning of what she said.

'OK, we have to do that then, how I don't know, but Cormac is out there in the water and the fight is between Magh and Irnan now, not you and her,' he said, regretting immediately thinking out loud.

'What do you mean Matt, should I distract the witch, get into the water?' she asked, as perplexed as he felt.

'No, no, not at all, the current is too powerful, and anyway Magh is lying low, gathering strength and giving her mind time to outwit the witch, just wait… wait a little longer… let's see what she does,' he said, hoping his words would steady her mind and her impulses, realising why Magh had insisted Kate take him with them.

COMING OF AGE

MATT WATCHED KATE quieten herself and after a little while she moved towards one of the oak trunks.

'Matt, stay here with me, I'm going towards the other-world for a while. I'll be back shortly. Don't worry, just watch Cormac and the sparrow hawk,' she said firmly and sat down.

He pulled at one of her arms the moment she sat down. She had leaded back against the trunk as a back support.

'Leave me alone Matt, what are you doing? Let me help her.' She was her bossy self, snappy, almost overruling him but he knew instinctively that Magh would want her to stay in this world. So he ignored the anger coming out of her.

'She wants you here; I will not let you go…' he grabbed her other arm in an effort to stop her relaxing her body.

'You have no right…' she kicked him in the knee with her boot.

'I'm stronger than you think; go on, keep on fighting me…' he shouted, holding tight to the arms inside the sleeves of her anorak.

She toppled him over and he was forced to let go of her. He quickly gathered himself up from the damp leaves, some clinging to their clothes. He grabbed the shoulders of her anorak, pulling, partly from behind, preventing her from sitting down again. It was a desperate battle; she had regained her strength and was much taller than him. Suddenly she stopped fighting him. For a second he felt he had lost the battle, he looked at her face; she was alert and staring at the river. He only let go of her when she moved away from the trees.

It was so murky and dark that he had to squint to distinguish the forms in the water. It was easier to make out the shape of Cormac's head; beside him there was a smaller shape, a human head, sometimes submerged and sometimes above the current.

'It's her,' he heard Kate say to herself.

They both moved closer to the river and could just differentiate a slight form pulling itself onto Cormac's back.

'No,' wailed Kate.

Matty stood still, paralysed, eye muscles aching as he examined the two dark forms in the middle of the current which had melded into one, half of Magh above the water near to and slightly above Cormac's head. They both heard the screech of the bird of prey at the same time, searching upwards in the darkness and descending they found no bird. Two pairs of eyes searched the turbulence, looking again for Magh and her Cormac... he would never forget the gasp and sound that emanated from Kate, like a fatally wounded animal. She bent over and began to cry, as if she was doubled over in pain.

'No, oh no, no, no...' It ended in a roar.

Matty found himself physically shivering, particularly his knees: *they seem to give way under pressure first*, he momentarily considered. A figure had appeared behind Magh in the current; it was so obviously the witch. Two slight figures behind the jennet's head, it could only be two ancient women.

'You expect me to do nothing?' she straightened up and turned on him.

'Watch Kate, look at what's happening... Out there, Kate, in the waves,' he insisted.

She turned just in time to see the three barely discernible dark forms disappear beneath the water. They stood, both of them, stunned, helpless. Time went by, it was pitch dark. There was only the sound of the current. No shadows appeared out in the middle of the river. Matty recalled Jack's retelling of the night Girija disappeared beneath the water on a calm lake. Kate had to be reliving it again.

'We've got to get out of here,' he urged.

She ignored him, standing as still as a statue.

'I can't see my way back to where we left our bags,' he said, looking behind them, 'it's just too dark.'

'Kate,' he raised his voice. A light breeze moved strands of her hair which were free of her cap.

Still nothing from her.

'We are going to be in big trouble,' he made his voice more insistent; he really didn't have to, the thought of dealing with Gran and Uncle Liam only added to the panic he was already feeling for the consequences of Magh.

'You expect me to walk away and leave her here... is that what you want to do... just leave...?' she spat the accusatory words out at him; he could feel her anger and frustration and loss.

'Staying here... will not get her back, she's gone... maybe, maybe for a short time...' he tried, but couldn't even convince himself.

'Stop it!' she shouted and then roaring cries emanated from her, like a wild being, walking in circles just emitting anguished sounds.

And then as he watched her, a figure moved towards them out of the darkness.

'Ailill,' she greeted him. An exchange took place in Irish, choppy, short sentences. This didn't seem to placate her at all. She continued in the circles.

'Kate… we must go home,' Matty reminded her again; obviously there was to be no good ending to this day.

Ailill nodded his head and led them into the wood. They came to the place where their bags lay. She gathered up her paraphernalia and pulled her bag on one shoulder as if she was in physical pain, then the ancient warrior led them through the dark grove. Matty got his trusty pen torch out before slinging on his Crane Bag, regretting the weightlessness of it and the memory of earlier. As they neared the bridge, Matty could just about distinguish something underneath the street light, he became aware of the sound of adult voices. One said, 'There are two children's bicycles here.'

The warrior disappeared and they trudged up the muddy bank which was visible in the headlights of cars parked both on the steep hill and the village side of the bridge. Uncle Liam's large frame greeted them at the top of the bank and even Kate looked astounded at the number of adults gathered, Wellingtons and anoraks and stout sticks in their hands.

'What are you doing in the grove this time of night?' demanded Uncle Liam.

'What's all the fuss about?' she replied, rude and dismissive and Matty knew she didn't care.

Liam yanked Matty's upstretched arm onto the bank, Kate turned down his extended arm. Just behind his uncle, Matty noticed a familiar form; he wasn't sure if he was imagining it or not. She was leaning, searching from the only space available above the slippery path on the bank. He was aware of Aunt Bernie's voice announcing, 'False alarm everyone, they are safe, thanks for coming out in the cold.'

'Yes, thanks everyone, sorry to trouble you all, appreciate your concern,' came from Uncle Liam and he moved back onto the safety of the footpath.

The figure behind him advanced on Matty, who stood on the tiny piece of bank just beside the footpath, mesmerised in the darkness which descended again as soon as the cars moved away with their headlights.

'Mum,' he finally managed to say.

SOUL

 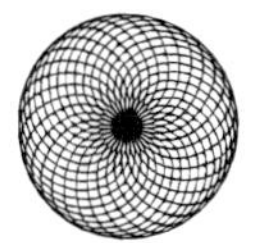

MATTY HAD A restless night, waking several times having to untangle his dreams from what he had seen in the woods the previous day. Alarmingly, there was little difference. The only comfort he felt was that he wasn't alone with the sudden appearance of his mother; the comfortable feeling that his little family was coming back together again reinforced his steadfastness. He got up early and dressed; normally he lazed around in a dressing gown and pyjamas having breakfast at one end of the kitchen table which provided an excellent view of the TV. He found his mother in the kitchen with a mug of tea, watching the news.

She rose and hugged him, enquiring why he was up so early.

'I thought I'd check on Kate, she was upset, Magh did not turn up yesterday,' he half-lied.

'Why were you meeting her in the village, why not meet up at her house?' she asked.

'Kate wanted to show me the game of conkers and everyone said we wouldn't find any chestnuts at this time of year but Magh said she knew where the squirrels hid them,' he hoped this would get past the jet-lagged, sleep-deprived brain.

'They may not be up yet,' she said, on her way back to the corner of the sofa.

'I'll see if the outside light is still on,' he said as he headed for the back door, taking its key from the nail in the upper cross plank. He had a sudden flashback to the shed where Jack and he were held, remembering how he had to cling on the two unpainted planks, of a prison door. *This miserable situation started back then, why?* His heart sunk as he stepped outside and into a white frost.

He could just about distinguish two figures against the pale coral of a new day and the fading night sky. It was Kate and Macha at the top of the lane directly in the centre of the T junction and they had bicycles with them. They appeared to be talking. Matty quickly went inside the porch, pulled on his anorak and trainers, stuck his head around the kitchen door, making sure he had his woollen cap on and announced he was going to see Kate.

'What about something to eat?' came her protest. 'You need something warm inside.'

'Nicky has rice crispies,' he answered before closing the outer door.

Once inside the barn, he was forced to take time to forage in his pockets for gloves; even the grips on the handlebars of the bicycle were so cold his skin felt as if it was sticking to the plastic or rubber or whatever it was.

He knew Brandy would try to escape once he opened the gate so he went over to the back door and let him into the kitchen with his mother where he knew he would be welcome, she called him Biddle and an animated one-way conversation started mainly informing the dog that his stay would be short, just until Gran got up, then it would be the barn for him until after supper when he was allowed in for a few hours but never on the furniture.

By the time all this had taken place and Matty had taken the bicycle onto the lane, the two figures were no longer to be seen. Matty peddled as fast as he could to the T junction, just in time to see the two disappear around a bend in the main road leading to the village. *They are going back to the wood beside the river.* He mounted again and followed at first with speed, avoiding potholes which were covered with ice. But intuition informed him not to be too reckless: there was bound to be black ice and he may end up in a skid. The cold air seemed to be forming a layer of invisible ice over his face but there was more and more light and it was going to be a beautiful morning. He could see their heads and bent shoulders cross the bridge when he reached that first bend, so he was a little behind, he would *catch them on the river bank, better be safe.* A mile further on and he came past the shop in the village, he could see them at the bottom of the hill leading down to the pubs and the post office. They were walking. Cleverly he dismounted: *the hill must be too slippery to ride down.* He carefully and slowly moved on to the slope and chose the verge where road chippings gave more grip. They had not mounted again; as he rounded the bend halfway down the village he still had sight of them walking towards the bridge over the river.

Kate was the first to spot him after propping her bicycle against the wall. She stood waiting for him; gloved hands shot into her pockets after she had blown warm air on to them. Macha disappeared down the path to the river bank.

'You're up early,' she said, looking into his face with her examining look.

'Didn't sleep very well… I am worried, could she be…?' he couldn't finish.

'Me too,' she replied swiftly as if to banish the idea. She moved on to follow Macha. 'I planned to go to see if Magh had come back but met Macha at the top of the lane,' she said while easing herself on to the rough path leading from the hill down by the side of the bridge, puffs of warm air visible when she spoke. Her words were without enthusiasm, her mood was low.

They tramped on following Macha, the beauty of the winter scene adding pathos to their despair. Matty had an urge to ask Kate what they were looking for but knew how futile it was before it emerged, he kept quiet.

'Where were you yesterday?' Macha asked, stopping but not turning back towards them, as if minimising his movements would minimise his pain.

'A little further on, the circle should still be there,' Kate answered, taking big steps forward and passing him.

After about four minutes she stopped, there was a half-cry, 'O God!' She collapsed down on her knees on the frost-covered leaves. Macha hovered beside her, his tall, thin, frame bent looking gloomy in his dark, long winter coat. When Matty was close enough to see he squatted to look for signs of life.

'Can I touch…?' Kate extended a hand, pulled out of a mitten, she turned her head and looked up at Macha, 'how do we know it is her?'

'It's her alright,' he said almost inaudibly, 'but only a little bit of her soul.'

'How do we know, though?' she whispered, her hand now across the middle of the squirrel.

'Look at the second last digit of the left paw,' he indicated with his hand, still looming from his gloomy height.

Sure enough, barely visible, for those with good eyesight, a tiny band of what looked like moonstone or a sky at dawn on a cloudy day pulsated.

'It's pulsating,' Kate said excitedly and Macha drew from the pocket of his coat what Matty recognised as the giant's slipper, the tears visible and running down his cheeks.

'Lift her into it,' he sobbed gently.

Kate stood and stepped purposefully into the circle, she squatted and with both hands lifted the lifeless body of the squirrel and gently laid it on the fabric of the slipper. Macha opened his great, dark coat and in a large pocket in its lining he placed the slipper. He began walking in the direction of the bridge, instructing Kate to take down her circle without turning his head.

Matty watched them both alternately, Kate going through a ritual she seemed familiar with and the old man-faerie trod homeward with his dearest dead or near-death tucked in from the cold that had either preserved her or destroyed her.

'Is she alive, Kate?' Matty asked once she finished and covered the marks she had made the previous evening with the crisp leaves.

'I don't know Matt, I think Macha doesn't know either,' she said almost in tears.

'Why the slipper?' he asked after they had walked briskly for a few minutes following Macha.

'He said the energies in it might help her, I think… I think he hoped to find her in human form and use it to get her home quickly,' she said, stopping and facing him for a few seconds and then back to the persistent pace of catching up with Macha, their breaths like intermittent productive chimneys.

'Could he not wear it and transport her quickly?' Matty asked.

'Macha is only half-faerie, he can't do what she can do… could do,' she answered, her voice breaking. He watched her swipe her sleeve across her eyes and knew she was on a funeral walk.

'But Kate, the pulse.' He, being as upset as her, still he kept searching for hope.

'Matt, that is from an etheric world, it may be the other part of her soul,' – more sobbing – 'something left for Macha, it's not a pulse… a heartbeat pulse…' She had turned to him and the tears streamed down her cheeks. It was so cold that Matty felt for one frantic and non-pertinent minute that the tears may freeze. She did a double swipe, first one sleeve which was still wet from the first swipe, then she did the second sleeve across her eyes, finishing off with the back of her mitten.

'This is all because of something that happened in India.' The guilt dominated his whole being.

THE SIDHE

CHRISTMAS CAME AND went and they all had Christmas dinner at Kate's house and except for Nicky's excitement, gloom predominated. It was the first Christmas for Matty that he had not been with Jack and celebration was no fun if he couldn't share it with Jack – and even if Jack had been with him his mood would have mirrored Kate's, he reasoned. Uncle Liam was off work for St Stephen's Day and the adults sat about talking; Matty's mother, being so out of touch with local people, listened to Uncle Liam's stories, some of which she realised later were fabricated and heavily interspersed with fun. Gran had been scheduled for more tests at the local hospital right after Christmas so there was an extra layer of fatalism emanating from her, her fear of hospitals almost tangible. After being tucked into bed and wallowing in the tiredness just before sleep Matty had a sudden realisation. For several days over the holidays Kate had been too quiet. Fully awake he considered this; she admitted that she visited Hedge Cottage and got no response and assumed that Macha did not want to be disturbed and on Christmas Day while he helped her clear the table and wash up they both had come to the conclusion that there was no change.

Next morning, while Matty munched his way through a bowl of chocolate rice crispies, staring into the middle distance outside the kitchen window, on his usual chair, Kate sped past on her bicycle. He jumped up went to his room and dressed quickly; he was right – *things had been too quiet for a proactive type like Kate.* He became frustrated at how many layers of clothing he had to contend with until fighting with the zipper in his anorak he realised there was only one of three lanes Kate would use and they were all dead ends. Finally, fully puffed out with warm clothing, he announced he was going cycling with Kate. He had ensured that his clothing would pass censorship. Protests were made about the half-finished breakfast; he hadn't thought about the breakfast.

'Finish your breakfast first,' insisted Gran.

'I'll have it later,' he replied.

'It'll be all soggy,' his mother added.

'I like it soggy,' he answered as he closed the kitchen door.

His first thought was to go to the gap which led into the lagoon, so he ignored the little lanes. He considered that it must be low tide if she needed to get to the sandy banks on the St George's Channel side. He was right; her bicycle was propped against a sandy bank as soon as he reached the gap. He dismounted and watched from the sea wall. The tide was out and he could see a figure almost across from him heading for the tall mounds covered with long sea grass and reeds. It was a grey day but he could make out the figure in the distance: it was Kate. He moved down onto the sand and stone-strewn beach and attempted to cross the slime through the car track but his trainers sank immediately he stepped into the wet sand. He contented himself with the fact that Kate seemed to be staying on the far shore; she did not move up into the dunes. Standing watching her in the cold was more than uncomfortable so he walked back and forth on the concrete in front of the sea defences, never losing sight of her. He considered that his grey anorak was good camouflage against the grey stone walls and boulders and so removed his bright red woolly cap, pulling up the hood of the anorak to protect his head from the cold.

Suddenly there was another figure about Kate's height. The figure was not compact, bound tightly with an anorak for example. Matty stood still, straining his eyes: the clothing was loose, could that be a cloak…? More like a blanket. Matty gasped, his hand went automatically to his chest and then he felt the wool of his Christmas gloves on his lips. *She is in touch with the Tuatha dé Danann. How dangerous was this, no Magh to protect and advise her?* He continued watching, ignoring his pounding heartbeat. The other figure disappeared from sight as quickly as he had seen it and as he watched Kate move ever so slightly back and forth, the figure appeared and disappeared from his sight.

Matty was so engrossed in the activities across the lagoon that he only became aware of the sound of hooves and soft chatter when it felt as though the horses were just above him. He moved slowly onto the sand to give the jockeys time to control the horses, for they would surely scare if he was suddenly to appear below the sea wall. He saw them tighten their reins and slow the animals, they bid him hello and entered the slimy track. There were five of them. Matty moved up onto the sea wall for a better view of Kate. He could see her move along the sand at the far side and then begin to cross the first channel of salty water. When the horses and jockeys met her they stopped momentarily; Matty considered she would have another white lie ready for them. They mostly teased her anyway, which irritated her.

By the time she reached the gap, drizzle had begun to fall. Matty had replaced his bright red woollen cap but kept the hood on too. He could see the weather front moving in from the bay, heavy, dark clouds laden with rain.

'Not much gets past you Matt,' she said. It was difficult for him to hide his disapproval, he hadn't planned on lecturing her, but Kate could sense more than other people.

'You have no back up,' was all he could reply.

'What do you expect me to do?' she asked angrily. 'I can't just do nothing.'

'I understand that… but… you have no help, either here or… in their world,' he replied.

'I know,' was all she said.

The drizzle had turned into soft rain and although gentle, was persistent; they wiped the saddles of the bicycles with their gloves and rode silently home.

DUNG

SHE DISMOUNTED OUTSIDE the garden gate and opened the gate leading to the sheep house and stable situated on the opposite side of the lane. Matty was glad; he didn't want to part with a negative atmosphere prevailing.

'Give them a wave,' she instructed.

'What?' he asked as he watched her wave at his grandmother's kitchen window.

He did as he was told and saw his mother raise the net curtain and wave back.

'They'll leave us alone once they know we are in out of the rain,' she explained as if no bad atmosphere had ever materialised between them. That was one thing among many others that Matty liked so much about Kate. She either forgot about or ignored the disagreements.

'They will leave us alone and we can talk in peace,' she added conspiratorially.

She parked her bicycle against the half wall with tubing set into it beside the gate leading to the high field where Finn's jumps were arranged. Matty followed and did the same with the red and white bicycle. He thought about the saddle getting wet but considered they were hardly likely to go cycling again that day.

'Did you see something, Matt?' she enquired as she walked towards the stable and opened its door.

'A cloaked figure,' he replied.

'That's Maeve, I've known her for ages,' she explained as she caught hold of Finn's mane and lead him into the unoccupied stall.

'Is she a Tuatha?' asked Matty unnecessarily, appearing more relaxed.

'Yes, you know I can see them without being my etheric self,' she urged him inside the stable door.

'Yes, I know that... but I thought it was Ailill... I never gave it much thought, I didn't know you were friends with...' and he just stopped talking, he couldn't think clearly, it was difficult to fully understand her. The sudden awareness that she was in touch with these beings after what had happened to her astounded his brain.

'Jack knows; maybe we forgot to tell you, there was so much you had to catch up on last year. Matt, can you wait here a moment?' She indicated that he should stand still just inside the stable door. He watched her pat Finn on the rump and gently catch hold of his mane again and guide his back legs into a position more aligned with the food trough, while conversing with him from the adjoining stall, then she said, 'Matt, carefully step through the straw, avoiding Finn's pooh and climb up there, and sit on the edge of the trough while I change the bedding', she indicated before disappearing. She parked a wheelbarrow outside the door on her return.

Matty climbed onto the edge of the concrete trough, holding onto the wood slats in the hay rack above it to balance himself on the narrow ledge. The concrete, like that which divided both stalls, was worn smooth over the years by heavy, working horses who were stabled in winter when his grandfather was young. It smelled of Finn and the gloomy space within, once Kate closed the half stable door, had a strong smell of horse pooh and urine-soaked straw.

'Matt you have got to trust me, give me a little credit for intelligence, I'm not going into their world until I know it is safe.' She said this while lifting the straw bedding scattered with horse manure into the wheelbarrow with a fork which she and everyone else there referred to as a sprong – an old Danish word, originating from the time of the Vikings, Matty had been reliably informed by one of the older cousins who was documenting a family history. 'I met her to have a chat, maybe get advice,' she added breathlessly as she leaned on the fork, resting from the exertion.

'What did she say,' he asked 'and how could I see her?'

'You're not old enough to have lost the sight, I guess,' she replied, scooping great fork-loads of dungy straw again.

'The news is out, though,' she said, standing still again. 'Everyone seems to be talking about a great fight between two witches.'

'Really? I didn't know Magh was a witch,' Matty exclaimed.

'She was, though; think about it, Matt,' she replied, continuing to scoop up a mixture of crisp and sodden straw with the sprong.

'What else, did she say... who won?' asked Matty anxiously.

'Only that they both put *Mallachti* on each other,' she replied breathlessly.

'*Mallachti*?' asked Matty.

'Curses,' replied Kate, placing her fork against the partition and sliding up onto the trough ledge beside Matty.

'Do you know how Magh was cursed?' enquired Matty hopefully.

'No, and Macha is still not answering his door,' she replied thoughtfully.

'Did the girl, what's her name again? Did she have any suggestions… how you could help Magh? Is she is still alive,' he asked. This stuck in his throat, it just slipped out. He felt and knew Kate avoided the question too.

'Maeve, Medb in Irish, yeah… but I'm not… I don't think I want to embroil myself in rituals involving the Morrigan,' she said pensively.

'What's the Morrigan?' he asked, he could feel the trepidation building up inside again.

'She's a very powerful Goddess, like Kali… No, I've decided not to get involved in that type of energy,' she said pensively, as if mulling it over to herself, both hands holding her balance on the narrow ledge of the trough.

'I don't know much about Kali,' he said. 'There are no statues or pictures of her in the prayer room or in the temple in Kerala,' he added.

'No, I know, she's the type of Goddess people pray to when they need something really badly,' she said, still thinking.

'But don't we need something badly?' He regretted the words before he finished saying them; his feelings for Magh and the help she had given his family countered against Kate's safety for just one unreasoned second.

'Magh told me never to invoke her energy… unless…' she said quietly as if sensing his feelings. 'I'll talk to Ailill again,' she said, jumping down on to the strawless floor.

They closed the stable half-doors and headed through the drizzle into the heat of the kitchen.

DRUID

SEVERAL DAYS WENT by during which Matty kept a close eye on Kate. His excuse to go to his cousins was to play games with Nicky on his Xbox. When he was there he persuaded him to watch his tape of *Jurassic Park* for the hundredth time. Nicky argued every time: being the owner of the tape, he stated, entitled him to decide when it should be watched, if at all, but he always gave in and Matty couldn't get enough of it. That way Matty spent every day at his cousins' and could find out what Kate had done in the morning and what her plans were for the very short afternoons of the holidays. The light disappeared around three-thirty and she was never allowed out after dark; even Matty was escorted home or collected by an adult on those short winter days. In order to get these privileges he had argued that he should be given the same study break as his cousins and his mother conceded. However, his grandmother had not made it easy; she appeared behind him as he discussed it with his mother's back while she did the washing up in the back kitchen. She expressed doubt as to how much he would be behind his class in India as his study had not been consistently intense, especially before his mother had arrived. In Matty's head the words appeared: *who needs an enemy when one has a grandmother like Gran?* But he kept quiet. Matty had developed a mixture of local and American language during his stay in Ireland, mostly from watching so many more TV programmes that they had on Star Plus at home.

By the end of the Christmas holidays Matty was contented that the surveillance of his cousin showed that she was not spending any time ethereally in the other-world. She took Finn out most mornings but was confined to the high field with the jumps due to bad weather.

One Saturday afternoon after the schools had opened and while Matty was slowly absorbing the excitement of *Jurassic Park* yet again and Nicky had given up and parked himself on his bedroom floor attached to the handset of one of his game players, Kate softly slid on to the sofa beside him. He only noticed her when a soup bowl of ice cream appeared right in front of his face.

'Enjoy,' she ordered, 'the parents and your mum and Gran have gone to visit someone; we're on our own for the evening.'

'Thanks, Kate,' Matty said, gratefully accepting the cold soup bowl.

'I have some news,' she said conspiratorially, getting up and closing the sitting room door with a socked foot while delivering a spoon of ice cream to her mouth.

Matty got the remote control and began lowering the volume.

'No, Matt, leave it as it was, I don't want Nicky to hear,' she commanded.

So he did as he was told.

'What's up?' he asked.

'Macha let me in this morning,' she said.

'Really?' Matty was eager for positive news. 'Did you see her?'

'No Matt, she's still in her squirrel form but she looks more alive, I could see her chest moving up and down as if she was breathing… so that's something… I guess,' she said, staring at the slowly melting ice cream in the bowl resting on the leg of her jeans, the half-sunken spoon forgotten as the gloom of the predicament filled both their minds. Matty said nothing, there was nothing to be said; the urge to eat ice cream had gone too.

However, as is always the way with Kate, gloom had to be brushed away; as she carefully positioned her spoon for another scoop of ice cream she looked at him from the downward position of her head and he knew she had a plan. Her eyes twinkled with an assuredness, but he only felt trepidation.

'Kate…' he began.

'Before you say anything…' The spoon rested on the soup bowl and the free hand rose slightly. 'The situation is different, my contacts are safe… Ailill, you know Ailill?'

'What is the plan?' Matty demanded. He put down his ice cream, stood up and began to pace. He felt agitated, he knew she outranked him and his powerlessness frustrated him.

'Matt, Matt,' she countered. 'OK, if you are going to be like that then I'll do it on my own.' She pushed herself back against the cushions of the sofa and began to eat the ice cream but certainly didn't appear as if she was enjoying it.

He knew this and how she hated a negative atmosphere and so he sat down again.

'Alright, tell me,' he said in a voice that conveyed his exasperation.

She sprung forward, the twinkle was back; she scooped the last of the ice cream and placed her empty bowl on the coffee table.

'Finish your ice cream,' she ordered, indicating the bowl with igloo shapes surrounded by a sea of melted ice cream.

'Now listen, I have discussed all of what I am about to say in detail with Macha. He knows a lot more than I do and he feels it is safe for me to meet the Druids.'

Matty's mouth opened. He could think of nothing useful to say and closed it again.

'It's worth a try, Matt, they may be able to lift the curse,' she said. He did note that her enthusiasm was restrained this time.

Matty picked up the bowl and started with the melted ice cream which was not too bad, like drinking vanilla and chocolate which was smooth, but not nearly as enjoyable as soggy rice crispies.

Kate rose, went through the sitting room door and returned apparently satisfied that Nicky was preoccupied, giving Matty a chance to consider what she had revealed. She sat once again beside him, with one leg curled underneath.

'Do you know what happened to Cruachain, does anyone know where she went?' he asked.

'Like Magh… she's just banished,' she replied with a barely perceptible shrug.

'Kate, you know where Magh is and she is banished. Cruachain will be somewhere in the other-world and it will only take the appearance of someone like you to rouse her into life or activity again,' he said slowly and with as much emphasis as he could.

'I have thought about that, Matt,' she said with a light-bulb expression. She slid along the sofa to be nearer to him and his bowl of completely melted ice cream, which he placed on the low table for fear of spilling it.

'I tend to travel as I am… in my body shape. When Magh first taught me how to travel I went out as a sphere… like a ball,' she began to explain; her hands automatically made a sphere shape. 'I have been going as myself because I want to be recognised; especially when I was in Kerala on my first holiday I needed to be a human shape… to become familiar to the Danavas.'

'And as a ball shape no being will recognise you, is that what you are saying…?' He found this incredible: surely the other beings would be aware there was someone in their midst.

'What's the matter, Matt?' she queried.

'The beings of the other-world are intelligent, Kate, they will be aware of you.' He looked directly into her eyes, having no proof of what he had said, only a belief, only common sense.

'You're right, you're right, Matt, the perceptible ones will become aware of my energy immediately, but they will not know it is *my* energy. I can hide my identity… stay safe,' she said, as if she was convincing herself as well as Matty.

'And, these priests, they will know the energy is yours?' he asked.

'Druids, yes, they will expect me in whatever form I decide on before the day, with Maeve and Ailill,' she said, head bowed, fingers interlocking and unlocking.

The trepidation was palpable in the room. They became aware of the sound of the unsettling film music: it was the kitchen scene, and the children were hiding from the swift, snippety, meat-eating dinosaurs. The pathos was too much. Matty had such an urge to turn off the film. He got up and paced.

'Don't use a squirrel shape,' he said after a long pause.

'That's her totem, may well be recognised in the other world,' she agreed uneasily.

'I was thinking of Ganesh...' She looked up at him.

'No Kate, as a symbol... that would be instantaneously recognisable as related to you... no...' He stood over her as if to emphasise the point. 'You must think of something that is not related to your life with us or even... with your own family... it could be traced.'

'It needs thinking about, Matt, I can see that,' she replied in a low voice.

KELLY'S BARN

TO PEOPLE WHO live in Blackstone, especially those of Matty's mother's age and older, referred to present-day life as if it was the same as when they were young. The farmstead where the Kelly family lived was known as Kelly's even though the land had been sold and the house bought by a family from Dublin who used it as a holiday cottage. Some of the outbuildings were leased to local farmers for animal winter feed and bedding storage. One of these buildings, set to the front of the property, was a tiny one-storey barn. It had a broad and heavy ladder which lay on the ground alongside the building unless it was needed for access. Kate had confided in Matty her worries about the ladder leaning against the whitewashed walls of the barn and being seen from the lane, leaning up to a closed barn door on the first floor. This annoyed him intensely: *why did she wait until the last minute to confide her problems with him? He had no time to think of a solution.* They stood surveying the barn from the lane side of the stone wall after walking down the lane, which was also whitewashed, she with an enormous backpack. His grandmother had asked where he was going when Kate arrived and he replied he was going out with Kate. Kate kept herself well-hidden from the lane side of the yard wall, calling into the back kitchen window to her grandmother that they were going exploring.

'Exploring what?' came her query. But Kate signalled to Matty to run and they did, down the hill and were very quickly hidden by the hedgerows beyond the bend despite the lack of foliage; they had the advantage of the dip in the road.

'If we throw the ladder away from the barn door once we are inside we would not be able to get out, it's far too high to jump down,' she said staring at the door high up on the building.

'What about Mebh, or Ailill?' he asked. 'Could they prop the ladder against the wall for us?'

'Yeah…' she replied, 'it's just that sometimes they disappear without warning and I'd be happier with a backup plan.'

'Well tell them beforehand then,' he said, still a little bothered with her minimal interaction.

Matty's mood softened a little with the thrill of climbing up to the hayloft and the darken interior. It was the last Saturday in January and Matty was a very long way from his relaxed zone, something he consciously tried to cultivate especially as it was much easier to achieve. His Mother's appearance and the definite news that he would return home with her contributed greatly to this new state of mind. However, the situation he found himself in felt much more uncomfortable mentally than even the experience in the grove before Christmas. In fact, he felt his feelings were verging on those he experienced in the woods in the autumn, running for his life… saved by one of those beings from another place. He told himself he was exaggerating.

'Maitiu, Matt, that's your name in Irish, that's what she is asking you, what your name is?' Kate said, so at ease with the… being from another world.

'Why the grinning… and the endless staring?' he asked.

'Matt, she has never seen anyone like you before, well… a human who can see her too… so she is fascinated, she thinks you are cute.' Kate had stood upright, sensing his discomfort; she had been yanking a bale of hay out of the only partially unoccupied corner.

She surveyed the bales which were tightly packed right up to the rafters 'Obviously plenty of winter feed still in this barn,' she said aloud to herself.

'I need to make a bed Matt, somewhere to lie down, but that's the only loose bale,' she said, pointing to the one she had pulled out of a corner.

'Ask her for help,' Matty said, unconsciously throwing an eye in the direction of the young Tuatha dé Danann, thinking it may stop her ceaseless staring.

'Good idea Matt,' she said and thereafter a conversation in Gaelic ensued. Mebh appeared confused and Kate continued to gesture towards the roof of the barn.

'What's the matter?' Matty enquired.

'I can't think of the words for making a bed or like a bed… *on leaba a choiriu*,' she said with relief.

Mebh seemed to understand the bed and looked up as Kate pointed and continued to speak in Gaelic. Then Mebh began to climb, like an experienced mountain climber.

'I'm normally lying on my bed when I go travelling with her, no wonder she is confused with me today,' Kate mused while they watched her place her hands and feet methodically in the tiny spaces between bales, gaining height bit by bit.

'Wait a minute, you have been in the other-world… with her… since Christmas?' he turned towards the upturned chin.

'Matt, I couldn't just go today for the first time, this is a big meeting today, I needed to… to familiarise myself with them again,' she faced him, mostly placating and partially explaining.

'So why do you need me here… if you are in and out all the time…?' He began walking to and fro in the small space near the door.

'I need you… in case anything goes wrong… nobody would be able to find me…' she pleaded.

'And what about the times you went before… who would find you then?' he demanded, stepping in front of her.

'I was at home… in my bed… Mammy would find me in the morning if something was wrong,' she explained with her sensible, 'in control' face on.

'Oh, so you are going from home now?' he asked.

'Yes, do you think I am stupid? I'm not taking risks Matt… not any more,' she said.

'What if you go into a coma?' he persisted.

'If I become cataleptic you watch my chest to see if it goes up and down; it will be very slow, much slower than your breaths. If you can't see any movement with my anorak… just place your hand near my mouth, be patient, though; the breaths, like I said, will be very slow,' she explained. *As if it was as easy as riding a bicycle*, he thought.

'What if there is nothing… no breaths?' he asked.

'Forget that Matt, it will not happen,' she dismissed the question. *A little too hasty*, he thought.

'How long do I leave you in the cataleptic, coma state?' he asked.

'Really, we have only got two hours: it's one now, I should be back by three. You know time moves very slowly in the other-world. If we are not home by three-thirty, latest, the adults will start looking for us and we will be in trouble. Fortunately it's a little bright today so we will have light till maybe three-forty-five,' she said, all this while opening the door a crack and looking at the sky. Then, opening the door wider, she knelt down and pushed the ladder to the ground. He heard a thud and felt the cold air. Silence followed but, as always, not for long.

'What are the sleeping bags for?' he asked; she had pulled one out of her rucksack and he could see another.

'Matt, it's only four degrees outside and we cannot let our temperatures drop. I will use one bag, but keep an eye on me; I should not get too hot or I will be pulled back into my body before I am ready, just pull the zip down a bit if you think I feel very warm. The other bag is for you. Sitting still will make you cold too.' This was all said with a mittened hand on his shoulder.

'*Fear*,' came a shout from the rafters.

Matty was startled; he had momentarily forgotten about the Tuatha.

'What did she say?' he asked as Kate pulled him into the corner, a second before a large bale of hay landed on the wood floor.

'*Fear*,' he repeated.

'It means hay,' she explained. A smile had reappeared on her face.

'*Do*,' came another shout from the rafters.

'*Tri*,' Kate shouted upwards. 'Matt, stay in the corner, she's throwing down two more bales.'

Perhaps, he considered, it was the dark space they were in, confined in a hayloft with no place to move for hay bales that made him reflect. Kate was on par with Jack in Matty's estimation of closeness but with the addition of magic. Unfortunately, she could be equally frustrating. They were both headstrong and reacted to situations in a way that Matty found difficult to understand. Jack did outrageous things at times but nothing like her and because of her abilities she was beyond control. Matty was thankful that Jack did not have Kate's gifts.

By the time Mebh had climbed down on to the floorboards again and Kate had arranged four bales of hay in a bed formation, Matty had overcome the disappointment of Kate failing to confide her etheric travels with him. A conversation was ongoing in Irish again. He caught the words *Ailill* and *Draiocht*.

THE WATCH

MATTY REALISED, YET again, how unused he was to experiences he had with Kate. Afterwards the events faded a little and his mind seemed to accept what he had seen and felt. She on the other hand appeared to accept them as part of her life most of the time. He considered but he knew her fears; he could feel her disquiet, especially at a time like this. As he sat next to her head on the fourth bale of hay he had indeed began to feel the chill of winter. He lifted the flap of her sleeping bag and pulled up the sleeve of her anorak very gently and checked her wristwatch: only ten minutes had passed.

He slid off the bale and pulled out the remaining sleeping bag, remembering her instructions. *Pull it up around you, Matt, before your feet begin to get cold, otherwise you will never warm up.* When he got to the end of the bag – which was a struggle, she had stuffed it into her backpack so tightly – he realised there was something else in the bag; it made a thud sound when it fell to the floor as he fought to release the remainder of the sleeping bag. He let go of the red sleeping bag and opened the backpack. At the very bottom was a small Thermos flask and half a packet of milk biscuits with its wrap twisted to prevent the biscuits scattering into the bag. He couldn't help smiling: *she thought of everything.* He certainly did not feel like eating anything; his grandmother continued the tradition of having the main meal at lunchtime and he had eaten well as per Kate's instructions and this was not the time for milk biscuits, however much he liked them. He did feel it was necessary to have a little warm liquid before wrapping up in the sleeping bag and as he undid the cup and screw cover the smell of drinking chocolate greeted his nostrils. This evoked another smile. He poured himself half of the cup of what seemed like really hot chocolate and searched for a place near his position on the bales to place it while he eased himself into to the grey inside of the red sleeping bag. Wrapped up, knees bent with plastic cup in gloved hands he resumed his watch.

He examined her: she was breathing but much more slowly than he was, just as she had said. He compared the rate of the breaths. At first he became alarmed waiting for the front of her anorak to rise and then fall again, she was so still, and then it rose a little, only four or six breaths a minute. He counted his own: he noted that when he was anxious he took sixteen or more breaths. He sipped on the still hot liquid and let practicalities run through his mind. He must not startle when Mebh or Ailill suddenly appear in the tiny space: *expect them*, he told himself. Then he remembered, he had forgotten to ask her what shape she had decided her etheric form would take. He realised he had forgotten to look once she lay still, he was so preoccupied with the two beings taking up the entire tiny space. Perhaps if he had not been so focused on them – *and they did appear very intent*, he remembered – he would have been aware of Kate's matter leaving her body. After all, he could actually see the beings from another time and place. And then he remembered Jack once saw Ailill too, at the cold store in Madras, while they waited for their father in the car outside. What news he would have to tell Jack about the warrior.

Time dragged, Matty slipped his hand out of one glove and slid a couple of fingers inside one of Kate's mittens to see if she was cold. It was difficult to decide; she certainly was not too hot. He decided to bring the flap of her sleeping bag across her chest, right up to her chin; there was enough light to see if her cheeks began to flush if it caused her to be too warm and then there was his trusty torch as well. The thought of when he should call for help also crossed his mind; he dismissed this, reassuring himself it was still too early.

While doing this Matty became startled with a movement he noticed from the side of his eye. He told himself it may be a being from the other-world, maybe a sylph. Whenever the Tuatha were involved all sorts of unexpected happenings occurred in the vicinity. He turned his head but stayed partially leaning over Kate. It was a cat. She stood, like him, momentarily frozen on three legs, one paw raised as if to flee. He very slowly moved his shoulders back into his watch position, against the bales. After hesitating for much longer than he had, the cat moved across the floor boards in front of him, cautiously, watching him all the while. When she disappeared out of sight Matty became aware of mewlings, snufflings and in the silence, sounds the hay made when touched. He just couldn't resist. He slid out the sleeping bag as quietly as he could and tiptoed in the direction the cat went. He was in front of the barn wall in a couple of feet and could see nothing. He took out his torch and examined the bales of hay, high up and then lower down. There they were, mother and three kittens in a hollowed-out nest in the space made where the tightly packed bales met the floorboards. The cat raised her head, eyes shining in the torch light while three little kittens suckled her milk. Matty turned off his torch and squatted, taking in the sight in the dim light afforded by the slits in the high barn door. After spending some time watching and he hoped reassuring the mother there was no danger, he crept back to his place on the bale of hay and slipped back inside his sleeping bag, pulling it up over his shoulders this time and pulling down his woollen cap over his ears, the tips of which felt cold. His shoulders, too, felt chilly.

He once again tried to bring his mind back to practicalities and the first thought which loomed large was what if the light faded and Kate had not returned. He dismissed that and how long he would leave it, *etc. etc. etc.* He wrapped his arms around his chest inside the sleeping bag and had to admit how cold he was becoming.

He was considering unzipping Kate's bag to check if her legs and feet were very cold when he was once again startled by the cat. She had leaped up onto a ledge of bale where Matty had placed his mug of drinking chocolate and she began to lap the remainder up. She was obviously thirsty and maybe hungry, she certainly looked very thin. Matty slowly undid his sleeping bag; she looked up and watched him, he stayed still and slid out of the bag once she appeared satisfied he was no threat. He carefully reached for the Thermos on the floor, undid the lid and reached up to the ledge, and tried pouring hot chocolate into the mug.

'Move, cat,' he said to her, but she was so hungry and thirsty that she allowed him to push her head away enough to pour in more hot liquid. She put her head in again but quickly withdrew it shaking it rapidly from side to side and licking her snout with her tongue. It was then that Matty had a brainwave: *why not dissolve some of the biscuits in the drinking chocolate*? He carefully took the mug away and, squatting on the floor, found the packet of biscuits and began crumbling them into the hot drink. She joined him beside the mug and attempted to push her nose into it again, he gave her a corner of the biscuit he was crumbling which she took and ate. When he had a sort of biscuit porridge made he took the mug and sat back on the bale beside Kate and pulled the sleeping bag halfway up. The cat followed him and allowed him to touch the fur on her back as she ate the unsuitable cat food.

'This is not good for you,' he told her as he smoothed the fur on her back. She was a lovely ginger colour from what he could see in the dim light.

While he was contemplating should he give her more, Mebh suddenly appeared in front of him; the cat squealed and leaped away. The young Tuatha bent towards him, laughing and speaking in Gaelic to him, obviously something to do with the cat. He was startled but recovered quickly: *why is everything so funny to her*? In an instant she had disappeared.

The cat leaped up on the bales at the far side of the barn, perched with all four paws close together on the tiny space she found among the bales of hay.

She appeared to be calculating where her next landing spot would be as she leaped from one squeezed space to the next; quickly she disappeared. Matty pulled off his sleeping bag and climbed down on to the floorboards. He backed towards the wall with the door in it, trying to get a better view of the top of the barn. The cat had found a way in and out, somewhere up high. He could see no chink of light on the bales higher up. He took out his torch and looked. Nothing. Time was dragging for him. He went in search of the kittens and spent some time watching them. Mostly they were asleep, snuggled in together in the nest. He noticed even when they were awake and moving their heads, their eyes remained closed.

He went back to Kate on her bed of hay bales. He pulled back the sleeping bag a little and taking his hand out of his glove he decided to check her temperature and the time on her watch. Her arm felt about the same as before, not particularly hot or cold. But then his fingers were bordering on cold so he was not sure what he was feeling. He needed his torch to check the hands on the dial of the watch. *The light must be fading,* he thought. He was surprised to find it was three-fifteen. *She needs to be back.*

He went to the door and opened it a crack: the sun had begun to set. He closed it again; it was really getting very cold. Just as he was contemplating drinking the remainder of the warm chocolate directly from the flask he heard her.

'Matt,' came her faint voice.

'I'm here, Kate,' he said and moved into her line of vision.

'I'm so cold, Matt, and I can't move,' she said anxiously.

'Can I pull on your arms and get you sitting up?' he asked and peeled back the sleeping bag from her shoulders.

He caught both her wrists and pulled the upper part of her forward. He needed to prop himself behind her as she was unable to sit upright. He waited.

'How does that feel?' he asked.

'I feel dizzy, sitting up,' she said.

Then he remembered, in Madras Jack needed to bring her a lot of food after one of her unconscious periods.

'Kate can you stay upright while I get the flask? There is some hot chocolate still left, that will bring you back,' he asked, hoping this suggestion would be the solution.

'You're right, Matt, I need to eat and drink, just let me grab the twine on that bale and I'll manage, it's only for a second,' she said. 'I'll be alright.'

He quickly reached down for the flask, grabbing the biscuits as well. Kneeling on the bale behind her he reached over her shoulder and offered her the flask after unscrewing the lid.

'Where's the cup?' she asked.

'I fed a cat with it,' he said. 'I'll tell you later, there are three little kittens in a nest in here.'

He pulled out a rectangular biscuit from the packet: there were only four left, not meat and potato like Jack had fed her.

'Eat this,' he said, taking the flask and offering her the biscuit from behind.

'Thanks, Matt,' she said and ate it quickly. 'Any more left?'

He fed her the last of the biscuits and made sure she drank all the chocolate. By then she had turned and was able to lower her legs in the sleeping back over the edge of the bales. Matty busied himself rolling up his sleeping bag and stuffing it into the back pack with the Thermos as tightly as he could, remembering the lid had the remainder of the biscuit porridge on it. Kate, he noticed, had peeled off the sleeping bag but lay back against the bales, pale and exhausted after her effort. He rolled that sleeping bag too and pushed it into the rucksack, clipped in the plastic fasteners and heaved the bag on to his back, securing it at the front. It was much bigger than his Crane Bag and he needed to climb down the ladder.

'Can you get on your feet?' he asked.

She slid towards the edge of the bed of bales and stood up; he needed to hold her arm to steady her.

'Still dizzy?' he asked.

She nodded but placed one foot in front of the other until they reached the barn door. To Matty's relief the ladder was propped against the wall just below the threshold.

'I'll go first,' he said, 'you follow.' All of this was said without the slightest bit of confidence in her abilities and he watched as she knelt and dropped one leg and then another on to the top rung of the ladder. Once she was at ground level she slid on to the grass with her back against the barn wall. She was alarmingly pale, Matty noticed.

'Give me a minute, Matt,' she said disjointedly.

He nodded and busied himself with the task of replacing the ladder, with which he had great difficulty. It was a heavy, old ladder and trying to manoeuvre it away from the wall was almost impossible due to its weight. Eventually Matty decided to get behind the angle it made with the wall and just push it forward, hoping it would not break when it hit the ground. It made a very loud thud and even bounced once. He looked at Kate who was dragging herself up from the ground using the wall for support. He hauled the ladder up on one of its sides and dragged it alongside the long wall of the barn which was next to a hedge and hidden from the road, then he propped it there on its side.

By then Kate had walked like someone who was learning to walk for the first time out onto the road. They began their slow journey home.

QUESTIONS

'WHAT'S WRONG WITH her?' demanded his grandmother.

'She… was tired… and pale…' Matt looked at Kate, sprawled across the sofa in the kitchen. His mother was checking her pulse.

'She needs food, she needs to eat meat,' he said.

'He's right,' Kate managed to say; she was so pale and the skin on her forehead was glistening.

'She was like this in Madras once, Mum,' Matty directed the urgent words towards his mother.

'Really? I don't remember that,' his mother said, thinking.

'Are you unwell, Kate?' Gran asked quietly of Kate. It seemed to be a confidential question; Matty felt it had another meaning.

'No, Gran, I need a sandwich. Have you any meat?' she managed to say.

'Jack gave her lamb cutlets with tomato ketchup and she was alright.' Matty's words were insistent.

'We had ham for dinner, will I make a ham and tomato sandwich?' his mother asked her while Gran hovered with an anxious look.

Kate nodded, she tried to unzip her anorak but her hands fell limp on the sofa. Matty undid the zip and pulled off her gloves and cap.

'Better?' he asked. She nodded.

'Where were you two?' asked Gran, busying herself at the kitchen table. Matty looked at Kate who rolled her eyes, indicating she could not cope.

'We were in Kelly's Barn,' Matty replied, unclipping the rucksack. Kate looked alarmed.

'Kelly's Barn?' his grandmother repeated.

'The high barn?' she asked.

'Yes,' replied Matty, removing his gloves, cap and anorak. He avoided looking directly at Kate. Startlingly the lie emerged as he progressed.

'Did you have permission to be in there?' she asked the rhetorical question.

His mother appeared with a sandwich on a place and helped Kate take off her anorak.

'Would you like tea, Kate, or a glass of milk or hot chocolate?' his mother enquired while Kate bit her way hungrily into the bread and meat. She nodded while chewing a massive mouthful.

'Hot chocolate – make it with milk,' she managed to say weakly after a long pause while all watched her push a bolus of food to one side of her mouth. It was as if she had to be economical with physical activities.

All the while Matty was aware he had not answered his grandmother's question, hoping it would dissipate.

'Why Kelly's barn?' Gran asked as she sat at the far end of the kitchen table, smoothing creases that did not exist in the tablecloth.

'Because of the kittens,' he replied as nonchalantly as possible.

He sat down beside Kate on the sofa avoiding her.

'Kittens, are there kittens in the barn?' enquired his grandmother.

'Yes, three,' he replied.

After a little while Matty's mother arrived with the drink and placed it on the wooden arm of the sofa.

'Aunt Elizabeth, can I have another sandwich?' enquired Kate.

'Of course,' she replied and disappeared into the dining room. 'Is the life force coming back?' she called out.

'Yes, I think so,' Kate replied, lifting the mug of hot chocolate to her mouth.

'Did you not have your dinner today?' enquired Gran.

'We don't eat our dinner till night, Gran,' Kate replied with a slight sarcasm as Gran knew that already. Matty could tell from her voice her energy had returned partially and she was part of the evasion. A quick glance reassured him: her cheeks had a pink tinge as the heat from the fire warmed her outside and the drink warmed her inside. The food nourished her, fastening her to this world.

'What's in the bag?' Matty's mother enquired when she arrived with more ham and bread.

"Sleeping blankets,' Matty quickly answered, 'we had to wait in the cold for ages waiting for the cat so that we could find out where she hid the kittens.'

'Why would you want to know that?' *Gran was not to be convinced*, thought Matty and he had run out of white lies.

'Because I'm going to take one for myself,' Kate came to his rescue, so unexpected but yet typical.

'Your daddy will never allow that,' Gran said assuredly.

'He hates cats,' added Matty's mother who had seated herself in the large leather grandfather's chair opposite the sofa, 'he once threw mud from the guttering into a tea chest I had with four kittens in.'

Kate did not reply; she finished her sandwich and chocolate and asked if Matty's mother would drive her home.

'No skipping meals Kate, you are not overweight. Your aunt started slimming at your age; you get enough exercise, do you hear me?' her grandmother said while helping Kate on with her anorak.

'Yes, Gran,' she replied, obviously too tired to protest.

'See you tomorrow for Sunday dinner, Matt,' and she was gone. He would have to wait to find out what if anything had happened.

MAGH MELL

 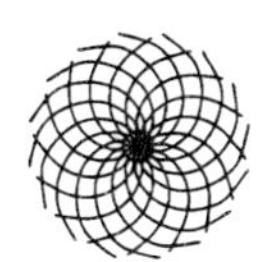

MATTY WAS ACCUSTOMED to Sunday dinner at his uncle's house. It tended to be more lively than usual with his mother there: Uncle Liam monopolised the conversation with tall tales. Kate dutifully helped their grandmother prepare the vegetables and wash up afterwards and when all the adults were resting and chatting in the sitting room she announced that she and Matty were taking a little stroll.

'Not too long,' reminded Gran, 'remember what happened yesterday.'

'What happened yesterday?' enquired Uncle Liam, propelling himself upright in his armchair.

'Nothing, they just stayed out too long…' Matty's mother quickly added, Matty felt that being a cat lover she automatically came to their defence. '… and they got a little cold, that's all.'

'It's a lovely day, we'll just go down to see Finn, maybe let him out while the sun is up,' Kate added reassuringly.

'Be sure to put his cover on,' instructed Uncle Liam, resting his body back against the leather chair again.

But they didn't go to the stable. Instead, Kate manoeuvred her way into the yard through the gate where the Jack Russell was desperately trying to make his escape from.

'We're going in here?' Matty asked.

'It's a lot warmer and I'm still a little shaky,' she replied, pawing in a round hole high up in the barn wall while standing on the toes of her trainers.

She produced the large key to the back door. Once in the kitchen they settled in beside the fire which had been banked up with coal and logs.

'Did you see her? You were gone just over two hours,' Matty began sitting on the edge of the grandfather's chair, anorak halfway down his arms.

'The plan was that I should not go too far and Tykillen, Crossabeg is the nearest and largest settlement,' she began.

'What settlement?' he asked, extracting his sweater-covered arms from the sleeves of the anorak with difficulty. His mother had added another layer underneath since she arrived.

'One with a druidess, I'm totally reliant on Maeve and Ailill now... now that Magh has gone...' she began, unzipping her own anorak.

'How far is that?' enquired Matty.

'Just at the far side of Wexford town, not far compared with journeys I have done with Magh,' she answered. 'Maeve and Ailill in particular had located a Tuatha woman who is the guardian of a stone they call the Neevougi. She can request help from it or pray to it to change weather patterns, that sort of thing.'

'A stone?' Matty asked.

'Yes, it reminded me of some of the idols in the temples in India, especially the older ones, where the carvings are worn away by veneration. This stone was dressed like the temple idols after being unwrapped,' she explained.

'You were not in a temple?' he asked. 'You said the stone was unwrapped.'

'No, we were in a grove and the old woman brought the stone and set it up on the stump of a dead oak tree,' she said.

Kate moved to the edge of the sofa and began rubbing the palms of her hands together thoughtfully and slowly.

'What's the matter?' he asked.

'She reminded me so much of Cruachain, the way she stared at me. I was so scared I really wanted to leave and if it wasn't for Maeve holding on to my entity I just might have,' she said, the unease visible on her face, in her gestures and in the force of her words.

Matty remained silent; lots of what he considered to be comforting words were on the tip of his tongue like *maybe she is not used to people from this dimension* came into his mind, which he did not use.

'Anyway, she did a rite and asked me who I wanted to contact. Ailill spoke on my behalf,' she continued, somewhat recovered, staring at the window as she remembered. 'He told her Magh's full name and after some time she directed my entity to a small pool of water next to the oak stump.'

'Why the pool?' he asked quietly; he noticed she was becoming upset.

'Have you heard of divination, Matt?' she asked, looking at him but still lost in thought.

'No,' he replied as quietly, as he did not want to disturb her recollections.

'It's a bit like a fortune teller looking into a glass ball at the fairs,' she said, still in a dreamy voice.

'Yes,' he replied, 'I have read about it.'

'She asked me to look into it, only me,' she emphasised as if she was reliving the experience. 'I had to come forward and stand beside her... and she, knowing everything… could sense my fear.' She pushed her anorak to one side and sat back against the cushions as if she was very tired.

Matty remained quiet.

'There… in the pool I saw her, Matt.' The statement was deathly serious and she looked directly at him.

'Magh, you saw Magh?' he asked keeping his voice quiet.

'Yes, but not as we know her, Matt… I didn't recognise her at first until the old woman said her name and looked at me right in the eyes… and then I knew it must be her.' She was still in a dreamy state and began looking at the kitchen window again which she was not seeing.

Matty stayed quiet for a while, collecting what she had said in his mind.

'Was it because she was young?' he ventured. 'Jack told me that people do not age in Tir na Og,' he added. 'Was she in Tir na Og?'

'Yes Matt, how did you know?' she asked.

'Because I hoped she would be there and not…' he wished he hadn't thought about the alternative and now it was out and he knew she would ask for an answer.

'You said you hoped she was in Tir na Og and not where, Matt?' she repeated, insisting that he must express what was in his mind. 'Matt,' she said again firmly, her eyes right on his and her voice was not to be ignored; he considered how weak she was.

'A captive of Cruachain,' he answered, his voice low.

'But she wouldn't be, would she?' she said, sitting upright again, in the present and maintaining the look, straight at him. 'They put curses on each other, remember, each other. Magh must have found her way to this place,' she said as if talking to herself and fell back on the cushions.

'The curse stopped her resuming her life with Macha… and with me…' she trailed off, eyes set on the window again. 'I just assumed… I never thought… I thought she would always be here for me… with me…'

Matty stayed still, consuming the new information: if the curse was to end her life here and in the present, then… they would never see her again.

There was silence for a very long time; the sun disappeared from the kitchen window, a log spat on the fire. Matty had the feeling of experiencing time and space, being part of an immense universe in which he was connected to everything, even things and places he could not see or even imagine. When he looked up he found her staring at him.

'She will not come back, will she?' he stated rather than asked. Their thoughts were so synchronised at that moment they could tell that they were thinking and mourning together.

'She can, I have given her the option,' she replied, looking very serious. 'Maybe I shouldn't have... but I did,' she said pulling at the sleeve of her sweater.

'But...' he began.

'Yes, I know what happens, but I thought for Macha's sake... and maybe my own... Oh I just don't know...' She was in despair and got up and began pacing the kitchen floor.

'By the way, Matt, she is not in Tir na Og, she is in Magh Mell,' she said standing over him still frustrated as if it was his fault. And of course it was, it all started in India and it seemed a long time ago.

'I'm sorry, Kate,' he said after watching her pace like a caged animal, feeling the weight of the decision she obviously had to make quickly and among unknown beings the previous day.

'No Matt, I'm sorry, it's not anyone's fault,' she said exhausted and resumed her place on the sofa.

Again he was silent. He kept an eye on her; it looked like she was flung back against the back of the sofa, tense and tired. *Maybe it would help to talk about what happened yesterday*, and he wanted to know too.

'You said you didn't recognise Magh yesterday,' he ventured quietly. 'Why did you believe it was her, then?

'I watched her walk around a market place... a young woman walking around a market place centuries ago, she moved here and there...' she trailed off she appeared to be experiencing what she had seen.

'It's a good place this, Magh...?' he asked quietly.

'It seems to be like Tir na Og but according to Maeve life is not as perfect there,' she answered, still far away in her thoughts.

Tears began running down her cheeks. Matty did not know what to do. He joined her quietly on the sofa and touched her arm while she sobbed and sobbed.

'She turned around after standing still for a moment and then... she looked right at me and said my name... that's how I know...' she sobbed and he reached over to the cupboard and got his grandmother's paper tissue box. 'It was like you and me Matt, looking into someone's eyes and knowing exactly who they are.' She blew her nose and wiped her cheeks and eventually after much rubbing interspersed with talk she pushed the hanky up one of the sleeves of her sweater.

'You said you gave her the option of coming back?' Matty enquired, still using a quiet voice. 'Did you talk to her?'

'No Matt, the fact that I went searching for her was a reminder of her life here... maybe I shouldn't have done it... but Macha was all for it... we had to know find out where she was...' she replied, assuring herself.

'Yes, you are right, we wanted to know… that she was safe… and all you have done is find it out for Macha and us,' he said as logically as he could and hoped it came across as such.

Within moments they heard the back door open, his mother and grandmother appeared, pulling off their heavy winter clothing the moment they entered the heat of the kitchen.

'No television,' remarked their Grandmother.

'No, we were just talking,' replied Kate, who got up and began pulling on her anorak.

Matty fetched his and pulled on the obligatory woolly cap.

'Where are you two off to now?' enquired their grandmother as she poked the fire.

'Home,' replied Kate, hand already on the door knob.

'Did you let Finn out?' Grandmother asked.

'No, it was too cold,' she said and started out of the door.

'I'm just going to see *Jurassic Park* for an hour,' Matty said to his mother.

'You will drive Nicky mad,' she said.

'I'll be back before dark.' He knew all the right things to say to reassure them so that he could make his escape.

They walked silently up the lane. As they neared Kate's house she stood still and turned to him. He knew she had something serious to say.

'Matt, you know I didn't recognise Magh at first,' she began.

'Yes,' he said, recalling her recollections.

'It was because… she looked like Aillien,' she said and there was a look of surprise on her face as if she only realised it there and then.

'The faerie queen… who we met in…' he trailed off thinking it did not make sense.

'Yes, her, I wonder…' and she stopped. 'But then,' she stopped again and a hand was raised and she had the light-bulb expression.

'What?' he asked.

'Could Magh be her mother?'

BLESSINGS

IT WAS MID-FEBRUARY and although La Feale Brede was on February first it did not feel like spring; the weather was cold, wet and dreary. Despite the greyness of the weather Matty felt excited and nervous all at once. He was going home: return flights had been booked for a week before his eleventh birthday, he would be home and the family would be together for his birthday… and more than that, safe. He was nervous as he rode the little red and white bicycle along the quiet road towards Hedge Cottage; hardly any traffic, just one tractor. Everyone had gone back to school, he never did join and although he didn't have to contend with catching up with an Irish language class his mother had been particularly diligent, he considered, possibly severe on how many hours a day he spent on the homework set in India. Still, he put that out of his mind for the moment, being allowed out for a break.

He had been invited to visit Magh; the relief was so great, he had been afraid he would never see her again. When Kate told him he felt lucky. For once every wish he had was slipping into place, coming together like a jigsaw puzzle: in his mind, that's what it looked like. And more than that, even, Kate was confident of getting in and out of the other-world safely. She was less proactive, more measured in her approach and undoubtedly had success. That, he felt, was because she now had the right contacts on the other side. There was a sadness, though, as Magh had decided to come back and would pass away like any human.

He parked his bike as was usual for him, by the hawthorn hedge which was bereft of leaves and approached the little green door; the thatch of the roof almost reached the lintel. He didn't need to knock, Macha opened the door before he reached its step. He wasn't exactly smiling, Matty noted, but there were no unfriendly vibrations either. He stood aside to allow Matty entry. Matty realised he had not greeted Macha, but the moment had passed so he just crossed the threshold. The cottage interior was gloomy. Matty waited while

Macha closed the door. He gestured with his hand that Matty should move on into the living room. He did and found Magh on a bed-like structure near the inglenook; one of the high-backed benches had been removed and there she rested. Kate had prepared him: she said Magh looked old and was very, very weak. However that description was not at all adequate for the sight Matty encountered. In retrospect, he thought that he had taken too casually Kate's actual words, brushed aside, lost in the pleasure of the chance to see Magh before he left Ireland.

She greeted him warmly, stretching up both arms towards him. He held her tiny, skinny hands, noticing the shape of the bones in her arms which were visible underneath a thin layer of skin, while she rubbed his reassuringly.

'Sit, sit,' she said gently, indicating the long stool in front of the fire.

Matty stepped back a pace or two without looking and sat down, still with his eyes on hers; he knew this place, he didn't need to look. Macha loomed nearby, vigilant.

'Thank you, for what you have done for us… and I'm sorry…' he couldn't continue, tears welled up annoyingly. He took one hand away from hers and swiped his tears with his sleeve, seeing the state of her physical deterioration, her face shrunken – she was always quite slim but now she looked devastated, her nose just a cartilage covered with tissue paper-like skin and her cheekbones sharp, like her arms, all the skeleton visible. The vision of an unbound mummy arose in Matty's mind; this lovely creature was little more.

'Shee, shee,' and she shushed him gently. 'You are not responsible. I'm her guardian, it was my job, I did it for her, she chose the cause; if it was not you it would be someone else.'

He looked at her again, while feeling the gentle reassurance of her on his other hand.

She smiled, watching him for what seemed a long time.

'You are leaving us soon?' she said.

He nodded his head.

'I want you to remember something.' She looked directly at his eyes.

He nodded again.

'Will you take care of her, make sure she is always grounded?' she increased the pressure on his hand, her voice scarcely audible.

'Like in the grove, when she wanted to follow you into the river,' he confirmed.

'Exactly, that is exactly what she needs, will need…' She released his hand and withdrew hers and slipped from her side onto her back as if exhausted.

Macha moved forward, touching Matty's shoulder. Matty stood up; he felt that Magh's obvious exhaustion was a signal to leave. He knew too that no mortal left Tir na Og and returned to life in this dimension, she returned just to say goodbye and Macha wanted every single second of that time.

'You will move to England in two years… you and your brother will be her guardians…' came the faint words between difficult in-breaths from the cot bed.

Macha urged Matty away from the inglenook fireplace and into the little passage.

Whilst approaching the hedge to retrieve his bicycle Matty turned to thank Macha but he had already closed out the world and returned to his watch; his wife was dying, that was obvious.

Move to England, two years, she had said; he pondered as he turned his bicycle towards Blackstone.

But she did say, *you and your brother will be her guardians.*

THE STOLEN CHILD

by William Butler Yeats

Where dips the rocky highland
Of Sleuth Wood in the lake,
There lies a leafy island
Where flapping herons wake
The drowsy water rats;
There we've hid our faery vats,
Full of berrys
And of reddest stolen cherries.
Come away, O human child!
To the waters and the wild
With a faery, hand in hand.
For the world's more full of weeping than you can understand.

Where the wave of moonlight glosses
The dim gray sands with light,
Far off by furthest Rosses
We foot it all the night,
Weaving olden dances
Mingling hands and mingling glances
Till the moon has taken flight;
To and fro we leap
And chase the frothy bubbles,
While the world is full of troubles
And anxious in its sleep.
Come away, O human child!
To the waters and the wild
With a faery, hand in hand,
For the world's more full of weeping than you can understand.

Where the wandering water gushes
From the hills above Glen-Car,
In pools among the rushes
That scarce could bathe a star,
We seek for slumbering trout
And whispering in their ears
Give them unquiet dreams;
Leaning softly out
From ferns that drop their tears
Over the young streams.
Come away, O human child!
To the waters and the wild
With a faery, hand in hand,
For the world's more full of weeping than you can understand.

Away with us he's going,
The solemn-eyed -
He'll hear no more the lowing
Of the calves on the warm hillside
Or the kettle on the hob
Sing peace into his breast,
Or see the brown mice bob
Round and round the oatmeal chest
For he comes the human child,
To the waters and the wild
With a faery, hand in hand,
From a world more full of weeping than he can understand.